PENGUIN

THE PORTABLE D

Diana Trilling was born
She was graduated from Radcliffe
and in 1940 began her literary career as fiction critic of *The Nation*. A free-lance writer after 1949, she explored political and sociological as well as literary subjects in *Partisan Review, American Scholar, Encounter, Commentary*, and other publications. In 1964 she published *Claremont Essays*, a collection of essays named for the New York street where she lived with her husband, Lionel Trilling, and their son, James Lionel. Describing her as Arnoldian, the critic Frank Kermode wrote: "Mrs. Trilling's virtues are great; she argues clearly and is as explicit as anybody could well be about her beliefs and methods, advantages and limitations. She therefore requires one to be with her or against her, and one's disagreements are tributes to her skill and integrity."

THE PORTABLE
D. H. LAWRENCE

EDITED AND
WITH AN INTRODUCTION
BY DIANA TRILLING

PENGUIN BOOKS

Penguin Books Ltd, Harmondsworth,
Middlesex, England
Penguin Books, 625 Madison Avenue,
New York, New York 10022, U.S.A.
Penguin Books Australia Ltd, Ringwood,
Victoria, Australia
Penguin Books Canada Limited, 2801 John Street,
Markham, Ontario, Canada L3R 1B4
Penguin Books (N.Z.) Ltd, 182–190 Wairau Road,
Auckland 10, New Zealand

First published in the United States of America
by The Viking Press 1947
Paperbound edition published 1955
Reprinted 1956, 1957, 1958, 1959 (twice), 1960, 1961, 1962, 1963,
1964, 1965, 1966, 1967, 1968 (twice), 1969 (three times),
1971 (twice), 1972, 1973, 1974, 1975, 1976.
Published in Penguin Books 1977
Reprinted 1978, 1980

LIBRARY OF CONGRESS CATALOGING IN PUBLICATION DATA
Lawrence, David Herbert, 1885-1930.
The portable D. H. Lawrence.
I. Trilling, Diana. II. Title.
PR6023.A93A6 1977   828'.9'1209   76-54705
ISBN 0 14 015.028 5

Printed in the United States of America by
Kingsport Press, Inc., Kingsport, Tennessee
Set in Linotype Caledonia

Contents

v

Editor's Introduction

D. H. LAWRENCE was only forty-five when he died in Vence, in the south of France, of the tuberculosis that had long been threatening him. His life, although relatively short, had been strikingly active and full of dramatic contrasts. Born in a small English mining-town, he had travelled over a large part of the world—on the Continent, in Australia, India, the United States, and Mexico. The son of a coal-miner, he had married Frieda von Richthofen, of an old German feudal family. Brought up in the confines of an inordinately tight family group, he had come to know people of many nationalities and distinctions. Never robust, he had lived with titanic energy and produced an enormous quantity of work.

At his death in 1930, Lawrence left behind him close to fifty volumes of novels, long and short stories, plays, poems, essays, and travel journals, not to mention an extensive personal correspondence and a mass of material that has been published posthumously. It is an unusually large production, among the largest in English letters. It is also an unusually varied and fascinating body of work, the fruit of one of the very great literary talents of our time.

If Lawrence had been only a novelist, he would still claim a permanent place in literary history for his ten full-length novels alone. Or if he had written nothing except his long and short stories, not even his novels, he

would still have made a major contribution to modern
fiction. But apart from the novels and stories, there is
Lawrence's poetry—some of it, it is true, careless or uninteresting, but a good part of it of extraordinary quality and there are his critical writings which offer an
embarrassment of riches to the editor who would choose
among them.

The abundance of Lawrence's production is not the
result of merely a literary impulse—the desire of the
artist to multiply his creations. It is the expression of
Lawrence's urgent temperament, and of the immediacy
with which he responded to the world. Lawrence lived,
of course, in the years which gave birth to so many of
our present-day social and political confusions. What he
saw around him drove him to extremes of loathing and
fear: writing was his means of exorcizing his own
demons and of trying to exorcize the demons of the rest
of mankind. It was a work to which he brought an ec-
centric but remarkably acute intelligence. He saw and
recorded the first appearance of the telephone, the
motor-car, the movies, the airplane, the radio—and had
a deep, bitter intuition of their role in our culture. He
reached the height of his powers during the First World
War, to which he was opposed with more than con-
scientious objections. He estimated, more accurately
than any of his contemporaries, the social and moral cost
of an increasingly dominant industrialism, and the price
the modern "free" spirit must pay for its assertions.

There have been few writers in any era, and certainly
none in ours, who have combined as Lawrence did the
gifts of the creative heart and the penetrations of the
critical intellect. Poet and prophet, novelist and polemicist, mystic and pamphleteer, he was a richly complicated human being, profoundly committed to the life
of the Word at the same time that he so rigorously

attacked the perversions of life that have been communicated in language.

In view of Lawrence's unique interest, the condition of his literary reputation requires explanation. For between his achievement and his fate as a writer there is certainly a serious disproportion. Even while he lived, Lawrence met great popular and critical resistance. He was never read as widely as he deserved and seldom read properly; he had many difficulties of publication; the problem of earning a living was a constant harassment. In fact, I suppose that of all modern authors Lawrence has generated most prejudice and suspicion. And since his death, his fate has become even worse. A literary position that was never secure seems to be steadily weakening. In the short space of a decade and a half, a writer of the first rank gives evidence of becoming a peripheral figure—someone whom the younger readers among us neither know nor feel they need to know and whom the older readers among us remember with a touch of awkward indulgence for their own youth.

No doubt accident has played its part in this history of a reputation. A very uneven writer, Lawrence is peculiarly at the mercy of where we chance to make his acquaintance. His work varies considerably in the success of its art and, what is even more important, it gives an often disturbing play to Lawrence's temporary moods. The non-mystical reader who first meets Lawrence when he is very advanced in mysticism is little likely to search for the reality from which this mysticism derives and to which it was directed; or the reader who comes on certain of Lawrence's political ideas before he has a context for them, will scarcely seek out a context before formulating judgment. Nor does Lawrence ever suggest that a first acquaintance is a sampling. His personality is so pronounced that he seems always to be making final pronouncements, and we do not look for the corrections and modifications that would be expectable in a person of less passion.

But the misunderstanding of Lawrence's intention that arises from inadequate knowledge cannot alone explain the antagonism his work has roused. This must in large share be accounted for by the character of the work itself. And even an admirer must admit the justice in some of the charges that have been made against Lawrence. But what anyone who recognizes his enormous interest and value as well as his faults and shortcomings is also aware of, is the illegitimate uses to which his weaknesses have been put, the way in which criticism has concentrated on his shortcomings in order not to have to see his truth. Measured against his achievements, his faults make but a poor indictment. One need not hesitate to name them. Lawrence, in fact, is pre-eminently the kind of writer who can only profit from objective appraisal.

The first, and probably the most justified, reason for distrust or dislike of Lawrence is his intemperate tone. It is not to be denied that Lawrence often presents himself as an emotionally undisciplined writer, especially in the work of his middle and late years. There are the pages of black mood in such novels as *The Rainbow*, *Women in Love*, and *Aaron's Rod*; the extravagance of conception and statement in the novels *The Lost Girl*, *Kangaroo*, *The Plumed Serpent*; the aggressiveness of much of his poetry; the too-great intensity of much of his critical writing. His emotional excess and the nature of his fantasy are bound to disturb the unoriented reader; even to the reader schooled in Lawrence, they are uncongenial. By offering his startling ideas in such a startling manner, Lawrence gives an easy handle to disapprobation.

But if this intemperateness is the first cause of hostility, I think it is also the most superficial cause. I suspect Lawrence's extravagances could be edited out of his work and the work would still excite a quick antagonism. For the real source of our hostility lies well beneath the surface of Lawrence's eccentricity, at the very heart of his genius. We could no doubt forgive him the excess of his virtues if we could but forgive the virtues themselves, which so disquietingly challenge all our accepted ways of thinking and feeling.

From the very start of his career, already in *The White Peacock*, published when he was only twenty-six, Lawrence sounded the revolutionary note in his art which was to be emphasized until, by the end of his career, one would be hard put to it to name another writer, unless among the extreme *avant-garde* of this century, who so thoroughly rejects the moral and emotional premises of modern life—not alone the traditional literary forms, but also the whole modern Christian ethos. The mature James Joyce, for example, is far more revolutionary in technique than Lawrence, but except in so far as any technical innovation must be regarded as a new moral assumption, Joyce's work does not break with the moral assumptions of the past; it is a commonplace to speak of Joyce as a Catholic writer. It is only the post-Joycean writers, the formulated aim of whose technical innovations, unlike that of Joyce, is complete discontinuity with the modern tradition rather than a renewal or renovation of our awareness of the traditional, who can be said to bear any inner moral kinship with Lawrence.

But these innovators turn their backs on the past, whereas Lawrence confronts it in a fierce and fearless attack, carrying the ark into battle against all our modern imperatives. The assault that Lawrence makes upon the imperative of the modern individual will, of the modern social will, of the modern Christian will, is wide and relentless, unalleviated by any real hope of change, improvement, or reform. It is therefore misleading even to speak of him as a revolutionary—since in our present-day society it is the revolutionaries who are the great guardians and proselytizers of hope. And certainly in the limited contemporary political use of the word, Lawrence, who saw so little tò please him in the Russian Revolution or in any projected uprising of the proletariat, was anything but a revolutionary. On the other hand, neither was he a reactionary, or any other order of political man. He canvassed the modern social-political organization because he wished to search out as many as possible of the origins and manifestations of the modern spirit, but he never deceived himself that the new form of *being* which he demanded could be legislated into existence. Like his inquiry into Freudian doctrine, his research into various kinds of political doctrine had its conclusion as its point of departure.

Lawrence studied the contemporary politic as he studied the contemporary psychology, the more surely to be able to discard it as incompatible with his personal vision. Whatever sympathy for one social order as against another he may temporarily indicate, there is finally no new order he would substitute for our present order; there is no new political system with which he would replace any of the familiar systems; no reform program for the reconstitution of a civilization. To Lawrence, all orders, systems, programs are equally suspect as mere reshufflings of the modes of a worn and fruitless way of being. For what he is seeking is not a new form of organization, but an entirely new form of consciousness. He sees a terrible error in our modern institutions, but he is certain that our institutions only reflect our erroneous conception of man's nature. For a new form of consciousness, man requires a new notion of the self; or, to take it the other way round, a new self can be created only out of an entirely new form of consciousness. Because all of modern civilization as we have known it in the Christian era is founded on "ideal" values, on mental consciousness and the denial of the body, on a denial of the "blood-consciousness," he is sure it must be destroyed if man is ever to realize his human possibilities.

In *Kangaroo*, his Australian novel, Lawrence describes himself as "a kind of human bomb." The figure is an accurate one; the bomb-like effect is the effect to which he aspires. Like his talismanic symbol of the Phoenix which rises to a new life from its ashes, Lawrence's bomb image suggests the total annihilation of Christian civilization which is his condition for a new birth. And his instrument, both for this act of destruction and the act of re-creation, is the sexual mystery. It is in man's sexual impulse, taken out of the mental consciousness and returned to the body and the blood where it belongs, that Lawrence finds the clue to salvation. Not the "sex in the head" of "advanced" people, of the modern theorists of sex; not the sensation of sex, which is what is sought in the decadence of civilization; not idealized sex, as it is allowed by the Christian religions; but sex as it is understood by primitive peoples, before the body has been "purified" and de-energized, civilized out of existence. According to Lawrence it is when man fulfills his sexual nature that he attains his highest human destiny, and achieves godhood.

"I am a profoundly religious man," Lawrence wrote in a letter. But his religion is, of course, as little connected with religion as we commonly know it as his revolution is connected with our usual notions of political change. It has nothing at all to do with organized faith, with a religion of doctrine, covenants, and churches. It derives from neither the Old Testament nor the New; quite the contrary; it is deeply opposed to both Hebraism and Christianity. Indeed, Lawrence concentrates most of the blame for our basic ills upon Christianity. It is because modern man follows the word of Jesus that he lives by a false prophecy. Seeking a new revelation for the world, Lawrence finds it in the religion of the pre-Christian, pre-Judaic mysteries, in an invocation of the "dark gods" of certain primitive civilizations.

The relation between Lawrence's religious ideas and the whole of his personal, social, and political thinking is integral. Just as his only god is the god of the sexual mystery, the god in man's own blood, so his only social and political criterion is whether man is permitted his godhood or robbed of it. This is the test by which Lawrence appraises us in our private lives, and finds *us* wanting, and it is the test by which he judges, and condemns, both our social theory and our social practice. The revolution to which all of his work is dedicated is a revolution of our inner values, out of which will naturally spring a thorough revision of political and social institutions. It is an attitude so deeply antithetical to the spirit of our time, to our modern faith in social progress, as to suggest not revolution but counter-revolution. And when we confront, as well, Lawrence's conviction that the modern democratic ideal destroys rather than creates this spiritual revolution, we begin to glimpse some part of our present-day need to stand firmly against his ideas.

Yet the fact is that Lawrence's thinking is intended less to offer us a set of new ideas than a totally new experience—the experience of a wholly new way of feeling. It is a distinction to which Lawrence himself is very alert as he writes: "The world doesn't fear a new idea. It can pigeonhole any idea. But it can't pigeonhole a real new experience." But the world can of course try to destroy a new and fearful experience by trying to pigeonhole the ideas which are the vehicle of its expression—and this is exactly what has happened in Lawrence's case.

Lawrence's ideas are essentially poetic ideas, by which I mean that they suggest more than they state and that, read literally, they are read mistakenly or inadequately. But Lawrence is always being taken as literally as if he were a systematic thinker—a philosopher, a theologian, a political theorist, or a theoretical psychologist. The responsibility for this mistaken approach is not ours alone; Lawrence invites us to it. He himself constantly confuses us as to whether he is talking poetry or hard, polemical prose. All but his young works, *The White Peacock*, *The Trespasser*, *Sons and Lovers*, the early poems and stories, hover on the edge of social-political formulation, and some of them, such as the play *Touch and Go* or the novel *Kangaroo* or the novel *The Plumed Serpent*, go well over the edge. There are few controversial issues of his and our day—the relation of capital and labor, the ideologies of communism and socialism, Freudianism, sexual problems, feminism, education—to which he fails to address himself. Surrounding and supporting his poetic insights are opinions in our immediate world of reality with which we may sometimes agree but which frequently do violence to our own most cherished opinions. Thus, he will discuss democracy in terms that are bound to offend the modern democratic spirit; or he investigates the class structure of our society with all the bias of his own disquiet about his proletarian origin. And if there is nevertheless a truth in his analysis of our democratic assumptions that democrats of any spirit do well to ponder, and a profound perceptiveness in his anatomy of the master-man relationship, we can benefit by these insights only by making a separation that Lawrence himself never finally makes—between his poetic vision and its application.

In other words, himself far too passionate to be very elastic, Lawrence requires a great elasticity of his reader. He demands a double approach—to the polemicist and to the poet. And this demand must surely generate much of our suspicion of him. For the current of modern feeling is peculiarly against the making of double judgments. We want both our literature and our politics to deal in absolutes. We want truth all in one piece, and we resent having to pick our way to it, taking a bit here and a bit there, or being compelled to admit that a subtle truth can inhere in what has all the appearance of falsehood. We prefer to discard truth with untruth, especially when, as in Lawrence, the truth itself is of such a disturbing kind. And Lawrence's poetic perceptions touch the very quick of the modern sensibility, penetrating all the layers of disguise and self-deception with which we cover our personal and social fears. It is because Lawrence hits so directly at our weaknesses that we rush to the attack upon *his* weaknesses, manifest or imagined, and try to dismiss him as reactionary, as fascist, as death-worshipping, as sexually abnormal.

The last is the most frequent avenue of attack—naturally, since it is in the sexual sphere, where we are most self-protective, that Lawrence speaks to us most often and pointedly. We may dismiss a public which, never having read Lawrence, yet disapproves of him as a sexual writer, as even a sort of shady character. Or we may dismiss the people who have read *Lady Chatterley's Lover* as a work of pornography. There still remains the large group of presumably responsible readers who, though they may grant Lawrence a seriousness which should preclude sensationalism, themselves sensationalize or otherwise distort his sexual content. No aspect of Lawrence's thought has been more over-responded to, or more misrepresented, than his sexual ideas. On the one hand, he is accused of an absurd, almost obscene, emphasis upon the physical act of sex—an advocacy of "more and better copulation," as one critic has recently put it; on the other, he is denounced for rarefying sex out of any possibility of ordinary normal enjoyment; and between these two extremes, he is made the victim of almost all our modern sexual confusions. The Lawrence record is combed for evidences of personal abnormality, and where any hint is found or guessed at, it is presented no for the better understanding of his work, but against his sexual authority.

Only less common than the attack upon Lawrence for his sexual ideas, and equally ungrounded, is the attack upon him as a death-worshipper, as a negator of our life energies.

Turn away, friend, from a man who fled from himself, in a
  year
When the nations were turning like giants in slumber, O far
  and near
For the mythological war of the world, and this one with a
  sneer
Sailed away to a Mexican death which was all that his genius
  held dear.

The lines are from a poem called "D.H.L.," by one of our younger poets. They expose as much ignorance of Lawrence as hatred of him. For the "otherness" of which Lawrence was so sensible, his invocation of the dark, hidden forces of the universe, may borrow—in the

orthodox way of mysticism—from the imagined experience of death what it needs as a counter to overly
conscious modern life. But it is still an invocation of
life, not of death. It does not wish to put an end to
mortal man; on the contrary, its aim is to alter man's
condition here on earth, with himself, his wife, and
his fellow mortals. Lawrence is, if you will, a great
pessimist. That is very different from being destructive
of life; for pessimism, when it has stature, is a form of
tragic affirmation.

There is his extravagance, then, to explain our impulse to reject Lawrence. There is the provocation in
his doctrine. There is the demand he makes on us for
the exercise of a double judgment. There is his talent
for striking at us where we are most vulnerable and
defensive. Four such breaches of literary propriety
would be sufficient to explain why his way has been
so hazardous, without our having, in addition, to take
into account his personality, which, as it comes through
his books, is not always an ingratiating one. We are
repeatedly told of Lawrence, by people who knew him,
that he was a lovable and charming man. But while
this charm does sometimes appear in his work—in *The
White Peacock*, in parts of *Sons and Lovers*, in parts
of *The Rainbow*, and of *Women in Love*, in much of
his shorter fiction and travel writing, in most of the
fugitive pieces that are gathered together in the volume
Pheonix, in many of his letters—in other places, particularly in the work of his middle and late years, his
personality can be very rasping and irritating. And it
is not only very difficult to separate what Lawrence
says from the way in which he says it, but almost impossible to put any distance between him and ourselves. Lawrence the man is everywhere in his writings.
To make even a superficial acquaintance with a Law-

rence book is to be immediately in an extraordinarily close connection with its author—to be, indeed, in all the intimacy of a familial relationship with him. We respond to Lawrence as we respond to our connections by blood: just as there would seem to be no such thing as a neutral family emotion, there would seem to be no such thing as a neutral Lawrence emotion.

Such is the nature of his genius—and clearly it is of a type that is profoundly unsympathetic to the literary temper of the last ten to fifteen years. It is not given to many writers to die with their times, but ironical as it may appear in view of Lawrence's struggles while he lived, I think we can yet say that he died with the end of the period that could give him his fullest expression. For in the years since 1930, a political, social, and moral situation which Lawrence thought almost as bad as it could be, has become immeasurably worse. Lawrence was already mortally ill when the economic depression of the nineteen-thirties began. And a new world war, while something Lawrence could imagine, actually achieved horrors beyond the vision of even this prophet of doom, whose experience of the First World War, described in the chapter called "The Nightmare" in *Kangaroo*, was so awful. Into the last decade and a half we have crowded ages of catastrophe. And correlatively, we have put an unprecedented burden upon our writers. We have insisted that our renovators of the spirit—our poets, novelists, and critics—renovate, instead, the body politic, that they be public health officers, criers of economic and political cures, anything except, like Lawrence, spokesmen for the self and the self's mysterious possibilities.

Then, too, a world that has again gone to war in the name of a democratic ideal and for which the very word democracy is charged with a religious significance is scarcely to be expected to give an easy tolerance to a writer who defines democracy not in terms of political constitution but in terms of the emotional requirements of individuals; a writer who, like Lawrence, can compare aristocracy and democracy, "the two sorts of human nature," all to the favor of the former because the natural aristocrats are "those that feel themselves strong in their souls" and the natural democrats are "those that feel themselves weak."

One hesitates to conjecture what would have happened to Lawrence had he lived through these last fifteen years. But as one confronts the principal directions of his thought and its dominant tone, it is not hard to understand why his work has always encountered so hostile a response, and why it has come to be less and less read and talked about. A writer of extraordinary courage, he asks for readers who match him a little in daring, who are willing to suffer a certain outrage to their accustomed feelings, for the sake of a large new poetic experience.

David Herbert Lawrence was born in 1885 in the little town of Eastwood, near Nottingham, England. From *Sons and Lovers*, his autobiographical novel, we learn the conditions of his childhood and early manhood: that his father was a coal-miner, uncouth and unambitious; that his mother was a woman of some education and much ambition, with a strong conviction of superiority to her husband; that the childhood home was tormented by poverty, by the father's drinking and the unhappy relationship of the parents. Lawrence gave early promise of his talents: he was quick at school, fond of reading and drawing. After the death of an older son, it was upon the younger boy that Mrs. Lawrence centred her fierce maternal affections, looking to him to justify her bad marriage. When Lawrence had completed his primary education, he worked for several months in a local warehouse. This was followed by three years of teaching. Then, at twenty-one, a scholarship took him to Nottingham University for two years. He had already begun to write; now came another period of teaching, near London. But with the death of his mother and the publication of his first work, Lawrence gave up teaching to devote himself entirely to literature.

It is to this stage in his career—just over the threshold of manhood—that *Sons and Lovers* carries us. And in addition to a handful of autobiographical sketches and the later first-person travel journals, only *Sons and Lovers,* among Lawrence's books, is based on the actual events of his life. This does not mean, however, that Lawrence's personal history ends with *Sons and Lovers.* Every word he wrote was an unusually direct reflection of his emotional life, and all his books can therefore be read into the autobiographical record. As a matter of fact, Lawrence's own writings, taken in order of composition, are still the best biography we have of him.

The main outlines of the self-portrait are supplied by the novels. Lawrence's approach to short fiction is as subjective as his approach to the novel, but the short stories are less revealing if only because they are more concentrated. It is in the novels that we best observe how much of his driving power is the force of his personal conflicts rather than of the conventional fictional imagination. By any orthodox standard, there is little characterization in a Lawrence novel and even less plot. Even within a single volume, the people are often indistinguishable from one another except by name, for they are most of them, whether men or women, but slightly modified projections of Lawrence himself: it is impossible, for instance, for Lawrence, who was of medium height, to conceive of a tall hero. The most significant encounters in a Lawrence novel are encounters of the spirit. The things that happen are largely devices for transmitting Lawrence's own subjective states.

But if Lawrence's fiction supplies the broad outlines of his emotional progress, it is his poetry that gives us the most pertinent detail. Although the best of Lawrence's poems are not the ones that speak directly to the private occasion, those that do are extraordinarily informative. All the later developments of the long quarrel with his childhood sweetheart, the Miriam of *Sons and Lovers,* are recorded in Lawrence's verse. Or it is among his poems that we find the nakedest statement of his feelings upon the death of his mother:

> And so, my love, my mother,
> I shall always be true to you;
> Twice I am born, my dearest,
> To life, and to death, in you;
> And this is the life hereafter
> Wherein I am true.

Again, it is in his poetry that we best follow the changing moods of Lawrence's marriage, and his developing social responses.

And even his critical writing is part of Lawrence's spiritual autobiography. For his criticism makes no effort to stand at the conventional distance from the book or idea it is discussing. Whatever Lawrence is writing about, he is first and always writing from and about himself. For example, the two books *Fantasia of the Unconscious* and *Psychoanalysis and the Unconscious,* both excursions into Freudian theory, scarcely make the attempt of objectivity; and they misrepresent as well as misunderstand Freud. Or his *Studies in Classic Ameri-*

can Literature, while moving forward by way of certain outstanding figures in American literary history, never moves far from the author himself; a study in the history of the democratic ideal, it is also a vivid portrait of Lawrence the anti-democrat.

An author in a better-proportioned relation to the external world would probably neither desire, nor be capable of, such an insistent self-reference. The element of personal determination in all of Lawrence's work is uncommonly large—enough to constitute, if you will, an abnormal approach to the art of literary creation or even to the art of thinking. The evidence of a driven, at times of almost an obsessed, personality makes it difficult to hypothesize, in Lawrence's case, a free creative will. He can write in a letter: "It [the book that was later called *The Rainbow*] is *very* different from *Sons and Lovers:* written in another language almost . . . I shan't write in the same manner as *Sons and Lovers* again, I think— in that hard violent style full of sensation and presentation." And he would seem to be voicing a reasoned preference. But the suspicion is bound to occur to us that however much he may protest his freedom of choice, he is actually rationalizing a choice forced on him by his emotional nature.

Yet Lawrence's books will be full of surprises for the reader who, because he recognizes the urgency of Lawrence's temperament, assumes that Lawrence is a novelist only by virtue of emotional necessity, and that he came to his method of abstraction in fiction because he lacked the ability to create character and situation in the traditional manner. Whatever may have influenced him to discard traditional fictional means, he at least started with as much of a traditional endowment as a novelist could wish; and this original gift can always reassert itself. There are pages in Lawrence—the early chapters of *The Lost Girl* are a notable instance—which for wit, color, and dramatic visualization compare with the best of Dickens. He was also a very careful craftsman despite his precipitousness, profoundly sensitive to the beauties of expression. Indeed, Lawrence is one of the very great stylists of English letters, his prose consistently the prose of a master, taut, vivid, capable of evoking every subtlety of his thought and feeling, endlessly quotable for its sharp epigrammatic accuracy.

Particularly his descriptions of nature rank with the finest nature-writing in our language. Long before Lawrence had completely formulated his distaste for modern civilized life, he had an acute awareness of non-human life, a specialist's knowledge of trees, flowers, animals. Born in the country, he remained a country person—a great walker, despite his unsound health, a tireless traveller through the little-known countrysides as well as through cities, who seemed to learn the way of a new place not only by human encounter, but almost by the feel of the earth under his feet or by a sense of the currents with which the new air was charged. Lawrence's responses to nature vary, however, with his mood. Among his novels, it is *The White Peacock* that contains his loveliest descriptions of the out-of-door world. *The White Peacock* is a novel of his native countryside, a book of glittering weather and the marked procession of the seasons. Its natural environment is almost wholly benevolent; the pain of nature is present only by short, sharp intimation. Lawrence's first work is his most sunlit work, as if here were the record only of the sweet youthful wonder and promise of nature, with none of the wild conflicts and deep mysteries with which, in the main, he later matched the increasing stress of his own spirit. From *The White Peacock*, however, we move to *The Trespasser*, his second novel, much of it set by the sea,

to hear the untranquil ocean echoing the mounting un-
ease in his own heart. And by the time we come to the
third novel, *Sons and Lovers*, the radiance of the outdoor
world has begun to dim. We are back in the Derbyshire
of *The White Peacock*, but now the sunlight fights to
penetrate the thick enveloping fog from the mine-fields
in whose reach Lawrence had passed his childhood and
youth.

Of all Lawrence's work, *Sons and Lovers* tells us most
about the emotional source of his ideas. It was after its
publication that Lawrence wrote to a friend: "One sheds
one's sicknesses in books—repeats and presents again
one's emotions, to be master of them." This must not be
taken to mean that Lawrence considered the therapeu-
tic purpose the aim of book-writing, but merely that he
recognized therapy as a natural consequence of the
process of creation. Still, in *Sons and Lovers* therapy
and narrative are hard to separate. *Sons and Lovers* is a
developmental novel, the story of the coming of age of a
hero. The efforts of its protagonist, Paul Morel, to come
to terms with himself within the love-bond to his mother
is Lawrence's effort to shed the sickness he can most
easily acknowledge, to master the strongest of the emotions of which he is aware.

But anyone who reads Lawrence's account of his
family situation and then reads Lawrence on Freud, anyone who compares the conscious with the unconscious
revelations of *Sons and Lovers*, must be struck by
Lawrence's capacity (shared, of course, with the rest of
mankind) most to deceive himself at the very moment
he would seem to be most rigorously striving for honesty.
For it is almost in the degree that Lawrence's research
into his childhood is a page-by-page substantiation of
the Oedipal situation that Lawrence disputes the Freudian Oedipal hypothesis. Almost in the measure that he

tries to tell the whole truth of his family experience, he himself suggests that the truth actually lies in a quite different direction. In a pair of little-known short pieces, "Adolf" and "Rex," which Lawrence was to write some years later, he could show a very altered attitude toward his parents. But now, in *Sons and Lovers,* his conscious feelings are only of love for his mother and hatred for his father. Of the love that underlies his hatred for the original of Mr. Morel, and of the animus against the original of Mrs. Morel which underlies his love for her, he is apparently wholly unaware. Yet the artist perceives and divulges what the man must hide from himself. Lawrence's conflicting sentiments about his parents emerge clearly from beneath the surface of his picture of the Morel family; his over-statements of both love and hate carry their immediate unconscious correction.

More than that of any writer one can name, Lawrence's mature thinking is a monolithic structure raised square upon the ground of his childhood circumstances. All of his ideas derive from his sexual premise, and *Sons and Lovers* uncovers the source of this sexual premise in his early life. In the unequal mating of Mr. and Mrs. Morel and in Paul's ardently confused response to his ascendant mother and his dominated father lies the chief clue to Lawrence's feeling nature. The famous Lawrence theme of the struggle for sexual power—and he is sure that all the struggles of civilized life have their root in this primary contest—is the constantly elaborated statement of the fierce battle which tore Lawrence's family. Just as Mrs. Morel, with her tough realism, her high energy, and her bitter anger at being married to a man who imposes himself upon her without equalling or mastering her, is the prefiguration of the long line of desperate women who people Lawrence's fiction, so Morel, the coal-miner whose manliness is so mute and embattled, is the prefiguration of all the darkly self-protective men of Lawrence's novels and stories. But if all Lawrence's heroes and heroines are variants of his father and mother, so too are they all variants of himself. Identifying himself now with the one parent, now with the other, all his life Lawrence tried, in his own person, to understand and reconstitute their unhappy marriage.

To speak of Lawrence as a writer of triangle stories, in the vulgar connotation, is patently absurd. Nevertheless, almost all his fiction either directly concerns, or works around the edges of, a triangular love situation of two men and a woman. In *The White Peacock*, the triangle may appear only in the constant presence of the male narrator, himself inactive, at the crucial love moments between the other men and the women of the story. By the time we reach *Women in Love*, however, Lawrence has begun to work perfectly explicitly with the problem of a male relationship to supplement the male-female relationship: it is not only that Birkin's connection with Ursula, and Gerald's with Gudrun, are reinforced by the connection between Birkin and Gerald, but that Lawrence in large part ascribes Gerald's final destruction to his refusal of a "blood-friendship" with the other man. And in *Aaron's Rod*, in *The Lost Girl*, in *Kangaroo*, in *The Plumed Serpent*, he continues to stress the need of a relation between man and man in order that the relation between man and woman be spared a weight too heavy for it. We must wait for *Lady Chatterley's Lover*, near the close of Lawrence's career, to encounter, for the first time in his full-length fiction, a comparatively orthodox triangle, in which a woman chooses between husband and lover with no indication given of any affectional line between the two male characters.

The latent homosexuality, or rather, the ambivalence of homosexual and heterosexual impulse, implied in such a persistent triangulation is at once apparent. But—and this must be said quite simply—Lawrence was not a homosexual, nor was he seeking a license for homosexuality for his male characters. On the other hand, if to interpret the male relationships in Lawrence as sexually perverse is to distort them, then to rob them of their physical dimension is to falsify them no less. Perhaps the most convenient terms in which to distinguish between the homosexuality of Lawrence's fiction and ordinary perverse sexuality are the terms of the child-state in which so many of his sexual emotions remained. In order to recognize his sexual ideas without the shadow of perversity, we must accept the bisexuality of our own infant pasts.

The triangle of Lawrence's fiction is the triangle of Mr. and Mrs. Morel and Paul—the triangle of Lawrence's formative years. And it is to this original family situation that we trace, as well, Lawrence's concern with manliness and his bitterness against the assertions of the will. One of the sadly amusing contradictions in Lawrence is between his youthful approval of his mother, so peculiarly dominating a woman, and his lifelong battle against the dominating maternal will wherever else it might expose itself. One has the impression of all Lawrence's work after Sons and Lovers that it is an effort not to let happen again what he shows to have happened both to his father and himself in his autobiographical novel.

But of course it is not alone the maternal will that Lawrence combats throughout his career. It is all the manifestations of mental consciousness. As far back as his first novel, Lawrence had discovered what it is that the Mr. and Mrs. Morels of this world—and who of us does not share their sexual fate, if only in some part?—substitute for the life of the body which is the life of our

deepest needs and satisfactions. It is the ambitions of the
ego, the urge to power and pride, which Lettie and
George, in *The White Peacock,* allow to interfere with
their true mating—to an outcome of tragedy and waste.
As he continues writing, Lawrence grows ever more
certain that when the mental-consciousness replaces the
blood-consciousness the outcome is always tragic and
wasteful, and not alone in our personal lives but also in
our social lives.

Politics, commerce, the flummery, the enslavement,
the rapacity of our civilization—these, to Lawrence,
are all merely extensions of man's private disposition.
And man's disposition has been hopelessly warped by
Christian idealism. Lawrence sees the whole functioning
of society as a fool's game, a giant conspiracy to put first
things last and to exalt principles of conduct which are
the very negation of any true principle of being and becoming. And sometimes it is the wilfulness of men that
Lawrence blames for the defeat of women; other times,
it is the wilfulness of women that he holds responsible
for the fate of men. Since both sexes have been equally
educated out of their animal natures, neither sex is
spared his anger. In piece after piece, whether fiction
or essay, he attacks the modern woman for her false
feminity, her feminism, for the various possessivenesses
of mother- and wife-love; and equally he attacks the
modern man, at the one extreme, for his fraudulent
motor-car masculinity, and at the other extreme, for his
Christ-ideal of paternalism and selfless love for his
fellow-man. They are all manifestations of the personal
will and to them Lawrence opposes the individual's
sexual mystery. Similarly, to all the manifestations of the
corporate will he opposes the ways of primitive societies,
before Christianity thinned out the blood with ideal
love.

It is this persistent attack upon the life of mental-con-sciousness that has been made the basis for the counter-attack upon Lawrence as an anti-intellectual. Actually, however, it must be understood that Lawrence is not at all against the intellect as such, but only against what he sees as the perverted uses of intellect. He was himself the most thoughtful of men, and a continuously self-educating one. Our trouble, in his opinion, is not that we know too much but that we do not know enough, or the right things, or in the right way. To accuse Lawrence of anti-intellectualism in, say, the fascist sense, is as ill-founded as to accuse him of savage-worship or of child-worship. On the subject of "going savage," for instance, Lawrence is very explicit. Of Melville's savages he writes, "We can be in sympathy with them. We can take a great curve in their direction, onwards. But we cannot turn the current of our life backwards." He is equally explicit on the subject of child-worship: "Every woman expects her baby to be a Messiah. It takes a man, not a baby." It is true that over and over again in Lawrence we find the phrase "lapsing back." And because Law-rence is so fixed by, even *in*, his own childhood ex-perience, we might expect that by "lapsing back" he means a regression to the earliest conditions of the in-dividual's experience. But whatever equivalence we our-selves may make between the child-state and the primitive experience of the race, Lawrence himself is clear and insistent that the only condition for sexuality is full maturity. Far from making a cult of childhood, he attacks most of the civilized activities of mankind for their infantilism.

If there is anything of which Lawrence does make a cult, it is manhood. Just as his hatred of the will is the negative program forged in his childhood experience, so the phallic quest is the positive program. It is man in the full assurance of his sexual self that Lawrence sets up for worship. The dark god of his mystical universe is the phallic god, and he is certain that when Christianity raised, in place of the dark gods of our blood, the God of light, it conspired at the death of life. For light is the mind triumphing over the body; light is the will that man substitutes for his phallic strength and that woman substitutes for her female mystery. The struggle of will against will is the great sterilizing and enervating force of the modern world. The roar of the battle of wills is the sole music of our idealistic universe.

It was after his marriage that Lawrence began clearly to formulate his mystical phallus-worship. Although it is beyond the scope of this short essay even to attempt an estimate of the influence of Frieda Lawrence upon her husband's writing, it must at least suggest the large and open role his marriage played in his work. It is not only that Frieda Lawrence actually figures in *Kangaroo* and in the travel books, but that Lawrence's work, after his marriage, shows a far greater sexual emphasis, a greater intellectual conviction, and much more emotional exacerbation than it did before, and that it also begins to take a new social direction. Lawrence's "natural aristocracy" had been carefully nurtured by his mother from his earliest childhood: it was one of Mrs. Lawrence's major determinations to pass on to her son her own emotion of superiority to the coal-mining people among whom she lived. Now Lawrence's marriage, coinciding with his first establishment as a literary man, opened social doors which had previously been closed to him and inevitably confirmed his early distaste for the mean sterile ways of the class in which he had been born.

A great deal of nonsense is written about snobbery in general, and in particular about a snobbery like Lawrence's. All artists are snobs, whatever the social group with which they make common cause, if only to the extent that they live by discriminations. Since all art represents a privileged view of life, all artists are privileged members of society by assumption. And there is a great flaw in the reasoning whereby we constantly demand the advantages of a higher class for the members of a less privileged group, at the same time that we rush to condemn any lower-class person who gains these advantages for himself. This illogic, and ungenerosity, is demonstrated, for instance, in our attitude toward certain Negro artists who make their way successfully in the white world: as soon as they give signs of enjoying the privileges we have presumably been seeking for them, we censure them as traitors to their race. There is no denying that Lawrence was "disloyal" to the proletarian class of his origin. But whatever snobbery may be implied in his rejection of this class, it is well to remember that there would have been an equal, if perhaps less obvious, snobbery—the snobbery of condescension —in his maintaining a false identification with it. This does not mean, however, that Lawrence is not to be criticized for the pitilessness of his treatment of his coal-miners in this period after his marriage, or for the political extravagances to which he was tempted. There are an ignorance and cruelty in Lawrence's work of his middle years, a blindness to the economic realities, which cannot be ignored and are not easily forgiven.

Lawrence's heated indictments of the English working-class for its lack of manhood and its bottom-dog humility, which he ascribes to a lack of physical-moral pride, have their undeniable soundness as evaluations of working-class psychology. What we must object to is the sort of thing we find in Touch and Go, where Lawrence demonstrates the sexual pride of a mine-owner by

having him kick the representative of the workers. We
are moved to remind him that only the rich can afford
such shows of sexual strength, and that, even among the
rich, conduct of this kind is bullying and not a decent
pride. That the class struggle is first an economic struggle, that financial insecurity is scarcely the condition in
which pride flourishes, that money is power, and that
his worker would not only be out of a job but in jail if
he took the mine-owner's way of "manliness," Lawrence
now chooses not to see. And at moments of such wilful
blindness, it is extremely difficult to appreciate Lawrence's flashes of sound poetic insight—his perception
that a people's leadership can be no bigger than the
people themselves, his understanding of the likely emotional basis and fruits of a paternalistic capitalism, his
observation of the satisfactions which a subdued people
take in their subjugation.

Obviously there is involved here a good deal more
than simple social ambition, if social ambition is ever
simple. The venomousness with which Lawrence at this
period turned against the class of his father is surely of
the kind reserved for our self-hatreds. From the Morel
household Lawrence had learned that when man is
robbed of his sexual dignity, he is robbed also of authority. Authority, in other words, has become incor-
porated into the male principle, and lack of authority has
become synonymous, for Lawrence, with lack of manhood. The restoration of manhood requires, then, the
restoration of authority; and because authority was so
absent from the Morel class, Lawrence assumes it must
reside in the upper class.

The whole burden of a group of poems Lawrence
wrote in his last years is a confession of, and apology for,
this earlier belief in the inherent virtue of the upper
classes.

And so there came the saddest day
When I had to tell myself plain:
the upper classes are just a fraud,
you'd better get down again.

There is something deeply touching in this poetry of recantation. And I think that *Lady Chatterley's Lover* must also be read as a work of atonement: for here it is an aristocrat, Sir Clifford, against whom Lawrence turns his pitiless scorn; the ruthless money-making which is Sir Clifford's compensation for sexual impotence is the upper-class analogue to the money-grubbing of an emasculated proletariat. But before Lawrence makes this restitution, his social and political investigations have been undermined by his readiness to confuse worldly with sexual power, and probably nowhere so distressingly as in *The Plumed Serpent*. In Lawrence's Mexican novel, both Ramón, who is a present-day personification of the god Quetzalcoatl, and Cipriano, Ramón's chief adjutant, are engaged in a revival of the religion of their primitive forbears. They are metaphors for the pre-Christian life of the blood-consciousness. But unfortunately Lawrence's metaphors in *The Plumed Serpent* are rather mixed figures of speech. Tyrannical, vain, wise in the ways of worldly intrigue, Ramón is the archetype of fascist dictator, and Cipriano, a military man, is the perfect satellite to power. Although, to himself, Lawrence can justify their methods because they operate in the name of the phallic mystery, he fails to justify them to the modern reader, trained by the experience of recent years especially to beware the political dangers of a power-urge wrapped round with mystical language. In the way of the creative mind, Lawrence has no doubt come to a true knowledge of the passivity of others out of the knowledge of his own passivity. But however correct he may be in supposing that a large part of mankind wishes to be relieved of the responsibility of self-government, we shrink from his willingness to cede this responsibility to a Ramón or a Cipriano, and even to arm them for it. When Lawrence writes, "There is no liberty for a man, apart from the god of his manhood," but then adds, "All we can do is choose our master," and himself chooses a Ramón, we have at best a reductio ad absurdum of the integral connection between his religious and political ideas.

Unquestionably both Lawrence's anti-Christian emotions and his anti-democratic emotions can lead him far afield. A parallel, in what might be called the theological sphere, to the political excesses of *The Plumed Serpent* is the novelette *The Man Who Died*, in which Lawrence resurrects Christ to have him reassess his prophecy and, by mating with a priestess of Isis, discover that a love which refuses the body refuses life itself. But the mythological hodge-podge of *The Man Who Died* should not be allowed to obscure its chief poetic point —Lawrence's conviction that spiritual love is a profanation of our humanity—any more than the extremes to which Lawrence is carried in his Mexican novel can be allowed to obscure the poetic truth that resides in his anti-egalitarianism.

This truth has perhaps its best statement in *Studies in Classic American Literature*, the volume in which Lawrence traces the outcome, in our culture, of the American democratic sentiment. The history of American literature, he finds, is the history of two things—of our ever-increasing mental-consciousness and of our ever-increasing desire to be masterless. "Which is all very well," Lawrence comments of the latter, "but it isn't freedom. Rather the reverse. A hopeless sort of constraint. It is never freedom till you find something you really *positively want to be*. And people in America

have always been shouting about the things they are
not." He defines American liberty as a "thing of sheer
will . . . a liberty of THOU SHALT NOT . . . THOU
SHALT NOT PRESUME TO BE A MASTER. Hence democracy." And he goes on, "Men are less free than they
imagine. . . . The freest are perhaps least free. . . .
Men are free when they are obeying some deep inward
voice of religious belief . . . when they belong to a
living, organic, *believing* community, active in fulfilling
some unfulfilled, perhaps unrealized, purpose. . . .
Men are freest when they are most unconscious of freedom. The shout is a rattling of chains, always was."

It was this rattling of chains that Lawrence had of
course heard behind the Italian shout of freedom after
the war (he records it in *Sea and Sardinia*), and behind
the shouting of the Russian Revolution. To the man who
measures the individual by the amount of "dark god" in
him, and the political purpose by what it adds up to in
terms of individuals, the ideals of socialism and communism have never presented themselves as anything
except new forms of self-deception. "When man has
nothing but his *will* to assert—even his good will—it is
always bullying. Bolshevism is one sort of bullying,
capitalism another." And, according to Lawrence, perhaps Bolshevism is the worse of the two because, looked
to as a step-in-progress, it is that much more than
capitalism a step in the progression of our civilized consciousness. Lawrence has his own idea of revolution:

> O! Start a revolution, somebody!
> not to get the money
> but to lose it all for ever.
> O! Start a revolution, somebody!
> not to instal the working classes
> but to abolish the working classes for ever
> and have a world of men.

Lawrence's "world of men" would very likely be a world peopled with Mellorses. Mellors is the hero of *Lady Chatterley's Lover;* he is the gamekeeper for whom Lady Constance leaves the impotent aristocrat, Sir Clifford. It is interesting that in an earlier version of the Chatterley story, recently published, the whole tenor of the novel is political, but that as Lawrence re-wrote the book the labor-capital situation disappeared as a prime motif, to be replaced by the sexual motif; that it is now Mellors's very classlessness that Lawrence offers as assurance of his manliness. The figure of the gamekeeper has of course appeared long before this in Lawrence's fiction—as far back, indeed, as *The White Peacock.* In fact, in all his heroes there has always been some touch of Mellors, if only of his anger, his sullen aloneness, his sexual sense of himself, his authority. But now, finally, Lawrence has arrived at his complete pro-tagonist—the solitary man, free of social commitment and sure in his sexual strength—just as, now, he seems to have transcended the need to support heroism with religion. *Lady Chatterley's Lover* has no mystical para-phernalia. A wholly naturalistic book, its revelation is the revelation only of biology.

Lady Chatterley's Lover is the boldest and clearest statement of Lawrence's sexual ideas. The whole of his evolution can be thought of as a great musical composi-tion in reverse: first it was the myriad variations on his theme that Lawrence stated, and now he announces the basic theme itself. One has the impression that with ap-proaching death he perhaps felt that there was no more time for elaboration and fantasy, that he must come down to immediate domestic fact and try to explain the working of his idea among actual human beings in a familiar environment. Except for *Sons and Lovers* in its early scenes, no other novel or story of Lawrence's deals in such recognizable commonplaces of daily life. And although the portrait of the crippled Sir Clifford is probably the cruelest thing Lawrence ever wrote, his account of the relationship of Constance and Mellors is probably the tenderest. Despite its didacticism, *Lady Chatterley's Lover* has a quality both of reality and humanity that is not often present in Lawrence's fiction.

The quick warm touch of instinctive sympathy for his fellow-man is indeed what we have always most missed in Lawrence's work—this and its counterpart, humor. Their absence is bound to be regretted. One of the things we all of us unconsciously seek in art, particularly in fiction, is the knowledge of ready love and forgiveness, the promise of the kind of understanding that is shared in laughter. But if, himself too tortured by life to be in the business of dispensing benevolences, Lawrence gives us no such reassurance, he surely does give us what is often indicated instead of palliatives but almost never made available to us in art—a possible procedure for a fierce surgery upon our ailing world and selves. In the degree that our civilization daily comes closer to the point where perhaps only the most drastic therapy can be hoped to save it, his work has an extraordinary poetic significance. It is a metaphor against doom.

DIANA TRILLING

STORIES
AND NOVELETTES

EDITOR'S PREFACE

ALTHOUGH Lawrence is usually first thought of as a novelist, I think the best introduction to him is through his stories. If we include the novelettes— "The Woman Who Rode Away," "The Captain's Doll," "The Fox," "The Ladybird," "The Man Who Died," "The Virgin and the Gipsy"—and what is really a short novel, "St. Mawr," he wrote more than half a hundred short pieces of fiction. They prove him to be one of the very great masters of the story form, sharing with Chekhov a genius for using the briefer medium not merely anecdotally, as in the contemporary manner, or for a swift glimpse into one aspect of character, but for a complete statement of dramatic human conflict. There are only a few occasions—"The Woman Who Rode Away" is one, "The Man Who Died" is another—where the stories approach the emotional or imaginative extremes of the novels. From the point of view both of situation and emotional attitude, the short fiction is more conventional than the long and more easily received by the naturalistic-minded modern reader. It is also quicker and wittier, and the personality of its author is more consistently attractive.

"The Prussian Officer," one of Lawrence's earliest stories, is also one of his best-known; but I reprint it nonetheless—and not only because it so manifestly deserves its reputation but because, a fierce negative response to power, it should stand as a good corrective

34

to the many instances in which Lawrence seemed over-receptive to authority. "Tickets, Please" and "The Blind Man" are also fairly early works; but together with "The Rocking-Horse Winner," a later story, these of all Lawrence's narratives have reverberated in my memory longest and with most meaning. I find "Two Blue Birds" and "The Lovely Lady" especially appealing because of their tone of worldliness: Lawrence seldom writes in this vein, but it is somehow pleasant to know he was capable of it.

Of the novelettes, I reprint "The Princess" (if it *is* a novelette; it strikes me as being, rather, only a more-than-usually-long story) and "The Fox" instead of the more popular "The Captain's Doll" or "The Ladybird." With each re-reading, I become increasingly disturbed by a note of contrivance in "The Captain's Doll," and its ending is surely a major weakness; as for "The Ladybird," in addition to its being sluggish in pace, it impresses me as a dim, first, unconscious projection of *Lady Chatterley's Lover* rather than as a fully-inspired entity. "The Princess," on the other hand, seems to me to be entirely successful in itself as well as the most compelling piece of fiction produced by Lawrence's visit to Mexico and New Mexico. And "The Fox" I find the most perfectly conceived and sustained of any of the novelettes.

The Prussian Officer

THEY had marched more than thirty kilometres since dawn, along the white, hot road where occasional thickets of trees threw a moment of shade, then out into the glare again. On either hand, the valley, wide and shallow, glittered with heat; dark green patches of rye, pale young corn, fallow and meadow and black pine woods spread in a dull, hot diagram under a glistening sky. But right in front the mountains ranged across, pale blue and very still, snow gleaming gently out of the deep atmosphere. And towards the mountains, on and on, the regiment marched between the rye fields and the meadows, between the scraggy fruit trees set regularly on either side the high road. The burnished, dark green rye threw off a suffocating heat, the mountains drew gradually nearer and more distinct. While the feet of the soldiers grew hotter, sweat ran through their hair under their helmets, and their knapsacks could burn no more in contact with their shoulders, but seemed instead to give off a cold, prickly sensation.

He walked on and on in silence, staring at the mountains ahead, that rose sheer out of the land and stood fold behind fold, half earth, half heaven, the heaven, the barrier with slits of soft snow, in the pale, bluish peaks.

He could now walk almost without pain. At the start, he had determined not to limp. It had made him sick to take the first steps, and during the first mile or so, he

had compressed his breath, and the cold drops of sweat
had stood on his forehead. But he had walked it off.
What were they after all but bruises! He had looked at
them, as he was getting up: deep bruises on the backs of
his thighs. And since he had made his first step in the
morning, he had been conscious of them, till now he had
a tight, hot place in his chest, with suppressing the pain,
and holding himself in. There seemed no air when he
breathed. But he walked almost lightly.

The Captain's hand had trembled at taking his coffee
at dawn: his orderly saw it again. And he saw the fine
figure of the Captain wheeling on horseback at the farm-
house ahead, a handsome figure in pale blue uniform
with facings of scarlet, and the metal gleaming on the
black helmet and the sword-scabbard, and dark streaks
of sweat coming on the silky bay horse. The orderly felt
he was connected with that figure moving so suddenly
on horseback: he followed it like a shadow, mute and inevitable and damned by it. And the officer was always
aware of the tramp of the company behind, the march
of his orderly among the men.

The Captain was a tall man of about forty, grey at the
temples. He had a handsome, finely knit figure, and was
one of the best horsemen in the West. His orderly,
having to rub him down, admired the amazing riding-
muscles of his loins.

For the rest, the orderly scarcely noticed the officer
any more than he noticed himself. It was rarely he saw
his master's face: he did not look at it. The Captain had
reddish-brown, stiff hair that he wore short upon his
skull. His moustache was also cut short and bristly over
a full, brutal mouth. His face was rather rugged, the
cheeks thin. Perhaps the man was the more handsome
for the deep lines in his face, the irritable tension of his
brow, which gave him the look of a man who fights with

life. His fair eyebrows stood bushy over light blue eyes that were always flashing with cold fire.

He was a Prussian aristocrat, haughty and overbearing. But his mother had been a Polish Countess. Having made too many gambling debts when he was young, he had ruined his prospects in the Army, and remained an infantry captain. He had never married: his position did not allow of it, and no woman had ever moved him to it. His time he spent riding—occasionally he rode one of his own horses at the races—and at the officers' club. Now and then he took himself a mistress. But after such an event, he returned to duty with his brow still more tense, his eyes still more hostile and irritable. With the men, however, he was merely impersonal, though a devil when roused; so that, on the whole, they feared him, but had no great aversion from him. They accepted him as the inevitable.

To his orderly he was at first cold and just and indifferent: he did not fuss over trifles. So that his servant knew practically nothing about him, except just what orders he would give, and how he wanted them obeyed. That was quite simple. Then the change gradually came.

The orderly was a youth of about twenty-two, of medium height, and well built. He had strong, heavy limbs, was swarthy, with a soft, black, young moustache. There was something altogether warm and young about him. He had firmly marked eye-brows over dark, expressionless eyes that seemed never to have thought, only to have received life direct through his senses, and acted straight from instinct.

Gradually the officer had become aware of his servant's young, vigorous, unconscious presence about him. He could not get away from the sense of the youth's person, while he was in attendance. It was like a warm flame upon the older man's tense, rigid body, that had become almost unliving, fixed. There was something so free and self-contained about him, and something in the young fellow's movement, that made the officer aware of him. And this irritated the Prussian. He did not choose to be touched into life by his servant. He might easily have changed his man, but he did not. He now very rarely looked direct at his orderly, but kept his face averted, as if to avoid seeing him. And yet as the young soldier moved unthinking about the apartment, the elder watched him, and would notice the movement of his strong young shoulders under the blue cloth, the bend of his neck. And it irritated him. To see the soldier's young, brown, shapely peasant's hand grasp the loaf or the wine-bottle sent a flash of hate or of anger through the elder man's blood. It was not that the youth was clumsy: it was rather the blind, instinctive sureness of movement of an unhampered young animal that irritated the officer to such a degree.

Once, when a bottle of wine had gone over, and the red gushed out on to the tablecloth, the officer had started up with an oath, and his eyes, bluey like fire, had held those of the confused youth for a moment. It was a shock for the young soldier. He felt something sink deeper, deeper into his soul, where nothing had ever gone before. It left him rather blank and wondering. Some of his natural completeness in himself was gone, a little uneasiness took its place. And from that time an undiscovered feeling had held between the two men.

Henceforward the orderly was afraid of really meeting his master. His subconsciousness remembered those steely blue eyes and the harsh brows, and did not intend to meet them again. So he always stared past his master and avoided him. Also, in a little anxiety, he waited for the three months to have gone, when his time would be up. He began to feel a constraint in the Captain's presence, and the soldier even more than the officer wanted to be left alone, in his neutrality as servant.

He had served the Captain for more than a year, and knew his duty. This he performed easily, as if it were natural to him. The officer and his commands he took for granted, as he took the sun and the rain, and he served as a matter of course. It did not implicate him personally.

But now if he were going to be forced into a personal interchange with his master he would be like a wild thing caught, he felt he must get away.

But the influence of the young soldier's being had penetrated through the officer's stiffened discipline, and perturbed the man in him. He, however, was a gentleman, with long, fine hands and cultivated movements, and was not going to allow such a thing as the stirring of his innate self. He was a man of passionate temper, who had always kept himself suppressed. Occasionally there had been a duel, an outburst before the soldiers. He knew himself to be always on the point of breaking out. But he kept himself hard to the idea of the Service. Whereas the young soldier seemed to live out his warm, full nature, to give it off in his very movements, which had a certain zest, such as wild animals have in free movement. And this irritated the officer more and more.

In spite of himself, the Captain could not regain his neutrality of feeling towards his orderly. Nor could he leave the man alone. In spite of himself, he watched him, gave him sharp orders, tried to take up as much of his time as possible. Sometimes he flew into a rage with the young soldier, and bullied him. Then the orderly shut himself off, as it were out of earshot, and waited, with sullen, flushed face, for the end of the noise. The words never pierced to his intelligence, he made himself, protectively, impervious to the feelings of his master.

He had a scar on his left thumb, a deep seam going across the knuckle. The officer had long suffered from it, and wanted to do something to it. Still it was there, ugly and brutal on the young, brown hand. At last the Captain's reserve gave way. One day, as the orderly was smoothing out the tablecloth, the officer pinned down his thumb with a pencil, asking:

"How did you come by that?"

The young man winced and drew back at attention. "A wood axe, Herr Hauptmann," he answered.

The officer waited for further explanation. None came. The orderly went about his duties. The elder man was sullenly angry. His servant avoided him. And the next day he had to use all his will-power to avoid seeing the scarred thumb. He wanted to get hold of it and—— A hot flame ran in his blood.

He knew his servant would soon be free, and would be glad. As yet, the soldier had held himself off from the elder man. The Captain grew madly irritable. He could not rest when the soldier was away, and when he was present, he glared at him with tormented eyes. He hated those fine black brows over the unmeaning dark eyes, he was infuriated by the free movement of the handsome limbs, which no military discipline could make stiff. And he became harsh and cruelly bullying, using contempt and satire. The young soldier only grew more mute and expressionless.

"What cattle were you bred by, that you can't keep straight eyes? Look me in the eyes when I speak to you."

And the soldier turned his dark eyes to the other's face, but there was no sight in them: he stared with the slightest possible cast, holding back his sight, perceiving the blue of his master's eyes, but receiving no look from them. And the elder man went pale, and his reddish eyebrows twitched. He gave his order, barrenly.

Once he flung a heavy military glove into the young soldier's face. Then he had the satisfaction of seeing the black eyes flare up into his own, like a blaze when straw is thrown on a fire. And he had laughed with a little tremor and a sneer.

But there were only two months more. The youth instinctively tried to keep himself intact: he tried to serve the officer as if the latter were an abstract authority and not a man. All his instinct was to avoid personal contact, even definite hate. But in spite of himself the hate grew, responsive to the officer's passion. However, he put it in the background. When he had left the Army he could dare acknowledge it. By nature he was active, and had many friends. He thought what amazing good fellows they were. But, without knowing it, he was alone. Now this solitariness was intensified. It would carry him through his term. But the officer seemed to be going irritably insane, and the youth was deeply frightened.

The soldier had a sweetheart, a girl from the mountains, independent and primitive. The two walked together, rather silently. He went with her, not to talk, but to have his arm round her, and for the physical contact. This eased him, made it easier for him to ignore the Captain; for he could rest with her held fast against his chest. And she, in some unspoken fashion, was there for him. They loved each other.

The Captain perceived it, and was mad with irritation. He kept the young man engaged all the evenings long, and took pleasure in the dark look that came on his face. Occasionally, the eyes of the two men met, those of the younger sullen and dark, doggedly unalterable, those of the elder sneering with restless contempt.

The officer tried hard not to admit the passion that had got hold of him. He would not know that his feeling for his orderly was anything but that of a man incensed by his stupid, perverse servant. So, keeping quite justified and conventional in his consciousness, he let the other thing run on. His nerves, however, were suffering. At last he slung the end of a belt in his servant's face. When he saw the youth start back, the pain-tears in his eyes and the blood on his mouth, he had felt at once a thrill of deep pleasure and of shame.

But this, he acknowledged to himself, was a thing he had never done before. The fellow was too exasperating. His own nerves must be going to pieces. He went away for some days with a woman.

It was a mockery of pleasure. He simply did not want the woman. But he stayed on for his time. At the end of it, he came back in an agony of irritation, torment, and misery. He rode all the evening, then came straight in to supper. His orderly was out. The officer sat with his long, fine hands lying on the table, perfectly still, and all his blood seemed to be corroding.

At last his servant entered. He watched the strong, easy young figure, the fine eyebrows, the thick black hair. In a week's time the youth had got back his old well-being. The hands of the officer twitched and seemed to be full of mad flame. The young man stood at attention, unmoving, shut off.

The meal went in silence. But the orderly seemed eager. He made a clatter with the dishes.

"Are you in a hurry?" asked the officer, watching the intent, warm face of his servant. The other did not reply.

"Will you answer my question?" said the Captain.

"Yes, sir," replied the orderly, standing with his pile of deep Army plates. The Captain waited, looked at him, then asked again:

"Are you in a hurry?"

"Yes, sir," came the answer, that sent a flash through the listener.

"For what?"

"I was going out, sir."

"I want you this evening."

There was a moment's hesitation. The officer had a curious stiffness of countenance.

"Yes, sir," replied the servant, in his throat.

"I want you tomorrow evening also—in fact, you may consider your evenings occupied, unless I give you leave."

The mouth with the young moustache set close.

"Yes, sir," answered the orderly, loosening his lips for a moment.

He again turned to the door.

"And why have you a piece of pencil in your ear?"

The orderly hesitated, then continued on his way without answering. He set the plates in a pile outside the door, took the stump of pencil from his ear, and put it in his pocket. He had been copying a verse for his sweetheart's birthday card. He returned to finish clearing the table. The officer's eyes were dancing, he had a little, eager smile.

"Why have you a piece of pencil in your ear?" he asked.

The orderly took his hands full of dishes. His master was standing near the great green stove, a little smile on his face, his chin thrust forward. When the young soldier saw him his heart suddenly ran hot. He felt blind. Instead of answering, he turned dazedly to the door. As he was crouching to set down the dishes, he was pitched forward by a kick from behind. The pots went in a stream down the stairs, he clung to the pillar of the banisters. And as he was rising he was kicked heavily again, and again, so that he clung sickly to the post for some moments. His master had gone swiftly into the room and closed the door. The maid-servant downstairs looked up the staircase and made a mocking face at the crockery disaster.

The officer's heart was plunging. He poured himself a glass of wine, part of which he spilled on the floor, and gulped the remainder, leaning against the cool, green stove. He heard his man collecting the dishes from the stairs. Pale, as if intoxicated, he waited. The servant entered again. The Captain's heart gave a pang, as of pleasure, seeing the young fellow bewildered and uncertain on his feet, with pain.

"Schöner!" he said.

The soldier was a little slower in coming to attention.

"Yes, sir!"

The youth stood before him, with pathetic young moustache, and fine eyebrows very distinct on his forehead of dark marble.

"I asked you a question."

"Yes, sir."

The officer's tone bit like acid.

"Why had you a pencil in your ear?"

Again the servant's heart ran hot, and he could not breathe. With dark, strained eyes, he looked at the officer, as if fascinated. And he stood there sturdily planted, unconscious. The withering smile came into the Captain's eyes, and he lifted his foot.

"I—I forgot it—sir," panted the soldier, his dark eyes fixed on the other man's dancing blue ones.

"What was it doing there?"

He saw the young man's breast heaving as he made an effort for words.

"I had been writing."

"Writing what?"

Again the soldier looked him up and down. The officer could hear him panting. The smile came into the blue eyes. The soldier worked his dry throat, but could not speak. Suddenly the smile lit like a flame on the officer's face, and a kick came heavily against the orderly's thigh. The youth moved a pace sideways. His face went dead, with two black, staring eyes.

"Well?" said the officer.

The orderly's mouth had gone dry, and his tongue rubbed in it as on dry brown-paper. He worked his throat. The officer raised his foot. The servant went stiff.

"Some poetry, sir," came the crackling, unrecognizable sound of his voice.

"Poetry, what poetry?" asked the Captain, with a sickly smile.

Again there was the working in the throat. The Captain's heart had suddenly gone down heavily, and he stood sick and tired.

"For my girl, sir," he heard the dry, inhuman sound.

"Oh!" he said, turning away. "Clear the table."

"Click!" went the soldier's throat; then again, "Click!" and then the half-articulate:

"Yes, sir."

The young soldier was gone, looking old, and walking heavily.

The officer, left alone, held himself rigid, to prevent himself from thinking. His instinct warned him that he must not think. Deep inside him was the intense gratification of his passion, still working powerfully. Then there was a counter-action, a horrible breaking down of something inside him, a whole agony of reaction. He stood there for an hour motionless, a chaos of sensations, but rigid with a will to keep blank his consciousness, to prevent his mind grasping. And he held himself so until the worst of the stress had passed, when he began to drink, drank himself to an intoxication, till he slept obliterated. When he woke in the morning he was shaken to the base of his nature. But he had fought off the realization of what he had done. He had prevented his mind from taking it in, had suppressed it along with his instincts, and the conscious man had nothing to do with it. He felt only as after a bout of intoxication, weak, but the affair itself all dim and not to be recovered. Of the drunkenness of his passion he successfully refused remembrance. And when his orderly appeared with coffee, the officer assumed the same self he had had the morning before. He refused the event of the past night —denied it had ever been—and was successful in his denial. He had not done any such thing—not he himself. Whatever there might be, lay at the door of a stupid, insubordinate servant.

The orderly had gone about in a stupor all the evening. He drank some beer because he was parched, but not much, the alcohol made his feeling come back, and he could not bear it. He was dulled, as if nine-tenths of the ordinary man in him were inert. He crawled about disfigured. Still, when he thought of the kicks, he went sick, and when he thought of the threat of more kicking, in the room afterwards, his heart went hot and faint, and he panted, remembering the one that had come. He had been forced to say, "For my girl." He was much too done even to want to cry. His mouth hung slightly open, like an idiot's. He felt vacant, and wasted. So, he wandered at his work, painfully, and very slowly and clumsily, fumbling blindly with the brushes, and finding it difficult, when he sat down, to summon the energy to move again. His limbs, his jaw, were slack and nerveless. But he was very tired. He got to bed at last, and slept inert, relaxed, in a sleep that was rather stupor than slumber, a dead night of stupefaction shot through with gleams of anguish.

In the morning were the manœuvres. But he woke even before the bugle sounded. The painful ache in his chest, the dryness of his throat, the awful steady feeling of misery made his eyes come awake and dreary at once. He knew, without thinking, what had happened. And he knew that the day had come again, when he must go on with his round. The last bit of darkness was being pushed out of the room. He would have to move his inert body and go on. He was so young, and had known so little trouble, that he was bewildered. He only wished it would stay night, so that he could lie still, covered up by the darkness. And yet nothing would prevent the day from coming, nothing would save him from having to get up and saddle the Captain's horse, and make the Captain's coffee. It was there, inevitable. And then, he thought, it was impossible. Yet they would not leave him free. He must go and take the coffee to the Captain. He was too stunned to understand it. He only knew it was inevitable—inevitable, however long he lay inert.

At last, after heaving at himself, for he seemed to be a mass of inertia, he got up. But he had to force every one of his movements from behind, with his will. He felt lost, and dazed, and helpless. Then he clutched hold of the bed, the pain was so keen. And looking at his thighs, he saw the darker bruises on his swarthy flesh and he knew that, if he pressed one of his fingers on one of the bruises, he should faint. But he did not want to faint— he did not want anybody to know. No one should ever know. It was between him and the Captain. There were only the two people in the world now—himself and the Captain.

Slowly, economically, he got dressed and forced himself to walk. Everything was obscure, except just what he had his hands on. But he managed to get through his work. The very pain revived his dull senses. The worst remained yet. He took the tray and went up to the Captain's room. The officer, pale and heavy, sat at the table. The orderly, as he saluted, felt himself put out of existence. He stood still for a moment submitting to his own nullification—then he gathered himself, seemed to regain himself, and then the Captain began to grow vague, unreal, and the younger soldier's heart beat up. He clung to this situation—that the Captain did not exist—so that he himself might live. But when he saw his officer's hand tremble as he took the coffee, he felt everything falling shattered. And he went away, feeling as if he himself were coming to pieces, disintegrated. And when the Captain was there on horseback, giving orders, while he himself stood, with rifle and knapsack, sick with pain, he felt as if he must shut his eyes—as if he must shut his eyes on everything. It was only the long agony of marching with a parched throat that filled him with one single, sleep-heavy intention: to save himself.

II

He was getting used even to his parched throat. That the snowy peaks were radiant among the sky, that the whity-green glacier-river twisted through its pale shoals in the valley below, seemed almost supernatural. But he was going mad with fever and thirst. He plodded on uncomplaining. He did not want to speak, not to anybody. There were two gulls, like flakes of water and snow, over the river. The scent of green rye soaked in sunshine came like a sickness. And the march continued, monotonously, almost like a bad sleep.

At the next farm-house, which stood low and broad near the high road, tubs of water had been put out. The

soldiers clustered round to drink. They took off their
helmets, and the steam mounted from their wet hair.
The Captain sat on horseback, watching. He needed to
see his orderly. His helmet threw a dark shadow over
his light, fierce eyes, but his moustache and mouth and
chin were distinct in the sunshine. The orderly must
move under the presence of the figure of the horseman.
It was not that he was afraid, or cowed. It was as if he
was disembowelled, made empty, like an empty shell.
He felt himself as nothing, a shadow creeping under the
sunshine. And, thirsty as he was, he could scarcely drink,
feeling the Captain near him. He would not take off his
helmet to wipe his wet hair. He wanted to stay in
shadow, not to be forced into consciousness. Starting, he
saw the light heel of the officer prick the belly of the
horse; the Captain cantered away, and he himself could
relapse into vacancy.

Nothing, however, could give him back his living
place in the hot, bright morning. He felt like a gap
among it all. Whereas the Captain was prouder, overriding. A hot flash went through the young servant's
body. The Captain was firmer and prouder with life, he
himself was empty as a shadow. Again the flash went
through him, dazing him out. But his heart ran a little
firmer.

The company turned up the hill, to make a loop for
the return. Below, from among the trees, the farm-bell
clanged. He saw the labourers, mowing barefoot at the
thick grass, leave off their work and go downhill, their
scythes hanging over their shoulders, like long, bright
claws curving down behind them. They seemed like
dream-people, as if they had no relation to himself. He
felt as in a blackish dream: as if all the other things were
there and had form, but he himself was only a consciousness, a gap that could think and perceive.

The soldiers were tramping silently up the glaring hillside. Gradually his head began to revolve, slowly, rhythmically. Sometimes it was dark before his eyes, as if he saw this world through a smoked glass, frail shadows and unreal. It gave him a pain in his head to walk.

The air was too scented, it gave no breath. All the lush green-stuff seemed to be issuing its sap, till the air was deathly, sickly with the smell of greenness. There was the perfume of clover, like pure honey and bees. Then there grew a faint acrid tang—they were near the beeches; and then a queer clattering noise, and a suffocating, hideous smell; they were passing a flock of sheep, a shepherd in a black smock, holding his crook. Why should the sheep huddle together under this fierce sun? He felt that the shepherd would not see him, though he could see the shepherd.

At last there was the halt. They stacked rifles in a conical stack, put down their kit in a scattered circle around it, and dispersed a little, sitting on a small knoll high on the hillside. The chatter began. The soldiers were steaming with heat, but were lively. He sat still, seeing the blue mountains rising upon the land, twenty kilometres away. There was a blue fold in the ranges, then out of that, at the foot, the broad, pale bed of the river, stretches of whity-green water between pinkish-grey shoals among the dark pine woods. There it was, spread out a long way off. And it seemed to come down-hill, the river. There was a raft being steered, a mile away. It was a strange country. Nearer, a red-roofed, broad farm with white base and square dots of windows crouched beside the wall of beech foliage on the wood's edge. There were long strips of rye and clover and pale green corn. And just at his feet, below the knoll, was a darkish bog, where globe flowers stood breathless still on their slim stalks. And some of the pale gold bubbles were burst, and a broken fragment hung in the air. He thought he was going to sleep.

Suddenly something moved into this coloured mirage before his eyes. The Captain, a small, light-blue and scarlet figure, was trotting evenly between the strips of corn, along the level brow of the hill. And the man making flag-signals was coming on. Proud and sure moved the horseman's figure, the quick, bright thing, in which was concentrated all the light of this morning, which for the rest lay a fragile, shining shadow. Submissive, apathetic, the young soldier sat and stared. But as the horse slowed to a walk, coming up the last steep path, the great flash flared over the body and soul of the orderly. He sat waiting. The back of his head felt as if it were weighted with a heavy piece of fire. He did not want to eat. His hands trembled slightly as he moved them. Meanwhile the officer on horseback was approaching slowly and proudly. The tension grew in the orderly's soul. Then again, seeing the Captain ease himself on the saddle, the flash blazed through him.

The Captain looked at the patch of light blue and scarlet, and dark heads, scattered closely on the hill-side. It pleased him. The command pleased him. And he was feeling proud. His orderly was among them in common subjection. The officer rose a little on his stirrups to look. The young soldier sat with averted, dumb face. The Captain relaxed on his seat. His slim-legged, beautiful horse, brown as a beech nut, walked proudly uphill. The Captain passed into the zone of the company's atmosphere: a hot smell of men, of sweat, of leather. He knew it very well. After a word with the lieutenant, he went a few paces higher, and sat there, a dominant figure, his sweat-marked horse swishing its tail, while he looked down on his men, on his orderly, a nonentity among the crowd.

The young soldier's heart was like fire in his chest, and he breathed with difficulty. The officer, looking downhill, saw three of the young soldiers, two pails of water between them, staggering across a sunny green field. A table had been set up under a tree, and there the slim lieutenant stood, importantly busy. Then the Captain summoned himself to an act of courage. He called his orderly.

The flame leapt into the young soldier's throat as he heard the command, and he rose blindly, stifled. He saluted, standing below the officer. He did not look up. But there was the flicker in the Captain's voice.

"Go to the inn and fetch me . . ." the officer gave his commands. "Quick!" he added.

At the last word, the heart of the servant leapt with a flash, and he felt the strength come over his body. But he turned in mechanical obedience, and set off at a heavy run downhill, looking almost like a bear, his trousers bagging over his military boots. And the officer watched this blind, plunging run all the way.

But it was only the outside of the orderly's body that was obeying so humbly and mechanically. Inside had gradually accumulated a core into which all the energy of that young life was compact and concentrated. He executed his commission, and plodded quickly back uphill. There was a pain in his head, as he walked, that made him twist his features unknowingly. But hard there in the centre of his chest was himself, himself, firm, and not to be plucked to pieces.

The Captain had gone up into the wood. The orderly plodded through the hot, powerfully smelling zone of the company's atmosphere. He had a curious mass of energy inside him now. The Captain was less real than himself. He approached the green entrance to the wood. There, in the half-shade, he saw the horse standing, the sunshine and the flickering shadow of leaves dancing over his brown body. There was a clearing where timber had lately been felled. Here, in the gold-green shade beside the brilliant cup of sunshine, stood two figures, blue and pink, the bits of pink showing out plainly. The Captain was talking to his lieutenant.

The orderly stood on the edge of the bright clearing, where great trunks of trees, stripped and glistening, lay stretched like naked, brown-skinned bodies. Chips of wood littered the trampled floor, like splashed light, and the bases of the felled trees stood here and there, with their raw, level tops. Beyond was the brilliant, sunlit green of a beech.

"Then I will ride forward," the orderly heard his Captain say. The lieutenant saluted and strode away. He himself went forward. A hot flash passed through his belly, as he tramped towards his officer.

The Captain watched the rather heavy figure of the young soldier stumble forward, and his veins, too, ran hot. This was to be man to man between them. He yielded before the solid, stumbling figure with bent head. The orderly stooped and put the food on a level-sawn tree-base. The Captain watched the glistening, sun-inflamed, naked hands. He wanted to speak to the young soldier but could not. The servant propped a bottle against his thigh, pressed open the cork, and poured out the beer into the mug. He kept his head bent. The Captain accepted the mug.

"Hot!" he said, as if amiably.

The flame sprang out of the orderly's heart, nearly suffocating him.

"Yes, sir," he replied, between shut teeth.

And he heard the sound of the Captain's drinking, and he clenched his fists, such a strong torment came into his wrists. Then came the faint clang of the closing of the pot-lid. He looked up. The Captain was watching him. He glanced swiftly away. Then he saw the officer stoop and take a piece of bread from the tree-base. Again the flash of flame went through the young soldier, seeing the stiff body stoop beneath him, and his hands jerked. He looked away. He could feel the officer was nervous. The bread fell as it was being broken. The officer ate the other piece. The two men stood tense and still, the master laboriously chewing his bread, the serv- ant staring with averted face, his fist clenched.

Then the young soldier started. The officer had pressed open the lid of the mug again. The orderly watched the lid of the mug, and the white hand that clenched the handle, as if he were fascinated. It was raised. The youth followed it with his eyes. And then he saw the thin, strong throat of the elder man moving up and down as he drank, the strong jaw working. And the instinct which had been jerking at the young man's wrists suddenly jerked free. He jumped, feeling as if it were rent in two by a strong flame.

The spur of the officer caught in a tree-root, he went down backwards with a crash, the middle of his back thudding sickeningly against a sharp-edged tree-base, the pot flying away. And in a second the orderly, with serious, earnest young face, and underlip between his teeth, had got his knee in the officer's chest and was pressing the chin backward over the farther edge of the tree-stump, pressing, with all his heart behind in a pas- sion of relief, the tension of his wrists exquisite with re- lief. And with the base of his palms he shoved at the chin, with all his might. And it was pleasant, too, to have that chin, that hard jaw already slightly rough with beard, in his hands. He did not relax one hair's breadth, but, all the force of all his blood exulting in his thrust, he shoved back the head of the other man, till there was a little "cluck" and a crunching sensation. Then he felt as if his head went to vapour. Heavy convulsions shook the body of the officer, frightening and horrifying the young soldier. Yet it pleased him, too, to repress them. It pleased him to keep his hands pressing back the chin, to feel the chest of the other man yield in expiration to the weight of his strong, young knees, to feel the hard twitchings of the prostrate body jerking his own whole frame, which was pressed down on it.

But it went still. He could look into the nostrils of the other man, the eyes he could scarcely see. How curiously the mouth was pushed out, exaggerating the full lips, and the moustache bristling up from them. Then, with a start, he noticed the nostrils gradually filled with blood. The red brimmed, hesitated, ran over, and went in a thin trickle down the face to the eyes.

It shocked and distressed him. Slowly, he got up. The body twitched and sprawled there, inert. He stood and looked at it in silence. It was a pity *it* was broken. It represented more than the thing which had kicked and bullied him. He was afraid to look at the eyes. They were hideous now, only the whites showing, and the blood running to them. The face of the orderly was drawn with horror at the sight. Well, it was so. In his heart he was satisfied. He had hated the face of the Captain. It was extinguished now. There was a heavy relief in the orderly's soul. That was as it should be. But he could not bear to see the long, military body lying broken over the tree-base, the fine fingers crisped. He wanted to hide it away.

Quickly, busily, he gathered it up and pushed it under the felled tree-trunks, which rested their beautiful, smooth length either end on logs. The face was horrible with blood. He covered it with the helmet. Then he pushed the limbs straight and decent, and brushed the dead leaves off the fine cloth of the uniform. So, it lay quite still in the shadow under there. A little strip of sunshine ran along the breast, from a chink between the logs. The orderly sat by it for a few moments. Here his own life also ended.

Then, through his daze, he heard the lieutenant, in a loud voice, explaining to the men outside the wood, that they were to suppose the bridge on the river below was held by the enemy. Now they were to march to the attack in such and such a manner. The lieutenant had no gift of expression. The orderly, listening from habit, got muddled. And when the lieutenant began it all again he ceased to hear.

He knew he must go. He stood up. It surprised him that the leaves were glittering in the sun, and the chips of wood reflecting white from the ground. For him a change had come over the world. But for the rest it had not—all seemed the same. Only he had left it. And he could not go back. It was his duty to return with the beer-pot and the bottle. He could not. He had left all that. The lieutenant was still hoarsely explaining. He must go, or they would overtake him. And he could not bear contact with anyone now.

He drew his fingers over his eyes, trying to find out where he was. Then he turned away. He saw the horse standing in the path. He went up to it and mounted. It hurt him to sit in the saddle. The pain of keeping his seat occupied him as they cantered through the wood. He would not have minded anything, but he could not get away from the sense of being divided from the others. The path led out of the trees. On the edge of the wood he pulled up and stood watching. There in the spacious sunshine of the valley soldiers were moving in a little swarm. Every now and then, a man harrowing on a strip of fallow shouted to his oxen, at the turn. The

village and the white-towered church was small in the
sunshine. And he no longer belonged to it—he sat there,
beyond, like a man outside in the dark. He had gone out
from everyday life into the unknown, and he could not,
he even did not want to go back.

Turning from the sun-blazing valley, he rode deep
into the wood. Tree-trunks, like people standing grey
and still, took no notice as he went. A doe, herself a moving bit of sunshine and shadow, went running through
the flecked shade. There were bright green rents in the
foliage. Then it was all pine wood, dark and cool. And
he was sick with pain, he had an intolerable great pulse
in his head, and he was sick. He had never been ill in
his life. He felt lost, quite dazed with all this.

Trying to get down from the horse, he fell, astonished
at the pain and his lack of balance. The horse shifted uneasily. He jerked its bridle and sent it cantering jerkily
away. It was his last connection with the rest of things.

But he only wanted to lie down and not be disturbed.
Stumbling through the trees, he came on a quiet place
where beeches and pine trees grew on a slope. Immediately he had lain down and closed his eyes, his consciousness went racing on without him. A big pulse of
sickness beat in him as if it throbbed through the whole
earth. He was burning with dry heat. But he was too
busy, too tearingly active in the incoherent race of delirium to observe.

III

He came to with a start. His mouth was dry and hard,
his heart beat heavily, but he had not the energy to get
up. His heart beat heavily. Where was he?—the barracks—at home? There was something knocking. And,
making an effort, he looked round—trees, and litter of

greenery, and reddish, bright, still pieces of sunshine on
the floor. He did not believe he was himself, he did not
believe what he saw. Something was knocking. He made
a struggle towards consciousness, but relapsed. Then he
struggled again. And gradually his surroundings fell into
relationship with himself. He knew, and a great pang of
fear went through his heart. Somebody was knocking.
He could see the heavy, black rags of a fir tree overhead. Then everything went black. Yet he did not believe he had closed his eyes. He had not. Out of the
blackness sight slowly emerged again. And someone was
knocking. Quickly, he saw the blood-disfigured face of
his Captain, which he hated. And he held himself still
with horror. Yet, deep inside him, he knew that it was
so, the Captain should be dead. But the physical delirium got hold of him. Someone was knocking. He lay
perfectly still, as if dead, with fear. And he went unconscious.

When he opened his eyes again, he started, seeing
something creeping swiftly up a tree-trunk. It was a little
bird. And the bird was whistling overhead. Tap-tap-tap
—it was the small, quick bird rapping the tree-trunk
with its beak, as if its head were a little round hammer.
He watched it curiously. It shifted sharply, in its creeping fashion. Then, like a mouse, it slid down the bare
trunk. Its swift creeping sent a flash of revulsion through
him. He raised his head. It felt a great weight. Then,
the little bird ran out of the shadow across a still patch
of sunshine, its little head bobbing swiftly, its white legs
twinkling brightly for a moment. How neat it was in its
build, so compact, with pieces of white on its wings.
There were several of them. They were so pretty—but
they crept like swift, erratic mice, running here and
there among the beech-mast.

He lay down again exhausted, and his consciousness

lapsed. He had a horror of the little creeping birds. All his blood seemed to be darting and creeping in his head. And yet he could not move.

He came to with a further ache of exhaustion. There was the pain in his head, and the horrible sickness, and his inability to move. He had never been ill in his life. He did not know where he was or what he was. Probably he had got sunstroke. Or what else?—he had silenced the Captain for ever—some time ago—oh, a long time ago. There had been blood on his face, and his eyes had turned upwards. It was all right, somehow. It was peace. But now he had got beyond himself. He had never been here before. Was it life, or not life? He was by himself. They were in a big, bright place, those others, and he was outside. The town, all the country, a big bright place of light: and he was outside, here, in the darkened open beyond, where each thing existed alone. But they would all have to come out there sometime, those others. Little, and left behind him, they all were. There had been father and mother and sweetheart. What did they all matter? This was the open land.

He sat up. Something scuffled. It was a little brown squirrel running in lovely, undulating bounds over the floor, its red tail completing the undulation of its body —and then, as it sat up, furling and unfurling. He watched it, pleased. It ran on again, friskily, enjoying itself. It flew wildly at another squirrel, and they were chasing each other, and making little scolding, chattering noises. The soldier wanted to speak to them. But only a hoarse sound came out of his throat. The squirrels burst away—they flew up the trees. And then he saw the one peeping round at him, half-way up a tree-trunk. A start of fear went through him, though, in so far as he was conscious, he was amused. It still stayed, its little, keen face staring at him half-way up the tree-trunk, its little ears pricked up, its clawey little hands clinging to the bark, its white breast reared. He started from it in panic.

Struggling to his feet, he lurched away. He went on walking, walking, looking for something—for a drink. His brain felt hot and inflamed for want of water. He stumbled on. Then he did not know anything. He went unconscious as he walked. Yet he stumbled on, his mouth open.

When, to his dumb wonder, he opened his eyes on the world again, he no longer tried to remember what it was. There was thick, golden light behind golden-green glitterings, and tall, grey-purple shafts, and darknesses further off, surrounding him, growing deeper. He was conscious of a sense of arrival. He was amid the reality, on the real, dark bottom. But there was the thirst burning in his brain. He felt lighter, not so heavy. He supposed it was newness. The air was muttering with thunder. He thought he was walking wonderfully swiftly and was coming straight to relief—or was it to water?

Suddenly he stood still with fear. There was a tremendous flare of gold, immense—just a few dark trunks like bars between him and it. All the young level wheat was burnished gold glaring on its silky green. A woman, full-skirted, a black cloth on her head for head-dress, was passing like a block of shadow through the glistening green corn, into the full glare. There was a farm, too, pale blue in shadow, and the timber black. And there was a church spire, nearly fused away in the gold. The woman moved on, away from him. He had no language with which to speak to her. She was the bright, solid unreality. She would make a noise of words that would confuse him, and her eyes would look at him without seeing him. She was crossing there to the other side. He stood against a tree.

When at last he turned, looking down the long, bare grove whose flat bed was already filling dark, he saw the mountains in a wonder-light, not far away, and radiant. Behind the soft, grey ridge of the nearest range the further mountains stood golden and pale grey, the snow all radiant like pure, soft gold. So still, gleaming in the sky, fashioned pure out of the ore of the sky, they shone in their silence. He stood and looked at them, his face illuminated. And like the golden, lustrous gleaming of the snow he felt his own thirst bright in him. He stood and gazed, leaning against a tree. And then everything slid away into space.

During the night the lightning fluttered perpetually, making the whole sky white. He must have walked again. The world hung livid round him for moments, fields a level sheen of grey-green light, trees in dark bulk, and the range of clouds black across a white sky. Then the darkness fell like a shutter, and the night was whole. A faint flutter of a half-revealed world, that could not quite leap out of the darkness!—Then there again stood a sweep of pallor for the land, dark shapes looming, a range of clouds hanging overhead. The world was a ghostly shadow, thrown for a moment upon the pure darkness, which returned ever whole and complete.

And the mere delirium of sickness and fever went on inside him—his brain opening and shutting like the night—then sometimes convulsions of terror from something with great eyes that stared round a tree—then the long agony of the march, and the sun decomposing his blood—then the pang of hate for the Captain, followed by a pang of tenderness and ease. But everything was distorted, born of an ache and resolving into an ache.

In the morning he came definitely awake. Then his brain flamed with the sole horror of thirstiness! The sun was on his face, the dew was steaming from his wet clothes. Like one possessed, he got up. There, straight in front of him, blue and cool and tender, the mountains ranged across the pale edge of the morning sky. He wanted them—he wanted them alone—he wanted to leave himself and be identified with them. They did not move, they were still and soft, with white, gentle markings of snow. He stood still, mad with suffering, his hands crisping and clutching. Then he was twisting in a paroxysm on the grass.

He lay still, in a kind of dream of anguish. His thirst seemed to have separated itself from him, and to stand apart, a single demand. Then the pain he felt was another single self. Then there was the clog of his body, another separate thing. He was divided among all kinds of separate beings. There was some strange, agonized connection between them, but they were drawing further apart. Then they would all split. The sun, drilling down on him, was drilling through the bond. Then they would all fall, fall through the everlasting lapse of space. Then again, his consciousness reasserted itself. He roused on to his elbow and stared at the gleaming mountains. There they ranked, all still and wonderful between earth and heaven. He stared till his eyes went black, and the mountains, as they stood in their beauty, so clean and cool, seemed to have it, that which was lost in him.

IV

When the soldiers found him, three hours later, he was lying with his face over his arm, his black hair giving off heat under the sun. But he was still alive. Seeing the open, black mouth, the young soldiers dropped him in horror.

He died in the hospital at night, without having seen again.

The doctors saw the bruises on his legs, behind, and were silent.

The bodies of the two men lay together, side by side, in the mortuary, the one white and slender, but laid rigidly at rest, the other looking as if every moment it must rouse into life again, so young and unused, from a slumber.

Tickets, Please

THERE is in the Midlands a single-line tramway system which boldly leaves the county town and plunges off into the black, industrial countryside, up hill and down dale, through the long, ugly villages of workmen's houses, over canals and railways, past churches perched high and nobly over the smoke and shadows through stark, grimy, cold little market-places, tilting away in a rush past cinemas and shops down to the hollow where the collieries are, then up again, past a little rural church, under the ash trees, on in a rush to the terminus, the last little ugly place of industry, the cold little town that shivers on the edge of the wild, gloomy country beyond. There the green and creamy coloured tram-car seems to pause and purr with curious satisfaction. But in a few minutes—the clock on the turret of the Co-operative Wholesale Society's Shops gives the time—away it starts once more on the adventure. Again there are the reckless swoops downhill, bouncing the loops: again the chilly wait in the hill-top market-place: again the breathless slithering round the precipitous drop under the church: again the patient halts at the loops, waiting for the outcoming car: so on and on, for two long hours, till at last the city looms beyond the fat gas-works, the narrow factories draw near, we are in the sordid streets of the great town, once more we sidle to a standstill at our terminus, abashed by the great crimson and cream-coloured city cars, but still perky, jaunty, somewhat dare-devil, green as a jaunty sprig of parsley out of a black colliery garden.

To ride on these cars is always an adventure. Since we are in war-time, the drivers are men unfit for active service: cripples and hunchbacks. So they have the spirit of the devil in them. The ride becomes a steeple-chase. Hurray! we have leapt in a clear jump over the canal bridges —now for the four-lane corner. With a shriek and a trail of sparks we are clear again. To be sure, a tram often leaps the rails—but what matter! It sits in a ditch till other trams come to haul it out. It is quite common for a car, packed with one solid mass of living people, to come to a dead halt in the midst of unbroken blackness, the heart of nowhere on a dark night, and for the driver and the girl conductor to call, "All get off—car's on fire!" Instead, however, of rushing out in a panic, the passengers stolidly reply: "Get on—get on! We're not coming out. We're stopping where we are. Push on, George." So till flames actually appear.

The reason for this reluctance to dismount is that the nights are howlingly cold, black, and windswept, and a car is a haven of refuge. From village to village the miners travel, for a change of cinema, of girl, of pub. The trams are desperately packed Who is going to risk himself in the black gulf outside, to wait perhaps an hour for another tram, then to see the forlorn notice "Depot Only," because there is something wrong! or to greet a unit of three bright cars all so tight with people that they sail past with a howl of derision. Trams that pass in the night.

This, the most dangerous tram-service in England, as

the authorities themselves declare, with pride, is entirely
conducted by girls, and driven by rash young men, a
little crippled, or by delicate young men, who creep forward in terror. The girls are fearless young hussies. In
their ugly blue uniform, skirts up to their knees, shape-
less old peaked caps on their heads, they have all the
sang-froid of an old non-commissioned officer. With a
tram packed with howling colliers, roaring hymns downstairs and a sort of antiphony of obscenities upstairs, the
lasses are perfectly at their ease. They pounce on the
youths who try to evade their ticket-machine. They push
off the men at the end of their distance. They are not
going to be done in the eye—not they. They fear nobody—and everybody fears them.

"Hello, Annie!"

"Hello, Ted!"

"Oh, mind my corn, Miss Stone. It's my belief you've
got a heart of stone, for you've trod on it again."

"You should keep it in your pocket," replies Miss
Stone, and she goes sturdily upstairs in her high boots.

"Tickets, please."

She is peremptory, suspicious, and ready to hit first.
She can hold her own against ten thousand. The step of
that tram-car is her Thermopylæ.

Therefore, there is a certain wild romance aboard
these cars—and in the sturdy bosom of Annie herself.
The time for soft romance is in the morning, between
ten o'clock and one, when things are rather slack: that
is, except market-day and Saturday. Thus Annie has
time to look about her. Then she often hops off her car
and into a shop where she has spied something, while
the driver chats in the main road. There is very good
feeling between the girls and the drivers. Are they not
companions in peril, shipments aboard this careering

vessel of a tram-car, for ever rocking on the waves of a stormy land.

Then, also, during the easy hours, the inspectors are most in evidence. For some reason, everybody employed in this tram-service is young: there are no grey heads. It would not do. Therefore the inspectors are of the right age, and one, the chief, is also good-looking. See him stand on a wet, gloomy morning, in his long oilskin, his peaked cap well down over his eyes, waiting to board a car. His face is ruddy, his small brown moustache is weathered, he has a faint impudent smile. Fairly tall and agile, even in his waterproof, he springs aboard a car and greets Annie.

"Hello, Annie! Keeping the wet out?"

"Trying to."

There are only two people in the car. Inspecting is soon over. Then for a long and impudent chat on the footboard, a good, easy, twelve-mile chat.

The inspector's name is John Thomas Raynor—always called John Thomas, except sometimes, in malice, Coddy. His face sets in fury when he is addressed, from a distance, with this abbreviation. There is considerable scandal about John Thomas in half a dozen villages. He flirts with the girl conductors in the morning and walks out with them in the dark night, when they leave their tram-car at the depot. Of course, the girls quit the service frequently. Then he flirts and walks out with the newcomer: always providing she is sufficiently attractive, and that she will consent to walk. It is remarkable, however, that most of the girls are quite comely, they are all young, and this roving life aboard the car gives them a sailor's dash and recklessness. What matter how they behave when the ship is in port. Tomorrow they will be aboard again.

Annie, however, was something of a Tartar, and her sharp tongue had kept John Thomas at arm's length for many months. Perhaps, therefore, she liked him all the more: for he always came up smiling, with impudence. She watched him vanquish one girl, then another. She could tell by the movement of his mouth and eyes, when he flirted with her in the morning, that he had been walking out with this lass, or the other, the night before. A fine cock-of-the-walk he was. She could sum him up pretty well.

In this subtle antagonism they knew each other like old friends, they were as shrewd with one another almost as man and wife. But Annie had always kept him sufficiently at arm's length. Besides, she had a boy of her own.

The Statutes fair, however, came in November, at Bestwood. It happened that Annie had the Monday night off. It was a drizzling ugly night, yet she dressed herself up and went to the fair ground. She was alone, but she expected soon to find a pal of some sort.

The roundabouts were veering round and grinding out their music, the side shows were making as much commotion as possible. In the cocoanut shies there were no cocoanuts, but artificial war-time substitutes, which the lads declared were fastened into the irons. There was a sad decline in brilliance and luxury. None the less, the ground was muddy as ever, there was the same crush, the press of faces lighted up by the flares and the electric lights, the same smell of naphtha and a few fried potatoes, and of electricity.

Who should be the first to greet Miss Annie, on the show ground, but John Thomas. He had a black overcoat buttoned up to his chin, and a tweed cap pulled down over his brows, his face between was ruddy and smiling and handy as ever. She knew so well the way his mouth moved.

She was very glad to have a "boy." To be at the Statutes without a fellow was no fun. Instantly, like the gallant he was, he took her on the Dragons, grim-toothed, roundabout switchbacks. It was not nearly so exciting as a tram-car actually. But, then, to be seated in a shaking green dragon, uplifted above the sea of bubble faces, careering in a rickety fashion in the lower heavens, whilst John Thomas leaned over her, his cigarette in his mouth, was after all the right style. She was a plump, quick, alive little creature. So she was quite excited and happy.

John Thomas made her stay on for the next round. And therefore she could hardly for shame repulse him when he put his arm round her and drew her a little nearer to him, in a very warm and cuddly manner. Besides, he was fairly discreet, he kept his movement as hidden as possible. She looked down and saw that his red, clean hand was out of sight of the crowd. And they knew each other so well. So they warmed up to the fair.

After the dragons they went on the horses. John Thomas paid each time, so she could but be complaisant. He, of course, sat astride on the outer horse—named "Black Bess"—and she sat sideways, towards him, on the inner horse—named "Wildfire." But of course John Thomas was not going to sit discreetly on "Black Bess," holding the brass bar. Round they spun and heaved, in the light. And round he swung on his wooden steed, flinging one leg across her mount, and perilously tipping up and down, across the space, half lying back, laughing at her. He was perfectly happy; she was afraid her hat was on one side, but she was excited.

He threw quoits on a table and won for her two large,

pale-blue hat-pins. And then, hearing the noise of the cinemas, announcing another performance, they climbed the boards and went in.

Of course, during these performances pitch darkness falls from time to time, when the machine goes wrong. Then there is a wild whooping, and a loud smacking of simulated kisses. In these moments John Thomas drew Annie towards him. After all, he had a wonderfully warm, cosy way of holding a girl with his arm, he seemed to make such a nice fit. And after all, it was pleasant to be so held: so very comforting and cosy and nice. He leaned over her and she felt his breath on her hair; she knew he wanted to kiss her on the lips. And after all, he was so warm and she fitted in to him so softly. After all, she wanted him to touch her lips.

But the light sprang up; she also started electrically, and put her hat straight. He left his arm lying non-chalantly behind her. Well, it was fun, it was exciting to be at the Statutes with John Thomas.

When the cinema was over they went for a walk across the dark, damp fields. He had all the arts of love-making. He was especially good at holding a girl, when he sat with her on a stile in the black, drizzling dark-ness. He seemed to be holding her in space, against his own warmth and gratification. And his kisses were soft and slow and searching.

So Annie walked out with John Thomas, though she kept her own boy dangling in the distance. Some of the tram-girls chose to be huffy. But there, you must take things as you find them, in this life.

There was no mistake about it, Annie liked John Thomas a good deal. She felt so rich and warm in herself wherever he was near. And John Thomas really liked Annie more than usual. The soft, melting way in which she could flow into a fellow, as if she melted into his very

bones, was something rare and good. He fully appreci-
ated this.

But with a developing acquaintance there began a developing intimacy. Annie wanted to consider him a person, a man; she wanted to take an intelligent interest in
him, and to have an intelligent response. She did not
want a mere nocturnal presence, which was what he was
so far. And she prided herself that he could not leave
her.

Here she made a mistake. John Thomas intended to
remain a nocturnal presence; he had no idea of becoming an all-round individual to her. When she started to
take an intelligent interest in him and his life and his
character, he sheered off. He hated intelligent interest.
And he knew that the only way to stop it was to avoid
it. The possessive female was aroused in Annie. So he
left her.

It is no use saying she was not surprised. She was at
first startled, thrown out of her count. For she had been
so *very* sure of holding him. For a while she was stag-
gered, and everything became uncertain to her. Then
she wept with fury, indignation, desolation, and misery.
Then she had a spasm of despair. And then, when he
came, still impudently, on to her car, still familiar, but
letting her see by the movement of his head that he had
gone away to somebody else for the time being and was
enjoying pastures new, then she determined to have her
own back.

She had a very shrewd idea what girls John Thomas
had taken out. She went to Nora Purdy. Nora was a tall,
rather pale, but well-built girl, with beautiful yellow
hair. She was rather secretive.

"Hey!" said Annie, accosting her; then softly, "Who's
John Thomas on with now?"

"I don't know," said Nora.

"Why tha does," said Annie, ironically lapsing into dialect. "Tha knows as well as I do."

"Well, I do, then," said Nora. "It isn't me, so don't bother."

"It's Cissy Meakin, isn't it?"

"It is, for all I know."

"Hasn't he got a face on him!" said Annie. "I don't half like his cheek. I could knock him off the footboard when he comes round at me."

"He'll get dropped-on one of these days," said Nora.

"Ay, he will when somebody makes up their mind to drop it on him. I should like to see him taken down a peg or two, shouldn't you?"

"I shouldn't mind," said Nora.

"You've got quite as much cause to as I have," said Annie. "But we'll drop on him one of these days, my girl. What? Don't you want to?"

"I don't mind," said Nora.

But as a matter of fact, Nora was much more vindictive than Annie.

One by one Annie went the round of the old flames. It so happened that Cissy Meakin left the tramway service in quite a short time. Her mother made her leave. Then John Thomas was on the qui-vive. He cast his eyes over his old flock. And his eyes lighted on Annie. He thought she would be safe now. Besides, he liked her.

She arranged to walk home with him on Sunday night. It so happened that her car would be in the depot at half-past nine: the last car would come in at ten-fifteen. So John Thomas was to wait for her there.

At the depot the girls had a little waiting-room of their own. It was quite rough, but cosy, with a fire and an oven and a mirror, and table and wooden chairs. The half dozen girls who knew John Thomas only too well had arranged to take service this Sunday afternoon. So, as the cars began to come in, early, the girls dropped into the waiting-room. And instead of hurrying off home, they sat around the fire and had a cup of tea. Outside was the darkness and lawlessness of war-time.

John Thomas came on the car after Annie, at about a quarter to ten. He poked his head easily into the girls' waiting-room.

"Prayer-meeting?" he asked.

"Ay," said Laura Sharp. "Ladies only."

"That's me!" said John Thomas. It was one of his favourite exclamations.

"Shut the door, boy," said Muriel Baggaley.

"On which side of me?" said John Thomas.

"Which tha likes," said Polly Birkin.

He had come in and closed the door behind him. The girls moved in their circle, to make a place for him near the fire. He took off his great-coat and pushed back his hat.

"Who handles the teapot?" he said.

Nora Purdy silently poured him out a cup of tea.

"Want a bit o' my bread and drippin'?" said Muriel Baggaley to him.

"Ay, give us a bit."

And he began to eat his piece of bread.

"There's no place like home, girls," he said.

They all looked at him as he uttered this piece of impudence. He seemed to be sunning himself in the presence of so many damsels.

"Especially if you're not afraid to go home in the dark," said Laura Sharp.

"Me! By myself I am."

They sat till they heard the last tram come in. In a few minutes Emma Houselay entered.

"Come on, my old duck!" cried Polly Birkin.

"It *is* perishing," said Emma, holding her fingers to the fire.

"But—I'm afraid to, go home in, the dark," sang Laura Sharp, the tune having got into her mind.

"Who're you going with tonight, John Thomas?" asked Muriel Baggaley, coolly.

"Tonight?" said John Thomas. "Oh, I'm going home by myself tonight—all on my lonely-O."

"That's me!" said Nora Purdy, using his own ejaculation.

The girls laughed shrilly.

"Me as well, Nora," said John Thomas.

"Don't know what you mean," said Laura.

"Yes, I'm toddling," said he, rising and reaching for his overcoat.

"Nay," said Polly. "We're all here waiting for you."

"We've got to be up in good time in the morning," he said in the benevolent official manner.

They all laughed.

"Nay," said Muriel. "Don't leave us all lonely, John Thomas. Take one!"

"I'll take the lot, if you like," he responded gallantly.

"That you won't, either," said Muriel. "Two's company; seven's too much of a good thing."

"Nay—take one," said Laura. "Fair and square, all above board, and say which."

"Ay," cried Annie, speaking for the first time. "Pick, John Thomas; let's hear thee."

"Nay," he said. "I'm going home quiet tonight. Feeling good, for once."

"Whereabouts?" said Annie. "Take a good un, then. But tha's got to take one of us!"

"Nay, how can I take one," he said, laughing uneasily. "I don't want to make enemies."

"You'd only make *one*," said Annie.

"The chosen *one*," added Laura.

"Oh, my! Who said girls!" exclaimed John Thomas, again turning, as if to escape. "Well—good-night."

"Nay, you've got to make your pick," said Muriel. "Turn your face to the wall and say which one touches you. Go on—we shall only just touch your back—one of us. Go on—turn your face to the wall, and don't look, and say which one touches you."

He was uneasy, mistrusting them. Yet he had not the courage to break away. They pushed him to a wall and stood him there with his face to it. Behind his back they all grimaced, tittering. He looked so comical. He looked around uneasily.

"Go on!" he cried.

"You're looking—you're looking!" they shouted.

He turned his head away. And suddenly, with a movement like a swift cat, Annie went forward and fetched him a box on the side of the head that set his cap flying, and himself staggering. He started round.

But at Annie's signal they all flew at him, slapping him, pinching him, pulling his hair, though more in fun than in spite or anger. He, however, saw red. His blue eyes flamed with strange fear as well as fury, and he butted through the girls to the door. It was locked. He wrenched at it. Roused, alert, the girls stood round and looked at him. He faced them, at bay. At that moment they were rather horrifying to him, as they stood in their short uniforms. He was distinctly afraid.

"Come on, John Thomas! Come on! Choose!" said Annie.

"What are you after? Open the door," he said.

"We sha'n't—not till you've chosen!" said Muriel.

"Chosen what?" he said.

"Chosen the one you're going to marry," she replied.

He hesitated a moment.

"Open the blasted door," he said, "and get back to your senses." He spoke with official authority.

"You've got to choose!" cried the girls.

"Come on!" cried Annie, looking him in the eye. "Come on! Come on!"

He went forward, rather vaguely. She had taken off her belt, and swinging it, she fetched him a sharp blow over the head with the buckle end. He sprang and seized her. But immediately the other girls rushed upon him, pulling and tearing and beating him. Their blood was now thoroughly up. He was their sport now. They were going to have their own back, out of him. Strange, wild creatures, they hung on him and rushed at him to bear him down. His tunic was torn right up the back, Nora had hold at the back of his collar, and was actually strangling him. Luckily the button burst. He struggled in a wild frenzy of fury and terror, almost mad terror. His tunic was simply torn off his back, his shirt-sleeves were torn away, his arms were naked. The girls rushed at him, clenched their hands on him and pulled at him: or they rushed at him and pushed him, butted him with all their might: or they struck him wild blows. He ducked and cringed and struck sideways. They became more intense.

At last he was down. They rushed on him, kneeling on him. He had neither breath nor strength to move. His face was bleeding with a long scratch, his brow was bruised.

Annie knelt on him, the other girls knelt and hung on to him. Their faces were flushed, their hair wild, their eyes were all glittering strangely. He lay at last quite still, with face averted, as an animal lies when it is defeated and at the mercy of the captor. Sometimes his

eye glanced back at the wild faces of the girls. His breast
rose heavily, his wrists were torn.

"Now, then, my fellow!" gasped Annie at length.
"Now then—now——"

At the sound of her terrifying, cold triumph, he suddenly started to struggle as an animal might, but the
girls threw themselves upon him with unnatural strength
and power, forcing him down.

"Yes—now, then!" gasped Annie at length.

And there was a dead silence, in which the thud of
heart-beating was to be heard. It was a suspense of pure
silence in every soul.

"Now you know where you are," said Annie.

The sight of his white, bare arm maddened the girls.
He lay in a kind of trance of fear and antagonism. They
felt themselves filled with supernatural strength.

Suddenly Polly started to laugh—to giggle wildly—
helplessly—and Emma and Muriel joined in. But Annie
and Nora and Laura remained the same, tense, watchful, with gleaming eyes. He winced away from these
eyes.

"Yes," said Annie, in a curious low tone, secret and
deadly. "Yes! You've got it now! You know what you've
done, don't you? You know what you've done."

He made no sound nor sign, but lay with bright,
averted eyes, and averted, bleeding face.

"You ought to be *killed*, that's what you ought," said
Annie tensely. "You ought to be *killed*." And there was
a terrifying lust in her voice.

Polly was ceasing to laugh, and giving long-drawn
oh-h-hs and sighs as she came to herself.

"He's got to choose," she said vaguely.

"Oh, yes, he has," said Laura, with vindictive decision.

"Do you hear—do you hear?" said Annie. And with a sharp movement that made him wince, she turned his face to her.

"Do you hear?" she repeated, shaking him.

But he was quite dumb. She fetched him a sharp slap on the face. He started, and his eyes widened. Then his face darkened with defiance, after all.

"Do you hear?" she repeated.

He only looked at her with hostile eyes.

"Speak!" she said, putting her face devilishly near his.

"What?" he said, almost overcome.

"You've got to *choose!*" she cried, as if it were some terrible menace, and as if it hurt her that she could not exact more.

"What?" he said in fear.

"Choose your girl, Coddy. You've got to choose her now. And you'll get your neck broken if you play any more of your tricks, my boy. You're settled now."

There was a pause. Again he averted his face. He was cunning in his overthrow. He did not give in to them really—no, not if they tore him to bits.

"All right, then," he said, "I choose Annie." His voice was strange and full of malice. Annie let go of him as if he had been a hot coal.

"He's chosen Annie!" said the girls in chorus.

"Me!" cried Annie. She was still kneeling, but away from him. He was still lying prostrate, with averted face. The girls grouped uneasily around.

"Me!" repeated Annie, with a terrible bitter accent.

Then she got up, drawing away from him with strange disgust and bitterness.

"I wouldn't touch him," she said.

But her face quivered with a kind of agony, she seemed as if she would fall. The other girls turned aside.

He remained lying on the floor, with his torn clothes and bleeding, averted face.

"Oh, if he's chosen——" said Polly.

"I don't want him—he can choose again," said Annie, with the same rather bitter hopelessness.

"Get up," said Polly, lifting his shoulder. "Get up."

He rose slowly, a strange, ragged, dazed creature. The girls eyed him from a distance, curiously, furtively, dangerously.

"Who wants him?" cried Laura roughly.

"Nobody," they answered with contempt. Yet each one of them waited for him to look at her, hoped he would look at her. All except Annie, and something was broken in her.

He, however, kept his face closed and averted from them all. There was a silence of the end. He picked up the torn pieces of his tunic, without knowing what to do with them. The girls stood about uneasily, flushed, panting, tidying their hair and their dress unconsciously, and watching him. He looked at none of them. He espied his cap in a corner and went and picked it up. He put it on his head, and one of the girls burst into a shrill, hysteric laugh at the sight he presented. He, however, took no heed but went straight to where his overcoat hung on a peg. The girls moved away from contact with him as if he had been an electric wire. He put on his coat and buttoned it down. Then he rolled his tunic-rags into a bundle, and stood before the locked door, dumbly.

"Open the door, somebody," said Laura.

"Annie's got the key," said one.

Annie silently offered the key to the girls. Nora unlocked the door.

"Tit for tat, old man," she said. "Show yourself a man, and don't bear a grudge."

But without a word or sign he had opened the door and gone, his face closed, his head dropped.

"That'll learn him," said Laura.

"Coddy!" said Nora.

"Shut up, for God's sake!" cried Annie fiercely, as if in torture.

"Well, I'm about ready to go, Polly. Look sharp!" said Muriel.

The girls were all anxious to be off. They were tidying themselves hurriedly, with mute, stupefied faces.

The Blind Man

ISABEL PERVIN was listening for two sounds— for the sound of wheels on the drive outside and for the noise of her husband's footsteps in the hall. Her dearest and oldest friend, a man who seemed almost indispensable to her living, would drive up in the rainy dusk of the closing November day. The trap had gone to fetch him from the station. And her husband, who had been blinded in Flanders, and who had a disfiguring mark on his brow, would be coming in from the outhouses.

He had been home for a year now. He was totally blind. Yet they had been very happy. The Grange was Maurice's own place. The back was a farmstead, and the Wernhams, who occupied the rear premises, acted as farmers. Isabel lived with her husband in the handsome rooms in front. She and he had been almost entirely alone together since he was wounded. They talked and sang and read together in a wonderful and unspeakable intimacy. Then she reviewed books for a Scottish newspaper, carrying on her old interest, and he occupied himself a good deal with the farm. Sightless, he could still discuss everything with Wernham, and he could also do a good deal of work about the place—menial work, it is true, but it gave him satisfaction. He milked the cows, carried in the pails, turned the separator, attended to the pigs and horses. Life was still very full and strangely serene for the blind man, peaceful with the almost incomprehensible peace of immediate contact in darkness. With his wife he had a whole world, rich and real and invisible.

They were newly and remotely happy. He did not even regret the loss of his sight in these times of dark, palpable joy. A certain exultance swelled his soul.

But as time wore on, sometimes the rich glamour would leave them. Sometimes, after months of this intensity, a sense of burden overcame Isabel, a weariness, a terrible *ennui*, in that silent house approached between a colonnade of tall-shafted pines. Then she felt she would go mad, for she could not bear it. And sometimes he had devastating fits of depression, which seemed to lay waste his whole being. It was worse than depression —a black misery, when his own life was a torture to him, and when his presence was unbearable to his wife. The dread went down to the roots of her soul as these black days recurred. In a kind of panic she tried to wrap herself up still further in her husband. She forced the old spontaneous cheerfulness and joy to continue. But the effort it cost her was almost too much. She knew she could not keep it up. She felt she would scream with the strain, and would give anything, anything, to escape. She longed to possess her husband utterly; it gave her inordinate joy to have him entirely to herself. And yet, when again he was gone in a black and massive misery, she could not bear him, she could not bear herself; she wished she could be snatched away off the earth altogether, anything rather than live at this cost.

Dazed, she schemed for a way out. She invited friends, she tried to give him some further connection with the outer world. But it was no good. After all their joy and suffering, after their dark, great year of blindness and solitude and unspeakable nearness, other people seemed to them both shallow, rattling, rather impertinent. Shallow prattle seemed presumptuous. He became impatient and irritated, she was wearied. And so they lapsed into their solitude again. For they preferred it.

But now, in a few weeks' time, her second baby would be born. The first had died, an infant, when her husband first went out to France. She looked with joy and relief to the coming of the second. It would be her salvation. But also she felt some anxiety. She was thirty years old, her husband was a year younger. They both wanted the child very much. Yet she could not help feeling afraid. She had her husband on her hands, a terrible joy to her, and a terrifying burden. The child would occupy her love and attention. And then, what of Maurice? What would he do? If only she could feel that he, too, would be at peace and happy when the child came! She did so want to luxuriate in a rich, physical satisfaction of maternity. But the man, what would he do? How could she provide for him, how avert those shattering black moods of his, which destroyed them both?

She sighed with fear. But at this time Bertie Reid wrote to Isabel. He was her old friend, a second or third cousin, a Scotchman, as she was a Scotchwoman. They had been brought up near to one another, and all her life he had been her friend, like a brother, but better than her own brothers. She loved him—though not in the marrying sense. There was a sort of kinship between them, an affinity. They understood one another instinctively. But Isabel would never have thought of marrying Bertie. It would have seemed like marrying in her own family.

Bertie was a barrister and a man of letters, a Scotchman of the intellectual type, quick, ironical, sentimental, and on his knees before the woman he adored but did not want to marry. Maurice Pervin was different. He came of a good old country family—the Grange was not a very great distance from Oxford. He was passionate, sensitive, perhaps over-sensitive, wincing—a big fellow with heavy limbs and a forehead that flushed painfully. For his mind was slow, as if drugged by the strong provincial blood that beat in his veins. He was very sensitive to his own mental slowness, his feelings being quick and acute. So that he was just the opposite to Bertie, whose mind was much quicker than his emotions, which were not so very fine.

From the first the two men did not like each other. Isabel felt that they *ought* to get on together. But they did not. She felt that if only each could have the clue to the other there would be such a rare understanding between them. It did not come off, however. Bertie adopted a slightly ironical attitude, very offensive to Maurice, who returned the Scotch irony with English resentment, a resentment which deepened sometimes into stupid hatred.

This was a little puzzling to Isabel. However, she accepted it in the course of things. Men were made freakish and unreasonable. Therefore, when Maurice was going out to France for the second time, she felt that, for her husband's sake, she must discontinue her

friendship with Bertie. She wrote to the barrister to
this effect. Bertram Reid simply replied that in this, as
in all other matters, he must obey her wishes, if these
were indeed her wishes.

For nearly two years nothing had passed between the
two friends. Isabel rather gloried in the fact; she had no
compunction. She had one great article of faith, which
was, that husband and wife should be so important to
one another, that the rest of the world simply did not
count. She and Maurice were husband and wife. They
loved one another. They would have children. Then let
everybody and everything else fade into insignificance
outside this connubial felicity. She professed herself
quite happy and ready to receive Maurice's friends. She
was happy and ready: the happy wife, the ready woman
in possession. Without knowing why, the friends retired
abashed, and came no more. Maurice, of course, took as
much satisfaction in this connubial absorption as Isabel
did.

He shared in Isabel's literary activities, she cultivated
a real interest in agriculture and cattle-raising. For she,
being at heart perhaps an emotional enthusiast, always
cultivated the practical side of life and prided herself on
her mastery of practical affairs. Thus the husband and
wife had spent the five years of their married life. The
last had been one of blindness and unspeakable intimacy. And now Isabel felt a great indifference coming
over her, a sort of lethargy. She wanted to be allowed
to bear her child in peace, to nod by the fire and drift
vaguely, physically, from day to day. Maurice was like
an ominous thunder-cloud. She had to keep waking up
to remember him.

When a little note came from Bertie, asking if he were
to put up a tombstone to their dead friendship, and

speaking of the real pain he felt on account of her husband's loss of sight, she felt a pang, a fluttering agitation of re-awakening. And she read the letter to Maurice.

"Ask him to come down," he said.

"Ask Bertie to come here!" she re-echoed.

"Yes—if he wants to."

Isabel paused for a few moments.

"I know he wants to—he'd only be too glad," she replied. "But what about you, Maurice? How would you like it?"

"I should like it."

"Well—in that case—— But I thought you didn't care for him——"

"Oh, I don't know. I might think differently of him now," the blind man replied. It was rather abstruse to Isabel.

"Well, dear," she said, "if you're quite sure——"

"I'm sure enough. Let him come," said Maurice.

So Bertie was coming, coming this evening, in the November rain and darkness. Isabel was agitated, racked with her old restlessness and indecision. She had always suffered from this pain of doubt, just an agonizing sense of uncertainty. It had begun to pass off, in the lethargy of maternity. Now it returned, and she resented it. She struggled as usual to maintain her calm, composed, friendly bearing, a sort of mask she wore over all her body.

A woman had lighted a tall lamp beside the table and spread the cloth. The long dining-room was dim, with its elegant but rather severe pieces of old furniture. Only the round table glowed softly under the light. It had a rich, beautiful effect. The white cloth glistened and dropped its heavy, pointed lace corners almost to the carpet, the china was old and handsome, creamy-yellow, with a blotched pattern of harsh red and deep blue, the cups large and bell-shaped, the teapot gallant. Isabel looked at it with superficial appreciation.

Her nerves were hurting her. She looked automatically again at the high, uncurtained windows. In the last dusk she could just perceive outside a huge fir-tree swaying its boughs: it was as if she thought it rather than saw it. The rain came flying on the window panes. Ah, why had she no peace? These two men, why did they tear at her? Why did they not come—why was there this suspense?

She sat in a lassitude that was really suspense and irritation. Maurice, at least, might come in—there was nothing to keep him out. She rose to her feet. Catching sight of her reflection in a mirror, she glanced at herself with a slight smile of recognition, as if she were an old friend to herself. Her face was oval and calm, her nose a little arched. Her neck made a beautiful line down to her shoulder. With hair knotted loosely behind, she had something of a warm, maternal look. Thinking this of herself, she arched her eyebrows and her rather heavy eyelids, with a little flicker of a smile, and for a moment her grey eyes looked amused and wicked, a little sardonic, out of her transfigured Madonna face.

Then, resuming her air of womanly patience—she was really fatally self-determined—she went with a little jerk towards the door. Her eyes were slightly reddened.

She passed down the wide hall and through a door at the end. Then she was in the farm premises. The scent of dairy, and of farm-kitchen, and of farm-yard and of leather almost overcame her: but particularly the scent of dairy. They had been scalding out the pans. The flagged passage in front of her was dark, puddled, and wet. Light came out from the open kitchen door. She went forward and stood in the doorway. The farm-people were at tea, seated at a little distance from her, round a long, narrow table, in the centre of which stood a white lamp. Ruddy faces, ruddy hands holding food, red mouths working, heads bent over the tea-cups: men, land-girls, boys: it was tea-time, feeding-time. Some faces caught sight of her. Mrs. Wernham, going round behind the chairs with a large black teapot, halting slightly in her walk, was not aware of her for a moment. Then she turned suddenly.

"Oh, is it Madam!" she exclaimed. "Come in, then, come in! We're at tea." And she dragged forward a chair.

"No, I won't come in," said Isabel. "I'm afraid I interrupt your meal."

"No—no—not likely, Madam, not likely."

"Hasn't Mr. Pervin come in, do you know?"

"I'm sure I couldn't say! Missed him, have you, Madam?"

"No, I only wanted him to come in," laughed Isabel, as if shyly.

"Wanted him, did ye? Get up, boy—get up, now——"

Mrs. Wernham knocked one of the boys on the shoulder. He began to scrape to his feet, chewing largely.

"I believe he's in top stable," said another face from the table.

"Ah! No, don't get up. I'm going myself," said Isabel.

"Don't you go out of a dirty night like this. Let the lad go. Get along wi' ye, boy," said Mrs. Wernham.

"No, no," said Isabel, with a decision that was always obeyed. "Go on with your tea, Tom. I'd like to go across to the stable, Mrs. Wernham."

"Did ever you hear tell!" exclaimed the woman.

"Isn't the trap late?" asked Isabel.

"Why, no," said Mrs. Wernham, peering into the distance at the tall, dim clock. "No, Madam—we can give it another quarter or twenty minutes yet, good—yes, every bit of a quarter."

"Ah! It seems late when darkness falls so early," said Isabel.

"It do, that it do. Bother the days, that they draw in so," answered Mrs. Wernham. "Proper miserable!"

"They are," said Isabel, withdrawing.

She pulled on her overshoes, wrapped a large tartan shawl around her, put on a man's felt hat, and ventured out along the causeways of the first yard. It was very dark. The wind was roaring in the great elms behind the outhouses. When she came to the second yard the darkness seemed deeper. She was unsure of her footing. She wished she had brought a lantern. Rain blew against her. Half she liked it, half she felt unwilling to battle.

She reached at last the just visible door of the stable. There was no sign of a light anywhere. Opening the upper half, she looked in: into a simple well of darkness. The smell of horses, and ammonia, and of warmth was startling to her, in that full night. She listened with all her ears but could hear nothing save the night, and the stirring of a horse.

"Maurice!" she called, softly and musically, though she was afraid. "Maurice—are you there?"

Nothing came from the darkness. She knew the rain and wind blew in upon the horses, the hot animal life. Feeling it wrong, she entered the stable and drew the lower half of the door shut, holding the upper part close. She did not stir, because she was aware of the presence of the dark hind-quarters of the horses, though she could not see them, and she was afraid. Something wild stirred in her heart.

She listened intensely. Then she heard a small noise

in the distance—far away, it seemed—the chink of a pan, and a man's voice speaking a brief word. It would be Maurice, in the other part of the stable. She stood motionless, waiting for him to come through the partition door. The horses were so terrifyingly near to her, in the invisible.

The loud jarring of the inner door-latch made her start; the door was opened. She could hear and feel her husband entering and invisibly passing among the horses near to her, darkness as they were, actively intermingled. The rather low sound of his voice as he spoke to the horses came velvety to her nerves. How near he was, and how invisible! The darkness seemed to be in a strange swirl of violent life, just upon her. She turned giddy.

Her presence of mind made her call, quietly and musically:

"Maurice! Maurice—dea-ar!"

"Yes," he answered. "Isabel?"

She saw nothing, and the sound of his voice seemed to touch her.

"Hello!" she answered cheerfully, straining her eyes to see him. He was still busy, attending to the horses near her, but she saw only darkness. It made her almost desperate

"Won't you come in, dear?" she said.

"Yes, I'm coming. Just half a minute. *Stand over— now!* Trap's not come, has it?"

"Not yet," said Isabel.

His voice was pleasant and ordinary, but it had a slight suggestion of the stable to her. She wished he would come away. Whilst he was so utterly invisible, she was afraid of him.

"How's the time?" he asked.

"Not yet six," she replied. She disliked to answer into the dark. Presently he came very near to her, and she retreated out of doors.

"The weather blows in here," he said, coming steadily forward, feeling for the doors. She shrank away. At last she could dimly see him.

"Bertie won't have much of a drive," he said, as he closed the doors.

"He won't indeed!" said Isabel calmly, watching the dark shape at the door.

"Give me your arm, dear," she said.

She pressed his arm close to her, as she went. But she longed to see him, to look at him. She was nervous. He walked erect, with face rather lifted, but with a curious tentative movement of his powerful, muscular legs. She could feel the clever, careful, strong contact of his feet with the earth, as she balanced against him. For a moment he was a tower of darkness to her, as if he rose out of the earth.

In the house-passage he wavered and went cautiously, with a curious look of silence about him as he felt for the bench. Then he sat down heavily. He was a man with rather sloping shoulders, but with heavy limbs, powerful legs that seemed to know the earth. His head was small, usually carried high and light. As he bent down to unfasten his gaiters and boots he did not look blind. His hair was brown and crisp, his hands were large, reddish, intelligent, the veins stood out in the wrists; and his thighs and knees seemed massive. When he stood up his face and neck were surcharged with blood, the veins stood out on his temples. She did not look at his blindness.

Isabel was always glad when they had passed through the dividing door into their own regions of repose and beauty. She was a little afraid of him, out there in the animal grossness of the back. His bearing also changed, as he smelt the familiar indefinable odour that pervaded his wife's surroundings, a delicate, refined scent, very faintly spicy. Perhaps it came from the potpourri bowls.

He stood at the foot of the stairs, arrested, listening. She watched him, and her heart sickened. He seemed to be listening to fate.

"He's not here yet," he said. "I'll go up and change."

"Maurice," she said, "you're not wishing he wouldn't come, are you?"

"I couldn't quite say," he answered. "I feel myself rather on the qui vive."

"I can see you are," she answered. And she reached up and kissed his cheek. She saw his mouth relax into a slow smile.

"What are you laughing at?" she said roguishly.

"You consoling me," he answered.

"Nay," she answered. "Why should I console you? You know we love each other—you know *how* married we are! What does anything else matter?"

"Nothing at all, my dear."

He felt for her face and touched it, smiling.

"*You're* all right, aren't you?" he asked anxiously.

"I'm wonderfully all right, love," she answered. "It's you I am a little troubled about, at times."

"Why me?" he said, touching her cheeks delicately with the tips of his fingers. The touch had an almost hypnotizing effect on her.

He went away upstairs. She saw him mount into the darkness, unseeing and unchanging. He did not know that the lamps on the upper corridor were unlighted. He went on into the darkness with unchanging step. She heard him in the bath-room.

Pervin moved about almost unconsciously in his familiar surroundings, dark though everything was. He seemed to know the presence of objects before he touched them. It was a pleasure to him to rock thus through a world of things, carried on the flood in a sort of blood-prescience. He did not think much or trouble much. So long as he kept this sheer immediacy of blood-contact with the substantial world he was happy, he wanted no intervention of visual consciousness. In this state there was a certain rich positivity, bordering sometimes on rapture. Life seemed to move in him like a tide lapping, lapping, and advancing, enveloping all things darkly. It was a pleasure to stretch forth the hand and meet the unseen object, clasp it, and possess it in pure contact. He did not try to remember, to visualize. He did not want to. The new way of consciousness substituted itself in him.

The rich suffusion of this state generally kept him happy, reaching its culmination in the consuming passion for his wife. But at times the flow would seem to be checked and thrown back. Then it would beat inside him like a tangled sea, and he was tortured in the shattered chaos of his own blood. He grew to dread this arrest, this throw-back, this chaos inside himself, when he seemed merely at the mercy of his own powerful and conflicting elements. How to get some measure of control or surety, this was the question. And when the question rose maddening in him, he would clench his fists as if he would *compel* the whole universe to submit to him. But it was in vain. He could not even compel himself.

Tonight, however, he was still serene, though little tremors of unreasonable exasperation ran through him. He had to handle the razor very carefully, as he shaved, for it was not at one with him, he was afraid of it. His hearing also was too much sharpened. He heard the woman lighting the lamps on the corridor, and attending to the fire in the visitors' room. And then, as he went to his room, he heard the trap arrive. Then came Isabel's voice, lifted and calling, like a bell ringing:

"Is it you, Bertie? Have you come?"

And a man's voice answered out of the wind:

"Hello, Isabel! There you are."

"Have you had a miserable drive? I'm so sorry we couldn't send a closed carriage. I can't see you at all, you know."

"I'm coming. No, I liked the drive—it was like Perth-shire. Well, how are you? You're looking fit as ever, as far as I can see."

"Oh, yes," said Isabel. "I'm wonderfully well. How are you? Rather thin, I think——"

"Worked to death—everybody's old cry. But I'm all right, Ciss. How's Pervin?—isn't he here?"

"Oh, yes, he's upstairs changing. Yes, he's awfully well. Take off your wet things; I'll send them to be dried."

"And how are you both, in spirits? He doesn't fret?"

"No—no, not at all. No, on the contrary, really. We've been wonderfully happy, incredibly. It's more than I can understand—so wonderful: the nearness, and the peace——"

"Ah! Well, that's awfully good news——"

They moved away. Pervin heard no more. But a childish sense of desolation had come over him, as he heard their brisk voices. He seemed shut out—like a child that is left out. He was aimless and excluded, he did not know what to do with himself. The helpless desolation came over him. He fumbled nervously as he dressed himself, in a state almost of childishness. He disliked the Scotch accent in Bertie's speech, and the slight response it found on Isabel's tongue. He disliked the slight purr of complacency in the Scottish speech. He disliked intensely the glib way in which Isabel spoke of

their happiness and nearness. It made him recoil. He
was fretful and beside himself like a child, he had almost
a childish nostalgia to be included in the life circle. And
at the same time he was a man, dark and powerful and
infuriated by his own weakness. By some fatal flaw, he
could not be by himself, he had to depend on the support of another. And this very dependence enraged him.
He hated Bertie Reid, and at the same time he knew the
hatred was nonsense, he knew it was the outcome of his
own weakness.

He went downstairs. Isabel was alone in the dining-
room. She watched him enter, head erect, his feet tentative. He looked so strong-blooded and healthy and, at
the same time, cancelled. Cancelled—that was the word
that flew across her mind. Perhaps it was his scar suggested it.

"You heard Bertie come, Maurice?" she said.

"Yes—isn't he here?"

"He's in his room. He looks very thin and worn."

"I suppose he works himself to death."

A woman came in with a tray—and after a few
minutes Bertie came down. He was a little dark man,
with a very big forehead, thin, wispy hair, and sad, large
eyes. His expression was inordinately sad—almost
funny. He had odd, short legs.

Isabel watched him hesitate under the door, and
glance nervously at her husband. Pervin heard him and
turned.

"Here you are, now," said Isabel. "Come, let us eat."

Bertie went across to Maurice.

"How are you, Pervin?" he said, as he advanced.

The blind man stuck his hand out into space, and
Bertie took it.

"Very fit. Glad you've come," said Maurice.

Isabel glanced at them, and glanced away, as if she could not bear to see them.

"Come," she said. "Come to table. Aren't you both awfully hungry? I am, tremendously."

"I'm afraid you waited for me," said Bertie, as they sat down.

Maurice had a curious monolithic way of sitting in a chair, erect and distant. Isabel's heart always beat when she caught sight of him thus.

"No," she replied to Bertie. "We're very little later than usual. We're having a sort of high tea, not dinner. Do you mind? It gives us such a nice long evening, un-interrupted."

"I like it," said Bertie.

Maurice was feeling, with curious little movements, almost like a cat kneading her bed, for his plate, his knife and fork, his napkin. He was getting the whole geography of his cover into his consciousness. He sat erect and inscrutable, remote-seeming. Bertie watched the static figure of the blind man, the delicate tactile discernment of the large, ruddy hands, and the curious mindless silence of the brow, above the scar. With difficulty he looked away, and without knowing what he did, picked up a little crystal bowl of violets from the table, and held them to his nose.

"They are sweet-scented," he said. "Where do they come from?"

"From the garden—under the windows," said Isabel.

"So late in the year—and so fragrant! Do you remember the violets under Aunt Bell's south wall?"

The two friends looked at each other and exchanged a smile, Isabel's eyes lighting up.

"Don't I?" she replied. "*Wasn't* she queer!"

"A curious old girl," laughed Bertie. "There's a streak of freakishness in the family, Isabel."

"Ah—but not in you and me, Bertie," said Isabel. "Give them to Maurice, will you?" she added, as Bertie was putting down the flowers. "Have you smelled the violets, dear? Do!—they are so scented."

Maurice held out his hand, and Bertie placed the tiny bowl against his large, warm-looking fingers. Maurice's hand closed over the thin white fingers of the barrister. Bertie carefully extricated himself. Then the two watched the blind man smelling the violets. He bent his head and seemed to be thinking. Isabel waited.

"Aren't they sweet, Maurice?" she said at last, anxiously.

"Very," he said. And he held out the bowl. Bertie took it. Both he and Isabel were a little afraid, and deeply disturbed.

The meal continued. Isabel and Bertie chatted spasmodically. The blind man was silent. He touched his food repeatedly, with quick, delicate touches of his knife-point, then cut irregular bits. He could not bear to be helped. Both Isabel and Bertie suffered: Isabel wondered why. She did not suffer when she was alone with Maurice. Bertie made her conscious of a strangeness.

After the meal the three drew their chairs to the fire, and sat down to talk. The decanters were put on a table near at hand. Isabel knocked the logs on the fire, and clouds of brilliant sparks went up the chimney. Bertie noticed a slight weariness in her bearing.

"You will be glad when your child comes now, Isabel?" he said.

She looked up to him with a quick wan smile.

"Yes, I shall be glad," she answered. "It begins to seem long. Yes, I shall be very glad. So will you, Maurice, won't you?" she added.

"Yes, I shall," replied her husband.

"We are both looking forward so much to having it," she said.

"Yes, of course," said Bertie.

He was a bachelor, three or four years older than Isabel. He lived in beautiful rooms overlooking the river, guarded by a faithful Scottish man-servant. And he had his friends among the fair sex—not lovers, friends. So long as he could avoid any danger of court- ship or marriage, he adored a few good women with constant and unfailing homage, and he was chivalrously fond of quite a number. But if they seemed to encroach on him, he withdrew and detested them.

Isabel knew him very well, knew his beautiful con- stancy, and kindness, also his incurable weakness, which made him unable ever to enter into close contact of any sort. He was ashamed of himself because he could not marry, could not approach women physically. He wanted to do so. But he could not. At the centre of him he was afraid, helplessly and even brutally afraid. He had given up hope, had ceased to expect any more that he could escape his own weakness. Hence he was a brilliant and successful barrister, also a *littérateur* of high repute, a rich man, and a great social success. At the centre he felt himself neuter, nothing.

Isabel knew him well. She despised him even while she admired him. She looked at his sad face, his little short legs, and felt contempt of him. She looked at his dark grey eyes, with their uncanny, almost childlike, in- tuition, and she loved him. He understood amazingly— but she had no fear of his understanding. As a man she patronized him.

And she turned to the impassive, silent figure of her husband. He sat leaning back, with folded arms, and face a little uptilted. His knees were straight and mas- sive. She sighed, picked up the poker, and again began to prod the fire, to rouse the clouds of soft brilliant sparks.

"Isabel tells me," Bertie began suddenly, "that you have not suffered unbearably from the loss of sight."

Maurice straightened himself to attend but kept his arms folded.

"No," he said, "not unbearably. Now and again one struggles against it, you know. But there are compensations."

"They say it is much worse to be stone deaf," said Isabel.

"I believe it is," said Bertie. "Are there compensations?" he added, to Maurice.

"Yes. You cease to bother about a great many things." Again Maurice stretched his figure, stretched the strong muscles of his back, and leaned backwards, with uplifted face.

"And that is a relief," said Bertie. "But what is there in place of the bothering? What replaces the activity?"

There was a pause. At length the blind man replied, as out of a negligent, unattentive thinking:

"Oh, I don't know. There's a good deal when you're not active."

"Is there?" said Bertie. "What, exactly? It always seems to me that when there is no thought and no action, there is nothing."

Again Maurice was slow in replying.

"There is something," he replied. "I couldn't tell you what it is."

And the talk lapsed once more, Isabel and Bertie chatting gossip and reminiscence, the blind man silent.

At length Maurice rose restlessly, a big obtrusive figure. He felt tight and hampered. He wanted to go away.

"Do you mind," he said, "if I go and speak to Wernham?"

"No—go along, dear," said Isabel.

And he went out. A silence came over the two friends. At length Bertie said:

"Nevertheless, it is a great deprivation, Cissie."

"It is, Bertie. I know it is."

"Something lacking all the time," said Bertie.

"Yes, I know. And yet—and yet—Maurice is right. There is something else, something *there*, which you never knew was there, and which you can't express."

"What is there?" asked Bertie.

"I don't know—it's awfully hard to define it—but something strong and immediate. There's something strange in Maurice's presence—indefinable—but I couldn't do without it. I agree that it seems to put one's mind to sleep. But when we're alone I miss nothing; it seems awfully rich, almost splendid, you know."

"I'm afraid I don't follow," said Bertie.

They talked desultorily. The wind blew loudly outside, rain chattered on the window-panes, making a sharp drum-sound because of the closed, mellow-golden shutters inside. The logs burned slowly, with hot, almost invisible small flames. Bertie seemed uneasy, there were dark circles round his eyes. Isabel, rich with her approaching maternity, leaned looking into the fire. Her hair curled in odd, loose strands, very pleasing to the man. But she had a curious feeling of old woe in her heart, old, timeless night-woe.

"I suppose we're all deficient somewhere," said Bertie.

"I suppose so," said Isabel wearily.

"Damned, sooner or later."

"I don't know," she said, rousing herself. "I feel quite all right, you know. The child coming seems to make me indifferent to everything, just placid. I can't feel that there's anything to trouble about, you know."

"A good thing, I should say," he replied slowly.

"Well, there it is. I suppose it's just Nature. If only I felt I needn't trouble about Maurice, I should be perfectly content——"

"But you feel you must trouble about him?"

"Well—I don't know——" She even resented this much effort.

The night passed slowly. Isabel looked at the clock. "I say," she said. "It's nearly ten o'clock. Where can Maurice be? I'm sure they're all in bed at the back. Excuse me a moment."

She went out, returning almost immediately.

"It's all shut up and in darkness," she said. "I wonder where he is. He must have gone out to the farm——"

Bertie looked at her.

"I suppose he'll come in," he said.

"I suppose so," she said. "But it's unusual for him to be out now."

"Would you like me to go out and see?"

"Well—if you wouldn't mind. I'd go, but——" She did not want to make the physical effort.

Bertie put on an old overcoat and took a lantern. He went out from the side door. He shrank from the wet and roaring night. Such weather had a nervous effect on him: too much moisture everywhere made him feel almost imbecile. Unwilling, he went through it all. A dog barked violently at him. He peered in all the buildings. At last, as he opened the upper door of a sort of intermediate barn, he heard a grinding noise, and looking in, holding up his lantern, saw Maurice, in his shirt-sleeves, standing listening, holding the handle of a turnip-pulper. He had been pulping sweet roots, a pile of which lay dimly heaped in a corner behind him.

"That you, Wernham?" said Maurice, listening.

"No, it's me," said Bertie.

A large, half-wild grey cat was rubbing at Maurice's leg. The blind man stooped to rub its sides. Bertie watched the scene, then unconsciously entered and shut the door behind him. He was in a high sort of barn-place, from which, right and left, ran off the corridors in front of the stalled cattle. He watched the slow, stooping motion of the other man, as he caressed the great cat.

Maurice straightened himself.

"You came to look for me?" he said.

"Isabel was a little uneasy," said Bertie.

"I'll come in. I like messing about doing these jobs."

The cat had reared her sinister, feline length against his leg, clawing at his thigh affectionately. He lifted her claws out of his flesh.

"I hope I'm not in your way at all at the Grange here," said Bertie, rather shy and stiff.

"My way? No, not a bit. I'm glad Isabel has some-body to talk to. I'm afraid it's I who am in the way. I know I'm not very lively company. Isabel's all right, don't you think? She's not unhappy, is she?"

"I don't think so."

"What does she say?"

"She says she's very content—only a little troubled about you."

"Why me?"

"Perhaps afraid that you might brood," said Bertie, cautiously.

"She needn't be afraid of that." He continued to caress the flattened grey head of the cat with his fingers. "What I am a bit afraid of," he resumed, "is that she'll find me a dead weight, always alone with me down here."

"I don't think you need think that," said Bertie, though this was what he feared himself.

"I don't know," said Maurice. "Sometimes I feel it isn't fair that she's saddled with me." Then he dropped his voice curiously. "I say," he asked, secretly struggling, "is my face much disfigured? Do you mind telling me?"

"There is the scar," said Bertie, wondering. "Yes, it is a disfigurement. But more pitiable than shocking."

"A pretty bad scar, though," said Maurice.

"Oh, yes."

There was a pause.

"Sometimes I feel I am horrible," said Maurice, in a low voice, talking as if to himself. And Bertie actually felt a quiver of horror.

"That's nonsense," he said.

Maurice again straightened himself, leaving the cat.

"There's no telling," he said. Then again, in an odd tone, he added: "I don't really know you, do I?"

"Probably not," said Bertie.

"Do you mind if I touch you?"

The lawyer shrank away instinctively. And yet, out of very philanthropy, he said, in a small voice: "Not at all."

But he suffered as the blind man stretched out a strong, naked hand to him. Maurice accidentally knocked off Bertie's hat.

"I thought you were taller," he said, starting. Then he laid his hand on Bertie Reid's head, closing the dome of the skull in a soft, firm grasp, gathering it, as it were; then, shifting his grasp and softly closing again, with a fine, close pressure, till he had covered the skull and the face of the smaller man, tracing the brows, and touching the full, closed eyes, touching the small nose and the nostrils, the rough, short moustache, the mouth, the rather strong chin. The hand of the blind man grasped the shoulder, the arm, the hand of the other man. He seemed to take him, in the soft, travelling grasp.

"You seem young," he said quietly, at last.

The lawyer stood almost annihilated, unable to answer.

"Your head seems tender, as if you were young," Maurice repeated. "So do your hands. Touch my eyes, will you?—touch my scar."

Now Bertie quivered with revulsion. Yet he was under the power of the blind man, as if hypnotized. He lifted his hand, and laid the fingers on the scar, on the scarred eyes. Maurice suddenly covered them with his own hand, pressed the fingers of the other man upon his disfigured eye-sockets, trembling in every fibre, and rocking slightly, slowly, from side to side. He remained thus for a minute or more, whilst Bertie stood as if in a swoon, unconscious, imprisoned.

Then suddenly Maurice removed the hand of the other man from his brow, and stood holding it in his own.

"Oh, my God," he said, "we shall know each other now, shan't we? We shall know each other now."

Bertie could not answer. He gazed mute and terror-struck, overcome by his own weakness. He knew he could not answer. He had an unreasonable fear, lest the other man should suddenly destroy him. Whereas Maurice was actually filled with hot, poignant love, the passion of friendship. Perhaps it was this very passion of friendship which Bertie shrank from most.

"We're all right together now, aren't we?" said Maurice. "It's all right now, as long as we live, so far as we're concerned?"

"Yes," said Bertie, trying by any means to escape.

Maurice stood with head lifted, as if listening. The new delicate fulfilment of mortal friendship had come as a revelation and surprise to him, something exquisite and unhoped-for. He seemed to be listening to hear if it were real.

Then he turned for his coat.

"Come," he said, "we'll go to Isabel."

Bertie took the lantern and opened the door. The cat disappeared. The two men went in silence along the causeways. Isabel, as they came, thought their footsteps sounded strange. She looked up pathetically and anxiously for their entrance. There seemed a curious elation about Maurice. Bertie was haggard, with sunken eyes.

"What is it?" she asked.

"We've become friends," said Maurice, standing with his feet apart, like a strange colossus.

"Friends!" re-echoed Isabel. And she looked again at Bertie. He met her eyes with a furtive, haggard look; his eyes were as if glazed with misery.

"I'm so glad," she said, in sheer perplexity.

"Yes," said Maurice.

He was indeed so glad. Isabel took his hand with both hers, and held it fast.

"You'll be happier now, dear," she said.

But she was watching Bertie. She knew that he had one desire—to escape from this intimacy, this friendship, which had been thrust upon him. He could not bear it that he had been touched by the blind man, his insane reserve broken in. He was like a mollusc whose shell is broken.

Two Blue Birds

THERE was a woman who loved her husband, but she could not live with him. The husband, on his side, was sincerely attached to his wife, yet he could not live with her. They were both under forty, both hand-

some and both attractive. They had the most sincere
regard for one another, and felt, in some odd way,
eternally married to one another. They knew one another more intimately than they knew anybody else,
they felt more known to one another than to any other
person.

Yet they could not live together. Usually, they kept a
thousand miles apart, geographically. But when he sat in
the greyness of England, at the back of his mind, with a
certain grim fidelity, he was aware of his wife, her
strange yearning to be loyal and faithful, having her
gallant affairs away in the sun, in the south. And she,
as she drank her cocktail on the terrace over the sea, and
turned her grey, sardonic eyes on the heavy dark face
of her admirer, whom she really liked quite a lot, she
was actually preoccupied with the clear-cut features
of her handsome young husband, thinking of how he
would be asking his secretary to do something for him,
asking in that good-natured, confident voice of a man
who knows that his request will be only too gladly fulfilled.

The secretary, of course, adored him. She was *very*
competent, quite young, and quite good-looking. She
adored him. But then all his servants always did, particularly his women-servants. His men-servants were
likely to swindle him.

When a man has an adoring secretary, and you are
the man's wife, what are you to do? Not that there was
anything "wrong"—if you know what I mean!—between them. Nothing you could call adultery, to come
down to brass tacks. No, no! They were just the young
master and his secretary. He dictated to her, she slaved
for him and adored him, and the whole thing went on
wheels.

He didn't "adore" her. A man doesn't need to adore

his secretary. But he depended on her. "I simply rely on Miss Wrexall." Whereas he could never rely on his wife. The one thing he knew finally about *her* was that she didn't intend to be relied on.

So they remained friends, in the awful unspoken intimacy of the once-married. Usually each year they went away together for a holiday, and, if they had not been man and wife, they would have found a great deal of fun and stimulation in one another. The fact that they were married, had been married for the last dozen years, and couldn't live together for the last three or four, spoilt them for one another. Each had a private feeling of bitterness about the other.

However, they were awfully kind. He was the soul of generosity, and held her in real, tender esteem, no matter how many gallant affairs she had. Her gallant affairs were part of her modern necessity. "After all, I've got to *live*. I can't turn into a pillar of salt in five minutes just because you and I can't live together! It takes years for a woman like me to turn into a pillar of salt. At least I hope so!"

"Quite!" he replied. "Quite! By all means put them in pickle, make pickled cucumbers of them, before you crystallize out. That's my advice."

He was like that: so awfully clever and enigmatic. She could more or less fathom the idea of the pickled cucumbers, but the "crystallizing out"—what did that signify?

And did he mean to suggest that he himself had been well pickled and that further immersion was for him unnecessary, would spoil his flavour? Was that what he meant? And herself, was she the brine and the vale of tears?

You never knew how catty a man was being, when he was really clever and enigmatic, withal a bit whimsical.

He was adorably whimsical, with a twist of his flexible, vain mouth, that had a long upper lip, so fraught with vanity! But then a handsome, clear-cut, histrionic young man like that, how could he help being vain? The women made him so.

Ah, the women! How nice men would be if there were no other women!

And how nice the women would be if there were no other men! That's the best of a secretary. She may have a husband, but a husband is the mere shred of a man compared to a boss, a chief, a man who dictates to you and whose words you faithfully write down and then transcribe. Imagine a wife writing down anything her husband said to her! But a secretary! Every *and* and *but* of his she preserves for ever. What are candied violets in comparison!

Now it is all very well having gallant affairs under the southern sun, when you know there is a husband whom you adore dictating to a secretary whom you are too scornful to hate yet whom you rather despise, though you allow she has her good points, away north in the place you ought to regard as home. A gallant affair isn't much good when you've got a bit of grit in your eye. Or something at the back of your mind.

What's to be done? The husband, of course, did not send his wife away.

"You've got your secretary and your work," she said. "There's no room for me."

"There's a bedroom and a sitting-room exclusively for you," he replied. "And a garden and half a motor-car. But please yourself entirely. Do what gives you most pleasure."

"In that case," she said, "I'll just go south for the winter."

"Yes, do!" he said. "You always enjoy it."

"I always do," she replied.

They parted with a certain relentlessness that had a touch of wistful sentiment behind it. Off she went to her gallant affairs, that were like the curate's egg, palatable in parts. And he settled down to work. He said he hated working, but he never did anything else. Ten or eleven hours a day. That's what it is to be your own master!

So the winter wore away, and it was spring, when the swallows homeward fly, or northward, in this case. This winter, one of a series similar, had been rather hard to get through. The bit of grit in the gallant lady's eye had worked deeper in the more she blinked. Dark faces might be dark, and icy cocktails might lend a glow; she blinked her hardest to blink that bit of grit away, without success. Under the spicy balls of the mimosa she thought of that husband of hers in his library, and of that neat, competent but *common* little secretary of his, forever taking down what he said!

"How a man can *stand* it! How *she* can stand it, common little thing as she is, I don't know!" the wife cried to herself.

She meant this dictating business, this ten hours a day intercourse, *à deux*, with nothing but a pencil between them, and a flow of words.

What was to be done? Matters, instead of improving, had grown worse. The little secretary had brought her mother and sister into the establishment. The mother was a sort of cook-housekeeper, the sister was a sort of upper maid—she did the fine laundry, and looked after "his" clothes, and valeted him beautifully. It was really an excellent arrangement. The old mother was a splendid plain cook, the sister was all that could be desired as a valet de chambre, a fine laundress, an upper parlour-maid, and a table-waiter. And all economical to a degree. They knew his affairs by heart. His secretary flew to town when a creditor became dangerous, and she *always* smoothed over the financial crisis.

"He," of course, had debts, and he was working to pay them off. And if he had been a fairy prince who could call the ants to help him, he would not have been more wonderful than in securing this secretary and her family. They took hardly any wages. And they seemed to perform the miracle of loaves and fishes daily.

"She," of course, was the wife who loved her husband, but helped him into debt, and she still was an expensive item. Yet when she appeared at her "home," the secretarial family received her with most elaborate attentions and deference. The knight returning from the Crusades didn't create a greater stir. She felt like Queen Elizabeth at Kenilworth, a sovereign paying a visit to her faithful subjects. But perhaps there lurked always this hair in her soup! Won't they be glad to be rid of me again!

But they protested No! No! They had been waiting and hoping and praying she would come. They had been pining for her to be there, in charge: the mistress, "his" wife. Ah, "his" wife!

"His" wife! His halo was like a bucket over her head.

The cook-mother was "of the people," so it was the upper-maid daughter who came for orders.

"What will you order for tomorrow's lunch and dinner, Mrs. Gee?"

"Well, what do you usually have?"

"Oh, we want *you* to say."

"No, what do you *usually* have?"

"We don't have anything fixed. Mother goes out and chooses the best she can find, that is nice and fresh. But she thought you would tell her now what to get."

"Oh, I don't know! I'm not very good at that sort of thing. Ask her to go on just the same; I'm quite sure she knows best."

"Perhaps you'd like to suggest a sweet?"

"No, I don't care for sweets—and you know Mr. Gee doesn't. So don't make one for me."

Could anything be more impossible! They had the house spotless and running like a dream; how could an incompetent and extravagant wife dare to interfere, when she saw their amazing and almost inspired economy! But they ran the place on simply nothing!

Simply marvellous people! And the way they strewed palm-branches under her feet!

But that only made her feel ridiculous.

"Don't you think the family manage very well?" he asked her tentatively.

"Awfully well! Almost romantically well!" she replied. "But I suppose you're perfectly happy?"

"I'm perfectly comfortable," he replied.

"I can see you are," she replied. "Amazingly so! I never knew such comfort! Are you sure it isn't bad for you?"

She eyed him stealthily. He looked very well, and extremely handsome, in his histrionic way. He was shockingly well-dressed and valeted. And he had that air of easy *aplomb* and good humour which is so becoming to a man, and which he only acquires when he is cock of his own little walk, made much of by his own hens.

"No!" he said, taking his pipe from his mouth and smiling whimsically round at her. "Do I look as if it were bad for me?"

"No, you don't," she replied promptly: thinking, naturally, as a woman is supposed to think nowadays, of his health and comfort, the foundation, apparently, of all happiness.

Then, of course, away she went on the backwash.

"Perhaps for your work, though, it's not so good as it is for *you*," she said in a rather small voice. She knew he couldn't bear it if she mocked at his work for one moment. And he knew that rather small voice of hers.

"In what way?" he said, bristles rising.

"Oh, I don't know," she answered indifferently. "Perhaps it's not good for a man's work if he is too comfortable."

"I don't know about *that!*" he said, taking a dramatic turn round the library and drawing at his pipe. "Considering I work, actually, by the clock, for twelve hours a day, and for ten hours when it's a short day, I don't think you can say I am deteriorating from easy comfort."

"No, I suppose not," she admitted.

Yet she did think it, nevertheless. His comfortableness didn't consist so much in good food and a soft bed, as in having nobody, absolutely nobody and nothing, to contradict him. "I do like to think he's got nothing to aggravate him," the secretary had said to the wife.

"Nothing to aggravate him!" What a position for a man! Fostered by women who would let nothing "aggravate" him. If anything would aggravate his wounded vanity, this would!

So thought the wife. But what was to be done about it? In the silence of midnight she heard his voice in the distance, dictating away, like the voice of God to Samuel, alone and monotonous, and she imagined the little figure of the secretary busily scribbling shorthand. Then in the sunny hours of morning, while he was still in bed—he never rose till noon—from another distance came that sharp insect-noise of the typewriter, like some immense grasshopper chirping and rattling. It was the secretary, poor thing, typing out his notes.

That girl—she was only twenty-eight—really slaved herself to skin and bone. She was small and neat, but she was actually worn out. She did far more work than he did, for she had not only to take down all those words he uttered, she had to type them out, make three copies, while he was still resting.

"What on earth she gets out of it," thought the wife, "I don't know. She's simply worn to the bone, for a very poor salary, and he's never kissed her, and never will, if I know anything about him."

Whether his never kissing her—the secretary, that is —made it worse or better, the wife did not decide. He never kissed anybody. Whether she herself—the wife, that is—wanted to be kissed by him, even that she was not clear about. She rather thought she didn't.

What on earth did she want then? She was his wife. What on earth did she want of him?

She certainly didn't want to take him down in short-hand and type out again all those words. And she didn't really want him to kiss her; she knew him too well. Yes, she knew him too well. If you know a man too well, you don't want him to kiss you.

What then? What did she want? Why had she such an extraordinary hang-over about him? Just because she was his wife? Why did she rather "enjoy" other men— and she was relentless about enjoyment—without ever taking them seriously? And why must she take him so damn seriously, when she never really "enjoyed" him?

Of course she *had* had good times with him, in the past, before—ah! before a thousand things, all amounting really to nothing. But she enjoyed him no more. She never even enjoyed being with him. There was a silent, ceaseless tension between them, that never broke, even when they were a thousand miles apart.

Awful! That's what you call being married! What's to be done about it? Ridiculous, to know it all and not do anything about it!

She came back once more, and there she was, in her own house, a sort of super-guest, even to him. And the secretarial family devoting their lives to him.

Devoting their lives to him! But actually! Three women pouring out their lives for him day and night! And what did they get in return? Not one kiss! Very little money, because they knew all about his debts, and had made it their life-business to get them paid off! No expectations! Twelve hours' work a day! Comparative isolation, for he saw nobody!

And beyond that? Nothing! Perhaps a sense of uplift and importance because they saw his name and photograph in the newspapers sometimes. But would anybody believe that it was good enough?

Yet they adored it! They seemed to get a deep satisfaction out of it, like people with a mission. Extraordinary!

Well, if they did, let them. They were, of course, rather common, "of the people"; there might be a sort of glamour in it for them.

But it was bad for him. No doubt about it. His work was getting diffuse and poor in quality—and what wonder! His whole tone was going down—becoming commoner. Of course it was bad for him.

Being his wife, she felt she ought to do something to save him. But how could she? That perfectly devoted, marvellous secretarial family, how could she make an attack on them? Yet she'd love to sweep them into oblivion. Of course they were bad for him: ruining his work, ruining his reputation as a writer, ruining his life. Ruining him with their slavish service.

Of course she ought to make an onslaught on them! But how *could* she? Such devotion! And what had she herself to offer in their place? Certainly not slavish devotion to him, nor to his flow of words! Certainly not!

She imagined him stripped once more naked of secretary and secretarial family, and she shuddered. It was like throwing the naked baby in the dust-bin. Couldn't do that!

Yet something must be done. She felt it. She was almost tempted to get into debt for another thousand pounds and send in the bill, or have it sent in to him, as usual.

But no! Something more drastic!

Something more drastic, or perhaps more gentle. She wavered between the two. And wavering, she first did nothing, came to no decision, dragged vacantly on from day to day, waiting for sufficient energy to take her departure once more.

It was spring! What a fool she had been to come up in spring! And she was forty! What an idiot of a woman to go and be forty! ⸳

She went down the garden in the warm afternoon, when birds were whistling loudly from the cover, the sky being low and warm, and she had nothing to do. The garden was full of flowers: he loved them for their theatrical display. Lilac and snowball bushes, and laburnum and red may, tulips and anemones and coloured daisies. Lots of flowers! Borders of forget-me-nots! Bachelor's buttons! What absurd names flowers had! She would have called them blue dots and yellow blobs and white frills. Not so much sentiment, after all!

There is a certain nonsense, something showy and stagey, about spring, with its pushing leaves and chorus-girl flowers, unless you have something corresponding inside you. Which she hadn't.

Oh, heaven! Beyond the hedge she heard a voice, a steady rather theatrical voice. Oh, heaven! He was dictating to his secretary, in the garden. Good God, was there nowhere to get away from it!

She looked around: there was indeed plenty of escape. But what was the good of escaping? He would go on and on. She went quietly towards the hedge, and listened.

He was dictating a magazine article about the modern novel. "What the modern novel lacks is architecture." Good God! Architecture! He might just as well say: What the modern novel lacks is whalebone, or a tea-spoon, or a tooth stopped.

Yet the secretary took it down, took it down, took it down! No, this could not go on! It was more than flesh and blood could bear.

She went quietly along the hedge, somewhat wolf-like in her prowl, a broad, strong woman in an expensive mustard-coloured silk jersey and cream-coloured pleated skirt. Her legs were long and shapely, and her shoes were expensive.

With a curious wolf-like stealth she turned the hedge and looked across at the small, shaded lawn where the daisies grew impertinently. "He" was reclining in a coloured hammock under the pink-flowering horse-chestnut tree, dressed in white serge with a fine yellow-coloured linen shirt. His elegant hand dropped over the side of the hammock and beat a sort of vague rhythm to his words. At a little wicker table the little secretary, in a green knitted frock, bent her dark head over her note-book, and diligently made those awful shorthand marks. He was not difficult to take down, as he dictated slowly, and kept a sort of rhythm, beating time with his dangling hand.

"In every novel there must be one outstanding character with which we always sympathize—with *whom* we always sympathize—even though we recognize its— even when we are most aware of the human frailties——"

Every man his own hero, thought the wife grimly, forgetting that every woman is intensely her own heroine.

But what did startle her was a blue bird dashing about near the feet of the absorbed, shorthand-scribbling little secretary. At least it was a blue-tit, blue with grey and some yellow. But to the wife it seemed blue, that juicy spring day, in the translucent afternoon. The blue bird, fluttering round the pretty but rather *common* little feet of the little secretary.

The blue bird! The blue bird of happiness! Well, I'm blest, thought the wife. Well, I'm blest!

And as she was being blest, appeared another blue bird—that is, another blue-tit—and began to wrestle with the first blue-tit. A couple of blue birds of happiness, having a fight over it! Well, I'm blest!

She was more or less out of sight of the human preoccupied pair. But "he" was disturbed by the fighting blue birds, whose little feathers began to float loose.

"Get out!" he said to them mildly, waving a dark-yellow handkerchief at them. "Fight your little fight, and settle your private affairs, elsewhere, my dear little gentlemen."

The little secretary looked up quickly, for she had already begun to write it down. He smiled at her his twisted whimsical smile.

"No, don't take that down," he said affectionately.

"Did you see those two tits laying into one another?"

"No!" said the little secretary, gazing brightly round, her eyes half-blinded with work.

But she saw the queer, powerful, elegant, wolf-like figure of the wife, behind her, and terror came into her eyes.

"I did!" said the wife, stepping forward with those curious, shapely, she-wolf legs of hers, under the very short skirt.

"Aren't they extraordinarily vicious little beasts?" said he.

"Extraordinarily!" she re-echoed, stooping and picking up a little breast-feather. "Extraordinarily! See how the feathers fly!"

And she got the feather on the tip of her finger, and looked at it. Then she looked at the secretary, then she looked at him. She had a queer, werwolf expression between her brows.

"I think," he began, "these are the loveliest afternoons, when there's no direct sun, but all the sounds and the colours and the scents are sort of dissolved, don't you know, in the air, and the whole thing is steeped, steeped in spring. It's like being on the inside; you know how I mean, like being inside the egg and just ready to chip the shell."

"Quite like that!" she assented without conviction.

There was a little pause. The secretary said nothing. They were waiting for the wife to depart again.

"I suppose," said the latter, "you're awfully busy, as usual?"

"Just about the same," he said, pursing his mouth deprecatingly.

Again the blank pause, in which he waited for her to go away again.

"I know I'm interrupting you," she said.

"As a matter of fact," he said, "I was just watching those two blue-tits."

"Pair of little demons!" said the wife, blowing away the yellow feather from her finger-tip.

"Absolutely!" he said.

"Well, I'd better go, and let you get on with your work," she said.

"No hurry!" he said, with benevolent nonchalance. "As a matter of fact, I don't think it's a great success, working out of doors."

"What made you try it?" said the wife. "You know you never could do it."

"Miss Wrexall suggested it might make a change. But I don't think it altogether helps, do you, Miss Wrexall?"

"I'm sorry," said the little secretary.

"Why should *you* be sorry?" said the wife, looking down at her as a wolf might look down half-benignly at a little black-and-tan mongrel. "You only suggested it for his good, I'm sure!"

"I thought the air might be good for him," the secretary admitted.

"Why do people like you never think about your-selves?" the wife asked.

The secretary looked her in the eye.

"I suppose we do, in a different way," she said.

"A *very* different way!" said the wife ironically. "Why don't you make *him* think about *you?*" she added slowly, with a sort of drawl. "On a soft spring afternoon like this, you ought to have him dictating poems to you, about the blue birds of happiness fluttering round your dainty little feet. I know *I* would, if I were his secretary."

There was a dead pause. The wife stood immobile and statuesque, in an attitude characteristic of her, half turn-

ing back to the little secretary, half averted. She half
turned her back on everything.

The secretary looked at him.

"As a matter of fact," he said, "I was doing an article
on the Future of the Novel."

"I know that," said the wife. "That's what's so awful!
Why not something lively in the life of the novelist?"

There was a prolonged silence, in which he looked
pained, and somewhat remote, statuesque. The little
secretary hung her head. The wife sauntered slowly
away.

"Just where were we, Miss Wrexall?" came the sound
of his voice.

The little secretary started. She was feeling profoundly indignant. Their beautiful relationship, his and
hers, to be so insulted!

But soon she was veering downstream on the flow of
his words, too busy to have any feelings, except one of
elation at being so busy.

Tea-time came; the sister brought out the tea-tray
into the garden. And immediately, the wife appeared.
She had changed, and was wearing a chicory-blue dress
of fine cloth. The little secretary had gathered up her
papers and was departing, on rather high heels.

"Don't go, Miss Wrexall," said the wife.

The little secretary stopped short, then hesitated.

"Mother will be expecting me," she said.

"Tell her you're not coming. And ask your sister to
bring another cup. I want you to have tea with us."

Miss Wrexall looked at the man, who was reared on
one elbow in the hammock, and was looking enigmati-
cal, Hamletish.

He glanced at her quickly, then pursed his mouth in
a boyish negligence.

"Yes, stay and have tea with us for once," he said. "I see strawberries, and I know you're the bird for them."

She glanced at him, smiled wanly, and hurried away to tell her mother. She even stayed long enough to slip on a silk dress.

"Why, how smart you are!" said the wife, when the little secretary reappeared on the lawn, in chicory-blue silk.

"Oh, don't look at my dress, compared to yours!" said Miss Wrexall. They were of the same colour, indeed!

"At least you earned yours, which is more than I did mine," said the wife, as she poured tea. "You like it strong?"

She looked with her heavy eyes at the smallish, birdy, blue-clad, overworked young woman, and her eyes seemed to speak many inexplicable dark volumes.

"Oh, as it comes, thank you," said Miss Wrexall, leaning nervously forward.

"It's coming pretty black, if you want to ruin your digestion," said the wife.

"Oh, I'll have some water in it, then."

"Better, I should say."

"How'd the work go—all right?" asked the wife, as they drank tea, and the two women looked at each other's blue dresses.

"Oh!" he said. "As well as you can expect. It was a piece of pure flummery. But it's what they want. Awful rot, wasn't it, Miss Wrexall?"

Miss Wrexall moved uneasily on her chair.

"It interested me," she said, "though not so much as the novel."

"The novel? Which novel?" said the wife. "Is there another new one?"

Miss Wrexall looked at him. Not for words would she give away any of his literary activities.

"Oh, I was just sketching out an idea to Miss Wrexall," he said.

"Tell us about it!" said the wife. "Miss Wrexall, *you* tell us what it's about."

She turned on her chair and fixed the little secretary.

"I'm afraid"—Miss Wrexall squirmed—"I haven't got it very clearly myself, yet."

"Oh, go along! Tell us what you *have* got then!"

Miss Wrexall sat dumb and very vexed. She felt she was being baited. She looked at the blue pleatings of her skirt.

"I'm afraid I can't," she said.

"Why are you afraid you can't? You're so *very* competent. I'm sure you've got it all at your finger-ends. I expect you write a good deal of Mr. Gee's books for him, really. He gives you the hint, and you fill it all in. Isn't that how you do it?" She spoke ironically, and as if she were teasing a child. And then she glanced down at the fine pleatings of her own blue skirt, very fine and expensive.

"Of course you're not speaking seriously?" said Miss Wrexall, rising on her mettle.

"Of course I am! I've suspected for a long time—at least, for some time—that you write a good deal of Mr. Gee's books for him, from his hints."

It was said in a tone of raillery, but it was cruel.

"I should be terribly flattered," said Miss Wrexall, straightening herself, "if I didn't know you were only trying to make me feel a fool."

"Make you feel a fool? My dear child!—why, nothing could be farther from me! You're twice as clever and a million times as competent as I am. Why, my dear child, I've the greatest admiration for you! I wouldn't do what you do, not for all the pearls in India. I *couldn't*, anyhow——"

Miss Wrexall closed up and was silent.

"Do you mean to say my books read as if——" he began, rearing up and speaking in a harrowed voice.

"I do!" said the wife. "*Just* as if Miss Wrexall had written them from your hints. I *honestly* thought she did —when you were too busy——"

"How very clever of you!" he said.

"Very!" she cried. "Especially if I was wrong!"

"Which you were," he said.

"How very extraordinary!" she cried. "Well, I am once more mistaken!"

There was a complete pause.

It was broken by Miss Wrexall, who was nervously twisting her fingers.

"You want to spoil what there is between me and him, I can see that," she said bitterly.

"My dear, but what *is* there between you and him?" asked the wife.

"I was *happy* working with him, working for him! I was *happy* working for him!" cried Miss Wrexall, tears of indignant anger and chagrin in her eyes.

"My dear child!" cried the wife, with simulated excitement, "go *on* being happy working with him, go on being happy while you can! If it makes you happy, why then, enjoy it! Of course! Do you think I'd be so cruel as to want to take it away from you?—working with him? *I* can't do shorthand and typewriting and double-entrance book-keeping, or whatever it's called. I tell you, I'm utterly incompetent. I never earn anything. I'm the parasite on the British oak, like the mistletoe. The blue bird doesn't flutter round my feet. Perhaps they're too big and trampling."

She looked down at her expensive shoes.

"If I *did* have a word of criticism to offer," she said,

turning to her husband, "it would be to you, Cameron, for taking so much from her and giving her nothing."

"But he gives me everything, everything!" cried Miss Wrexall. "He gives me everything!"

"What do you mean by everything?" said the wife, turning on her sternly.

Miss Wrexall pulled up short. There was a snap in the air and a change of currents.

"I mean nothing that *you* need begrudge me," said the little secretary rather haughtily. "I've never made myself cheap."

There was a blank pause.

"My God!" said the wife. "You don't call that being cheap? Why, I should say you got nothing out of him at all, you only give! And if you don't call that making yourself cheap—my God!"

"You see, we see things different," said the secretary.

"I should say we do!—*thank God!*" rejoined the wife.

"On whose behalf are you thanking God?" he asked sarcastically.

"Everybody's, I suppose! Yours, because you get everything for nothing, and Miss Wrexall's, because she seems to like it, and mine because I'm well out of it all."

"You *needn't* be out of it all," cried Miss Wrexall magnanimously, "if you didn't *put* yourself out of it all."

"Thank you, my dear, for your offer," said the wife, rising. "But I'm afraid no man can expect *two* blue birds of happiness to flutter round his feet, tearing out their little feathers!"

With which she walked away.

After a tense and desperate interim, Miss Wrexall cried:

"And *really*, need any woman be jealous of *me?*"

"Quite!" he said.

And that was all he did say.

The Lovely Lady

AT SEVENTY-TWO, Pauline Attenborough could still sometimes be mistaken, in the half-light, for thirty. She really was a wonderfully preserved woman, of perfect chic. Of course, it helps a great deal to have the right frame. She would be an exquisite skeleton, and her skull would be an exquisite skull, like that of some Etruscan woman, with feminine charm still in the swerve of the bone and the pretty naïve teeth.

Mrs. Attenborough's face was of the perfect oval and slightly flat type that wears best. There is no flesh to sag. Her nose rode serenely in its finely bridged curve. Only her big grey eyes were a tiny bit prominent on the surface of her face, and they gave her away most. The bluish lids were heavy, as if they ached sometimes with the strain of keeping the eyes beneath them arch and bright; and at the corners of the eyes were fine little wrinkles which would slacken with haggardness, then be pulled up tense again, to that bright, gay look, like a Leonardo woman who really could laugh outright.

Her niece Cecilia was perhaps the only person in the world who was aware of the invisible little wire which connected Pauline's eye-wrinkles with Pauline's will power. Only Cecilia *consciously* watched the eyes go haggard and old and tired, and remain so, for hours; until Robert came home. Then, ping!—the mysterious little wire that worked between Pauline's will and her face went taut; the weary, haggard, prominent eyes suddenly began to gleam; the eyelids arched; the queer curved eye-brows, which floated in such frail arches on Pauline's forehead, began to gather a mocking significance, and you had the *real* lovely lady, in all her charm.

She really had the secret of everlasting youth; that is to say, she could don her youth again like an eagle. But she was sparing of it. She was wise enough not to try being young for too many people. Her son Robert, in the evenings, and Sir Wilfred Knipe sometimes in the afternoon to tea; then occasional visitors on Sunday, when Robert was home; for these she was her lovely and changeless self, that age could not wither, nor custom stale; so bright and kindly and yet subtly mocking, like Mona Lisa who knew a thing or two. But Pauline knew more, so she needn't be smug at all, she could laugh that lovely mocking Bacchante laugh of hers, which was at the same time never malicious, always good-naturedly tolerant, both of virtues and vices. The former, of course, taking much more tolerating. So she suggested, roguishly.

Only with her niece Cecilia she did not trouble to keep up the glamour. Ciss was not very observant, anyhow; and more than that, she was plain; more still, she was in love with Robert; and most of all, she was thirty, and dependent on her Aunt Pauline. Oh, Cecilia! Why make music for her!

Cecilia, called by her aunt and by her cousin Robert just Ciss, like a cat spitting, was a big dark-complexioned pug-faced young woman who very rarely spoke, and, when she did, couldn't get it out. She was the daughter of a poor Congregational minister who had been, while he lived, brother to Ronald, Aunt Pauline's husband. Ronald and the Congregational minister were both well dead, and Aunt Pauline had had charge of Ciss for the last five years.

They lived all together in a quite exquisite though rather small Queen Anne house some twenty-five miles out of town, secluded in a little dale, and surrounded by small but very quaint and pleasant grounds. It was an ideal place and an ideal life for Aunt Pauline, at the age of seventy-two. When the kingfishers flashed up the little stream in the garden, going under the alders, something still flashed in her heart. She was that kind of woman.

Robert, who was two years older than Ciss, went every day to town, to his chambers in one of the Inns. He was a barrister, and, to his secret but very deep mortification, he earned about a hundred pounds a year. He simply *couldn't* get above that figure, though it was rather easy to get below it. Of course, it didn't matter. Pauline had money. But then what was Pauline's was Pauline's, and, though she could give almost lavishly, still, one was always aware of having a *lovely* and *undeserved* present made to one: presents are so much nicer when they are undeserved, Aunt Pauline would say.

Robert too was plain and almost speechless. He was medium-sized, rather broad and stout, though not fat. Only his creamy, clean-shaven face was rather fat and sometimes suggestive of an Italian priest, in its silence and its secrecy. But he had grey eyes like his mother but very shy and uneasy, not bold like hers. Perhaps Ciss was the only person who fathomed his awful shyness and *malaise,* his habitual feeling that he was in the wrong place: almost like a soul that has got into the wrong body. But he never did anything about it. He went up to his chambers, and read law. It was, however, all the weird old processes that interested him. He had, unknown to everybody but his mother, a quite extraordinary collection of old Mexican legal documents, reports of processes and trials, pleas, accusations, the weird and awful mixture of ecclesiastical law and com-

mon law in seventeenth-century Mexico. He had started
a study in this direction through coming across a report
of a trial of two English sailors, for murder, in Mexico
in 1620, and he had gone on, when the next document
was an accusation against a Don Miguel Estrada for
seducing one of the nuns of the Sacred Heart Convent
in Oaxaca in 1680.

Pauline and her son Robert had wonderful evenings
with these old papers. The lovely lady knew a little
Spanish. She even looked a trifle Spanish herself, with
a high comb and a marvellous dark brown shawl embroidered in thick silvery silk embroidery. So she would
sit at the perfect old table, soft as velvet in its deep
brown surface, a high comb in her hair, ear-rings with
dropping pendants in her ears, her arms bare and still
beautiful, a few strings of pearls round her throat, a
puce velvet dress on, and this or another beautiful
shawl, and by candlelight she looked, yes, a Spanish
high-bred beauty of thirty-two or three. She set the
candles to give her face just the chiaroscuro she knew
suited her; her high chair that rose behind her face was
done in old green brocade, against which her face
emerged like a Christmas rose.

They were always three at table; and they always
drank a bottle of champagne: Pauline two glasses, Ciss
two glasses, Robert the rest. The lovely lady sparkled
and was radiant. Ciss, her black hair bobbed, her broad
shoulders in a very nice and becoming dress that Aunt
Pauline had helped her to make, stared from her aunt to
her cousin and back again, with rather confused, mute,
hazel eyes, and played the part of an audience suitably
impressed. She *was* impressed, somewhere, all the time.
And even rendered speechless by Pauline's brilliancy,
even after five years. But at the bottom of her conscious-

ness were the data of as weird a document as Robert
ever studied: all the things she knew about her aunt
and cousin.

Robert was always a gentleman, with an old-fashioned
punctilious courtesy that covered his shyness quite completely. He was, and Ciss knew it, more confused than
shy. He was worse than she was. Cecilia's own confusion dated from only five years back—Robert's must
have started before he was born. In the lovely lady's
womb he must have felt *very* confused.

He paid all his attention to his mother, drawn to her
as a humble flower to the sun. And yet, priestlike, he
was all the time aware, with the tail of his consciousness,
that Ciss was there, and that she was a bit shut out of
it, and that something wasn't right. He was aware of the
third consciousness in the room. Whereas, to Pauline,
her niece Cecilia was an appropriate part of her own
setting, rather than a distinct consciousness.

Robert took coffee with his mother and Ciss in the
warm drawing-room, where all the furniture was so
lovely, all collectors' pieces—Mrs. Attenborough had
made her own money, dealing privately in pictures and
furniture and rare things from barbaric countries—and
the three talked desultorily till about eight or half-past.
It was very pleasant, very cosy, very homely even: Pauline made a real home cosiness out of so much elegant
material. The chat was simple and nearly always bright.
Pauline was her *real* self, emanating a friendly mockery
and an odd, ironic gaiety. Till there came a little pause.

At which Ciss always rose and said good night and
carried out the coffee tray, to prevent Burnett from in-
truding any more.

And then! Oh, then, the lovely glowing intimacy of
the evening, between mother and son, when they de-
ciphered manuscripts and discussed points, Pauline with

that eagerness of a girl, for which she was famous. And it was quite genuine. In some mysterious way she had *saved up* her power for being thrilled, in connexion with a man. Robert, solid, rather quiet and subdued, seemed like the elder of the two: almost like a priest with a young girl pupil. And that was rather how he felt.

Ciss had a flat for herself just across the court-yard, over the old coachhouse and stables. There were no horses. Robert kept his car in the coach-house. Ciss had three very nice rooms up there, stretching along in a row one after another, and she had got used to the ticking of the stable clock.

But sometimes she did not go up to her rooms. In the summer she would sit on the lawn, and from the open window of the drawing-room upstairs she would hear Pauline's wonderful heart-searching laugh. And in the winter the young woman would put on a thick coat and walk slowly to the little balustraded bridge over the stream, and then look back at the three lighted windows of that drawing-room where mother and son were so happy together.

Ciss loved Robert, and she believed that Pauline intended the two of them to marry: when she was dead. But poor Robert, he was so convulsed with shyness already, with man or woman. What would he be when his mother was dead?—in a dozen more years. He would be just a shell, the shell of a man who had never lived.

The strange unspoken sympathy of the young with one another, when they are overshadowed by the old, was one of the bonds between Robert and Ciss. But another bond, which Ciss did not know how to draw tight, was the bond of passion. Poor Robert was by nature a passionate man. His silence and his agonized, though hidden, shyness were both the result of a secret physical passionateness. And how Pauline could play on this! Ah, Ciss was not blind to the eyes which he fixed on his mother, eyes fascinated yet humiliated, full of shame. He was ashamed that he was not a man. And he did not love his mother. He was fascinated by her. Completely fascinated. And for the rest, paralyzed in a life-long confusion.

Ciss stayed in the garden till the lights leapt up in Pauline's bedroom—about ten o'clock. The lovely lady had retired. Robert would now stay another hour or so, alone. Then he too would retire. Ciss, in the dark outside, sometimes wished she could creep up to him and say: "Oh, Robert! It's all wrong!" But Aunt Pauline would hear. And anyhow, Ciss couldn't do it. She went off to her own rooms, once more, and so for ever.

In the morning, coffee was brought up on a tray to each of the three relatives. Ciss had to be at Sir Wilfred Knipe's at nine o'clock, to give two hours' lessons to his little granddaughter. It was her sole serious occupation, except that she played the piano for the love of it. Robert set off to town about nine. And, as a rule, Aunt Pauline appeared to lunch, though sometimes not until tea-time. When she appeared, she looked fresh and young. But she was inclined to fade rather quickly, like a flower without water, in the daytime. Her hour was the candle hour.

So she always rested in the afternoon. When the sun shone, if possible she took a sun bath. This was one of her secrets. Her lunch was very light, she could take her sun-and-air bath before noon or after, as it pleased her. Often it was in the afternoon, when the sun shone very warmly into a queer little yew-walled square just behind the stables. Here Ciss stretched out the lying-chair and rugs, and put the light parasol handy in the silent little enclosure of thick dark yew hedges beyond the red

walls of the unused stables. And hither came the lovely
lady with her book. Ciss then had to be on guard in one
of her own rooms, should her aunt, who was very keen-
eared, hear a footstep.

One afternoon it occurred to Cecilia that she herself
might while away this rather long afternoon by taking a
sun bath. She was growing restive. The thought of the
flat roof of the stable buildings, to which she could climb
from a loft at the end, started her on a new adventure.
She often went on to the roof: she had to, to wind up the
stable clock, which was a job she had assumed to herself. Now she took a rug, climbed out under the heavens,
looked at the sky and the great elm-tops, looked at the
sun, then took off her things and lay down perfectly
serenely, in a corner of the roof under the parapet, full
in the sun.

It was rather lovely, to bask all one's length like this
in warm sun and air. Yes, it was very lovely! It even
seemed to melt some of the hard bitterness of her heart,
some of that core of unspoken resentment which never
dissolved. Luxuriously, she spread herself, so that the
sun should touch her limbs fully, fully. If she had no
other lover, she should have the sun! She rolled volup-
tuously. And suddenly, her heart stood still in her body,
and her hair almost rose on end as a voice said very
softly, musingly in her ear:

"No, Henry dear! It was not my fault you died instead of marrying that Claudia. No, darling. I was quite,
quite willing for you to marry her, unsuitable though she
was."

Cecilia sank down on her rug powerless and perspir-
ing with dread. That awful voice, so soft, so musing, yet
so unnatural. Not a human voice at all. Yet there must,
there must be someone on the roof! Oh! how unspeakably awful!

She lifted her weak head and peeped across the sloping leads. Nobody! The chimneys were far too narrow to shelter anybody. There was nobody on the roof. Then it must be someone in the trees, in the elms. Either that, or terror unspeakable, a bodiless voice! She reared her head a little higher.

And as she did so, came the voice again:

"No, darling! I told you you would tire of her in six months. And you see, it was true, dear. It was true, true, true! I wanted to spare you that. So it wasn't I who made you feel weak and disabled, wanting that very silly Claudia; poor thing, she looked so woebegone afterwards! Wanting her and not wanting her, you got *yourself* into that perplexity, my dear. I only warned you. What else could I do? And you lost your spirit and died without ever knowing me again. It was bitter, bitter——"

The voice faded away. Cecilia subsided weakly on to her rug, after the anguished tension of listening. Oh, it was awful. The sun shone, the sky was blue, all seemed so lovely and afternoony and summery. And yet, oh, horror!—she was going to be forced to believe in the supernatural! And she loathed the supernatural, ghosts and voices and rappings and all the rest.

But that awful creepy bodiless voice, with its rusty sort of whisper of an overtone! It had something so fearfully familiar in it too! and yet was so utterly uncanny. Poor Cecilia could only lie there unclothed, and so all the more agonizingly helpless, inert, collapsed in sheer dread.

And then she heard the thing sigh! A deep sigh that seemed weirdly familiar, yet was not human. "Ah, well; ah, well, the heart must bleed! Better it should bleed than break. It is grief, grief! But it wasn't my fault, dear. And Robert could marry our poor dull Ciss tomorrow, if he wanted her. But he doesn't care about it, so why force him into anything!" The sounds were very uneven, sometimes only a husky sort of whisper. Listen! Listen!

Cecilia was about to give vent to loud and piercing screams of hysteria, when the last two sentences arrested her. All her caution and her cunning sprang alert. It was Aunt Pauline! It must be Aunt Pauline, practising ventriloquism or something like that! What a devil she was!

Where was she? She must be lying down there, right below where Cecilia herself was lying. And it was either some fiend's trick of ventriloquism, or else thought transference that conveyed itself like sound. The sounds were very uneven. Sometimes quite inaudible, sometimes only a brushing sort of noise. Ciss listened intently. No, it could not be ventriloquism. It was worse, some form of thought transference. Some horror of that sort. Cecilia still lay weak and inert, terrified to move, but she was growing calmer, with suspicion. It was some diabolic trick of that unnatural woman.

But *what a devil* of a woman! She even knew that she, Cecilia, had mentally accused her of killing her son Henry. Poor Henry was Robert's elder brother, twelve years older than Robert. He had died suddenly when he was twenty-two, after an awful struggle with himself, because he was passionately in love with a young and very good-looking actress, and his mother had humorously despised him for the attachment. So he had caught some sudden ordinary disease, but the poison had gone to his brain and killed him, before he ever regained consciousness. Ciss knew the few facts from her own father. And lately, she had been thinking that Pauline was going to kill Robert as she had killed Henry. It was clear murder: a mother murdering her sensitive sons, who were fascinated by her: the Circe!

"I suppose I may as well get up," murmured the dim unbreaking voice. "Too much sun is as bad as too little. Enough sun, enough love thrill, enough proper food, and not too much of any of them, and a woman might live for ever. I verily believe for ever. If she absorbs as much vitality as she expends! Or perhaps a trifle more!"

It was certainly Aunt Pauline! How, how horrible! She, Ciss, was hearing Aunt Pauline's thoughts. Oh, how ghastly! Aunt Pauline was sending out her thoughts in a sort of radio, and she, Ciss, had to *hear* what her aunt was thinking. How ghastly! How insufferable! One of them would surely have to die.

She twisted and she lay inert and crumpled, staring vacantly in front of her. Vacantly! Vacantly! And her eyes were staring almost into a hole. She was staring into it unseeing, a hole going down in the corner from the lead gutter. It meant nothing to her. Only it frightened her a little more.

When suddenly out of the hole came a sigh and a last whisper. "Ah, well! Pauline! Get up, it's enough for today!"—Good God! Out of the hole of the rain-pipe! The rain-pipe was acting as a speaking-tube! Impossible! No, quite possible. She had read of it even in some book. And Aunt Pauline, like the old and guilty woman she was, talked aloud to herself. That was it!

A sullen exultance sprang into Ciss's breast. *That* was why she would never have anybody, not even Robert, in her bedroom. That was why she never dozed in a chair, never sat absent-minded anywhere, but went to her room, and kept to her room, except when she roused herself to be alert. When she slackened off, she talked to herself! She talked in a soft little crazy voice, to herself. But she was not crazy. It was only her thoughts murmuring themselves aloud.

So she had qualms about poor Henry! Well she might

have! Ciss believed that Aunt Pauline had loved her big, handsome, brilliant first-born much more than she loved Robert, and that his death had been a terrible blow and a chagrin to her. Poor Robert had been only ten years old when Henry died. Since then he had been the substitute.

Ah, how awful!

But Aunt Pauline was a strange woman. She had left her husband when Henry was a small child, some years even before Robert was born. There was no quarrel. Sometimes she saw her husband again, quite amicably, but a little mockingly. And she even gave him money.

For Pauline earned all her own. Her father had been a Consul in the East and in Naples, and a devoted collector of beautiful and exotic things. When he died, soon after his grandson Henry was born, he left his collection of treasures to his daughter. And Pauline, who had really a passion and a genius for loveliness, whether in texture or form or colour, had laid the basis of her fortune on her father's collection. She had gone on collecting, buying where she could, and selling to collectors and to museums. She was one of the first to sell old, weird African wooden figures to the museums, and ivory carvings from New Guinea. She bought Renoir as soon as she saw his pictures. But not Rousseau. And all by herself, she made a fortune.

After her husband died, she had not married again. She was not even *known* to have had lovers. If she did have lovers, it was not among the men who admired her most and paid her devout and open attendance. To these she was a "friend."

Cecilia slipped on her clothes and caught up her rug, hastening carefully down the ladder to the loft. As she descended she heard the ringing musical call: "All right, Ciss!" which meant that the lovely lady was finished, and returning to the house. Even her voice was marvellously young and sonorous, beautifully balanced and self-possessed. So different from the little voice in which she talked to herself. *That* was much more the voice of an old woman.

Ciss hastened round to the yew enclosure, where lay the comfortable chaise-longue with the various delicate rugs. Everything Pauline had was choice, to the fine straw mat on the floor. The great yew walls were beginning to cast long shadows. Only in the corner, where the rugs tumbled their delicate colours, was there hot, still sunshine.

The rugs folded up, the chair lifted away, Cecilia stooped to look at the mouth of the rain-pipe. There it was, in the corner, under a little hood of masonry and just projecting from the thick leaves of the creeper on the wall. If Pauline, lying there, turned her face towards the wall, she would speak into the very mouth of the hole. Cecilia was reassured. She had heard her aunt's thoughts indeed, but by no uncanny agency.

That evening, as if aware of something, Pauline was a little quicker than usual, though she looked her own serene, rather mysterious self. And after coffee she said to Robert and Ciss: "I'm so sleepy. The sun has made me so sleepy. I feel full of sunshine like a bee. I shall go to bed, if you don't mind. You two sit and have a talk."

Cecilia looked quickly at her cousin.

"Perhaps you would rather be alone," she said to him.

"No, no," he replied. "Do keep me company for a while, if it doesn't bore you."

The windows were open, the scent of the honeysuckle wafted in, with the sound of an owl. Robert smoked in silence. There was a sort of despair in the motionless, rather squat body. He looked like a caryatid bearing a weight.

"Do you remember Cousin Henry?" Cecilia asked him suddenly.

He looked up in surprise.

"Yes, very well," he said.

"What did he look like?" she said, glancing into her cousin's big secret-troubled eyes, in which there was so much frustration.

"Oh, he was handsome; tall and fresh-coloured, with mother's soft brown hair." As a matter of fact, Pauline's hair was grey. "The ladies admired him very much; he was at all the dances."

"And what kind of character had he?"

"Oh, very good-natured and jolly. He liked to be amused. He was rather quick and clever, like mother, and very good company."

"And did he love your mother?"

"Very much. She loved him too—better than she does me, as a matter of fact. He was so much more nearly her idea of a man."

"Why was he more her idea of a man?"

"Tall—handsome—attractive, and very good company —and would, I believe, have been very successful at law. I'm afraid I am merely negative in all those respects."

Ciss looked at him attentively, with her slow-thinking hazel eyes. Under his impassive mask, she knew he suffered.

"Do you think you are so much more negative than he?" she said.

He did not lift his face. But after a few moments he replied:

"My life, certainly, is a negative affair."

She hesitated before she dared ask him:

"And do you mind?"

He did not answer her at all. Her heart sank.

"You see, I am afraid my life is as negative as yours is," she said. "And I'm beginning to mind bitterly. I'm thirty."

She saw his creamy, well-bred hand tremble.

"I suppose," he said, without looking at her, "one will rebel when it is too late."

That was queer, from him.

"Robert," she said, "do you like me at all?"

She saw his dusky creamy face, so changeless in its folds, go pale.

"I am very fond of you," he murmured.

"Won't you kiss me? Nobody ever kisses me," she said pathetically.

He looked at her, his eyes strange with fear and a certain haughtiness. Then he rose and came softly over to her, and kissed her gently on the cheek.

"It's an awful shame, Ciss!" he said softly.

She caught his hand and pressed it to her breast.

"And sit with me sometime in the garden," she said, murmuring with difficulty. "Won't you?"

He looked at her anxiously and searchingly.

"What about mother?" he said.

Ciss smiled a funny little smile, and looked into his eyes. He suddenly flushed crimson, turning aside his face. It was a painful sight.

"I know," he said, "I am no lover of women."

He spoke with sarcastic stoicism against himself, but even she did not know the shame it was to him.

"You never try to be!" she said.

Again his eyes changed uncannily.

"Does one have to try?" he said.

"Why, yes! One never does anything if one doesn't try."

He went pale again.

"Perhaps you are right," he said.

In a few minutes she left him, and went to her rooms. At least, she had tried to take off the everlasting lid from things.

The weather continued sunny, Pauline continued her sun baths, and Ciss lay on the roof eavesdropping in the literal sense of the word. But Pauline was not to be heard. No sound came up the pipe. She must be lying with her face away into the open. Ciss listened with all her might. She could just detect the faintest, faintest murmur away below, but no audible syllable.

And at night, under the stars, Cecilia sat and waited in silence, on the seat which kept in view the drawing-room windows and the side door into the garden. She saw the light go up in her aunt's room. She saw the lights at last go out in the drawing-room. And she waited. But he did not come. She stayed on in the darkness half the night, while the owl hooted. But she stayed alone.

Two days she heard nothing, her aunt's thoughts were not revealed, and at evening nothing happened. Then the second night, as she sat with heavy, helpless persistence in the garden, suddenly she started. He had come out. She rose and went softly over the grass to him.

"Don't speak," he murmured.

And in silence, in the dark, they walked down the garden and over the little bridge to the paddock, where the hay, cut very late, was in cock. There they stood disconsolate under the stars.

"You see," he said, "how can I ask for love, if I don't feel any love in myself. You know I have a real regard for you——"

"How can you feel any love, when you never feel anything?" she said.

"That is true," he replied.

And she waited for what next.

"And how can I marry?" he said. "I am a failure even at making money. I can't ask my mother for money."

She sighed deeply.

"Then don't bother yet about marrying," she said. "Only love me a little. Won't you?"

He gave a short laugh.

"It sounds so atrocious, to say it is hard to begin," he said.

She sighed again. He was so stiff to move.

"Shall we sit down a minute?" she said. And then as they sat on the hay, she added: "May I touch you? Do you mind?"

"Yes, I mind! But do as you wish," he replied, with that mixture of shyness and queer candour which made him a little ridiculous, as he knew quite well. But in his heart there was almost murder.

She touched his black, always tidy hair with her fingers.

"I suppose I shall rebel one day," he said again, suddenly.

They sat some time till it grew chilly. And he held her hand fast, but he never put his arms round her. At last she rose and went indoors, saying good night.

The next day, as Cecilia lay stunned and angry on the roof, taking her sun bath, and becoming hot and fierce with sunshine, suddenly she started. A terror seized her in spite of herself. It was the voice.

"Caro, caro, tu non l'hai visto!" it was murmuring away, in a language Cecilia did not understand. She lay and writhed her limbs in the sun, listening intently to words she could not follow. Softly, whisperingly, with infinite caressiveness and yet with that subtle, insidious arrogance under its velvet, came the voice, murmuring in Italian: "Bravo, si, molto bravo, poverino, ma uomo

come te non lo sara mai, mai, mai!" Oh, especially in
Italian Cecilia heard the poisonous charm of the voice,
so caressive, so soft and flexible, yet so utterly egoistic.
She hated it with intensity as it sighed and whispered
out of nowhere. Why, why should it be so delicate, so
subtle and flexible and beautifully controlled, while she
herself was so clumsy! Oh, poor Cecilia, she writhed in
the afternoon sun, knowing her own clownish clumsiness and lack of suavity, in comparison.

"No, Robert dear, you will never be the man your
father was, though you have some of his looks. He was
a marvellous lover, soft as a flower yet piercing as a
humming-bird. No, Robert dear, you will never know
how to serve a woman as Monsignor Mauro did. Cara,
cara mia bellisima, ti ho aspettato come l'agonizzante
aspetta la morte, morte deliziosa, quasi quasi troppo
deliziosa per un' anima humana—Soft as a flower, yet
probing like a humming-bird. He gave himself to a
woman as he gave himself to God. Mauro! Mauro! How
you loved me!"

The voice ceased in reverie, and Cecilia knew what
she had guessed before, that Robert was not the son of
her Uncle Ronald, but of some Italian.

"I am disappointed in you, Robert. There is no poign-
ancy in you. Your father was a Jesuit, but he was the
most perfect and poignant lover in the world. You are a
Jesuit like a fish in a tank. And that Ciss of yours is the
cat fishing for you. It is less edifying even than poor
Henry."

Cecilia suddenly bent her mouth down to the tube,
and said in a deep voice:

"Leave Robert alone! Don't kill him as well."

There was a dead silence, in the hot July afternoon
that was lowering for thunder. Cecilia lay prostrate, her

heart beating in great thumps. She was listening as if her whole soul were an ear. At last she caught the whisper:

"Did someone speak?"

She leaned again to the mouth of the tube.

"Don't kill Robert as you killed me," she said with slow enunciation, and a deep but small voice.

"Ah!" came the sharp little cry. "Who is that speaking?"

"Henry!" said the deep voice.

There was dead silence. Poor Cecilia lay with all the use gone out of her. And there was dead silence. Till at last came the whisper:

"I didn't kill Henry. No, NO! Henry, surely you can't blame me! I loved you, dearest. I only wanted to help you."

"You killed me!" came the deep, artificial, accusing voice. "Now, let Robert live. Let him go! Let him marry!"

There was a pause.

"How very, very awful!" mused the whispering voice. "Is it possible, Henry, you are a spirit, and you condemn me?"

"Yes! I condemn you!"

Cecilia felt all her pent-up rage going down that rain-pipe. At the same time, she almost laughed. It was awful.

She lay and listened and listened. No sound! As if time had ceased, she lay inert in the weakening sun. The sky was yellowing. Quickly she dressed herself, went down, and out to the corner of the stables.

"Aunt Pauline!" she called discreetly. "Did you hear thunder?"

"Yes! I am going in. Don't wait," came a feeble voice.

Cecilia retired, and from the loft watched, spying, as

the figure of the lovely lady, wrapped in a lovely wrap of old blue silk, went rather totteringly to the house.

The sky gradually darkened, Cecilia hastened in with the rugs. Then the storm broke. Aunt Pauline did not appear to tea. She found the thunder trying. Robert also did not arrive till after tea, in the pouring rain. Cecilia went down the covered passage to her own house, and dressed carefully for dinner, putting some white columbines at her breast.

The drawing-room was lit with a softly shaded lamp. Robert, dressed, was waiting, listening to the rain. He too seemed strangely crackling and on edge. Cecilia came in, with the white flowers nodding at her breast. Robert was watching her curiously, a new look on his face. Cecilia went to the bookshelves near the door and was peering for something, listening acutely. She heard a rustle, then the door softly opening. And as it opened, Ciss suddenly switched on the strong electric light by the door.

Her aunt, in a dress of black lace over ivory colour, stood in the doorway. Her face was made up, but haggard with a look of unspeakable irritability, as if years of suppressed exasperation and dislike of her fellow-men had suddenly crumpled her into an old witch.

"Oh, aunt!" cried Cecilia.

"Why, mother, you're a little old lady!" came the astounded voice of Robert; like an astonished boy; as if it were a joke.

"Have you only just found it out?" snapped the old woman venomously.

"Yes! Why, I thought——" his voice trailed out in misgiving.

The haggard, old Pauline, in a frenzy of exasperation, said:

"Aren't we going down?"

She had never even noticed the excess of light, a thing she shunned. And she went downstairs almost tottering.

At table she sat with her face like a crumpled mask of unspeakable irritability. She looked old, very old, and like a witch. Robert and Cecilia fetched furtive glances at her. And Ciss, watching Robert, saw that he was so astonished and repelled by his mother's looks that he was another man.

"What kind of a drive home did you have?" snapped Pauline, with an almost gibbering irritability.

"It rained, of course," he said.

"How clever of you to have found that out!" said his mother, with the grisly grin of malice that had succeeded her arch smirk.

"I don't understand," he said with quiet suavity.

"It's apparent," said his mother, rapidly and sloppily eating her food.

She rushed through the meal like a crazy dog, to the utter consternation of the servant. And the moment it was over, she darted in a queer, crab-like way upstairs. Robert and Cecilia followed her, thunderstruck, like two conspirators.

"You pour the coffee. I loathe it! I'm going! Good night!" said the old woman, in a succession of sharp shots. And she scrambled out of the room.

There was a dead silence. At last he said:

"I'm afraid mother isn't well. I must persuade her to see a doctor."

"Yes!" said Cecilia.

The evening passed in silence. Robert and Ciss stayed on in the drawing-room, having lit a fire. Outside was cold rain. Each pretended to read. They did not want to separate. The evening passed with ominous mysteriousness, yet quickly.

At about ten o'clock, the door suddenly opened, and

Pauline appeared, in a blue wrap. She shut the door behind her and came to the fire. Then she looked at the two young people in hate, real hate.

"You two had better get married quickly," she said in an ugly voice. "It would look more decent; such a passionate pair of lovers!"

Robert looked up at her quietly.

"I thought you believed that cousins should not marry, mother," he said.

"I do! But you're not cousins. Your father was an Italian priest." Pauline held her daintily slippered foot to the fire, in an old coquettish gesture. Her body tried to repeat all the old graceful gestures. But the nerve had snapped, so it was a rather dreadful caricature.

"Is that really true, mother?" he asked.

"True! What do you think? He was a distinguished man, or he wouldn't have been my lover. He was far too distinguished a man to have had you for a son. But that joy fell to me."

"How unfortunate all round," he said slowly.

"Unfortunate for you? *You* were lucky. It was *my* misfortune," she said acidly to him.

She was really a dreadful sight, like a piece of lovely Venetian glass that has been dropped, and gathered up again in horrible, sharp edged fragments.

Suddenly she left the room again.

For a week it went on. She did not recover. It was as if every nerve in her body had suddenly started screaming in an insanity of discordance. The doctor came, and gave her sedatives, for she never slept. Without drugs, she never slept at all, only paced back and forth in her room, looking hideous and evil, reeking with malevolence. She could not bear to see either her son or her niece. Only when either of them came, she asked in pure malice:

"Well! When's the wedding? Have you celebrated the nuptials yet?"

At first Cecilia was stunned by what she had done. She realized vaguely that her aunt, once a definite thrust of condemnation had penetrated her beautiful armour, had just collapsed, squirming inside her shell. It was too terrible. Ciss was almost terrified into repentance. Then she thought: This is what she always was. Now let her live the rest of her days in her true colours.

But Pauline would not live long. She was literally shrivelling away. She kept her room, and saw no one. She had her mirrors taken away.

Robert and Cecilia sat a good deal together. The jeering of the mad Pauline had not driven them apart, as she had hoped. But Cecilia dared not confess to him what she had done.

"Do you think your mother ever loved anybody?" Ciss asked him tentatively, rather wistfully, one evening.

He looked at her fixedly.

"Herself!" he said at last.

"She didn't even *love* herself," said Ciss. "It was something else—what was it?" She lifted a troubled, utterly puzzled face to him.

"Power!" he said curtly.

"But what power?" she asked. "I don't understand."

"Power to feed on other lives," he said bitterly. "She was beautiful, and she fed on life. She has fed on me as she fed on Henry. She put a sucker into one's soul, and sucked up one's essential life."

"And don't you forgive her?"

"No."

"Poor Aunt Pauline!"

But even Ciss did not mean it. She was only aghast.

"I *know* I've got a heart," he said, passionately striking his breast. "But it's almost sucked dry. I *know* people who want power over others."

Ciss was silent; what was there to say?

And two days later, Pauline was found dead in her bed, having taken too much veronal, for her heart was weakened. From the grave even she hit back at her son and her niece. She left Robert the noble sum of one thousand pounds; and Ciss one hundred. All the rest, with the nucleus of her valuable antiques, went to form the "Pauline Attenborough Museum."

The Rocking-Horse Winner

THERE was a woman who was beautiful, who started with all the advantages, yet she had no luck. She married for love, and the love turned to dust. She had bonny children, yet she felt they had been thrust upon her, and she could not love them. They looked at her coldly, as if they were finding fault with her. And hurriedly she felt she must cover up some fault in herself. Yet what it was that she must cover up she never knew. Nevertheless, when her children were present, she always felt the centre of her heart go hard. This troubled her, and in her manner she was all the more gentle and anxious for her children, as if she loved them very much. Only she herself knew that at the centre of her heart was a hard little place that could not feel love, no, not for anybody. Everybody else said of her: "She is such a good mother. She adores her children." Only she herself, and her children themselves, knew it was not so. They read it in each other's eyes.

There were a boy and two little girls. They lived in a

pleasant house, with a garden, and they had discreet
servants, and felt themselves superior to anyone in the
neighbourhood.

Although they lived in style, they felt always an anxiety in the house. There was never enough money. The
mother had a small income, and the father had a small
income, but not nearly enough for the social position
which they had to keep up. The father went in to town
to some office. But though he had good prospects, these
prospects never materialized. There was always the
grinding sense of the shortage of money, though the
style was always kept up.

At last the mother said: "I will see if *I* can't make
something." But she did not know where to begin. She
racked her brains, and tried this thing and the other, but
could not find anything successful. The failure made
deep lines come into her face. Her children were growing up, they would have to go to school. There must be
more money, there must be more money. The father, who
was always very handsome and expensive in his tastes,
seemed as if he never *would* be able to do anything
worth doing. And the mother, who had a great belief
in herself, did not succeed any better, and her tastes
were just as expensive.

And so the house came to be haunted by the unspoken phrase: *There must be more money! There must
be more money!* The children could hear it all the time,
though nobody said it aloud. They heard it at Christmas,
when the expensive and splendid toys filled the nursery.
Behind the shining modern rocking-horse, behind the
smart doll's-house, a voice would start whispering:
"There *must* be more money! There *must* be more
money!" And the children would stop playing, to listen
for a moment. They would look into each other's eyes,
to see if they had all heard. And each one saw in the

eyes of the other two that they too had heard. "There *must* be more money! There *must* be more money!"

It came whispering from the springs of the still-swaying rocking-horse, and even the horse, bending his wooden, champing head, heard it. The big doll, sitting so pink and smirking in her new pram, could hear it quite plainly, and seemed to be smirking all the more self-consciously because of it. The foolish puppy, too, that took the place of the teddy-bear, he was looking so extraordinarily foolish for no other reason but that he heard the secret whisper all over the house: "There *must* be more money!"

Yet nobody ever said it aloud. The whisper was everywhere, and therefore no one spoke it. Just as no one ever says: "We are breathing!" in spite of the fact that breath is coming and going all the time.

"Mother," said the boy Paul one day, "why don't we keep a car of our own? Why do we always use uncle's, or else a taxi?"

"Because we're the poor members of the family," said the mother.

"But why *are* we, mother?"

"Well—I suppose," she said slowly and bitterly, "it's because your father has no luck."

The boy was silent for some time.

"Is luck money, mother?" he asked rather timidly.

"No, Paul. Not quite. It's what causes you to have money."

"Oh!" said Paul vaguely. "I thought when Uncle Oscar said *filthy lucker*, it meant money."

"*Filthy lucre* does mean money," said the mother. "But it's lucre, not luck."

"Oh!" said the boy. "Then what *is* luck, mother?"

"It's what causes you to have money. If you're lucky you have money. That's why it's better to be born lucky than rich. If you're rich, you may lose your money. But if you're lucky, you will always get more money."

"Oh! Will you? And is father not lucky?"

"Very unlucky, I should say," she said bitterly.

The boy watched her with unsure eyes.

"Why?" he asked.

"I don't know. Nobody ever knows why one person is lucky and another unlucky."

"Don't they? Nobody at all? Does *nobody* know?"

"Perhaps God. But He never tells."

"He ought to, then. And aren't you lucky either, mother?"

"I can't be, if I married an unlucky husband."

"But by yourself, aren't you?"

"I used to think I was, before I married. Now I think I am very unlucky indeed."

"Why?"

"Well—never mind! Perhaps I'm not really," she said.

The child looked at her, to see if she meant it. But he saw, by the lines of her mouth, that she was only trying to hide something from him.

"Well, anyhow," he said stoutly, "I'm a lucky person."

"Why?" said his mother, with a sudden laugh.

He stared at her. He didn't even know why he had said it.

"God told me," he asserted, brazening it out.

"I hope He did, dear!" she said, again with a laugh, but rather bitter.

"He did, mother!"

"Excellent!" said the mother, using one of her husband's exclamations.

The boy saw she did not believe him; or, rather, that she paid no attention to his assertion. This angered him somewhat, and made him want to compel her attention.

He went off by himself, vaguely, in a childish way,

seeking for the clue to "luck." Absorbed, taking no heed of other people, he went about with a sort of stealth, seeking inwardly for luck. He wanted luck, he wanted it, he wanted it. When the two girls were playing dolls in the nursery, he would sit on his big rocking-horse, charging madly into space, with a frenzy that made the little girls peer at him uneasily. Wildly the horse careered, the waving dark hair of the boy tossed, his eyes had a strange glare in them. The little girls dared not speak to him.

When he had ridden to the end of his mad little journey, he climbed down and stood in front of his rocking-horse, staring fixedly into its lowered face. Its red mouth was slightly open, its big eye was wide and glassy-bright.

"Now!" he would silently command the snorting steed. "Now, take me to where there is luck! Now take me!"

And he would slash the horse on the neck with the little whip he had asked Uncle Oscar for. He *knew* the horse could take him to where there was luck, if only he forced it. So he would mount again, and start on his furious ride, hoping at last to get there. He knew he could get there.

"You'll break your horse, Paul!" said the nurse.

"He's always riding like that! I wish he'd leave off!" said his elder sister Joan.

But he only glared down on them in silence. Nurse gave him up. She could make nothing of him. Anyhow he was growing beyond her.

One day his mother and his Uncle Oscar came in when he was on one of his furious rides. He did not speak to them.

"Hallo, you young jockey! Riding a winner?" said his uncle.

"Aren't you growing too big for a rocking-horse? You're not a very little boy any longer, you know," said his mother.

But Paul only gave a blue glare from his big, rather close-set eyes. He would speak to nobody when he was in full tilt. His mother watched him with an anxious expression on her face.

At last he suddenly stopped forcing his horse into the mechanical gallop, and slid down.

"Well, I got there!" he announced fiercely, his blue eyes still flaring, and his sturdy long legs straddling apart.

"Where did you get to?" asked his mother.

"Where I wanted to go," he flared back at her.

"That's right, son!" said Uncle Oscar. "Don't you stop till you get there. What's the horse's name?"

"He doesn't have a name," said the boy.

"Gets on without all right?" asked the uncle.

"Well, he has different names. He was called Sansovino last week."

"Sansovino, eh? Won the Ascot. How did you know his name?"

"He always talks about horse-races with Bassett," said Joan.

The uncle was delighted to find that his small nephew was posted with all the racing news. Bassett, the young gardener, who had been wounded in the left foot in the war and had got his present job through Oscar Cresswell, whose batman he had been, was a perfect blade of the "turf." He lived in the racing events, and the small boy lived with him.

Oscar Cresswell got it all from Bassett.

"Master Paul comes and asks me, so I can't do more than tell him, sir," said Bassett, his face terribly serious, as if he were speaking of religious matters.

"And does he ever put anything on a horse he. fancies?"

"Well—I don't want to give him away—he's a young sport, a fine sport, sir. Would you mind asking him himself? He sort of takes a pleasure in it, and perhaps he'd feel I was giving him away, sir, if you don't mind."

Bassett was serious as a church.

The uncle went back to his nephew and took him off for a ride in the car.

"Say, Paul, old man, do you ever put anything on a horse?" the uncle asked.

The boy watched the handsome man closely.

"Why, do you think I oughtn't to?" he parried.

"Not a bit of it! I thought perhaps you might give me a tip for the Lincoln."

The car sped on into the country, going down to Uncle Oscar's place in Hampshire.

"Honour bright?" said the nephew.

"Honour bright, son!" said the uncle.

"Well, then, Daffodil."

"Daffodil! I doubt it, sonny. What about Mirza?"

"I only know the winner," said the boy. "That's Daffodil."

"Daffodil, eh?"

There was a pause. Daffodil was an obscure horse comparatively.

"Uncle!"

"Yes, son?"

"You won't let it go any further, will you? I promised Bassett."

"Bassett be damned, old man! What's he got to do with it?"

"We're partners. We've been partners from the first. Uncle, he lent me my first five shillings, which I lost. I promised him, honour bright, it was only between me

and him; only you gave me that ten-shilling note I
started winning with, so I thought you were lucky. You
won't let it go any further, will you?"

The boy gazed at his uncle from those big, hot, blue
eyes, set rather close together. The uncle stirred and
laughed uneasily.

"Right you are, son! I'll keep your tip private. Daffodil, eh? How much are you putting on him?"

"All except twenty pounds," said the boy. "I keep
that in reserve."

The uncle thought it a good joke.

"You keep twenty pounds in reserve, do you, you
young romancer? What are you betting, then?"

"I'm betting three hundred," said the boy gravely.
"But it's between you and me, Uncle Oscar! Honour
bright?"

The uncle burst into a roar of laughter.

"It's between you and me all right, you young Nat
Gould," he said, laughing. "But where's your three hundred?"

"Bassett keeps it for me. We're partners."

"You are, are you! And what is Bassett putting on
Daffodil?"

"He won't go quite as high as I do, I expect. Perhaps
he'll go a hundred and fifty."

"What, pennies?" laughed the uncle.

"Pounds," said the child, with a surprised look at his
uncle. "Bassett keeps a bigger reserve than I do."

Between wonder and amusement Uncle Oscar was
silent. He pursued the matter no further, but he determined to take his nephew with him to the Lincoln races.

"Now, son," he said, "I'm putting twenty on Mirza,
and I'll put five for you on any horse you fancy. What's
your pick?"

"Daffodil, uncle."

"No, not the fiver on Daffodil!"

"I should if it was my own fiver," said the child.

"Good! Good! Right you are! A fiver for me and a fiver for you on Daffodil."

The child had never been to a race-meeting before, and his eyes were blue fire. He pursed his mouth tight, and watched. A Frenchman just in front had put his money on Lancelot. Wild with excitement, he flayed his arms up and down, yelling *"Lancelot! Lancelot!"* in his French accent.

Daffodil came in first, Lancelot second, Mirza third. The child, flushed and with eyes blazing, was curiously serene. His uncle brought him four five-pound notes, four to one.

"What am I to do with these?" he cried, waving them before the boy's eyes.

"I suppose we'll talk to Bassett," said the boy. "I expect I have fifteen hundred now; and twenty in reserve; and this twenty."

His uncle studied him for some moments.

"Look here, son!" he said. "You're not serious about Bassett and that fifteen hundred, are you?"

"Yes, I am. But it's between you and me, uncle. Honour bright!"

"Honour bright all right, son! But I must talk to Bassett."

"If you'd like to be a partner, uncle, with Bassett and me, we could all be partners. Only, you'd have to promise, honour bright, uncle, not to let it go beyond us three. Bassett and I are lucky, and you must be lucky, because it was your ten shillings I started winning with. . . ."

Uncle Oscar took both Bassett and Paul into Richmond Park for an afternoon, and there they talked.

"It's like this, you see, sir," Bassett said. "Master Paul

would get me talking about racing events, spinning yarns, you know, sir. And he was always keen on knowing if I'd made or if I'd lost. It's about a year since, now, that I put five shilling on Blush of Dawn for him—and we lost. Then the luck turned, with that ten shillings he had from you, that we put on Singhalese. And since that time, it's been pretty steady, all things considering. What do you say, Master Paul?"

"We're all right when we're sure," said Paul. "It's when we're not quite sure that we go down."

"Oh, but we're careful then," said Bassett.

"But when are you *sure?*" smiled Uncle Oscar.

"It's Master Paul, sir," said Bassett, in a secret, religious voice. "It's as if he had it from heaven. Like Daffodil, now, for the Lincoln. That was as sure as eggs."

"Did you put anything on Daffodil?" asked Oscar Cresswell.

"Yes, sir. I made my bit."

"And my nephew?"

Bassett was obstinately silent, looking at Paul.

"I made twelve hundred, didn't I, Bassett? I told uncle I was putting three hundred on Daffodil."

"That's right," said Bassett, nodding.

"But where's the money?" asked the uncle.

"I keep it safe locked up, sir. Master Paul he can have it any minute he likes to ask for it."

"What, fifteen hundred pounds?"

"And twenty! And *forty,* that is, with the twenty he made on the course."

"It's amazing!" said the uncle.

"If Master Paul offers you to be partners, sir, I would, if I were you; if you'll excuse me," said Bassett.

Oscar Cresswell thought about it.

"I'll see the money," he said.

They drove home again, and sure enough, Bassett came round to the garden-house with fifteen hundred pounds in notes. The twenty pounds reserve was left with Joe Glee, in the Turf Commission deposit.

"You see, it's all right, uncle, when I'm *sure!* Then we go strong, for all we're worth. Don't we, Bassett?"

"We do that, Master Paul."

"And when are you sure?" said the uncle, laughing.

"Oh, well, sometimes I'm *absolutely* sure, like about Daffodil," said the boy; "and sometimes I have an idea; and sometimes I haven't even an idea, have I, Bassett? Then we're careful, because we mostly go down."

"You do, do you! And when you're sure, like about Daffodil, what makes you sure, sonny?"

"Oh, well, I don't know," said the boy uneasily. "I'm sure, you know, uncle; that's all."

"It's as if he had it from heaven, sir," Bassett reiterated.

"I should say so!" said the uncle.

But he became a partner. And when the Leger was coming on, Paul was "sure" about Lively Spark, which was a quite inconsiderable horse. The boy insisted on putting a thousand on the horse, Bassett went for five hundred, and Oscar Cresswell two hundred. Lively Spark came in first, and the betting had been ten to one against him. Paul had made ten thousand.

"You see," he said, "I was absolutely sure of him."

Even Oscar Cresswell had cleared two thousand.

"Look here, son," he said, "this sort of thing makes me nervous."

"It needn't, uncle! Perhaps I shan't be sure again for a long time."

"But what are you going to do with your money?" asked the uncle.

"Of course," said the boy, "I started it for mother. She said she had no luck, because father is unlucky, so I thought if *I* was lucky, it might stop whispering."

"What might stop whispering?"

"Our house. I *hate* our house for whispering."

"What does it whisper?"

"Why—why"—the boy fidgeted—"why, I don't know. But it's always short of money, you know, uncle."

"I know it, son, I know it."

"You know people send mother writs, don't you, uncle?"

"I'm afraid I do," said the uncle.

"And then the house whispers, like people laughing at you behind your back. It's awful, that is! I thought if I was lucky . . ."

"You might stop it," added the uncle.

The boy watched him with big blue eyes, that had an uncanny cold fire in them, and he said never a word.

"Well, then!" said the uncle. "What are we doing?"

"I shouldn't like mother to know I was lucky," said the boy.

"Why not, son?"

"She'd stop me."

"I don't think she would."

"Oh!"—and the boy writhed in an odd way—"I *don't* want her to know, uncle."

"All right, son! We'll manage it without her knowing."

They managed it very easily. Paul, at the other's suggestion, handed over five thousand pounds to his uncle, who deposited it with the family lawyer, who was then to inform Paul's mother that a relative had put five thousand pounds into his hands, which sum was to be paid out a thousand pounds at a time, on the mother's birthday, for the next five years.

"So she'll have a birthday present of a thousand pounds for five successive years," said Uncle Oscar. "I hope it won't make it all the harder for her later."

Paul's mother had her birthday in November. The house had been "whispering" worse than ever lately, and, even in spite of his luck, Paul could not bear up against it. He was very anxious to see the effect of the birthday letter, telling his mother about the thousand pounds.

When there were no visitors, Paul now took his meals with his parents, as he was beyond the nursery control. His mother went into town nearly every day. She had discovered that she had an odd knack of sketching furs and dress materials, so she worked secretly in the studio of a friend who was the chief "artist" for the leading drapers. She drew the figures of ladies in furs and ladies in silk and sequins for the newspaper advertisements. This young woman artist earned several thousand pounds a year, but Paul's mother only made several hundreds, and she was again dissatisfied. She so wanted to be first in something, and she did not succeed, even in making sketches for drapery advertisements.

She was down to breakfast on the morning of her birthday. Paul watched her face as she read her letters. He knew the lawyer's letter. As his mother read it, her face hardened and became more expressionless. Then a cold, determined look came on her mouth. She hid the letter under the pile of others, and said not a word about it.

"Didn't you have anything nice in the post for your birthday, mother?" said Paul.

"Quite moderately nice," she said, her voice cold and absent.

She went away to town without saying more.

But in the afternoon Uncle Oscar appeared. He said Paul's mother had had a long interview with the lawyer, asking if the whole five thousand could not be advanced at once, as she was in debt.

"What do you think, uncle?" said the boy.

"I leave it to you, son."

"Oh, let her have it, then! We can get some more with the other," said the boy.

"A bird in the hand is worth two in the bush, laddie!" said Uncle Oscar.

"But I'm sure to *know* for the Grand National; or the Lincolnshire; or else the Derby. I'm sure to know for *one* of them," said Paul.

So Uncle Oscar signed the agreement, and Paul's mother touched the whole five thousand. Then something very curious happened. The voices in the house suddenly went mad, like a chorus of frogs on a spring evening. There were certain new furnishings, and Paul had a tutor. He was *really* going to Eton, his father's school, in the following autumn. There were flowers in the winter, and a blossoming of the luxury Paul's mother had been used to. And yet the voices in the house, behind the sprays of mimosa and almond blossom, and from under the piles of iridescent cushions, simply trilled and screamed in a sort of ecstasy: "There *must* be more money! Oh-h-h; there *must* be more money. Oh, now, now-w! Now-w-w—there *must* be more money!—more than ever! More than ever!"

It frightened Paul terribly. He studied away at his Latin and Greek with his tutors. But his intense hours were spent with Bassett. The Grand National had gone by: he had not "known," and had lost a hundred pounds. Summer was at hand. He was in agony for the Lincoln. But even for the Lincoln he didn't "know," and he lost fifty pounds. He became wild-eyed and strange, as if something were going to explode in him.

"Let it alone, son! Don't you bother about it!" urged Uncle Oscar. But it was as if the boy couldn't really hear what his uncle was saying.

"I've got to know for the Derby! I've got to know for the Derby!" the child reiterated, his big blue eyes blazing with a sort of madness.

His mother noticed how overwrought he was.

"You'd better go to the seaside. Wouldn't you like to go now to the seaside, instead of waiting? I think you'd better," she said, looking down at him anxiously, her heart curiously heavy because of him.

But the child lifted his uncanny blue eyes.

"I couldn't possibly go before the Derby, mother!" he said. "I couldn't possibly!"

"Why not?" she said, her voice becoming heavy when she was opposed. "Why not? You can still go from the seaside to see the Derby with your Uncle Oscar, if that's what you wish. No need for you to wait here. Besides, I think you care too much about these races. It's a bad sign. My family has been a gambling family, and you won't know till you grow up how much damage it has done. But it has done damage. I shall have to send Bassett away, and ask Uncle Oscar not to talk racing to you, unless you promise to be reasonable about it; go away to the seaside and forget it. You're all nerves!"

"I'll do what you like, mother, so long as you don't send me away till after the Derby," the boy said.

"Send you away from where? Just from this house?"

"Yes," he said, gazing at her.

"Why, you curious child, what makes you care about this house so much, suddenly? I never knew you loved it."

He gazed at her without speaking. He had a secret within a secret, something he had not divulged, even to Bassett or to his Uncle Oscar.

But his mother, after standing undecided and a little bit sullen for some moments, said:

"Very well, then! Don't go to the seaside till after the Derby, if you don't wish it. But promise me you won't let your nerves go to pieces. Promise you won't think so much about horse-racing and *events*, as you call them!"

"Oh, no," said the boy casually. "I won't think much about them, mother. You needn't worry. I wouldn't worry, mother, if I were you."

"If you were me and I were you," said his mother, "I wonder what we *should* do!"

"But you know you needn't worry, mother, don't you?" the boy repeated.

"I should be awfully glad to know it," she said wearily.

"Oh, well, you *can*, you know. I mean, you *ought* to know you needn't worry," he insisted.

"Ought I? Then I'll see about it," she said.

Paul's secret of secrets was his wooden horse, that which had no name. Since he was emancipated from a nurse and a nursery-governess, he had had his rocking-horse removed to his own bedroom at the top of the house.

"Surely, you're too big for a rocking-horse!" his mother had remonstrated.

"Well, you see, mother, till I can have a *real* horse, I like to have *some* sort of animal about," had been his quaint answer.

"Do you feel he keeps you company?" she laughed.

"Oh, yes! He's very good, he always keeps me company, when I'm there," said Paul.

So the horse, rather shabby, stood in an arrested prance in the boy's bedroom.

The Derby was drawing near, and the boy grew more and more tense. He hardly heard what was spoken to him, he was very frail, and his eyes were really uncanny. His mother had sudden strange seizures of uneasiness about him. Sometimes, for half-an-hour, she would feel a sudden anxiety about him that was almost anguish. She wanted to rush to him at once, and know he was safe.

Two nights before the Derby, she was at a big party in town, when one of her rushes of anxiety about her boy, her first-born, gripped her heart till she could hardly speak. She fought with the feeling, might and main, for she believed in common-sense. But it was too strong. She had to leave the dance and go downstairs to telephone to the country. The children's nursery-governess was terribly surprised and startled at being rung up in the night.

"Are the children all right, Miss Wilmot?"

"Oh, yes, they are quite all right."

"Master Paul? Is he all right?"

"He went to bed as right as a trivet. Shall I run up and look at him?"

"No," said Paul's mother reluctantly. "No! Don't trouble. It's all right. Don't sit up. We shall be home fairly soon." She did not want her son's privacy intruded upon.

"Very good," said the governess.

It was about one o'clock when Paul's mother and father drove up to their house. All was still. Paul's mother went to her room and slipped off her white fur cloak. She had told her maid not to wait up for her. She heard her husband downstairs, mixing a whisky-and-soda.

And then, because of the strange anxiety at her heart, she stole upstairs to her son's room. Noiselessly she went along the upper corridor. Was there a faint noise? What was it?

She stood, with arrested muscles, outside his door, listening. There was a strange, heavy, and yet not loud noise. Her heart stood still. It was a soundless noise, yet rushing and powerful. Something huge, in violent, hushed motion. What was it? What in God's name was it? She ought to know. She felt that she knew the noise. She knew what it was.

Yet she could not place it. She couldn't say what it was. And on and on it went, like a madness.

Softly, frozen with anxiety and fear, she turned the door-handle.

The room was dark. Yet in the space near the window, she heard and saw something plunging to and fro. She gazed in fear and amazement.

Then suddenly she switched on the light, and saw her son, in his green pyjamas, madly surging on the rocking-horse. The blaze of light suddenly lit him up, as he urged the wooden horse, and lit her up, as she stood, blonde, in her dress of pale green and crystal, in the doorway.

"Paul!" she cried. "Whatever are you doing?"

"It's Malabar!" he screamed, in a powerful, strange voice. "It's Malabar!"

His eyes blazed at her for one strange and senseless second, as he ceased urging his wooden horse. Then he fell with a crash to the ground, and she, all her tormented motherhood flooding upon her, rushed to gather him up.

But he was unconscious, and unconscious he remained, with some brain-fever. He talked and tossed, and his mother sat stonily by his side.

"Malabar! It's Malabar! Bassett, Bassett, I *know!* It's Malabar!"

So the child cried, trying to get up and urge the rocking-horse that gave him his inspiration.

"What does he mean by Malabar?" asked the heart-frozen mother.

"I don't know," said the father stonily.

"What does he mean by Malabar?" she asked her brother Oscar.

"It's one of the horses running for the Derby," was the answer.

And, in spite of himself, Oscar Cresswell spoke to Bassett, and himself put a thousand on Malabar: at fourteen to one.

The third day of the illness was critical: they were waiting for a change. The boy, with his rather long, curly hair, was tossing ceaselessly on the pillow. He neither slept nor regained consciousness, and his eyes were like blue stones. His mother sat, feeling her heart had gone, turned actually into a stone.

In the evening, Oscar Cresswell did not come, but Bassett sent a message, saying could he come up for one moment, just one moment? Paul's mother was very angry at the intrusion, but on second thought she agreed. The boy was the same. Perhaps Bassett might bring him to consciousness.

The gardener, a shortish fellow with a little brown moustache, and sharp little brown eyes, tip-toed into the room, touched his imaginary cap to Paul's mother, and stole to the bedside, staring with glittering, smallish eyes, at the tossing, dying child.

"Master Paul!" he whispered. "Master Paul! Malabar came in first all right, a clean win. I did as you told me. You've made over seventy thousand pounds, you have; you've got over eighty thousand. Malabar came in all right, Master Paul.".

"Malabar! Malabar! Did I say Malabar, mother? Did

I say Malabar? Do you think I'm lucky, mother? I knew Malabar, didn't I? Over eighty thousand pounds! I call that lucky, don't you, mother? Over eighty thousand pounds! I knew, didn't I know I knew? Malabar came in all right. If I ride my horse till I'm sure, then I tell you, Bassett, you can go as high as you like. Did you go for all you were worth, Bassett?"

"I went a thousand on it, Master Paul."

"I never told you, mother, that if I can ride my horse, and *get there*, then I'm absolutely sure—oh, absolutely! Mother, did I ever tell you? I *am* lucky!"

"No, you never did," said the mother.

But the boy died in the night.

And even as he lay dead, his mother heard her brother's voice saying to her: "My God, Hester, you're eighty-odd thousand to the good, and a poor devil of a son to the bad. But, poor devil, poor devil, he's best gone out of a life where he rides his rocking-horse to find a winner."

The Princess

TO HER father, she was The Princess. To her Boston aunts and uncles she was just "Dollie Urquhart, poor little thing."

Colin Urquhart was just a bit mad. He was of an old Scottish family, and he claimed royal blood. The blood of Scottish kings flowed in his veins. On this point, his American relatives said, he was just a bit "off." They could not bear any more to be told *which* royal blood of Scotland blued his veins. The whole thing was rather ridiculous and a sore point. The only fact they remembered was that it was not Stuart.

He was a handsome man, with a wide-open blue eye that seemed sometimes to be looking at nothing, soft black hair brushed rather low on his low, broad brow, and a very attractive body. Add to this a most beautiful speaking voice, usually rather hushed and diffident, but sometimes resonant and powerful like bronze, and you have the sum of his charms. He looked like some old Celtic hero. He looked as if he should have worn a greyish kilt and a sporran, and shown his knees. His voice came direct out of the hushed Ossianic past.

For the rest, he was one of those gentlemen of sufficient but not excessive means who fifty years ago wandered vaguely about, never arriving anywhere, never doing anything, and never definitely being anything, yet well received and familiar in the good society of more than one country.

He did not marry till he was nearly forty, and then it was a wealthy Miss Prescott, from New England. Hannah Prescott at twenty-two was fascinated by the man with the soft black hair not yet touched by grey, and the wide, rather vague, blue eyes. Many women had been fascinated before her. But Colin Urquhart, by his very vagueness, had avoided any decisive connection.

Mrs. Urquhart lived three years in the mist and glamour of her husband's presence. And then it broke her. It was like living with a fascinating spectre. About most things he was completely, even ghostly, oblivious. He was always charming, courteous, perfectly gracious in that hushed, musical voice of his. But absent. When all came to all, he just wasn't there. "Not all there," as the vulgar say.

He was the father of the little girl she bore at the end of the first year. But this did not substantiate him the more. His very beauty and his haunting musical quality became dreadful to her after the first few months. The strange echo: he was like a living echo! His very flesh, when you touched it, did not seem quite the flesh of a real man.

Perhaps it was that he was a little bit mad. She thought it definitely the night her baby was born.

"Ah, so my little princess has come at last!" he said, in his throaty, singing Celtic voice, like a glad chant, swaying absorbed.

It was a tiny, frail baby, with wide, amazed blue eyes. They christened it Mary Henrietta. She called the little thing My Dollie. He called it always My Princess.

It was useless to fly at him. He just opened his wide blue eyes wider, and took a childlike, silent dignity there was no getting past.

Hannah Prescott had never been robust. She had no great desire to live. So when the baby was two years old she suddenly died.

The Prescotts felt a deep but unadmitted resentment against Colin Urquhart. They said he was selfish. Therefore they discontinued Hannah's income, a month after her burial in Florence, after they had urged the father to give the child over to them, and he had courteously, musically, but quite finally refused. He treated the Prescotts as if they were not of his world, not realities to him: just casual phenomena, or gramophones, talking-machines that had to be answered. He answered them. But of their actual existence he was never once aware.

They debated having him certified unsuitable to be guardian of his own child. But that would have created a scandal. So they did the simplest thing, after all—washed their hands of him. But they wrote scrupulously to the child, and sent her modest presents of money at Christmas, and on the anniversary of the death of her mother.

To The Princess her Boston relatives were for many years just a nominal reality. She lived with her father, and he travelled continually, though in a modest way, living on his moderate income. And never going to America. The child changed nurses all the time. In Italy it was a contadina; in India she had an ayah; in Germany she had a yellow-haired peasant girl.

Father and child were inseparable. He was not a recluse. Wherever he went he was to be seen paying formal calls, going out to luncheon or to tea, rarely to dinner. And always with the child. People called her Princess Urquhart, as if that were her christened name.

She was a quick, dainty little thing with dark gold hair that went a soft brown, and wide, slightly prominent blue eyes that were at once so candid and so knowing. She was always grown up; she never really grew up. Always strangely wise, and always childish.

It was her father's fault.

"My little Princess must never take too much notice of people and the things they say and do," he repeated to her. "People don't know what they are doing and saying. They chatter-chatter, and they hurt one another, and they hurt themselves very often, till they cry. But don't take any notice, my little Princess. Because it is all nothing. Inside everybody there is another creature, a demon which doesn't care at all. You peel away all the things they say and do and feel, as cook peels away the outside of the onions. And in the middle of everybody there is a green demon which you can't peel away. And this green demon never changes, and it doesn't care at all about all the things that happen to the outside leaves of the person, all the chatter-chatter, and all the husbands and wives and children, and troubles and fusses. You peel everything away from people, and there is a green, upright demon in every man and woman; and this demon is a man's real self, and a woman's real self. It doesn't really care about anybody, it belongs to the demons and the primitive fairies, who never care. But, even so, there are big demons and mean demons, and splendid demonish fairies, and vulgar ones. But there are no royal fairy women left. Only you, my little Princess. You are the last of the royal race of the old people; the last, my Princess. There are no others. You and I are the last. When I am dead there will be only you. And that is why, darling, you will never care for any of the people in the world very much. Because their demons are all dwindled and vulgar. They are not royal. Only you are royal, after me. Always remember that. And always remember, it is a *great secret*. If you tell people, they will try to kill you, because they will envy you for being a Princess. It is our great secret, darling. I am a prince, and you a princess, of the old, old blood. And we keep our secret between us, all alone. And so, darling, you must treat all people very politely, because *noblesse oblige*. But you must never forget that you alone are the last of Princesses, and that all others are less than you are, less noble, more vulgar. Treat them politely and gently and kindly, darling. But you are the Princess, and they are commoners. Never try to think of them as if they were like you. They are not. You will find, always, that they are lacking, lacking in the royal touch, which only you have——"

The Princess learned her lesson early—the first lesson, of absolute reticence, the impossibility of intimacy with any other than her father; the second lesson, of naïve, slightly benevolent politeness. As a small child, something crystallized in her character, making her clear and finished, and as impervious as crystal.

"Dear child!" her hostesses said of her. "She is so quaint and old-fashioned; such a lady, poor little mite!"

She was erect, and very dainty. Always small, nearly tiny in physique, she seemed like a changeling beside her big, handsome, slightly mad father. She dressed very simply, usually in blues or delicate greys, with little collars of old Milan point, or very finely-worked linen. She had exquisite little hands, that made the piano sound like a spinet when she played. She was rather given to wearing cloaks and capes, instead of coats, out of doors, and little eighteenth-century sort of hats. Her complexion was pure apple-blossom.

She looked as if she had stepped out of a picture. But no one, to her dying day, ever knew exactly the strange picture her father had framed her in, and from which she never stepped.

Her grandfather and grandmother and her Aunt Maud demanded twice to see her, once in Rome and once in Paris. Each time they were charmed, piqued, and annoyed. She was so exquisite and such a little virgin. At the same time so knowing and so oddly assured. That odd, assured touch of condescension, and the inward coldness, infuriated her American relations.

Only she really fascinated her grandfather. He was spellbound; in a way, in love with the little faultless thing. His wife would catch him brooding, musing over his grandchild, long months after the meeting, and craving to see her again. He cherished to the end the fond hope that she might come to live with him and her grandmother.

"Thank you so much, grandfather. You are so very kind. But papa and I are such an old couple, you see, such a crotchety old couple, living in a world of our own."

Her father let her see the world—from the outside. And he let her read. When she was in her teens she read Zola and Maupassant, and with the eyes of Zola and Maupassant she looked on Paris. A little later she read Tolstoy and Dostoevsky. The latter confused her. The others, she seemed to understand with a very shrewd, canny understanding, just as she understood the Decameron stories as she read them in their old Italian, or the Nibelung poems. Strange and *uncanny*, she seemed to understand things in a cold light perfectly, with all the flush of fire absent. She was something like a changeling, not quite human.

This earned her, also, strange antipathies. Cabmen and railway-porters, especially in Paris and Rome, would suddenly treat her with brutal rudeness, when she was alone. They seemed to look on her with sudden violent antipathy. They sensed in her curious impertinence, an easy, sterile impertinence towards the things *they* felt most. She was so assured, and her flower of maidenhood was so scentless. She could look at a lusty, sensual Roman cabman as if he were a sort of grotesque, to make her smile. She knew all about him, in Zola. And the peculiar condescension with which she would give him her order, as if she, frail, beautiful thing, were the only reality, and he, coarse monster, were a sort of Caliban floundering in the mud on the margin of the pool of the perfect lotus, would suddenly enrage the fellow, the real Mediterranean who prided himself on his *beauté male*, and to whom the phallic mystery was still the only mystery. And he would turn a terrible face on her, bully her in a brutal, coarse fashion—hideous. For to him she had only the blasphemous impertinence of her own sterility.

Encounters like these made her tremble, and made her know she must have support from the outside. The power of her spirit did not extend to these low people, and they had all the physical power. She realized an implacability of hatred in their turning on her. But she did not lose her head. She quietly paid out money and turned away.

Those were dangerous moments, though, and she learned to be prepared for them. The Princess she was, and the fairy from the North, and could never understand the volcanic phallic rage with which coarse people could turn on her in a paroxysm of hatred. They never turned on her father like that. And quite early she decided it was the New England mother in her whom they hated. Never for one minute could she see with the old Roman eyes, see herself as sterility, the barren flower taking on airs and an intolerable impertinence. This was what the Roman cabman saw in her. And he longed to crush the barren blossom. Its sexless beauty and its authority put him in a passion of brutal revolt.

When she was nineteen her grandfather died, leaving her a considerable fortune in the safe hands of responsible trustees. They would deliver her her income, but only on condition that she resided for six months in the year in the United States.

"Why should they make me conditions?" she said to her father. "I refuse to be imprisoned six months in the year in the United States. We will tell them to keep their money."

"Let us be wise, my little Princess, let us be wise. No, we are almost poor, and we are never safe from rudeness. I cannot allow anybody to be rude to me. I hate it, I hate it!" His eyes flamed as he said it. "I could kill any man or woman who is rude to me. But we are in exile in the world. We are powerless. If we were really poor, we should be quite powerless, and then I should die. No, my Princess. Let us take their money, then they will not dare to be rude to us. Let us take it, as we put on clothes to cover ourselves from their aggressions."

There began a new phase, when the father and daughter spent their summers on the Great Lakes or in California, or in the South-West. The father was something of a poet, the daughter something of a painter. He wrote poems about the lakes or the red-wood trees, and she made dainty drawings. He was physically a strong man, and he loved the out-of-doors. He would go off with her for days, paddling in a canoe and sleeping by a camp-fire. Frail little Princess, she was always undaunted, always undaunted. She would ride with him on horseback over the mountain trails till she was so tired she was nothing but a bodiless consciousness sitting astride her pony. But she never gave in. And at night he folded her in her blankets on a bed of balsam-pine twigs, and she lay and looked at the stars unmurmuring. She was fulfilling her role.

People said to her as the years passed, and she was a woman of twenty-five, then a woman of thirty, and always the same virgin dainty Princess, "knowing" in a dispassionate way, like an old woman, and utterly intact:

"Don't you ever think what you will do when your father is no longer with you?"

She looked at her interlocutor with that cold, elfin detachment of hers:

"No, I never think of it," she said.

She had a tiny but exquisite little house in London, and another small, perfect house in Connecticut, each with a faithful housekeeper. Two homes, if she chose. And she knew many interesting literary and artistic people. What more?

So the years passed imperceptibly. And she had that quality of the sexless fairies, she did not change. At thirty-three she looked twenty-three.

Her father, however, was ageing, and becoming more and more queer. It was now her task to be his guardian in his private madness. He spent the last three years of life in the house in Connecticut. He was very much estranged, sometimes had fits of violence which almost killed the little Princess. Physical violence was horrible to her; it seemed to shatter her heart. But she found a woman a few years younger than herself, well-educated and sensitive, to be a sort of nurse-companion to the mad old man. So the fact of madness was never openly admitted. Miss Cummins, the companion, had a passionate loyalty to the Princess, and a curious affection, tinged with love, for the handsome, white-haired, courteous old man, who was never at all aware of his fits of violence once they had passed.

The Princess was thirty-eight years old when her father died. And quite unchanged. She was still tiny, and like a dignified, scentless flower. Her soft brownish hair, almost the colour of beaver fur, was bobbed, and fluffed softly round her apple-blossom face, that was modelled with an arched nose like a proud old Florentine portrait. In her voice, manner and bearing she was exceedingly still, like a flower that has blossomed in a shadowy place. And from her blue eyes looked out the Princess's eternal laconic challenge, that grew almost sardonic as the years passed. She was the Princess, and sardonically she looked out on a princeless world.

She was relieved when her father died, and at the same time it was as if everything had evaporated around her. She had lived in a sort of hot-house, in the aura of her father's madness. Suddenly the hot-house had been removed from around her, and she was in the raw, vast, vulgar open air.

Quoi faire? What was she to do? She seemed faced with absolute nothingness. Only she had Miss Cummins, who shared with her the secret, and almost the passion for her father. In fact the Princess felt that her passion for her mad father had in some curious way transferred itself largely to Charlotte Cummins during the last years. And now Miss Cummins was the vessel that held the passion for the dead man. She herself, the Princess, was an empty vessel.

An empty vessel in the enormous warehouse of the world.

Quoi faire? What was she to do? She felt that, since she could not evaporate into nothingness, like alcohol from an unstoppered bottle, she must *do* something. Never before in her life had she felt the incumbency. Never, never had she felt she must *do* anything. That was left to the vulgar.

Now her father was dead, she found herself on the *fringe* of the vulgar crowd, sharing their necessity to *do* something. It was a little humiliating. She felt herself becoming vulgarized. At the same time she found herself looking at men with a shrewder eye: an eye to marriage. Not that she felt any sudden interest in men, or attraction towards them. No. She was still neither interested nor attracted towards men vitally. But "marriage," that peculiar abstraction, had imposed a sort of spell on her. She thought that "marriage," in the blank abstract, was the thing she ought to *do*. That "marriage" implied a man she also knew. She knew all the facts. But the man seemed a property of her own mind rather than a thing in himself, another being.

His father died in the summer, the month after her thirty-eighth birthday. When all was over, the obvious thing to do, of course, was to travel. With Miss Cummins. The two women knew each other intimately, but they were always Miss Urquhart and Miss Cummins to one another, and a certain distance was instinctively maintained. Miss Cummins, from Philadelphia, of scholastic stock, and intelligent but untravelled, four years younger than the Princess, felt herself immensely the junior of her "lady." She had a sort of passionate veneration for the Princess, who seemed to her ageless, timeless. She could not see the rows of tiny, dainty, exquisite shoes in the Princess's cupboard without feeling a stab at the heart, a stab of tenderness and reverence, almost of awe.

Miss Cummins also was virginal, but with a look of puzzled surprise in her brown eyes. Her skin was pale and clear, her features well modelled, but there was a certain blankness in her expression, where the Princess had an odd touch of Renaissance grandeur. Miss Cummins' voice also hushed almost to a whisper; it was the inevitable effect of Colin Urquhart's room. But the hushedness had a hoarse quality.

The Princess did not want to go to Europe. Her face seemed turned west. Now her father was gone, she felt she would go west, westwards, as if for ever. Following, no doubt, the March of Empire, which is brought up rather short on the Pacific coast, among swarms of wallowing bathers.

No, not the Pacific coast. She would stop short of that. The South-West was less vulgar. She would go to New Mexico.

She and Miss Cummins arrived at the Rancho del Cerro Gordo towards the end of August, when the crowd was beginning to drift back east. The ranch lay by a stream on the desert some four miles from the foot of the mountains, a mile away from the Indian pueblo of San Cristobal. It was a ranch for the rich; the Princess paid thirty dollars a day for herself and Miss Cummins. But then she had a little cottage to herself, among the apple-trees of the orchard, with an excellent cook. She and Miss Cummins, however, took dinner at evening in the large guest-house. For the Princess still entertained the idea of "marriage."

The guests at the Rancho del Cerro Gordo were of all sorts, except the poor sort. They were practically all rich, and many were romantic. Some were charming, others were vulgar, some were movie people, quite quaint and not unattractive in their vulgarity, and many were Jews. The Princess did not care for Jews, though they were usually the most interesting to *talk* to. So she talked a good deal with the Jews, and painted with the artists, and rode with the young men from college, and had altogether quite a good time. And yet she felt something of a fish out of water, or a bird in the wrong forest. And "marriage" remained still completely in the abstract. No connecting it with any of these young men, even the nice ones.

The Princess looked just twenty-five. The freshness of her mouth, the hushed, delicate-complexioned virginity of her face, gave her not a day more. Only a certain laconic look in her eyes was disconcerting. When she was *forced* to write her age, she put twenty-eight, making the figure *two* rather badly, so that it just avoided being a three.

Men hinted marriage at her. Especially boys from college suggested it from a distance. But they all failed before the look of sardonic ridicule in the Princess's eyes. It always seemed to her rather preposterous, quite ridiculous, and a tiny bit impertinent on their part.

The only man that intrigued her at all was one of the guides, a man called Romero—Domingo Romero. It was he who had sold the ranch itself to the Wilkiesons, ten years before, for two thousand dollars. He had gone away, then reappeared at the old place. For he was the son of the old Romero, the last of the Spanish family that had owned miles of land around San Cristobal. But the coming of the white man and the failure of the vast flocks of sheep, and the fatal inertia which overcomes all men, at last, on the desert near the mountains, had finished the Romero family. The last descendants were just Mexican peasants.

Domingo, the heir, had spent his two thousand dollars, and was working for white people. He was now about thirty years old, a tall, silent fellow, with a heavy closed mouth and black eyes that looked across at one almost sullenly. From behind he was handsome, with a strong, natural body, and the back of his neck very dark and well-shapen, strong with life. But his dark face was long and heavy, almost sinister, with that peculiar heavy meaninglessness in it characteristic of the Mexicans of his own locality. They are strong, they seem healthy. They laugh and joke with one another. But their physique and their natures seem static, as if there were nowhere, nowhere at all tor their energies to go, and their faces, degenerating to misshapen heaviness, seem to have no *raison d'être*, no radical meaning. Waiting either to die or to be aroused into passion and hope. In some of the black eyes a queer, haunting mystic qual- ity, sombre and a bit gruesome, the skull-and-cross- bones look of the Penitentes. They had found their *raison d'être* in self-torture and death-worship. Unable to wrest a *positive* significance for themselves from the vast, beautiful, but vindictive landscape they were born into, they turned on their own selves, and worshipped death through self-torture. The mystic gloom of this showed in their eyes.

But as a rule the dark eyes of the Mexicans were heavy and half-alive, sometimes hostile, sometimes kindly, often with the fatal Indian glaze on them, or the fatal Indian glint.

Domingo Romero was *almost* a typical Mexican to look at, with the typical heavy, dark, long face, clean-shaven, with an almost brutally heavy mouth. His eyes were black and Indian-looking. Only, at the centre of their hopelessness was a spark of pride, or self-confidence, or dauntlessness. Just a spark in the midst of the blackness of static despair.

But this spark was the difference between him and the mass of men. It gave a certain alert sensitiveness to his bearing and a certain beauty to his appearance. He wore a low-crowned black hat, instead of the ponderous headgear of the usual Mexican, and his clothes were thinnish and graceful. Silent, aloof, almost imperceptible in the landscape, he was an admirable guide, with a startling quick intelligence that anticipated difficulties about to arise. He could cook, too, crouching over the camp-fire and moving his lean deft brown hands. The only fault he had was that he was not forthcoming, he wasn't chatty and cosy.

"Oh, don't send Romero with us," the Jews would say. "One can't get any response from him."

Tourists come and go, but they rarely *see* anything, inwardly. None of them ever saw the spark at the middle of Romero's eye; they were not alive enough to see it.

The Princess caught it one day, when she had him for a guide. She was fishing for trout in the canyon, Miss Cummins was reading a book, the horses were tied under the trees, Romero was fixing a proper fly on her line. He fixed the fly and handed her the line, looking up at her. And at that moment she caught the spark in his eye. And instantly she knew that he was a gentleman, that his "demon," as her father would have said, was a fine demon. And instantly her manner towards him changed.

He had perched her on a rock over a quiet pool, be-

yond the cotton-wood trees. It was early September,
and the canyon already cool, but the leaves of the
cotton-woods were still green. The Princess stood on her
rock, a small but perfectly-formed figure, wearing a soft,
close grey sweater and neatly-cut grey riding breeches,
with tall black boots, her fluffy brown hair straggling
from under a little grey felt hat. A woman? Not quite.
A changeling of some sort, perched in outline tnere on
the rock, in the bristling wild canyon. She knew perfectly well how to handle a line. Her father had made a
fisherman of her.

Romero, in a black shirt and with loose black trousers
pushed into wide black riding boots, was fishing a little
further down. He had put his hat on a rock behind him;
his dark head was bent a little forward, watching the
water. He had caught three trout. From time to time he
glanced upstream at the Princess, perched there so
daintily. He saw she had caught nothing.

Soon he quietly drew in his line and came up to her.
His keen eye watched her line, watched her position.
Then, quietly, he suggested certain changes to her,
putting his sensitive brown hand before her. And he
withdrew a little, and stood in silence, leaning against a
tree, watching her. He was helping her across the distance. She knew it and thrilled. And in a moment she
had a bite. In two minutes she landed a good trout. She
looked round at him quickly, her eyes sparkling, the
colour heightened in her cheeks. And as she met his eyes
a smile of greeting went over his dark face, very sudden,
with an odd sweetness.

She knew he was helping her. And she felt in his presence a subtle, insidious male *kindliness* she had never
known before waiting upon her. Her cheek flushed, and
her blue eyes darkened.

After this, she always looked for him, and for that

curious dark beam of a man's kindliness which he could give her, as it were, from his chest, from his heart. It was something she had never known before.

A vague, unspoken intimacy grew up between them. She liked his voice, his appearance, his presence. His natural language was Spanish; he spoke English like a foreign language, rather slow, with a slight hesitation, but with a sad, plangent sonority lingering over from his Spanish. There was a certain subtle correctness in his appearance; he was always perfectly shaved; his hair was thick and rather long on top, but always carefully groomed behind. And his fine black cashmere shirt, his wide leather belt, his well-cut, wide black trousers going into the embroidered cowboy boots had a certain inextinguishable elegance. He wore no silver rings or buckles. Only his boots were embroidered and decorated at the top with an inlay of white suede. He seemed elegant, slender, yet he was very strong.

And at the same time, curiously, he gave her the feeling that death was not far from him. Perhaps he too was half in love with death. However that may be, the sense she had that death was not far from him made him "possible" to her.

Small as she was, she was quite a good horsewoman. They gave her at the ranch a sorrel mare, very lovely in colour, and well-made, with a powerful broad neck and the hollow back that betokens a swift runner. Tansy, she was called. Her only fault was the usual mare's failing, she was inclined to be hysterical.

So that every day the Princess set off with Miss Cummins and Romero, on horseback, riding into the mountains. Once they went camping for several days, with two more friends in the party.

"I think I like it better," the Princess said to Romero, "when we three go alone."

And he gave her one of his quick, transfiguring smiles.

It was curious no white man had ever showed her this capacity for subtle gentleness, this power to *help* her in silence across a distance, if she were fishing without success, or tired of her horse, or if Tansy suddenly got scared. It was as if Romero could send her *from his heart* a dark beam of succour and sustaining. She had never known this before, and it was very thrilling.

Then the smile that suddenly creased his dark face, showing the strong white teeth. It creased his face almost into a savage grotesque. And at the same time there was in it something so warm, such a dark flame of kindliness for her, she was elated into her true Princess self.

Then that vivid, latent spark in his eye, which she had seen, and which she knew he was aware she had seen. It made an inter-recognition between them, silent and delicate. Here he was delicate as a woman in this subtle inter-recognition.

And yet his presence only put to flight in her the *idée fixe* of "marriage." For some reason, in her strange little brain, the idea of *marrying* him could not enter. Not for any definite reason. He was in himself a gentleman, and she had plenty of money for two. There was no actual obstacle. Nor was she conventional.

No, now she came down to it, it was as if their two "demons" could marry, were perhaps married. Only their two *selves*, Miss Urquhart and Señor Domingo Romero, were for some reason incompatible. There was a peculiar subtle intimacy of inter-recognition between them. But she did not see in the least how it would lead to marriage. Almost she could more easily marry one of the nice boys from Harvard or Yale.

The time passed, and she let it pass. The end of

September came, with aspens going yellow on the mountain heights, and oak-scrub going red. But as yet the cottonwoods in the valley and canyons had not changed.

"When will you go away?" Romero asked her, looking at her fixedly, with a blank black eye.

"By the end of October," she said. "I have promised to be in Santa Barbara at the beginning of November."

He was hiding the spark in his eye from her. But she saw the peculiar sullen thickening of his heavy mouth.

She had complained to him many times that one never saw any wild animals, except chipmunks and squirrels, and perhaps a skunk and a porcupine. Never a deer, or a bear, or a mountain lion.

"Are there no bigger animals in these mountains?" she asked, dissatisfied.

"Yes," he said. "There are deer—I see their tracks. And I saw the tracks of a bear."

"But why can one never see the animals themselves?" She looked dissatisfied and wistful like a child.

"Why, it's pretty hard for you to see them. They won't let you come close. You have to keep still, in a place where they come. Or else you have to follow their tracks a long way."

"I can't bear to go away till I've seen them: a bear, or a deer——"

The smile came suddenly on his face, indulgent.

"Well, what do you want? Do you want to go up into the mountains to some place, to wait till they come?"

"Yes," she said, looking up at him with a sudden naïve impulse of recklessness.

And immediately his face became sombre again, responsible.

"Well," he said, with slight irony, a touch of mockery of her. "You will have to find a house. It's very cold at night now. You would have to stay all night in a house."

"And there are no houses up there?" she said.

"Yes," he replied. "There is a little shack that belongs to me, that a miner built a long time ago, looking for gold. You can go there and stay one night, and maybe you see something. Maybe! I don't know. Maybe nothing come."

"How much chance is there?"

"Well, I don't know. Last time when I was there I see three deer come down to drink at the water, and I shot two raccoons. But maybe this time we don't see anything."

"Is there water there?" she asked.

"Yes, there is a little round pond, you know, below the spruce trees. And the water from the snow runs into it."

"Is it far away?" she asked.

"Yes, pretty far. You see that ridge there"—and turning to the mountains he lifted his arm in the gesture which is somehow so moving, out in the West, pointing to the distance—"that ridge where there are no trees, only rock"—his black eyes were focussed on the distance, his face impassive, but as if in pain—"you go round that ridge, and along, then you come down through the spruce trees to where that cabin is. My father bought that placer claim from a miner who was broke, but nobody ever found any gold or anything, and nobody ever goes there. Too lonesome!"

The Princess watched the massive, heavy-sitting, beautiful bulk of the Rocky Mountains. It was early in October, and the aspens were already losing their gold leaves; high up, the spruce and pine seemed to be growing darker; the great flat patches of oak-scrub on the heights were red like gore.

"Can I go over there?" she asked, turning to him and meeting the spark in his eye.

His face was heavy with responsibility.

"Yes," he said, "you can go. But there'll be snow over the ridge, and it's awful cold, and awful lonesome."

"I should like to go," she said, persistent.

"All right," he said. "You can go if you want to."

She doubted, though, if the Wilkiesons would let her go; at least alone with Romero and Miss Cummins.

Yet an obstinacy characteristic of her nature, an obstinacy tinged perhaps with madness, had taken hold of her. She wanted to look over the mountains into their secret heart. She wanted to descend to the cabin below the spruce trees, near the tarn of bright green water. She wanted to see the wild animals move about in their wild unconsciousness.

"Let us say to the Wilkiesons that we want to make the trip round the Frijoles canyon," she said.

The trip round the Frijoles canyon was a usual thing. It would not be strenuous, nor cold, nor lonely: they could sleep in the log house that was called an hotel.

Romero looked at her quickly.

"If you want to say that," he replied, "you can tell Mrs. Wilkieson. Only I know she'll be mad with me if I take you up in the mountains to that place. And I've got to go there first with a pack-horse, to take lots of blankets and some bread. Maybe Miss Cummins can't stand it. Maybe not. It's a hard trip."

He was speaking, and thinking, in the heavy, disconnected Mexican fashion.

"Never mind!" The Princess was suddenly very decisive and stiff with authority. "I want to do it. I will arrange with Mrs. Wilkieson. And we'll go on Saturday."

He shook his head slowly.

"I've got to go up on Sunday with a pack-horse and blankets," he said. "Can't do it before."

"Very well!" she said, rather piqued. "Then we'll start on Monday."

She hated being thwarted even the tiniest bit.

He knew that if he started with the pack on Sunday at dawn he would not be back until late at night. But he consented that they should start on Monday morning at seven. The obedient Miss Cummins was told to prepare for the Frijoles trip. On Sunday Romero had his day off. He had not put in an appearance when the Princess retired on Sunday night, but on Monday morning, as she was dressing, she saw him bringing in the three horses from the corral. She was in high spirits.

The night had been cold. There was ice at the edges of the irrigation ditch, and the chipmunks crawled into the sun and lay with wide, dumb, anxious eyes, almost too numb to run.

"We may be away two or three days," said the Princess.

"Very well. We won't begin to be anxious about you before Thursday, then," said Mrs. Wilkieson, who was young and capable: from Chicago. "Anyway," she added, "Romero will see you through. He's so trustworthy."

The sun was already on the desert as they set off towards the mountains, making the greasewood and the sage pale as pale-grey sands, luminous the great level around them. To the right glinted the shadows of the adobe pueblo, flat and almost invisible on the plain, earth of its earth. Behind lay the ranch and the tufts of tall, plumy cottonwoods, whose summits were yellowing under the perfect blue sky.

Autumn breaking into colour in the great spaces of the South-West.

But the three trotted gently along the trail, towards the sun that sparkled yellow just above the dark bulk of the ponderous mountains. Side-slopes were already gleaming yellow, flaming with a second light, under the coldish blue of the pale sky. The front slopes were in shadow, with submerged lustre of red oak-scrub and dull-gold aspens, blue-black pines and grey-blue rock. While the canyon was full of a deep blueness.

They rode single file, Romero first, on a black horse. Himself in black, he made a flickering black spot in the delicate pallor of the great landscape, where even pine-trees at a distance take a film of blue paler than their green. Romero rode on in silence past the tufts of furry greasewood. The Princess came next, on her sorrel mare. And Miss Cummins, who was not quite happy on horse-back, came last, in the pale dust that the others kicked up. Sometimes her horse sneezed, and she started.

But on they went, at a gentle trot. Romero never looked round. He could hear the sound of the hoofs following, and that was all he wanted.

For the rest, he held ahead. And the Princess, with that black, unheeding figure always travelling away from her, felt strangely helpless, withal elated.

They neared the pale, round foot-hills, dotted with the round dark piñon and cedar shrubs. The horses clinked and clattered among stones. Occasionally a big round greasewood held out fleecy tufts of flowers, pure gold. They wound into blue shadow, then up a steep stony slope, with the world lying pallid away behind and below. Then they dropped into the shadow of the San Cristobal canyon.

The stream was running full and swift. Occasionally the horses snatched at a tuft of grass. The trail narrowed and became rocky; the rocks closed in; it was dark and cool as the horses climbed and climbed upwards, and the tree-trunks crowded in in the shadowy, silent tightness of the canyon. They were among cottonwood trees that ran straight up and smooth and round to an extra-ordinary height. Above, the tips were gold, and it was sun. But away below, where the horses struggled up the rocks and wound among the trunks, there was still blue shadow by the sound of waters and an occasional grey festoon of old man's beard, and here and there a pale, dipping crane's-bill flower among the tangle and the debris of the virgin place. And again the chill entered the Princess's heart as she realized what a tangle of decay and despair lay in the virgin forests.

They scrambled downwards, splashed across stream, up rocks and along the trail of the other side. Romero's black horse stopped, looked down quizzically at the fallen trees, then stepped over lightly. The Princess's sorrel followed, carefully. But Miss Cummins's buckskin made a fuss, and had to be got round.

In the same silence, save for the clinking of the horses and the splashing as the trail crossed stream, they worked their way upwards in the tight, tangled shadow of the canyon. Sometimes, crossing stream, the Princess would glance upwards, and then always her heart caught in her breast. For high up, away in heaven, the mountain heights shone yellow, dappled with dark spruce firs, clear almost as speckled daffodils against the pale turquoise blue lying high and serene above the dark-blue shadow where the Princess was. And she would snatch at the blood-red leaves of the oak as her horse crossed a more open slope, not knowing what she felt.

They were getting fairly high, occasionally lifted above the canyon itself, in the low groove below the speckled, gold-sparkling heights which towered beyond. Then again they dipped and crossed stream, the horses stepping gingerly across a tangle of fallen, frail aspen stems, then suddenly floundering in a mass of rocks. The black emerged ahead, his black tail waving. The Princess let her mare find her own footing; then she too emerged from the clatter. She rode on after the black. Then came a great frantic rattle of the buckskin behind. The Princess was aware of Romero's dark face looking round, with a strange, demon-like watchfulness, before she herself looked round, to see the buckskin scrambling rather lamely beyond the rocks, with one of his pale buff knees already red with blood.

"He almost went down!" called Miss Cummins.

But Romero was already out of the saddle and hastening down the path. He made quiet little noises to the buckskin, and began examining the cut knee.

"Is he hurt?" cried Miss Cummins anxiously, and she climbed hastily down.

"Oh, my goodness!" she cried, as she saw the blood running down the slender buff leg of the horse in a thin trickle. "Isn't that *awful?*" She spoke in a stricken voice, and her face was white.

Romero was still carefully feeling the knee of the buckskin. Then he made him walk a few paces. And at last he stood up straight and shook his head.

"Not very bad!" he said. "Nothing broken."

Again he bent and worked at the knee. Then he looked up at the Princess.

"He can go on," he said. "It's not bad."

The Princess looked down at the dark face in silence.

"What, go on right up here?" cried Miss Cummins. "How many hours?"

"About five," said Romero simply.

"Five hours!" cried Miss Cummins. "A horse with a lame knee! And a steep mountain! Why-y!"

"Yes, it's pretty steep up there," said Romero, pushing back his hat and staring fixedly at the bleeding knee. The buckskin stood in a stricken sort of dejection. "But I think he'll make it all right," the man added.

"Oh!" cried Miss Cummins, her eyes bright with sudden passion of unshed tears. "I wouldn't think of it. I wouldn't ride him up there, not for any money."

"Why wouldn't you?" asked Romero.

"It *hurts* him."

Romero bent down again to the horse's knee.

"Maybe it hurts him a little," he said. "But he can make it all right, and his leg won't get stiff."

"What! Ride him five hours up the steep mountains?" cried Miss Cummins. "I couldn't. I just couldn't do it. I'll lead him a little way and see if he can go. But I *couldn't* ride him again. I couldn't. Let me walk."

"But Miss Cummins, dear, if Romero says he'll be all right?" said the Princess.

"I know it hurts him. Oh, I just couldn't bear it."

There was no doing anything with Miss Cummins. The thought of a hurt animal always put her into a sort of hysterics.

They walked forward a little, leading the buckskin. He limped rather badly. Miss Cummins sat on a rock.

"Why, it's agony to see him!" she cried. "It's *cruel!*"

"He won't limp after a bit, if you take no notice of him," said Romero. "Now he plays up, and limps very much, because he wants to make you see."

"I don't think there can be much playing up," said Miss Cummins bitterly. "We can *see* how it must hurt him."

"It don't hurt much," said Romero.

But now Miss Cummins was silent with antipathy.

It was a deadlock. The party remained motionless on the trail, the Princess in the saddle, Miss Cummins seated on a rock, Romero standing black and remote near the drooping buckskin.

"Well!" said the man suddenly at last. "I guess we go back, then."

And he looked up swiftly at his horse, which 'was

cropping at the mountain herbage and treading on the trailing reins.

"No!" cried the Princess. "Oh no!" Her voice rang with a great wail of disappointment and anger. Then she checked herself.

Miss Cummins rose with energy.

"Let me lead the buckskin home," she said, with cold dignity, "and you two go on."

This was received in silence. The Princess was looking down at her with a sardonic, almost cruel gaze.

"We've only come about two hours," said Miss Cummins. "I don't mind a bit leading him home. But I *couldn't* ride him. I *couldn't* have him ridden with that knee."

This again was received in dead silence. Romero remained impassive, almost inert.

"Very well, then," said the Princess. "You lead him home. You'll be quite all right. Nothing can happen to you, possibly. And say to them that we have gone on and shall be home tomorrow—or the day after."

She spoke coldly and distinctly. For she could not bear to be thwarted.

"Better all go back, and come again another day," said Romero—non-committal.

"There will never *be* another day," cried the Princess. "I want to go on."

She looked at him square in the eyes, and met the spark in his eye.

He raised his shoulders slightly.

"If you want it," he said. "I'll go with you. But Miss Cummins can ride my horse to the end of the canyon, and I lead the buckskin. Then I come back to you."

It was arranged so. Miss Cummins had her saddle put on Romero's black horse, Romero took the buckskin's

bridle, and they started back. The Princess rode very
slowly on, upwards, alone. She was at first so angry with
Miss Cummins that she was blind to everything else.
She just let her mare follow her own inclinations.

The peculiar spell of anger carried the Princess on,
almost unconscious, for an hour or so. And by this time
she was beginning to climb pretty high. Her horse
walked steadily all the time. They emerged on a bare
slope, and the trail wound through frail aspen-stems.
Here a wind swept, and some of the aspens were already
bare. Others were fluttering their discs of pure, solid
yellow leaves, so *nearly* like petals, while the slope
ahead was one soft, glowing fleece of daffodil yellow;
fleecy like a golden foxskin, and yellow as daffodils alive
in the wind and the high mountain sun.

She paused and looked back. The near great slopes
were mottled with gold and the dark hue of spruce, like
some unsinged eagle, and the light lay gleaming upon
them. Away through the gap of the canyon she could see
the pale blue of the egg-like desert, with the crumpled
dark crack of the Rio Grande Canyon. And far, far off,
the blue mountains like a fence of angels on the horizon.

And she thought of her adventure. She was going on
alone with Romero. But then she was very sure of herself, and Romero was not the kind of man to do anything to her against her will. This was her first thought.
And she just had a fixed desire to go over the brim of the
mountains, to look into the inner chaos of the Rockies.
And she wanted to go with Romero, because he had
some peculiar kinship with her; there was some peculiar
link between the two of them. Miss Cummins anyhow
would have been only a discordant note.

She rode on, and emerged at length in the lap of the
summit. Beyond her was a great concave of stone and
stark, dead-grey trees, where the mountain ended

against the sky. But nearer was the dense black, bristling
spruce, and at her feet was the lap of the summit, a flat
little valley of sere grass and quiet-standing yellow
aspens, the stream trickling like a thread across.

It was a little valley or shell from which the stream
was gently poured into the lower rocks and trees of the
canyon. Around her was a fairy-like gentleness, the delicate sere grass, the groves of delicate-stemmed aspens
dropping their flakes of bright yellow. And the delicate,
quick little stream threading through the wild, sere
grass.

Here one might expect deer and fawns and wild
things, as in a little paradise. Here she was to wait for
Romero, and they were to have lunch.

She unfastened her saddle and pulled it to the ground
with a crash, letting her horse wander with a long rope.
How beautiful Tansy looked, sorrel, among the yellow
leaves that lay like a patina on the sere ground. The
Princess herself wore a fleecy sweater of a pale, sere
buff, like the grass, and riding breeches of a pure
orange-tawny colour. She felt quite in the picture.

From her saddle pouches she took the packages of
lunch, spread a little cloth, and sat to wait for Romero.
Then she made a little fire. Then she ate a devilled egg.
Then she ran after Tansy, who was straying across-
stream. Then she sat in the sun, in the stillness near the
aspens, and waited.

The sky was blue. Her little alp was soft and delicate
as fairy-land. But beyond and up jutted the great slopes,
dark with the pointed feathers of spruce, bristling with
grey dead trees among grey rock, or dappled with dark
and gold. The beautiful, but fierce, heavy, cruel mountains, with their moments of tenderness.

She saw Tansy start, and begin to run. Two ghost-like
figures on horseback emerged from the black of the

spruce across the stream. It was two Indians on horse-back, swathed like seated mummies in their pale-grey cotton blankets. Their guns jutted beyond the saddles. They rode straight towards her, to her thread of smoke.

As they came near, they unswathed themselves and greeted her, looking at her curiously from their dark eyes. Their black hair was somewhat untidy, the long rolled plaits on their shoulders were soiled. They looked tired.

They got down from their horses near her little fire—a camp was a camp—swathed their blankets round their hips, pulled the saddles from their ponies and turned them loose, then sat down. One was a young Indian whom she had met before, the other was an older man.

"You all alone?" said the younger man.

"Romero will be here in a minute," she said, glancing back along the trail.

"Ah, Romero! You with him? Where are you going?"

"Round the ridge," she said. "Where are you going?"

"We going down to Pueblo."

"Been out hunting? How long have you been out?"

"Yes. Been out five days." The young Indian gave a little meaningless laugh.

"Got anything?"

"No. We see tracks of two deer—but not got noth-ing."

The Princess noticed a suspicious-looking bulk under one of the saddles—surely a folded-up deer. But she said nothing.

"You must have been cold," she said.

"Yes, very cold in the night. And hungry. Got nothing to eat since yesterday. Eat it all up." And again he laughed his little meaningless laugh. Under their dark skins, the two men looked peaked and hungry. The Princess rummaged for food among the saddle-bags.

There was a lump of bacon—the regular stand-back—
and some bread. She gave them this, and they began
toasting slices of it on long sticks at the fire. Such was
the little camp Romero saw as he rode down the slope:
the Princess in her orange breeches, her head tied in a
blue-and-brown silk kerchief, sitting opposite the two
dark-headed Indians across the camp-fire, while one of
the Indians was leaning forward toasting bacon, his two
plaits of braid-swathed hair dangling as if wearily.

Romero rode up, his face expressionless. The Indians
greeted him in Spanish. He unsaddled his horse, took
food from the bags, and sat down at the camp to eat.
The Princess went to the stream for water, and to wash
her hands.

"Got coffee?" asked the Indians.

"No coffee this outfit," said Romero.

They lingered an hour or more in the warm midday
sun. Then Romero saddled the horses. The Indians
still squatted by the fire. Romero and the Princess rode
away, calling *Adios!* to the Indians, over the stream and
into the dense spruce whence the two strange figures
had emerged.

When they were alone, Romero turned and looked at
her curiously, in a way she could not understand, with
such a hard glint in his eyes. And for the first time she
wondered if she was rash.

"I hope you don't mind going alone with me," she
said.

"If you want it," he replied.

They emerged at the foot of the great bare slope of
rocky summit, where dead spruce-trees stood sparse and
bristling like bristles on a grey dead hog. Romero said
the Mexicans, twenty years back, had fired the mountains, to drive out the whites. This grey concave slope
of summit was corpse-like.

The trail was almost invisible. Romero watched for the trees which the Forest Service had blazed. And they climbed the stark corpse slope, among dead spruce, fallen and ash-grey, into the wind. The wind came rushing from the west, up the funnel of the canyon, from the desert. And there was the desert, like a vast mirage tilting slowly upwards towards the west, immense and pallid, away beyond the funnel of the canyon. The Princess could hardly look.

For an hour their horses rushed the slope, hastening with a great working of the haunches upwards, and halting to breathe, scrambling again, and rowing their way up length by length, on the livid, slanting wall. While the wind blew like some vast machine.

After an hour they were working their way on the incline, no longer forcing straight up. All was grey and dead around them; the horses picked their way over the silver-grey corpses of the spruce. But they were near the top, near the ridge.

Even the horses made a rush for the last bit. They had worked round to a scrap of spruce forest near the very top. They hurried in, out of the huge, monstrous, mechanical wind, that whistled inhumanly and was palely cold. So, stepping through the dark screen of trees, they emerged over the crest.

In front now was nothing but mountains, ponderous, massive, down-sitting mountains, in a huge and intricate knot, empty of life or soul. Under the bristling black feathers of spruce near by lay patches of white snow. The lifeless valleys were concaves of rock and spruce, the rounded summits and the hog-backed summits of grey rock crowded one behind the other like some monstrous herd in arrest.

It frightened the Princess, it was so inhuman. She had not thought it could be so inhuman, so, as it were, anti-life. And yet now one of her desires was fulfilled. She had seen it, the massive, gruesome, repellent core of the Rockies. She saw it there beneath her eyes, in its gigantic, heavy gruesomeness.

And she wanted to go back. At this moment she wanted to turn back. She had looked down into the intestinal knot of these mountains. She was frightened. She wanted to go back.

But Romero was riding on, on the lee side of the spruce forest, above the concaves of the inner mountains. He turned round to her and pointed at the slope with a dark hand.

"Here a miner has been trying for gold," he said. It was a grey, scratched-out heap near a hole—like a great badger hole. And it looked quite fresh.

"Quite lately?" said the Princess.

"No, long ago—twenty, thirty years." He had reined in his horse and was looking at the mountains. "Look!" he said. "There goes the Forest Service trail—along those ridges, on the top, way over there till it comes to Lucytown, where is the Government road. We go down there—no trail—see behind that mountain—you see the top, no trees, and some grass?"

His arm was lifted, his brown hand pointing, his dark eyes piercing into the distance, as he sat on his black horse twisting round to her. Strange and ominous, only the demon of himself, he seemed to her. She was dazed and a little sick, at that height, and she could not see any more. Only she saw an eagle turning in the air beyond, and the light from the west showed the pattern on him underneath.

"Shall I ever be able to go so far?" asked the Princess faintly, petulantly.

"Oh yes! All easy now. No more hard places."

They worked along the ridge, up and down, keeping

on the lee side, the inner side, in the dark shadow. It
was cold. Then the trail laddered up again, and they
emerged on a narrow ridge-track, with the mountain
slipping away enormously on either side. The Princess
was afraid. For one moment she looked out, and saw the
desert, the desert ridges, more desert, more blue ridges,
shining pale and very vast, far below, vastly palely tilting to the western horizon. It was ethereal and terrifying
in its gleaming, pale, half-burnished immensity, tilted
at the west. She could not bear it. To the left was the
ponderous, involved mass of mountains all kneeling
heavily.

She closed her eyes and let her consciousness evaporate away. The mare followed the trail. So on and on, in
the wind again.

They turned their backs to the wind, facing inwards
to the mountains. She thought they had left the trail; it
was quite invisible.

"No," he said, lifting his hand and pointing. "Don't
you see the blazed trees?"

And making an effort of consciousness, she was able to
perceive on a pale-grey dead spruce stem the old marks
where an axe had chipped a piece away. But with the
height, the cold, the wind, her brain was numb.

They turned again and began to descend; he told her
they had left the trail. The horses slithered in the loose
stones, picking their way downward. It was afternoon,
the sun stood obtrusive and gleaming in the lower heavens—about four o'clock. The horses went steadily,
slowly, but obstinately onwards. The air was getting
colder. They were in among the lumpish peaks and steep
concave valleys. She was barely conscious at all of Romero.

He dismounted and came to help her from her saddle.
She tottered, but would not betray her feebleness.

"We must slide down here," he said. "I can lead the horses."

They were on a ridge, and facing a steep bare slope of pallid, tawny mountain grass on which the western sun shone full. It was steep and concave. The Princess felt she might start slipping, and go down like a toboggan into the great hollow.

But she pulled herself together. Her eye blazed up again with excitement and determination. A wind rushed past her; she could hear the shriek of spruce trees far below. Bright spots came on her cheeks as her hair blew across. She looked a wild, fairy-like little thing.

"No," she said. "I will take my horse."

"Then mind she doesn't slip down on top of you," said Romero. And away he went, nimbly dropping down the pale, steep incline, making from rock to rock, down the grass, and following any little slanting groove. His horse hopped and slithered after him, and sometimes stopped dead, with forefeet pressed back, refusing to go further. He, below his horse, looked up and pulled the reins gently, and encouraged the creature. Then the horse once more dropped his forefeet with a jerk, and the descent continued.

The Princess set off in blind, reckless pursuit, tottering and yet nimble. And Romero, looking constantly back to see how she was faring, saw her fluttering down like some queer little bird, her orange breeches twinkling like the legs of some duck, and her head, tied in the blue and buff kerchief, bound round and round like the head of some blue-topped bird. The sorrel mare rocked and slipped behind her. But down came the Princess in a reckless intensity, a tiny, vivid spot on the great hollow flank of the tawny mountain. So tiny! Tiny as a frail bird's egg. It made Romero's mind go blank, with wonder.

But they had to get down, out of that cold and dragging wind. The spruce trees stood below, where a tiny
stream emerged in stones. Away plunged Romero, zig-
zagging down. And away behind, up the slope, fluttered
the tiny, bright-coloured Princess, holding the end of
the long reins, and leading the lumbering, four-footed,
sliding mare.

At last they were down. Romero sat in the sun, below
the wind, beside some squaw-berry bushes. The Princess
came near, the colour flaming in her cheeks, her eyes
dark blue, much darker than the kerchief on her head,
and glowing unnaturally.

"We make it," said Romero.

"Yes," said the Princess, dropping the reins and sub-
siding on to the grass, unable to speak, unable to think.

But, thank heaven, they were out of the wind and in
the sun.

In a few minutes her consciousness and her control
began to come back. She drank a little water. Romero
was attending to the saddles. Then they set off again,
leading the horses still a little further down the tiny
stream-bed. Then they could mount.

They rode down a bank and into a valley grove dense
with aspens. Winding through the thin, crowding, pale-
smooth stems, the sun shone flickering beyond them, and
the disc-like aspen leaves, waving queer mechanical
signals, seemed to be splashing the gold light before her
eyes. She rode on in a splashing dazzle of gold.

Then they entered shadow and the dark, resinous
spruce trees. The fierce boughs always wanted to sweep
her off her horse. She had to twist and squirm past.

But there was a semblance of an old trail. And all at
once they emerged in the sun on the edge of the spruce-
grove, and there was a little cabin, and the bottom of a
small, naked valley with grey rock and heaps of stones,

and a round pool of intense green water, dark green. The sun was just about to leave it.

Indeed, as she stood, the shadow came over the cabin and over herself; they were in the lower gloom, a twilight. Above, the heights still blazed.

It was a little hole of a cabin, near the spruce trees, with an earthen floor and an unhinged door. There was a wooden bed-bunk, three old sawn-off log-lengths to sit on as stools, and a sort of fire-place; no room for anything else. The little hole would hardly contain two people. The roof had gone—but Romero had laid on thick spruce-boughs.

The strange squalor of the primitive forest pervaded the place, the squalor of animals and their droppings, the squalor of the wild. The Princess knew the peculiar repulsiveness of it. She was tired and faint.

Romero hastily got a handful of twigs, set a little fire going in the stove grate, and went out to attend to the horses. The Princess vaguely, mechanically, put sticks on the fire, in a sort of stupor, watching the blaze, stupefied and fascinated. She could not make much fire—it would set the whole cabin alight. And smoke oozed out of the dilapidated mud-and-stone chimney.

When Romero came in with the saddle-pouches and saddles, hanging the saddles on the wall, there sat the little Princess on her stump of wood in front of the dilapidated fire-grate, warming her tiny hands at the blaze, while her orange breeches glowed almost like another fire. She was in a sort of stupor.

"You have some whisky now, or some tea? Or wait for some soup?" he asked.

She rose and looked at him with bright, dazed eyes, half comprehending; the colour glowing hectic in her cheeks.

"Some tea," she said, "with a little whisky in it. Where's the kettle?"

"Wait," he said. "I'll bring the things."

She took her cloak from the back of her saddle, and followed him into the open. It was a deep cup of shadow. But above the sky was still shining, and the heights of the mountains were blazing with aspen like fire blazing.

Their horses were cropping the grass among the stones. Romero clambered up a heap of grey stones and began lifting away logs and rocks, till he had opened the mouth of one of the miner's little old workings. This was his cache. He brought out bundles of blankets, pans for cooking, a little petrol camp-stove, an axe, the regular camp outfit. He seemed so quick and energetic and full of force. This quick force dismayed the Princess a little.

She took a saucepan and went down the stones to the water. It was very still and mysterious, and of a deep green colour, yet pure, transparent as glass. How cold the place was! How mysterious and fearful.

She crouched in her dark cloak by the water, rinsing the saucepan, feeling the cold heavy above her, the shadow like a vast weight upon her, bowing her down. The sun was leaving the mountain tops, departing, leaving her under profound shadow. Soon it would crush her down completely.

Sparks? Or eyes looking at her across the water? She gazed, hypnotized. And with her sharp eyes she made out in the dusk the pale form of a bob-cat crouching by the water's edge, pale as the stones among which it crouched, opposite. And it was watching her with cold, electric eyes of strange intentness, a sort of cold, icy wonder and fearlessness. She saw its *museau* pushed forward, its tufted ears pricking intensely up. It was watch-

ing her with cold, animal curiosity, something demonish
and conscienceless.

She made a swift movement, spilling her water. And
in a flash the creature was gone, leaping like a cat that
is escaping; but strange and soft in its motion, with its
little bob-tail. Rather fascinating. Yet that cold, intent,
demonish watching! She shivered with cold and fear.
She knew well enough the dread and repulsiveness of
the wild.

Romero carried in the bundles of bedding and the
camp outfit. The windowless cabin was already dark inside. He lit a lantern, and then went out again with the
axe. She heard him chopping wood as she fed sticks to
the fire under her water. When he came in with an armful of oak-scrub faggots, she had just thrown the tea into
the water.

"Sit down," she said, "and drink tea."

He poured a little bootleg whisky into the enamel
cups, and in the silence the two sat on the log-ends, sip-
ping the hot liquid and coughing occasionally from the
smoke.

"We burn these oak sticks," he said. "They don't make
hardly any smoke."

Curious and remote he was, saying nothing except
what had to be said. And she, for her part, was as remote from him. They seemed far, far apart, worlds
apart, now they were so near.

He unwrapped one bundle of bedding, and spread the
blankets and the sheepskin in the wooden bunk.

"You lie down and rest," he said, "and I make the
supper."

She decided to do so. Wrapping her cloak round her,
she lay down in the bunk, turning her face to the wall.
She could hear him preparing supper over the little pet-

rol stove. Soon she could smell the soup he was heating; and soon she heard the hissing of fried chicken in a pan.

"You eat your supper now?" he said.

With a jerky, despairing movement, she sat up in the bunk, tossing back her hair. She felt cornered.

"Give it me here," she said.

He handed her first the cupful of soup. She sat among the blankets, eating it slowly. She was hungry. Then he gave her an enamel plate with pieces of fried chicken and currant jelly, butter and bread. It was very good. As they ate the chicken he made the coffee. She said never a word. A certain resentment filled her. She was cornered.

When supper was over he washed the dishes, dried them, and put everything away carefully, else there would have been no room to move in the hole of a cabin. The oak-wood gave out a good bright heat.

He stood for a few moments at a loss. Then he asked her:

"You want to go to bed soon?"

"Soon," she said. "Where are you going to sleep?"

"I make my bed here——" he pointed to the floor along the wall. "Too cold out of doors."

"Yes," she said. "I suppose it is."

She sat immobile, her cheeks hot, full of conflicting thoughts. And she watched him while he folded the blankets on the floor, a sheepskin underneath. Then she went out into the night.

The stars were big. Mars sat on the edge of a mountain, for all the world like the blazing eye of a crouching mountain lion. But she herself was deep, deep below in a pit of shadow. In the intense silence she seemed to hear the spruce forest crackling with electricity and cold. Strange, foreign stars floated on that unmoving water.

The night was going to freeze. Over the hills came the far sobbing-singing howling of the coyotes. She wondered how the horses would be.

Shuddering a little, she turned to the cabin. Warm light showed through its chinks. She pushed at the rickety, half-opened door.

"What about the horses?" she said.

"My black, he won't go away. And your mare will stay with him. You want to go to bed now?"

"I think I do."

"All right. I feed the horses some oats."

And he went out into the night.

He did not come back for some time. She was lying wrapped up tight in the bunk.

He blew out the lantern, and sat down on his bedding to take off his clothes. She lay with her back turned. And soon, in the silence, she was asleep.

She dreamed it was snowing, and the snow was falling on her through the roof, softly, softly, helplessly, and she was going to be buried alive. She was growing colder and colder, the snow was weighing down on her. The snow was going to absorb her.

She awoke with a sudden convulsion, like pain. She was really very cold; perhaps the heavy blankets had numbed her. Her heart seemed unable to beat, she felt she could not move.

With another convulsion she sat up. It was intensely dark. There was not even a spark of fire, the light wood had burned right away. She sat in thick oblivious darkness. Only through a chink she could see a star.

What did she want? Oh, what did she want? She sat in bed and rocked herself woefully. She could hear the steady breathing of the sleeping man. She was shivering with cold; her heart seemed as if it could not beat. She wanted warmth, protection, she wanted to be taken away from herself. And at the same time, perhaps more deeply than anything, she wanted to keep herself intact, intact, untouched, that no one should have any power over her, or rights to her. It was a wild necessity in her that no one, particularly no man, should have any rights or power over her, that no one and nothing should possess her.

Yet that other thing! And she was so cold, so shivering, and her heart could not beat. Oh, would not someone help her heart to beat?

"I want a fire," she said.

She tried to speak, and could not. Then she cleared her throat.

"Romero," she said strangely, "it is so· cold."

Where did her voice come from, and whose voice was it, in the dark?

She heard him at once sit up, and his voice, startled, with a resonance that seemed to vibrate against her, saying:

"You want me to make you warm?"

"Yes."

As soon as he had lifted her in his arms, she wanted to scream to him not to touch her. She stiffened herself. Yet she was dumb.

And he was warm, but with a terrible animal warmth that seemed to annihilate her. He panted like an animal with desire. And she was given over to this thing.

She had never, never wanted to be given over to this. But she had *willed* that it should happen to her. And according to her will, she lay and let it happen. But she never wanted it. She never wanted to be thus assailed and handled and mauled. She wanted to keep herself to herself.

However, she had willed it to happen, and it had happened. She panted with relief when it was over.

Yet even now she had to lie within the hard, powerful clasp of this other creature, this man. She dreaded to struggle to go away. She dreaded almost too much the icy cold of that other bunk.

"Do you want to go away from me?" asked his strange voice. Oh, if it could only have been a thousand miles away from her! Yet she had willed to have it thus close.

"No," she said.

And she could feel a curious joy and pride surging up again in him: at her expense. Because he had got her. She felt like a victim there. And he was exulting in his power over her, his possession, his pleasure.

When dawn came, he was fast asleep. She sat up suddenly.

"I want a fire," she said.

He opened his brown eyes wide and smiled with a curious tender luxuriousness.

"I want you to make a fire," she said.

He glanced at the chinks of light. His brown face hardened to the day.

"All right," he said. "I'll make it."

She hid her face while he dressed. She could not bear to look at him. He was so suffused with pride and luxury. She hid her face almost in despair. But feeling the cold blast of air as he opened the door, she wriggled down into the warm place where he had been. How soon the warmth ebbed, when he had gone!

He made a fire and went out, returning after a while with water.

"You stay in bed till the sun comes," he said. "It very cold."

"Hand me my cloak."

She wrapped the cloak fast round her, and sat up among the blankets. The warmth was already spreading from the fire.

"I suppose we will start back as soon as we've had breakfast?"

He was crouching at his camp-stove making scrambled eggs. He looked up suddenly, transfixed, and his brown eyes, so soft and luxuriously widened, looked straight at her.

"You want to?" he said.

"We'd better get back as soon as possible," she said, turning aside from his eyes.

"You want to get away from me?" he asked, repeating the question of the night in a sort of dread.

"I want to get away from here," she said decisively. And it was true. She wanted supremely to get away, back to the world of people.

He rose slowly to his feet, holding the aluminium frying-pan.

"Don't you like last night?" he asked.

"Not really," she said. "Why? Do you?"

He put down the frying-pan and stood staring at the wall. She could see she had given him a cruel blow. But she did not relent. She was getting her own back. She wanted to regain possession of all herself, and in some mysterious way she felt that he possessed some part of her still.

He looked round at her slowly, his face greyish and heavy.

"You Americans," he said, "you always want to do a man down."

"I am not American," she said. "I am British. And I don't want to do any man down. I only want to go back, now."

"And what will you say about me, down there?"

"That you were very kind to me, and very good."

He crouched down again and went on turning the

eggs. He gave her her plate, and her coffee, and sat down to his own food.

But again he seemed not to be able to swallow. He looked up at her.

"You don't like last night?" he asked.

"Not really," she said, though with some difficulty. "I don't care for that kind of thing."

A blank sort of wonder spread over his face, at these words, followed immediately by a black look of anger, and then a stony, sinister despair.

"You don't?" he said, looking her in the eyes.

"Not really," she replied, looking back with steady hostility into his eyes.

Then a dark flame seemed to come from his face.

"I make you," he said, as if to himself.

He rose and reached her clothes, that hung on a peg: the fine linen underwear, the orange breeches, the fleecy jumper, the blue-and-buff kerchief; then he took up her riding boots and her bead moccasins. Crushing everything in his arms, he opened the door. Sitting up, she saw him stride down to the dark-green pool in the frozen shadow of that deep cup of a valley. He tossed the clothing and the boots out on the pool. Ice had formed. And on the pure, dark green mirror, in the slaty shadow, the Princess saw her things lying, the white linen, the orange breeches, the black boots, the blue moccasins, a tangled heap of colour. Romero picked up rocks and heaved them out at the ice, till the surface broke and the fluttering clothing disappeared in the rattling water, while the valley echoed and shouted again with the sound.

She sat in despair among the blankets, hugging tight her pale-blue cloak. Romero strode straight back to the cabin.

"Now you stay here with me," he said.

She was furious. Her blue eyes met his. They were like two demons watching one another. In his face, beyond a sort of unrelieved gloom, was a demonish desire for death.

He saw her looking round the cabin, scheming. He saw her eyes on his rifle. He took the gun and went out with it. Returning, he pulled out her saddle, carried it to the tarn, and threw it in. Then he fetched his own saddle, and did the same.

"Now will you go away?" he said, looking at her with a smile.

She debated within herself whether to coax him and wheedle him. But she knew he was already beyond it. She sat among her blankets in a frozen sort of despair, hard as hard ice with anger.

He did the chores, and disappeared with the gun. She got up in her blue pyjamas, huddled in her cloak, and stood in the doorway. The dark-green pool was motionless again, the stony slopes were pallid and frozen. Shadow still lay, like an after-death, deep in this valley. Always in the distance she saw the horses feeding. If she could catch one! The brilliant yellow sun was halfway down the mountain. It was nine o'clock.

All day she was alone, and she was frightened. What she was frightened of she didn't know. Perhaps the crackling in the dark spruce wood. Perhaps just the savage, heartless wildness of the mountains. But all day she sat in the sun in the doorway of the cabin, watching, watching for hope. And all the time her bowels were cramped with fear.

She saw a dark spot that probably was a bear, roving across the pale grassy slope in the far distance, in the sun.

When, in the afternoon, she saw Romero approaching, with silent suddenness, carrying his gun and a dead deer, the cramp in her bowels relaxed, then became colder. She dreaded him with a cold dread.

"There is deer-meat," he said, throwing the dead doe at her feet.

"You don't want to go away from here," he said. "This is a nice place."

She shrank into the cabin.

"Come into the sun," he said, following her. She looked up at him with hostile, frightened eyes.

"Come into the sun," he repeated, taking her gently by the arm, in a powerful grasp.

She knew it was useless to rebel. Quietly he led her out, and seated himself in the doorway, holding her still by the arm.

"In the sun it is warm," he said. "Look, this is a nice place. You are such a pretty white woman, why do you want to act mean to me? Isn't this a nice place? Come! Come here! It is sure warm here."

He drew her to him, and in spite of her stony resistance, he took her cloak from her, holding her in her thin blue pyjamas.

"You sure are a pretty little white woman, small and pretty," he said. "You sure won't act mean to me—you don't want to, I know you don't."

She, stony and powerless, had to submit to him. The sun shone on her white, delicate skin.

"I sure don't mind hell fire," he said. "After this."

A queer, luxurious good-humour seemed to possess him again. But though outwardly she was powerless, inwardly she resisted him, absolutely and stonily.

When later he was leaving her again, she said to him suddenly:

"You think you can conquer me this way. But you can't. You can never conquer me."

He stood arrested, looking back at her, with many emotions conflicting in his face—wonder, surprise, a touch of horror, and an unconscious pain that crumpled his face till it was like a mask. Then he went out without saying a word, hung the dead deer on a bough, and started to flay it. While he was at this butcher's work, the sun sank and cold night came on again.

"You, see," he said to her as he crouched, cooking the supper, "I ain't going to let you go. I reckon you called to me in the night, and I've some right. If you want to fix it up right now with me, and say you want to be with me, we'll fix it up now and go down to the ranch tomorrow and get married or whatever you want. But you've got to say you want to be with me. Else I shall stay right here, till something happens."

She waited a while before she answered:

"I don't want to be with anybody against my will. I don't dislike you; at least, I didn't, till you tried to put your will over mine. I won't have anybody's will put over me. You can't succeed. Nobody could. You can never get me under your will. And you won't have long to try, because soon they will send someone to look for me."

He pondered this last, and she regretted having said it. Then, sombre, he bent to the cooking again.

He could not conquer her, however much he violated her. Because her spirit was hard and flawless as a diamond. But he could shatter her. This she knew. Much more, and she would be shattered.

In a sombre, violent excess he tried to expend his desire for her. And she was racked with agony, and felt each time she would die. Because, in some peculiar way, he had got hold of her, some unrealized part of her which she never wished to realize. Racked with a burning, tearing anguish, she felt that the thread of her being would break, and she would die. The burning heat that racked her inwardly.

If only, only she could be alone again, cool and intact! If only she could recover herself again, cool and intact! Would she ever, ever, ever be able to bear herself again?

Even now she did not hate him. It was beyond that. Like some racking, hot doom. Personally he hardly existed.

The next day he would not let her have any fire, because of attracting attention with the smoke. It was a grey day, and she was cold. He stayed around and heated soup on the petrol stove. She lay motionless in the blankets.

And in the afternoon she pulled the clothes over her head and broke into tears. She had never really cried in her life. He dragged the blankets away and looked to see what was shaking her. She sobbed in helpless hysterics. He covered her over again and went outside, looking at the mountains, where clouds were dragging and leaving a little snow. It was a violent, windy, horrible day, the evil of winter rushing down.

She cried for hours. And after this a great silence came between them. They were two people who had died. He did not touch her any more. In the night she lay and shivered like a dying dog. She felt that her very shivering would rupture something in her body, and she would die.

At last she had to speak.

"Could you make a fire? I am so cold," she said, with chattering teeth.

"Want to come over here?" came his voice.

"I would rather you made me a fire," she said, her teeth knocking together and chopping the words in two.

He got up and kindled a fire. At last the warmth spread, and she could sleep.

The next day was still chilly, with some wind. But the sun shone. He went about in silence, with a dead-looking face. It was now so dreary and so like death she wished he would do anything rather than continue in this negation. If now he asked her to go down with him to the world and marry him, she would do it. What did it matter? Nothing mattered any more.

But he would not ask her. His desire was dead and heavy like ice within him. He kept watch around the house.

On the fourth day as she sat huddled in the doorway in the sun, hugged in a blanket, she saw two horsemen come over the crest of the grassy slope—small figures. She gave a cry. He looked up quickly and saw the figures. The men had dismounted. They were looking for the trail.

"They are looking for me," she said.

"Muy bien," he answered in Spanish.

He went and fetched his gun, and sat with it across his knees.

"Oh!" she said. "Don't shoot!"

He looked across at her.

"Why?" he said. "You like staying with me?"

"No," she said. "But don't shoot."

"I ain't going to Pen," he said.

"You won't have to go to Pen," she said. "Don't shoot!"

"I'm going to shoot," he muttered.

And straightaway he kneeled and took very careful aim. The Princess sat on in an agony of helplessness and hopelessness.

The shot rang out. In an instant she saw one of the horses on the pale grassy slope rear and go rolling down. The man had dropped in the grass, and was invisible.

The second man clambered on his horse, and on that precipitous place went at a gallop in a long swerve towards the nearest spruce-tree cover. Bang! Bang! went Romero's shots. But each time he missed, and the running horse leaped like a kangaroo towards cover.

It was hidden. Romero now got behind a rock; tense silence, in the brilliant sunshine. The Princess sat on the bunk inside the cabin, crouching, paralysed. For hours, it seemed, Romero knelt behind this rock, in his black shirt, bare-headed, watching. He had a beautiful, alert figure. The Princess wondered why she did not feel sorry for him. But her spirit was hard and cold, her heart could not melt. Though now she would have called him to her, with love.

But no, she did not love him. She would never love any man. Never! It was fixed and sealed in her, almost vindictively.

Suddenly she was so startled she almost fell from the bunk. A shot rang out quite close from behind the cabin. Romero leaped straight into the air, his arms fell outstretched, turning as he leaped. And even while he was in the air, a second shot rang out, and he fell with a crash, squirming, his hands clutching the earth towards the cabin door.

The Princess sat absolutely motionless, transfixed, staring at the prostrate figure. In a few moments the figure of a man in the Forest Service appeared close to the house; a young man in a broad-brimmed Stetson hat, dark flannel shirt, and riding-boots, carrying a gun. He strode over to the prostrate figure.

"Got you, Romero!" he said aloud. And he turned the dead man over. There was already a little pool of blood where Romero's breast had been.

"H'm!" said the Forest Service man. "Guess I got you nearer than I thought."

And he squatted there, staring at the dead man.

The distant calling of his comrade aroused him. He stood up.

"Hullo, Bill!" he shouted. "Yep! Got him! Yep! Done him in, apparently."

The second man rode out of the forest on a grey horse. He had a ruddy, kind face, and round brown eyes, dilated with dismay.

"He's not passed out?" he asked anxiously.

"Looks like it," said the first young man, coolly.

The second dismounted and bent over the body. Then he stood up again and nodded.

"Yea-a!" he said. "He's done in all right. It's him all right, boy! It's Domingo Romero."

"Yep! I know it!" replied the other.

Then in perplexity he turned and looked into the cabin, where the Princess squatted, staring with big owl eyes from her red blanket.

"Hello!" he said, coming towards the hut. And he took his hat off. Oh, the sense of ridicule she felt! Though he did not mean any.

But she could not speak, no matter what she felt.

"What'd this man start firing for?" he asked.

She fumbled for words, with numb lips.

"He had gone out of his mind!" she said, with solemn, stammering conviction.

"Good Lord! You mean to say he'd gone out of his mind? Whew! That's pretty awful! That explains it then. H'm!"

He accepted the explanation without more ado.

With some difficulty they succeeded in getting the Princess down to the ranch. But she, too, was not a little mad.

"I'm not quite sure where I am," she said to Mrs. Wilkieson, as she lay in bed. "Do you mind explaining?"

Mrs. Wilkieson explained tactfully.

"Oh, yes!" said the Princess. "I remember. And I had an accident in the mountains, didn't I? Didn't we meet a man who'd gone mad, and who shot my horse from under me?"

"Yes, you met a man who had gone out of his mind."

The real affair was hushed up. The Princess departed east in a fortnight's time, in Miss Cummins's care. Apparently she had recovered herself entirely. She was the Princess, and a virgin intact.

But her bobbed hair was grey at the temples, and her eyes were a little mad. She was slightly crazy.

"Since my accident in the mountains, when a man went mad and shot my horse from under me, and my guide had to shoot him dead, I have never felt quite myself."

So she put it.

Later, she married an elderly man, and seemed pleased.

The Fox

THE two girls were usually known by their surnames, Banford and March. They had taken the farm together, intending to work it all by themselves: that is, they were going to rear chickens, make a living by poultry, and add to this by keeping a cow, and raising one or two young beasts. Unfortunately things did not turn out well.

Banford was a small, thin, delicate thing with spectacles. She, however, was the principal investor, for March had little or no money. Banford's father, who was a tradesman in Islington, gave his daughter the start, for

her health's sake, and because he loved her, and because
it did not look as if she would marry. March was more
robust. She had learned carpentry and joinery at the
evening classes in Islington. She would be the man about
the place. They had, moreover, Banford's old grandfather living with them at the start. He had been a
farmer. But unfortunately the old man died after he had
been at Bailey Farm for a year. Then the two girls were
left alone.

They were neither of them young: that is, they were
near thirty. But they certainly were not old. They set
out quite gallantly with their enterprise. They had numbers of chickens, black Leghorns and white Leghorns,
Plymouths and Wyandots; also some ducks; also two
heifers in the fields. One heifer, unfortunately, refused
absolutely to stay in the Bailey Farm closes. No matter
how March made up the fences, the heifer was out, wild
in the woods, or trespassing on the neighbouring pas-
ture, and March and Banford were away, flying after
her, with more haste than success. So this heifer they
sold in despair. And just before the other beast was expecting her first calf, the old man died, and the girls,
afraid of the coming event, sold her in a panic, and
limited their attentions to fowls and ducks.

In spite of a little chagrin, it was a relief to have no
more cattle on hand. Life was not made merely to be
slaved away. Both girls agreed in this. The fowls were
quite enough trouble. March had set up her carpenter's
bench at the end of the open shed. Here she worked,
making coops and doors and other appurtenances. The
fowls were housed in the bigger building, which had
served as barn and cowshed in old days. They had a
beautiful home, and should have been perfectly content. Indeed, they looked well enough. But the girls were
disgusted at their tendency to strange illnesses, at their

exacting way of life, and at their refusal, obstinate refusal, to lay eggs.

March did most of the outdoor work. When she was out and about, in her puttees and breeches, her belted coat and her loose cap, she looked almost like some graceful, loose-balanced young man, for her shoulders were straight, and her movements easy and confident, even tinged with a little indifference, or irony. But her face was not a man's face, ever. The wisps of her crisp dark hair blew about her as she stooped, her eyes were big and wide and dark, when she looked up again, strange, startled, shy and sardonic at once. Her mouth, too, was almost pinched as if in pain and irony. There was something odd and unexplained about her. She would stand balanced on one hip, looking at the fowls pottering about in the obnoxious fine mud of the sloping yard, and calling to her favourite white hen, which came in answer to her name. But there was an almost satirical flicker in March's big, dark eyes as she looked at her three-toed flock pottering about under her gaze, and the same slight dangerous satire in her voice as she spoke to the favoured Patty, who pecked at March's boot by way of friendly demonstration.

Fowls did not flourish at Bailey Farm, in spite of all that March did for them. When she provided hot food for them, in the morning, according to rule, she noticed that it made them heavy and dozy for hours. She expected to see them lean against the pillars of the shed in their languid processes of digestion. And she knew quite well that they ought to be busily scratching and foraging about, if they were to come to any good. So she decided to give them their hot food at night, and let them sleep on it. Which she did. But it made no difference.

War conditions, again, were very unfavourable to poultry keeping. Food was scarce and bad. And when

the Daylight Saving Bill was passed, the fowls obstinately refused to go to bed as usual, about nine o'clock
in the summer time. That was late enough, indeed, for
there was no peace till they were shut up and asleep.
Now they cheerfully walked around, without so much as
glancing at the barn, until ten o'clock or later. Both Banford and March disbelieved in living for work alone.
They wanted to read or take a cycle-ride in the evening,
or perhaps March wished to paint curvilinear swans on
porcelain, with green background, or else make a marvellous fire-screen by processes of elaborate cabinet
work. For she was a creature of odd whims and unsatisfied tendencies. But from all these things she was prevented by the stupid fowls.

One evil there was greater than any other. Bailey
Farm was a little homestead, with ancient wooden barn
and low gabled farm-house, lying just one field removed
from the edge of the wood. Since the War the fox was a
demon. He carried off the hens under the very noses of
March and Banford. Banford would start and stare
through her big spectacles with all her eyes, as another
squawk and flutter took place at her heels. Too late! Another white Leghorn gone. It was disheartening.

They did what they could to remedy it. When it became permitted to shoot foxes, they stood sentinel with
their guns, the two of them, at the favoured hours. But
it was no good. The fox was too quick for them. So another year passed, and another, and they were living on
their losses, as Banford said. They let their farm-house
one summer, and retired to live in a railway-carriage that
was deposited as a sort of out-house in a corner of the
field. This amused them, and helped their finances.
None the less, things looked dark.

Although they were usually the best of friends, because Banford, though nervous and delicate, was a

warm, generous soul, and March, though so odd and absent in herself, had a strange magnanimity, yet, in the long solitude, they were apt to become a little irritable with one another, tired of one another. March had four-fifths of the work to do, and though she did not mind, there seemed no relief, and it made her eyes flash curiously sometimes. Then Banford, feeling more nerve-worn than ever, would become despondent, and March would speak sharply to her. They seemed to be losing ground, somehow, losing hope as the months went by. There alone in the fields by the wood, with the wide country stretching hollow and dim to the round hills of the White Horse, in the far distance, they seemed to have to live too much off themselves. There was nothing to keep them up—and no hope.

The fox really exasperated them both. As soon as they had let the fowls out, in the early summer mornings, they had to take their guns and keep guard; and then again, as soon as evening began to mellow, they must go once more. And he was so sly. He slid along in the deep grass, he was difficult as a serpent to see. And he seemed to circumvent the girls deliberately. Once or twice March had caught sight of the white tip of his brush, or the ruddy shadow of him in the deep grass, and she had let fire at him. But he made no account of this.

One evening March was standing with her back to the sunset, her gun under her arm, her hair pushed under her cap. She was half watching, half musing. It was her constant state. Her eyes were keen and observant, but her inner mind took no notice of what she saw. She was always lapsing into this odd, rapt state, her mouth rather screwed up. It was a question whether she was there, actually consciously present, or not.

The trees on the wood-edge were a darkish, brownish green in the full light—for it was the end of August.

Beyond, the naked, copper-like shafts and limbs of the pine-trees shone in the air. Nearer, the rough grass, with its long brownish stalks all agleam, was full of light. The fowls were round about—the ducks were still swimming on the pond under the pine-trees. March looked at it all, saw it all, and did not see it. She heard Banford speaking to the fowls, in the distance—and she did not hear. What was she thinking about? Heaven knows. Her consciousness was, as it were, held back.

She lowered her eyes and suddenly saw the fox. He was looking up at her. His chin was pressed down, and his eyes were looking up. They met her eyes. And he knew her. She was spell-bound—she knew he knew her. So he looked into her eyes, and her soul failed her. He knew her, he was not daunted.

She struggled, confusedly she came to herself, and saw him making off, with slow leaps over some fallen boughs, slow, impudent jumps. Then he glanced over his shoulder, and ran smoothly away. She saw his brush held smooth like a feather, she saw his white buttocks twinkle. And he was gone, softly, soft as the wind.

She put her gun to her shoulder, but even then pursed her mouth, knowing it was nonsense to pretend to fire. So she began to walk slowly after him, in the direction he had gone, slowly, pertinaciously. She expected to find him. In her heart she was determined to find him. What she would do when she saw him again she did not consider. But she was determined to find him. So she walked abstractedly about on the edge of the wood, with wide, vivid dark eyes, and a faint flush in her cheeks. She did not think. In strange mindlessness she walked hither and thither.

At last she became aware that Banford was calling her. She made an effort of attention, turned, and gave some sort of screaming call in answer. Then again she was striding off towards the homestead. The red sun was setting, the fowls were retiring towards their roost. She watched them, white creatures, black creatures, gathering to the barn. She watched them spell-bound, without seeing them. But her automatic intelligence told her when it was time to shut the door.

She went indoors to supper, which Banford had set on the table. Banford chatted easily. March seemed to listen, in her distant, manly way. She answered a brief word now and then. But all the time she was as if spell-bound. And as soon as supper was over, she rose again to go out, without saying why.

She took her gun again and went to look for the fox. For he had lifted his eyes upon her, and his knowing look seemed to have entered her brain. She did not so much think of him: she was possessed by him. She saw his dark, shrewd, unabashed eye looking into her, knowing her. She felt him invisibly master her spirit. She knew the way he lowered his chin as he looked up, she knew his muzzle, the golden brown, and the greyish white. And again, she saw him glance over his shoulder at her, half-inviting, half-contemptuous and cunning. So she went, with her great startled eyes glowing, her gun under her arm, along the wood-edge. Meanwhile the night fell, and a great moon rose above the pine-trees. And again Banford was calling.

So she went indoors. She was silent and busy. She examined her gun, and cleaned it, musing abstractedly by the lamp-light. Then she went out again, under the great moon, to see if everything was right. When she saw the dark crests of the pine-trees against the blood-red sky, again her heart beat to the fox, the fox. She wanted to follow him, with her gun.

It was some days before she mentioned the affair to Banford. Then suddenly, one evening, she said:

"The fox was right at my feet on Saturday night."

"Where?" said Banford, her eyes opening behind her spectacles.

"When I stood just above the pond."

"Did you fire?" cried Banford.

"No, I didn't."

"Why not?"

"Why, I was too much surprised, I suppose."

It was the same old, slow, laconic way of speech March always had. Banford stared at her friend for a few moments.

"You saw him?" she cried.

"Oh, yes! He was looking up at me, cool as anything."

"I tell you," cried Banford, "the cheek!—They're not afraid of us, Nellie."

"Oh, no," said March.

"Pity you didn't get a shot at him," said Banford.

"Isn't it a pity! I've been looking for him ever since. But I don't suppose he'll come so near again."

"I don't suppose he will," said Banford.

And she proceeded to forget about it, except that she was more indignant than ever at the impudence of the beggars. March also was not conscious that she thought of the fox. But whenever she fell into her half-musing, when she was half-rapt and half-intelligently aware of what passed under her vision, then it was the fox which somehow dominated her unconsciousness, possessed the blank half of her musing. And so it was for weeks, and months. No matter whether she had been climbing the trees for the apples, or boating down the last of the damsons, or whether she had been digging out the ditch from the duck-pond, or clearing out the barn, when she had finished, or when she straightened herself, and pushed the wisps of hair away again from her forehead, and pursed up her mouth again in an odd, screwed fash-

ion, much too old for her years, there was sure to come
over her mind the old spell of·the fox, as it came when
he was looking at her. It was as if she could smell him at
these times. And it always recurred at unexpected moments, just as she was going to sleep at night, or just
as she was pouring the water into the tea-pot, to make
tea—it was the fox, it came over her like a spell.

So the months passed. She still looked for him unconsciously when she went towards the wood. He had become a settled effect in her spirit, a state permanently
established, not continuous, but always recurring. She
did not know what she felt or thought: only the state
came over her, as when he looked at her.

The months passed, the dark evenings came, heavy,
dark November, when March went about in high boots,
ankle deep in mud, when the night began to fall at four
o'clock, and the day never properly dawned. Both girls
dreaded these times. They dreaded the almost continuous darkness that enveloped them on their desolate little
farm near the wood. Banford was physically afraid. She
was afraid of tramps, afraid lest someone should come
prowling round. March was not so much afraid, as uncomfortable, and disturbed. She felt discomfort and
gloom in all her physique.

Usually the two girls had tea in the sitting room.
March lighted a fire at dusk, and put on the wood she
had chopped and sawed during the day. Then the long
evening was in front, dark, sodden, black outside, lonely
and rather oppressive inside, a little dismal. March was
content not to talk, but Banford could not keep still.
Merely listening to the wind in the pines outside, or the
drip of water, was too much for her.

One evening the girls had washed up the tea-things in
the kitchen, and March had put on her house-shoes, and

taken up a roll of crochet-work, which she worked at slowly from time to time. So she lapsed into silence. Banford stared at the red fire, which, being of wood, needed constant attention. She was afraid to begin to read too early, because her eyes would not bear any strain. So she sat staring at the fire, listening to the distant sounds, sound of cattle lowing, of a dull, heavy moist wind, of the rattle of the evening train on the little railway not far off. She was almost fascinated by the red glow of the fire.

Suddenly both girls started, and lifted their heads. They heard a footstep—distinctly a footstep. Banford recoiled in fear. March stood listening. Then rapidly she approached the door that led into the kitchen. At the same time they heard the footsteps approach the back door. They waited a second. The back door opened softly. Banford gave a loud cry. A man's voice said softly:

"Hello!"

March recoiled and took a gun from a corner.

"What do you want?" she cried, in a sharp voice.

Again the soft, softly vibrating man's voice said:

"Hello! What's wrong?"

"I shall shoot!" cried March. "What do you want?"

"Why, what's wrong? What's wrong?" came the soft, wondering, rather scared voice: and a young soldier, with his heavy kit on his back, advanced into the dim light. "Why," he said, "who lives here then?"

"We live here," said March. "What do you want?"

"Oh!" came the long, melodious, wonder-note from the young soldier. "Doesn't William Grenfel live here then?"

"No—you know he doesn't."

"Do I?—Do I? I don't, you see.—He *did* live here,

because he was my grandfather, and I lived here myself five years ago. What's become of him then?"

The young man—or youth, for he would not be more than twenty—now advanced and stood in the inner doorway. March, already under the influence of his strange, soft, modulated voice, stared at him spellbound. He had a ruddy, roundish face, with fairish hair, rather long, flattened to his forehead with sweat. His eyes were blue, and very bright and sharp. On his cheeks, on the fresh ruddy skin, were fine, fair hairs, like a down, but sharper. It gave him a slightly glistening look. Having his heavy sack on his shoulders, he stooped, thrusting his head forward. His hat was loose in one hand. He stared brightly, very keenly from girl to girl, particularly at March, who stood pale, with great dilated eyes, in her belted coat and puttees, her hair knotted in a big crisp knot behind. She still had the gun in her hand. Behind her, Banford, clinging to the sofa-arm, was shrinking away, with half-averted head.

"I thought my grandfather still lived here?—I wonder if he's dead."

"We've been here for three years," said Banford, who was beginning to recover her wits, seeing something boyish in the round head with its rather long sweaty hair.

"Three years! You don't say so!—And you don't know who was here before you?"

"I know it was an old man, who lived by himself."

"Ay! Yes, that's him!—And what became of him then?"

"He died. I know he died——"

"Ay! He's dead then!"

The youth stared at them without changing colour or expression. If he had any expression, besides a slight

baffled look of wonder, it was one of sharp curiosity con-
cerning the two girls; sharp impersonal curiosity, the
curiosity of that round young head.

But to March he was the fox. Whether it was the
thrusting forward of his head, or the glisten of fine whitish hairs on the ruddy cheek-bones, or the bright, keen
eyes, that can never be said: but the boy was to her the
fox, and she could not see him otherwise.

"How is it you didn't know if your grandfather was
alive or dead?" asked Banford, recovering her natural
sharpness.

"Ay, that's it," replied the softly-breathing youth.
"You see I joined up in Canada, and I hadn't heard for
three or four years—I ran away to Canada."

"And now have you just come from France?"

"Well—from Salonika really."

There was a pause, nobody knowing quite what to
say.

"So you've nowhere to go now?" said Banford rather
lamely.

"Oh, I know some people in the village. Anyhow, I
can go to the Swan."

"You came on the train, I suppose.—Would you like
to sit down a bit?"

"Well—I don't mind."

He gave an odd little groan as he swung off his kit.
Banford looked at March.

"Put the gun down," she said. "We'll make a cup of
tea."

"Ay," said the youth. "We've seen enough of rifles."

He sat down rather tired on the sofa, leaning forward.

March recovered her presence of mind and went into
the kitchen. There she heard the soft young voice musing:

"Well, to think I should come back and find it like this!" He did not seem sad, not at all—only rather interestedly surprised.

"And what a difference in the place, eh?" he continued, looking round the room.

"You see a difference, do you?" said Banford.

"Yes, don't I!"

His eyes were unnaturally clear and bright, though it was the brightness of abundant health.

March was busy in the kitchen preparing another meal. It was about seven o'clock. All the time, while she was active, she was attending to the youth in the sitting-room, not so much listening to what he said, as feeling the soft run of his voice. She primmed up her mouth tighter and tighter, puckering it as if it was sewed, in her effort to keep her will uppermost. Yet her large eyes dilated and glowed in spite of her, she lost herself. Rapidly and carelessly she prepared the meal, cutting large chunks of bread and margarine—for there was no butter. She racked her brain to think of something else to put on the tray—she had only bread, margarine, and jam, and the larder was bare. Unable to conjure anything up, she went into the sitting-room with her tray.

She did not want to be noticed. Above all, she did not want him to look at her. But when she came in, and was busy setting the table just behind him, he pulled himself up from his sprawling and turned and looked over his shoulder. She became pale and wan.

The youth watched her as she bent over the table, looked at her slim, well-shapen legs, at the belted coat dropping around her thighs, at the knot of dark hair, and his curiosity, vivid and widely alert, was again arrested by her.

The lamp was shaded with a dark-green shade, so that the light was thrown downwards, the upper half of the room was dim. His face moved bright under the light, but March loomed shadowy in the distance.

She turned round, but kept her eyes sideways, dropping and lifting her dark lashes. Her mouth unpuckered, as she said to Banford:

"Will you pour out?"

Then she went into the kitchen again.

"Have your tea where you are, will you?" said Banford to the youth, "unless you'd rather come to the table."

"Well," said he, "I'm nice and comfortable here, aren't I? I will have it here, if you don't mind."

"There's nothing but bread and jam," she said. And she put his plate on a stool by him. She was very happy now, waiting on him. For she loved company. And now she was no more afraid of him than if he were her own younger brother. He was such a boy.

"Nellie," she cried. "I've poured you a cup out."

March appeared in the doorway, took her cup, and sat down in a corner, as far from the light as possible. She was very sensitive in her knees. Having no skirts to cover them, and being forced to sit with them boldly exposed, she suffered. She shrank and shrank, trying not to be seen. And the youth, sprawling low on the couch, glanced up at her, with long, steady, penetrating looks, till she was almost ready to disappear. Yet she held her cup balanced, she drank her tea, screwed up her mouth and held her head averted. Her desire to be invisible was so strong that it quite baffled the youth. He felt he could not see her distinctly. She seemed like a shadow within the shadow. And ever his eyes came back to her, searching, unremitting, with unconscious fixed attention.

Meanwhile he was talking softly and smoothly to Banford, who loved nothing so much as gossip, and who was

full of perky interest, like a bird. Also he ate largely
and quickly and voraciously, so that March had to cut
more chunks of bread and margarine, for the roughness
of which Banford apologized.

"Oh, well," said March, suddenly speaking, "if there's
no butter to put on it, it's no good trying to make dainty
pieces."

Again the youth watched her, and he laughed, with a
sudden, quick laugh, showing his teeth and wrinkling
his nose.

"It isn't, is it?" he answered, in his soft, near voice.

It appeared he was Cornish by birth and upbringing.
When he was twelve years old he had come to Bailey
Farm with his grandfather, with whom he had never
agreed very well. So he had run away to Canada, and
worked far away in the West. Now he was here—and
that was the end of it.

He was very curious about the girls, to find out exactly
what they were doing. His questions were those of a
farm youth; acute, practical, a little mocking. He was
very much amused by their attitude to their losses: for
they were amusing on the score of heifers and fowls.

"Oh, well," broke in March, "we don't believe in living
for nothing but work."

"Don't you?" he answered. And again the quick
young laugh came over his face. He kept his eyes steadily on the obscure woman in the corner.

"But what will you do when you've used up all your
capital?" he said.

"Oh, I don't know," answered March laconically.
"Hire ourselves out for landworkers, I suppose."

"Yes, but there won't be any demand for women land-
workers, now the war's over," said the youth.

"Oh, we'll see. We shall hold on a bit longer yet,"

said March, with a plangent, half-sad, half-ironical in-difference.

"There wants a man about the place," said the youth softly. Banford burst out laughing.

"Take care what you say," she interrupted. "We con-sider ourselves quite efficient."

"Oh," came March's slow, plangent voice, "it isn't a case of efficiency, I'm afraid. If you're going to do farm-ing you must be at it from morning till night, and you might as well be a beast yourself."

"Yes, that's it," said the youth. "You aren't willing to put yourselves into it."

"We aren't," said March, "and we know it."

"We want some of our time for ourselves," said Ban-ford.

The youth threw himself back on the sofa, his face tight with laughter, and laughed silently but thoroughly. The calm scorn of the girls tickled him tremendously.

"Yes," he said, "but why did you begin then?"

"Oh," said March, "we had a better opinion of the nature of fowls then than we have now."

"Of Nature altogether, I'm afraid," said Banford. "Don't talk to me about Nature."

Again the face of the youth tightened with delighted laughter.

"You haven't a very high opinion of fowls and cattle, have you?" he said.

"Oh, no—quite a low one," said March.

He laughed out.

"Neither fowls nor heifers," said Banford, "nor goats nor the weather."

The youth broke into a sharp yap of laughter, de-lighted. The girls began to laugh too, March turning aside her face and wrinkling her mouth in amusement.

"Oh, well," said Banford, "we don't mind, do we, Nellie?"

"No," said March, "we don't mind."

The youth was very pleased. He had eaten and drunk his fill. Banford began to question him. His name was Henry Grenfel—no, he was not called Harry, always Henry. He continued to answer with courteous simplicity, grave and charming. March, who was not included, cast long, slow glances at him from her recess, as he sat there on the sofa, his hands clasping his knees, his face under the lamp bright and alert, turned to Banford. She became almost peaceful, at last. He was identified with the fox—and he was here in full presence. She need not go after him any more. There in the shadow of her corner she gave herself up to a warm, relaxed peace, almost like sleep, accepting the spell that was on her. But she wished to remain hidden. She was only fully at peace whilst he forgot her, talking with Banford. Hidden in the shadow of the corner, she need not any more be divided in herself, trying to keep up two planes of consciousness. She could at last lapse into the odour of the fox.

For the youth, sitting before the fire in his uniform, sent a faint but distinct odour into the room, indefinable, but something like a wild creature. March no longer tried to reserve herself from it. She was still and soft in her corner like a passive creature in its cave.

At last the talk dwindled. The youth relaxed his clasp of his knees, pulled himself together a little, and looked round. Again he became aware of the silent, half-invisible woman in the corner.

"Well," he said, unwillingly, "I suppose I'd better be going, or they'll be in bed at the Swan."

"I'm afraid they're in bed anyhow," said Banford. "They've all got this influenza."

"Have they!" he exclaimed. And he pondered. "Well," he continued, "I shall find a place somewhere."

"I'd say you could stay here, only—" Banford began.

He turned and watched her, holding his head forward. "What—?" he asked.

"Oh, well," she said, "propriety, I suppose—" She was rather confused.

"It wouldn't be improper, would it?" he said, gently surprised.

"Not as far as we're concerned," said Banford.

"And not as far as *I'm* concerned," he said, with grave naïveté. "After all, it's my own home, in a way."

Banford smiled at this.

"It's what the village will have to say," she said.

There was a moment's blank pause.

"What do you say, Nellie?" asked Banford.

"I don't mind," said March, in her distinct tone. "The village doesn't matter to me, anyhow."

"No," said the youth, quick and soft. "Why should it?—I mean, what should they say?"

"Oh, well," came March's piangent, laconic voice, "they'll easily find something to say. But it makes no difference what they say. We can look after ourselves."

"Of course you can," said the youth.

"Well then, stop if you like," said Banford. "The spare room is quite ready."

His face shone with pleasure.

"If you're quite sure it isn't troubling you too much," he said, with that soft courtesy which distinguished him.

"Oh, it's no trouble," they both said.

He looked, smiling with delight, from one to another.

"It's awfully nice not to have to turn out again, isn't it?" he said gratefully.

"I suppose it is," said Banford.

March disappeared to attend to the room. Banford

was as pleased and thoughtful as if she had her own
young brother home from France. It gave her just the
same kind of gratification to attend on him, to get out the
bath for him, and everything. Her natural warmth and
kindliness had now an outlet. And the youth luxuriated
in her sisterly attention. But it puzzled him slightly to
know that March was silently working for him too. She
was so curiously silent and obliterated. It seemed to him
he had not really seen her. He felt he should not know
her if he met her in the road.

That night March dreamed vividly. She dreamed she
heard a singing outside, which she could not understand,
a singing that roamed round the house, in the fields and
in the darkness. It moved her so, that she felt she must
weep. She went out, and suddenly she knew it was the
fox singing. He was very yellow and bright, like corn.
She went nearer to him, but he ran away and ceased
singing. He seemed near, and she wanted to touch him.
She stretched out her hand, but suddenly he bit her
wrist, and at the same instant, as she drew back, the fox,
turning round to bound away, whisked his brush across
her face, and it seemed his brush was on fire, for it
seared and burned her mouth with a great pain. She
awoke with the pain of it, and lay trembling as if she
were really seared.

In the morning, however, she only remembered it as
a distant memory. She arose and was busy preparing
the house and attending to the fowls. Banford flew into
the village on her bicycle, to try and buy food. She was
a hospitable soul. But alas in the year 1918 there was
not much food to buy. The youth came downstairs in
his shirt-sleeves. He was young and fresh, but he walked
with his head thrust forward, so that his shoulders
seemed raised and rounded, as if he had a slight curva-
ture of the spine. It must have been only a manner of

bearing himself, for he was young and vigorous. He washed himself and went outside, whilst the women were preparing breakfast.

He saw everything, and examined everything. His curiosity was quick and insatiable. He compared the state of things with that which he remembered before, and cast over in his mind the effect of the changes. He watched the fowls and the ducks, to see their condition, he noticed the flight of wood-pigeons overhead: they were very numerous; he saw the few apples high up, which March had not been able to reach; he remarked that they had borrowed a draw-pump, presumably to empty the big soft-water cistern which was on the north side of the house.

"It's a funny, dilapidated old place," he said to the girls, as he sat at breakfast.

His eyes were wise and childish with thinking about things. He did not say much, but ate largely. March kept her face averted. She, too, in the early morning, could not be aware of him, though something about the glint of his khaki reminded her of the brilliance of her dream-fox.

During the day the girls went about their business. In the morning, he attended to the guns, shot a rabbit and a wild duck that was flying high, towards the wood. That was a great addition to the empty larder. The girls felt that already he had earned his keep. He said nothing about leaving, however. In the afternoon he went to the village. He came back at tea-time. He had the same alert, forward-reaching look on his roundish face. He hung his hat on a peg with a little swinging gesture. He was thinking about something.

"Well," he said to the girls, as he sat at table. "What am I going to do?"

"How do you mean—what are you going to do?" said Banford.

"Where am I going to find a place in the village, to stay?" he said.

"I don't know," said Banford. "Where do you think of staying?"

"Well—" he hesitated, "at the Swan they've got this flu, and at the Plough and Harrow they've got the soldiers who are collecting the hay for the army: besides in the private houses, there's ten men and a corporal altogether billeted in the village, they tell me. I'm not sure where I could get a bed."

He left the matter to them. He was rather calm about it. March sat with her elbows on the table, her two hands supporting her chin, looking at him unconsciously. Suddenly he lifted his clouded blue eyes, and unthinking looked straight into March's eyes. He was startled as well as she. He, too, recoiled a little. March felt the same sly, taunting, knowing spark leap out of his eyes as he turned his head aside, and fall into her soul, as had fallen from the dark eyes of the fox. She pursed her mouth as if in pain, as if asleep too.

"Well, I don't know—" Banford was saying. She seemed reluctant, as if she were afraid of being imposed upon. She looked at March. But, with her weak, troubled sight, she only saw the usual semi-abstraction on her friend's face. "Why don't you speak, Nellie?" she said.

But March was wide-eyed and silent, and the youth, as if fascinated, was watching her without moving his eyes.

"Go on—answer something," said Banford. And March turned her head slightly aside, as if coming to consciousness, or trying to come to consciousness.

"What do you expect me to say?" she asked automatically.

"Say what you think," said Banford.

"It's all the same to me," said March.

And again there was silence. A pointed light seemed to be on the boy's eyes, penetrating like a needle.

"So it is to me," said Banford. "You can stop on here if you like."

A smile like a cunning little flame came over his face, suddenly and involuntarily. He dropped his head quickly to hide it and remained with his head dropped, his face hidden.

"You can stop on here if you like. You can please yourself, Henry," Banford concluded.

Still he did not reply but remained with his head dropped. Then he lifted his face. It was bright with a curious light, as if exultant, and his eyes were strangely clear as he watched March. She turned her face aside, her mouth suffering as if wounded, and her consciousness dim.

Banford became a little puzzled. She watched the steady, pellucid gaze of the youth's eyes as he looked at March, with the invisible smile gleaming on his face. She did not know how he was smiling, for no feature moved. It seemed only in the gleam, almost the glitter of the fine hairs on his cheeks. Then he looked, with quite a changed look, at Banford.

"I'm sure," he said in his soft, courteous voice, "you're awfully good. You're too good. You don't want to be bothered with me, I'm sure."

"Cut a bit of bread, Nellie," said Banford uneasily; adding: "It's no bother, if you like to stay. It's like having my own brother here for a few days. He's a boy like you are."

"That's awfully kind of you," the lad repeated. "I should like to stay, ever so much, if you're sure I'm not a trouble to you."

"No, of course you're no trouble. I tell you, it's a pleasure to have somebody in the house besides ourselves," said warm-hearted Banford.

"But Miss March?" he said in his soft voice, looking at her.

"Oh, it's quite all right as far as I'm concerned," said March vaguely.

His face beamed, and he almost rubbed his hands with pleasure.

"Well, then," he said, "I should love it, if you'd let me pay my board and help with the work."

"You've no need to talk about board," said Banford.

One or two days went by, and the youth stayed on at the farm. Banford was quite charmed by him. He was so soft and courteous in speech, not wanting to say much himself, preferring to hear what she had to say, and to laugh in his quick, half-mocking way. He helped readily with the work—but not too much. He loved to be out alone with the gun in his hands, to watch, to see. For his sharp-eyed, impersonal curiosity was insatiable, and he was most free when he was quite alone, half-hidden, watching.

Particularly he watched March. She was a strange character to him. Her figure, like a graceful young man's, piqued him. Her dark eyes made something rise in his soul, with a curious elate excitement, when he looked into them, an excitement he was afraid to let be seen, it was so keen and secret. And then her odd, shrewd speech made him laugh outright. He felt he must go further, he was inevitably impelled. But he put away the thought of her, and went off towards the wood's edge with the gun.

The dusk was falling as he came home, and with the dusk a fine, late November rain. He saw the fire-light leaping in the window of the sitting-room, a leaping light in the little cluster of the dark buildings. And he thought to himself, it would be a good thing to have this place for his own. And then the thought entered him shrewdly: why not marry March? He stood still in the middle of the field for some moments, the dead rabbit hanging still in his hand, arrested by this thought. His mind waited in amazement—it seemed to calculate—— then he smiled curiously to himself in acquiescence. Why not? Why not, indeed? It was a good idea. What if it was rather ridiculous? What did it matter? What if she was older than he? It didn't matter. When he thought of her dark, startled, vulnerable eyes he smiled subtly to himself. He was older than she, really. He was master of her.

He scarcely admitted his intention even to himself. He kept it as a secret even from himself. It was all too uncertain as yet. He would have to see how things went. Yes, he would have to see how things went. If he wasn't careful, she would just simply mock at the idea. He knew, sly and subtle as he was, that if he went to her plainly and said: "Miss March, I love you and want you to marry me," her inevitable answer would be: "Get out. I don't want any of that tomfoolery." This was her attitude to men and their "tomfoolery." If he was not careful, she would turn round on him with her savage, sardonic ridicule and dismiss him from the farm and from her own mind, for ever. He would have to go gently. He would have to catch her as you catch a deer or a wood-cock when you go out shooting. It's no good walking out into the forest and saying to the deer: "Please fall to my gun." No, it is a slow, subtle battle. When you really go out to get a deer, you gather yourself together, you coil yourself inside yourself, and you advance secretly, before dawn, into the mountains. It is not so much what you do, when you go out hunting, as how

you feel. You have to be subtle and cunning and absolutely fatally ready. It becomes like a fate. Your own fate
overtakes and determines the fate of the deer you are
hunting. First of all, even before you come in sight
of your quarry, there is a strange battle, like mesmerism.
Your own soul, as a hunter, has gone out to fasten on the
soul of the deer, even before you see any deer. And the
soul of the deer fights to escape. Even before the deer
has any wind of you, it is so. It is a subtle, profound
battle of wills, which takes place in the invisible. And
it is a battle never finished till your bullet goes home.
When you are *really* worked up to the true pitch, and
you come at last into range, you don't then aim as you
do when you are firing at a bottle. It is your own *will*
which carries the bullet into the heart of your quarry.
The bullet's flight home is a sheer projection of your
own fate into the fate of the deer. It happens like a
supreme wish, a supreme act of volition, not as a
dodge of cleverness.

He was a huntsman in spirit, not a farmer, and not
a soldier stuck in a regiment. And it was as a young
hunter that he wanted to bring down March as his
quarry, to make her his wife. So he gathered himself
subtly together, seemed to withdraw into a kind of in-
visibility. He was not quite sure how he would go on.
And March was suspicious as a hare. So he remained in
appearance just the nice, odd stranger-youth, staying for
a fortnight on the place.

He had been sawing logs for the fire, in the afternoon.
Darkness came very early. It was still a cold, raw mist.
It was getting almost too dark to see. A pile of short
sawed logs lay beside the trestle. March came to carry
them indoors, or into the shed, as he was busy sawing
the last log. He was working in his shirt-sleeves, and
did not notice her approach. She came unwillingly, as if

shy. He saw her stooping to the bright-ended logs, and he stopped sawing. A fire like lightning flew down his legs in the nerves.

"March?" he said, in his quiet young voice.

She looked up from the logs she was piling.

"Yes!" she said.

He looked down on her in the dusk. He could see her not too distinctly.

"I wanted to ask you something," he said.

"Did you? What was it?" she said. Already the fright was in her voice. But she was too much mistress of herself.

"Why"—his voice seemed to draw out soft and subtle, it penetrated her nerves—"why, what do you think it is?"

She stood up, placed her hands on her hips, and stood looking at him transfixed, without answering. Again he burned with a sudden power.

"Well," he said and his voice was so soft it seemed rather like a subtle touch, like the merest touch of a cat's paw, a feeling rather than a sound. "Well—I wanted to ask you to marry me."

March felt rather than heard him. She was trying in vain to turn aside her face. A great relaxation seemed to have come over her. She stood silent, her head slightly on one side. He seemed to be bending towards her, invisibly smiling. It seemed to her fine sparks came out of him.

Then very suddenly, she said:

"Don't try any of your tomfoolery on me."

A quiver went over his nerves. He had missed. He waited a moment to collect himself again. Then he said, putting all the strange softness into his voice, as if he were imperceptibly stroking her:

"Why, it's not tomfoolery. It's not tomfoolery. I mean it. I mean it. What makes you disbelieve me?"

He sounded hurt. And his voice had such a curious power over her; making her feel loose and relaxed. She struggled somewhere for her own power. She felt for a moment that she was lost—lost—lost. The word seemed to rock in her as if she were dying. Suddenly again she spoke.

"You don't know what you are talking about," she said, in a brief and transient stroke of scorn. "What nonsense! I'm old enough to be your mother."

"Yes, I do know what I'm talking about. Yes, I do," he persisted softly, as if he were producing his voice in her blood. "I know quite well what I'm talking about. You're not old enough to be my mother. That isn't true. And what does it matter even if it was? You can marry me whatever age we are. What is age to me? And what is age to you! Age is nothing."

A swoon went over her as he concluded. He spoke rapidly—in the rapid Cornish fashion—and his voice seemed to sound in her somewhere where she was helpless against it. "Age is nothing!" The soft, heavy insistence of it made her sway dimly out there in the darkness. She could not answer.

A great exultance leaped like fire over his limbs. He felt he had won.

"I want to marry you, you see. Why shouldn't I?" he proceeded, soft and rapid. He waited for her to answer. In the dusk he saw her almost phosphorescent. Her eyelids were dropped, her face half-averted and unconscious. She seemed to be in his power. But he waited, watchful. He dared not yet touch her.

"Say then," he said. "Say then you'll marry me. Say —say?" He was softly insistent.

"What?" she asked, faint, from a distance, like one in

pain. His voice was now unthinkably near and soft. He drew very near to her.

"Say yes."

"Oh, I can't," she wailed helplessly, half articulate, as if semi-conscious, and as if in pain, like one who dies. "How can I?"

"You can," he said softly, laying his hand gently on her shoulder as she stood with her head averted and dropped, dazed. "You can. Yes, you can. What makes you say you can't? You can. You can." And with awful softness he bent forward and just touched her neck with his mouth and his chin.

"Don't!" she cried, with a faint mad cry like hysteria, starting away and facing round on him. "What do you mean?" But she had no breath to speak with. It was as if she were killed.

"I mean what I say," he persisted softly and cruelly. "I want you to marry me. I want you to marry me. You know that, now, don't you? You know that, now? Don't you? Don't you?"

"What?" she said.

"Know," he replied.

"Yes," she said. "I know you say so."

"And you know I mean it, don't you?"

"I know you say so."

"You believe me?" he said.

She was silent for some time. Then she pursed her lips.

"I don't know what I believe," she said.

"Are you out there?" came Banford's voice, calling from the house.

"Yes, we're bringing in the logs," he answered.

"I thought you'd gone lost," said Banford disconsolately. "Hurry up, do, and come and let's have tea. The kettle's boiling."

He stooped at once, to take an armful of little logs and carry them into the kitchen, where they were piled in a corner. March also helped, filling her arms and carrying the logs on her breast as if they were some heavy child. The night had fallen cold.

When the logs were all in, the two cleaned their boots noisily on the scraper outside, then rubbed them on the mat. March shut the door and took off her old felt hat —her farm-girl hat. Her thick, crisp black hair was loose, her face was pale and strained. She pushed back her hair vaguely and washed her hands. Banford came hurrying into the dimly-lighted kitchen to take from the oven the scones she was keeping hot.

"Whatever have you been doing all this time?" she asked fretfully. "I thought you were never coming in. And it's ages since you stopped sawing. What were you doing out there?"

"Well," said Henry, "we had to stop that hole in the barn, to keep the rats out."

"Why, I could see you standing there in the shed. I could see your shirt-sleeves," challenged Banford.

"Yes, I was just putting the saw away."

They went in to tea. March was quite mute. Her face was pale and strained and vague. The youth, who always had the same ruddy, self-contained look on his face, as though he were keeping himself to himself, had come to tea in his shirt-sleeves as if he were at home. He bent over his plate as he ate his food.

"Aren't you cold?" said Banford spitefully. "In your shirt-sleeves."

He looked up at her, with his chin near his plate, and his eyes very clear, pellucid, and unwavering as he watched her.

"No, I'm not cold," he said with his usual soft courtesy. "It's much warmer in here than it is outside, you see."

"I hope it is," said Banford, feeling nettled by him. He had a strange suave assurance and a wide-eyed bright look that got on her nerves this evening.

"But perhaps," he said softly and courteously, "you don't like me coming to tea without my coat. I forgot that."

"Oh, I don't mind," said Banford: although she *did.*

"I'll go and get it, shall I?" he said.

March's dark eyes turned slowly down to him.

"No, don't you bother," she said in her queer, twanging tone. "If you feel all right as you are, stop as you are." She spoke with a crude authority.

"Yes," said he, "I *feel* all right, if I'm not rude."

"It's usually considered rude," said Banford. "But we don't mind."

"Go along, 'considered rude,'" ejaculated March. "Who considers it rude?"

"Why you do, Nellie, in anybody else," said Banford, bridling a little behind her spectacles and feeling her food stick in her throat.

But March had again gone vague and unheeding, chewing her food as if she did not know she was eating at all. And the youth looked from one to another, with bright, watchful eyes.

Banford was offended. For all his suave courtesy and soft voice, the youth seemed to her impudent. She did not like to look at him. She did not like to meet his clear, watchful eyes, she did not like to see the strange glow in his face, his cheeks with their delicate fine hair, and his ruddy skin that was quite dull and yet which seemed to burn with a curious heat of life. It made her feel a little ill to look at him: the quality of his physical presence was too penetrating, too hot.

After tea the evening was very quiet. The youth rarely went into the village. As a rule he read: he was a great reader, in his own hours. That is, when he did begin, he read absorbedly. But he was not very eager to begin. Often he walked about the fields and along the hedges alone in the dark at night, prowling with a queer instinct for the night, and listening to the wild sounds.

Tonight, however, he took a Captain Mayne Reid book from Banford's shelf and sat down with knees wide apart and immersed himself in his story. His brownish fair hair was long and lay on his head like a thick cap, combed sideways. He was still in his shirt-sleeves and, bending forward under the lamp-light, with his knees stuck wide apart and the book in his hand and his whole figure absorbed in the rather strenuous business of reading, he gave Banford's sitting-room the look of a lumber-camp. She resented this. For on her sitting-room floor she had a red Turkey rug and dark stain round, the fire-place had fashionable green tiles, the piano stood open with the latest dance-music: she played quite well: and on the walls were March's hand-painted swans and water-lilies. Moreover, with the logs nicely, tremulously burning in the grate, the thick curtains drawn, the doors all shut, and the pine-trees hissing and shuddering in the wind outside, it was cosy, it was refined and nice. She resented the big, raw, long-legged youth sticking his khaki knees out and sitting there with his soldier's shirt-cuffs buttoned on his thick red wrists. From time to time he turned a page, and from time to time he gave a sharp look at the fire, settling the logs. Then he immersed himself again in the intense and isolated business of reading.

March, on the far side of the table, was spasmodically crocheting. Her mouth was pursed in an odd way, as when she had dreamed the fox's brush burned it, her beautiful, crisp black hair strayed in wisps. But her whole figure was absorbed in its bearing, as if she herself were miles away. In a sort of semi-dream she seemed to be hearing the fox singing round the house in the wind, singing wildly and sweetly and like a madness. With red but well-shaped hands she slowly crocheted the white cotton, very slowly, awkwardly.

Banford was also trying to read, sitting in her low chair. But between those two she felt fidgety. She kept moving and looking round and listening to the wind and glancing secretly from one to the other of her companions. March, seated on a straight chair, with her knees in their close breeches crossed, and slowly, laboriously crocheting, was also a trial.

"Oh, dear!" said Banford. "My eyes are bad tonight." And she pressed her fingers on her eyes.

The youth looked up at her with his clear bright look but did not speak.

"Are they, Jill?" said March absently.

Then the youth began to read again, and Banford perforce returned to her book. But she could not keep still. After a while she looked up at March, and a queer, almost malignant, little smile was on her thin face.

"A penny for them, Nell," she said suddenly.

March looked round with big, startled black eyes and went pale as if with terror. She had been listening to the fox singing so tenderly, so tenderly, as he wandered round the house.

"What?" she said vaguely.

"A penny for them," said Banford sarcastically. "Or twopence, if they're as deep as all that."

The youth was watching with bright clear eyes from beneath the lamp.

"Why," came March's vague voice, "what do you want to waste your money for?"

"I thought it would be well spent," said Banford.

"I wasn't thinking of anything except the way the wind was blowing," said March.

"Oh, dear," replied Banford. "I could have had as original thoughts as that myself. I'm afraid I *have* wasted my money this time."

"Well, you needn't pay," said March.

The youth suddenly laughed. Both women looked at him: March rather surprised-looking, as if she had hardly known he was there.

"Why, do you ever pay up on these occasions?" he asked.

"Oh, yes," said Banford. "We always do. I've sometimes had to pass a shilling a week to Nellie, in the winter time. It costs much less in summer."

"What, paying for each other's thoughts?" he laughed.

"Yes, when we've absolutely come to the end of everything else."

He laughed quickly, wrinkling his nose sharply like a puppy and laughing with quick pleasure, his eyes shining.

"It's the first time I ever heard of that," he said.

"I guess you'd hear of it often enough if you stayed a winter on Bailey Farm," said Banford lamentably.

"Do you get so tired, then?" he asked.

"So bored," said Banford.

"Oh!" he said gravely. "But why should you be bored?"

"Who wouldn't be bored?" said Banford.

"I'm sorry to hear that," he said gravely.

"You must be, if you were hoping to have a lively time here," said Banford.

He looked at her long and gravely.

"Well," he said, with his odd young seriousness, "it's quite lively enough for me."

"I'm glad to hear it," said Banford.

And she returned to her book. In her thin, frail hair were already many threads of grey, though she was not yet thirty. The boy did not look down but turned his eyes to March, who was sitting with pursed mouth laboriously crocheting, her eyes wide and absent. She had a warm, pale, fine skin, and a delicate nose. Her pursed mouth looked shrewish. But the shrewish look was contradicted by the curious lifted arch of her dark brows, and the wideness of her eyes; a look of startled wonder and vaguenes. She was listening again for the fox, who seemed to have wandered farther off into the night.

From under the edge of the lamp-light the boy sat with his face looking up, watching her silently, his eyes round and very clear and intent. Banford, biting her fingers irritably, was glancing at him under her hair. He sat there perfectly still, his ruddy face tilted up from the low level under the light, on the edge of the dimness, and watching with perfect abstract intentness. March suddenly lifted her great dark eyes from her crocheting, and saw him. She started, giving a little exclamation.

"There he is!" she cried, involuntarily, as if terribly startled.

Banford looked around in amazement, sitting up straight.

"Whatever has got you, Nellie?" she cried.

But March, her face flushed a delicate rose colour, was looking away to the door.

"Nothing! Nothing!" she said crossly. "Can't one speak?"

"Yes, if you speak sensibly," said Banford. "Whatever did you mean?"

"I don't know what I meant," cried March testily.

"Oh, Nellie, I hope you aren't going jumpy and nervy. I feel I can't stand another *thing!*—Whoever did you mean? Did you mean Henry?" cried poor frightened Banford.

"Yes. I suppose so," said March laconically. She would never confess to the fox.

"Oh, dear, my nerves are all gone for tonight," wailed Banford.

At nine o'clock March brought in a tray with bread and cheese and tea—Henry had confessed that he liked a cup of tea. Banford drank a glass of milk and ate a little bread. And soon she said:

"I'm going to bed, Nellie. I'm all nerves tonight. Are you coming?"

"Yes, I'm coming the minute I've taken the tray away," said March.

"Don't be long then," said Banford fretfully. "Good night, Henry. You'll see the fire is safe, if you come up last, won't you?"

"Yes, Miss Banford, I'll see it's safe," he replied in his reassuring way.

March was lighting the candle to go to the kitchen. Banford took her candle and went upstairs. When March came back to the fire she said to him:

"I suppose we can trust you to put out the fire and everything?" She stood there with her hand on her hip, and one knee loose, her head averted shyly, as if she could not look at him. He had his face lifted, watching her.

"Come and sit down a minute," he said softly.

"No, I'll be going. Jill will be waiting, and she'll get upset if I don't come."

"What made you jump like that this evening?" he asked.

"When did I jump?" she retorted, looking at him.

"Why, just now you did," he said. "When you cried out."

"Oh!" she said. "Then!—Why, I thought you were the fox!" And her face screwed into a queer smile, half ironic.

"The fox! Why the fox?" he asked softly.

"Why, one evening last summer when I was out with the gun I saw the fox in the grass nearly at my feet, looking straight up at me. I don't know—I suppose he made an impression on me." She turned aside her head again, and let one foot stray loose, self-consciously.

"And did you shoot him?" asked the boy.

"No, he gave me such a start, staring straight at me as he did, and then stopping to look back at me over his shoulder with a laugh on his face."

"A laugh on his face!" repeated Henry, also laughing. "He frightened you, did he?"

"No, he didn't frighten me. He made an impression on me, that's all."

"And you thought I was the fox, did you?" he laughed, with the same queer quick little laugh, like a puppy wrinkling its nose.

"Yes, I did, for the moment," she said. "Perhaps he'd been in my mind without my knowing."

"Perhaps you think I've come to steal your chickens or something," he said, with the same young laugh.

But she only looked at him with a wide, dark, vacant eye.

"It's the first time," he said, "that I've ever been taken for a fox. Won't you sit down for a minute?" His voice was very soft and cajoling.

"No," she said. "Jill will be waiting." But still she did not go, but stood with one foot loose and her face turned aside, just outside the circle of light.

"But won't you answer my question?" he said, lowering his voice still more.

"I don't know what question you mean."

"Yes, you do. Of course you do. I mean the question of you marrying me."

"No, I shan't answer that question," she said flatly.

"Won't you?" The queer young laugh came on his nose again. "Is it because I'm like the fox? Is that why?" And still he laughed.

She turned and looked at him with a long, slow look.

"I wouldn't let that put you against me," he said. "Let me turn the lamp low, and come and sit down a minute."

He put his red hand under the glow of the lamp, and suddenly made the light very dim. March stood there in the dimness quite shadowy, but unmoving. He rose silently to his feet, on his long legs. And now his voice was extraordinarily soft and suggestive, hardly audible.

"You'll stay a moment," he said. "Just a moment." And he put his hand on her shoulder. She turned her face from him. "I'm sure you don't really think I'm like the fox," he said, with the same softness and with a suggestion of laughter in his tone, a subtle mockery. "Do you now?"—And he drew her gently towards him and kissed her neck, softly. She winced and trembled and hung away. But his strong young arm held her, and he kissed her softly again, still on the neck, for her face was averted.

"Won't you answer my question? Won't you now?" came his soft, lingering voice. He was trying to draw her near to kiss her face. And he kissed her cheek softly, near the ear.

At that moment Banford's voice was heard calling fretfully, crossly, from upstairs.

"There's Jill!" cried March, starting and drawing erect.

And as she did so, quick as lightning he kissed her on the mouth, with a quick brushing kiss. It seemed to burn through her every fibre. She gave a queer little cry.

"You will, won't you? You will?" he insisted softly.

"Nellie! *Nellie!* Whatever are you so long for?" came Banford's faint cry from the outer darkness.

But he held her fast and was murmuring with that intolerable softness and insistency:

"You will, won't you? Say yes! Say yes!"

March, who felt as if the fire had gone through her and scathed her, and as if she could do no more, murmured:

"Yes! Yes! Anything you like! Anything you like! Only let me go! Only let me go! Jill's calling."

"You know you've promised," he said insidiously.

"Yes! Yes! I do!—" Her voice suddenly rose into a shrill cry. "All right, Jill, I'm coming."

Startled, he let her go, and she went straight upstairs.

In the morning at breakfast, after he had looked round the place and attended to the stock and thought to himself that one could live easily enough here, he said to Banford:

"Do you know what, Miss Banford?"

"Well, what?" said the good-natured, nervy Banford.

He looked at March, who was spreading jam on her bread.

"Shall I tell?" he said to her.

She looked up at him, and a deep pink colour flushed over her face.

"Yes, if you mean Jill," she said. "I hope you won't go talking all over the village, that's all." And she swallowed her dry bread with difficulty.

"Whatever's coming?" said Banford, looking up with wide, tired, slightly reddened eyes. She was a thin, frail little thing, and her hair, which was delicate and thin, was bobbed, so it hung softly by her worn face in its faded brown and grey.

"Why, what do you think?" he said, smiling like one who has a secret.

"How do I know!" said Banford.

"Can't you guess?" he said, making bright eyes, and smiling, pleased with himself.

"I'm sure I can't. What's more, I'm not going to try."

"Nellie and I are going to be married."

Banford put down her knife, out of her thin, delicate fingers, as if she would never take it up to eat any more. She stared with blank, reddened eyes.

"You what?" she exclaimed.

"We're going to get married. Aren't we, Nellie?" and he turned to March.

"You say so, anyway," said March laconically. But again she flushed with an agonized flush. She, too, could swallow no more.

Banford looked at her like a bird that has been shot: a poor little sick bird. She gazed at her with all her wounded soul in her face, at the deep-flushed March.

"Never!" she exclaimed, helpless.

"It's quite right," said the bright and gloating youth.

Banford turned aside her face, as if the sight of the food on the table made her sick. She sat like this for some moments, as if she were sick. Then, with one hand on the edge of the table, she rose to her feet.

"I'll *never* believe it, Nellie," she cried. "It's absolutely impossible!"

Her plaintive, fretful voice had a thread of hot anger and despair.

"Why? Why shouldn't you believe it?" asked the youth, with all his soft, velvety impertinence in his voice.

Banford looked at him from her wide vague eyes, as if he were some creature in a museum.

"Oh," she said languidly, "because she can never be such a fool. She can't lose her self-respect to such an extent." Her voice was cold and plaintive, drifting.

"In what way will she lose her self-respect?" asked the boy.

Banford looked at him with vague fixity from behind her spectacles.

"If she hasn't lost it already," she said.

He became very red, vermilion, under the slow vague stare from behind the spectacles.

"I don't see it at all," he said.

"Probably you don't. I shouldn't expect you would," said Banford, with that straying mild tone of remoteness which made her words even more insulting.

He sat stiff in his chair, staring with hot blue eyes from his scarlet face. An ugly look had come on his brow.

"My word, she doesn't know what she's letting herself in for," said Banford, in her plaintive, drifting, insulting voice.

"What has it got to do with you, anyway?" said the youth in a temper.

"More than it has to do with you, probably," she replied, plaintive and venomous.

"Oh, has it! I don't see that at all," he jerked out.

"No, you wouldn't," she answered, drifting.

"Anyhow," said March, pushing back her chair and rising uncouthly, "it's no good arguing about it." And she seized the bread and the tea-pot, and strode away to the kitchen.

Banford let her fingers stray across her brow and along her hair, like one bemused. Then she turned and went away upstairs.

Henry sat stiff and sulky in his chair, with his face and his eyes on fire. March came and went, clearing the table. But Henry sat on, stiff with temper. He took no notice of her. She had regained her composure and her soft, even, creamy complexion. But her mouth was pursed up. She glanced at him each time as she came to take things from the table, glanced from her large, curious eyes, more in curiosity than anything. Such a long, red-faced sulky boy! That was all he was. He seemed as remote from her as if his red face were a red chimney-pot on a cottage across the fields, and she looked at him just as objectively, as remotely.

At length he got up and stalked out into the fields with the gun. He came in only at dinner-time, with the devil still in his face, but his manners quite polite. Nobody said anything particular: they sat each one at the sharp corner of a triangle, in obstinate remoteness. In the afternoon he went out again at once with the gun. He came in at nightfall with a rabbit and a pigeon. He stayed in all evening but hardly opened his mouth. He was in the devil of a temper, feeling he had been insulted.

Banford's eyes were red, she had evidently been crying. But her manner was more remote and supercilious than ever, the way she turned her head if he spoke at all, as if he were some tramp or inferior intruder of that sort, made his blue eyes go almost black with rage. His face looked sulkier. But he never forgot his polite intonation, if he opened his mouth to speak.

March seemed to flourish in this atmosphere. She seemed to sit between the two antagonists with a little wicked smile on her face, enjoying herself. There was even a sort of complacency in the way she laboriously crocheted, this evening.

When he was in bed, the youth could hear the two women talking and arguing in their room. He sat up in bed and strained his ears to hear what they said. But he could hear nothing, it was too far off. Yet he could hear the soft, plaintive drip of Banford's voice, and March's deeper note.

The night was quiet, frosty. Big stars were snapping outside, beyond the ridge-tops of the pine-trees. He listened and listened. In the distance he heard a fox yelping: and the dogs from the farms barking in answer. But it was not that he wanted to hear. It was what the two women were saying.

He got stealthily out of bed and stood by his door. He could hear no more than before. Very, very carefully he began to lift the door-latch. After quite a time he had his door open. Then he stepped stealthily out into the passage. The old oak planks were cold under his feet, and they creaked preposterously. He crept very, very gently up the one step, and along by the wall, till he stood outside their door. And there he held his breath and listened. Banford's voice:

"No, I simply couldn't stand it. I should be dead in a month. Which is just what he would be aiming at, of course. That would just be his game, to see me in the churchyard. No, Nellie, if you were to do such a thing as to marry him, you could never stop here. I couldn't, I couldn't live in the same house with him. Oh-h! I feel quite sick with the smell of his clothes. And his red face simply turns me over. I can't eat my food when he's at the table. What a fool I was ever to let him stop. One ought *never* to try to do a kind action. It always flies back in your face like a boomerang."

"Well, he's only got two more days," said March.

"Yes, thank heaven. And when he's gone he'll never come in this house again. I feel so bad while he's here. And I know, I know he's only counting what he can get out of you. I know that's all it is. He's just a good-for-nothing, who doesn't want to work, and who thinks he'll

live on us. But he won't live on me. If you're such a
fool, then it's your own lookout. Mrs. Burgess knew him
all the time he was here. And the old man could never
get him to do any steady work. He was off with the gun
on every occasion, just as he is now. Nothing but the
gun! Oh, I do hate it. You don't know what you're doing,
Nellie, you don't. If you marry him he'll just make a fool
of you. He'll go off and leave you stranded. I know he
will. If he can't get Bailey Farm out of us—and he's
not going to, while I live. While I live he's never going
to set foot here. I know what it would be. He'd soon
think he was master of both of us, as he thinks he's master of you already."

"But he isn't," said Nellie.

"He thinks he is, anyway. And that's what he wants:
to come and be master here. Yes, imagine it! That's
what we've got the place together for, is it, to be bossed
and bullied by a hateful red-faced boy, a beastly labourer? Oh, we *did* make a mistake when we let him
stop. We ought never to have lowered ourselves. And
I've had such a fight with all the people here, not to be
pulled down to their level. No, he's not coming here—
and then you see. If he can't have the place, he'll run
off to Canada or somewhere again, as if he'd never
known you. And here you'll be, absolutely ruined and
made a fool of. I know I shall never have any peace of
mind again."

"We'll tell him he can't come here. We'll tell him
that," said March.

"Oh, don't you bother, I'm going to tell him that, and
other things as well, before he goes. He's not going to
have all his own way, while I've got the strength left to
speak. Oh, Nellie, he'll despise you, he'll despise you
like the awful little beast he is, if you give way to him.
I'd no more trust him than I'd trust a cat not to steal.

He's deep, he's deep, and he's bossy, and he's selfish through and through, as cold as ice. All he wants is to make use of you. And when you're no more use to him, then I pity you."

"I don't think he's as bad as all that," said March.

"No, because he's been playing up to you. But you'll find out, if you see much more of him. Oh, Nellie, I can't bear to think of it."

"Well, it won't hurt you, Jill darling."

"Won't it! Won't it! I shall never know a moment's peace again while I live, nor a moment's happiness. No, Nellie—" and Banford began to weep bitterly.

The boy outside could hear the stifled sound of the woman's sobbing and could hear March's soft, deep, tender voice comforting, with wonderful gentleness and tenderness, the weeping woman.

His eyes were so round and wide that he seemed to see the whole night, and his ears were almost jumping off his head. He was frozen stiff. He crept back to bed, but felt as if the top of his head were coming off. He could not sleep. He could not keep still. He rose, quietly dressed himself, and crept out on to the landing once more. The women were silent. He went softly downstairs and out to the kitchen.

Then he put on his boots and his overcoat and took the gun. He did not think to go away from the farm. No, he only took the gun. As softly as possible he unfastened the door and went out into the frosty December night. The air was still, the stars bright, the pine-trees seemed to bristle audibly in the sky. He went stealthily away down a fence-side, looking for something to shoot. At the same time he remembered that he ought not to shoot and frighten the women.

So he prowled round the edge of the gorse cover, and through the grove of tall old hollies, to the woodside.

There he skirted the fence, peering through the darkness with dilated eyes that seemed to be able to grow black and full of sight in the dark, like a cat's. An owl was slowly and mournfully whooing round a great oak tree. He stepped stealthily with his gun, listening, listening, watching.

As he stood under the oaks of the wood-edge he heard the dogs from the neighbouring cottage, up the hill, yelling suddenly and startlingly, and the wakened dogs from the farms around barking answer. And suddenly, it seemed to him England was little and tight, he felt the landscape was constricted even in the dark, and that there were too many dogs in the night, making a noise like a fence of sound, like the network of English hedges netting the view. He felt the fox didn't have a chance. For it must be the fox that had started all this hullabaloo.

Why not watch for him, anyhow! He would no doubt be coming sniffing round. The lad walked downhill to where the farmstead with its few pine-trees crouched blackly. In the angle of the long shed, in the black dark, he crouched down. He knew the fox would be coming. It seemed to him it would be the last of the foxes in this loudly barking, thick-voiced England, tight with innumerable little houses.

He sat a long time with his eyes fixed unchanging upon the open gateway, where a little light seemed to fall from the stars or from the horizon, who knows? He was sitting on a log in a dark corner with the gun across his knees. The pine-trees snapped. Once a chicken fell off its perch in the barn, with a loud crawk and cackle and commotion that startled him, and he stood up, watching with all his eyes, thinking it might be a rat. But he *felt* it was nothing. So he sat down again with the gun on his knees and his hands tucked in to keep them warm, and his eyes fixed unblinking on the pale reach of the open gateway. He felt he could smell the hot, sickly, rich smell of live chickens on the cold air.

And then—a shadow. A sliding shadow in the gate-way. He gathered all his vision into a concentrated spark and saw the shadow of the fox, the fox creeping on his belly through the gate. There he went, on his belly like a snake. The boy smiled to himself and brought the gun to his shoulder. He knew quite well what would happen. He knew the fox would go to where the fowl-door was boarded up, and sniff there. He knew he would lie there for a minute, sniffing the fowls within. And then he would start again prowling under the edge of the old barn, waiting to get in.

The fowl-door was at the top of a slight incline. Soft, soft as a shadow the fox slid up this incline, and crouched with his nose to the boards. And at the same moment there was the awful crash of a gun reverberat-ing between the old buildings, as if all the night had gone smash. But the boy watched keenly. He saw even the white belly of the fox as the beast beat his paws in death. So he went forward.

There was a commotion everywhere. The fowls were scuffling and crawking, the ducks were quark-quarking, the pony had stamped wildly to his feet. But the fox was on his side, struggling in his last tremors. The boy bent over him and smelt his foxy smell.

There was a sound of a window opening upstairs, then March's voice calling:

"Who is it?"

"It's me," said Henry; "I've shot the fox."

"Oh, goodness! You nearly frightened us to death."

"Did I? I'm awfully sorry."

"Whatever made you get up?"

"I heard him about."

"And have you shot him?"

"Yes, he's here," and the boy stood in the yard hold-ing up the warm, dead brute. "You can't see, can you? Wait a minute." And he took his flash-light from his pocket, and flashed it on to the dead animal. He was holding it by the brush. March saw, in the middle of the darkness, just the reddish fleece and the white belly and the white underneath of the pointed chin, and the queer, dangling paws. She did not know what to say.

"He's a beauty," he said. "He will make you a lovely fur."

"You don't catch me wearing a fox fur," she replied.

"Oh!" he said. And he switched off the light.

"Well, I should think you'd come in and go to bed again now," she said.

"Probably I shall. What time is it?"

"What time is it, Jill?" called March's voice. It was a quarter to one.

That night March had another dream. She dreamed that Banford was dead, and that she, March, was sob-bing her heart out. Then she had to put Banford into her coffin. And the coffin was the rough wood-box in which the bits of chopped wood were kept in the kitchen, by the fire. This was the coffin, and there was no other, and March was in agony and dazed bewilderment, look-ing for something to line the box with, something to make it soft with, something to cover up the poor dead darling. Because she couldn't lay her in there just in her white thin nightdress, in the horrible wood-box. So she hunted and hunted, and picked up thing after thing, and threw it aside in the agony of dream-frustration. And in her dream-despair all she could find that would do was a fox-skin. She knew that it wasn't right, that this was not what she could have. But it was all she could find. And so she folded the brush of the fox, and laid her darling Jill's head on this, and she brought round the skin of the fox and laid it on the top of the body, so that it seemed to make a whole ruddy, fiery coverlet, and she cried and cried and woke to find the tears streaming down her face.

The first thing that both she and Banford did in the morning was to go out to see the fox. He had hung it up by the heels in the shed, with its poor brush falling backwards. It was a lovely dog-fox in its prime, with a handsome thick winter coat: a lovely golden-red colour, with grey as it passed to the belly, and belly all white, and a great full brush with a delicate black and grey and pure white tip.

"Poor brute!" said Banford. "If it wasn't such a thieving wretch, you'd feel sorry for it."

March said nothing, but stood with her foot trailing aside, one hip out; her face was pale and her eyes big and black, watching the dead animal that was suspended upside down. White and soft as snow his belly: white and soft as snow. She passed her hand softly down it. And his wonderful black-glinted brush was full and frictional, wonderful. She passed her hand down this also, and quivered. Time after time she took the full fur of that thick tail between her hand, and passed her hand slowly downwards. Wonderful sharp thick splendour of a tail! And he was dead! She pursed her lips, and her eyes went black and vacant. Then she took the head in her hand.

Henry was sauntering up, so Banford walked rather pointedly away. March stood there bemused, with the head of the fox in her hand. She was wondering, wondering, wondering over his long fine muzzle. For some reason it reminded her of a spoon or a spatula. She felt she could not understand it. The beast was a strange beast to her, incomprehensible, out of her range. Wonderful silver whiskers he had, like ice-threads. And pricked ears with hair inside—but that long, long slender spoon of a nose!—and the marvellous white teeth beneath! It was to thrust forward and bite with,—deep, deep into the living prey, to bite and bite the blood.

"He's a beauty, isn't he?" said Henry, standing by.

"Oh, yes, he's a fine big fox. I wonder how many chickens he's responsible for," she replied.

"A good many. Do you think he's the same one you saw in the summer?"

"I should think very likely he is," she replied.

He watched her, but he could make nothing of her. Partly she was so shy and virgin, and partly she was so grim, matter-of-fact, shrewish. What she said seemed to him so different from the look of her big, queer dark eyes.

"Are you going to skin him?" she asked.

"Yes, when I've had breakfast and got a board to peg him on."

"My word, what a strong smell he's got! Pooo!—It'll take some washing off one's hands. I don't know why I was so silly as to handle him."—And she looked at her right hand, that had passed down his belly and along his tail, and had even got a tiny streak of blood from one dark place in his fur.

"Have you seen the chickens when they smell him, how frightened they are?" he said.

"Yes, aren't they!"

"You must mind you don't get some of his fleas."

"Oh, fleas!" she replied, nonchalant.

Later in the day she saw the fox's skin nailed flat on a board, as if crucified. It gave her an uneasy feeling.

The boy was angry. He went about with his mouth shut, as if he had swallowed part of his chin. But in behaviour he was polite and affable. He did not say anything about his intentions. And he left March alone.

That evening they sat in the dining-room. Banford wouldn't have him in her sitting-room any more. There was a very big log on the fire. And everybody was busy. Banford had letters to write, March was sewing a dress, and he was mending some little contrivance.

Banford stopped her letter-writing from time to time to look round and rest her eyes. The boy had his head down, his face hidden over his job.

"Let's see," said Banford. "What train do you go by, Henry?"

He looked up straight at her.

"The morning train. In the morning," he said.

"What, the eight-ten or the eleven-twenty?"

"The eleven-twenty, I suppose," he said.

"That is the day after tomorrow?" said Banford.

"Yes, the day after tomorrow."

"Mmm!" murmured Banford, and she returned to her writing. But as she was licking her envelope, she asked:

"And what plans have you made for the future, if I may ask?"

"Plans?" he said, his face very bright and angry.

"I mean about you and Nellie, if you are going on with this business. When do you expect the wedding to come off?" She spoke in a jeering tone.

"Oh, the wedding!" he replied. "I don't know."

"Don't you know anything?" said Banford. "Are you going to clear out on Friday and leave things no more settled than they are?"

"Well, why shouldn't I? We can always write letters."

"Yes, of course you can. But I wanted to know because of this place. If Nellie is going to get married all of a sudden, I shall have to be looking round for a new partner."

"Couldn't she stay on here if she was married?" he said. He knew quite well what was coming.

"Oh," said Banford, "this is no place for a married couple. There's not enough work to keep a man going, for one thing. And there's no money to be made. It's quite useless your thinking of staying on here if you marry. Absolutely!"

"Yes, but I wasn't thinking of staying on here," he said.

"Well, that's what I want to know. And what about Nellie, then? How long is *she* going to be here with me, in that case?"

The two antagonists looked at one another.

"That I can't say," he answered.

"Oh, go along," she cried petulantly. "You must have some idea what you are going to do, if you ask a woman to marry you. Unless it's all a hoax."

"Why should it be a hoax?—I am going back to Canada."

"And taking her with you?"

"Yes, certainly."

"You hear that, Nellie?" said Banford.

March, who had had her head bent over her sewing, now looked up with a sharp pink blush on her face and a queer, sardonic laugh in her eyes and on her twisted mouth.

"That's the first time I've heard that I was going to Canada," she said. .

"Well, you have to hear it for the first time, haven't you?" said the boy.

"Yes, I suppose I have," she said nonchalantly. And she went back to her sewing.

"You're quite ready, are you, to go to Canada? Are you, Nellie?" asked Banford.

March looked up again. She let her shoulders go slack, and let her hand that held the needle lie loose in her lap.

"It depends on *how* I'm going," she said. "I don't think I want to go jammed up in the steerage, as a soldier's wife. I'm afraid I'm not used to that way."

The boy watched her with bright eyes.

"Would you rather stay over here while I go first?" he asked.

"I would, if that's the only alternative," she replied.

"That's much the wisest. Don't make it any fixed engagement," said Banford. "Leave yourself free to go or not after he's got back and found you a place, Nellie. Anything else is madness, madness."

"Don't you think," said the youth, "we ought to get married before I go—and then go together, or separate, according to how it happens?"

"I think it's a terrible idea," cried Banford.

But the boy was watching March.

"What do you think?" he asked her.

She let her eyes stray vaguely into space.

"Well, I don't know," she said. "I shall have to think about it."

"Why?" he asked, pertinently.

"Why?" She repeated his question in a mocking way, and looked at him laughing, though her face was pink again. "I should think there's plenty of reasons why."

He watched her in silence. She seemed to have escaped him. She had got into league with Banford against him. There was again the queer sardonic look about her, she would mock stoically at everything he said or which life offered.

"Of course," he said, "I don't want to press you to do anything you don't wish to do."

"I should think not, indeed," cried Banford indignantly.

At bedtime Banford said plaintively to March:

"You take my hot bottle up for me, Nellie, will you?"

"Yes, I'll do it," said March, with the kind of willing
unwillingness she so often showed towards her beloved
but uncertain Jill.

The two women went upstairs. After a time March
called from the top of the stairs: "Good night, Henry. I
shan't be coming down. You'll see to the lamp and the
fire, won't you?"

The next day Henry went about with the cloud on his
brow and his young cub's face shut up tight. He was
cogitating all the time. He had wanted March to marry
him and go back to Canada with him. And he had been
sure she would do it. Why he wanted her he didn't know.
But he did want her. He had set his mind on her. And
he was convulsed with a youth's fury at being thwarted.
To be thwarted, to be thwarted! It made him so furious
inside, that he did not know what to do with himself.
But he kept himself in hand. Because even now things
might turn out differently. She might come over to him.
Of course she might. It was her business to do so.

Things drew to a tension again towards evening. He
and Banford had avoided each other all day. In fact
Banford went in to the little town by the 11:20 train. It
was market day. She arrived back on the 4:25. Just as
the night was falling Henry saw her little figure in a
dark-blue coat and a dark-blue tam-o'-shanter hat crossing the first meadow from the station. He stood under
one of the wild pear trees, with the old dead leaves
round his feet. And he watched the little blue figure
advancing persistently over the rough winter-ragged
meadow. She had her arms full of parcels, and advanced
slowly, frail thing she was, but with that devilish little
certainty which he so detested in her. He stood invisible
under the pear tree, watching her every step. And if
looks could have affected her, she would have felt a log
of iron on each of her ankles as she made her way for-

ward. "You're a nasty little thing, you are," he was saying softly, across the distance. "You're a nasty little thing.
I hope you'll be paid back for all the harm you've done
me for nothing. I hope you will—you nasty little thing. I
hope you'll have to pay for it. You will, if wishes are
anything. You nasty little creature that you are."

She was toiling slowly up the slope. But if she had
been slipping back at every step towards the Bottomless
Pit, he would not have gone to help her with her parcels.
Aha! there went March, striding with her long land stride
in her breeches and her short tunic! Striding downhill
at a great pace, and even running a few steps now and
then, in her great solicitude and desire to come to the
rescue of the little Banford. The boy watched her with
rage in his heart. See her leap a ditch, and run, run as
if a house was on fire, just to get to that creeping dark
little object down there! So, the Banford just stood still
and waited. And March strode up and took *all* the
parcels except a bunch of yellow chrysanthemums.
These the Banford still carried—yellow chrysanthemums!

"Yes, you look well, don't you," he said softly into the
dusk air. "You look well, pottering up there with a bunch
of flowers, you do. I'd make you eat them for your tea,
if you hug them so tight. And I'd give them you for
breakfast again, I would. I'd give you flowers. Nothing
but flowers."

He watched the progress of the two women. He could
hear their voices: March always outspoken and rather
scolding in her tenderness, Banford murmuring rather
vaguely. They were evidently good friends. He could
not hear what they said till they came to the fence of the
home meadow, which they must climb. Then he saw
March manfully climbing over the bars with all her pack-

ages in her arms, and on the still air he heard Banford's fretful:

"Why don't you let me help you with the parcels?" She had a queer plaintive hitch in her voice. Then came March's robust and reckless:

"Oh, I can manage. Don't you bother about me. You've all you can do to get yourself over."

"Yes, that's all very well," said Banford fretfully. "You say 'Don't you bother about me' and then all the while you feel injured because nobody thinks of you."

"When do I feel injured?" said March.

"Always. You always feel injured. Now you're feeling injured because I won't have that boy to come and live on the farm."

"I'm not feeling injured at all," said March.

"I know you are. When he's gone you'll sulk over it. I know you will."

"Shall I?" said March. "We'll see."

"Yes, we *shall* see, unfortunately. I can't think how you can make yourself so cheap. I can't *imagine* how you can lower yourself like it."

"I haven't lowered myself," said March.

"I don't know what you call it, then. Letting a boy like that come so cheeky and impudent and make a mug of you. I don't know what you think of yourself. How much respect do you think he's going to have for you afterwards? My word, I wouldn't be in your shoes, if you married him."

"Of course you wouldn't. My boots are a good bit too big for you, and not half dainty enough," said March, with rather a miss-fire sarcasm.

"I thought you had too much pride, really I did. A woman's got to hold herself high, especially with a youth like that. Why, he's impudent. Even the way he forced himself on us at the start."

"We asked him to stay," said March.

"Not till he'd almost forced us to. And then he's so cocky and self-assured. My word, he puts my back up. I simply can't imagine how you can let him treat you so cheaply."

"I don't let him treat me cheaply," said March. "Don't you worry yourself, nobody's going to treat me cheaply. And even you aren't, either." She had a tender defiance, and a certain fire in her voice.

"Yes, it's sure to come back to me," said Banford bitterly. "That's always the end of it. I believe you only do it to spite me."

They went now in silence up the steep grassy slope and over the brow through the gorse bushes. On the other side the hedge the boy followed in the dusk, at some little distance. Now and then, through the huge ancient hedge of hawthorn, risen into trees, he saw the two dark figures creeping up the hill. As he came to the top of the slope he saw the homestead dark in the twilight, with a huge old pear tree leaning from the near gable, and a little yellow light twinkling in the small side windows of the kitchen. He heard the clink of the latch and saw the kitchen door open into light as the two women went indoors. So, they were at home.

And so!—this was what they thought of him. It was rather in his nature to be a listener, so he was not at all surprised whatever he heard. The things people said about him always missed him personally. He was only rather surprised at the women's way with one another. And he disliked the Banford with an acid dislike. And he felt drawn to the March again. He felt again irresistibly drawn to her. He felt there was a secret bond, a secret thread between him and her, something very exclusive, which shut out everybody else and made him and her possess each other in secret.

He hoped again that she would have him. He hoped with his blood suddenly firing up that she would agree to marry him quite quickly: at Christmas, very likely. Christmas was not far off. He wanted, whatever else happened, to snatch her into a hasty marriage and a consummation with him. Then for the future, they could arrange later. But he hoped it would happen as he wanted it. He hoped that tonight she would stay a little while with him, after Banford had gone upstairs. He hoped he could touch her soft, creamy cheek, her strange, frightened face. He hoped he could look into her dilated, frightened dark eyes, quite near. He hoped he might even put his hand on her bosom and feel her soft breasts under her tunic. His heart beat deep and powerful as he thought of that. He wanted very much to do so. He wanted to make sure of her soft woman's breasts under her tunic. She always kept the brown linen coat buttoned so close up to her throat. It seemed to him like some perilous secret, that her soft woman's breasts must be buttoned up in that uniform. It seemed to him moreover that they were so much softer, tenderer, more lovely and lovable, shut up in that tunic, than were the Banford's breasts, under her soft blouses and chiffon dresses. The Banford would have little iron breasts, he said to himself. For all her frailty and fretfulness and delicacy, she would have tiny iron breasts. But March under her crude, fast, workman's tunic, would have soft white breasts, white and unseen. So he told himself, and his blood burned.

When he went in to tea, he had a surprise. He appeared at the inner door, his face very ruddy and vivid and his blue eyes shining, dropping his head forward as he came in, in his usual way, and hesitating in the doorway to watch the inside of the room, keenly and cautiously, before he entered. He was wearing a long-sleeved waistcoat. His face seemed extraordinarily a piece of the out-of-doors come indoors: as holly-berries do. In his second of pause in the doorway he took in the two women sitting at table, at opposite ends, saw them sharply. And to his amazement March was dressed in a dress of dull green silk crape. His mouth came open in surprise. If she had suddenly grown a moustache he could not have been more surprised.

"Why," he said, "do you wear a dress, then?"

She looked up, flushing a deep rose colour, and twisting her mouth with a smile, said:

"Of course I do. What else do you expect me to wear, but a dress?"

"A land girl's uniform, of course," said he.

"Oh," she cried nonchalant, "that's only for this dirty mucky work about here."

"Isn't it your proper dress, then?" he said.

"No, not indoors it isn't," she said. But she was blushing all the time as she poured out his tea. He sat down in his chair at table, unable to take his eyes off her. Her dress was a perfectly simple slip of bluey-green crape, with a line of gold stitching round the top and round the sleeves, which came to the elbow. It was cut just plain, and round at the top, and showed her white soft throat. Her arms he knew. strong and firm muscled, for he had often seen her with her sleeves rolled up. But he looked her up and down, up and down.

Banford, at the other end of the table, said not a word, but piggled with the sardine on her plate. He had forgotten her existence. He just simply stared at March, while he ate his bread and margarine in huge mouthfuls, forgetting even his tea.

"Well, I never knew anything make such a difference!" he murmured, across his mouthfuls.

"Oh, goodness!" cried March, blushing still more. "I might be a pink monkey!"

And she rose quickly to her feet and took the teapot to the fire, to the kettle. And as she crouched on the hearth with her green slip about her, the boy stared more wide-eyed than ever. Through the crape her woman's form seemed soft and womanly. And when she stood up and walked he saw her legs move soft within her modernly short skirt. She had on black silk stockings and small, patent-leather shoes with little gold buckles.

No, she was another being. She was something quite different. Seeing her always in the hard-cloth breeches, wide on the hips, buttoned on the knee, strong as armour, and in the brown puttees and thick boots, it had never occurred to him that she had a woman's legs and feet. Now it came upon him. She had a woman's soft, skirted legs, and she was accessible. He blushed to the roots of his hair, shoved his nose in his tea-cup and drank his tea with a little noise that made Banford simply squirm: and strangely, suddenly he felt a man, no longer a youth. He felt a man, with all a man's grave weight of responsibility. A curious quietness and gravity came over his soul. He felt a man, quiet, with a little of the heaviness of male destiny upon him.

She was soft and accessible in her dress. The thought went home in him like an everlasting responsibility.

"Oh, for goodness sake, say something, somebody," cried Banford fretfully. "It might be a funeral." The boy looked at her, and she could not bear his face.

"A funeral!" said March, with a twisted smile. "Why, that breaks my dream."

Suddenly she had thought of Banford in the wood-box for a coffin.

"What, have you been dreaming of a wedding?" said Banford sarcastically.

"Must have been," said March.

"Whose wedding?" asked the boy.

"I can't remember," said March.

She was shy and rather awkward that evening, in spite of the fact that, wearing a dress, her bearing was much more subdued than in her uniform. She felt unpeeled and rather exposed. She felt almost improper.

They talked desultorily about Henry's departure next morning and made the trivial arrangement. But of the matter on their minds, none of them spoke. They were rather quiet and friendly this evening; Banford had practically nothing to say. But inside herself she seemed still, perhaps kindly.

At nine o'clock March brought in the tray with the everlasting tea and a little cold meat which Banford had managed to procure. It was the last supper, so Banford did not want to be disagreeable. She felt a bit sorry for the boy, and felt she must be as nice as she could.

He wanted her to go to bed. She was usually the first. But she sat on in her chair under the lamp, glancing at her book now and then, and staring into the fire. A deep silence had come into the room. It was broken by March asking, in a rather small tone:

"What time is it, Jill?"

"Five past ten," said Banford, looking at her wrist.

And then not a sound. The boy had looked up from the book he was holding between his knees. His rather wide, cat-shaped face had its obstinate look, his eyes were watchful.

"What about bed?" said March at last.

"I'm ready when you are," said Banford.

"Oh, very well," said March. "I'll fill your bottle."

She was as good as her word. When the hot-water bottle was ready, she lit a candle and went upstairs with it. Banford remained in her chair, listening acutely. March came downstairs again.

"There you are then," she said. "Are you going up?"

"Yes, in a minute," said Banford. But the minute passed, and she sat on in her chair under the lamp.

Henry, whose eyes were shining like a cat's as he watched from under his brows, and whose face seemed wider, more chubbed and cat-like with unalterable obstinacy, now rose to his feet to try his throw.

"I think I'll go and look if I can see the she-fox," he said. "She may be creeping round. Won't you come as well for a minute, Nellie, and see if we see anything?"

"Me!" cried March, looking up with her startled, wondering face.

"Yes. Come on," he said. It was wonderful how soft and warm and coaxing his voice could be, how near. The very sound of it made Banford's blood boil.

"Come on for a minute," he said, looking down into her uplifted, unsure face.

And she rose to her feet as if drawn up by his young, ruddy face that was looking down on her.

"I should think you're never going out at this time of night, Nellie!" cried Banford.

"Yes, just for a minute," said the boy, looking round on her, and speaking with an odd sharp yelp in his voice.

March looked from one to the other, as if confused, vague. Banford rose to her feet for a battle.

"Why, it's ridiculous. It's bitter cold. You'll catch your death in that thin frock. And in those slippers. You're not going to do any such thing."

There was a moment's pause. Banford turtled up like a little fighting cock, facing March and the boy.

"Oh, I don't think you need worry yourself," he replied. "A moment under the stars won't do anybody any damage. I'll get the rug off the sofa in the dining-room. You're coming, Nellie."

His voice had so much anger and contempt and fury in it as he spoke to Banford: and so much tenderness and proud authority as he spoke to March, that the latter answered:

"Yes, I'm coming."

And she turned with him to the door.

Banford, standing there in the middle of the room, suddenly burst into a long wail and a spasm of sobs. She covered her face with her poor thin hands, and her thin shoulders shook in an agony of weeping. March looked back from the door.

"Jill!" she cried in a frantic tone, like someone just coming awake. And she seemed to start towards her darling.

But the boy had March's arm in his grip, and she could not move. She did not know why she could not move. It was as in a dream when the heart strains and the body cannot stir.

"Never mind," said the boy, softly. "Let her cry. Let her cry. She will have to cry sooner or later. And the tears will relieve her feelings. They will do her good."

So he drew March slowly through the doorway. But her last look was back to the poor little figure which stood in the middle of the room with covered face and thin shoulders shaken with bitter weeping.

In the dining-room he picked up the rug and said:

"Wrap yourself up in this."

She obeyed—and they reached the kitchen door, he holding her soft and firm by the arm, though she did not know it. When she saw the night outside she started back.

"I must go back to Jill," she said. "I *must!* Oh, yes, I must!"

Her tone sounded final. The boy let go of her and she turned indoors. But he seized her again and arrested her.

"Wait a minute," he said. "Wait a minute. Even if you go you're not going yet."

"Leave go! Leave go!" she cried. "My place is at Jill's side. Poor little thing, she's sobbing her heart out."

"Yes," said the boy bitterly. "And your heart, too, and mine as well."

"Your heart?" said March. He still gripped her and detained her.

"Isn't it as good as her heart?" he said. "Or do you think it's not?"

"Your heart?" she said again, incredulous.

"Yes, mine! Mine! Do you think I haven't *got* a heart?" And with his hot grasp he took her hand and pressed it under his left breast. "There's my heart," he said, "if you don't believe in it."

It was wonder which made her attend. And then she felt the deep, heavy, powerful stroke of his heart, terrible, like something from beyond. It was like something from beyond, something awful from outside, signalling to her. And the signal paralysed her. It beat upon her very soul, and made her helpless. She forgot Jill. She could not think of Jill any more. She could not think of her. That terrible signalling from outside!

The boy put his arm round her waist.

"Come with me," he said gently. "Come and let us say what we've got to say."

And he drew her outside, closed the door. And she went with him darkly down the garden path. That he should have a beating heart! And that he should have his arm round her, outside the blanket! She was too confused to think who he was or what he was.

He took her to a dark corner of the shed, where there was a tool-box with a lid, long and low.

"We'll sit here a minute," he said.

And obediently she sat down by his side.

"Give me your hand," he said.

She gave him both her hands, and he held them between his own. He was young, and it made him tremble.

"You'll marry me. You'll marry me before I go back, won't you?" he pleaded.

"Why, aren't we both a pair of fools!" she said.

He had put her in the corner, so that she should not look out and see the lighted window of the house, across the dark yard and garden. He tried to keep her all there inside the shed with him.

"In what way a pair of fools?" he said. "If you go back to Canada with me, I've got a job and a good wage waiting for me, and it's a nice place, near the mountains. Why shouldn't you marry me? Why shouldn't we marry? I should like to have you there with me. I should like to feel I'd got somebody there, at the back of me, all my life."

"You'd easily find somebody else, who'd suit you better," she said.

"Yes, I might easily find another girl. I know I could. But not one I really wanted. I've never met one I really wanted, for good. You see, I'm thinking of all my life. If I marry, I want to feel it's for all my life. Other girls: well, they're just girls, nice enough to go a walk with now and then. Nce enough for a bit of play. But when I think of my life, then I should be very sorry to have to marry one of them, I should indeed."

"You mean they wouldn't make you a good wife."

"Yes, I mean that. But I don't mean they wouldn't do their duty by me. I mean—I don't know what I mean. Only when I think of my life, and of you, then the two things go together."

"And what if they didn't?" she said, with her odd sardonic touch.

"Well, I think they would."

They sat for some time silent. He held her hands in his, but he did not make love to her. Since he had realized that she was a woman, and vulnerable, accessible, a certain heaviness had possessed his soul. He did not want to make love to her. He shrank from any such performance, almost with fear. She was a woman, and vulnerable, accessible to him finally, and he held back from that which was ahead, almost with dread. It was a kind of darkness he knew he would enter finally, but of which he did not want as yet even to think. She was the woman, and he was responsible for the strange vulnerability he had suddenly realized in her.

"No," she said at last, "I'm a fool. I know I'm a fool."

"What for?" he asked.

"To go on with this business."

"Do you mean me?" he asked.

"No, I mean myself. I'm making a fool of myself, and a big one."

"Why, because you don't want to marry me, really?"

"Oh, I don't know whether I'm against it, as a matter of fact. That's just it. I don't know."

He looked at her in the darkness, puzzled. He did not in the least know what she meant.

"And don't you know whether you like to sit here with me this minute, or not?" he asked.

"No, I don't, really. I don't know whether I wish I was somewhere else, or whether I like being here. I don't know, really."

"Do you wish you were with Miss Banford? Do you

wish you'd gone to bed with her?" he asked, as a challenge.

She waited a long time before she answered:

"No," she said at last. "I don't wish that."

"And do you think you would spend all your life with her—when your hair goes white, and you are old?" he said.

"No," she said, without much hesitation. "I don't see Jill and me two old women together."

"And don't you think, when I'm an old man, and you're an old woman, we might be together still, as we are now?" he said.

"Well, not as we are now," she replied. "But I could imagine—no, I can't. I can't imagine you an old man. Besides, it's dreadful!"

"What, to be an old man?"

"Yes, of course."

"Not when the time comes," he said. "But it hasn't come. Only it will. And when it does, I should like to think you'd be there as well."

"Sort of old age pensions," she said dryly.

Her kind of witless humour always startled him. He never knew what she meant. Probably she didn't quite know herself.

"No," he said, hurt.

"I don't know why you harp on old age," she said. "I'm not ninety."

"Did anybody ever say you were?" he asked, offended.

They were silent for some time, pulling different ways in the silence.

"I don't want you to make fun of me," he said.

"Don't you?" she replied, enigmatic.

"No, because just this minute I'm serious. And when I'm serious, I believe in not making fun of it."

"You mean nobody else must make fun of you," she replied.

"Yes, I mean that. And I mean I don't believe in making fun of it myself. When it comes over me so that I'm serious, then—there it is, I don't want it to be laughed at."

She was silent for some time. Then she said, in a vague, almost pained voice:

"No, I'm not laughing at you."

A hot wave rose in his heart.

"You believe me, do you?" he asked.

"Yes, I believe you," she replied, with a twang of her old tired nonchalance, as if she gave in because she was tired. But he didn't care. His heart was hot and clamorous.

"So you agree to marry me before I go?—perhaps at Christmas?"

"Yes, I agree."

"There!" he exclaimed. "That's settled it."

And he sat silent, unconscious, with all the blood burning in all his veins, like fire in all the branches and twigs of him. He only pressed her two hands to his chest, without knowing. When the curious passion began to die down, he seemed to come awake to the world.

"We'll go in, shall we?" he said: as if he realized it was cold.

She rose without answering.

"Kiss me before we go, now you've said it," he said.

And he kissed her gently on the mouth, with a young, frightened kiss. It made her feel so young, too, and frightened, and wondering: and tired, tired, as if she were going to sleep.

They went indoors. And in the sitting-room, there, crouched by the fire like a queer little witch, was Banford. She looked round with reddened eyes as they entered, but did not rise. He thought she looked frightening, unnatural, crouching there and looking round at them. Evil he thought her look was, and he crossed his fingers.

Banford saw the ruddy, elate face of the youth: he seemed strangely tall and bright and looming. And March had a delicate look on her face, she wanted to hide her face, to screen it, to let it not be seen.

"You've come at last," said Banford uglily.

"Yes, we've come," said he.

"You've been long enough for anything," she said.

"Yes, we have. We've settled it. We shall marry as soon as possible," he replied.

"Oh, you've settled it, have you! Well, I hope you won't live to repent it," said Banford.

"I hope so too," he replied.

"Are you going to bed *now*, Nellie?" said Banford.

"Yes, I'm going now."

"Then for goodness' sake come along."

March looked at the boy. He was glancing with his very bright eyes at her and at Banford. March looked at him wistfully. She wished she could stay with him. She wished she had married him already, and it was all over. For oh, she felt suddenly so safe with him. She felt so strangely safe and peaceful in his presence. If only she could sleep in his shelter, and not with Jill. She felt afraid of Jill. In her dim, tender state, it was agony to have to go with Jill and sleep with her. She wanted the boy to save her. She looked again at him.

And he, watching with bright eyes, divined something of what she felt. It puzzled and distressed him that she must go with Jill.

"I shan't forget what you've promised," he said, looking clear into her eyes, right into her eyes, so that he seemed to occupy all her self with his queer, bright look.

She smiled to him, faintly, gently. She felt safe again
—safe with him.

But in spite of all the boy's precautions, he had a set-
back. The morning he was leaving the farm he got
March to accompany him to the market-town, about six
miles away, where they went to the registrar and had
their names stuck up as two people who were going to
marry. He was to come at Christmas, and the wedding
was to take place then. He hoped in the spring to be
able to take March back to Canada with him, now the
war was really over. Though he was so young, he had
saved some money.

"You never have to be without *some* money at the
back of you, if you can help it," he said.

So she saw him off in the train that was going west:
his camp was on Salisbury plains. And with big dark
eyes she watched him go, and it seemed as if everything
real in life was retreating as the train retreated with his
queer, chubby, ruddy face, that seemed so broad across
the cheeks, and which never seemed to change its expression, save when a cloud of sulky anger hung on the
brow, or the bright eyes fixed themselves in their stare.
This was what happened now. He leaned there out of
the carriage window as the train drew off, saying good-
bye and staring back at her, but his face quite unchanged. There was no emotion on his face. Only his
eyes tightened and became fixed and intent in their
watching, as a cat when suddenly she sees something
and stares. So the boy's eyes stared fixedly as the train
drew away, and she was left feeling intensely forlorn.
Failing his physical presence, she seemed to have nothing of him. And she had nothing of anything. Only his
face was fixed in her mind: the full, ruddy, unchanging
cheeks, and the straight snout of a nose, and the two

eyes staring above. All she could remember was how he suddenly wrinkled his nose when he laughed, as a puppy does when he is playfully growling. But him, himself, and what he was—she knew nothing, she had nothing of him when he left her.

On the ninth day after he had left her he received this letter:

DEAR HENRY,

I have been over it all again in my mind, this business of me and you, and it seems to me impossible. When you aren't there I see what a fool I am. When you are there you seem to blind me to things as they actually are. You make me see things all unreal and I don't know what. Then when I am alone again with Jill I seem to come to my own senses and realize what a fool I am making of myself and how I am treating you unfairly. Because it must be unfair to you for me to go on with this affair when I can't feel in my heart that I really love you. I know people talk a lot of stuff and nonsense about love, and I don't want to do that. I want to keep to plain facts and act in a sensible way. And that seems to me what I'm not doing. I don't see on what grounds I am going to marry you. I know I am not head over heels in love with you, as I have fancied myself to be with fellows when I was a young fool of a girl. You are an absolute stranger to me, and it seems to me you will always be one. So on what grounds am I going to marry you? When I think of Jill she is ten times more real to me. I know her and I'm awfully fond of her and I hate myself for a beast if I ever hurt her little finger. We have a life together. And even if it can't last for ever, it is a life while it does last. And it might last as long as either of us lives. Who knows how long we've got to live? She is a delicate little thing, perhaps nobody but me knows how delicate. And as for me, I feel I might fall down the well any day. What I don't seem to see at all is you. When I think of what I've been and what I've done with you I'm afraid I am a few screws loose. I should be sorry to think that softening of the brain is setting in so soon, but that is what it seems like. You are such an absolute stranger and so different from what I'm used to and we don't seem to have a thing in common. As for love the very word seems impossible. I know what love means even in Jill's case, and I know that in this affair with you it's an absolute impossibility. And then going to Canada. I'm sure I must have been clean off my chump when I promised such a thing. It makes me feel fairly frightened of myself. I feel I might do something really silly, that I wasn't responsible for. And end my days in a lunatic asylum. You may think that's all I'm fit for after the way I've gone on, but it isn't a very nice thought for me. Thank goodness Jill is here and her being here makes me feel sane again, else I don't know what I might do, I might have an accident with the gun one evening. I love Jill and she makes me feel safe and sane, with her loving anger against me for being such a fool. Well, what I want to say is won't you let us cry the whole thing off? I can't marry you, and really, I won't do such a thing if it seems to me wrong. It is all a great mistake. I've made a complete fool of myself, and all I can do is to apologize to you and ask you please to forget it and please to take no further notice of me. Your fox skin is nearly ready and seems all right. I will post it to you if you will let me know if this address is still right, and if you will accept my apology for the awful and lunatic way I have behaved with you, and then let the matter rest.

Jill sends her kindest regards. Her mother and father are staying with us over Christmas.

Yours very sincerely,
ELLEN MARCH.

The boy read this letter in camp as he was cleaning his kit. He set his teeth and for a moment went almost pale, yellow round the eyes with fury. He said nothing and saw nothing and felt nothing but a livid rage that was quite unreasoning. Balked! Balked again! Balked! He wanted the woman, he had fixed like doom upon having her. He felt that was his doom, his destiny, and his reward, to have this woman. She was his heaven and hell on earth, and he would have none elsewhere. Sightless with rage and thwarted madness, he got through the morning. Save that in his mind he was lurking and scheming towards an issue, he would have committed some insane act. Deep in himself he felt like roaring and howling and gnashing his teeth and breaking things. But he was too intelligent. He knew society was on top of him, and he must scheme. So with his teeth bitten together and his nose curiously slightly lifted, like some creature that is vicious, and his eyes fixed and staring, he went through the morning's affairs drunk with anger and suppression. In his mind was one thing—Banford. He took no heed of all March's outpouring: none. One thorn rankled, stuck in his mind. Banford. In his mind, in his soul, in his whole being, one thorn rankling to insanity. And he would have to get it out. He would have to get the thorn of Banford out of his life, if he died for it.

With this one fixed idea in his mind, he went to ask for twenty-four hours' leave of absence. He knew it was not due to him. His consciousness was supernaturally keen. He knew where he must go—he must go to the Captain. But how could he get at the Captain? In that great camp of wooden huts and tents, he had no idea where his Captain was.

But he went to the officers' canteen. There was his Captain standing talking with three other officers. Henry stood in the doorway at attention.

"May I speak to Captain Berryman?" The Captain was Cornish like himself.

"What do you want?" called the Captain.

"May I speak to you, Captain?"

"What do you want?" replied the Captain, not stirring from among his group of fellow officers.

Henry watched his superior for a minute without speaking.

"You won't refuse me, sir, will you?" he asked gravely.

"It depends what it is."

"Can I have twenty-four hours' leave?"

"No, you've no business to ask."

"I know I haven't. But I must ask you."

"You've had your answer."

"Don't send me away, Captain."

There was something strange about the boy as he stood there so everlasting in the doorway. The Cornish Captain felt the strangeness at once, and eyed him shrewdly.

"Why, what's afoot?" he said, curious.

"I'm in trouble about something. I must go to Blewbury," said the boy.

"Blewbury, eh? After the girls?"

"Yes, it is a woman, Captain." And the boy, as he stood there with his head reaching forward a little, went suddenly terribly pale, or yellow, and his lips seemed to give off pain. The Captain saw and paled a little also. He turned aside.

"Go on then," he said. "But for God's sake don't cause any trouble of any sort."

"I won't, Captain, thank you."

He was gone. The Captain, upset, took a gin and bitters. Henry managed to hire a bicycle. It was twelve o'clock when he left the camp. He had sixty miles of wet and muddy crossroads to ride. But he was in the saddle and down the road without a thought of food.

At the farm, March was busy with a work she had had some time in hand. A bunch of Scotch fir trees stood at the end of the open shed, on a little bank where ran the fence between two of the gorse-shaggy meadows. The furthest of these trees was dead—it had died in the summer and stood with all its needles brown and sere in the air. It was not a very big tree. And it was absolutely dead. So March determined to have it, although they were not allowed to cut any of the timber. But it would make such splendid firing, in these days of scarce fuel.

She had been giving a few stealthy chops at the trunk

for a week or more, every now and then hacking away
for five minutes, low down, near the ground, so no one
should notice. She had not tried the saw, it was such
hard work, alone. Now the tree stood with a great yawn-
ing gap in his base, perched as it were on one sinew, and
ready to fall. But he did not fall.

It was late in the damp December afternoon, with
cold mists creeping out of the woods and up the hollows,
and darkness waiting to sink in from above. There was a
bit of yellowness where the sun was fading away beyond
the low woods of the distance. March took her axe and
went to the tree. The small thud-thud of her blows re-
sounded rather ineffectual about the wintry homestead.
Banford came out wearing her thick coat, but with no
hat on her head, so that her thin, bobbed hair blew on
the uneasy wind that sounded in the pines and in the
wood.

"What I'm afraid of," said Banford, "is that it will
fall on the shed and we'll have another job repairing
that."

"Oh, I don't think so," said March, straightening herself and wiping her arm over her hot brow. She was
flushed red, her eyes were very wide-open and queer,
her upper lip lifted away from her two white front teeth
with a curious, almost rabbit-look.

A little stout man in a black overcoat and a bowler hat
came pottering across the yard. He had a pink face and
a white beard and smallish, pale-blue eyes. He was not
very old, but nervy, and he walked with little short steps.

"What do you think, father?" said Banford. "Don't
you think it might hit the shed in falling?"

"Shed, no!" said the old man. "Can't hit the shed.
Might as well say the fence."

"The fence doesn't matter," said March, in her high
voice.

"Wrong as usual, am I?" said Banford, wiping her straying hair from her eyes.

The tree stood as it were on one spelch of itself, leaning, and creaking in the wind. It grew on the bank of a little dry ditch between the two meadows. On the top of the bank straggled one fence, running to the bushes uphill. Several trees clustered there in the corner of the field near the shed and near the gate which led into the yard. Towards this gate, horizontal across the weary meadows came the grassy, rutted approach from the highroad. There trailed another rickety fence, long split poles joining the short, thick, wide-apart uprights. The three people stood at the back of the tree, in the corner of the shed meadow, just above the yard gate. The house with its two gables and its porch stood tidy in a little grassed garden across the yard. A little stout rosy-faced woman in a little red woollen shoulder shawl had come and taken her stand in the porch.

"Isn't it down yet?" she cried, in a high little voice.

"Just thinking about it," called her husband. His tone towards the two girls was always rather mocking and satirical. March did not want to go on with her hitting while he was there. As for him, he wouldn't lift a stick from the ground if he could help it, complaining, like his daughter, of rheumatics in his shoulder. So the three stood there a moment silent in the cold afternoon, in the bottom corner near the yard.

They heard the far-off taps of a gate and craned to look. Away across, on the green horizontal approach, a figure was just swinging on to a bicycle again, and lurching up and down over the grass, approaching.

"Why it's one of our boys—it's Jack," said the old man.

"Can't be," said Banford.

March craned her head to look. She alone recognized the khaki figure. She flushed but said nothing.

"No, it isn't Jack, I don't think," said the old man, staring with little round blue eyes under his white lashes.

In another moment the bicycle lurched into sight, and the rider dropped off at the gate. It was Henry, his face wet and red and spotted with mud. He was altogether a muddy sight.

"Oh!" cried Banford, as if afraid. "Why, it's Henry!"

"What!" muttered the old man. He had a thick, rapid, muttering way of speaking, and was slightly deaf. "What? What? Who is it? Who is it do you say? That young fellow? That young fellow of Nellie's? Oh! Oh!" And the satiric smile came on his pink face and white eyelashes.

Henry, pushing the wet hair off his steaming brow, had caught sight of them and heard what the old man said. His hot young face seemed to flame in the cold light.

"Oh, are you all there!" he said, giving his sudden, puppy's little laugh. He was so hot and dazed with cycling he hardly knew where he was. He leaned the bicycle against the fence and climbed over into the corner on to the bank, without going in to the yard.

"Well, I must say, we weren't expecting *you,*" said Banford laconically.

"No, I suppose not," said he, looking at March.

She stood aside, slack, with one knee drooped and the axe resting its head loosely on the ground. Her eyes were wide and vacant, and her upper lip lifted from her teeth in that helpless, fascinated rabbit-look. The moment she saw his glowing red face it was all over with her. She was as helpless as if she had been bound. The moment she saw the way his head seemed to reach forward.

"Well, who is it? Who is it, anyway?" asked the smiling, satiric old man in his muttering voice.

"Why, Mr. Grenfel, whom you've heard us tell about, father," said Banford coldly.

"Heard you tell about, I should think so. Heard of nothing else practically," muttered the elderly man with his queer little jeering smile on his face. "How do you do," he added, suddenly reaching out his hand to Henry.

The boy shook hands just as startled. Then the two men fell apart.

"Cycled over from Salisbury Plain, have you?" asked the old man.

"Yes."

"Ha! Longish ride. How long d'it take you, eh? Some time, eh? Several hours, I suppose."

"About four."

"Eh? Four! Yes, I should have thought so. When are you going back then?"

"I've got till tomorrow evening."

"Till tomorrow evening, eh? Yes. Ha! Girls weren't expecting you, were they?"

And the old man turned his pale-blue, round little eyes under their white lashes mockingly towards the girls. Henry also looked round. He had become a little awkward. He looked at March, who was still staring away into the distance as if to see where the cattle were. Her hand was on the pommel of the axe, whose head rested loosely on the ground.

"What were you doing there?" he asked in his soft, courteous voice. "Cutting a tree down?"

March seemed not to hear, as if in a trance.

"Yes," said Banford. "We've been at it for over a week."

"Oh! And have you done it all by yourselves, then?"

"Nellie's done it all, I've done nothing," said Banford.

"Really! You must have worked quite hard," he said, addressing himself in a curious gentle tone direct to March. She did not answer, but remained half averted, staring away towards the woods above as if in a trance.

"*Nellie!*" cried Banford sharply. "Can't you answer?"

"What—me?" cried March starting round, and looking from one to the other. "Did anyone speak to me?"

"Dreaming!" muttered the old man, turning aside to smile. "Must be in love, eh, dreaming in the daytime!"

"Did you say anything to me?" said March, looking at the boy as from a strange distance, her eyes wide and doubtful, her face delicately flushed.

"I said you must have worked hard at the tree," he replied courteously.

"Oh, that! Bit by bit. I thought it would have come down by now."

"I'm thankful it hasn't come down in the night, to frighten us to death," said Banford.

"Let me just finish it for you, shall I?" said the boy. March slanted the axe-shaft in his direction.

"Would you like to?" she said.

"Yes, if you wish it," he said.

"Oh, I'm thankful when the thing's down, that's all," she replied, nonchalant.

"Which way is it going to fall?" said Banford. "Will it hit the shed?"

"No, it won't hit the shed," he said. "I should think it will fall there—quite clear. Though it might give a twist and catch the fence."

"Catch the fence!" cried the old man. "What, catch the fence! When it's leaning at that angle? Why it's further off than the shed. It won't catch the fence."

"No," said Henry, "I don't suppose it will. It has plenty of room to fall quite clear, and I suppose it will fall clear."

"Won't tumble backwards on top of *us*, will it!" asked the old man sarcastic.

"No, it won't do that," said Henry, taking off his short overcoat and his tunic. "Ducks! Ducks! Go back!"

A line of four brown-speckled ducks led by a brown-and-green drake were stemming away downhill from the upper meadow, coming like boats running on a ruffled sea, cackling their way top speed downwards towards the fence and towards the little group of people, and cackling as excitedly as if they brought news of the Spanish Armada.

"Silly things! Silly things!" cried Banford going forward to turn them off. But they came eagerly towards her, opening their yellow-green beaks and quacking as if they were so excited to say something.

"There's no food. There's nothing here. You must wait a bit," said Banford to them. "Go away. Go away. Go round to the yard."

They didn't go, so she climbed the fence to swerve them round under the gate and into the yard. So off they waggled in an excited string once more, wagging their rumps like the sterns of little gondolas ducking under the bar of the gate. Banford stood on the top of the bank, just over the fence, looking down on the other three.

Henry looked up at her, and met her queer, round-pupilled, weak eyes staring behind her spectacles. He was perfectly still. He looked away, up at the weak, leaning tree. And as he looked into the sky, like a huntsman who is watching a flying bird, he thought to himself: "If the tree falls in just such a way, and spins just so much as it falls, then the branch there will strike her exactly as she stands on top of that bank."

He looked at her again. She was wiping the hair from her brow again, with that perpetual gesture. In his heart he had decided her death. A terrible still force seemed in him, and a power that was just his. If he turned even a hair's breadth in the wrong direction, he would lose the power.

"Mind yourself, Miss Banford," he said. And his heart held perfectly still, in the terrible pure will that she should not move.

"Who me, mind myself?" she cried, her father's jeering tone in her voice. "Why, do you think you might hit me with the axe?"

"No, it's just possible the tree might, though," he answered soberly. But the tone of his voice seemed to her to imply that he was only being falsely solicitous and trying to make her move because it was his will to move her.

"Absolutely impossible," she said.

He heard her. But he held himself icy still, lest he should lose his power.

"No, it's just possible. You'd better come down this way."

"Oh, all right. Let us see some crack Canadian tree felling," she retorted.

"Ready then," he said, taking the axe, looking round to see he was clear.

There was a moment of pure, motionless suspense, when the world seemed to stand still. Then suddenly his form seemed to flash up enormously tall and fearful, he gave two swift, flashing blows, in immediate succession, the tree was severed, turning slowly, spinning strangely in the air and coming down like a sudden darkness on the earth. No one saw what was happening except himself. No one heard the strange little cry which the Banford gave as the dark end of the bough swooped down, down on her. No one saw her crouch a little and receive the blow on the back of the neck. No one saw her flung outwards and laid, a little twitching heap, at the foot of the fence. No one except the boy. And he watched with intense bright eyes, as he would watch a wild goose he had shot. Was it winged, or dead? Dead!

Immediately he gave a loud cry. Immediately March gave a wild shriek that went far, far down the afternoon. And the father started a strange bellowing sound.

The boy leapt the fence and ran to the figure. The back of the neck and head was a mass of blood, of horror. He turned it over. The body was quivering with little convulsions. But she was dead really. He knew it, that it was so. He knew it in his soul and his blood. The inner necessity of his life was fulfilling itself, it was he who was to live. The thorn was drawn out of his bowels. So, he put her down gently, she was dead.

He stood up. March was standing there petrified and absolutely motionless. Her face was dead white, her eyes big black pools. The old man was scrambling horribly over the fence.

"I'm afraid it's killed her," said the boy.

The old man was making curious, blubbering noises as he huddled over the fence.

"What!" cried March, starting electric.

"Yes, I'm afraid," repeated the boy.

March was coming forward. The boy was over the fence before she reached it.

"What do you say, killed her?" she asked in a sharp voice.

"I'm afraid so," he answered softly.

She went still whiter, fearful. The two stood facing each other. Her black eyes gazed on him with the last look of resistance. And then in a last agonized failure she began to grizzle, to cry in a shivery little fashion of a child that doesn't want to cry, but which is beaten from within, and gives that little first shudder of sobbing which is not yet weeping, dry and fearful.

He had won. She stood there absolutely helpless, shuddering her dry sobs and her mouth trembling rapidly. And then, as in a child, with a little crash came the tears and the blind agony of sightless weeping. She sank down on the grass and sat there with her hands on her breast and her face lifted in sightless, convulsed weeping. He stood above her, looking down on her, mute, pale, and everlasting seeming. He never moved, but looked down on her. And among all the torture of the scene, the torture of his own heart and bowels, he was glad, he had won.

After a long time he stooped to her and took her hands.

"Don't cry," he said softly. "Don't cry."

She looked up at him with tears running from her eyes, a senseless look of helplessness and submission. So she gazed on him as if sightless, yet looking up to him. She would never leave him again. He had won her. And he knew it and was glad, because he wanted her for his life. His life must have her. And now he had won her. It was what his life must have.

But if he had won her, he had not yet got her. They were married at Christmas as he had planned, and he got again ten days leave. They went to Cornwall, to his own village, on the sea. He realized that it was awful for her to be at the farm any more.

But though she belonged to him, though she lived in his shadow, as if she could not be away from him, she was not happy. She did not want to leave him: and yet she did not feel free with him. Everything around her seemed to watch her, seemed to press on her. He had won her, he had her with him, she was his wife. And she—she belonged to him, she knew it. But she was not glad. And he was still foiled. He realized that though he was married to her and possessed her in every possible way, apparently, and though she *wanted* him to possess her, she wanted it, she wanted nothing else, now, still he did not quite succeed.

Something was missing. Instead of her soul swaying with new life, it seemed to droop, to bleed, as if it were wounded. She would sit for a long time with her hand in his, looking away at the sea. And in her dark, vacant eyes was a sort of wound, and her face looked a little peaked. If he spoke to her, she would turn to him with a faint new smile, the strange, quivering little smile of a woman who has died in the old way of love, and can't quite rise to the new way. She still felt she ought to *do* something, to strain herself in some direction. And there was nothing to do, and no direction in which to strain herself. And she could not quite accept the submergence which his new love put upon her. If she was in love, she ought to *exert* herself, in some way, loving. She felt the weary need of our day to *exert* herself in love. But she knew that in fact she must no more exert herself in love. He would not have the love which exerted itself towards him. It made his brow go black. No, he wouldn't let her exert her love towards him. No, she had to be passive, to acquiesce, and to be submerged under the surface of love. She had to be like the seaweed she saw as she peered down from the boat, swaying for ever delicately under water, with all their delicate fibrils put tenderly out upon the flood, sensitive, utterly sensitive and receptive within the shadowy sea, and never, never rising and looking forth above water while they lived. Never. Never looking forth from the water until they died, only then washing, corpses, upon the surface. But while they lived, always submerged, always beneath the wave. Beneath the wave they might have powerful roots, stronger than iron, they might be tenacious and dangerous in their soft waving within the flood. Beneath the water

they might be stronger, more indestructible, than resistant oak trees are on land. But it was always under-water,
always under-water. And she, being a woman, must be
like that.

And she had been so used to the very opposite. She
had had to take all the thought for love and for life, and
all the responsibility. Day after day she had been responsible for the coming day, for the coming year: for her
dear Jill's health and happiness and well-being. Verily,
in her own small way, she had felt herself responsible
for the well-being of the world. And this had been her
great stimulant, this grand feeling that, in her own small
sphere, she was responsible for the well-being of the
world.

And she had failed. She knew that, even in her small
way, she had failed. She had failed to satisfy her own
feeling of responsibility. It was so difficult. It seemed
so grand and easy at first. And the more you tried, the
more difficult it became. It had seemed so easy to make
one beloved creature happy. And the more you tried,
the worse the failure. It was terrible. She had been all
her life reaching, reaching, and what she reached for
seemed so near, until she had stretched to her utmost
limit. And then it was always beyond her.

Always beyond her, vaguely, unrealizably beyond
her, and she was left with nothingness at last. The life
she reached for, the happiness she reached for, the well-
being she reached for, all slipped back, became unreal,
the further she stretched her hand. She wanted some
goal, some finality—and there was none. Always this
ghastly reaching, reaching, striving for something that
might be just beyond. Even to make Jill happy. She was
glad Jill was dead. For she had realized that she could
never make her happy. Jill would always be fretting herself thinner and thinner, weaker and weaker. Her pains

grew worse instead of less. It would be so for ever. She was glad she was dead.

And if she had married a man it would have been just the same. The woman striving, striving to make the man happy, striving within her own limits for the well-being of her world. And always achieving failure. Little, foolish successes in money or in ambition. But at the very point where she most wanted success, in the anguished effort to make some one beloved human being happy and perfect, there the failure was almost catastrophic. You wanted to make your beloved happy, and his happiness seemed always achievable. If only you did just this, that and the other. And you did this, that, and the other, in all good faith, and every time the failure became a little more ghastly. You could love yourself to ribbons, and strive and strain yourself to the bone, and things would go from bad to worse, bad to worse, as far as happiness went. The awful mistake of happiness.

Poor March, in her goodwill and her responsibility, she had strained herself till it seemed to her that the whole of life and everything was only a horrible abyss of nothingness. The more you reached after the fatal flower of happiness, which trembles so blue and lovely in a crevice just beyond your grasp, the more fearfully you become aware of the ghastly and awful gulf of the precipice below you, into which you will inevitably plunge, as into the bottomless pit, if you reach any further. You pluck flower after flower—it is never *the* flower. The flower itself—its calyx is a horrible gulf, it is the bottomless pit.

That is the whole history of the search for happiness, whether it be your own or somebody else's that you want to win. It ends, and it always ends, in the ghastly sense of the bottomless nothingness into which you will inevitably fall if you strain any further.

And women?—what goal can any woman conceive, except happiness? Just happiness, for herself and the whole world. That, and nothing else. And so, she assumes the responsibility, and sets off towards her goal. She can see it there, at the foot of the rainbow. Or she can see it a little way beyond, in the blue distance. Not far, not far.

But the end of the rainbow is a bottomless gulf down which you can fall for ever without arriving, and the blue distance is a void pit which can swallow you and all your efforts into its emptiness, and still be no emptier. You and all your efforts. So, the illusion of attainable happiness!

Poor March, she had set off so wonderfully, towards the blue goal. And the further and further she had gone, the more fearful had become the realization of emptiness. An agony, an insanity at last.

She was glad it was over. She was glad to sit on the shore and look westwards over the sea, and know the great strain had ended. She would never strain for love and happiness any more. And Jill was safely dead. Poor Jill, poor Jill. It must be sweet to be dead.

For her own part, death was not her destiny. She would have to leave her destiny to the boy. But then, the boy. He wanted more than that. He wanted her to give herself without defences, to sink and become submerged in him. And she—she wanted to sit still, like a woman on the last milestone, and watch. She wanted to see, to know, to understand. She wanted to be alone: with him at her side.

And he! He did not want her to watch any more, to see any more, to understand any more. He wanted to veil her woman's spirit, as Orientals veil the woman's face. He wanted her to commit herself to him, and to put her independent spirit to sleep. He wanted to take

away from her all her effort, all that seemed her very
raison d'être. He wanted to make her submit, yield,
blindly pass away out of all her strenuous consciousness.
He wanted to take away her consciousness, and make
her just his woman. Just his woman.

And she was so tired, so tired, like a child that wants
to go to sleep, but which fights against sleep as if sleep
were death. She seemed to stretch her eyes wider in the
obstinate effort and tension of keeping awake. She
would keep awake. She *would* know. She *would* consider and judge and decide. She *would* have the reins of
her own life between her own hands. She *would* be an
independent woman, to the last. But she was so tired, so
tired of everything. And sleep seemed near. And there
was such rest in the boy.

Yet there, sitting in a niche of the high wild cliffs of
West Cornwall, looking over the westward sea, she
stretched her eyes wider and wider. Away to the West,
Canada, America. She *would* know and she *would* see
what was ahead. And the boy, sitting beside her staring
down at the gulls, had a cloud between his brows and
the strain of discontent in his eyes. He wanted her
asleep, at peace in him. He wanted her at peace, asleep
in him. And *there* she was, dying with the strain of her
own wakefulness. Yet she would not sleep: no, never.
Sometimes he thought bitterly that he ought to have left
her. He ought never to have killed Banford. He should
have left Banford and March to kill one another.

But that was only impatience: and he knew it. He
was waiting, waiting to go west. He was aching almost
in torment to leave England, to go west, to take March
away. To leave this shore! He believed that as they
crossed the seas, as they left this England which he so
hated, because in some way it seemed to have stung him

with poison, she would go to sleep. She would close her eyes at last, and give in to him.

And then he would have her and he would have his own life at last. He chafed, feeling he hadn't got his own life. He would never have it till she yielded and slept in him. Then he would have all his own life as a young man and a male, and she would have all her own life as a woman and a female. There would be no more of this awful straining. She would not be a man any more, an independent woman with a man's responsibility. Nay, even the responsibility for her own soul she would have to commit to him. He knew it was so, and obstinately held out against her, waiting for the surrender.

"You'll feel better when once we get over the seas, to Canada, over there," he said to her as they sat among the rocks on the cliff.

She looked away to the sea's horizon, as if it were not real. Then she looked round at him, with the strained, strange look of a child that is struggling against sleep.

"Shall I?" she said.

"Yes," he answered quietly.

And her eyelids dropped with the slow motion, sleep weighing them unconscious. But she pulled them open again to say:

"Yes, I may. I can't tell. I can't tell what it will be like over there."

"If only we could go soon!" he said, with pain in his voice.

NOVELS

EDITOR'S PREFACE

ANY editor must feel deeply guilty who, attempting to represent Lawrence, fails to represent him with one of the complete novels. Lawrence himself wrote, "Being a novelist, I consider myself superior to the saint, the scientist, the philosopher and the poet. The novel is the one bright book of life." But unfortunately all the novels, and especially the best of them—*The White Peacock, Sons and Lovers, The Rainbow, Women in Love, Lady Chatterley's Lover*—are so long that it is impossible to include one in a volume which would also contain anything else. I have therefore been forced to limit this sampling of Lawrence's full-length fiction to excerpts from it.

The two excerpts I reprint here—one from *The Rainbow,* the other from *Women in Love*—while not exactly complete in themselves, can, I think, be comfortably read without reference to what precedes or follows them. *The Rainbow* was Lawrence's fourth, *Women in Love* his fifth, novel. They were written at the height of his powers, but in a period of darkening emotion. Particularly *Women in Love* has a pervasive note of gloom which no doubt reflects Lawrence's response to the war situation in which it was composed, although the war itself is never mentioned in the story: as he was finishing it, Lawrence wrote in a letter, "The book frightens me. It is so end-of-the-world."

The Rainbow deals with three generations of the

Brangwen family. Anna, the daughter of the Polish wife of Tom Brangwen, is the heroine of the second generation, and it is her girlhood and marriage that is described in the selection that follows. I think these pages are the most beautiful that Lawrence ever wrote.

Ursula and Gudrun Brangwen, the daughters of Anna and Will, command not only the last section of *The Rainbow* but all of *Women in Love,* which is therefore often referred to as a sequel of the earlier book. But actually both novels are entirely self-contained: indeed, if the names of the two girls had been changed, I think the reader would make little connection between the pair of sisters of the second book and the first. The continuity between the two volumes would seem to be chiefly a matter of Lawrence's feeling that he had not explored the fictional possibilities of two such girls as fully as he would like.

Of all Lawrence's novels, *Women in Love* is the most thickly textured. No other of the novels spreads so wide a physical canvas. If this is a dark spiritual time for its author—and there is more than a hint of emotional and intellectual crisis even in the few chapters I reprint—it is also a time of many new experiences, when Lawrence's world had opened far beyond the Nottinghamshire of his boyhood and of such novels as *The White Peacock* and *Sons and Lovers,* even of *The Rainbow.*

FROM *The Rainbow*

IV. GIRLHOOD OF ANNA BRANGWEN

WHEN Anna was nine years old, Brangwen sent her to the dames' school in Cossethay. There she went, flipping and dancing in her inconsequential fashion, doing very much as she liked, disconcerting old Miss Coates by her indifference to respectability and by her lack of reverence. Anna only laughed at Miss Coates, liked her, and patronized her in superb, childish fashion.

The girl was at once shy and wild. She had a curious contempt for ordinary people, a benevolent superiority. She was very shy, and tortured with misery when people did not like her. On the other hand, she cared very little for anybody save her mother, whom she still rather resentfully worshipped, and her father, whom she loved and patronized, but upon whom she depended. These two, her mother and father, held her still in fee. But she was free of other people, towards whom, on the whole, she took the benevolent attitude. She deeply hated ugliness or intrusion or arrogance, however. As a child, she was as proud and shadowy as a tiger, and as aloof. She could confer favours, but, save from her mother and father, she could receive none. She hated people who came too near to her. Like a wild thing, she wanted her distance. She mistrusted intimacy.

In Cossethay and Ilkeston she was always an alien. She had plenty of acquaintances, but no friends. Very few people whom she met were significant to her. They seemed part of a herd, undistinguished. She did not take people very seriously.

She had two brothers, Tom, dark-haired, small, volatile, whom she was intimately related to but whom she never mingled with, and Fred, fair and responsive, whom she adored but did not consider as a real, separate being. She was too much the centre of her own universe, too little aware of anything outside.

The first *person* she met, who affected her as a real, living person, whom she regarded as having definite existence, was Baron Skrebensky, her mother's friend. He also was a Polish exile, who had taken orders, and had received from Mr. Gladstone a small country living in Yorkshire.

When Anna was about ten years old, she went with her mother to spend a few days with the Baron Skrebensky. He was very unhappy in his red-brick vicarage. He was vicar of a country church, a living worth a little over two hundred pounds a year, but he had a large parish containing several collieries, with a new, raw, heathen population. He went to the north of England expecting homage from the common people, for he was an aristocrat. He was roughly, even cruelly, received. But he never understood it. He remained a fiery aristocrat. Only he had to learn to avoid his parishioners.

Anna was very much impressed by him. He was a smallish man with a rugged, rather crumpled face and blue eyes set very deep and glowing. His wife was a tall thin woman, of noble Polish family, mad with pride. He still spoke broken English, for he had kept very close to his wife, both of them forlorn in this strange, inhospitable country, and they always spoke in Polish together.

He was disappointed with Mrs. Brangwen's soft, natural English, very disappointed that her child spoke no Polish.

Anna loved to watch him. She liked the big, new, rambling vicarage, desolate and stark on its hill. It was so exposed, so bleak and bold after the Marsh. The Baron talked endlessly in Polish to Mrs. Brangwen; he made furious gestures with his hands, his blue eyes were full of fire. And to Anna, there was a significance about his sharp, flinging movements. Something in her responded to his extravagance and his exuberant manner. She thought him a very wonderful person. She was shy of him, she liked him to talk to her. She felt a sense of freedom near him.

She never could tell how she knew it, but she did know that he was a knight of Malta. She could never remember whether she had seen his star, or cross, of his order or not, but it flashed in her mind, like a symbol. He at any rate represented to the child the real world, where kings and lords and princes moved and fulfilled their shining lives, whilst queens and ladies and princesses upheld the noble order.

She had recognized the Baron Skrebensky as a real person, he had had some regard for her. But when she did not see him any more, he faded and became a memory. But as a memory he was always alive to her.

Anna became a tall, awkward girl. Her eyes were still very dark and quick, but they had grown careless, they had lost their watchful, hostile look. Her fierce, spun hair turned brown, it grew heavier and was tied back. She was sent to a young ladies' school in Nottingham.

And at this period she was absorbed in becoming a young lady. She was intelligent enough but not interested in learning. At first, she thought all the girls at school very ladylike and wonderful, and she wanted to be like them. She came to a speedy disillusion: they galled and maddened her, they were petty and mean. After the loose, generous atmosphere of her home, where little things did not count, she was always uneasy in the world, that would snap and bite at every trifle.

A quick change came over her. She mistrusted herself, she mistrusted the outer world. She did not want to go on, she did not want to go out into it, she wanted to go no further.

"What do *I* care about that lot of girls?" she would say to her father, contemptuously. "They are nobody."

The trouble was that the girls would not accept Anna at her measure. They would have her according to themselves or not at all. So she was confused, seduced, she became as they were for a time, and then, in revulsion, she hated them furiously.

"Why don't you ask some of your girls here?" her father would say.

"They're not coming here," she cried.

"And why not?"

"They're bagatelle," she said, using one of her mother's rare phrases.

"Bagatelles or billiards, it makes no matter, they're nice young lasses enough."

But Anna was not to be won over. She had a curious shrinking from commonplace people, and particularly from the young lady of her day. She would not go into company because of the ill-at-ease feeling other people brought upon her. And she never could decide whether it were her fault or theirs. She half respected these other people, and continuous disillusion maddened her. She wanted to respect them. Still she thought the people she did not *know* were wonderful. Those she knew seemed always to be limiting her, tying her up in little falsities that irritated her beyond bearing. She would rather stay at home and avoid the rest of the world, leaving it illusory.

For at the Marsh life had indeed a certain freedom and largeness. There was no fret about money, no mean little precedence, nor care for what other people thought, because neither Mrs. Brangwen nor Brangwen could be sensible of any judgment passed on them from outside. Their lives were too separate.

So Anna was only easy at home, where the common sense and the supreme relation between her parents produced a freer standard of being than she could find outside. Where, outside the Marsh, could she find the tolerant dignity she had been brought up in? Her parents stood undiminished and unaware of criticism. The people she met outside seemed to begrudge her her very existence. They seemed to want to belittle her also. She was exceedingly reluctant to go amongst them. She depended upon her mother and her father. And yet she wanted to go out.

At school, or in the world, she was usually at fault, she felt usually that she ought to be slinking in disgrace. She never felt quite sure, in herself, whether she were wrong, or whether the others were wrong. She had not done her lessons: well, she did not see any reason why she *should* do her lessons, if she did not want to. Was there some occult reason why she should? Were these people, schoolmistresses, representatives of some mystic Right, some Higher Good? They seemed to think so themselves. But she could not for her life see why a woman should bully and insult her because she did not know thirty lines of *As You Like It*. After all, *what* did it matter if she knew them or not? Nothing could persuade her that it was of the slightest importance. Because she despised inwardly the coarsely working nature of the mistress. Therefore she was always at outs with

authority. From constant telling, she came almost to believe in her own badness, her own intrinsic inferiority.
She felt that she ought always to be in a state of slinking
disgrace, if she fulfilled what was expected of her. But
she rebelled. She never really believed in her own badness. At the bottom of her heart she despised the other
people, who carped and were loud over trifles. She despised them, and wanted revenge on them. She hated
them whilst they had power over her.

Still she kept an ideal: a free, proud lady absolved
from the petty ties, existing beyond petty considerations.
She would see such ladies in pictures: Alexandra, Princess of Wales, was one of her models. This lady was
proud and royal, and stepped indifferently over all
small, mean desires: so thought Anna, in her heart. And
the girl did up her hair high under a little slanting hat,
her skirts were fashionably bunched up, she wore an
elegant, skin-fitting coat.

Her father was delighted. Anna was very proud in her
bearing, too naturally indifferent to smaller bonds to
satisfy Ilkeston, which would have liked to put her
down. But Brangwen was having no such thing. If she
chose to be royal, royal she should be. He stood like a
rock between her and the world.

After the fashion of his family, he grew stout and
handsome. His blue eyes were full of light, twinkling
and sensitive, his manner was deliberate, but hearty,
warm. His capacity for living his own life without attention from his neighbours made them respect him. They
would run to do anything for him. He did not consider
them, but was open-handed towards them, so they made
profit of their willingness. He liked people, so long as
they remained in the background.

Mrs. Brangwen went on in her own way, following
her own devices. She had her husband, her two sons and

Anna. These staked out and marked her horizon. The
other people were outsiders. Inside her own world, her
life passed along like a dream for her, it lapsed, and she
lived within its lapse, active and always pleased, intent.
She scarcely noticed the outer things at all. What was
outside was outside, nonexistent. She did not mind if
the boys fought, so long as it was out of her presence.
But if they fought when she was by, she was angry, and
they were afraid of her. She did not care if they broke a
window of a railway carriage or sold their watches to
have a revel at the Goose Fair. Brangwen was perhaps
angry over these things. To the mother they were insignificant. It was odd little things that offended her.
She was furious if the boys hung round the slaughter-
house, she was displeased when the school reports were
bad. It did not matter how many sins her boys were accused of, so long as they were not stupid, or inferior. If
they seemed to brook insult, she hated them. And it was
only a certain *gaucherie*, a gawkiness on Anna's part
that irritated her against the girl. Certain forms of clumsiness, grossness, made the mother's eyes glow with
curious rage. Otherwise she was pleased, indifferent.

Pursuing her splendid-lady ideal, Anna became a
lofty demoiselle of sixteen, plagued by family shortcomings. She was very sensitive to her father. She knew
if he had been drinking, were he ever so little affected,
and she could not bear it. He flushed when he drank,
the veins stood out on his temples, there was a twinkling,
cavalier boisterousness in his eyes, his manner was jovi-
ally overbearing and mocking. And it angered her.
When she heard his loud, roaring, boisterous mockery,
an anger of resentment filled her. She was quick to fore-
stall him, the moment he came in.

"You look a sight, you do, red in the face," she cried.

"I might look worse if I was green," he answered.

"Boozing in Ilkeston."

"And what's wrong wi' Il'son?"

She flounced away. He watched her with amused, twinkling eyes, yet in spite of himself said that she flouted him.

They were a curious family, a law to themselves, separate from the world, isolated, a small republic set in invisible bounds. The mother was quite indifferent to Ilkeston and Cossethay, to any claims made on her from outside, she was very shy of any outsider, exceedingly courteous, winning even. But the moment a visitor had gone, she laughed and dismissed him, he did not exist. It had been all a game to her. She was still a foreigner, unsure of her ground. But alone with her own children and husband at the Marsh, she was mistress of a little native land that lacked nothing.

She had some beliefs somewhere, never defined. She had been brought up a Roman Catholic. She had gone to the Church of England for protection. The outward form was a matter of indifference to her. Yet she had some fundamental religion. It was as if she worshipped God as a mystery, never seeking in the least to define what He was.

And inside her, the subtle sense of the Great Absolute wherein she had her being was very strong. The English dogma never reached her: the language was too foreign. Through it all she felt the great Separator who held life in His hands, gleaming, imminent, terrible, the Great Mystery, immediate beyond all telling.

She shone and gleamed to the Mystery, Whom she knew through all her senses, she glanced with strange, mystic superstitions that never found expression in the English language, never mounted to thought in English. But so she lived, within a potent, sensuous belief that included her family and contained her destiny.

To this she had reduced her husband. He existed with
her entirely indifferent to the general values of the
world. Her very ways, the very mark of her eyebrows
were symbols and indication to him. There, on the farm
with her, he lived through a mystery of life and death
and creation, strange, profound ecstasies and incom-
municable satisfactions, of which the rest of the world
knew nothing; which made the pair of them apart and
respected in the English village, for they were also well-
to-do.

But Anna was only half safe within her mother's unthinking knowledge. She had a mother-of-pearl rosary
that had been her own father's. What it meant to her
she could never say. But the string of moonlight and silver, when she had it between her fingers, filled her with
strange passion. She learned at school a little Latin, she
learned an Ave Maria and a Pater Noster, she learned
how to say her rosary. But that was no good. "Ave
Maria, gratia plena, Dominus tecum, Benedicta tu in
mulieribus et benedictus fructus ventris tui Jesus. Ave
Maria, Sancta Maria, ora pro nobis peccatoribus, nunc
et in hora mortis nostrae, Amen."

It was not right, somehow. What these words meant
when translated was not the same as the pale rosary
meant. There was a discrepancy, a falsehood. It irritated
her to say, "Dominus tecum," or, "benedicta tu in mulieribus." She loved the mystic words, "Ave Maria, Sancta
Maria;" she was moved by "benedictus fructus ventris
tui Jesus," and by "nunc et in hora mortis nostrae." But
none of it was quite real. It was not satisfactory, somehow.

She avoided her rosary, because, moving her with
curious passion as it did, it *meant* only these not very
significant things. She put it away. It was her instinct to

put all these things away. It was her instinct to avoid thinking, to avoid it, to save herself.

She was seventeen, touchy, full of spirits, and very moody: quick to flush, and always uneasy, uncertain. For some reason or other, she turned more to her father, she felt almost flashes of hatred for her mother. Her mother's dark muzzle and curiously insidious ways, her mother's utter surety and confidence, her strange satisfaction, even triumph, her mother's way of laughing at things and her mother's silent overriding of vexatious propositions, most of all her mother's triumphant power, maddened the girl.

She became sudden and incalculable. Often she stood at the window, looking out, as if she wanted to go. Sometimes she went, she mixed with people. But always she came home in anger, as if she were diminished, belittled, almost degraded.

There was over the house a kind of dark silence and intensity, in which passion worked its inevitable conclusions. There was in the house a sort of richness, a deep, inarticulate interchange which made other places seem thin and unsatisfying. Brangwen could sit silent, smoking in his chair, the mother could move about in her quiet, insidious way, and the sense of the two presences was powerful, sustaining. The whole intercourse was wordless, intense and close.

But Anna was uneasy. She wanted to get away. Yet wherever she went, there came upon her that feeling of thinness, as if she were made smaller, belittled. She hastened home.

There she raged and interrupted the strong, settled interchange. Sometimes her mother turned on her with a fierce, destructive anger, in which was no pity or consideration. And Anna shrank, afraid. She went to her father.

He would still listen to the spoken word, which fell
sterile on the unheeding mother. Sometimes Anna talked
to her father. She tried to discuss people, she wanted to
know what was meant. But her father became uneasy.
He did not want to have things dragged into consciousness. Only out of consideration for her he listened. And
there was a kind of bristling rousedness in the room. The
cat got up and, stretching itself, went uneasily to the
door. Mrs. Brangwen was silent, she seemed ominous.
Anna could not go on with her fault-finding, her criticism, her expression of dissatisfactions. She felt even
her father against her. He had a strong, dark bond with
her mother, a potent intimacy that existed inarticulate
and wild, following its own course, and savage if interrupted, uncovered.

Nevertheless Brangwen was uneasy about the girl,
the whole house continued to be disturbed. She had a
pathetic, baffled appeal. She was hostile to her parents,
even whilst she lived entirely with them, within their
spell.

Many ways she tried, of escape. She became an as-
siduous church-goer. But the *language* meant nothing to
her: it seemed false. She hated to hear things expressed,
put into words. Whilst the religious feelings were inside
her they were passionately moving. In the mouth of the
clergyman, they were false, indecent. She tried to read.
But again the tedium and the sense of the falsity of the
spoken word put her off. She went to stay with girl
friends. At first she thought it splendid. But then the
inner boredom came on, it seemed to her all nothingness. And she felt always belittled, as if never, never
could she stretch her length and stride her stride.

Her mind reverted often to the torture cell of a certain
Bishop of France, in which the victim could neither
stand nor lie stretched out, never. Not that she thought

of herself in any connection with this. But often there came into her mind the wonder, how the cell was built, and she could feel the horror of the crampedness, as something very real.

She was, however, only eighteen when a letter came from Mrs. Alfred Brangwen, in Nottingham, saying that her son William was coming to Ilkeston to take a place as junior draughtsman, scarcely more than apprentice, in a lace factory. He was twenty years old, and would the Marsh Brangwens be friendly with him.

Tom Brangwen at once wrote offering the young man a home at the Marsh. This was not accepted, but the Nottingham Brangwens expressed gratitude.

There had never been much love lost between the Nottingham Brangwens and the Marsh. Indeed, Mrs. Alfred, having inherited three thousand pounds, and having occasion to be dissatisfied with her husband, held aloof from all the Brangwens whatsoever. She affected, however, some esteem of Mrs. Tom, as she called the Polish woman, saying that at any rate she was a lady.

Anna Brangwen was faintly excited at the news of her Cousin Will's coming to Ilkeston. She knew plenty of young men, but they had never become real to her. She had seen in this young gallant a nose she liked, in that a pleasant moustache, in the other a nice way of wearing clothes, in one a ridiculous fringe of hair, in another a comical way of talking. They were objects of amusement and faint wonder to her, rather than real beings, the young men.

The only man she knew was her father; and, as he was something large, looming, a kind of Godhead, he embraced all manhood for her, and other men were just incidental.

She remembered her Cousin Will. He had town clothes and was thin, with a very curious head, black as jet, with hair like sleek, thin fur. It was a curious head; it reminded her she knew not of what; of some animal, some mysterious animal that lived in the darkness under the leaves and never came out, but which lived vividly, swift and intense. She always thought of him with that black, keen, blind head. And she considered him odd.

He appeared at the Marsh one Sunday morning: a rather long, thin youth with a bright face and a curious self-possession among his shyness, a native unawareness of what other people might be, since he was himself.

When Anna came downstairs in her Sunday clothes, ready for church, he rose and greeted her conventionally, shaking hands. His manners were better than hers. She flushed. She noticed that he now had a black fledge on his upper lip, a black, finely-shapen line marking his wide mouth. It rather repelled her. It reminded her of the thin, fine fur of his hair. She was aware of something strange in him.

His voice had rather high upper notes and very resonant middle notes. It was queer. She wondered why he did it. But he sat very naturally in the Marsh living-room. He had some uncouthness, some natural self-possession of the Brangwens, that made him at home there.

Anna was rather troubled by the strangely intimate, affectionate way her father had towards this young man. He seemed gentle towards him, he put himself aside in order to fill out the young man. This irritated Anna.

"Father," she said abruptly, "give me some collection."

"What collection?" asked Brangwen.

"Don't be ridiculous," she cried, flushing.

"Nay," he said, "what collection's this?"

"You know it's the first Sunday of the month."

Anna stood confused. Why was he doing this, why was he making her conspicuous before this stranger!

"I want some collection," she reasserted.

"So tha says," he replied indifferently, looking at her, then turning again to his nephew.

She went forward, and thrust her hand into his breeches pocket. He smoked stolidly, making no resistance, talking to his nephew. Her hand groped about in his pocket, and then drew out his leathern purse. Her colour was bright in her clear cheeks, her eyes shone. Brangwen's eyes were twinkling. The nephew sat sheepishly. Anna, in her finery, sat down and slid all the money into her lap. There was silver and gold. The youth could not help watching her. She was bent over the heap of money, fingering the different coins.

"I've a good mind to take half-a-sovereign," she said, and she looked up with glowing dark eyes. She met the light-brown eyes of her cousin, close and intent upon her. She was startled. She laughed quickly, and turned to her father.

"I've a good mind to take half-a-sovereign, our Dad," she said.

"Yes, nimble fingers," said her father. "You take what's your own."

"Are you coming, our Anna?" asked her brother from the door.

She suddenly chilled to normal, forgetting both her father and her cousin.

"Yes, I'm ready," she said, taking sixpence from the heap of money and sliding the rest back into the purse, which she laid on the table.

"Give it here," said her father.

Hastily she thrust the purse into his pocket and was going out.

"You'd better go wi' 'em, lad, hadn't you?" said the father to the nephew.

Will Brangwen rose uncertainly. He had golden-brown, quick, steady eyes, like a bird's, like a hawk's, which cannot look afraid.

"Your Cousin Will 'll come with you," said the father.

Anna glanced at the strange youth again. She felt him waiting there for her to notice him. He was hovering on the edge of her consciousness, ready to come in. She did not want to look at him. She was antagonistic to him.

She waited without speaking. Her cousin took his hat and joined her. It was summer outside. Her brother Fred was plucking a sprig of flowering currant to put in his coat, from the bush at the angle of the house. She took no notice. Her cousin followed just behind her.

They were on the highroad. She was aware of a strangeness in her being. It made her uncertain. She caught sight of the flowering currant in her brother's buttonhole.

"Oh, our Fred," she cried. "Don't wear that stuff to go to church."

Fred looked down protectively at the pink adornment on his breast.

"Why, I like it," he said.

"Then you're the only one who does, I'm sure," she said. And she turned to her cousin.

"Do *you* like the smell of it?" she asked.

He was there beside her, tall and uncouth and yet self-possessed. It excited her.

"I can't say whether I do or not," he replied.

"Give it here, Fred, don't have it smelling in church," she said to the little boy, her page.

Her fair, small brother handed her the flower dutifully. She sniffed it and gave it without a word to her cousin, for his judgment. He smelled the dangling flower curiously.

"It's a funny smell," he said.

And suddenly she laughed, and a quick light came on

all their faces, there was a blithe trip in the small boy's walk.

The bells were ringing, they were going up the summery hill in their Sunday clothes. Anna was very fine in a silk frock of brown and white stripes, tight along the arms and the body, bunched up very elegantly behind the skirt. There was something of the cavalier about Will Brangwen, and he was well dressed.

He walked along with the sprig of currant-blossom dangling between his fingers, and none of them spoke. The sun shone brightly on little showers of buttercup down the bank, in the fields the fool's-parsley was foamy, held very high and proud above a number of flowers that flitted in the greenish twilight of the mowing-grass below.

They reached the church. Fred led the way to the pew, followed by the cousin, then Anna. She felt very conspicuous and important. Somehow, this young man gave her away to other people. He stood aside and let her pass to her place, then sat next to her. It was a curious sensation, to sit next to him.

The colour came streaming from the painted window above her. It lit on the dark wood of the pew, on the stone, worn aisle, on the pillar behind her cousin, and on her cousin's hands, as they lay on his knees. She sat amid illumination, illumination and luminous shadow all around her, her soul very bright. She sat, without knowing it, conscious of the hands and motionless knees of her cousin. Something strange had entered into her world, something entirely strange and unlike what she knew.

She was curiously elated. She sat in a glowing world of unreality, very delightful. A brooding light, like laughter, was in her eyes. She was aware of a strange influence entering in to her, which she enjoyed. It was a dark

enrichening influence she had not known before. She did
not think of her cousin. But she was startled when his
hands moved.

She wished he would not say the responses so plainly.
It diverted her from her vague enjoyment. Why would
he obtrude and draw notice to himself? It was bad taste.
But she went on all right till the hymn came. He stood
up beside her to sing, and that pleased her. Then suddenly, at the very first word, his voice came strong and
overriding, filling the church. He was singing the tenor.
Her soul opened in amazement. His voice filled the
church! It rang out like a trumpet, and rang out again.
She started to giggle over her hymn-book. But he went
on, perfectly steady. Up and down rang his voice, going
its own way. She was helplessly shocked into laughter.
Between moments of dead silence in herself she shook
with laughter. On came the laughter, seized her and
shook her till the tears were in her eyes. She was amazed
and rather enjoyed it. And still the hymn rolled on, and
still she laughed. She bent over her hymn-book crimson
with confusion, but still her sides shook with laughter.
She pretended to cough, she pretended to have a crumb
in her throat. Fred was gazing up at her with clear blue
eyes. She was recovering herself. And then a slur in the
strong, blind voice at her side brought it all on again, in
a gust of mad laughter.

She bent down to prayer in cold reproof of herself.
And yet, as she knelt, little eddies of giggling went over
her. The very sight of his knees on the praying cushion
sent the little shock of laughter over her.

She gathered herself together and sat with prim, pure
face, white and pink and cold as a Christmas rose, her
hands in her silk gloves folded on her lap, her dark eyes
all vague, abstracted in a sort of dream, oblivious of
everything.

The sermon rolled on vaguely, in a tide of pregnant peace.

Her cousin took out his pocket-handkerchief. He seemed to be drifted absorbed into the sermon. He put his handkerchief to his face. Then something dropped on to his knee. There lay the bit of flowering currant! He was looking down at it in real astonishment. A wild snirt of laughter came from Anna. Everybody heard: it was torture. He had shut the crumpled flower in his hand and was looking up again with the same absorbed attention to the sermon. Another snirt of laughter from Anna. Fred nudged her remindingly. Her cousin sat motionless. Somehow she was aware that his face was red. She could feel him. His hand, closed over the flower, remained quite still, pretending to be normal. Another wild struggle in Anna's breast, and the snirt of laughter. She bent forward shaking with laughter. It was now no joke. Fred was nudge-nudging at her. She nudged him back fiercely. Then another vicious spasm of laughter seized her. She tried to ward it off in a little cough. The cough ended in a suppressed whoop. She wanted to die. And the closed hand crept away to the pocket. Whilst she sat in taut suspense, the laughter rushed back at her, knowing he was fumbling in his pocket to shove the flower away.

In the end, she felt weak, exhausted, and thoroughly depressed. A blankness of wincing depression came over her. She hated the presence of the other people. Her face became quite haughty. She was unaware of her cousin any more.

When the collection arrived with the last hymn, her cousin was again singing resoundingly. And still it amused her. In spite of the shameful exhibition she had made of herself, it amused her still. She listened to it in a spell of amusement. And the bag was thrust in front of her, and her sixpence was mingled in the folds of her glove. In her haste to get it out, it flipped away and went twinkling in the next pew. She stood and giggled. She could not help it: she laughed outright, a figure of shame.

"What were you laughing about, our Anna?" asked Fred, the moment they were out of the church.

"Oh, I couldn't help it," she said, in her careless, half-mocking fashion. "I don't know *why* Cousin Will's singing set me off."

"What was there in my singing to make you laugh?" he asked.

"It was so loud," she said.

They did not look at each other, but they both laughed again, both reddening.

"What were you snorting and laughing for, our Anna?" asked Tom, the elder brother, at the dinner table, his hazel eyes bright with joy. "Everybody stopped to look at you." Tom was in the choir.

She was aware of Will's eyes shining steadily upon her, waiting for her to speak.

"It was Cousin Will's singing," she said.

At which her cousin burst into a suppressed, chuckling laugh, suddenly showing all his small, regular, rather sharp teeth, and just as quickly closing his mouth again.

"Has he got such a remarkable voice on him then?" asked Brangwen.

"No, it's not that," said Anna. "Only it tickled me—I couldn't tell you why."

And again a ripple of laughter went down the table.

Will Brangwen thrust forward his dark face, his eyes dancing, and said:

"I'm in the choir of St. Nicholas."

"Oh, you go to church then!" said Brangwen.

"Mother does—father doesn't," replied the youth.

It was the little things, his movement, the funny tones of his voice, that showed up big to Anna. The matter-of-fact things he said were absurd in contrast. The things her father said seemed meaningless and neutral.

During the afternoon they sat in the parlour that smelled of geranium and they ate cherries and talked. Will Brangwen was called on to give himself forth. And soon he was drawn out.

He was interested in churches, in church architecture. The influence of Ruskin had stimulated him to a pleasure in the medieval forms. His talk was fragmentary, he was only half articulate. But listening to him, as he spoke of church after church, of nave and chancel and transept, of rood-screen and font, of hatchet-carving and moulding and tracery, speaking always with close passion of particular things, particular places, there gathered in her heart a pregnant hush of churches, a mystery, a ponderous significance of bowed stone, a dim-coloured light through which something took place obscurely, passing into darkness: a high, delighted framework of the mystic screen, and beyond, in the furthest beyond, the altar. It was a very real experience. She was carried away. And the land seemed to be covered with a vast, mystic church, reserved in gloom, thrilled with an unknown Presence.

Almost it hurt her, to look out of the window and see the lilacs towering in the vivid sunshine. Or was this the jewelled glass?

He talked of Gothic and Renaissance and Perpendicular, and Early English and Norman. The words thrilled her.

"Have you been to Southwell?" he said. "I was there at twelve o'clock at midday, eating my lunch in the churchyard. And the bells played a hymn.

"Ay, it's a fine Minster, Southwell, heavy. It's got

heavy, round arches, rather low, on thick pillars. It's grand, the way those arches travel forward.

"There's a sedilia as well—pretty. But I like the main body of the church—and that north porch——"

He was very much excited and filled with himself that afternoon. A flame kindled round him, making his experience passionate and glowing, burningly real.

His uncle listened with twinkling eyes, half-moved. His aunt bent forward her dark face, half-moved, but held by other knowledge. Anna went with him.

He returned to his lodging at night treading quick, his eyes glittering, and his face shining darkly as if he came from some passionate, vital tryst.

The glow remained in him, the fire burned, his heart was fierce like a sun. He enjoyed his unknown life and his own self. And he was ready to go back to the Marsh.

Without knowing it, Anna was wanting him to come. In him she had escaped. In him the bounds of her experience were transgressed: he was the hole in the wall, beyond which the sunshine blazed on an outside world.

He came. Sometimes, not often, but sometimes, talking again, there recurred the strange, remote reality which carried everything before it. Sometimes, he talked of his father, whom he hated with a hatred that was burningly close to love, of his mother, whom he loved with a love that was keenly close to hatred, or to revolt. His sentences were clumsy, he was only half articulate. But he had the wonderful voice, that could ring its vibration through the girl's soul, transport her into his feeling. Sometimes his voice was hot and declamatory, sometimes it had a strange, twanging, almost catlike sound, sometimes it hesitated, puzzled, sometimes there was the break of a little laugh. Anna was taken by him. She loved the running flame that coursed through her as she listened to him. And his mother and his father became to her two separate people in her life.

For some weeks the youth came frequently, and was received gladly by them all. He sat amongst them, his dark face glowing, an eagerness and a touch of derisiveness on his wide mouth, something grinning and twisted, his eyes always shining like a bird's, utterly without depth. There was no getting hold of the fellow, Brangwen irritably thought. He was like a grinning young tom-cat, that came when he thought he would, and without cognizance of the other person.

At first the youth had looked towards Tom Brangwen when he talked; and then he looked towards his aunt, for her appreciation, valuing it more than his uncle's; and then he turned to Anna, because from her he got what he wanted, which was not in the elder people.

So that the two young people, from being always attendant on the elder, began to draw apart and establish a separate kingdom. Sometimes Tom Brangwen was irritated. His nephew irritated him. The lad seemed to him too special, self-contained. His nature was fierce enough, but too much abstracted, like a separate thing, like a cat's nature. A cat could lie perfectly peacefully on the hearthrug whilst its master or mistress writhed in agony a yard away. It had nothing to do with other people's affairs. What did the lad really care about anything, save his own instinctive affairs?

Brangwen was irritated. Nevertheless he liked and respected his nephew. Mrs. Brangwen was irritated by Anna, who was suddenly changed, under the influence of the youth. The mother liked the boy: he was not quite an outsider. But she did not like her daughter to be so much under the spell.

So that gradually the two young people drew apart,

escaped from the elders, to create a new thing by themselves. He worked in the garden to propitiate his uncle. He talked churches to propitiate his aunt. He followed Anna like a shadow: like a long, persistent, unswerving black shadow he went after the girl. It irritated Brangwen exceedingly. It exasperated him beyond bearing, to see the lit up grin, the cat grin as he called it, on his nephew's face.

And Anna had a new reserve, a new independence. Suddenly she began to act independently of her parents, to live beyond them. Her mother had flashes of anger.

But the courtship went on. Anna would find occasion to go shopping in Ilkeston at evening. She always returned with her cousin; he walking with his head over her shoulder, a little bit behind her, like the Devil looking over Lincoln, as Brangwen noted angrily and yet with satisfaction.

To his own wonder, Will Brangwen found himself in an electric state of passion. To his wonder, he had stopped her at the gate as they came home from Ilkeston one night, and had kissed her, blocking her way and kissing her whilst he felt as if some blow were struck at him in the dark. And when they went indoors, he was acutely angry that her parents looked up scrutizingly at him and her. What right had they there: why should they look up! Let them remove themselves, or look elsewhere.

And the youth went home with the stars in heaven whirling fiercely about the blackness of his head, and his heart fierce, insistent, but fierce as if he felt something baulking him. He wanted to smash through something.

A spell was cast over her. And how uneasy her parents were, as she went about the house unnoticing, not noticing them, moving in a spell as if she were invisible to them. She *was* invisible to them. It made them angry.

Yet they had to submit. She went about absorbed, obscured for a while.

Over him too the darkness of obscurity settled. He seemed to be hidden in a tense, electric darkness, in which his soul, his life, was intensely active, but without his aid or attention. His mind was obscured. He worked swiftly and mechanically, and he produced some beautiful things.

His favourite work was woodcarving. The first thing he made for her was a butter-stamper. In it he carved a mythological bird, a phœnix, something like an eagle rising on symmetrical wings, from a circle of very beautiful flickering flames that rose upwards from the rim of the cup.

Anna thought nothing of the gift on the evening when he gave it to her. In the morning, however, when the butter was made, she fetched his seal in place of the old wooden stamper of oak-leaves and acorns. She was curiously excited to see how it would turn out. Strange, the uncouth bird moulded there, in the cup-like hollow, with curious, thick waverings running inwards from a smooth rim. She pressed another mould. Strange, to lift the stamp and see that eagle-beaked bird raising its breast to her. She loved creating it over and over again. And every time she looked, it seemed a new thing come to life. Every piece of butter became this strange, vital emblem.

She showed it to her mother and father.

"That is beautiful," said her mother, a little light coming on to her face.

"Beautiful!" exclaimed the father, puzzled, fretted. "Why, what sort of a bird does he call it?"

And this was the question put by the customers during the next weeks.

"What sort of a bird do you call *that*, as you've got on th' butter?"

When he came in the evening, she took him into the dairy to show him.

"Do you like it?" he asked, in his loud, vibrating voice that always sounded strange, re-echoing in the dark places of her being.

They very rarely touched each other. They liked to be alone together, near to each other, but there was still a distance between them.

In the cool dairy the candle-light lit on the large, white surfaces of the cream pans. He turned his head sharply. It was so cool and remote in there, so remote. His mouth was open in a little, strained laugh. She stood with her head bent, turned aside. He wanted to go near to her. He had kissed her once. Again his eye rested on the round blocks of butter, where the emblematic bird lifted its breast from the shadow cast by the candle flame. What was restraining him? Her breast was near him; his head lifted like an eagle's. She did not move. Suddenly, with an incredibly quick, delicate movement, he put his arms round her and drew her to him. It was quick, cleanly done, like a bird that swoops and sinks close, closer.

He was kissing her throat. She turned and looked at him. Her eyes were dark and flowing with fire. His eyes were hard and bright with a fierce purpose and gladness, like a hawk's. She felt him flying into the dark space of her flames, like a brand, like a gleaming hawk.

They had looked at each other, and seen each other strange, yet near, very near, like a hawk stooping, swooping, dropping into a flame of darkness. So she took the candle and they went back to the kitchen.

They went on in this way for some time, always coming together, but rarely touching, very seldom did they kiss. And then, often, it was merely a touch of the lips, a sign. But her eyes began to waken with a constant fire, she paused often in the midst of her transit, as if to recollect something, or to discover something.

And his face became sombre, intent, he did not readily hear what was said to him.

One evening in August he came when it was raining. He came in with his jacket collar turned up, his jacket buttoned close, his face wet. And he looked so slim and definite, coming out of the chill rain, she was suddenly blinded with love for him. Yet he sat and talked with her father and mother, meaninglessly, whilst her blood seethed to anguish in her. She wanted to touch him now, only to touch him.

There was the queer, abstract look on her silvery radiant face that maddened her father, her dark eyes were hidden. But she raised them to the youth. And they were dark with a flare that made him quail for a moment.

She went into the second kitchen and took a lantern. Her father watched her as she returned.

"Come with me, Will," she said to her cousin. "I want to see if I put the brick over where that rat comes in."

"You've no need to do that," retorted her father. She took no notice. The youth was between the two wills. The colour mounted into the father's face, his blue eyes stared. The girl stood near the door, her head held slightly back, like an indication that the youth must come. He rose, in his silent, intent way, and was gone with her. The blood swelled in Brangwen's forehead veins.

It was raining. The light of the lantern flashed on the cobbled path and the bottom of the wall. She came to a small ladder, and climbed up. He reached her the lantern and followed. Up there in the fowl-loft, the birds sat in fat bunches on the perches, the red combs shining like fire. Bright, sharp eyes opened. There was a sharp crawk of expostulation as one of the hens shifted over. The cock sat watching, his yellow neck-feathers bright as glass. Anna went across the dirty floor. Brangwen crouched in the loft watching. The light was soft under the red, naked tiles. The girl crouched in a corner. There was another explosive bustle of a hen springing from her perch.

Anna came back, stooping under the perches. He was waiting for her near the door. Suddenly she had her arms round him, was clinging close to him, cleaving her body against his, and crying, in a whispering, whimpering sound.

"Will, I love you, I love you, Will, I love you." It sounded as if it were tearing her.

He was not even very much surprised. He held her in his arms and his bones melted. He leaned back against the wall. The door of the loft was open. Outside, the rain slanted by in fine, steely, mysterious haste, emerging out of the gulf of darkness. He held her in his arms, and he and she together seemed to be swinging in big, swooping oscillations, the two of them clasped together up in the darkness. Outside the open door of the loft in which they stood, beyond them and below them, was darkness, with a travelling veil of rain.

"I love you, Will, I love you," she moaned, "I love you, Will."

He held her as though they were one, and was silent.

In the house, Tom Brangwen waited a while. Then he got up and went out. He went down the yard. He saw the curious misty shaft coming from the loft door. He scarcely knew it was the light in the rain. He went on till the illumination fell on him dimly. Then looking up, through the blurr, he saw the youth and the girl together, the youth with his back against the wall, his head sunk over the head of the girl. The elder man saw them, blurred through the rain, but lit up. They thought themselves so buried in the night. He even saw the lighted dryness of the loft behind, and shadows and bunches of roosting fowls, up in the night, strange shadows cast from the lantern on the floor.

And a black gloom of anger, and a tenderness of self-effacement, fought in his heart. She did not understand what she was doing. She betrayed herself. She was a child, a mere child. She did not know how much of herself she was squandering. And he was blackly and furiously miserable. Was he then an old man, that he should be giving her away in marriage? Was he old? He was not old. He was younger than that young thoughtless fellow in whose arms she lay. Who knew her—he or that blind-headed youth? To whom did she belong, if not to himself?

He thought again of the child he had carried out at night into the barn, whilst his wife was in labour with the young Tom. He remembered the soft, warm weight of the little girl on his arm, round his neck. Now she would say he was finished. She was going away, to deny him, to leave an unendurable emptiness in him, a void that he could not bear. Almost he hated her. How dared she say he was old. He walked on in the rain, sweating with pain, with the horror of being old, with the agony of having to relinquish what was life to him.

Will Brangwen went home without having seen his uncle. He held his hot face to the rain, and walked on in a trance. "I love you, Will, I love you." The words repeated themselves endlessly. The veils had ripped and issued him naked into the endless space, and he shuddered. The walls had thrust him out and given him a vast space to walk in. Whither, through this darkness of infinite space, was he walking blindly? Where, at the

end of all the darkness, was God the Almighty still
darkly seated, thrusting him on? "I love you, Will, I love
you." He trembled with fear as the words beat in his
heart again. And he dared not think of her face, of her
eyes which shone, and of her strange, transfigured face.
The hand of the Hidden Almighty, burning bright, had
thrust out of the darkness and gripped him. He went on
subject and in fear, his heart gripped and burning from
the touch.

The days went by, they ran on dark-padded feet in
silence. He went to see Anna, but again there had come
a reserve between them. Tom Brangwen was gloomy,
his blue eyes sombre. Anna was strange and delivered
up. Her face in its delicate colouring was mute, touched
dumb and poignant. The mother bowed her head and
moved in her own dark world, that was pregnant again
with fulfilment.

Will Brangwen worked at his woodcarving. It was a
passion, a passion for him to have the chisel under his
grip. Verily the passion of his heart lifted the fine bite of
steel. He was carving, as he had always wanted, the
Creation of Eve. It was a panel in low relief, for a
church. Adam lay asleep as if suffering, and God, a dim,
large figure, stooped towards him, stretching forward
His unveiled hand; and Eve, a small vivid, naked female
shape, was issuing like a flame towards the hand of God,
from the torn side of Adam.

Now, Will Brangwen was working at the Eve. She
was thin, a keen, unripe thing. With trembling passion,
fine as a breath of air, he sent the chisel over her belly,
her hard, unripe, small belly. She was a stiff little figure,
with sharp lines, in the throes and torture and ecstasy
of her creation. But he trembled as he touched her. He
had not finished any of his figures. There was a bird on
a bough overhead, lifting its wings for flight, and a ser-

pent wreathing up to it. It was not finished yet. He trembled with passion, at last able to create the new, sharp
body of his Eve.

At the sides, at the far sides, at either end, were two
Angels covering their faces with their wings. They were
like trees. As he went to the Marsh, in the twilight, he
felt that the Angels, with covered faces, were standing
back as he went by. The darkness was of their shadows
and the covering of their faces. When he went through
the Canal bridge, the evening glowed in its last deep
colours, the sky was dark blue, the stars glittered from
afar, very remote and approaching above the darkening
cluster of the farm, above the paths of crystal along the
edge of the heavens.

She waited for him like the glow of light, and as if his
face were covered. And he dared not lift his face to look
at her.

Corn harvest came on. One evening they walked out
through the farm buildings at nightfall. A large gold
moon hung heavily to the grey horizon, trees hovered
tall, standing back in the dusk, waiting. Anna and the
young man went on noiselessly by the hedge, along
where the farm-carts had made dark ruts in the grass.
They came through a gate into a wide open field where
still much light seemed to spread against their faces. In
the under-shadow the sheaves lay on the ground where
the reapers had left them, many sheaves like bodies
prostrate in shadowy bulk; others were riding hazily in
shocks, like ships in the haze of moonlight and of dusk,
further off.

They did not want to turn back, yet whither were
they to go, towards the moon? For they were separate,
single.

"We will put up some sheaves," said Anna. So they
could remain there in the broad, open place.

They went across the stubble to where the long rows of upreared shocks ended. Curiously populous that part of the field looked, where the shocks rode erect; the rest was open and prostrate.

The air was all hoary silver. She looked around her. Trees stood vaguely at their distance, as if waiting, like heralds, for the signal to approach. In this space of vague crystal her heart seemed like a bell ringing. She was afraid lest the sound should be heard.

"You take this row," she said to the youth, and passing on, she stooped in the next row of lying sheaves, grasping her hands in the tresses of the oats, lifting the heavy corn in either hand, carrying it, as it hung heavily against her, to the cleared space, where she set the two sheaves sharply down, bringing them·together with a faint, keen clash. Her two bulks stood leaning together. He was coming, walking shadowily with the gossamer dusk, carrying his two sheaves. She waited near by. He set his sheaves with a keen, faint clash, next to her sheaves. They rode unsteadily. He tangled the tresses of corn. It hissed like a fountain. He looked up and laughed.

Then she turned away towards the moon, which seemed glowingly to uncover her bosom every time she faced it. He went to the vague emptiness of the field opposite, dutifully.

They stooped, grasped the wet, soft hair of the corn, lifted the heavy bundles, and returned. She was always first. She set down her sheaves, making a pent house with those others. He was coming shadowy across the stubble, carrying his bundles. She turned away, hearing only the sharp hiss of his mingling corn. She walked between the moon and his shadowy figure.

She took her new two sheaves and walked towards him, as he rose from stooping over the earth. He was coming out of the near distance. She set down her sheaves to make a new stook. They were unsure. Her hands fluttered. Yet she broke away, and turned to the moon, which laid bare her bosom, so she felt as if her bosom were heaving and panting with moonlight. And he had to put up her two sheaves, which had fallen down. He worked in silence. The rhythm of the work carried him away again, as she was coming near.

They worked together, coming and going, in a rhythm, which carried their feet and their bodies in tune. She stooped, she lifted the burden of sheaves, she turned her face to the dimness where he was, and went with her burden over the stubble. She hesitated, set down her sheaves, there was a swish and hiss of mingling oats, he was drawing near, and she must turn again. And there was the flaring moon laying bare her bosom again, making her drift and ebb like a wave.

He worked steadily, engrossed, threading backwards and forwards like a shuttle across the strip of cleared stubble, weaving the long line of riding shocks, nearer and nearer to the shadowy trees, threading his sheaves with hers.

And always, she was gone before he came. As he came, she drew away, as he drew away, she came. Were they never to meet? Gradually a low, deep-sounding will in him vibrated to her, tried to set her in accord, tried to bring her gradually to him, to a meeting, till they should be together, till they should meet as the sheaves that swished together.

And the work went on. The moon grew brighter, clearer, the corn glistened. He bent over the prostrate bundles, there was a hiss as the sheaves left the ground, a trailing of heavy bodies against him, a dazzle of moonlight on his eyes. And then he was setting the corn together at the stook. And she was coming near.

He waited for her, he fumbled at the stook. She came.
But she stood back till he drew away. He saw her in
shadow, a dark column, and spoke to her, and she answered. She saw the moonlight flash question on his
face. But there was a space between them, and he went
away, the work carried them, rhythmic.

Why was there always a space between them, why
were they apart? Why, as she came up from under the
moon, would she halt and stand off from him? Why was
he held away from her? His will drummed persistently,
darkly, it drowned everything else.

Into the rhythm of his work there came a pulse and a
steadied purpose. He stooped, he lifted the weight, he
heaved it towards her, setting it as in her, under the
moonlit space. And he went back for more. Ever with increasing closeness he lifted the sheaves and swung striding to the centre with them, ever he drove her more
nearly to the meeting, ever he did his share, and drew
towards her, overtaking her. There was only the moving
to and fro in the moonlight, engrossed, the swinging in
the silence, that was marked only by the splash of
sheaves, and silence, and a splash of sheaves. And ever
the splash of his sheaves broke swifter, beating up to
hers, and ever the splash of her sheaves recurred monotonously, unchanging, and ever the splash of his
sheaves beat nearer.

Till at last, they met at the shock, facing each other,
sheaves in hand. And he was silvery with moonlight,
with a moonlit, shadowy face that frightened her. She
waited for him.

"Put yours down," she said.

"No, it's your turn." His voice was twanging and insistent.

She set her sheaves against the shock. He saw her
hands glisten among the spray of grain. And he dropped

his sheaves and he trembled as he took her in his arms. He had overtaken her, and it was his privilege to kiss her. She was sweet and fresh with the night air, and sweet with the scent of grain. And the whole rhythm of him beat into his kisses, and still he pursued her, in his kisses, and still she was not quite overcome. He wondered over the moonlight on her nose! All the moonlight upon her, all the darkness within her! All the night in his arms, darkness and shine, he possessed of it all! All the night for him now, to unfold, to venture within, all the mystery to be entered, all the discovery to be made.

Trembling with keen triumph, his heart was white as a star as he drove his kisses nearer.

"My love!" she called, in a low voice, from afar. The low sound seemed to call to him from far off, under the moon, to him who was unaware. He stopped, quivered, and listened.

"My love," came again the low, plaintive call, like a bird unseen in the night.

He was afraid. His heart quivered and broke. He was stopped.

"Anna," he said, as if he answered her from a distance, unsure.

"My love."

And he drew near, and she drew near.

"Anna," he said, in wonder and birthpain of love.

"My love," she said, her voice growing rapturous. And they kissed on the mouth, in rapture and surprise, long, real kisses. The kiss lasted, there among the moonlight. He kissed her again, and she kissed him. And again they were kissing together. Till something happened in him, he was strange. He wanted her. He wanted her exceedingl, She was something new. They stood there folded, suspended in the night. And his whole being quivered with surprise, as from a blow. He wanted her and he wanted to tell her so. But the shock was too great to him. He had never realized before. He trembled with irritation and unusedness, he did not know what to do. He held her more gently, gently, much more gently. The conflict was gone by. And he was glad, and breathless, and almost in tears. But he knew he wanted her. Something fixed in him for ever. He was hers. And he was very glad and afraid. He did not know what to do, as they stood there in the open, moonlit field. He looked through her hair at the moon, which seemed to swim liquid-bright.

She sighed, and seemed to wake up, then she kissed him again. Then she loosened herself away from him and took his hand. It hurt him when she drew away from his breast. It hurt him with a chagrin. Why did she draw away from him? But she held his hand.

"I want to go home," she said, looking at him in a way he could not understand.

He held close to her hand. He was dazed and he could not move, he did not know how to move. She drew him away.

He walked helplessly beside her, holding her hand. She went with bent head. Suddenly he said, as the simple solution stated itself to him:

"We'll get married, Anna."

She was silent.

"We'll get married, Anna, shall we?"

She stopped in the field again and kissed him, clinging to him passionately, in a way he could not understand. He could not understand. But he left it all now, to marriage. That was the solution now, fixed ahead. He wanted her, he wanted to be married to her, he wanted to have her altogether, as his own for ever. And he waited, intent, for the accomplishment. But there was all the while a slight tension of irritation.

He spoke to his uncle and aunt that night.

"Uncle," he said, "Anna and me think of getting married."

"Oh ay!" said Brangwen.

"But how, you have no money?" said the mother.

The youth went pale. He hated these words. But he was like a gleaming, bright pebble, something bright and inalterable. He did not think. He sat there in his hard brightness, and did not speak.

"Have you mentioned it to your own mother?" asked Brangwen.

"No—I'll tell her on Saturday."

"You'll go and see her?"

"Yes."

There was a long pause.

"And what are you going to marry on—your pound a week?"

Again the youth went pale, as if the spirit were being injured in him.

"I don't know," he said, looking at his uncle with his bright inhuman eyes, like a hawk's.

Brangwen stirred in hatred.

"It needs knowing," he said.

"I shall have the money later on," said the nephew. "I will raise some now, and pay it back then."

"Oh, ay! And why this desperate hurry? She's a child of eighteen, and you're a boy of twenty. You're neither of you of age to do as you like yet."

Will Brangwen ducked his head and looked at his uncle with swift, bright mistrustful eyes, like a caged hawk.

"What does it matter how old she is, and how old I am?" he said. "What's the difference between me now and when I'm thirty?"

"A big difference, let us hope."

"But you have no experience—you have no experience, and no money. Why do you want to marry, without experience or money?" asked the aunt.

"What experience do I want, Aunt?" asked the boy.

And if Brangwen's heart had not been hard and intact with anger, like a precious stone, he would have agreed.

Will Brangwen went home strange and untouched. He felt he could not alter from what he was fixed upon, his will was set. To alter it he must be destroyed. And he would not be destroyed. He had no money. But he would get some from somewhere, it did not matter. He lay awake for many hours, hard and clear and unthinking, his soul crystallizing more inalterably. Then he went fast asleep.

It was as if his soul had turned into a hard crystal. He might tremble and quiver and suffer, it did not alter.

The next morning Tom Brangwen, inhuman with anger, spoke to Anna.

"What's this about wanting to get married?" he said.

She stood, paling a little, her dark eyes springing to the hostile, startled look of a savage thing that will defend itself, but trembles with sensitiveness.

"I do," she said, out of her unconsciousness.

His anger rose, and he would have liked to break her.

"You do—you do—and what for?" he sneered with contempt. The old, childish agony, the blindness that could recognize nobody, the palpitating antagonism as of a raw, helpless, undefended thing, came back on her.

"I do because I do," she cried, in the shrill, hysterical way of her childhood. "*You* are not my father—my father is dead—*you* are not my father."

She was still a stranger. She did not recognize him The cold blade cut down, deep into Brangwen's soul. It cut him off from her.

"And what if I'm not?" he said.

But he could not bear it. It had been so passionately dear to him, her "Father—Daddy."

He went about for some days as if stunned. His wife was bemused. She did not understand. She only thought the marriage was impeded for want of money and position.

There was a horrible silence in the house. Anna kept out of sight as much as possible. She could be for hours alone.

Will Brangwen came back, after stupid scenes at Nottingham. He too was pale and blank, but unchanging. His uncle hated him. He hated this youth, who was so inhuman and obstinate. Nevertheless, it was to Will Brangwen that the uncle, one evening, handed over the shares which he had transferred to Anna Lensky. They were for two thousand five hundred pounds. Will Brangwen looked at his uncle. It was a great deal of the Marsh capital here given away. The youth, however, was only colder and more fixed. He was abstract, purely a fixed will. He gave the shares to Anna.

After which she cried for a whole day, sobbing her eyes out. And at night, when she had heard her mother go to bed, she slipped down and hung in the doorway. Her father sat in his heavy silence, like a monument. He turned his head slowly.

"Daddy," she cried from the doorway, and she ran to him sobbing as if her heart would break. "Daddy—daddy—daddy."

She crouched on the hearthrug with her arms round him and her face against him. His body was so big and comfortable. But something hurt her head intolerably. She sobbed almost with hysteria.

He was silent, with his hand on her shoulder. His heart was bleak. He was not her father. That beloved image she had broken. Who was he then? A man put apart with those whose life has no more developments. He was isolated from her. There was a generation between them, he was old, he had died out from hot life. A great deal of ash was in his fire, cold ash. He felt the inevitable coldness, and in bitterness forgot the fire. He sat in his coldness of age and isolation. He had his own wife. And he blamed himself, he sneered at himself, for this clinging to the young, wanting the young to belong to him.

The child who clung to him wanted her child-husband. As was natural. And from him, Brangwen, she wanted help, so that her life might be properly fitted out. But love she did not want. Why should there be love between them, between the stout, middle-aged man and this child? How could there be anything between them, but mere human willingness to help each other? He was her guardian, no more. His heart was like ice, his face cold and expressionless. She could not move him any more than a statue.

She crept to bed and cried. But she was going to be married to Will Brangwen, and then she need not bother any more. Brangwen went to bed with a hard, cold heart, and cursed himself. He looked at his wife. She was still his wife. Her dark hair was threaded with grey, her face was beautiful in its gathering age. She was just fifty. How poignantly he saw her! And he wanted to cut out some of his own heart, which was incontinent, and demanded still to share the rapid life of youth. How he hated himself.

His wife was so poignant and timely. She was still young and naïve, with some girl's freshness. But she did not want any more the fight, the battle, the control, as he, in his incontinence, still did. She was so natural, and he was ugly, unnatural, in his inability to yield place.

How hideous, this greedy middle-age, which must stand in the way of life, like a large demon.

What was missing in his life, that, in his ravening soul, he was not satisfied? He had had that friend at school, his mother, his wife, and Anna? What had he done? He had failed with his friend, he had been a poor son; but he had known satisfaction with his wife, let it be enough; he loathed himself for the state he was in over Anna. Yet he was *not* satisfied. It was agony to know it.

Was his life nothing? Had he nothing to show, no work? He did not count his work, anybody could have done it. What had he known but the long marital embrace with his wife! Curious, that this was what his life amounted to! At any rate, it was something, it was eternal. He would say so to anybody and be proud of it. He lay with his wife in his arms, and she was still his fulfilment, just the same as ever. And that was the be-all and the end-all. Yes, and he was proud of it.

But the bitterness, underneath, that there still remained an unsatisfied Tom Brangwen, who suffered agony, because a girl cared nothing for him. He loved his sons—he had them also. But it was the further, the creative life with the girl, he wanted as well. Oh, and he was ashamed. He trampled himself to extinguish himself.

What weariness! There was no peace, however old one grew! One was never right, never decent, never master of oneself. It was as if his hope had been in the girl.

Anna quickly lapsed again into her love for the youth. Will Brangwen had fixed his marriage for the Saturday before Christmas. And he waited for her, in his bright, unquestioning fashion, until then. He wanted her, she was his, he suspended his being till the day should come. The wedding day, December the twenty-third, had come into being for him as an absolute thing. He lived in it.

He did not count the days. But like a man who journeys in a ship, he was suspended till the coming to port.

He worked at his carving, he worked in his office, he came to see her; all was but a form of waiting, without thought or question.

She was much more alive. She wanted to enjoy courtship. He seemed to come and go like the wind, without asking why or whither. But she wanted to enjoy his presence. For her, he was the kernel of life, to touch him alone was bliss. But for him, she was the essence of life. She existed as much when he was at his carving in his lodging in Ilkeston, as when she sat looking at him in the Marsh kitchen. In himself, he knew her. But his outward faculties seemed suspended. He did not see her with his eyes, nor hear her with his voice.

And yet he trembled, sometimes into a kind of swoon, holding her in his arms. They would stand sometimes folded together in the barn, in silence. Then to her, as she felt his young, tense figure with her hands, the bliss was intolerable, intolerable the sense that she possessed him. For his body was so keen and wonderful, it was the only reality in her world. In her world, there was this one tense, vivid body of a man, and then many other shadowy men, all unreal. In him, she touched the centre of reality. And they were together, he and she, at the heart of the secret. How she clutched him to her, his body the central body of all life. Out of the rock of his form the very fountain of life flowed.

But to him, she was a flame that consumed him. The flame flowed up his limbs, flowed through him, till he was consumed, till he existed only as an unconscious, dark transit of flame, deriving from her.

Sometimes, in the darkness, a cow coughed. There was, in the darkness, a slow sound of cud chewing. And it all seemed to flow round them and upon them as the hot blood flows through the womb, laving the unborn young.

Sometimes, when it was cold, they stood to be lovers in the stables, where the air was warm and sharp with ammonia. And during these dark vigils, he learned to know her, her body against his, they drew nearer and nearer together, the kisses came more subtly close and fitting. So when in the thick darkness a horse suddenly scrambled to its feet, with a dull, thunderous sound, they listened as one person listening, they knew as one person, they were conscious of the horse.

Tom Brangwen had taken them a cottage at Cossethay, on a twenty-one years' lease. Will Brangwen's eyes lit up as he saw it. It was the cottage next the church, with dark yew trees, very black old trees, along the side of the house and the grassy front garden; a red, squarish cottage with a low slate roof, and low windows. It had a long dairy-scullery, a big flagged kitchen, and a low parlour, that went up one step from the kitchen. There were whitewashed beams across the ceilings, and odd corners with cupboards. Looking out through the windows, there was the grassy garden, the procession of black yew trees down one side, and along the other sides, a red wall with ivy separating the place from the highroad and the churchyard. The old, little church, with its small spire on a square tower, seemed to be looking back at the cottage windows.

"There'll be no need to have a clock," said Will Brangwen, peeping out at the white clock-face on the tower, his neighbour.

At the back of the house was a garden adjoining the paddock, a cowshed with standing for two cows, pig-cotes and fowl-houses. Will Brangwen was very happy. Anna was glad to think of being mistress of her own place.

Tom Brangwen was now the fairy godfather. He was never happy unless he was buying something. Will Brangwen, with his interest in all woodwork, was getting the furniture. He was left to buy tables and round-staved chairs and the dressers, quite ordinary stuff, but such as was identified with his cottage.

Tom Brangwen, with more particular thought, spied out what he called handy little things for her. He appeared with a set of new-fangled cooking-pans, with a special sort of hanging lamp, though the rooms were so low, with canny little machines for grinding meat or mashing potatoes or whisking eggs.

Anna took a sharp interest in what he bought, though she was not always pleased. Some of the little contrivances, which he thought so canny, left her doubtful. Nevertheless she was always expectant, on market days there was always a long thrill of anticipation. He arrived with the first darkness, the copper lamps of his cart glowing. And she ran to the gate, as he, a dark, burly figure up in the cart, was bending over his parcels.

"It's cupboard love as brings you out so sharp," he said, his voice resounding in the cold darkness. Nevertheless he was excited. And she, taking one of the cart lamps, poked and peered among the jumble of things he had brought, pushing aside the oil or implements he had got for himself.

She dragged out a pair of small, strong bellows, registered them in her mind, and then pulled uncertainly at something else. It had a long handle, and a piece of brown paper round the middle of it, like a waist-coat.

"What's this?" she said, poking.

He stopped to look at her. She went to the lamp-light by the horse, and stood there bent over the new thing, while her hair was like bronze, her apron white and cheerful. Her fingers plucked busily at the paper. She dragged forth a little wringer, with clean india-rubber rollers. She examined it critically, not knowing quite how it worked.

She looked up at him. He stood a shadowy presence beyond the light.

"How does it go?" she asked.

"Why, it's for pulpin' turnips," he replied.

She looked at him. His voice disturbed her.

"Don't be silly. It's a little mangle," she said. "How do you stand it, though?"

"You screw it on th' side o' your wash-tub." He came and held it out to her.

"Oh, yes!" she cried, with one of her little skipping movements, which still came when she was suddenly glad.

And without another thought she ran off into the house, leaving him to untackle the horse. And when he came into the scullery, he found her there, with the little wringer fixed on the dolly-tub, turning blissfully at the handle, and Tilly beside her, exclaiming:

"My word, that's a natty little thing! That'll save you luggin' your inside out. That's the latest contraption, that is."

And Anna turned away at the handle, with great gusto of possession. Then she let Tilly have a turn.

"It fair runs by itself," said Tilly, turning on and on. "Your clothes'll nip out on to th' line."

V. WEDDING AT THE MARSH

IT WAS a beautiful sunny day for the wedding, a muddy earth but a bright sky. They had three cabs and two big closed-in vehicles. Everybody crowded in the parlour in excitement. Anna was still upstairs. Her father kept taking a nip of brandy. He was handsome in his black coat and grey trousers. His voice was hearty but troubled. His wife came down in dark grey silk with lace, and a touch of peacock-blue in her bonnet. Her little body was very sure and definite. Brangwen was thankful she was there, to sustain him among all these people.

The carriages! The Nottingham Mrs. Brangwen, in silk brocade, stands in the doorway saying who must go with whom. There is a great bustle. The front door is opened, and the wedding guests are walking down the garden path, whilst those still waiting peer through the window, and the little crowd at the gate gorps and stretches. How funny such dressed-up people look in the winter sunshine!

They are gone—another lot! There begins to be more room. Anna comes down blushing and very shy, to be viewed in her white silk and her veil. Her mother-in-law surveys her objectively, twitches the white train, arranges the folds of the veil and asserts herself.

Loud exclamations from the window that the bridegroom's carriage has just passed.

"Where's your hat, father, and your gloves?" cries the bride, stamping her white slipper, her eyes flashing through her veil. He hunts round—his hair is ruffled. Everybody has gone but the bride and her father. He is ready—his face very red and daunted. Tilly dithers in the little porch, waiting to open the door. A waiting woman walks round Anna, who asks:

"Am I all right?"

She is ready. She bridles herself and looks queenly. She waves her hand sharply to her father:

"Come here!"

He goes. She puts her hand very lightly on his arm, and holding her bouquet like a shower, stepping, oh, very graciously, just a little impatient with her father for being so red in the face, she sweeps slowly past the fluttering Tilly, and down the path. There are hoarse shouts at the gate, and all her floating foamy whiteness passes slowly in to the cab.

Her father notices her slim ankle and foot as she steps up: a child's foot. His heart is hard with tenderness. But she is in ecstasies with herself for making such a lovely spectacle. All the way she sat flamboyant with bliss because it was all so lovely. She looked down solicitously at her bouquet: white roses and lilies-of-the-valley and tube-roses and maidenhair fern—very rich and cascade-like.

Her father sat bewildered with all this strangeness, his heart was so full it felt hard, and he couldn't think of anything.

The church was decorated for Christmas, dark with evergreens, cold and snowy with white flowers. He went vaguely down to the altar. How long was it since he had gone to be married himself? He was not sure whether he was going to be married now, or what he had come for. He had a troubled notion that he had to do something or other. He saw his wife's bonnet, and wondered why *she* wasn't there with him.

They stood before the altar. He was staring up at the east window, that glowed intensely, a sort of blue purple: it was deep blue glowing, and some crimson, and little yellow flowers held fast in veins of shadow, in a heavy web of darkness. How it burned alive in radiance among its black web.

"Who giveth this woman to be married to this man?" He felt somebody touch him. He started. The words still re-echoed in his memory, but were drawing off.

"Me," he said hastily.

Anna bent her head and smiled in her veil. How absurd he was!

Brangwen was staring away at the burning blue window at the back of the altar and wondering vaguely, with pain, if he ever should get old, if he ever should feel arrived and established. He was here at Anna's wedding. Well, what right had he to feel responsible, like a father? He was still as unsure and unfixed as when he had married himself. His wife and he! With a pang of anguish he realized what uncertainties they both were. He was a man of forty-five. Forty-five! In five more years fifty. Then sixty—then seventy—then it was finished. My God—and one still was so unestablished!

How did one grow old—how could one become confident? He wished he felt older. Why, what difference was there, as far as he felt matured or completed, between him now and him at his own wedding? He might be getting married over again—he and his wife. He felt himself tiny, a little, upright figure on a plain circled round with the immense, roaring sky: he and his wife, two little, upright figures walking across this plain, whilst the heavens shimmered and roared about them. When did one come to an end? In which direction was it finished? There was no end, no finish, only this roaring vast space. Did one never get old, never die? That was the clue. He exulted strangely, with torture. He would go on with his wife, he and she like two children camp-

ing in the plains. What was sure but the endless sky?
But that was so sure, so boundless.

Still the royal blue colour burned and blazed and
sported itself in the web of darkness before him, un-
wearyingly rich and splendid. How rich and splendid
his own life was, red and burning and blazing and sporting itself in the dark meshes of his body: and his wife,
how she glowed and burned dark within her meshes!
Always it was so unfinished and unformed!

There was a loud noise of the organ. The whole party
was trooping to the vestry. There was a blotted, scrawled
book—and that young girl putting back her veil in her
vanity, and laying her hand with the wedding-ring self-
consciously conspicuous, and signing her name proudly
because of the vain spectacle she made :

"Anna Theresa Lensky."

"Anna Theresa Lensky"—what a vain, independent
minx she was! The bridegroom, slender in his black
swallow-tail and grey trousers, solemn as a young solemn
cat, was writing seriously:

"William Brangwen."

That looked more like it.

"Come and sign, father," cried the imperious young
hussy.

"Thomas Brangwen—clumsy-fist," he said to himself
as he signed.

Then his brother, a big, sallow fellow with black side-
whiskers, wrote:

"Alfred Brangwen."

"How many more Brangwens?" said Tom Brangwen,
ashamed of the too-frequent recurrence of his family
name.

When they were out again in the sunshine, and he
saw the frost hoary and blue among the long grass under

the tombstones, the holly-berries overhead twinkling
scarlet as the bells rang, the yew trees hanging their
black, motionless, ragged boughs, everything seemed
like a vision.

The marriage party went across the graveyard to the
wall, mounted it by the little steps, and descended. Oh,
a vain white peacock of a bride perching herself on the
top of the wall and giving her hand to the bridegroom
on the other side, to be helped down! The vanity of her
white, slim, daintily-stepping feet, and her arched neck.
And the regal impudence with which she seemed to dismiss them all, the others, parents and wedding guests, as
she went with her young husband.

In the cottage big fires were burning, there were
dozens of glasses on the table, and holly and mistletoe
hanging up. The wedding party crowded in, and Tom
Brangwen, becoming roisterous, poured out drinks.
Everybody must drink. The bells were ringing away
against the windows.

"Lift your glasses up," shouted Tom Brangwen from
the parlour, "lift your glasses up, an' drink to the hearth
an' home—hearth an' home, an' may they enjoy it."

"Night an' day, an' may they enjoy it," shouted Frank
Brangwen, in addition.

"Hammer an' tongs, and may they enjoy it," shouted
Alfred Brangwen, the saturnine.

"Fill your glasses up, an' let's have it all over again,"
shouted Tom Brangwen.

"Hearth and home, an' may ye enjoy it."

There was a ragged shout of the company in response.

"Bed an' blessin', and may ye enjoy it," shouted Frank
Brangwen.

There was a swelling chorus in answer.

"Comin' and goin', an' may ye enjoy it," shouted the

saturnine Alfred Brangwen, and the men roared by now boldly, and the women said, "Just hark, now!"

There was a touch of scandal in the air.

Then the party rolled off in the carriages, full speed back to the Marsh, to a large meal of the high-tea order, which lasted for an hour and a half. The bride and bridegroom sat at the head of the table, very prim and shining both of them, wordless, whilst the company raged down the table.

The Brangwen men had brandy in their tea, and were becoming unmanageable. The saturnine Alfred had glittering, unseeing eyes, and a strange, fierce way of laughing that showed his teeth. His wife glowered at him and jerked her head at him like a snake. He was oblivious. Frank Brangwen, the butcher, flushed and florid and handsome, roared echoes to his two brothers. Tom Brangwen, in his solid fashion, was letting himself go at last.

These three brothers dominated the whole company. Tom Brangwen wanted to make a speech. For the first time in his life, he must spread himself wordily.

"Marriage," he began, his eyes twinkling and yet quite profound, for he was deeply serious and hugely amused at the same time, "Marriage," he said, speaking in the slow, full-mouthed way of the Brangwens, "is what we're made for——"

"Let him talk," said Alfred Brangwen, slowly and inscrutably, "let him talk." Mrs. Alfred darted indignant eyes at her husband.

"A man," continued Tom Brangwen, "enjoys being a man: for what purpose was he made a man, if not to enjoy it?"

"That a true word," said Frank, floridly.

"And likewise," continued Tom Brangwen, "a woman

enjoys being a woman: at least we surmise she does——"

"Oh, don't you bother——" called a farmer's wife.

"You may back your life they'd be summisin'," said Frank's wife.

"Now," continued Tom Brangwen, "for a man to be a man, it takes a woman——"

"It does that," said a woman grimly.

"And for a woman to be a woman, it takes a *man*——" continued Tom Brangwen.

"All speak up, men," chimed in a feminine voice.

"Therefore we have marriage," continued Tom Brangwen.

"Hold, hold," said Alfred Brangwen. "Don't run us off our legs."

And in dead silence the glasses were filled. The bride and bridegroom, two children, sat with intent, shining faces at the head of the table, abstracted.

"There's no marriage in heaven," went on Tom Brangwen; "but on earth there is marriage."

"That's the difference between 'em," said Alfred Brangwen, mocking.

"Alfred," said Tom Brangwen, "keep your remarks till afterwards, and then we'll thank you for them.—There's very little else, on earth, but marriage. You can talk about making money, or saving souls. You can save your own soul seven times over, and you may have a mint of money, but your soul goes gnawin', gnawin', gnawin', and it says there's something it must have. In heaven there is no marriage. But on earth there *is* marriage, else heaven drops out, and there's no bottom to it."

"Just hark you now," said Frank's wife.

"Go on, Thomas," said Alfred sardonically.

"*If* we've got to be Angels," went on Tom Brangwen, haranguing the company at large, "and if there is no such thing as a man nor a woman amongst them, then it seems to me as a married couple makes one Angel."

"It's the brandy," said Alfred Brangwen wearily.

"For," said Tom Brangwen, and the company was listening to the conundrum, "an Angel can't be *less* than a human being. And if it was only the soul of a man *minus* the man, then it would be less than a human being."

"Decidedly," said Alfred.

And a laugh went round the table. But Tom Brangwen was inspired.

"An Angel's got to be more than a human being," he continued. "So I say, an Angel is the soul of man and woman in one: they rise united at the Judgment Day, as one Angel——"

"Praising the Lord," said Frank.

"Praising the Lord," repeated Tom.

"And what about the women left over?" asked Alfred, jeering. The company was getting uneasy.

"That I can't tell. How do I know as there *is* anybody left over at the Judgment Day? Let that be. What I say is, that when a man's soul and a woman's soul unites together—that makes an Angel——"

"I dunno about souls. I know as one plus one makes three, sometimes," said Frank. But he had the laugh to himself.

"Bodies and souls, it's the same," said Tom.

"And what about your Missus, who was married afore you knew her?" asked Alfred, set on edge by this discourse.

"That I can't tell you. If I am to become an Angel, it'll be my married soul, and not my single soul. It'll not be the soul of me when I was a lad: for I hadn't a soul as would *make* an Angel then."

"I can always remember," said Frank's wife, "when our Harold was bad, he did nothink but see an Angel at th' back o' th' lookin' glass. 'Look, mother,' 'e said, 'at that Angel!' 'Theer isn't no Angel, my duck,' I said, but he wouldn't have it. I took th' lookin' glass off'n th' dressin' table, but it made no difference. He kep' on sayin' it was there. My word, it did give me a turn. I thought for sure as I'd lost him."

"I can remember," said another man, Tom's sister's husband, "my mother gave me a good hidin' once, for sayin' I'd got an Angel up my nose. She seed me pokin', an' she said: 'What are you pokin' at your nose for—give over.' 'There's an Angel up it,' I said, an' she fetched me such a wipe. But there was. We used to call them thistle things 'Angels' as wafts about. An' I'd pushed one o' these up my nose, for some reason or other."

"It's wonderful what children will get up their noses," said Frank's wife. "I c'n remember our Hemmie, she shoved one o' them bluebell things out o' th' middle of a bluebell, what they call 'candles,' up her nose, and oh, we had some work! I'd seen her stickin' 'em on the end of her nose, like, but I never thought she'd be so soft as to shove it right up. She was a gel of eight or more. Oh, my word, we got a crochet-hook an' I don't know what . . ."

Tom Brangwen's mood of inspiration began to pass away. He forgot all about it and was soon roaring and shouting with the rest. Outside the wake came, singing the carols. They were invited into the bursting house. They had two fiddles and a piccolo. There in the parlour they played carols, and the whole company sang them at the top of its voice. Only the bride and bridegroom sat with shining eyes and strange, bright faces, and scarcely sang, or only with just moving lips.

The wake departed, and the guysers came. There was

loud applause, and shouting and excitement as the old
mystery play of St. George, in which every man present
had acted as a boy, proceeded, with banging and thump-
ing of club and dripping pan.

"By Jove, I got a crack once, when I was playin'
Beelzebub," said Tom Brangwen, his eyes full of water
with laughing. "It knocked all th' sense out of me as
you'd crack an egg. But I tell you, when I come to, I
played Old Johnny Roger with St. George, I did that."

He was shaking with laughter. Another knock came
at the door. There was a hush.

"It's th' cab," said somebody from the door.

"Walk in," shouted Tom Brangwen, and a red-faced
grinning man entered.

"Now you two, get yourselves ready an' off to blanket
fair," shouted Tom Brangwen. "Strike a daisy, but if
you're not off like a blink o' lightnin', you shanna go, you
s'll sleep separate."

Anna rose silently and went to change her dress. Will
Brangwen would have gone out, but Tilly came with his
hat and coat. The youth was helped on.

"Well, here's luck, my boy," shouted his father.

"When th' fat's in th' fire, let it frizzle," admonished
his uncle Frank.

"Fair and *softly* does it, fair an' *softly* does it," cried
his aunt, Frank's wife, contrary.

"You don't want to fall over yourself," said his uncle
by marriage. "You're not a bull at a gate."

"Let a man have his own road," said Tom Brangwen
testily. "Don't be so free of your advice—it's his wedding
this time, not yours."

"'E won't want many sign-posts," said his father.
"There's some roads a man has to be led, an' there's
some roads a boss-eyed man can only follow wi' one eye
shut. But this road can't be lost by a blind man nor a

boss-eyed man nor a cripple—and he's neither, thank God."

"Don't you be so sure o' your walkin' powers," cried Frank's wife. "There's many a man gets no further than half-way, nor can't to save his life, let him live for ever."

"Why, how do you know?" said Alfred.

"It's plain enough in th' looks o' some," retorted Lizzie, his sister-in-law.

The youth stood with a faint, half-hearing smile on his face. He was tense and abstracted. These things, or anything, scarcely touched him.

Anna came down, in her day dress, very elusive. She kissed everybody, men and women, Will Brangwen shook hands with everybody, kissed his mother, who began to cry, and the whole party went surging out to the cab.

The young couple were shut up, last injunctions shouted at them.

"Drive on," shouted Tom Brangwen.

The cab rolled off. They saw the light diminish under the ash-trees. Then the whole party, quietened, went indoors.

"They'll have three good fires burning," said Tom Brangwen, looking at his watch. "I told Emma to make 'em up at nine, an' then leave the door on th' latch. It's only half-past. They'll have three fires burning, an' lamps lighted, an' Emma will ha' warmed th' bed wi' th' warmin' pan. So I s'd think they'll be all right."

The party was much quieter. They talked of the young couple.

"She said she didn't want a servant in," said Tom Brangwen. "The house isn't big enough, she'd always have the creature under her nose. Emma'll do what is wanted of her, an' they'll be to themselves."

"It's best," said Lizzie, "you're more free."

The party talked on slowly. Brangwen looked at his watch.

"Let's go an' give 'em a carol," he said. "We s'll find th' fiddles at the Cock an' Robin."

"Ay, come on," said Frank.

Alfred rose in silence. The brother-in-law and one of Will's brothers rose also.

The five men went out. The night was flashing with stars. Sirius blazed like a signal at the side of the hill, Orion, stately and magnificent, was sloping along.

Tom walked with his brother, Alfred. The men's heels rang on the ground.

"It's a fine night," said Tom.

"Ay," said Alfred.

"Nice to get out."

"Ay."

The brothers walked close together, the bond of blood strong between them. Tom always felt very much the junior to Alfred.

"It's a long while since you left home," he said.

"Ay," said Alfred. "I thought I was getting a bit oldish —but I'm not. It's the things you've got as gets worn out, it's not you yourself."

"Why, what's worn out?"

"Most folks as I've anything to do with—as has anything to do with me. They all break down. You've got to go on by yourself, if it's only to perdition. There's nobody going alongside even there."

Tom Brangwen meditated this.

"Maybe you was never broken in," he said.

"No, I never was," said Alfred proudly.

And Tom felt his elder brother despised him a little. He winced under it.

"Everybody's got a way of their own," he said, stubbornly. "It's only a dog as hasn't. An' them as can't take what they give an' give what they take, they must go by themselves, or get a dog as'll follow 'em."

"They can do without the dog," said his brother. And again Tom Brangwen was humble, thinking his brother was bigger than himself. But if he was, he was. And if it were finer to go alone, it was: he did not want to go for all that.

They went over the field, where a thin, keen wind blew round the ball of the hill, in the starlight. They came to the stile, and to the side of Anna's house. The lights were out, only on the blinds of the rooms downstairs, and of a bedroom upstairs, firelight flickered.

"We'd better leave 'em alone," said Alfred Brangwen.

"Nay, nay," said Tom. "We'll carol 'em, for th' last time."

And in a quarter-of-an-hour's time, eleven silent, rather tipsy men scrambled over the wall, and into the garden by the yew-trees, outside the windows where faint firelight glowered on the blinds. There came a shrill sound, two violins and a piccolo shrilling on the frosty air.

"In the fields with their flocks abiding." A commotion of men's voices broke out singing in ragged unison.

Anna Brangwen had started up, listening, when the music began. She was afraid.

"It's the wake," he whispered.

She remained tense, her heart beating heavily, possessed with strange, strong fear. Then there came the burst of men's singing, rather uneven. She strained still, listening.

"It's Dad," she said, in a low voice. They were silent, listening.

"And my father," he said.

She listened still. But she was sure. She sank down again into bed, into his arms. He held her very close, kissing her. The hymn rambled on outside, all the men singing their best, having forgotten everything else under the spell of the fiddles and the tune. The firelight glowed against the darkness in the room. Anna could hear her father singing with gusto.

"Aren't they silly," she whispered.

And they crept closer, closer together, hearts beating to one another. And even as the hymn rolled on, they ceased to hear it.

FROM *Women in Love*

XVI. MAN TO MAN

HE LAY sick and unmoved, in pure opposition to everything. He knew how near to breaking was the vessel that held his life. He knew also how strong and durable it was. And he did not care. Better a thousand times take one's chance with death, than accept a life one did not want. The best of all to persist and persist and persist for ever, till one were satisfied in life.

He knew that Ursula was referred back to him. He knew his life rested with her. But he would rather not live than accept the love she proffered. The old way of love seemed a dreadful bondage, a sort of conscription. What it was in him he did not know, but the thought of love, marriage, and children, and a life lived together, in the horrible privacy of domestic and connubial satisfaction, was repulsive. He wanted something clearer, more open, cooler, as it were. The hot narrow intimacy between man and wife was abhorrent. The way they shut their doors, these married people, and shut them-

selves in to their own exclusive alliance with each other,
even in love, disgusted him. It was a whole community
of mistrustful couples insulated in private houses or private rooms, always in couples, and no further life, no
further immediate, no disinterested relationship admitted: a kaleidoscope of couples, disjoined, separatist,
meaningless entities of married couples. True, he hated
promiscuity even worse than marriage, and a liaison was
only another kind of coupling, reactionary from the legal
marriage. Reaction was a greater bore than action.

On the whole, he hated sex, it was such a limitation.
It was sex that turned a man into a broken half of a
couple, the woman into the other broken half. And he
wanted to be single in himself, the woman single in herself. He wanted sex to revert to the level of the other
appetites, to be regarded as a functional process, not as a
fulfilment. He believed in sex marriage. But beyond this,
he wanted a further conjunction, where man had being
and woman had being, two pure beings, each constitut-
ing the freedom of the other, balancing each other like
two poles of one force, like two angels, or two demons.

He wanted so much to be free, not under the compulsion of any need for unification, or tortured by unsatisfied desire. Desire and aspiration should find their
object without all this torture, as now, in a world of
plenty of water, simple thirst is inconsiderable, satisfied
almost unconsciously. And he wanted to be with Ursula
as free as with himself, single and clear and cool, yet
balanced, polarized with her. The merging, the clutching, the mingling of love was become madly abhorrent
to him.

But it seemed to him, woman was always so horrible
and clutching, she had such a lust for possession, a greed
of self-importance in love. She wanted to have, to own,
to control, to be dominant. Everything must be referred

back to her, to Woman, the Great Mother of everything, out of whom proceeded everything and to whom everything must finally be rendered up.

It filled him with almost insane fury, this calm assumption of the Magna Mater, that all was hers, because she had borne it. Man was hers because she had borne him. A Mater Dolorosa, she had borne him, a Magna Mater, she now claimed him again, soul and body, sex, meaning, and all. He had a horror of the Magna Mater, she was detestable.

She was on a very high horse again, was woman, the Great Mother. Did he not know it in Hermione. Hermione, the humble, the subservient, what was she all the while but the Mater Dolorosa, in her subservience, claiming, with horrible, insidious arrogance and female tyranny, her own again, claiming back the man she had borne in suffering. By her very suffering and humility she bound her son with chains, she held him her everlasting prisoner.

And Ursula, Ursula was the same—or the inverse. She too was the awful, arrogant queen of life, as if she were a queen bee on whom all the rest depended. He saw the yellow flare in her eyes, he knew the unthinkable overweening assumption of primacy in her. She was unconscious of it herself. She was only too ready to knock her head on the ground before a man. But this was only when she was so certain of her man that she could worship him as a woman worships her own infant, with a worship of perfect possession.

It was intolerable, this possession at the hands of woman. Always a man must be considered as the broken-off fragment of a woman, and the sex was the still aching scar of the laceration. Man must be added on to a woman, before he had any real place or wholeness.

And why? Why should we consider ourselves, men

and women, as broken fragments of one whole? It is not true. We are not broken fragments of one whole. Rather we are the singling away into purity and clear being, of things that were mixed. Rather the sex is that which remains in us of the mixed, the unresolved. And passion is the further separating of this mixture, that which is manly being taken into the being of the man, that which is womanly passing to the woman, till the two are clear and whole as angels, the admixture of sex in the highest sense surpassed, leaving two single beings constellated together like two stars.

In the old age, before sex was, we were mixed, each one a mixture. The process of singling into individuality resulted into the great polarization of sex. The womanly drew to one side, the manly to the other. But the separation was imperfect even then. And so our world-cycle passes. There is now to come the new day, when we are beings each of us, fulfilled in difference. The man is pure man, the woman pure woman, they are perfectly polarized. But there is no longer any of the horrible merging, mingling self-abnegation of love. There is only the pure duality of polarization, each one free from any contamination of the other. In each, the individual is primal, sex is subordinate, but perfectly polarized. Each has a single, separate being, with its own laws. The man has his pure freedom, the woman hers. Each acknowledges the perfection of the polarized sex-circuit. Each admits the different nature in the other.

So Birkin meditated whilst he was ill. He liked sometimes to be ill enough to take to his bed. For then he got better very quickly, and things came to him clear and sure.

Whilst he was laid up, Gerald came to see him. The two men had a deep, uneasy feeling for each other.

Gerald's eyes were quick and restless, his whole manner tense and impatient, he seemed strung up to some activity. According to conventionality, he wore black clothes, he looked formal, handsome and *comme il faut*. His hair was fair almost to whiteness, sharp like splinters of light, his face was keen and ruddy, his body seemed full of northern energy.

Gerald really loved Birkin, thought he never quite believed in him. Birkin was too unreal; clever, whimsical, wonderful, but not practical enough. Gerald felt that his own understanding was much sounder and safer. Birkin was delightful, a wonderful spirit, but after all, not to be taken seriously, not quite to be counted as a man among men.

"Why are you laid up again?" he asked kindly, taking the sick man's hand. It was always Gerald who was protective, offering the warm shelter of his physical strength.

"For my sins, I suppose," Birkin said, smiling a little ironically.

"For your sins? Yes, probably that is so. You should sin less, and keep better in health."

"You'd better teach me."

He looked at Gerald with ironic eyes.

"How are things with you?" asked Birkin.

"With me?" Gerald looked at Birkin, saw he was serious, and a warm light came in to his eyes.

"I don't know that they're any different. I don't see how they could be. There's nothing to change."

"I suppose you are conducting the business as successfully as ever and ignoring the demand of the soul."

"That's it," said Gerald. "At least as far as the business is concerned. I couldn't say about the soul, I'm sure."

"No."

"Surely you don't expect me to?" laughed Gerald.

"No. How are the rest of your affairs progressing, apart from the business?"

"The rest of my affairs? What are those? I couldn't say; I don't know what you refer to."

"Yes, you do," said Birkin. "Are you gloomy or cheerful? And what about Gudrun Brangwen?"

"What about her?" A confused look came over Gerald. "Well," he added, "I don't know. I can only tell you she gave me a hit over the face last time I saw her."

"A hit over the face? What for?"

"That I couldn't tell you, either."

"Really! But when?"

"The night of the party—when Diana was drowned. She was driving the cattle up the hill, and I went after her—you remember."

"Yes, I remember. But what made her do that? You didn't definitely ask her for it, I suppose?"

"I? No, not that I know of. I merely said to her that it was dangerous to drive those Highland bullocks—as it *is*. She turned in such a way, and said—'I suppose you think I'm afraid of you and your cattle, don't you?' So I asked her 'why,' and for answer she flung me a backhander across the face."

Birkin laughed quickly, as if it pleased him. Gerald looked at him, wondering, and began to laugh as well, saying:

"I didn't laugh at the time, I assure you. I was never so taken aback in my life."

"And weren't you furious?"

"Furious? I should think I was. I'd have murdered her for two pins."

"H'm!" ejaculated Birkin. "Poor Gudrun, wouldn't she suffer afterwards for having given herself away!" He was hugely delighted.

"Would she suffer?" asked Gerald, also amused now.

Both men smiled in malice and amusement.

"Badly, I should think; seeing how self-conscious she is."

"She is self-conscious, is she? Then what made her do it? For I certainly think it was quite uncalled-for, and quite unjustified."

"I suppose it was a sudden impulse."

"Yes, but how do you account for her having such an impulse? I'd done her no harm."

Birkin shook his head.

"The Amazon suddenly came up in her, I suppose," he said.

"Well," replied Gerald, "I'd rather it had been the Orinoco."

They both laughed lightly at the poor joke. Gerald was thinking how Gudrun had said she would strike the last blow too. But some reserve made him keep this back from Birkin.

"And you resent it?" Birkin asked.

"I don't resent it. I don't care a tinker's curse about it." He was silent a moment, then he added, laughing, "No, I'll see it through, that's all. She seemed sorry afterwards."

"Did she? You've not met since that night?"

Gerald's face clouded.

"No," he said. "We've been—you can imagine how it's been, since the accident."

"Yes. Is it calming down?"

"I don't know. It's a shock, of course. But I don't believe mother minds. I really don't believe she takes any notice. And what's so funny, she used to be all for the children—nothing mattered, nothing whatever mattered but the children. And now, she doesn't take any more notice than if it was one of the servants."

"No? Did it upset *you* very much?"

"It's a shock. But I don't feel it very much, really. I don't feel any different. We've all got to die, and it doesn't seem to make any great difference, anyhow, whether you die or not. I can't feel any *grief*, you know. It leaves me cold. I can't quite account for it."

"You don't care if you die or not?" asked Birkin.

Gerald looked at him with eyes blue as the blue-fibred steel of a weapon. He felt awkward, but indifferent. As a matter of fact, he did care terribly, with a great fear.

"Oh," he said, "I don't want to die, why should I? But I never trouble. The question doesn't seem to be on the carpet for me at all. It doesn't interest me, you know."

"Timor mortis conturbat me," quoted Birkin, adding, "No, death doesn't really seem the point any more. It curiously doesn't concern one. It's like an ordinary to-morrow."

Gerald looked closely at his friend. The eyes of the two men met, and an unspoken understanding was exchanged.

Gerald narrowed his eyes, his face was cool and un-scrupulous as he looked at Birkin, impersonally, with a vision that ended in a point in space, strangely keen-eyed and yet blind.

"If death isn't the point," he said, in a strangely abstract, cold, fine voice—"what is?" He sounded as if he had been found out.

"What is?" re-echoed Birkin. And there was a mock-ing silence.

"There's a long way to go, after the point of intrinsic death, before we disappear," said Birkin.

"There is," said Gerald. "But what sort of way?" He seemed to press the other man for knowledge which he himself knew far better than Birkin did.

"Right down the slopes of degeneration—mystic, universal degeneration. There are many stages of pure degradation to go through: agelong. We live on long after our death and progressively, in progressive devolution."

Gerald listened with a faint, fine smile on his face, all the time, as if, somewhere, he knew so much better than Birkin, all about this: as if his own knowledge were direct and personal, whereas Birkin's was a matter of observation and inference, not quite hitting the nail on the head:—though aiming near enough at it. But he was not going to give himself away. If Birkin could get at the secrets, let him. Gerald would never help him. Gerald would be a dark horse to the end.

"Of course," he said, with a startling change of conversation, "it is father who really feels it. It will finish him. For him the world collapses. All his care now is for Winnie—he must save Winnie. He says she ought to be sent away to school, but she won't hear of it, and he'll never do it. Of course she *is* in rather a queer way. We're all of us curiously bad at living. We can do things—but we can't get on with life at all. It's curious—a family failing."

"She oughtn't to be sent away to school," said Birkin, who was considering a new proposition.

"She oughtn't? Why?"

"She's a queer child—a special child, more special even than you. And in my opinion special children should never be sent away to school. Only moderately ordinary children should be sent to school—so it seems to me."

"I'm inclined to think just the opposite. I think it would probably make her more normal if she went away and mixed with other children."

"She wouldn't mix, you see. *You* never really mixed,

did you? And she wouldn't be willing even to pretend
to. She's proud, and solitary, and naturally apart. If she
has a single nature, why do you want to make her gre-
garious?"

"No, I don't want to make her anything. But I think
school would be good for her."

"Was it good for you?"

Gerald's eyes narrowed uglily. School had been torture to him. Yet he had not questioned whether one
should go through this torture. He seemed to believe in
education through subjection and torment.

"I hated it at the time, but I can see it was necessary,"
he said. "It brought me into line a bit—and you can't
live unless you do come into line somewhere."

"Well," said Birkin, "I begin to think that you can't
live unless you keep entirely out of the line. It's no good
trying to toe the line, when your one impulse is to smash
up the line. Winnie is a special nature, and for special
natures you must give a special world."

"Yes, but where's your special world?" said Gerald.

"Make it. Instead of chopping yourself down to fit the
world, chop the world down to fit yourself. As a matter
of fact, two exceptional people make another world. You
and I, we make another, separate world. You don't *want*
a world same as your brothers-in-law. It's just the special
quality you value. Do you *want* to be normal or ordinary? It's a lie. You want to be free and extraordinary,
in an extraordinary world of liberty."

Gerald looked at Birkin with subtle eyes of knowledge.
But he would never openly admit what he felt. He knew
more than Birkin, in one direction—much more. And
this gave him his gentle love for the other man, as if
Birkin were in some way young, innocent, child-like: so
amazingly clever, but incurably innocent.

"Yet you are so banal as to consider me chiefly a freak," said Birkin pointedly.

"A freak!" exclaimed Gerald, startled. And his face opened suddenly, as if lighted with simplicity, as when a flower opens out of the cunning bud. "No—I never consider you a freak." And he watched the other man with strange eyes, that Birkin could not understand. "I feel," Gerald continued, "that there is always an element of uncertainty about you—perhaps you are uncertain about yourself. But I'm never sure of you. You can go away and change as easily as if you had no soul."

He looked at Birkin with penetrating eyes. Birkin was amazed. He thought he had all the soul in the world. He stared in amazement. And Gerald, watching, saw the amazing attractive goodliness of his eyes, a young, spontaneous goodness that attracted the other man infinitely, yet filled him with bitter chagrin, because he mistrusted it so much. He knew Birkin could do without him— could forget, and not suffer. This was always present in Gerald's consciousness, filling him with bitter unbelief: this consciousness of the young, animal-like spontaneity of detachment. It seemed almost like hypocrisy and lying, sometimes, oh, often, on Birkin's part, to talk so deeply and importantly.

Quite other things were going through Birkin's mind. Suddenly he saw himself confronted with another problem—the problem of love and eternal conjunction between two men. Of course this was necessary—it had been a necessity inside himself all his life—to love a man purely and fully. Of course he had been loving Gerald all along, and all along denying it.

He lay in the bed and wondered, whilst his friend sat beside him, lost in brooding. Each man was gone in his own thoughts.

"You know how the old German knights used to swear a Blutbruderschaft," he said to Gerald, with quite a new happy activity in his eyes.

"Make a little wound in their arms, and rub each other's blood into the cut?" said Gerald.

"Yes—and swear to be true to each other, of one blood, all their lives. That is what we ought to do. No wounds, that is obsolete. But we ought to swear to love each other, you and I, implicitly, and perfectly, finally, without any possibility of going back on it."

He looked at Gerald with clear, happy eyes of discovery. Gerald looked down at him, attracted, so deeply bondaged in fascinated attraction that he was mistrustful, resenting the bondage, hating the attraction.

"We will swear to each other, one day, shall we?" pleaded Birkin. "We will swear to stand by each other— be true to each other—ultimately—infallibly—given to each other, organically—without possibility of taking back."

Birkin sought hard to express himself. But Gerald hardly listened. His face shone with a certain luminous pleasure. He was pleased. But he kept his reserve. He held himself back.

"Shall we swear to each other, one day?" said Birkin, putting out his hand towards Gerald.

Gerald just touched the extended fine, living hand, as if withheld and afraid.

"We'll leave it till I understand it better," he said, in a voice of excuse.

Birkin watched him. A little sharp disappointment, perhaps a touch of contempt, came into his heart.

"Yes," he said. "You must tell me what you think, later. You know what I mean? Not sloppy emotionalism. An impersonal union that leaves one free."

They lapsed both into silence. Birkin was looking at

Gerald all the time. He seemed now to see, not the physical, animal man, which he usually saw in Gerald, and which usually he liked so much, but the man himself, complete, and as if fated, doomed, limited. This strange sense of fatality in Gerald, as if he were limited to one form of existence, one knowledge, one activity, a sort of fatal halfness, which to himself seemed wholeness, always overcame Birkin after their moments of passionate approach, and filled him with a sort of contempt, or boredom. It was the insistence on the limitation which so bored Birkin in Gerald. Gerald could never fly away from himself, in real indifferent gaiety. He had a clog, a sort of monomania.

There was silence for a time. Then Birkin said, in a lighter tone, letting the stress of the contact pass:

"Can't you get a good governess for Winifred?—somebody exceptional?"

"Hermione Roddice suggested we should ask Gudrun to teach her to draw and to model in clay. You know Winnie is astonishingly clever with that plasticine stuff. Hermione declares she is an artist." Gerald spoke in the usual animated, chatty manner, as if nothing unusual had passed. But Birkin's manner was full of reminder.

"Really! I didn't know that. Oh, well then, if Gudrun *would* teach her, it would be perfect—couldn't be anything better—if Winifred is an artist. Because Gudrun somewhere is one. And every true artist is the salvation of every other."

"I thought they got on so badly, as a rule."

"Perhaps. But only artists produce for each other the world that is fit to live in. If you can arrange *that* for Winifred, it is perfect."

"But you think she wouldn't come?"

"I don't know. Gudrun is rather self-opinionated. She won't go cheap anywhere. Or if she does, she'll pretty

soon take herself back. So whether she would conde-
scend to do private teaching, particularly here, in Beldover, I don't know. But it would be just the thing.
Winifred has got a special nature. And if you can put
into her way the means of being self-sufficient, that is
the best thing possible. She'll never get on with the ordinary life. You find it difficult enough yourself, and she
is several skins thinner than you are. It is awful to think
what her life will be like unless she does find a means
of expression, some way of fulfilment. You can see what
mere leaving it to fate brings. You can see how much
marriage is to be trusted to—look at your own mother."

"Do you think mother is abnormal?"

"No! I think she only wanted something more, or
other, than the common run of life. And not getting it,
she has gone wrong perhaps."

"After producing a brood of wrong children," said
Gerald gloomily.

"No more wrong than any of the rest of us," Birkin
replied. "The most normal people have the worst sub-
terranean selves, take them one by one."

"Sometimes I think it is a curse to be alive," said Gerald, with sudden impotent anger.

"Well," said Birkin, "why not? Let it be a curse sometimes to be alive—at other times it is anything but a
curse. You've got plenty of zest in it really."

"Less than you'd think," said Gerald, revealing a
strange poverty in his look at the other man.

There was silence, each thinking his own thoughts.

"I don't see what she has to distinguish between
teaching at the Grammar School, and coming to teach
Win," said Gerald.

"The difference between a public servant and a private one. The only nobleman today, king and only aris-

tocrat, is the public, the public. You are quite willing to serve the public—but to be a private tutor——"

"I don't want to serve either——"

"No! And Gudrun will probably feel the same."

Gerald thought for a few minutes. Then he said:

"At all events, father won't make her feel like a private servant. He will be fussy and grateful enough."

"So he ought. And so ought all of you. Do you think you can hire a woman like Gudrun Brangwen with money? She is your equal like anything—probably your superior."

"Is she?" said Gerald.

"Yes, and if you haven't the guts to know it, I hope she'll leave you to your own devices."

"Nevertheless," said Gerald, "if she is my equal, I wish she weren't a teacher, because I don't think teachers as a rule are my equal."

"Nor do I, damn them. But am I a teacher because I teach, or a parson because I preach?"

Gerald laughed. He was always uneasy on this score. He did not *want* to claim social superiority, yet he *would* not claim intrinsic personal superiority, because he would never base his standard of values on pure being. So he wobbled upon a tacit assumption of social standing. Now Birkin wanted him to accept the fact of intrinsic difference between human beings, which he did not intend to accept. It was against his social honour, his principle. He rose to go.

"I've been neglecting my business all this while," he said smiling.

"I ought to have reminded you before," Birkin replied, laughing and mocking.

"I knew you'd say something like that," laughed Gerald, rather uneasily.

"Did you?"

"Yes, Rupert. It wouldn't do for us all to be like you are—we should soon be in the cart. When I am above the world, I shall ignore all businesses."

"Of course, we're not in the cart now," said Birkin satirically.

"Not as much as you make out. At any rate, we have enough to eat and drink——"

"And be satisfied," added Birkin.

Gerald came near the bed and stood looking down at Birkin whose throat was exposed, whose tossed hair fell attractively on the warm brow, above the eyes that were so unchallenged and still in the satirical face. Gerald, full-limbed and turgid with energy, stood unwilling to go, he was held by the presence of the other man. He had not the power to go away.

"So," said Birkin. "Good-bye." And he reached out his hand from under the bed-clothes, smiling with a glimmering look.

"Good-bye," said Gerald, taking the warm hand of his friend in a firm grasp. "I shall come again. I miss you down at the mill."

"I'll be there in a few days," said Birkin.

The eyes of the two men met again. Gerald's, that were keen as a hawk's, were suffused now with warm light, and with unadmitted love, Birkin looked back as out of a darkness, unsounded and unknown, yet with a kind of warmth, that seemed to flow over Gerald's brain like a fertile sleep.

"Good-bye then. There's nothing I can do for you?"

"Nothing, thanks."

Birkin watched the black-clothed form of the other man move out of the door, the bright head was gone, he turned over to sleep.

XVII. THE INDUSTRIAL MAGNATE

IN BELDOVER, there was both for Ursula and
for Gudrun an interval. It seemed to Ursula as if
Birkin had gone out of her for the time, he had lost his
significance, he scarcely mattered in her world. She had
her own friends, her own activities, her own life. She
turned back to the old ways with zest, away from him.

And Gudrun, after feeling every moment in all her
veins conscious of Gerald Crich, connected even physically with him, was now almost indifferent to the thought
of him. She was nursing new schemes for going away
and trying a new form of life. All the time, there was
something in her urging her to avoid the final establishing of a relationship with Gerald. She felt it would be
wiser and better to have no more than a casual acquaintance with him.

She had a scheme for going to St. Petersburg, where
she had a friend who was a sculptor like herself, and
who lived with a wealthy Russian whose hobby was
jewel-making. The emotional, rather rootless life of the
Russians appealed to her. She did not want to go to
Paris. Paris was dry, and essentially boring. She would
like to go to Rome, Munich, Vienna, or to St. Petersburg
or Moscow. She had a friend in St. Petersburg and a
friend in Munich. To each of these she wrote, asking
about rooms.

She had a certain amount of money. She had come
home partly to save, and now she had sold several pieces
of work, she had been praised in various shows. She
knew she could become quite the "go" if she went to
London. But she knew London, she wanted something

else. She had seventy pounds, of which nobody knew anything. She would move soon, as soon as she heard from her friends. Her nature, in spite of her apparent placidity and calm, was profoundly restless.

The sisters happened to call in a cottage in Willey Green to buy honey. Mrs. Kirk, a stout, pale, sharp-nosed woman, sly, honied, with something shrewish and cat-like beneath, asked the girls into her too-cosy, too-tidy kitchen. There was a cat-like comfort and cleanliness everywhere.

"Yes, Miss Brangwen," she said, in her slightly whining, insinuating voice, "and how do you like being back in the old place, then?"

Gudrun, whom she addressed, hated her at once.

"I don't care for it," she replied abruptly.

"You don't? Ay, well, I suppose you found a difference from London. You like life, and big, grand places. Some of us has to be content with Willey Green and Beldover. And what do you think of our Grammar School, as there's so much talk about?"

"What do I think of it?" Gudrun looked round at her slowly. "Do you mean, do I think it's a good school?"

"Yes. What is your opinion of it?"

"I *do* think it's a good school."

Gudrun was very cold and repelling. She knew the common people hated the school.

"Ay, you do, then! I've heard so much, one way and the other. It's nice to know what those that's in it feel. But opinions vary, don't they? Mr. Crich up at High-close is all for it. Ay, poor man, I'm afraid he's not long for this world. He's very poorly."

"Is he worse?" asked Ursula.

"Eh, yes—since they lost Miss Diana. He's gone off to a shadow. Poor man, he's had a world of trouble."

"Has he?" asked Gudrun, faintly ironic.

"He has, a world of trouble. And as nice and kind a gentleman as ever you could wish to meet. His children don't take after him."

"I suppose they take after their mother?" said Ursula.

"In many ways." Mrs. Kirk lowered her voice a little. "She was a proud, haughty lady when she came into these parts—my word, she was that! She mustn't be looked at, and it was worth your life to speak to her." The woman made a dry, sly face.

"Did you know her when she was first married?"

"Yes, I knew her. I nursed three of her children. And proper little terrors they were, little fiends—that Gerald was a demon if ever there was one, a proper demon, ay, at six months old." A curious malicious, sly tone came into the woman's voice.

"Really," said Gudrun.

"That wilful, masterful—he'd mastered one nurse at six months. Kick, and scream, and struggle like a demon. Many's the time I've pinched his little bottom for him, when he was a child in arms. Ay, and he'd have been better if he'd had it pinched oftener. But she wouldn't have them corrected—no-o, wouldn't hear of it. I can remember the rows she had with Mr. Crich, my word. When he'd got worked up, properly worked up till he could stand no more, he'd lock the study door and whip them. But she paced up and down all the while like a tiger outside, like a tiger, with very murder in her face. She had a face that could *look* death. And when the door was opened, she'd go in with her hands lifted— 'What have you been doing to *my* children, you coward?' She was like one out of her mind. I believe he was frightened of her; he had to be driven mad before he'd lift a finger. Didn't the servants have a life of it! And didn't we used to be thankful when one of them caught it. They were the torment of your life."

"Really!" said Gudrun.

"In every possible way. If you wouldn't let them smash their pots on the table, if you wouldn't let them drag the kitten about with a string round its neck, if you wouldn't give them whatever they asked for, every mortal thing—then there was a shine on, and their mother coming in asking—'What's the matter with him? What have you done to him? What is it, Darling?' And then she'd turn on you as if she'd trample you under her feet. But she didn't trample on me. I was the only one that could do anything with her demons—for she wasn't going to be bothered with them herself. No, *she* took no trouble for them. But they must just have their way, they mustn't be spoken to. And Master Gerald was the beauty. I felt when he was a year and a half, I could stand no more. But I pinched his little bottom for him when he was in arms, I did, when there was no holding him, and I'm not sorry I did——"

Gudrun went away in fury and loathing. The phrase 'I pinched his little bottom for him,' sent her into a white, stony fury. She could not bear it, she wanted to have the woman taken out at once and strangled. And yet there the phrase was lodged in her mind for ever, beyond escape. She felt, one day, she would *have* to tell him, to see how he took it. And she loathed herself for the thought.

But at Shortlands the lifelong struggle was coming to a close. The father was ill and was going to die. He had bad internal pains, which took away all his attentive life, and left him with only a vestige of his consciousness. More and more a silence came over him, he was less and less acutely aware of his surroundings. The pain seemed to absorb his activity. He knew it was there, he knew it would come again. It was like something lurking in the

darkness within him. And he had not the power, or the
will, to seek it out and to know it. There it remained in
the darkness, the great pain, tearing him at times, and
then being silent. And when it tore him he crouched in
silent subjection under it, and when it left him alone
again, he refused to know of it. It was within the darkness, let it remain unknown. So he never admitted it,
except in a secret corner of himself, where all his never-
revealed fears and secrets were accumulated. For the
rest, he had a pain, it went away, it made no difference.
It even stimulated him, excited him.

But it gradually absorbed his life. Gradually it drew
away all his potentiality, it bled him into the dark, it
weaned him of life and drew him away into the darkness. And in this twilight of his life little remained visible to him. The business, his work, that was gone
entirely. His public interests had disappeared as if they
had never been. Even his family had become extraneous
to him, he could only remember, in some slight non-
essential part of himself, that such and such were his
children. But it was historical fact, not vital to him. He
had to make an effort to know their relation to him. Even
his wife barely existed. She indeed was like the darkness,
like the pain within him. By some strange association,
the darkness that contained the pain and the darkness
that contained his wife were identical. All his thoughts
and understandings became blurred and fused, and now
his wife and the consuming pain were the same dark
secret power against him, that he never faced. He never
drove the dread out of its lair within him. He only knew
that there was a dark place, and something inhabiting
this darkness which issued from time to time and rent
him. But he dared not penetrate and drive the beast into
the open. He had rather ignore its existence. Only, in

his vague way, the dread was his wife, the destroyer, and it was the pain, the destruction, a darkness which was one and both.

He very rarely saw his wife. She kept her room. Only occasionally she came forth, with her head stretched forward, and in her low, possessed voice, she asked him how he was. And he answered her, in the habit of more than thirty years: "Well, I don't think I'm any the worse, dear." But he was frightened of her, underneath this safeguard of habit, frightened almost to the verge of death.

But all his life, he had been so constant to his lights, he had never broken down. He would die even now without breaking down, without knowing what his feelings were, towards her. All his life, he had said: "Poor Christiana, she has such a strong temper." With unbroken will, he had stood by this position with regard to her, he had substituted pity for all his hostility, pity had been his shield and his safeguard, and his infallible weapon. And still, in his consciousness, he was sorry for her, her nature was so violent and so impatient.

But now his pity, with his life, was wearing thin, and the dread, almost amounting to horror, was rising into being. But before the armour of his pity really broke, he would die, as an insect when its shell is cracked. This was his final resource. Others would live on, and know the living death, the ensuing process of hopeless chaos. He would not. He denied death its victory.

He had been so constant to his lights, so constant to charity, and to his love for his neighbour. Perhaps he had loved his neighbour even better than himself—which is going one further than the commandment. Always, this flame had burned in his heart, sustaining him through everything, the welfare of the people. He was a large employer of labour, he was a great mine-owner.

And he had never lost this from his heart, that in Christ
he was one with his workmen. Nay, he had felt inferior
to them, as if they through poverty and labour were
nearer to God than he. He had always the unacknowl-
edged belief that it was his workmen, the miners, who
held in their hands the means of salvation. To move
nearer to God, he must move towards his miners, his
life must gravitate towards theirs. They were, unconsciously, his idol, his God made manifest. In them he
worshipped the highest, the great, sympathetic, mindless Godhead of humanity.

And all the while, his wife had opposed him like one
of the great demons of hell. Strange, like a bird of prey,
with the fascinating beauty and abstraction of a hawk,
she had beat against the bars of his philanthropy, and
like a hawk in a cage, she had sunk into silence. By force
of circumstance, because all the world combined to make
the cage unbreakable, he had been too strong for her, he
had kept her prisoner. And because she was his prisoner,
his passion for her had always remained keen as death.
He had always loved her, loved her with intensity.
Within the cage, she was denied nothing, she was given
all licence.

But she had gone almost mad. Of wild and overweening temper, she could not bear the humiliation of
her husband's soft, half-appealing kindness to everybody. He was not deceived by the poor. He knew they
came and sponged on him, and whined to him, the
worst sort; the majority, luckily for him, were much too
proud to ask for anything, much too independent to
come knocking at his door. But in Beldover, as everywhere else, there were the whining, parasitic, foul human beings who come crawling after charity, and
feeding on the living body of the public like lice. A kind
of fire would go over Christiana Crich's brain, as she

saw two more pale-faced, creeping women in objection-
able black clothes cringing lugubriously up the drive to
the door. She wanted to set the dogs on them, "Hi Rip!
Hi Ring! Ranger! At 'em boys, set 'em off." But Crowther, the butler, with all the rest of the servants, was
Mr. Crich's man. Nevertheless, when her husband was
away, she would come down like a wolf on the crawling
supplicants: "What do you people want? There is
nothing for you here. You have no business on the drive
at all. Simpson, drive them away and let no more of
them through the gate."

The servants had to obey her. And she would stand
watching with an eye like the eagle's, whilst the groom
in clumsy confusion drove the lugubrious persons down
the drive, as if they were rusty fowls, scuttling before
him.

But they learned to know, from the lodge-keeper,
when Mr. Crich was away, and they timed their visits.
How many times, in the first years, would Crowther
knock softly at the door: "Person to see you, sir."

"What name?"

"Grocock, sir."

"What do they want?" The question was half impatient, half gratified. He liked hearing appeals to his
charity.

"About a child, sir."

"Show them into the library, and tell them they
shouldn't come after eleven o'clock in the morning."

"Why do you get up from dinner?—send them off,"
his wife would say abruptly.

"Oh, I can't do that. It's no trouble just to hear what
they have to say."

"How many more have been here today? Why don't
you establish open house for them? They would soon
oust me and the children."

"You know, dear, it doesn't hurt me to hear what they have to say. And if they really are in trouble—well, it is my duty to help them out of it."

"It's your duty to invite all the rats in the world to gnaw at your bones."

"Come, Christiana, it isn't like that. Don't be uncharitable."

But she suddenly swept out of the room, and out to the study. There sat the meagre charity-seekers, looking as if they were at the doctor's.

"Mr. Crich can't see you. He can't see you at this hour. Do you think he is your property, that you can come whenever you like? You must go away, there is nothing for you here."

The poor people rose in confusion. But Mr. Crich, pale and black-bearded and deprecating, came behind her, saying:

"Yes, I don't like you coming as late as this. I'll hear any of you in the morning part of the day, but I can't really do with you after. What's amiss then, Gittens? How is your Missis?"

"Why, she's sunk very low, Mester Crich, she's a'most gone, she is——"

Sometimes, it seemed to Mrs. Crich as if her husband were some subtle funeral bird, feeding on the miseries of the people. It seemed to her he was never satisfied unless there was some sordid tale being poured out to him, which he drank in with a sort of mournful, sympathetic satisfaction. He would have no *raison d'être* if there were no lugubrious miseries in the world, as an undertaker would have no meaning if there were no funerals.

Mrs. Crich recoiled back upon herself, she recoiled away from this world of creeping democracy. A band of tight, baleful exclusion fastened round her heart, her isolation was fierce and hard, her antagonism was pas-

sive but terribly pure, like that of a hawk in a cage. As
the years went on, she lost more and more count of the
world, she seemed rapt in some glittering abstraction, almost purely unconscious. She would wander about the
house and about the surrounding country, staring keenly
and seeing nothing. She rarely spoke, she had no connection with the world. And she did not even think. She
was consumed in a fierce tension of opposition, like the
negative pole of a magnet.

And she bore many children. For, as time went on,
she never opposed her husband in word or deed. She
took no notice of him, externally. She submitted to him,
let him take what he wanted and do as he wanted with
her. She was like a hawk that sullenly submits to everything. The relation between her and her husband was
wordless and unknown, but it was deep, awful, a relation of utter interdestruction. And he, who triumphed in
the world, he became more and more hollow in his vitality, the vitality was bled from within him, as by some
hæmorrhage. She was hulked like a hawk in a cage, but
her heart was fierce and undiminished within her,
though her mind was destroyed.

So to the last he would go to her and hold her in his
arms sometimes, before his strength was all gone. The
terrible white, destructive light that burned in her eyes
only excited and roused him. Till he was bled to death,
and then he dreaded her more than anything. But he always said to himself, how happy he had been, how he
had loved her with a pure and consuming love ever since
he had known her. And he thought of her as pure,
chaste; the white flame which was known to him alone,
the flame of her sex, was a white flower of snow to his
mind. She was a wonderful white snow-flower, which he
had desired infinitely. And now he was dying with all
his ideas and interpretations intact. They would only

collapse when the breath left his body. Till then they
would be pure truths for him. Only death would show
the perfect completeness of the lie. Till death, she was
his white snow-flower. He had subdued her, and her
subjugation was to him an infinite chastity in her, a virginity which he could never break, and which dominated
him as by a spell.

She had let go the outer world, but within herself she
was unbroken and unimpaired. She only sat in her room
like a moping, dishevelled hawk, motionless, mindless.
Her children, for whom she had been so fierce in her
youth, now meant scarcely anything to her. She had lost
all that, she was quite by herself. Only Gerald, the
gleaming, had some existence for her. But of late years,
since he had become head of the business, he too was
forgotten. Whereas the father, now he was dying, turned
for compassion to Gerald. There had always been opposition between the two of them. Gerald had feared and
despised his father, and to a great extent had avoided
him all through boyhood and young manhood. And the
father had felt very often a real dislike of his eldest son,
which, never wanting to give way to, he had refused to
acknowledge. He had ignored Gerald as much as possible, leaving him alone.

Since, however, Gerald had come home and assumed
responsibility in the firm, and had proved such a wonderful director, the father, tired and weary of all outside
concerns, had put all his trust of these things in his son,
implicitly, leaving everything to him, and assuming a
rather touching dependence on the young enemy. This
immediately roused a poignant pity and allegiance in
Gerald's heart, always shadowed by contempt and by
unadmitted enmity. For Gerald was in reaction against
Charity; and yet he was dominated by it, it assumed
supremacy in the inner life, and he could not confute it.

So he was partly subject to that which his father stood for, but he was in reaction against it. Now he could not save himself. A certain pity and grief and tenderness for his father overcame him, in spite of the deeper, more sullen hostility.

The father won shelter from Gerald through compassion. But for love he had Winifred. She was his youngest child, she was the only one of his children whom he had ever closely loved. And her he loved with all the great, overweening, sheltering love of a dying man. He wanted to shelter her infinitely, infinitely, to wrap her in warmth and love and shelter, perfectly. If he could save her she should never know one pain, one grief. one hurt. He had been so right all his life, so constant in his kindness and his goodness. And this was his last passionate righteousness, his love for the child Winifred. Some things troubled him yet. The world had passed away from him, as his strength ebbed. There were no more poor and injured and humble to protect and succour. These were all lost to him. There were no more sons and daughters to trouble him, and to weigh on him as an unnatural responsibility. These too had faded out of reality. All these things had fallen out of his hands, and left him free.

There remained the covert fear and horror of his wife, as she sat mindless and strange in her room, or as she came forth with slow, prowling step, her head bent forward. But this he put away. Even his lifelong righteousness, however, would not quite deliver him from the inner horror. Still, he could keep it sufficiently at bay. It would never break forth openly. Death would come first.

Then there was Winifred! If only he could be sure about her, if only he could be sure. Since the death of Diana, and the development of his illness, his craving for surety with regard to Winifred amounted almost to obsession. It was as if, even dying, he must have some anxiety, some responsibility of love, of Charity, upon his heart.

She was an odd, sensitive, inflammable child, having her father's dark hair and quiet bearing, but being quite detached, momentaneous. She was like a changeling indeed, as if her feelings did not matter to her, really. She often seemed to be talking and playing like the gayest and most childish of children, she was full of the warmest, most delightful affection for a few things—for her father, and for her animals in particular. But if she heard that her beloved kitten Leo had been run over by the motor-car she put her head on one side, and replied, with a faint contraction like resentment on her face: "Has he?" Then she took no more notice. She only disliked the servant who would force bad news on her, and wanted her to be sorry. She wished not to know, and that seemed her chief motive. She avoided her mother, and most of the members of her family. She loved her Daddy, because he wanted her always to be happy, and because he seemed to become young again, and irresponsible, in her presence. She liked Gerald, because he was so self-contained. She loved people who would make life a game for her. She had an amazing instinctive critical faculty, and was a pure anarchist, a pure aristocrat at once. For she accepted her equals wherever she found them, and she ignored with blithe indifference her inferiors, whether they were her brothers and sisters, or whether they were wealthy guests of the house, or whether they were the common people or the servants. She was quite single and by herself, deriving from nobody. It was as if she were cut off from all purposes or continuity, and existed simply moment by moment.

The father, as by some strange final illusion, felt as if all his fate depended on his ensuring to Winifred her happiness. She who could never suffer, because she never formed vital connections, she who could lose the dearest things of her life and be just the same the next day, the whole memory dropped out, as if deliberately, she whose will was so strangely and easily free, anarchistic, almost nihilistic, who like a soulless bird flits on its own will, without attachment or responsibility beyond the moment, who in her every motion snapped the threads of serious relationship with blithe, free hands, really nihilistic, because never troubled, she must be the object of her father's final passionate solicitude.

When Mr. Crich heard that Gudrun Brangwen might come to help Winifred with her drawing and modelling he saw a road to salvation for his child. He believed that Winifred had talent, he had seen Gudrun, he knew that she was an exceptional person. He could give Winifred into her hands as into the hands of a right being. Here was a direction and a positive force to be lent to his child, he need not leave her directionless and defenceless. If he could but graft the girl on to some tree of utterance before he died, he would have fulfilled his responsibility. And here it could be done. He did not hesitate to appeal to Gudrun.

Meanwhile, as the father drifted more and more out of life, Gerald experienced more and more a sense of exposure. His father after all had stood for the living world to him. Whilst his father lived Gerald was not responsible for the world. But now his father was passing away, Gerald found himself left exposed and unready before the storm of living, like the mutinous first mate of a ship that has lost his captain, and who sees only a terrible chaos in front of him. He did not inherit an established order and a living idea. The whole unifying idea of mankind seemed to be dying with his father, the centralizing force that had held the whole together seemed to collapse with his father, the parts were ready to go asunder in terrible disintegration. Gerald was as if left on board of a ship that was going asunder beneath his feet, he was in charge of a vessel whose timbers were all coming apart.

He knew that all his life he had been wrenching at the frame of life to break it apart. And now, with something of the terror of a destructive child, he saw himself on the point of inheriting his own destruction. And during the last months, under the influence of death, and of Birkin's talk, and of Gudrun's penetrating being, he had lost entirely that mechanical certainty that had been his triumph. Sometimes spasms of hatred came over him, against Birkin and Gudrun and that whole set. He wanted to go back to the dullest conservatism, to the most stupid of conventional people. He wanted to revert to the strictest Toryism. But the desire did not last long enough to carry him into action.

During his childhood and his boyhood he had wanted a sort of savagedom. The days of Homer were his ideal, when a man was chief of an army of heroes, or spent his years in wonderful Odyssey. He hated remorselessly the circumstances of his own life, so much that he never really saw Beldover and the colliery valley. He turned his face entirely away from the blackened mining region that stretched away on the right hand of Shortlands, he turned entirely to the country and the woods beyond Willey Water. It was true that the panting and rattling of the coal mines could always be heard at Shortlands. But from his earliest childhood, Gerald had paid no heed to this. He had ignored the whole of the industrial sea which surged in coal-blackened tides against the grounds of the house. The world was really a wilderness where one hunted and swam and rode. He rebelled against all authority. Life was a condition of savage freedom.

Then he had been sent away to school, which was so much death to him. He refused to go to Oxford, choosing a German university. He had spent a certain time at Bonn, at Berlin, and at Frankfurt. There, a curiosity had been aroused in his mind. He wanted to see and to know, in a curious objective fashion, as if it were an amusement to him. Then he must try war. Then he must travel into the savage regions that had so attracted him.

The result was, he found humanity very much alike everywhere, and to a mind like his, curious and cold, the savage was duller, less exciting, than the European. So he took hold of all kinds of sociological ideas, and ideas of reform. But they never went more than skin-deep, they were never more than a mental amusement. Their interest lay chiefly in the reaction against the positive order, the destructive reaction.

He discovered at last a real adventure in the coal-mines. His father asked him to help in the firm. Gerald had been educated in the science of mining, and it had never interested him. Now, suddenly, with a sort of exultation, he laid hold of the world.

There was impressed photographically on his consciousness the great industry. Suddenly, it was real, he was part of it. Down the valley ran the colliery railway, linking mine with mine. Down the railway ran the trains, short trains of heavily laden trucks, long trains of empty wagons, each one bearing in big white letters the initials:
"C. B. & Co."

These white letters on all the wagons he had seen since his first childhood, and it was as if he had never seen them, they were so familiar, and so ignored. Now at last he saw his own name written on the wall. Now he had a vision of power.

So many wagons, bearing his initial, running all over the country. He saw them as he entered London in the train, he saw them at Dover. So far his power ramified. He looked at Beldover, at Selby, at Whatmore, at Lethley Bank, the great colliery villages which depended entirely on his mines. They were hideous and sordid, during his childhood they had been sores in his consciousness. And now he saw them with pride. Four raw new towns, and many ugly industrial hamlets, were crowded under his dependence. He saw the stream of miners flowing along the causeways from the mines at the end of the afternoon, thousands of blackened, slightly distorted human beings with red mouths, all moving subjugate to his will. He pushed slowly in his motor-car through the little market-top on Friday nights in Beldover, through a solid mass of human beings that were making their purchases and doing their weekly spending. They were all subordinate to him. They were ugly and uncouth, but they were his instruments. He was the God of the machine. They made way for his motor-car automatically, slowly.

He did not care whether they made way with alacrity, or grudgingly. He did not care what they thought of him. His vision had suddenly crystallized. Suddenly he had conceived the pure instrumentality of mankind. There had been so much humanitarianism, so much talk of sufferings and feelings. It was ridiculous. The sufferings and feelings of individuals did not matter in the least. They were mere conditions, like the weather. What mattered was the pure instrumentality of the individual. As a man as of a knife: does it cut well? Nothing else mattered.

Everything in the world has its function, and is good or not good in so far as it fulfils this function more or less perfectly. Was a miner a good miner? Then he was

complete. Was a manager a good manager? That was
enough. Gerald himself, who was responsible for all
this industry, was he a good director? If he were, he had
fulfilled his life. The rest was by-play.

The mines were there, they were old. They were giving out, it did not pay to work the seams. There was talk
of closing down two of them. It was at this point that
Gerald arrived on the scene.

He looked around. There lay the mines. They were
old, obsolete. They were like old lions, no more good.
He looked again. Pah! the mines were nothing but the
clumsy efforts of impure minds. There they lay, abor-
tions of a half-trained mind. Let the idea of them be
swept away. He cleared his brain of them, and thought
only of the coal in the under earth. How much was
there?

There was plenty of coal. The old workings could not
get at it, that was all. Then break the neck of the old
workings. The coal lay there in its seams, even though
the seams were thin. There it lay, inert matter, as it had
always lain, since the beginning of time, subject to the
will of man. The will of man was the determining factor.
Man was the arch-god of earth. His mind was obedient
to serve his will. Man's will was the absolute, the only
absolute.

And it was his will to subjugate Matter to his own
ends. The subjugation itself was the point, the fight was
the be-all, the fruits of victory were mere results. It was
not for the sake of money that Gerald took over the
mines. He did not care about money, fundamentally. He
was neither ostentatious nor luxurious, neither did he
care about social position, not finally. What he wanted
was the pure fulfilment of his own will in the struggle
with the natural conditions. His will was now, to take
the coal out of the earth, profitably. The profit was

merely the condition of victory, but the victory itself lay
in the feat achieved. He vibrated with zest before the
challenge. Every day he was in the mines, examining,
testing, he consulted experts, he gradually gathered the
whole situation into his mind, as a general grasps the
plan of his campaign.

Then there was need for a complete break. The mines
were run on an old system, an obsolete idea. The initial
idea had been to obtain as much money from the earth
as would make the owners comfortably rich, would allow
the workmen sufficient wages and good conditions, and
would increase the wealth of the country altogether.
Gerald's father, following in the second generation, having a sufficient fortune, had thought only of the men.
The mines, for him, were primarily great fields to produce bread and plenty for all the hundreds of human
beings gathered about them. He had lived and striven
with his fellow owners to benefit the men every time.
And the men had been benefited in their fashion. There
were few poor, and few needy. All was plenty, because
the mines were good and easy to work. And the miners,
in those days, finding themselves richer than they might
have expected, felt glad and triumphant. They thought
themselves well-off, they congratulated themselves on
their good fortune, they remembered how their fathers
had starved and suffered, and they felt that better times
had come. They were grateful to those others, the pio-
neers, the new owners, who had opened out the pits,
and let forth this stream of plenty.

But man is never satisfied, and so the miners, from
gratitude to their owners, passed on to murmuring. Their
sufficiency decreased with knowledge, they wanted
more. Why should the master be so out of all proportion
rich?

There was a crisis when Gerald was a boy, when the

Masters' Federation closed down the mines because the men would not accept a reduction. This lock-out had forced home the new conditions to Thomas Crich. Belonging to the Federation, he had been compelled by his honour to close the pits against his men. He, the father, the Patriarch, was forced to deny the means of life to his sons, his people. He, the rich man who would hardly enter heaven because of his possessions, must now turn upon the poor, upon those who were nearer Christ than himself, those who were humble and despised and closer to perfection, those who were manly and noble in their labours, and must say to them: "Ye shall neither labour nor eat bread."

It was this recognition of the state of war which really broke his heart. He wanted his industry to be run on love. Oh, he wanted love to be the directing power even of the mines. And now, from under the cloak of love, the sword was cynically drawn, the sword of mechanical necessity.

This really broke his heart. He must have the illusion and now the illusion was destroyed. The men were not against *him*, but they were against the masters. It was war, and willy nilly he found himself on the wrong side, in his own conscience. Seething masses of miners met daily, carried away by a new religious impulse. The idea flew through them: "All men are equal on earth," and they would carry the idea to its material fulfilment. After all, is it not the teaching of Christ? And what is an idea, if not the germ of action in the material world. "All men are equal in spirit, they are all sons of God. Whence then this obvious *disquality*?" It was a religious creed pushed to its material conclusion. Thomas Crich at least had no answer. He could but admit, according to his sincere tenets, that the disquality was wrong. But he could not give up his goods, which were the stuff of disquality. So the men would fight for their rights. The last impulses of the last religious passion left on earth, the passion for equality, inspired them.

Seething mobs of men marched about, their faces lighted up as for holy war, with a smoke of cupidity. How disentangle the passion for equality from the passion of cupidity, when begins the fight for equality of possessions? But the God was the machine. Each man claimed equality in the Godhead of the great productive machine. Every man equally was part of this Godhead. But somehow, somewhere, Thomas Crich knew this was false. When the machine is the Godhead, and production or work is worship, then the most mechanical mind is purest and highest, the representative of God on earth. And the rest are subordinate, each according to his degree.

Riots broke out, Whatmore pit-head was in flames. This was the pit furthest in the country, near the woods. Soldiers came. From the windows of Shortlands, on that fatal day, could be seen the flare of fire in the sky not far off, and now the little colliery train, with the workmen's carriages which were used to convey the miners to the distant Whatmore, was crossing the valley full of soldiers, full of redcoats. Then there was the far-off sound of firing, then the later news that the mob was dispersed, one man was shot dead, the fire was put out.

Gerald, who was a boy, was filled with the wildest excitement and delight. He longed to go with the soldiers to shoot the men. But he was not allowed to go out of the lodge gates. At the gates were stationed sentries with guns. Gerald stood near them in delight, whilst gangs of derisive miners strolled up and down the lanes, calling and jeering:

"Now then, three ha'porth o' coppers, let's see thee shoot thy gun." Insults were chalked on the walls and the fences, the servants left.

And all this while Thomas Crich was breaking his heart, and giving away hundreds of pounds in charity. Everywhere there was free food, a surfeit of free food. Anybody could have bread for asking, and a loaf cost only three-ha'pence. Every day there was a free tea somewhere, the children had never had so many treats in their lives. On Friday afternoon great basketfuls of buns and cakes were taken into the schools, and great pitchers of milk, the school-children had what they wanted. They were sick with eating too much cake and milk.

And then it came to an end, and the men went back to work. But it was never the same as before. There was a new situation created, a new idea reigned. Even in the machine, there should be equality. No part should be subordinate to any other part: all should be equal. The instinct for chaos had entered. Mystic equality lies in being, not in having or in doing, which are processes. In function and process, one man, one part, must of necessity be subordinate to another. It is a condition of being. But the desire for chaos had risen, and the idea of mechanical equality was the weapon of disruption which should execute the will of man, the will for chaos.

Gerald was a boy at the time of the strike, but he longed to be a man, to fight the colliers. The father however was trapped between two half-truths, and broken. He wanted to be a pure Christian, one and equal with all men. He even wanted to give away all he had, to the poor. Yet he was a great promoter of industry, and he knew perfectly that he must keep his goods and keep his authority. This was as divine a necessity in him as the need to give away all he possessed—more divine even, since this was the necessity he acted upon. Yet because

he did *not* act on the other ideal, it dominated him, he
was dying of chagrin because he must forfeit it. He
wanted to be a father of loving kindness and sacrificial
benevolence. The colliers shouted to him about his thousands a year. They would not be deceived.

When Gerald grew up in the ways of the world, he
shifted the position. He did not care about the equality.
The whole Christian attitude of love and self-sacrifice
was old hat. He knew that position and authority were
the right thing in the world, and it was useless to cant
about it. They were the right thing, for the simple reason that they were functionally necessary. They were not
the be-all and the end-all. It was like being part of a
machine. He himself happened to be a controlling, central part, the masses of men were the parts variously controlled. This was merely as it happened. As well get
excited because a central hub drives a hundred outer
wheels—or because the whole universe wheels round
the sun. After all, it would be mere silliness to say that
the moon and the earth and Saturn and Jupiter and
Venus have just as much right to be the centre of the
universe, each of them separately, as the sun. Such an
assertion is made merely in the desire of chaos.

Without bothering to *think* to a conclusion, Gerald
jumped to a conclusion. He abandoned the whole dem-
ocratic-equality problem as a problem of silliness. What
mattered was the great social productive machine. Let
that work perfectly, let it produce a sufficiency of everything, let every man be given a rational portion, greater
or less according to his functional degree or magnitude,
and then, provision made, let the devil supervene, let
every man look after his own amusements and appetites,
so long as he interfered with nobody.

So Gerald set himself to work, to put the great industry in order. In his travels, and in his accompanying

readings, he had come to the conclusion that the essential secret of life was harmony. He did not define to himself at all clearly what harmony was. The word pleased him, he felt he had come to his own conclusions. And he proceeded to put his philosophy into practice by forcing order into the established world, translating the mystic word harmony into the practical word organization.

Immediately he *saw* the firm, he realized what he could do. He had a fight to fight with Matter, with the earth and the coal it enclosed. This was the sole idea, to turn upon the inanimate matter of the underground, and reduce it to his will. And for this fight with Matter, one must have perfect instruments in perfect organization, a mechanism so subtle and harmonious in its workings that it represents the single mind of man, and by its relentless repetition of given movement will accomplish a purpose irresistibly, inhumanly. It was this inhuman principle in the mechanism he wanted to construct that inspired Gerald with an almost religious exaltation. He, the man, could interpose a perfect, changeless, godlike medium between himself and the Matter he had to subjugate. There were two opposites, his will and the resistant Matter of the earth. And between these he could establish the very expression of his will, the incarnation of his power, a great and perfect machine, a system, an activity of pure order, pure mechanical repetition, repetition ad infinitum, hence eternal and infinite. He found his eternal and his infinite in the pure machine-principle of perfect co-ordination into one pure, complex, infinitely repeated motion, like the spinning of a wheel; but a productive spinning, as the revolving of the universe may be called a productive spinning, a productive repetition through eternity, to infinity. And this is the God-motion, this productive repetition ad infinitum. And Gerald was the God of the machine, Deus ex Machina. And the whole productive will of man was the Godhead.

He had his life-work now, to extend over the earth a great and perfect system in which the will of man ran smooth and unthwarted, timeless, a Godhead in process. He had to begin with the mines. The terms were given: first the resistant Matter of the underground; then the instruments of its subjugation, instruments human and metallic; and finally his own pure will, his own mind. It would need a marvellous adjustment of myriad instruments, human, animal, metallic, kinetic, dynamic, a marvellous casting of myriad tiny wholes into one great perfect entirety. And then, in this case there was perfection attained, the will of the highest was perfectly fulfilled, the will of mankind was perfectly enacted; for was not mankind mystically contra-distinguished against inanimate Matter, was not the history of mankind just the history of the conquest of the one by the other?

The miners were overreached. While they were still in the toils of divine equality of man, Gerald had passed on, granted essentially their case, and proceeded in his quality of human being to fulfil the will of mankind as a whole. He merely represented the miners in a higher sense when he perceived that the only way to fulfil perfectly the will of man was to establish the perfect, inhuman machine. But he represented them very essentially, they were far behind, out of date, squabbling for their material equality. The desire had already transmuted into this new and greater desire, for a perfect intervening mechanism between man and Matter, the desire to translate the Godhead into pure mechanism.

As soon as Gerald entered the firm, the convulsion of death ran through the old system. He had all his life been tortured by a furious and destructive demon, which possessed him sometimes like an insanity. This temper now entered like a virus into the firm, and there were cruel eruptions. Terrible and inhuman were his examinations into every detail; there was no privacy he would spare, no old sentiment but he would turn it over. The old grey managers, the old grey clerks, the doddering old pensioners, he looked at them, and removed them as so much lumber. The whole concern seemed like a hospital of invalid employees. He had no emotional qualms. He arranged what pensions were necessary, he looked for efficient substitutes, and when these were found, he substituted them for the old hands.

"I've a pitiful letter here from Letherington," his father would say, in a tone of deprecation and appeal. "Don't you think the poor fellow might keep on a little longer? I always fancied he did very well."

"I've got a man in his place now, father. He'll be happier out of it, believe me. You think his allowance is plenty, don't you?"

"It's not the allowance that he wants, poor man. He feels it very much that he is superannuated. Says he thought he had twenty more years of work in him yet."

"Not of this kind of work I want. He doesn't understand."

The father sighed. He wanted not to know any more. He believed the pits would have to be overhauled if they were to go on working. And after all, it would be worse in the long run for everybody if they must close down. So he could make no answer to the appeals of his old and trusty servants, he could only repeat "Gerald says."

So the father drew more and more out of the light. The whole frame of the real life was broken for him. He had been right according to his lights. And his lights had been those of the great religion. Yet they seemed to have become obsolete, to be superseded in the world.

He could not understand. He only withdrew with his lights into an inner room, into the silence. The beautiful candles of belief, that would not do to light the world any more, they would still burn sweetly and sufficiently in the inner room of his soul, and in the silence of his retirement.

Gerald rushed into the reform of the firm, beginning with the office. It was needful to economize severely, to make possible the great alterations he must introduce.

"What are these widows' coals?" he asked.

"We have always allowed all widows of men who worked for the firm a load of coals every three months."

"They must pay cost price henceforward. The firm is not a charity institution, as everybody seems to think."

Widows, these stock figures of sentimental humanitarianism, he felt a dislike at the thought of them. They were almost repulsive. Why were they not immolated on the pyre of the husband, like the sati in India? At any rate, let them pay the cost of their coals.

In a thousand ways he cut down the expenditure, in ways so fine as to be hardly noticeable to the men. The miners must pay for the cartage of their coals, heavy cartage too; they must pay for their tools for the sharpening, for the care of lamps, for the many trifling things that made the bill of charges against every man mount up to a shilling or so in the week. It was not grasped very definitely by the miners, though they were sore enough. But it saved hundreds of pounds every week for the firm.

Gradually Gerald got hold of everything. And then began the great reform. Expert engineers were introduced in every department. An enormous electric plant was installed, both for lighting and for haulage underground, and for power. The electricity was carried into every mine. New machinery was brought from America, such as the miners had never seen before, great iron men, as the cutting machines were called, and unusual appliances. The working of the pits was thoroughly changed, all the control was taken out of the hands of the miners, the butty system was abolished. Everything was run on the most accurate and delicate scientific method, educated and expert men were in control everywhere, the miners were reduced to mere mechanical instruments. They had to work hard, much harder than before, the work was terrible and heart-breaking in its mechanicalness.

But they submitted to it all. The joy went out of their lives, the hope seemed to perish as they became more and more mechanized. And yet they accepted the new conditions. They even got a further satisfaction out of them. At first they hated Gerald Crich, they swore to do something to him, to murder him. But as time went on, they accepted everything with some fatal satisfaction. Gerald was their high priest, he represented the religion they really felt. His father was forgotten already. There was a new world, a new order, strict, terrible, inhuman, but satisfying in its very destructiveness. The men were satisfied to belong to the great and wonderful machine, even whilst it destroyed them. It was what they wanted. It was the highest that man had produced, the most wonderful and superhuman. They were exalted by belonging to this great and superhuman system which was beyond feeling or reason, something really godlike. Their hearts died within them, but their souls were satisfied. It was what they wanted. Otherwise Gerald could never have done what he did. He was just ahead of them in giving them what they wanted, this participation in a great and perfect system that subjected life to pure mathematical principles. This was a sort of freedom, the sort they really wanted. It was the first great step in

undoing, the first great phase of chaos, the substitution
of the mechanical principle for the organic, the destruction of the organic purpose, the organic unity, and the
subordination of every organic unit to the great mechanical purpose. It was pure organic disintegration and
pure mechanical organization. This is the first and finest
state of chaos.

Gerald was satisfied. He knew the colliers said they
hated him. But he had long ceased to hate them. When
they streamed past him at evening, their heavy boots
slurring on the pavement wearily, their shoulders
slightly distorted, they took no notice of him, they gave
him no greeting whatever, they passed in a grey-black
stream of unemotional acceptance. They were not important to him, save as instruments, nor he to them, save
as a supreme instrument of control. As miners they had
their being, he had his being as director. He admired
their qualities. But as men, personalities, they were just
accidents, sporadic little unimportant phenomena. And
tacitly, the men agreed to this. For Gerald agreed to it in
himself.

He had succeeded. He had converted the industry
into a new and terrible purity. There was a greater out-
put of coal than ever, the wonderful and delicate system
ran almost perfectly. He had a set of really clever
engineers, both mining and electrical, and they did not
cost much. A highly educated man cost very little more
than a workman. His managers, who were all rare men,
were no more expensive than the old bungling fools of
his father's days, who were merely colliers promoted.
His chief manager, who had twelve hundred a year,
saved the firm at least five thousand. The whole system
was now so perfect that Gerald was hardly necessary any
more.

It was so perfect that sometimes a strange fear came

over him, and he did not know what to do. He went on for some years in a sort of trance of activity. What he was doing seemed supreme, he was almost like a divinity. He was a pure and exalted activity.

But now he had succeeded—he had finally succeeded. And once or twice lately, when he was alone in the evening and had nothing to do, he had suddenly stood up in terror, not knowing what he was. And he went to the mirror and looked long and closely at his own face, at his own eyes, seeking for something. He was afraid, in mortal dry fear, but he knew not what of. He looked at his own face. There it was, shapely and healthy and the same as ever, yet somehow it was not real, it was a mask. He dared not touch it, for fear it should prove to be only a composition mask. His eyes were blue and keen as ever, and as firm in their look. Yet he was not sure that they were not blue false bubbles that would burst in a moment and leave clear annihilation. He could see the darkness in them, as if they were only bubbles of darkness. He was afraid that one day he would break down and be a purely meaningless bubble lapping round a darkness.

But his will yet held good, he was able to go away and read, and think about things. He liked to read books about the primitive man, books of anthropology, and also works of speculative philosophy. His mind was very active. But it was like a bubble floating in the darkness. At any moment it might burst and leave him in chaos. He would not die. He knew that. He would go on living, but the meaning would have collapsed out of him, his divine reason would be gone. In a strangely indifferent, sterile way, he was frightened. But he could not react even to the fear. It was as if his centres of feeling were drying up. He remained calm, calculative and healthy, and quite freely deliberate, even whilst he felt, with faint, small but final sterile horror, that his mystic reason was breaking, giving way now, at this crisis.

And it was a strain. He knew there was no equilibrium. He would have to go in some direction, shortly, to find relief. Only Birkin kept the fear definitely off him, saved him his quick sufficiency in life, by the odd mobility and changeableness which seemed to contain the quintessence of faith. But then Gerald must always come away from Birkin, as from a Church service, back to the outside real world of work and life. There it was, it did not alter, and words were futilities. He had to keep himself in reckoning with the world of work and material life. And it became more and more difficult, such a strange pressure was upon him, as if the very middle of him were a vacuum, and outside were an awful tension.

He had found his most satisfactory relief in women. After a debauch with some desperate woman, he went on quite easy and forgetful. The devil of it was, it was so hard to keep up his interest in women nowadays. He didn't care about them any more. A Pussum was all right in her way, but she was an exceptional case, and even she mattered extremely little. No, women, in that sense, were useless to him any more. He felt that his *mind* needed acute stimulation, before he could be physically roused.

XVIII. RABBIT

GUDRUN knew that it was a critical thing for her to go to Shortlands. She knew it was equivalent to accepting Gerald Crich as a lover. And though she hung back, disliking the condition, yet she knew she would go on. She equivocated. She said to herself, in torment recalling the blow and the kiss, "After all,

what is it? What is a kiss? What even is a blow? It is an
instant, vanished at once. I can go to Shortlands just for
a time, before I go away, if only to see what it is like."
For she had an insatiable curiosity to see and to know
everything.

She also wanted to know what Winifred was really
like. Having heard the child calling from the steamer in
the night, she felt some mysterious connection with her.

Gudrun talked with the father in the library. Then he
sent for his daughter. She came accompanied by Mademoiselle.

"Winnie, this is Miss Brangwen, who will be so kind
as to help you with your drawing and making models
of your animals," said the father.

The child looked at Gudrun for a moment with interest, before she came forward and with face averted
offered her hand. There was a complete sang-froid and
indifference under Winifred's childish reserve, a certain
irresponsible callousness.

"How do you do?" said the child, not lifting her face.

"How do you do?" said Gudrun.

Then Winifred stood aside, and Gudrun was introduced to Mademoiselle.

"You have a fine day for your walk," said Mademoiselle, in a bright manner.

"*Quite* fine," said Gudrun.

Winifred was watching from her distance. She was as
if amused, but rather unsure as yet what this new person
was like. She saw so many new persons, and so few who
became real to her. Mademoiselle was of no count whatever, the child merely put up with her, calmly and
easily, accepting her little authority with faint scorn,
compliant out of childish arrogance of indifference.

"Well, Winifred," said the father, "aren't you glad
Miss Brangwen has come? She makes animals and birds

in wood and in clay, that the people in London write
about in the papers, praising them to the skies."

Winifred smiled slightly.

"Who told you, Daddy?" she asked.

"Who told me? Hermione told me, and Rupert Birkin."

"Do you know them?" Winifred asked of Gudrun,
turning to her with faint challenge.

"Yes," said Gudrun.

Winifred readjusted herself a little. She had been
ready to accept Gudrun as a sort of servant. Now she
saw it was on terms of friendship they were intended to
meet. She was rather glad. She had so many half-
inferiors, whom she tolerated with perfect good-humour.

Gudrun was very calm. She also did not take these
things very seriously. A new occasion was mostly spec-
tacular to her. However, Winifred was a detached,
ironic child, she would never attach herself. Gudrun
liked her and was intrigued by her. The first meetings
went off with a certain humiliating clumsiness. Neither
Winifred nor her instructress had any social grace.

Soon, however, they met in a kind of make-belief
world. Winifred did not notice human beings unless they
were like herself, playful and slightly mocking. She
would accept nothing but the world of amusement, and
the serious people of her life were the animals she had
for pets. On those she lavished, almost ironically, her
affection and her companionship. To the rest of the
human scheme she submitted with a faint bored indifference.

She had a Pekinese dog called Looloo, which she
loved.

"Let us draw Looloo," said Gudrun, "and see if we
can get his Looliness, shall we?"

"Darling!" cried Winifred, rushing to the dog, that

sat with contemplative sadness on the hearth, and kissing its bulging brow. "Darling one, will you be drawn?
Shall its mummy draw its portrait?" Then she chuckled
gleefully, and turning to Gudrun, said: "Oh, let's!"

They proceeded to get pencils and paper, and were
ready.

"Beautifullest," cried Winifred, hugging the dog, "sit
still while its mummy draws its beautiful portrait." The
dog looked up at her with grievous resignation in its
large, prominent eyes. She kissed it fervently, and
said: "I wonder what mine will be like. It's sure to be
awful."

As she sketched she chuckled to herself, and cried out
at times:

"Oh, darling, you're so beautiful!"

And again chuckling, she rushed to embrace the dog,
in penitence, as if she were doing him some subtle in-
jury. He sat all the time with the resignation and fretfulness of ages on his dark velvety face. She drew slowly,
with a wicked concentration in her eyes, her head on one
side, an intense stillness over her. She was as if working
the spell of some enchantment. Suddenly she had
finished. She looked at the dog, and then at her drawing,
and then cried, with real grief for the dog, and at the
same time with a wicked exultation:

"My beautiful, why did they?"

She took her paper to the dog, and held it under his
nose. He turned his head aside as in chagrin and mortification, and she impulsively kissed his velvety bulging
forehead.

" 's a Loolie, 's a little Loozie! Look at his portrait,
darling, look at his portrait, that his mother has done of
him." She looked at her paper and chuckled. Then, kissing the dog once more, she rose and came gravely to
Gudrun, offering her the paper.

It was a grotesque little diagram of a grotesque little animal, so wicked and so comical, a slow smile came over Gudrun's face, unconsciously. And at her side Winifred chuckled with glee, and said:

"It isn't like him, is it? He's much lovelier than that. He's *so* beautiful—mmm, Looloo, my sweet darling." And she flew off to embrace the chagrined little dog. He looked up at her with reproachful, saturnine eyes, vanquished in his extreme agedness of being. Then she flew back to her drawing, and chuckled with satisfaction.

"It isn't like him, is it?" she said to Gudrun.

"Yes, it's very like him," Gudrun replied.

The child treasured her drawing, carried it about with her, and showed it, with a silent embarrassment, to everybody.

"Look," she said, thrusting the paper into her father's hand.

"Why, that's Looloo!" he exclaimed. And he looked down in surprise, hearing the almost inhuman chuckle of the child at his side.

Gerald was away from home when Gudrun first came to Shortlands. But the first morning he came back he watched for her. It was a sunny, soft morning, and he lingered in the garden paths, looking at the flowers that had come out during his absence. He was clean and fit as ever, shaven, his fair hair scrupulously parted at the side, bright in the sunshine, his short, fair moustache closely clipped, his eyes with their humorous kind twinkle, which was so deceptive. He was dressed in black, his clothes sat well on his well-nourished body. Yet as he lingered before the flower-beds in the morning sunshine, there was a certain isolation, a fear about him, as of something wanting.

Gudrun came up quickly, unseen. She was dressed in blue, with woollen yellow stockings, like the Bluecoat

boys. He glanced up in surprise. Her stockings always
disconcerted him, the pale-yellow stockings and the
heavy heavy black shoes. Winifred, who had been playing about the garden with Mademoiselle and the dogs,
came flitting towards Gudrun. The child wore a dress of
black-and-white stripes. Her hair was rather short, cut
round and hanging level in her neck.

"We're going to do Bismarck, aren't we?" she said,
linking her hand through Gudrun's arm.

"Yes, we're going to do Bismarck. Do you want to?"

"Oh yes—oh I do! I want most awfully to do Bismarck. He looks *so* splendid this morning, so *fierce*. He's
almost as big as a lion." And the child chuckled sardonically at her own hyperbole. "He's a real king, he
really is."

"Bon jour, Mademoiselle," said the little French
governess, wavering up with a slight bow, a bow of the
sort that Gudrun loathed, insolent.

"Winifred veut tant faire le portrait de Bismarck—!
Oh, mais toute le matinée—'We will do Bismarck this
morning!'—Bismarck, Bismarck, toujours Bismarck! C'est
un lapin, n'est-ce pas, mademoiselle?"

"Oui, c'est un grand lapin blanc et noir. Vous ne
l'avez pas vu?" said Gudrun in her good, but rather
heavy, French.

"Non, mademoiselle, Winifred n'a jamais voulu me le
faire voir. Tant de fois je le lui ai demandé, "Qu'est ce
donc que ce Bismarck, Winifred?' Mais elle n'a pas
voulu me le dire. Son Bismarck, c'était un mystère."

"Oui, c'est un mystère, vraiment un mystère! Miss
Brangwen, say that Bismarck is a mystery," cried Winifred.

"Bismarck is a mystery, Bismarck, c'est un mystère,
der Bismarck, er ist ein Wunder," said Gudrun, in mocking incantation.

"Ja er ist ein Wunder," repeated Winifred, with odd seriousness, under which lay a wicked chuckle.

"Ist er auch ein Wunder?" came the slightly insolent sneering of Mademoiselle.

"Doch!" said Winifred briefly, indifferent.

"Doch ist er nicht ein König. Beesmarck, he was not a king, Winifred, as you have said. He was only—il n'était que chancelier."

"Qu'est ce qu'un chancelier?" said Winifred, with slightly contemptuous indifference.

"A chancelier is a chancellor, and a chancellor is, I believe, a sort of judge," said Gerald, coming up and shaking hands with Gudrun. "You'll have made a song of Bismarck soon," said he.

Mademoiselle waited, and discreetly made her inclination, and her greeting.

"So they wouldn't let you see Bismarck, Mademoiselle?" he said.

"Non, Monsieur."

"Ay, very mean of them. What are you going to do to him, Miss Brangwen? I want him sent to the kitchen and cooked."

"Oh, no," cried Winifred.

"We're going to draw him," said Gudrun.

"Draw him and quarter him and dish him up," he said, being purposely fatuous.

"Oh, no," cried Winifred with emphasis, chuckling.

Gudrun detected the tang of mockery in him, and she looked up and smiled into his face. He felt his nerves caressed. Their eyes met in knowledge.

"How do you like Shortlands?" he asked.

"Oh, very much," she said, with nonchalance.

"Glad you do. Have you noticed these flowers?"

He led her along the path. She followed intently. Winifred came, and the governess lingered in the rear.

They stopped before some veined salpiglossis flowers.

"Aren't they wonderful!" she cried, looking at them absorbedly. Strange how her reverential, almost ecstatic admiration of the flowers caressed his nerves. She stooped down, and touched the trumpets, with infinitely fine and delicate-touching finger-tips. It filled him with ease to see her. When she rose, her eyes, hot with the beauty of the flowers, looked into his.

"What are they?" she asked.

"Sort of petunia, I suppose," he answered. "I don't really know them."

"They are quite strangers to me," she said.

They stood together in a false intimacy, a nervous contact. And he was in love with her.

She was aware of Mademoiselle standing near, like a little French beetle, observant and calculating. She moved away with Winifred, saying they would go to find Bismarck.

Gerald watched them go, looking all the while at the soft, full, still body of Gudrun, in its silky cashmere. How silky and rich and soft her body must be. An excess of appreciation came over his mind, she was the all-desirable, the all-beautiful. He wanted only to come to her, nothing more. He was only this, this being that should come to her, and be given to her.

At the same time he was finely and acutely aware of Mademoiselle's neat, brittle finality of form. She was like some elegant beetle with thin ankles, perched on her high heels, her glossy black dress perfectly correct, her dark hair done high and admirably. How repulsive her completeness and her finality was! He loathed her.

Yet he did admire her. She was perfectly correct. And it did rather annoy him that Gudrun came dressed in startling colours, like a macaw, when the family was in mourning. Like a macaw she was! He watched the lingering way she took her feet from the ground. And her ankles were pale yellow, and her dress a deep blue. Yet it pleased him. It pleased him very much. He felt the challenge in her very attire—she challenged the whole world. And he.smiled as to the note of a trumpet.

Gudrun and Winifred went through the house to the back, where were the stables and the out-buildings. Everywhere was still and deserted. Mr. Crich had gone out for a short drive, the stable-man had just led round Gerald's horse. The two girls went to the hutch that stood in a corner and looked at the great black-and-white rabbit.

"Isn't he beautiful! Oh, do look at him listening! Doesn't he look silly!" she laughed quickly, then added, "Oh, do let's do him listening, do let us, he listens with so much of himself;—don't you, darling Bismarck?"

"Can we take him out?" said Gudrun.

"He's very strong. He really is extremely strong." She looked at Gudrun, her head on one side, in odd calculating mistrust.

"But we'll try, shall we?"

"Yes, if you like. But he's a fearful kicker!"

They took the key to unlock the door. The rabbit exploded in a wild rush round the hutch.

"He scratches most awfully sometimes," cried Winifred in excitement. "Oh do look at him, isn't he wonderful!" The rabbit tore round the hutch in a flurry. "Bismarck!" cried the child, in rousing excitement. "How *dreadful* you are! You are beastly." Winifred looked up at Gudrun with some misgiving in her wild excitement. Gudrun smiled sardonically with her mouth. Winifred made a strange crooning noise of unaccountable excitement. "Now he's still!" she cried, seeing the rabbit settled down in a far corner of the hutch. "Shall we take him now?" she whispered excitedly, mysteriously, looking up at Gudrun and edging very close. "Shall we get him now?——" she chuckled wickedly to herself.

They unlocked the door of the hutch. Gudrun thrust in her arm and seized the great, lusty rabbit as it crouched still, she grasped its long ears. It set its four feet flat, and thrust back. There was a long scraping sound as it was hauled forward, and in another instant it was in mid-air, lunging wildly, its body flying like a spring coiled and released, as it lashed out, suspended from the ears. Gudrun held the black-and-white tempest at arms' length, averting her face. But the rabbit was magically strong, it was all she could do to keep her grasp. She almost lost her presence of mind.

"Bismarck, Bismarck, you are behaving terribly," said Winifred in a rather frightened voice, "Oh, do put him down, he's beastly."

Gudrun stood for a moment astounded by the thunderstorm that had sprung into being in her grip. Then her colour came up, a heavy rage came over her like a cloud. She stood shaken as a house in a storm, and utterly overcome. Her heart was arrested with fury at the mindlessness and the bestial stupidity of this struggle, her wrists were badly scored by the claws of the beast, a heavy cruelty welled up in her.

Gerald came round as she was trying to capture the flying rabbit under her arm. He saw, with subtle recognition, her sullen passion of cruelty.

"You should let one of the men do that for you," he said hurrying up.

"Oh, he's *so* horrid!" cried Winifred, almost frantic.

He held out his nervous, sinewy hand and took the rabbit by the ears, from Gudrun.

"It's most *fearfully* strong," she cried, in a high voice, like the crying of a seagull, strange and vindictive.

The rabbit made itself into a ball in the air, and lashed

out, flinging itself into a bow. It really seemed demonia-
cal. Gudrun saw Gerald's body tighten, saw a sharp
blindness come into his eyes.

"I know these beggars of old," he said.

The long, demon-like beast lashed out again, spread
on the air as if it were flying, looking something like a
dragon, then closing up again, inconceivably powerful
and explosive. The man's body, strung to its efforts, vibrated strongly. Then a sudden sharp, white-edged
wrath came upon him. Swift as lightning he drew back
and brought his free hand down like a hawk on the neck
of the rabbit. Simultaneously, there came the unearthly
abhorrent scream of a rabbit in the fear of death. It
made one immense writhe, tore his wrists and his sleeves
in a final convulsion, all its belly flashed white in a whirl-
wind of paws, and then he had slung it round and had it
under his arm, fast. It cowered and skulked. His face
was gleaming with a smile.

"You wouldn't think there was all that force in a
rabbit," he said, looking at Gudrun. And he saw her eyes
black as night in her pallid face, she looked almost unearthly. The scream of the rabbit, after the violent tussle,
seemed to have torn the veil of her consciousness. He
looked at her, and the whitish, electric gleam in his face
intensified.

"I don't really like him," Winifred was crooning. "I
don't care for him as I do for Loozie. He's hateful really."

A smile twisted Gudrun's face, as she recovered. She
knew she was revealed.

"Don't they make the most fearful noise when they
scream?" she cried, the high note in her voice, like a
seagull's cry.

"Abominable," he said.

"He shouldn't be so silly when he has to be taken
out," Winifred was saying, putting out her hand and

touching the rabbit tentatively, as it skulked under his arm, motionless as if it were dead.

"He's not dead, is he Gerald?" she asked.

"No, he ought to be," he said.

"Yes, he ought!" cried the child, with a sudden flush of amusement. And she touched the rabbit with more confidence. "His heart is beating *so* fast. Isn't he funny? He really is."

"Where do you want him?" asked Gerald.

"In the little green court," she said.

Gudrun looked at Gerald with strange, darkened eyes, strained with underworld knowledge, almost supplicating, like those of a creature which is at his mercy, yet which is his ultimate victor. He did not know what to say to her. He felt the mutual hellish recognition. And he felt he ought to say something, to cover it. He had the power of lightning in his nerves, she seemed like a soft recipient of his magical, hideous white fire. He was unconfident, he had qualms of fear.

"Did he hurt you?" he asked.

"No," she said.

"He's an insensible beast," he said, turning his face away.

They came to the little court, which was shut in by old red walls in whose crevices wall-flowers were growing. The grass was soft and fine and old, a level floor carpeting the court, the sky was blue overhead. Gerald tossed the rabbit down. It crouched still and would not move. Gudrun watched it with faint horror.

"Why doesn't it move?" she cried.

"It's skulking," he said.

She looked up at him, and a slight sinister smile contracted her white face.

"Isn't it a *fool!*" she cried. "Isn't it a sickening *fool?*" The vindictive mockery in her voice made his brain

quiver. Glancing up at him, into his eyes, she revealed
again the mocking, white-cruel recognition. There was a
league between them, abhorrent to them both. They
were implicated with each other in abhorrent mysteries.

"How many scratches have you?" he asked, showing
his hard forearm, white and hard and torn in red gashes.

"How really vile!" she cried, flushing with a sinister
vision. "Mine is nothing."

She lifted her arm and showed a deep red score down
the silken white flesh.

"What a devil!" he exclaimed. But it was as if he had
had knowledge of her in the long red rent of her forearm, so silken and soft. He did not want to touch her.
He would have to make himself touch her, deliberately.
The long, shallow red rip seemed torn across his own
brain, tearing the surface of his ultimate consciousness,
letting through the forever unconscious, unthinkable red
ether of the beyond, the obscene beyond.

"It doesn't hurt you very much, does it?" he asked
solicitous.

"Not at all," she cried.

And suddenly the rabbit, which had been crouching
as if it were a flower, so still and soft, suddenly burst
into life. Round and round the court it went, as if shot
from a gun, round and round like a furry meteorite, in
a tense hard circle that seemed to bind their brains.
They all stood in amazement, smiling uncannily, as if the
rabbit were obeying some unknown incantation. Round
and round it flew, on the grass under the old red walls
like a storm.

And then quite suddenly it settled down, hobbled
among the grass, and sat considering, its nose twitching
like a bit of fluff in the wind. After having considered for
a few minutes, a soft bunch with a black, open eye,
which perhaps was looking at them, perhaps was not, it

hobbled calmly forward and began to nibble the grass with that mean motion of a rabbit's quick eating.

"It's mad," said Gudrun. "It is most decidedly mad."

He laughed.

"The question is," he said, "what is madness? I don't suppose it is rabbit-mad."

"Don't you think it is?" she asked.

"No. That's what it is to be a rabbit."

There was a queer, faint, obscene smile over his face. She looked at him and saw him, and knew that he was initiate as she was initiate. This thwarted her, and contravened her, for the moment.

"God be praised we aren't rabbits," she said, in a high, shrill voice.

The smile intensified a little, on his face.

"Not rabbits?" he said, looking at her fixedly.

Slowly her face relaxed into a smile of obscene recognition.

"Ah Gerald," she said, in a strong, slow, almost man-like way. "—All that, and more." Her eyes looked up at him with shocking nonchalance.

He felt again as if she had hit him across the face— or rather, as if she had torn him across the breast, dully, finally. He turned aside.

"Eat, eat, my darling!" Winifred was softly conjuring the rabbit, and creeping forward to touch it. It hobbled away from her. "Let its mother stroke its fur then, darling, because it is so mysterious——"

XIX. MOONY

AFTER his illness Birkin went to the south of France for a time. He did not write, nobody heard anything of him. Ursula, left alone, felt as if everything were lapsing out. There seemed to be no hope in the world. One was a tiny little rock with the tide of nothingness rising higher and higher. She herself was real, and only herself—just like a rock in a wash of flood-water. The rest was all nothingness. She was hard and indifferent, isolated in herself.

There was nothing for it now but contemptuous, resistant indifference. All the world was lapsing into a grey wish-wash of nothingness, she had no contact and no connection anywhere. She despised and detested the whole show. From the bottom of her heart, from the bottom of her soul, she despised and detested people, adult people. She loved only children and animals: children she loved passionately, but coldly. They made her want to hug them, to protect them, to give them life. But this very love, based on pity and despair, was only a bondage and a pain to her. She loved best of all the animals, that were single and unsocial as she herself was. She loved the horses and cows in the field. Each was single and to itself, magical. It was not referred away to some detestable social principle. It was incapable of soulfulness and tragedy, which she detested so profoundly.

She could be very pleasant and flattering, almost subservient, to people she met. But no one was taken in. Instinctively each felt her contemptuous mockery of the human being in himself, or herself. She had a profound grudge against the human being. That which the word "human" stood for was despicable and repugnant to her.

Mostly her heart was closed in this hidden, unconscious strain of contemptuous ridicule. She thought she loved, she thought she was full of love. This was her idea of herself. But the strange brightness of her presence, a marvellous radiance of intrinsic vitality, was a luminousness of supreme repudiation, nothing but repudiation.

Yet, at moments, she yielded and softened, she wanted pure love, only pure love. This other, this state of constant unfailing repudiation, was a strain, a suffering also. A terrible desire for pure love overcame her again.

She went out one evening, numbed by this constant essential suffering. Those who are timed for destruction must die now. The knowledge of this reached a finality, a finishing in her. And the finality released her. If fate would carry off in death or downfall all those who were timed to go, why need she trouble, why repudiate any further. She was free of it all, she could seek a new union elsewhere.

Ursula set off to Willey Green, towards the mill. She came to Willey Water. It was almost full again, after its period of emptiness. Then she turned off through the woods. The night had fallen, it was dark. But she forgot to be afraid, she who had such great sources of fear. Among the trees, far from any human beings, there was a sort of magic peace. The more one could find a pure loneliness, with no taint of people, the better one felt. She was in reality terrified, horrified, in her apprehension of people.

She started, noticing something on her right hand, between the tree trunks. It was like a great presence, watching her, dodging her. She started violently. It was only the moon, risen through the thin trees. But it seemed so mysterious, with its white and deathly smile. And there was no avoiding it. Night or day, one could not escape the sinister face, triumphant and radiant like this moon, with a high smile. She hurried on, cowering from the white planet. She would just see the pond at the mill before she went home.

Not wanting to go through the yard, because of the dogs, she turned off along the hill-side to descend on the pond from above. The moon was transcendent over the bare, open space, she suffered from being exposed to it. There was a glimmer of nightly rabbits across the ground. The night was as clear as crystal, and very still. She could hear a distant coughing of a sheep.

So she swerved down to the steep, tree-hidden bank above the pond, where the alders twisted their roots. She was glad to pass into the shade out of the moon. There she stood, at the top of the fallen-away bank, her hand on the rough trunk of a tree, looking at the water, that was perfect in its stillness, floating the moon upon it. But for some reason she disliked it. It did not give her anything. She listened for the hoarse rustle of the sluice. And she wished for something else out of the night, she wanted another night, not this moon-brilliant hardness. She could feel her soul crying out in her, lamenting desolately.

She saw a shadow moving by the water. It would be Birkin. He had come back then, unawares. She accepted it without remark, nothing mattered to her. She sat down among the roots of the alder tree, dim and veiled, hearing the sound of the sluice like dew distilling audibly into the night. The islands were dark and half revealed, the reeds were dark also, only some of them had a little frail fire of reflection. A fish leaped secretly, revealing the light in the pond. This fire of the chill night breaking constantly on to the pure darkness repelled her. She wished it were perfectly dark, perfectly, and noiseless and without motion. Birkin, small and dark also, his hair tinged with moonlight, wandered nearer. He was quite near, and yet he did not exist in her. He did not know she was there. Supposing he did something he would not wish to be seen doing, thinking he was quite private? But there, what did it matter? What did the small privacies matter? How could it matter, what he did? How can there be any secrets, we are all the same organisms? How can there be any secrecy, when everything is known to all of us?

He was touching unconsciously the dead husks of flowers as he passed by, and talking disconnectedly to himself.

"You can't go away," he was saying. "There *is* no away. You only withdraw upon yourself."

He threw a dead flower-husk on to the water.

"An antiphony—they lie, and you sing back to them. There wouldn't have to be any truth, if there weren't any lies. Then one needn't assert anything——"

He stood still, looking at the water, and throwing upon it the husks of the flowers.

"Cybele—curse her! The accursed Syria Dea! Does one begrudge it her? What else is there——?"

Ursula wanted to laugh loudly and hysterically, hearing his isolated voice speaking out. It was so ridiculous.

He stood staring at the water. Then he stooped and picked up a stone, which he threw sharply at the pond. Ursula was aware of the bright moon leaping and swaying, all distorted, in her eyes. It seemed to shoot out arms of fire like a cuttlefish, like a luminous polyp, palpitating strongly before her.

And his shadow on the border of the pond was watching for a few moments, then he stooped and groped on the ground. Then again there was a burst of

sound, and a burst of brilliant light, the moon had exploded on the water, and was flying asunder in flakes of
white and dangerous fire. Rapidly, like white birds, the
fires all broken rose across the pond, fleeing in clamorous
confusion, battling with the flock of dark waves that
were forcing their way in. The furthest waves of light,
fleeing out, seemed to be clamouring against the shore
for escape, the waves of darkness came in heavily, running under towards the centre. But at the centre, the
heart of all, was still a vivid, incandescent quivering of
a white moon not quite destroyed, a white body of fire
writhing and striving and not even now broken open, not
yet violated. It seemed to be drawing itself together
with strange, violent pangs, in blind effort. It was getting
stronger, it was reasserting itself, the inviolable moon.
And the rays were hastening in in thin lines of light, to
return to the strengthened moon, that shook upon the
water in triumphant reassumption.

Birkin stood and watched, motionless, till the pond
was almost calm, the moon was almost serene. Then,
satisfied of so much, he looked for more stones. She felt
his invisible tenacity. And in a moment again, the
broken lights scattered in explosion over her face,
dazzling her; and then, almost immediately, came the
second shot. The moon leapt up white and burst through
the air. Darts of bright light shot asunder, darkness
swept over the centre. There was no moon, only a battle-
field of broken lights and shadows, running close together. Shadows, dark and heavy, struck again and again
across the place where the heart of the moon had been,
obliterating it altogether. The white fragments pulsed
up and down, and could not find where to go, apart
and brilliant on the water like the petals of a rose that a
wind has blown far and wide.

Yet again, they were flickering their way to the centre,

finding the path blindly, enviously. And again, all was still, as Birkin and Ursula watched. The waters were loud on the shore. He saw the moon regathering itself insidiously, saw the heart of the rose intertwining vigorously and blindly, calling back the scattered fragments, winning home the fragments, in a pulse and in effort of return.

And he was not satisfied. Like a madness, he must go on. He got large stones, and threw them, one after the other, at the white-burning centre of the moon, till there was nothing but a rocking of hollow noise, and a pond surged up, no moon any more, only a few broken flakes tangled and glittering broadcast in the darkness, without aim or meaning, a darkened confusion, like a black and white kaleidoscope tossed at random. The hollow night was rocking and crashing with noise, and from the sluice came sharp, regular flashes of sound. Flakes of light appeared here and there, glittering tormented among the shadows, far off, in strange places; among the dripping shadow of the willow on the island. Birkin stood and listened and was satisfied.

Ursula was dazed, her mind was all gone. She felt she had fallen to the ground and was spilled out, like water on the earth. Motionless and spent she remained in the gloom. Though even now she was aware, unseeing, that in the darkness was a little tumult of ebbing flakes of light, a cluster dancing secretly in a round, twining and coming steadily together. They were gathering a heart again, they were coming once more into being. Gradually the fragments caught together reunited, heaving, rocking, dancing, falling back as in panic, but working their way home again persistently, making semblance of fleeing away when they had advanced, but always flickering nearer, a little closer to the mark, the cluster growing mysteriously larger and brighter, as gleam after gleam fell in with the whole, until a ragged rose, a distorted, frayed moon was shaking upon the water again, reasserted, renewed, trying to recover from its convulsion, to get over the disfigurement and the agitation, to be whole and composed, at peace.

Birkin lingered vaguely by the water. Ursula was afraid that he would stone the moon again. She slipped from her seat and went down to him, saying:

"You won't throw stones at it any more, will you?"

"How long have you been there?"

"All the time. You won't throw any more stones, will you?"

"I wanted to see if I could make it be quite gone off the pond," he said.

"Yes, it was horrible, really. Why should you hate the moon? It hasn't done you any harm, has it?"

"Was it hate?" he said.

And they were silent for a few minutes.

"When did you come back?" she said.

"Today."

"Why did you never write?"

"I could find nothing to say."

"Why was there nothing to say?"

"I don't know. Why are there no daffodils now?"

"No."

Again there was a space of silence. Ursula looked at the moon. It had gathered itself together and was quivering slightly.

"Was it good for you, to be alone?" she asked.

"Perhaps. Not that I know much. But I got over a good deal. Did you do anything important?"

"No. I looked at England, and thought I'd done with it."

"Why England?" he asked in surprise.

"I don't know, it came like that."

"It 'isn't a question of nations," he said. "France is far worse."

"Yes, I know. I felt I'd done with it all."

They went and sat down on the roots of the trees, in the shadow. And being silent, he remembered the beauty of her eyes, which were sometimes filled with light, like spring, suffused with wonderful promise. So he said to her, slowly, with difficulty:

"There is a golden light in you, which I wish you would give me." It was as if he had been thinking of this for some time.

She was startled, she seemed to leap clear of him. Yet also she was pleased.

"What kind of a light?" she asked.

But he was shy, and did not say any more. So the moment passed for this time. And gradually a feeling of sorrow came over her.

"My life is unfulfilled," she said.

"Yes," he answered briefly, not wanting to hear this.

"And I feel as if nobody could ever really love me," she said.

But he did not answer.

"You think, don't you," she said slowly, "that I only want physical things? It isn't true. I want you to serve my spirit."

"I know you do. I know you don't want physical things by themselves. But, I want you to give me—to give your spirit to me—that golden light which is you— which you don't know—give it me——"

After a moment's silence she replied:

"But how can I, you don't love me! You only want your own ends. You don't want to serve *me*, and yet you want me to serve you. It is so one-sided!"

It was a great effort to him to maintain this conversation, and to press for the thing he wanted from her, the surrender of her spirit.

"It is different," he said. "The two kinds of service are so different. I serve you in another way—not through *yourself*—somewhere else. But I want us to be together without bothering about ourselves—to be really together because we *are* together, as if it were a phenomenon, not a thing we have to maintain by our own effort."

"No," she said, pondering. "You are just egocentric. You never have any enthusiasm, you never come out with any spark towards me. You want yourself, really, and your own affairs. And you want me just to be there, to serve you."

But this only made him shut off from her.

"Ah well," he said, "words make no matter, any way. The thing *is* between us, or it isn't."

"You don't even love me," she cried.

"I do," he said angrily. "But I want——" His mind saw again the lovely golden light of spring transfused through her eyes, as through some wonderful window. And he wanted her to be with him there, in this world of proud indifference. But what was the good of telling her he wanted this company in proud indifference? What was the good of talking, any way? It must happen beyond the sound of words. It was merely ruinous to try to work her by conviction. This was a paradisal bird that could never be netted, it must fly by itself to the heart.

"I always think I am going to be loved—and then I am let down. You *don't* love me, you know. You don't want to serve me. You only want yourself."

A shiver of rage went over his veins, at this repeated: "You don't want to serve me." All the paradisal disappeared from him.

"No," he said irritated, "I don't want to serve you, because there is nothing there to serve. What you want me
to serve, is nothing, mere nothing. It isn't even you, it is
your mere female quality. And I wouldn't give a straw
for your female ego—it's a rag doll."

"Ha!" she laughed in mockery. "That's all you think of
me, is it? And then you have the impudence to say you
love me!"

She rose in anger, to go home.

"You want the paradisal unknowing," she said, turning round on him as he still sat half-visible in the
shadow. "I know what that means, thank you. You want
me to be your thing, never to criticize you or to have
anything to say for myself. You want me to be a mere
thing for you! No thank you! If you want that, there are
plenty of women who will give it to you. There are
plenty of women who will lie down for you to walk
over them—*go* to them then, if that's what you want—
go to them."

"No," he said, outspoken with anger. "I want you to
drop your assertive *will*, your frightened apprehensive
self-insistence, that is what I want. I want you to trust
yourself so implicitly that you can let yourself go."

"Let myself go!" she re-echoed in mockery. "*I* can let
myself go, easily enough. It is you who can't let yourself
go, it is you who hang on to yourself as if it were your
only treasure. *You*—*you* are the Sunday school teacher
—*you*—you preacher."

The amount of truth that was in this made him stiff
and unheeding of her.

"I don't mean let yourself go in the Dionysiac ecstatic
way," he said. "I know you can do that. But I hate ecstasy, Dionysiac or any other. It's like going round in a
squirrel cage. I want you not to care about yourself, just

to be there and not to care about yourself, not to insist
—be glad and sure and indifferent."

"Who insists?" she mocked. "Who is it that keeps on
insisting? It isn't *me!*"

There was a weary, mocking bitterness in her voice.
He was silent for some time.

"I know," he said. "While ever either of us insists to
the other, we are all wrong. But there we are, the accord
doesn't come."

They sat in stillness under the shadow of the trees by
the bank. The night was white around them, they were
in the darkness, barely conscious.

Gradually, the stillness and peace came over them.
She put her hand tentatively on his. Their hands clasped
softly and silently, in peace.

"Do you really love me?" she said.

He laughed.

"I call that your war-cry," he replied, amused.

"Why!" she cried, amused and really wondering.

"Your insistence—Your war-cry—'A Brangwen, A
Brangwen,'—an old battle-cry. Yours is 'Do you love
me? Yield knave, or die.'"

"No," she said, pleading, "not like that. Not like that.
But I must know that you love me, mustn't I?"

"Well, then, know it and have done with it."

"But do you?"

"Yes, I do. I love you, and I know it's final. It is final,
so why say any more about it."

She was silent for some moments, in delight and
doubt.

"Are you sure?" she said, nestling happily near to him.

"Quite sure—so now have done—accept it and have
done."

She was nestled quite close to him.

"Have done with what?" she murmured, happily.

"With bothering," he said.

She clung nearer to him. He held her close and kissed her softly, gently. It was such peace and heavenly freedom, just to fold her and kiss her gently, and not to have any thoughts or any desires or any will, just to be still with her, to be perfectly still and together, in a peace that was not sleep, but content in bliss. To be content in bliss, without desire or insistence anywhere, this was heaven: to be together in happy stillness.

For a long time she nestled to him, and he kissed her softly, her hair, her face, her ears, gently, softly, like dew falling. But this warm breath on her ears disturbed her again, kindled the old destructive fires. She cleaved to him, and he could feel his blood changing like quicksilver.

"But we'll be still, shall we?" he said.

"Yes," she said, as if submissively.

And she continued to nestle against him.

But in a little while she drew away and looked at him.

"I must be going home," she said.

"Must you—how sad," he replied.

She leaned forward and put up her mouth to be kissed.

"Are you really sad?" she murmured, smiling.

"Yes," he said, "I wish we could stay as we were, always."

"Always! Do you?" she murmured, as he kissed her. And then, out of a full throat, she crooned "Kiss me! Kiss me!" And she cleaved close to him. He kissed her many times. But he too had his idea and his will. He wanted only gentle communion, no other, no passion now. So that soon she drew away, put on her hat and went home.

The next day, however, he felt wistful and yearning.

He thought he had been wrong, perhaps. Perhaps he had been wrong to go to her with an idea of what he wanted. Was it really only an idea, or was it the interpretation of a profound yearning? If the latter, how was it he was always talking about sensual fulfilment? The two did not agree very well.

Suddenly he found himself face to face with a situation. It was as simple as this: fatally simple. On the one hand, he knew he did not want a further sensual experience—something deeper, darker, than ordinary life could give. He remembered the African fetishes he had seen at Halliday's so often. There came back to him one, a statuette about two feet high, a tall, slim, elegant figure from West Africa, in dark wood, glossy and suave. It was a woman, with hair dressed high, like a melon-shaped dome. He remembered her vividly: she was one of his soul's intimates. Her body was long and elegant, her face was crushed tiny like a beetle's, she had rows of round heavy collars, like a column of quoits, on her neck. He remembered her: her astonishing cultured elegance, her diminished, beetle face, the astounding long elegant body, on short, ugly legs, with such protuberant buttocks, so weighty and unexpected below her slim long loins. She knew what he himself did not know. She had thousands of years of purely sensual, purely unspiritual knowledge behind her. It must have been thousands of years since her race had died, mystically: that is, since the relation between the senses and the outspoken mind had broken, leaving the experience all in one sort, mystically sensual. Thousands of years ago, that which was imminent in himself must have taken place in these Africans: the goodness, the holiness, the desire for creation and productive happiness must have lapsed, leaving the single impulse for knowledge in one sort, mindless progressive knowledge through the senses, knowledge arrested and ending in the senses, mystic knowledge in disintegration and dissolution, knowledge such as the beetles have, which live purely within the world of corruption and cold dissolution. This was why her face looked like a beetle's: this was why the Egyptians worshipped the ball-rolling scarab: because of the principle of knowledge in dissolution and corruption.

There is a long way we can travel, after the death-break: after that point when the soul in intense suffering breaks, breaks away from its organic hold like a leaf that falls. We fall from the connection with life and hope, we lapse from pure integral being, from creation and liberty, and we fall into the long, long African process of purely sensual understanding, knowledge in the mystery of dissolution.

He realized now that this is a long process—thousands of years it takes, after the death of the creative spirit. He realized that there were great mysteries to be unsealed, sensual, mindless, dreadful mysteries, far beyond the phallic cult. How far, in their inverted culture, had these West Africans gone beyond phallic knowledge? Very, very far. Birkin recalled again the female figure: the elongated, long, long body, the curious unexpected heavy buttocks, the long, imprisoned neck, the face with tiny features like a beetle's. This was far beyond any phallic knowledge, sensual subtle realities far beyond the scope of phallic investigation.

There remained this way, this awful African process, to be fulfilled. It would be done differently by the white races. The white races, having the arctic north behind them, the vast abstraction of ice and snow, would fulfil a mystery of ice-destructive knowledge, snow-abstract annihilation. Whereas the West Africans, controlled by the burning death-abstraction of the Sahara, had been fulfilled in sun-destruction, the putrescent mystery of sun-rays.

Was this then all that remained? Was there left now nothing but to break off from the happy creative being, was the time up? Is our day of creative life finished? Does there remain to us only the strange, awful after-wards of the knowledge in dissolution, the African knowledge, but different in us, who are blond and blue-eyed from the north?

Birkin thought of Gerald. He was one of these strange white wonderful demons from the north, fulfilled in the destructive frost mystery. And was he fated to pass away in this knowledge, this one process of frost-knowledge, death by perfect cold? Was he a messenger, an omen of the universal dissolution into whiteness and snow?

Birkin was frightened. He was tired, too, when he had reached this length of speculation. Suddenly his strange, strained attention gave way, he could not attend to these mysteries any more. There was another way, the way of freedom. There was the paradisal entry into pure, single being, the individual soul taking precedence over love and desire for union, stronger than any pangs of emo-tion, a lovely state of free proud singleness, which ac-cepted the obligation of the permanent connection with others, and with the other, submits to the yoke and leash of love, but never forfeits its own proud individual singleness, even while it loves and yields.

There was the other way, the remaining way. And he must run to follow it. He thought of Ursula, how sensi-tive and delicate she really was, her skin so over-fine, as if one skin were wanting. She was really so marvellously gentle and sensitive. Why did he ever forget it? He must go to her at once. He must ask her to marry him. They must marry at once, and so make a definite pledge, enter into a definite communion. He must set out at once and ask her, this moment. There was no moment to spare.

He drifted on swiftly to Beldover, half-unconscious of his own movement. He saw the town on the slope of the hill, not straggling, but as if walled-in with the straight, final streets of miners' dwellings, making a great square, and it looked like Jerusalem to his fancy. The world was all strange and transcendent.

Rosalind opened the door to him. She started slightly, as a young girl will, and said:

"Oh, I'll tell father."

With which she disappeared, leaving Birkin in the hall, looking at some reproductions from Picasso, lately introduced by Gudrun. He was admiring the almost wizard, sensuous apprehension of the earth, when Will Brangwen appeared, rolling down his shirt sleeves.

"Well," said Brangwen, "I'll get a coat." And he too disappeared for a moment. Then he returned, and opened the door of the drawing-room, saying:

"You must excuse me, I was just doing a bit of work in the shed. Come inside, will you."

Birkin entered and sat down. He looked at the bright, reddish face of the other man, at the narrow brow and the very bright eyes, and at the rather sensual lips that unrolled wide and expansive under the black cropped moustache. How curious it was that this was a human being! What Brangwen thought himself to be, how meaningless it was, confronted with the reality of him. Birkin could see only a strange, inexplicable almost patternless collection of passions and desires and suppressions and traditions and mechanical ideas, all cast unfused and disunited into this slender, bright-faced man of nearly fifty, who was as unresolved now as he was at twenty, and as uncreated. How could he be the parent of Ursula, when he was not created himself. He was not a parent. A slip of living flesh had been transmitted through him, but the spirit had not come from him. The spirit had not come from any ancestor, it had come out of the unknown. A child is the child of the mystery, or it is uncreated.

"The weather's not so bad as it has been," said Brangwen, after waiting a moment. There was no connection between the two men.

"No," said Birkin. "It was full moon two days ago."

"Oh! You believe in the moon then, affecting the weather?"

"No, I don't think I do. I don't really know enough about it."

"You know what they say? The moon and the weather may change together, but the change of the moon won't change the weather."

"Is that it?" said Birkin. "I hadn't heard it."

There was a pause. Then Birkin said:

"Am I hindering you? I called to see Ursula, really. Is she at home?"

"I don't believe she is. I believe she's gone to the library. I'll just see."

Birkin could hear him enquiring in the dining room.

"No," he said, coming back. "But she won't be long. You wanted to speak to her?"

Birkin looked across at the other man with curious calm, clear eyes.

"As a matter of fact," he said, "I wanted to ask her to marry me."

A point of light came on the golden-brown eyes of the elder man.

"O-oh?" he said, looking at Birkin, then dropping his eyes before the calm, steadily watching look of the other: "Was she expecting you then?"

"No," said Birkin.

"No? I didn't know anything of this sort was on foot——" Brangwen smiled awkwardly.

Birkin looked back at him, and said to himself: "I wonder why it should be 'on foot'!" Aloud he said:

"No, it's perhaps rather sudden." At which, thinking of his relationship with Ursula, he added—"But I don't know—"

"Quite sudden, is it? Oh!" said Brangwen, rather baffled and annoyed.

"In one way," replied Birkin, "not in another."

There was a moment's pause, after which Brangwen said:

"Well, she pleases herself——"

"Oh yes!" said Birkin, calmly.

A vibration came into Brangwen's strong voice, as he replied:

"Though I shouldn't want her to be in too big a hurry, either. It's no good looking round afterwards, when it's too late."

"Oh, it need never be too late," said Birkin, "as far as that goes."

"How do you mean?" asked the father.

"If one repents being married, the marriage is at an end," said Birkin.

"You think so?"

"Yes."

"Ay, well, that may be your way of looking at it."

Birkin, in silence, thought to himself: "So it may. As for *your* way of looking at it, William Brangwen, it needs a little explaining."

"I suppose," said Brangwen, "you know what sort of people we are? What sort of a bringing-up she's had?"

"'She,'" thought Birkin to himself, remembering his childhood's corrections, "is the cat's mother."

"Do I know what sort of a bringing-up she's had?" he said aloud.

He seemed to annoy Brangwen intentionally.

"Well," he said, "she's had everything that's right for a girl to have—as far as possible, as far as we could give it her."

"I'm sure she has," said Birkin, which caused a perilous full-stop. The father was becoming exasperated. There was something naturally irritant to him in Birkin's mere presence.

"And I don't want to see her going back on it all," he said, in a clanging voice.

"Why?" said Birkin.

This monosyllable exploded in Brangwen's brain like a shot.

"Why! *I* don't believe in your new-fangled ways and new-fangled ideas—in and out like a frog in a gallipot. It would never do for me."

Birkin watched him with steady emotionless eyes. The radical antagonism in the two men was rousing.

"Yes, but are my ways and ideas new-fangled?" asked Birkin.

"Are they?" Brangwen caught himself up. "I'm not speaking of you in particular," he said. "What I mean is that my children have been brought up to think and do according to the religion I was brought up in myself, and I don't want to see them going away from *that*."

There was a dangerous pause.

"And beyond that——?" asked Birkin.

The father hesitated, he was in a nasty position.

"Eh? What do you mean? All I want to say is that my daughter"—he tailed off into silence, overcome by futility. He knew that in some way he was off the track.

"Of course," said Birkin, "I don't want to hurt anybody or influence anybody. Ursula does exactly as she pleases."

There was a complete silence, because of the utter failure in mutual understanding. Birkin felt bored. Her father was not a coherent human being, he was a roomful of old echoes. The eyes of the younger man rested on the face of the elder. Brangwen looked up, and saw Birkin looking at him. His face was covered with inarticulate anger and humiliation and sense of inferiority in strength.

"And as for beliefs, that's one thing," he said. "But I'd rather see my daughters dead tomorrow than that they should be at the beck and call of the first man that likes to come and whistle for them."

A queer painful light came into Birkin's eyes.

"As to that," he said, "I only know that it's much more likely that it's I who am at the beck and call of the woman, than she at mine."

Again there was a pause. The father was somewhat bewildered.

"I know," he said, "she'll please herself—she always has done. I've done my best for them, but that doesn't matter. They've got themselves to please, and if they can help it they'll please nobody *but* themselves. But she's a right to consider her mother, and me as well——"

Brangwen was thinking his own thoughts.

"And I tell you this much, I would rather bury them, than see them getting into a lot of loose ways such as you see everywhere nowadays. I'd rather bury them——"

"Yes but, you see," said Birkin slowly, rather wearily, bored again by this new turn, "they won't give either you or me the chance to bury them, because they're not to be buried."

Brangwen looked at him in a sudden flare of impotent anger.

"Now, Mr. Birkin," he said, "I don't know what you've come here for, and I don't know what you're asking for. But my daughters are my daughters—and it's *my* business to look after them while I can."

Birkin's brows knitted suddenly, his eyes concentrated in mockery. But he remained perfectly stiff and still. There was a pause.

"I've nothing against your marrying Ursula," Brangwen began at length. "It's got nothing to do with me, she'll do as she likes, me or no me."

Birkin turned away, looking out of the window and letting go his consciousness. After all, what good was this? It was hopeless to keep it up. He would sit on till Ursula came home, then speak to her, then go away. He would not accept trouble at the hands of her father. It was all unnecessary, and he himself need not have provoked it.

The two men sat in complete silence, Birkin almost unconscious of his own whereabouts. He had come to ask her to marry him—well, then, he would wait on, and ask her. As for what she said, whether she accepted or not, he did not think about it. He would say what he had come to say, and that was all he was conscious of. He accepted the complete insignificance of this household, for him. But everything now was as if fated. He could see one thing ahead, and no more. From the rest, he was absolved entirely for the time being. It had to be left to fate and chance to resolve the issues.

At length they heard the gate. They saw her coming up the steps with a bundle of books under her arm. Her face was bright and abstracted as usual, with the abstraction, that look of being not quite *there*, not quite present to the facts of reality, that galled her father so much. She had a maddening faculty of assuming a light of her own, which excluded the reality, and within which she looked radiant as if in sunshine.

They heard her go into the dining-room, and drop her armful of books on the table.

"Did you bring me that Girl's Own?" cried Rosalind.

"Yes, I brought it. But I forgot which one it was you wanted."

"You would," cried Rosalind angrily. "It's right for a wonder."

Then they heard her say something in a lowered tone.

"Where?" cried Ursula.

Again her sister's voice was muffled.

Brangwen opened the door, and called, in his strong, brazen voice:

"Ursula."

She appeared in a moment, wearing her hat.

"Oh, how do you do!" she cried, seeing Birkin, and all dazzled as if taken by surprise. He wondered at her, knowing she was aware of his presence. She had her queer, radiant, breathless manner, as if confused by the actual world, unreal to it, having a complete bright world of her self alone.

"Have I interrupted a conversation?" she asked.

"No, only a complete silence," said Birkin.

"Oh," said Ursula, vaguely, absent. Their presence was not vital to her, she was withheld, she did not take them in. It was a subtle insult that never failed to exasperate her father.

"Mr. Birkin came to speak to *you*, not to me," said her father.

"Oh, did he!" she exclaimed vaguely, as if it did not concern her. Then, recollecting herself, she turned to him rather radiantly, but still quite superficially, and said: "Was it anything special?"

"I hope so," he said, ironically.

"—To propose to you, according to all accounts," said her father.

"Oh," said Ursula.

"Oh," mocked her father, imitating her. "Have you nothing more to say?"

She winced as if violated.

"Did you really come to propose to me?" she asked of Birkin, as if it were a joke.

"Yes," he said. "I suppose I came to propose." He seemed to fight shy of the last word.

"Did you?" she cried, with her vague radiance. He might have been saying anything whatsoever. She seemed pleased.

"Yes," he answered. "I wanted to—I wanted you to agree to marry me."

She looked at him. His eyes were flickering with mixed lights, wanting something of her, yet not wanting it. She shrank a little, as if she were exposed to his eyes, and as if it were a pain to her. She darkened, her soul clouded over, she turned aside. She had been driven out of her own radiant, single world. And she dreaded contact, it was almost unnatural to her at these times.

"Yes," she said vaguely, in a doubting, absent voice.

Birkin's heart contracted swiftly, in a sudden fire of bitterness. It all meant nothing to her. He had been mistaken again. She was in some self-satisfied world of her own. He and his hopes were accidentals, violations to her. It drove her father to a pitch of mad exasperation. He had had to put up with this all his life, from her.

"Well, what do you say?" he cried.

She winced. Then she glanced down at her father, half-frightened, and she said:

"I didn't speak, did I?" as if she were afraid she might have committed herself.

"No," said her father, exasperated. "But you needn't look like an idiot. You've got your wits, haven't you?"

She ebbed away in silent hostility.

"I've got my wits, what does that mean?" she repeated, in a sullen voice of antagonism.

"You heard what was asked you, didn't you?" cried her father in anger.

"Of course I heard."

"Well, then, can't you answer?" thundered her father.

"Why should I?"

At the impertinence of this retort, he went stiff. But he said nothing.

"No," said Birkin, to help out the occasion, "there's no need to answer at once. You can say when you like."

Her eyes flashed with a powerful light.

"Why should I say anything?" she cried. "You do this off your *own* bat, it has nothing to do with me. Why do you both want to bully me?"

"Bully you! Bully you!" cried her father, in bitter, rancorous anger. "Bully you! Why, it's a pity you can't be bullied into some sense and decency. Bully you! *You'll* see to that, you self-willed creature."

She stood suspended in the middle of the room, her face glimmering and dangerous. She was set in satisfied defiance. Birkin looked up at her. He too was angry.

"But no-one is bullying you," he said, in a very soft dangerous voice also.

"Oh, yes," she cried. "You both want to force me into something."

"That is an illusion of yours," he said ironically.

"Illusion!" cried her father. "A self-opinionated fool, that's what she is."

Birkin rose, saying:

"However, we'll leave it for the time being."

And without another word, he walked out of the house.

"You fool! You fool!" her father cried to her, with extreme bitterness. She left the room, and went upstairs, singing to herself. But she was terribly fluttered, as after some dreadful fight. From her window, she could see Birkin going up the road. He went in such a blithe drift of rage, that her mind wondered over him. He was ridiculous, but she was afraid of him. She was as if escaped from some danger.

Her father sat below, powerless in humiliation and chagrin. It was as if he were possessed with all the devils, after one of these unaccountable conflicts with Ursula. He hated her as if his only reality were in hating her to the last degree. He had all hell in his heart. But he went away, to escape himself. He knew he must despair, yield, give in to despair, and have done.

Ursula's face closed, she completed herself against them all. Recoiling upon herself, she became hard and self-completed, like a jewel. She was bright and invulnerable, quite free and happy, perfectly liberated in her self-possession. Her father had to learn not to see her blithe obliviousness, or it would have sent him mad. She was so radiant with all things, in her possession of perfect hostility.

She would go on now for days like this, in this bright frank state of seemingly pure spontaneity, so essentially oblivious of the existence of anything but herself, but so ready and facile in her interest. Ah it was a bitter thing for a man to be near her, and her father cursed his fatherhood. But he must learn not to see her, not to know.

She was perfectly stable in resistance when she was in this state: so bright and radiant and attractive in her

pure opposition, so very pure, and yet mistrusted by
everybody, disliked on every hand. It was her voice,
curiously clear and repellant, that gave her away. Only
Gudrun was in accord with her. It was at these times
that the intimacy between the two sisters was most complete, as if their intelligence were one. They felt a strong,
bright bond of understanding between them, surpassing
everything else. And during all these days of blind bright
abstraction and intimacy of his two daughters, the father
seemed to breathe an air of death, as if he were destroyed in his very being. He was irritable to madness,
he could not rest, his daughters seemed to be destroying
him. But he was inarticulate and helpless against them.
He was forced to breathe the air of his own death. He
cursed them in his soul, and only wanted that they
should be removed from him.

They continued radiant in their easy female tran-
scendancy, beautiful to look at. They exchanged confi-
dences, they were intimate in their revelations to the last
degree, giving each other at last every secret. They withheld nothing, they told everything, till they were over the
border of evil. And they armed each other with knowledge, they extracted the subtlest flavours from the apple
of knowledge. It was curious how their knowledge was
complementary, that of each to that of the other.

Ursula saw her men as sons, pitied their yearning and
admired their courage, and wondered over them as a
mother wonders over her child, with a certain delight in
their novelty. But to Gudrun, they were the opposite
camp. She feared them and despised them, and respected their activities even overmuch.

"Of course," she said easily, "there is a quality of life in
Birkin which is quite remarkable. There is an extraordinary rich spring of life in him, really amazing, the way
he can give himself to things. But there are so many

things in life that he simply doesn't know. Either he is not aware of their existence at all, or he dismisses them as merely negligible—things which are vital to the other person. In a way, he is not clever enough, he is too intense in spots."

"Yes," cried Ursula, "too much of a preacher. He is really a priest."

"Exactly! He can't hear what anybody else has to say —he simply cannot hear. His own voice is so loud."

"Yes. He cries you down."

"He cries you down," repeated Gudrun. "And by mere force of violence. And of course it is hopeless. Nobody is convinced by violence. It makes talking to him impossible—and living with him I should think would be more than impossible."

"You don't think one could live with him?" asked Ursula.

"I think it would be too wearing, too exhausting. One would be shouted down every time, and rushed into his way without any choice. He would want to control you entirely. He cannot allow that there is any other mind than his own. And then the real clumsiness of his mind, is his lack of self-criticism. No, I think it would be perfectly intolerable."

"Yes," assented Ursula vaguely. She only half agreed with Gudrun. "The nuisance is," she said, "that one would find almost any man intolerable after a fortnight."

"It's perfectly dreadful," said Gudrun. "But Birkin— he is too positive. He couldn't bear it if you called your soul your own. Of him that is strictly true."

"Yes," said Ursula. "You must have *his* soul."

"Exactly! And what can you conceive more deadly?" This was all so true that Ursula felt jarred to the bottom of her soul with ugly distaste.

She went on, with the discord jarring and jolting through her, in the most barren of misery.

Then there started a revulsion from Gudrun. She finished life off so thoroughly, she made things so ugly and so final. As a matter of fact, even if it were as Gudrun said, about Birkin, other things were true as well. But Gudrun would draw two lines under him and cross him out like an account that is settled. There he was, summed up, paid for, settled, done with. And it was such a lie. This finality of Gudrun's, this dispatching of people and things in a sentence, it was all such a lie. Ursula began to revolt from her sister.

One day as they were walking along the lane, they saw a robin sitting on the top twig of a bush, singing shrilly. The sisters stood to look at him. An ironical smile flickered on Gudrun's face.

"Doesn't he feel important?" smiled Gudrun.

"Doesn't he!" exclaimed Ursula, with a little ironical grimace. "Isn't he a little Lloyd George of the air!"

"Isn't he! Little Lloyd George of the air! That's just what they are," cried Gudrun in delight. Then for days Ursula saw the persistent, obtrusive birds as stout, short politicians lifting up their voices from the platform, little men who must make themselves heard at any cost.

But even from this there came the revulsion. Some yellow-hammers suddenly shot along the road in front of her. And they looked to her so uncanny and inhuman, like flaring yellow barbs shooting through the air on some weird, living errand, that she said to herself: "After all, it is impudence to call them little Lloyd Georges. They are really unknown to us, they are the unknown forces. It is impudence to look at them as if they were the same as human beings. They are of another world. How stupid anthropomorphism is! Gudrun is really impudent, insolent, making herself the measure

of everything, making everything come down to human
standards. Rupert is quite right, human beings are boring, painting the universe with their own image. The
universe is non-human, thank God." It seemed to her ir-
reverence, destructive of all true life, to make little
Lloyd Georges of the birds. It was such a lie towards
the robins, and such a defamation. Yet she had done it
herself. But under Gudrun's influence: so she exonerated
herself.

So she withdrew away from Gudrun and from that
which she stood for, she turned in spirit towards Birkin
again. She had not seen him since the fiasco of his proposal. She did not want to, because she did not want
the question of her acceptance thrust upon her. She
knew what Birkin meant when he asked her to marry
him; vaguely, without putting it into speech, she knew.
She knew what kind of love, what kind of surrender he
wanted. And she was not at all sure that this was the
kind of love that she herself wanted. She was not at all
sure that it was this mutual unison in separateness that
she wanted. She wanted unspeakable intimacies. She
wanted to have him, utterly, finally to have him as her
own, oh, so unspeakably, in intimacy. To drink him
down—ah, like a life-draught. She made great professions, to herself, of her willingness to warm his foot-soles
between her breasts, after the fashion of the nauseous
Meredith poem. But only on condition that he, her lover,
loved her absolutely, with complete self-abandon. And
subtly enough, she knew he would never abandon himself *finally* to her. He did not believe in final self-aban-
donment. He said it openly. It was his challenge. She
was prepared to fight him for it. For she believed that
love far surpassed the individual. He said the individual
was *more* than love, or than any relationship. For him,
the bright, single soul accepted love as one of its condi-

tions, a condition of its own equilibrium. She believed that love was *everything*. Man must render himself up to her. He must be quaffed to the dregs by her. Let him be *her man* utterly, and she in return would be his humble slave—whether she wanted it or not.

XX. GLADIATORIAL

AFTER the fiasco of the proposal, Birkin had hurried blindly away from Beldover, in a whirl of fury. He felt he had been a complete fool, that the whole scene had been a farce of the first water. But that did not trouble him at all. He was deeply, mockingly angry that Ursula persisted always in this old cry: "Why do you want to bully me?' and in her bright, insolent abstraction.

He went straight to Shortlands. There he found Gerald standing with his back to the fire, in the library, as motionless as a man is who is completely and emptily restless, utterly hollow. He had done all the work he wanted to do—and now there was nothing. He could go out in the car, he could run to town. But he did not want to go out in the car, he did not want to run to town, he did not want to call on the Thirlbys. He was suspended motionless, in an agony of inertia, like a machine that is without power.

This was very bitter to Gerald, who had never known what boredom was, who had gone from activity to activity, never at a loss. Now, gradually, everything seemed to be stopping in him. He did not want any more to do the things that offered. Something dead within him just refused to respond to any suggestion. He cast over in his mind what it would be possible to do, to save himself from this misery of nothingness, relieve the stress of this hollowness. And there were only three things left, that would rouse him, make him live. One was to drink or smoke hashish, the other was to be soothed by Birkin, and the third was women. And there was no one for the moment to drink with. Nor was there a woman. And he knew Birkin was out. So there was nothing to do but to bear the stress of his own emptiness.

When he saw Birkin his face lit up in a sudden, wonderful smile.

"By God, Rupert," he said, "I'd just come to the conclusion that nothing in the world mattered except somebody to take the edge off one's being alone: the right somebody."

The smile in his eyes was very astonishing, as he looked at the other man. It was the pure gleam of relief. His face was pallid and even haggard.

"The right woman, I suppose you mean," said Birkin spitefully.

"Of course, for choice. Failing that, an amusing man."

He laughed as he said it. Birkin sat down near the fire.

"What were you doing?" he asked.

"I? Nothing. I'm in a bad way just now, everything's on edge, and I can neither work nor play. I don't know whether it's a sign of old age, I'm sure."

"You mean you are bored?"

"Bored, I don't know. I can't apply myself. And I feel the devil is either very present inside me, or dead."

Birkin glanced up and looked in his eyes.

"You should try hitting something," he said.

Gerald smiled.

"Perhaps," he said. "So long as it was something worth hitting."

"Quite!" said Birkin, in his soft voice. There was a long pause during which each could feel the presence of the other.

"One has to wait," said Birkin.

"Ah God! Waiting! What are we waiting for?"

"Some old Johnny says there are three cures for ennui, sleep, drink, and travel," said Birkin.

"All cold eggs," said Gerald. "In sleep you dream, in drink you curse, and in travel you yell at a porter. No, work and love are the two. When you're not at work you should be in love."

"Be it then," said Birkin.

"Give me the object," said Gerald. "The possibilities of love exhaust themselves."

"Do they? And then what?"

"Then you die," said Gerald.

"So you ought," said Birkin.

"I don't see it," replied Gerald. He took his hands out of his trousers pockets, and reached for a cigarette. He was tense and nervous. He lit the cigarette over a lamp, reaching forward and drawing steadily. He was dressed for dinner, as usual in the evening, although he was alone.

"There's a third one even to your two," said Birkin. "Work, love, and fighting. You forget the fight."

"I suppose I do," said Gerald. "Did you ever do any boxing——?"

"No, I don't think I did," said Birkin.

"Ay——" Gerald lifted his head and blew the smoke slowly into the air.

"Why?" said Birkin.

"Nothing. I thought we might have a round. It is perhaps true that I want something to hit. It's a suggestion."

"So you think you might as well hit me?" said Birkin.

"You? Well—! Perhaps—! In a friendly kind of way, of course."

"Quite!" said Birkin, bitingly

Gerald stood leaning back against the mantelpiece. He looked down at Birkin, and his eyes flashed with a sort of terror like the eyes of a stallion, that are bloodshot and overwrought, turned glancing backwards in a stiff terror.

"I feel that if I don't watch myself, I shall find myself doing something silly," he said.

"Why not do it?" said Birkin coldly.

Gerald listened with quick impatience. He kept glancing down at Birkin, as if looking for something from the other man.

"I used to do some Japanese wrestling," said Birkin. "A Jap lived in the same house with me in Heidelberg, and he taught me a little. But I was never much good at it."

"You did!" exclaimed Gerald. "That's one of the things I've never even seen done. You mean jiu-jitsu, I suppose?"

"Yes. But I am no good at those things—they don't interest me."

"They don't? They do me. What's the start?"

"I'll show you what I can, if you like," said Birkin.

"You will?" A queer, smiling look tightened Gerald's face for a moment, as he said, "Well, I'd like it very much."

"Then we'll try jiu-jitsu. Only you can't do much in a starched shirt."

"Then let us strip, and do it properly. Hold a minute —" He rang the bell, and waited for the butler.

"Bring a couple of sandwiches and a syphon," he said to the man, "and then don't trouble me any more tonight —or let anybody else."

The man went. Gerald turned to Birkin with his eyes lighted.

"And you used to wrestle with a Jap?" he said. "Did you strip?"

"Sometimes."

"You did! What was he like then, as a wrestler?"

"Good, I believe. I am no judge. He was very quick and slippery and full of electric fire. It is a remarkable thing, what a curious sort of fluid force they seem to have in them, those people—not like a human grip—like a polyp——"

Gerald nodded.

"I should imagine so," he said, "to look at them. They repel me, rather."

"Repel and attract, both. They are very repulsive when they are cold, and they look grey. But when they are hot and roused, there is a definite attraction—a curious kind of full electric fluid—like eels."

"Well—yes—probably."

The man brought in the tray and set it down.

"Don't come in any more," said Gerald.

The door closed.

"Well, then," said Gerald, "shall we strip and begin? Will you have a drink first?"

"No, I don't want one."

"Neither do I."

Gerald fastened the door and pushed the furniture aside. The room was large, there was plenty of space, it was thickly carpeted. Then he quickly threw off his clothes, and waited for Birkin. The latter, white and thin, came over to him. Birkin was more a presence than a visible object; Gerald was aware of him completely, but not really visually. Whereas Gerald himself was concrete and noticeable, a piece of pure final substance.

"Now," said Birkin, "I will show you what I learned, and what I remember. You let me take you so——" And his hands closed on the naked body of the other man.

In another moment, he had Gerald swung over lightly and balanced against his knee, head downwards. Relaxed, Gerald sprang to his feet with eyes glittering.

"That's smart," he said. "Now try again."

So the two men began to struggle together. They were very dissimilar. Birkin was tall and narrow, his bones were very thin and fine. Gerald was much heavier and more plastic. His bones were strong and round, his limbs were rounded, all his contours were beautifully and fully moulded. He seemed to stand with a proper, rich weight on the face of the earth, whilst Birkin seemed to have the centre of gravitation in his own middle. And Gerald had a rich, frictional kind of strength, rather mechanical, but sudden and invincible, whereas Birkin was so abstract as to be almost intangible. He impinged invisibly upon the other man, scarcely seeming to touch him, like a garment, and then suddenly piercing in a tense fine grip that seemed to penetrate into the very quick of Gerald's being.

They stopped, they discussed methods, they practised grips and throws, they became accustomed to each other, to each other's rhythm, they got a kind of mutual physical understanding. And then again they had a real struggle. They seemed to drive their white flesh deeper and deeper against each other, as if they would break into a oneness. Birkin had a great subtle energy, that would press upon the other man with an uncanny force, weigh him like a spell put upon him. Then it would pass, and Gerald would heave free, with white, heaving, dazzling movements.

So the two men entwined and wrestled with each other, working nearer and nearer. Both were white and clear, but Gerald flushed smart red where he was touched, and Birkin remained white and tense. He seemed to penetrate into Gerald's more solid, more diffuse bulk, to interfuse his body through the body of the other, as if to bring it subtly into subjection, always seizing with some rapid necromantic foreknowledge every motion of the other flesh, converting and counteracting it, playing upon the limbs and trunk of Gerald like some hard wind. It was as if Birkin's whole physical intelligence interpenetrated into Gerald's body, as if his fine, sublimated energy entered into the flesh of the fuller man, like some potency, casting a fine net, a prison, through the muscles into the very depths of Gerald's physical being.

So they wrestled swiftly, rapturously, intent and mindless at last, two essential white figures working into a tighter closer oneness of struggle, with a strange, octopus-like knotting and flashing of limbs in the subdued light of the room; a tense white knot of flesh gripped in silence between the walls of old brown books. Now and again came a sharp gasp of breath, or a sound like a sigh, then the rapid thudding of movement on the thickly-carpeted floor, then the strange sound of flesh escaping under flesh. Often, in the white interlaced knot of violent living being that swayed silently, there was no head to be seen, only the swift, tight limbs, the solid white backs, the physical junction of two bodies clinched into oneness. Then would appear the gleaming, ruffled head of Gerald, as the struggle changed, then for a moment the dun-coloured, shadow-like head of the other man would lift up from the conflict, the eyes wide and dreadful and sightless.

At length Gerald lay back inert on the carpet, his breast rising in great slow panting, whilst Birkin knelt over him, almost unconscious. Birkin was much more exhausted. He caught little, short breaths, he could scarcely breathe any more. The earth seemed to tilt and sway, and a complete darkness was coming over his mind. He did not know what happened. He slid forward quite unconscious, over Gerald, and Gerald did not notice. Then he was half-conscious again, aware only of the strange tilting and sliding of the world. The world was sliding, everything was sliding off into the darkness. And he was sliding, endlessly, endlessly away.

He came to consciousness again, hearing an immense knocking outside. What could be happening, what was it, the great hammer-stroke resounding through the house? He did not know. And then it came to him that it was his own heart beating. But that seemed impossible, the noise was outside. No, it was inside himself, it was his own heart. And the beating was painful, so strained, surcharged. He wondered if Gerald heard it. He did not know whether he were standing or lying or falling.

When he realized that he had fallen prostrate upon Gerald's body he wondered, he was surprised. But he sat up, steadying himself with his hand and waiting for his heart to become stiller and less painful. It hurt very much, and took away his consciousness.

Gerald, however, was still less conscious than Birkin. They waited dimly, in a sort of not-being, for many uncounted, unknown minutes.

"Of course—" panted Gerald, "I didn't have to be rough—with you—I had to keep back—my force——"

Birkin heard the sound as if his own spirit stood behind him, outside him, and listened to it. His body was in a trance of exhaustion, his spirit heard thinly. His body could not answer. Only he knew his heart was getting quieter. He was divided entirely between his spirit, which stood outside, and knew, and his body, that was a plunging, unconscious stroke of blood.

"I could have thrown you—using violence—" panted Gerald. "But you beat me right enough."

"Yes," said Birkin, hardening his throat and producing the words in the tension there, "you're much stronger than I—you could beat me—easily."

Then he relaxed again to the terrible plunging of his heart and his blood.

"It surprised me," panted Gerald, "what strength you've got. Almost supernatural."

"For a moment," said Birkin.

He still heard as if it were his own disembodied spirit hearing, standing at some distance behind him. It drew nearer, however, his spirit. And the violent striking of blood in his chest was sinking quieter, allowing his mind to come back. He realized that he was leaning with all his weight on the soft body of the other man. It startled him, because he thought he had withdrawn. He recovered himself, and sat up. But he was still vague and unestablished. He put out his hand to steady himself. It touched the hand of Gerald, that was lying out on the floor. And Gerald's hand closed warm and sudden over Birkin's, they remained exhausted and breathless, the one hand clasped closely over the other. It was Birkin whose hand, in swift response, had closed in a strong, warm clasp over the hand of the other. Gerald's clasp had been sudden and momentaneous.

The normal consciousness, however, was returning, ebbing back. Birkin could breathe almost naturally again. Gerald's hand slowly withdrew, Birkin slowly, dazedly rose to his feet and went towards the table. He poured out a whisky and soda. Gerald also came for a drink.

"It was a real set-to, wasn't it?" said Birkin, looking at Gerald with darkened eyes.

"God, yes," said Gerald. He looked at the fine body of the other man, and added: "It wasn't too much for you, was it?"

"No. One ought to wrestle and strive and be physically close. It makes one sane."

"You do think so?"

"I do. Don't you?"

"Yes," said Gerald.

There were long spaces of silence between their words. The wrestling had some deep meaning to them—an unfinished meaning.

"We are mentally, spiritually intimate, therefore we should be more or less physically intimate too—it is more whole."

"Certainly it is," said Gerald. Then he laughed pleasantly, adding: "It's rather wonderful to me." He stretched out his arms handsomely.

"Yes," said Birkin. "I don't know why one should have to justify oneself."

"No."

The two men began to dress.

"I think also that you are beautiful," said Birkin to Gerald, "and that is enjoyable too. One should enjoy what is given."

"You think I am beautiful—how do you mean, physically?" asked Gerald, his eyes glistening.

"Yes. You have a northern kind of beauty, like light refracted from snow—and a beautiful, plastic form. Yes, that is there to enjoy as well. We should enjoy everything."

Gerald laughed in his throat, and said:

"That's certainly one way of looking at it. I can say this much, I feel better. It has certainly helped me. Is this the Bruderschaft you wanted?"

"Perhaps. Do you think this pledges anything?"

"I don't know," laughed Gerald.

"At any rate, one feels freer and more open now—and that is what we want."

"Certainly," said Gerald.

They drew to the fire, with the decanters and the glasses and the food.

"I always eat a little before I go to bed," said Gerald. "I sleep better."

"I should not sleep so well," said Birkin.

"No? There you are, we are not alike. I'll put a dressing-gown on." Birkin remained alone, looking at the fire. His mind had reverted to Ursula. She seemed to return again into his consciousness. Gerald came down wearing a gown of broad-barred, thick black-and-green silk, brilliant and striking.

"You are very fine," said Birkin, looking at the full robe.

"It was a caftan in Bokhara," said Gerald. "I like it."

"I like it too."

Birkin was silent, thinking how scrupulous Gerald was in his attire, how expensive too. He wore silk socks, and studs of fine workmanship, and silk underclothing, and silk braces. Curious! This was another of the differences between them. Birkin was careless and unimaginative about his own appearance.

"Of course you," said Gerald, as if he had been thinking; "there's something curious about you. You're curiously strong. One doesn't expect it, it is rather surprising."

Birkin laughed. He was looking at the handsome figure of the other man, blond and comely in the rich robe, and he was half thinking of the difference between it and himself—so different; as far, perhaps, apart as man from woman, yet in another direction. But really it was Ursula, it was the woman who was gaining ascendance over Birkin's being, at this moment. Gerald was becoming dim again, lapsing out of him.

"Do you know," he said suddenly, "I went and proposed to Ursula Brangwen tonight, that she should marry me."

He saw the blank shining wonder come over Gerald's face.

"You did?"

"Yes. Almost formally—speaking first to her father, as it should be, in the world—though that was accident —or mischief."

Gerald only stared in wonder, as if he did not grasp.

"You don't mean to say that you seriously went and asked her father to let you marry her?"

"Yes," said Birkin, "I did."

"What, had you spoken to her before about it, then?"

"No, not a word. I suddenly thought I would go there and ask her—and her father happened to come instead of her—so I asked him first."

"If you could have her?" concluded Gerald.

"Ye-es, that."

"And you didn't speak to her?"

"Yes. She came in afterwards. So it was put to her as well."

"It was! And what did she say then? You're an engaged man?"

"No—she only said she didn't want to be bullied into answering."

"She what?"

"Said she didn't want to be bullied into answering."

" 'Said she didn't want to be bullied into answering!' Why, what did she mean by that?"

Birkin raised his shoulders. "Can't say," he answered. "Didn't want to be bothered just then, I suppose."

"But is this really so? And what did you do then?"

"I walked out of the house and came here."

"You came straight here?"

"Yes."

Gerald stared in amazement and amusement. He could not take it in.

"But is this really true, as you say it now?"

"Word for word."

"It is?"

He leaned back in his chair, filled with delight and amusement.

"Well, that's good," he said. "And so you came here to wrestle with your good angel, did you?"

"Did I?" said Birkin.

"Well, it looks like it. Isn't that what you did?"

Now Birkin could not follow Gerald's meaning.

"And what's going to happen?" said Gerald. "You're going to keep open the proposition, so to speak?"

"I suppose so. I vowed to myself I would see them all to the devil. But I suppose I shall ask her again, in a little while."

Gerald watched him steadily.

"So you're fond of her then?" he asked.

"I think—I love her," said Birkin, his face going very still and fixed.

Gerald glistened for a moment with pleasure, as if it were something done specially to please him. Then his face assumed a fitting gravity, and he nodded his head slowly.

"You know," he said, "I always believed in love—true love. But where does one find it nowadays?"

"I don't know," said Birkin.

"Very rarely," said Gerald. Then, after a pause, "I've never felt it myself—not what I should call love. I've gone after women—and been keen enough over some of them. But I've never felt *love*. I don't believe I've ever felt as much *love* for a woman as I have for you—not *love*. You understand what I mean?"

"Yes. I'm sure you've never loved a woman."

"You feel that, do you? And do you think I ever shall? You understand what I mean?" He put his hand to his breast, closing his fist there, as if he would draw something out. "I mean that—that— I can't express what it is, but I know it."

"What is it, then?" asked Birkin.

"You see, I can't put it into words. I mean, at any rate, something abiding, something that can't change——"

His eyes were bright and puzzled.

"Now do you think I shall ever feel that for a woman?" he said, anxiously.

Birkin looked at him, and shook his head.

"I don't know," he said. "I could not say."

Gerald had been on the qui vive, as awaiting his fate. Now he drew back in his chair.

"No," he said, "and neither do I, and neither do I."

"We are different, you and I," said Birkin. "I can't tell your life."

"No," said Gerald, "no more can I. But I tell you—I begin to doubt it!"

"That you will ever love a woman?"

"Well—yes—what you would truly call love——"

"You doubt it?"

"Well—I begin to."

There was a long pause.

"Life has all kinds of things," said Birkin. "There isn't only one road."

"Yes, I believe that too. I believe it. And mind you, I don't care how it is with me—I don't care how it is—so long as I don't feel—" he paused, and a blank, barren look passed over his face, to express his feeling—"so long as I feel I've *lived*, somehow—and I don't care how it is —but I want to feel that——"

"Fulfilled," said Birkin.

"We-ell, perhaps it is, fulfilled; I don't use the same word: as you."

"It is the same."

POEMS

EDITOR'S PREFACE

ALL HIS life Lawrence wrote poetry. But curiously enough, his poetic inspiration, instead of diminishing with the years as so often happens, flowered steadily until in full maturity he shows himself transformed from a sentimental versifier into a poet of extraordinary power and distinction. This is not to say that his late poems are uniformly good. But the best of them are, with some of the stories, the best complete works of art Lawrence produced. The early poetry, on the other hand, is poor not only in comparison with what followed but in comparison with the prose he was writing at the same period. There is a softness of idiom, a banality of thought and expression, in much of Lawrence's youthful verse that has no parallel in the fiction that was contemporary with it. In even his earliest prose, Lawrence was able to rise above his youthful circumstances with all the sureness of born genius, but it took many years for his poetry to overcome its gaucherie.

Curious, too, about Lawrence's poetry is the general superiority of his poems of idea to what might be called his poems of experience. Although a genuineness of feeling does come through the poems which commemorate his mother, on the whole Lawrence's personal poetry is much less moving than his poetry of doctrinal inspiration. The emotions it communicates are likely to be shallow or shoddy, whereas the emotions of the more doctrinal poetry match their force of idea. For instance, of the volume *Look, We Have Come Through*, written out of the intense experience of the first months of Lawrence's marriage, only one poem, "Sunday Afternoon in Italy", seems to me to be worth inclusion in this limited selection; and "Sunday Afternoon in Italy" is one of the few poems in the book which is not immediately about Lawrence and his wife. But the volume *Birds, Beasts and Flowers* has poem after poem, all of them highly ideational in character, which I should have wished to reprint if space permitted; or it is with regret that I refrained from using in its entirety the cerebral little volume called *Tortoises;* or there is the volume *Pansies,* which, almost in the very measure that it speaks from its author's head as well as from his heart, strikes so much higher a poetic level than the volume *Bay* or the volume *New Poems.* The quality of Lawrence's poetry would seem to be in inverse proportion to its autobiographical interest.

As I look over the poems I have chosen, I am struck also by the fact that all but one are in free verse. Lawrence wrote a great deal of rhymed poetry, of course, and some of it is very grateful to the mind and ear. Nevertheless, his best achievement was not in metrical verse; free verse was far more congenial to his temperament. Lawrence describes the difference, as he sees it, between the two kinds of poetry in the Preface to *New Poems.* "There is poetry of the immediate present, instant poetry, as well as poetry of the infinite past and the infinite future. The seething poetry of the incarnate Now is supreme, beyond even the everlasting gems of the before and after." The poetry of the Now has "no goal in either eternity. . . . It does not want to get anywhere. It just takes place. For such utterance any externally applied law would be mere shackles and death." Although, as poetic theory, this is not sound, I think it accurately suggests the nature of the impulse behind Lawrence's unrestricted verse.

Sunday Afternoon in Italy

The man and the maid go side by side
With an interval of space between;
And his hands are awkward and want to hide,
She braves it out since she must be seen.

When some one passes he drops his head
Shading his face in his black felt hat,
While the hard girl hardens; nothing is said,
There is nothing to wonder or cavil at.

Alone on the open road again
With the mountain snows across the lake
Flushing the afternoon, they are uncomfortable,
The loneliness daunts them, their stiff throats ache.

And he sighs with relief when she parts from him;
Her proud head held in its black silk scarf
Gone under the archway, home, he can join
The men that lounge in a group on the wharf.

His evening is a flame of wine
Among the eager, cordial men.
And she with her women hot and hard
Moves at her ease again.

  She is marked, she is singled out
  For the fire:

The brand is upon him, look you!
    Of desire.

They are chosen, ah, they are fated
    For the fight!
Champion her, all you women! Men, menfolk
    Hold him your light!

Nourish her, train her, harden her
    Women all!
Fold him, be good to him, cherish him
    Men, ere he fall.

Women, another champion!
    This, men, is yours!
Wreathe and enlap and anoint them
    Behind separate doors.

Baby Tortoise

You know what it is to be born alone,
Baby tortoise!

The first day to heave your feet little by little from the
    shell,
Not yet awake,
And remain lapsed on earth,
Not quite alive.

A tiny, fragile, half-animate bean.

To open your tiny beak-mouth, that looks as if it would
    never open,

Like some iron door;
To lift the upper hawk-beak from the lower base
And reach your skinny little neck
And take your first bite at some dim bit of herbage,
Alone, small insect,
Tiny bright-eye,
Slow one.

To take your first solitary bite
And move on your slow, solitary hunt.
Your bright, dark little eye,
Your eye of a dark disturbed night,
Under its slow lid, tiny baby tortoise,
So indomitable.

No one ever heard you complain.

You draw your heard forward, slowly, from your little
    wimple
And set forward, slow-dragging, on your four-pinned
    toes,
Rowing slowly forward.
Whither away, small bird?

Rather like a baby working its limbs,
Except that you make slow, ageless progress
And a baby makes none.

The touch of sun excites you,
And the long ages, and the lingering chill
Make you pause to yawn,
Opening your impervious mouth,
Suddenly beak-shaped, and very wide, like some sud-
    denly gaping pincers;
Soft red tongue, and hard thin gums,

Then close the wedge of your little mountain front,
Your face, baby tortoise.

Do you wonder at the world, as slowly you turn your
     head in its wimple
And look with laconic, black eyes?
Or is sleep coming over you again,
The non-life?

You are so hard to wake.

Are you able to wonder?
Or is it just your indomitable will and pride of the first
     life
Looking round
And slowly pitching itself against the inertia
Which had seemed invincible?

The vast inanimate,
And the fine brilliance of your so tiny eye,
Challenger.

Nay, tiny shell-bird,
What a huge vast inanimate it is, that you must row
     against,
What an incalculable inertia.

Challenger,
Little Ulysses, fore-runner,
No bigger than my thumb-nail.
Buon viaggio.

All animate creation on your shoulder,
Set forth, little Titan, under your battle-shield.

The ponderous, preponderate,
Inanimate universe;
And you are slowly moving, pioneer, you alone.

How vivid your travelling seems now, in the troubled
    sunshine,
Stoic, Ulyssean atom;
Suddenly hasty, reckless, on high toes.

Voiceless little bird,
Resting your head half out of your wimple
In the slow dignity of your eternal pause.
Alone, with no sense of being alone,
And hence six times more solitary;
Fulfilled of the slow passion of pitching through im-
    memorial ages
Your little round house in the midst of chaos.

Over the garden earth,
Small bird.
Over the edge of all things.

Traveller,
With your tail tucked a little on one side
Like a gentleman in a long-skirted coat.

All life carried on your shoulder,
Invincible fore-runner.

Tortoise-Shell

The Cross, the Cross
Goes deeper in than we know,

Deeper into life;
Right into the marrow
And through the bone.

Along the back of the baby tortoise
The scales are locked in an arch like a bridge,
Scale-lapping, like a lobster's sections
Or a bee's.

Then crossways down his sides
Tiger-stripes and wasp-bands.

Five, and five again, and five again,
And round the edges twenty-five little ones,
The sections of the baby tortoise shell.

Four, and a keystone;
Four, and a keystone;
Four, and a keystone;
Then twenty-four, and a tiny little keystone.

It needed Pythagoras to see life placing her counters
        on the living back
Of the baby tortoise;
Life establishing the first eternal mathematical tablet,
Not in stone, like the Judean Lord, or bronze, but in
        life-clouded, life-rosy tortoise-shell.

The first little mathematical gentleman
Stepping, wee mite, in his loose trousers
Under all the eternal dome of mathematical law.

Fives, and tens,
Threes and fours and twelves,

All the volte face of decimals,
The whirligig of dozens and the pinnacle of seven.

Turn him on his back,
The kicking little beetle,
And there again, on his shell-tender, earth-touching
    belly,
The long cleavage of division, upright of the eternal
    cross
And on either side count five,
On each side, two above, on each side, two below
The dark bar horizontal.

The Cross!
It goes right through him, the sprottling insect,
Through his cross-wise cloven psyche,
Through his five-fold complex-nature.

So turn him over on his toes again;
Four pin-point toes, and a problematical thumb-piece,
Four rowing limbs, and one wedge-balancing head,
Four and one makes five, which is the clue to all mathe-
    matics.

The Lord wrote it all down on the little slate
Of the baby tortoise.
Outward and visible indication of the plan within,
The complex, manifold involvedness of an individual
    creature
Blotted out
On this small bird, this rudiment,
This little dome, this pediment
Of all creation,
This slow one.

Snake

A snake came to my water-trough
On a hot, hot day, and I in pyjamas for the heat,
To drink there.

In the deep, strange-scented shade of the great dark
        carob tree
I came down the steps with my pitcher
And must wait, must stand and wait, for there he was at
        the trough before me.

He reached down from a fissure in the earth-wall in the
        gloom
And trailed his yellow brown slackness soft-bellied
        down, over the edge of the stone trough
And rested his throat upon the stone bottom,
And where the water had dripped from the tap, in a
        small clearness,
He sipped with his straight mouth,
Softly drank through his straight gums, into his slack
        long body,
Silently.

Someone was before me at my water-trough,
And I, like a second-comer, waiting.

He lifted his head from his drinking, as cattle do,
And looked at me vaguely, as drinking cattle do,
And flickered his two-forked tongue from his lips, and
        mused a moment,

And stooped and drank a little more,
Being earth-brown, earth-golden from the burning
    bowels of the earth
On the day of Sicilian July, with Etna smoking.

The voice of my education said to me
He must be killed,
For in Sicily the black black snakes are innocent, the
    gold are venomous.

And voices in me said, If you were a man,
You would take a stick and break him now, and finish
    him off.

But must I confess how I liked him,
How glad I was he had come like a guest in quiet, to
    drink at my water-trough
And depart peaceful, pacified, and thankless
Into the burning bowels of this earth?

Was it cowardice, that I dared not kill him?
Was it perversity, that I longed to talk to him?
Was it humility, to feel so honoured?
I felt so honoured.

And yet those voices:
If you were not afraid, you would kill him!

And truly I was afraid, I was most afraid,
But even so, honoured still more
That he should seek my hospitality
From out the dark door of the secret earth.

He drank enough
And lifted his head, dreamily, as one who has drunken,

And flickered his tongue like a forked night on the air,
so black,
Seeming to lick his lips,
And looked around like a god, unseeing, into the air,
And slowly turned his head,
And slowly, very slowly, as if thrice adream
Proceeded to draw his slow length curving round
And climb again the broken bank of my wall-face.

And as he put his head into that dreadful hole,
And as he slowly drew up, snake-easing his shoulders,
and entered further,
A sort of horror, a sort of protest against his withdraw-
ing into that horrid black hole.
Deliberately going into the blackness, and slowly draw-
ing himself after,
Overcame me now his back was turned.

I looked round, I put down my pitcher,
I picked up a clumsy log
And threw it at the water-trough with a clatter.

I think it did not hit him;
But suddenly that part of him that was left behind con-
vulsed in undignified haste,
Writhed like lightning, and was gone
Into the black hole, the earth-lipped fissure in the wall-
front
At which, in the intense still noon, I stared with fascina-
tion.

And immediately I regretted it.
I thought how paltry, how vulgar, what a mean act!
I despised myself and the voices of my accursed human
education.

And I thought of the albatross,
And I wished he would come back, my snake.

For he seemed to me again like a king,
Like a king in exile, uncrowned in the underworld,
Now due to be crowned again.
And so, I missed my chance with one of the lords
Of life.
And I have something to expiate:
A pettiness.

Elephant

You go down shade to the river, where naked men sit
    on flat brown rocks, to watch the ferry, in the sun;
And you cross the ferry with the naked people, go up
    the tropical lane
Through the palm-trees and past hollow paddy-fields
    where naked men are threshing rice
And the monolithic water-buffaloes, like old, muddy
    stones with hair on them, are being idle;
And through the shadow of bread-fruit trees, with their
    dark green, glossy, fanged leaves
Very handsome, and some pure yellow fanged leaves;
Out into the open, where the path runs on the top of a
    dyke between paddy-fields:
And there, of course, you meet a huge and mud-grey
    elephant advancing his frontal bone, his trunk
    curled round a log of wood:
So you step down the bank, to make way.

Shuffle, shuffle, and his little wicked eye has seen you as
    he advances above you,

The slow beast curiously spreading his round feet for
the dust.
And the slim naked man slips down, and the beast
deposits the lump of wood, carefully.
The keeper hooks the vast knee, the creature salaams.

White man, you are saluted.
Pay a few cents.

But the best is the Pera-hera, at midnight, under the
tropical stars,
With a pale little wisp of a Prince of Wales, diffident,
up in a small pagoda on the temple side
And white people in evening dress buzzing and crowding the stand upon the grass below and opposite:
And at last the Pera-hera procession, flambeaux aloft in
the tropical night, of blazing cocoanut,
Naked dark men beneath,
And the huge frontal of three great elephants stepping
forth to the tom-tom's beat, in the torch-light,
Slowly sailing in gorgeous apparel through the flame-
light, in front of a towering, grimacing white image
of wood.

The elephant bells striking slow, tong-tong, tong-tong,
To music and queer chanting:
Enormous shadow-processions filing on in the flare of fire
In the fume of cocoanut oil, in the sweating tropical
night,
In the noise of the tom-toms and singers;
Elephants after elephants curl their trunks, vast
shadows, and some cry out
As they approach and salaam, under the dripping fire
of the torches

That pale fragment of a Prince up there, whose motto
 is *Ich dien.*

Pale, dispirited Prince, with his chin on his hands, his
 nerves tired out,
Watching and hardly seeing the trunk-curl approach and
 clumsy, knee-lifting salaam
Of the hugest, oldest of beasts, in the night and the fire-
 flare below.

He is white men's royalty, pale and dejected fragment
 up aloft.
And down below huge homage of shadowy beasts, barefoot and trunk-lipped in the night.

Chieftains, three of them abreast, on foot
Strut like peg-tops, wound around with hundreds of
 yards of fine linen.
They glimmer with tissue of gold, and golden threads
 on a jacket of velvet,
And their faces are dark, and fat, and important.

They are different royalty, dark-faced royalty, showing
 the conscious whites of their eyes
And stepping in homage, stubborn, to that nervous pale
 lad up there.

More elephants, tong, tong-tong, loom up,
Huge, more tassels swinging, more dripping fire of new
 cocoanut cressets
High, high flambeaux, smoking of the east;
And scarlet hot embers of torches knocked out of the
 sockets among bare feet of elephants and men on
 the path in the dark.

And devil dancers, luminous with sweat, dancing on to
    the shudder of drums,
Tom-toms, weird music of the devil, voices of men from
    the jungle singing;
Endless, under the Prince.

Towards the tail of the everlasting procession
In the long hot night, mere dancers from insignificant
    villages,
And smaller, more frightened elephants.

Men-peasants from jungle villages dancing and running
    with sweat and laughing,
Naked dark men with ornaments on, on their naked
    arms and their naked breasts, the grooved loins
Gleaming like metal with running sweat as they sud-
    denly turn, feet apart,
And dance and dance, forever dance, with breath half
    sobbing in dark, sweat-shining breasts,
And lustrous great tropical eyes unveiled now, gleam-
    ing a kind of laugh,
A naked, gleaming dark laugh, like a secret out in the
    dark,
And flare of a tropical energy, tireless, afire in the dark,
    slim limbs and breasts;
Perpetual, fire-laughing motion, among the slow shuffle
Of elephants,
The hot dark blood of itself a-laughing, wet, half-
    devilish, men all motion
Approaching under that small pavilion, and tropical eyes
    dilated turn up
Inevitably looking up
To the Prince,
To that tired remnant of white royalty up there
Whose motto is *Ich dien.*

As if the homage of the kindled blood of the east
Went up in wavelets to him, from the breasts and eyes
    of jungle torch-men.
And he couldn't take it.

What would they do, those jungle men running with
    sweat, with the strange dark laugh in their eyes,
    glancing up,
And the sparse-haired elephants slowly following,
If they knew that his motto was *Ich dien?*
And that he meant it.

They begin to understand,
The rickshaw boys begin to understand;
And then the devil comes into their faces,
But a different sort, a cold, rebellious, jeering devil.

In elephants and the east are two devils, in all men
    maybe.
The mystery of the dark mountain of blood, reeking
    in homage, in lust, in rage,
And passive with everlasting patience;
Then the little, cunning pig-devil of the elephant's lurk-
    ing eyes, the unbeliever.

We dodged, when the Pera-hera was finished, under the
    hanging, hairy pig's tails
And the flat, flaccid mountains of the elephants' stand-
    ing haunches,
Vast-blooded beasts,
Myself so little dodging rather scared against the eternal
    wrinkled pillars of their legs, as they were being
    dismantled;
Then I knew they were dejected, having come to hear
    the repeated

Royal summons: *Dient Ihr!*
Serve!
*Serve, vast mountainous blood, in submission and splen-
     dour, serve royalty.*
Instead of which, the silent, fatal emission from that
     nervous pale boy up there:
Ich dien.

That's why the night fell in frustration.
That's why, as the elephants ponderously, with unseem-
     ing swiftness galloped uphill in the night, going
     back to the jungle villages,
As the elephant bells sounded tong-tong-tong, bell of the
     temple of blood, in the night, swift-striking,
And the crowd like a field of rice in the dark gave way
     like liquid to the dark
Looming gallop of the beasts,
It was as if the great bare bulks of elephants in the
     festive night went over the hill-brow swiftly, with
     their tails between their legs, in haste to get away,
Their bells sounding frustrate and sinister.

And all the dark-faced, cotton-wrapped people, more
     numerous and whispering than grains of rice in a
     rice-field at night,
All the dark-faced, cotton-wrapped people, a countless
     host on the shores of the lake, like thick wild rice
     by the water's edge,
Waiting for the fireworks of the after-show;
As the rockets went up, and the glare passed over count-
     less faces, dark as black rice growing,
Showing a glint of teeth, and glancing tropical eyes
     aroused in the night,
There was the faintest twist of mockery in every face,
     across the hiss of wonders as the rocket burst

High, high up, in flakes, shimmering flakes of blue fire,
    above the palm trees of the islet in the lake.
Oh, faces upturned to the glare, oh, tropical wonder,
    wonder, a miracle in heaven!
And the shadow of a jeer, of underneath disappoint-
    ment, as the rocket-coruscation died, and shadow
    was the same as before.

They were foiled, the myriad whispering dark-faced
    cotton-wrapped people.
They had come to see royalty,
To bow before royalty, in the land of elephants, bow
    deep, bow deep.
Bow deep, for it's good as a draught of cool water to
    bow very, very low to the royal.

And all there was to bow to, an alien, diffident boy
    whose motto is *Ich dien.*
I serve! I serve! in all the weary irony of his mien—
    'Tis I who serve!
Drudge to the public.
I wish some dark-faced man could have taken the
    feathers three
And fearless gone up the pavilion, in that pepper-box
    aloft and alone
Held the three feathers out on the night, with a dark,
    fierce hand above the host,
Saying softly: *Dient Ihr! Dient!*
Omnes, vos omnes, servite.
Serve me, I am meet to be served.
Being royal of the gods.

I with the feathers.
I with the flower-de-luce.
I with the scarab-wings.

I from the marshes of blood,
Am back again.

And to the elephants:
First great beasts of the earth
A prince has come back to you,
Blood-mountains.
Crook the knee and be glad.

Won't It Be Strange—?

Won't it be strange, when the nurse brings the newborn
    infant
to the proud father, and shows its little, webbed greenish
    feet
made to smite the waters behind it?
or the round, wild vivid eye of a wild-goose staring
out of fathomless skies and seas?
or when it utters that undaunted little bird-cry
of one who will settle on ice-bergs, and honk across the
    Nile?—

And when the father says: This is none of mine!
Woman, where got you this little beast?—
will there be a whistle of wings in the air, and an icy
    draught?
will the singing of swans, high up, high up, invisible
break the drums of his ears
and leave him forever listening for the answer?

When I Went to the Circus—

When I went to the circus that had pitched on the waste
    lot
it was full of uneasy people
frightened of the bare earth and the temporary canvas
and the smell of horses and other beasts
instead of merely the smell of man.

Monkeys rode rather grey and wizened
on curly plump piebald ponies
and the children uttered a little cry—
and dogs jumped through hoops and turned somersaults
and then the geese scuttled in in a little flock
and round the ring they went to the sound of the whip
then doubled, and back, with a funny up-flutter of
    wings—
and the children suddenly shouted out.
Then came the hush again, like a hush of fear.

The tight-rope lady, pink and blonde and nude-looking,
    with a few gold spangles
footed cautiously out on the rope, turned prettily, spun
    round
bowed, and lifted her foot in her hand, smiled, swung
    her parasol
to another balance, tripped round, poised, and slowly
    sank
her handsome thighs down, down, till she slept her
    splendid body on the rope.
When she rose, tilting her parasol, and smiled at the
    cautious people
they cheered, but nervously.

The trapeze man, slim and beautiful and like a fish in
  the air
swung great curves through the upper space, and came
  down like a star
—And the people applauded, with hollow, frightened
  applause.

The elephants, huge and grey, loomed their curved bulk
  through the dusk
and sat up, taking strange postures, showing the pink
  soles of their feet
and curling their precious live trunks like ammonites
and moving always with soft slow precision
as when a great ship moves to anchor.
The people watched and wondered, and seemed to resent the mystery that lies in beasts.

Horse, gay horses, swirling round and plaiting
in a long line, their heads laid over each other's necks;
they were happy, they enjoyed it;
all the creatures seemed to enjoy the game
in the circus, with their circus people.

But the audience, compelled to wonder
compelled to admire the bright rhythms of moving
  bodies
compelled to see the delicate skill of flickering human
  bodies
flesh flamey and a little heroic, even in a tumbling
  clown,
they were not really happy.
There was no gushing response, as there is at the film.

When modern people see the carnal body dauntless and
  flickering gay

playing among the elements neatly, beyond competition
and displaying no personality,
modern people are depressed.

Modern people feel themselves at a disadvantage.
They know they have no bodies that could play among
    the elements.
They have only their personalities, that are best seen flat,
    on the film,
flat personalities in two dimensions, imponderable and
    touchless.

And they grudge the circus people the swooping gay
    weight of limbs
that flower in mere movement,
and they grudge them the immediate, physical under-
    standing they have with their circus beasts,
and they grudge them their circus-life altogether.

Yet the strange, almost frightened shout of delight that
    comes now and then from the children
shows that the children vaguely know how cheated they
    are of their birthright
in the bright wild circus flesh.

We Are Transmitters—

As we live, we are transmitters of life.
And when we fail to transmit life, life fails to flow
    through us.
That is part of the mystery of sex, it is a flow onwards.
Sexless people transmit nothing.

And if, as we work, we can transmit life into our work,
life, still more life, rushes into us to compensate, to be
    ready
and we ripple with life through the days.

Even if it is a woman making an apple dumpling, or a
    man a stool,
if life goes into the pudding, good is the pudding
good is the stool,
content is the woman, with fresh life rippling in to her,
content is the man.

Give, and it shall be given unto you
is still the truth about life.
But giving life is not so easy.
It doesn't mean handing it out to some mean fool, or
    letting the living dead eat you up.
It means kindling the life-quality where it was not,
even if it's only in the whiteness of a washed pocket-
    handkerchief.

The Gods! The Gods!

People were bathing and posturing themselves on the
    beach
and all was dreary, great robot limbs, robot breasts
robot voices, robot even the gay umbrellas.

But a woman, shy and alone, was washing herself under
    a tap
and the glimmer of the presence of the gods was like
    lilies,
and like water-lilies.

Retort to Whitman

And whoever walks a mile full of false sympathy
walks to the funeral of the whole human race.

Retort to Jesus

And whoever forces himself to love anybody
begets a murderer in his own body.

Whales Weep Not!

They say the sea is cold, but the sea contains
the hottest blood of all, and the wildest, the most urgent.

All the whales in the wider deeps, hot are they, as they
urge
on and on, and dive beneath the ice-bergs.
The right whales, the sperm-whales, the hammer-heads,
the killers
there they blow, there they blow, hot wild white breath
out of the sea!

And they rock and they rock, through the sensual ageless
ages
on the depths of the seven seas,
and through the salt they reel with drunk delight

and in the tropics tremble they with love
and roll with massive, strong desire, like gods.
Then the great bull lies up against his bride
in the blue deep of the sea
as mountain pressing on mountain, in the zest of life:
and out of the inward roaring of the inner red ocean of
    whale blood
the long tip reaches strong, intense, like the maelstrom-
    tip, and comes to rest
in the clasp and the soft, wild clutch of a she-whale's
    fathomless body.

And over the bridge of the whale's strong phallus, link-
    ing the wonder of whales
the burning archangels under the sea keep passing, back
    and forth,
keep passing archangels of bliss
from him to her, from her to him, great Cherubim
that wait on whales in mid-ocean, suspended in the
    waves of the sea
great heaven of whales in the waters, old hierarchies.
And enormous mother whales lie dreaming suckling
    their whale-tender young
and dreaming with strange whale eyes wide open in the
    waters of the beginning and the end.

And bull-whales gather their women and whale-calves in
    a ring
when danger threatens, on the surface of the ceaseless
    flood
and range themselves like great fierce Seraphim facing
    the threat
encircling their huddled monsters of love.
And all this happiness in the sea, in the salt

where God is also love, but without words:
and Aphrodite is the wife of whales
most happy, happy she!

and Venus among the fishes skips and is a she-dolphin
she is the gay, delighted porpoise sporting with love and
    the sea
she is the female tunny-fish, round and happy among
    the males
and dense with happy blood, dark rainbow bliss in the
    sea.

TRAVEL

EDITOR'S PREFACE

ALTHOUGH travel has always been a great subject for literature and an inspiration to writers, it would seem that in this century the impulse to keep moving has become more and more compelling in our literary life, until the phenomenon of the author who stays home and cultivates his garden is rather the exception than the rule. *A Passage to India,* produced by Forster's visit to India; *Travels in the Congo,* produced by Gide's African journey; *Man's Fate,* the product of Malraux's China experiences; *Black Lamb and Grey Falcon,* the report of Rebecca West's stay in Jugoslavia; Hemingway's books; many of Katherine Anne Porter's stories —here is but a sampling of the significant writing of our time which has grown out of the adventure into a new place and a new way of living.

Lawrence travelled constantly. In fact, after his mother's death he never again had a permanent home but moved, with his wife, in and out of England, in and out of Germany, Italy, France, Australia, India, Mexico, New Mexico. And even a temporary residence was a point of departure for incessant local excursion. On the other hand, despite their lack of permanent domestic attachment, both Lawrence and his wife were very home-making people. They shunned hotels; no matter how short their stay in new quarters, they did their own housekeeping. And they always carried with them a few personal belongings with which to put their own mark on the most temporary dwelling.

The most obvious expression of his restlessness of mind and spirit, Lawrence's movement from place to place is widely reflected in his fiction, his essays and poetry, where it accounts for the changes of background, for much of the fresh and colorful incident, for the new contexts in which he tested his social and political ideas. But in addition to this indirect part they played in his work, his travels were directly responsible for several volumes of reporting which are among Lawrence's most charming writing. The form of the travel books varies considerably. They are all of them expectably subjective and discursive, but whereas *Sea and Sardinia* more or less follows the diary form, *Mornings in Mexico* is a loosely-connected series of chapters of Mexican impressions, and *Twilight in Italy* is a quite random interweaving of personal experiences with character sketches which are virtually short pieces of fiction.

The casual ease of Lawrence's travel writing at first belies its exquisite precision and literary skill. I can think of nothing in literature to match his ability to evoke place or person in such brief space. What most writers fail to suggest at fullest length, Lawrence creates with almost a single stroke of the pen, so that we come away from a few sentences about a momentary meeting on the road, in an inn, on a bus, not with the sense of having made a fleeting acquaintance but with the conviction of having had a complete social, human experience.

To Sorgono

THE various trains in the junction squatted side by side and had long, long talks before at last we were off. It was wonderful to be running in the bright morning towards the heart of Sardinia, in the little train that seemed so familiar. We were still going third class, rather to the disgust of the railway officials at Mandas.

At first the country was rather open: always the long spurs of hills, steep-sided, but not high. And from our little train we looked across the country, across hill and dale. In the distance was a little town, on a low slope. But for its compact, fortified look it might have been a town on the English downs. A man in the carriage leaned out of the window holding out a white cloth, as a signal to someone in the far off town that he was coming. The wind blew the white cloth, the town in the distance glimmered small and alone in its hollow. And the little train pelted along.

It was rather comical to see it. We were always climb- ing. And the line curved in great loops. So that as one looked out of the window, time and again one started, seeing a little train running in front of us, in a diverging direction, making big puffs of steam. But lo, it was our own little engine pelting off around a loop away ahead. We were quite a long train, but all trucks in front, only our two passenger coaches hitched on behind. And for this reason our own engine was always running fussily into sight, like some dog scampering in front and swerving about us, while we followed at the tail end of the thin string of trucks.

I was surprised how well the small engine took the continuous steep slopes, how bravely it emerged on the sky-line. It is a queer railway. I would like to know who made it. It pelts up hill and down dale and round sudden bends in the most unconcerned fashion, not as proper big railways do, grunting inside deep cuttings and stinking their way through tunnels, but running up the hill like a panting, small dog, and having a look round, and starting off in another direction, whisking us behind unconcernedly. This is much more fun than the tunnel-and-cutting system.

They told me that Sadinia mines her own coal: and quite enough for her own needs: but very soft, not fit for steam-purposes. I saw heaps of it: small, dull, dirty-looking stuff. Truck-loads of it too. And truck-loads of grain.

At every station we were left ignominiously planted, while the little engines—they had gay gold names on their black little bodies—strolled about along the side-lines, and snuffed at the various trucks. There we sat, at every station, while some truck was discarded and some other sorted out like a branded sheep, from the sidings and hitched on to us. It took a long time, this did.

All the stations so far had had wire netting over the windows. This means malaria-mosquitoes. The malaria climbs very high in Sardinia. The shallow upland valleys, moorland with their intense summer sun and the riverless, boggy behaviour of the water breed the pest inevitably. But not very terribly, as far as one can make out: August and September being the danger months. The natives don't like to admit there is any malaria: a tiny bit, they say, a tiny bit. As soon as you come to the *trees* there is no more. So they say. For many miles the landscape is moorland and downlike, with no trees. But wait for the trees. Ah, the woods and forests of Gennargentu: the woods and forests higher up: no malaria there!

The little engine whisks up and up, around its loopy curves as if it were going to bite its own tail: we being the tail: then suddenly dives over the sky-line out of sight. And the landscape changes. The famous woods begin to appear. At first it is only hazel-thickets, miles of hazel-thickets, all wild, with a few black cattle trying to peep at us out of the green myrtle and arbutus scrub which forms the undergrowth; and a couple of rare, wild peasants peering at the train. They wear the black sheepskin tunic, with the wool outside, and the long stocking-caps. Like cattle they too peer out from between deep bushes. The myrtle scrub here rises man-high, and cattle and men are smothered in it. The big hazels rise bare above. It must be difficult getting about in these parts.

Sometimes in the distance one sees a black-and-white peasant riding lonely across a more open place, a tiny vivid figure. I like so much the proud instinct which makes a living creature distinguish itself from its background. I hate the rabbity khaki protection-colouration. A black-and-white peasant on his pony, only a dot in the distance beyond the foliage, still flashes and dominates the landscape. Ha-ha! proud mankind! There you ride! But alas, most of the men are still khaki-muffled, rabbit-indistinguishable, ignominious. The Italians look curiously rabbity in the grey-green uniform: just as our

sand-coloured khaki men look doggy. They seem to scuffle rather abased, ignominious on the earth. Give us back
the scarlet and gold, and devil take the hindmost.

The landscape really begins to change. The hillsides
tilt sharper and sharper. A man is ploughing with two
small red cattle on a craggy, tree-hanging slope as sharp
as a roof-side. He stoops at the small wooden plough,
and jerks the ploughlines. The oxen lift their noses to
heaven, with a strange and beseeching snake-like movement, and taking tiny little steps with their frail feet,
move slantingly across the slope-face, between rocks and
tree-roots. Little, frail, jerky steps the bullocks take, and
again they put their horns back and lift their muzzles
snakily to heaven, as the man pulls the line. And he
skids his wooden plough round another scoop of earth.
It is marvellous how they hang upon that steep, craggy
slope. An English labourer's eyes would bolt out of his
head at the sight.

There is a stream: actually a long tress of a water-
fall pouring into a little gorge, and a stream-bed that
opens a little, and shows a marvellous cluster of naked
poplars away below. They are like ghosts. They have a
ghostly, almost phosphorescent luminousness in the
shadow of the valley, by the stream of water. If not
phosphorescent, then incandescent: a grey, goldish-pale
incandescence of naked limbs and myriad cold-glowing
twigs, gleaming strangely. If I were a painter I would
paint them: for they seem to have living, sentient flesh.
And the shadow envelops them.

Another naked tree I would paint is the gleaming
mauve-silver fig, which burns its cold incandescence,
tangled, like some sensitive creature emerged from the
rock. A fig tree come forth in its nudity gleaming over
the dark winter-earth is a sight to behold. Like some

white, tangled sea anemone. Ah, if it could but answer!
or if we had tree-speech!

Yes, the steep valley sides become almost gorges, and
there are trees. Not forests such as I had imagined, but
scattered, grey, smallish oaks, and some lithe chestnuts.
Chestnuts with their long whips, and oaks with their
stubby boughs, scattered on steep hillsides where rocks
crop out. The train perilously winding round, half way
up. Then suddenly bolting over a bridge and into a completely unexpected station. What is more, men crowd in
—the station is connected with the main railway by a
post motor-omnibus.

An unexpected irruption of men—they may be miners
or navvies or land-workers. They all have huge sacks:
some lovely saddle-bags with rose-coloured flowers
across the darkness. One old man is in full black-and-
white costume, but very dirty and coming to pieces. The
others wear the tight madder-brown breeches and
sleeved waistcoats. Some have the sheepskin tunic, and
all wear the long stocking-cap. And how they smell! of
sheep-wool and of men and goat. A rank scent fills the
carriage.

They talk and are very lively. And they have mediæval faces, *rusé*, never really abandoning their defences
for a moment, as a badger or a pole-cat never abandons
its defences. There is none of the brotherliness and civilized simplicity. Each man knows he must guard himself
and his own: each man knows the devil is behind the
next bush. They have never known the post-Renaissance
Jesus. Which is rather an eye-opener.

Not that they are suspicious or uneasy. On the contrary, noisy, assertive, vigorous presences. But with
none of that implicit belief that everybody will be and
ought to be good to them which is the mark of our era.

They don't expect people to be good to them: they don't want it. They remind me of half-wild dogs that will love and obey, but which won't be handled. They won't have their heads touched. And they won't be fondled. One can almost hear the half-savage growl.

The long stocking caps they wear as a sort of crest, as a lizard wears his crest at mating time. They are always moving them, settling them on their heads. One fat fellow, young, with sly brown eyes and a young beard round his face, folds his stocking-foot in three, so that it rises over his brow martial and handsome. The old boy brings his stocking-foot over the left ear. A handsome fellow with a jaw of massive teeth pushes his cap back and lets it hang a long way down his back. Then he shifts it forward over his nose, and makes it have two sticking-out points, like fox-ears, above his temples. It is marvellous how much expression these caps can take on. They say that only those born to them can wear them. They seem to be just long bags, nearly a yard long, of black stockinette stuff.

The conductor comes to issue them their tickets. And they all take out rolls of paper money. Even a little mothy rat of a man who sits opposite me has quite a pad of ten-franc notes. Nobody seems short of a hundred francs nowadays: nobody.

They shout and expostulate with the conductor. Full of coarse life they are: but so coarse! The handsome fellow has his sleeved waistcoat open, and his shirt-breast has come unbuttoned. Not looking, it seems as if he wears a black undervest. Then suddenly, one sees it is his own hair. He is quite black inside his shirt, like a black goat.

But there is a gulf between oneself and them. They have no inkling of our crucifixion, our universal consciousness. Each of them is pivoted and limited to himself, as the wild animals are. They look out, and they see other objects, objects to ridicule or mistrust or to sniff curiously at. But "thou shalt love thy neighbour as thyself" has never entered their souls at all, not even the thin end of it. They might love their neighbour, with a hot, dark, unquestioning love. But the love would probably leave off abruptly. The fascination of what is beyond them has not seized on them. Their neighbour is a mere external. Their life is centripetal, pivoted inside itself, and does not run out towards others and mankind. One feels for the first time the real old mediæval life, which is enclosed in itself and has no interest in the world outside.

And so they lie about on the seats, play a game, shout, and sleep, and settle their long stocking-caps: and spit. It is wonderful in them that at this time of day they still wear the long stocking-caps as part of their inevitable selves. It is a sign of obstinate and powerful tenacity. They are not going to be broken in upon by worldconsciousness. They are not going into the world's common clothes. Coarse, vigorous, determined, they will stick to their own coarse dark stupidity and let the big world find its own way to its own enlightened hell. Their hell is their own hell, they prefer it unenlightened.

And one cannot help wondering whether Sardinia will resist right through. Will the last waves of enlightenment and world-unity break over them and wash away the stocking-caps? Or is the tide of enlightenment and world-unity already receding fast enough?

Certainly a reaction is setting in, away from the old universality, back, away from cosmopolitanism and internationalism. Russia, with her Third International, is at the same time reacting most violently away from all other contact, back, recoiling on herself, into a fierce, unapproachable Russianism. Which motion will conquer? The workman's International, or the centripetal movement into national isolation? Are we going to merge into one grey proletarian homogeneity?—or are we going to swing back into more-or-less isolated, separate, defiant communities?

Probably both. The workman's International movement will finally break the flow towards cosmopolitanism and world-assimilation, and suddenly in a crash the world will fly back into intense separations. The moment has come when America, that extremist in world-assimilation and world-oneness, is reacting into violent egocentricity, a truly Amerindian egocentricity. As sure as fate we are on the brink of American empire.

For myself, I am glad. I am glad that the era of love and oneness is over: hateful homogeneous world-oneness. I am glad that Russia flies back into savage Russianism, Scythism, savagely self-pivoting. I am glad that America is doing the same. I shall be glad when men hate their common, world-alike clothes, when they tear them up and clothe themselves fiercely for distinction, savage distinction, savage distinction against the rest of the creeping world: when America kicks the billy-cock and the collar-and-tie into limbo, and takes to her own national costume: when men fiercely react against looking all alike and being all alike, and betake themselves into vivid clan or nation-distinctions.

The era of love and oneness is over. The era of world-alike should be at an end. The other tide has set in. Men will set their bonnets at one another now, and fight themselves into separation and sharp distinction. The day of peace and oneness is over, the day of the great fight into multifariousness is at hand. Hasten the day, and save us from proletarian homogeneity and khaki all-alikeness.

I love my indomitable coarse men from mountain

Sardinia, for their stocking-caps and their splendid,
animal-bright stupidity. If only the last wave of all-
alikeness won't wash those superb crests, those caps,
away.

The Theatre

DURING carnival a company is playing in the
theatre. On Christmas Day the padrone came in
with the key of his box, and would we care to see the
drama? The theatre was small, a mere nothing, in fact;
a mere affair of peasants, you understand; and the
Signor Di Paoli spread his hands and put his head on
one side, parrot-wise; but we might find a little diver-
sion—"un peu de divertiment." With this he handed me
the key.

I made suitable acknowledgments, and was really impressed. To be handed the key of a box at the theatre,
so simply and pleasantly, in the large sitting-room looking over the grey lake of Christmas Day; it seemed to
me a very graceful event. The key had a chain and a
little shield of bronze, on which was beaten out a large
figure 8.

So the next day we went to see *I Spettri*, expecting
some good, crude melodrama. The theatre is an old
church. Since that triumph of the deaf and dumb, the
cinematograph, has come to give us the nervous excitement of speed—grimace, agitation, and speed, as of flying atoms, chaos—many an old church in Italy has taken
a new lease of life.

This cast-off church made a good theatre. I realized
how cleverly it had been constructed for the dramatic
presentation of religious ceremonies. The east end is
round, the walls are windowless, sound is well dis-

tributed. Now everything is theatrical, except the stone
floor and two pillars at the back of the auditorium, and
the slightly ecclesiastical seats below.

There are two tiers of little boxes in the theatre, some
forty in all, with fringe and red velvet, and lined with
dark red paper, quite like real boxes in a real theatre.
And the padrone's is one of the best. It just holds three
people.

We paid our threepence entrance fee in the stone hall
and went upstairs. I opened the door of Number 8, and
we were shut in our little cabin, looking down on all the
world. Then I found the barber, Luigi, bowing profusely
in a box opposite. It was necessary to make bows all
round: ah, the chemist, on the upper tier, near the barber; how-do-you-do to the padrona of the hotel, who is
our good friend, and who sits, wearing a little beaver
shoulder-cape, a few boxes off; very cold salutation to
the stout village magistrate with the long brown beard,
who leans forward in the box facing the stage, while a
grouping of faces look out from behind him; a warm
smile to the family of the Signora Gemma, across next to
the stage. Then we are settled.

I cannot tell why I hate the village magistrate. He
looks like a family portrait by a Flemish artist, he himself weighing down the front of the picture with his
portliness and his long brown beard, whilst the faces of
his family are arranged in two groups for the background. I think he is angry at our intrusion. He is very
republican and self-important. But we eclipse him easily,
with the aid of a large black velvet hat, and black furs,
and our Sunday clothes.

Downstairs the villagers are crowding, drifting like a
heavy current. The women are seated, by church instinct,
all together on the left, with perhaps an odd man at the
end of a row, beside his wife. On the right, sprawling in

the benches, are several groups of bersaglieri, in grey
uniforms and slanting cock's-feather hats; then peasants,
fishermen, and an odd couple or so of brazen girls taking
their places on the men's side.

At the back, lounging against the pillars or standing
very dark and sombre, are the more reckless spirits of
the village. Their black felt hats are pulled down, their
cloaks are thrown over their mouths, they stand very
dark and isolated in their moments of stillness, they
shout and wave to each other when anything occurs.

The men are clean, their clothes are all clean washed.
The rags of the poorest porter are always well washed.
But it is Sunday tomorrow, and they are shaved only on
a Sunday. So that they have a week's black growth on
their chins. But they have dark, soft eyes, unconscious
and vulnerable. They move and balance with loose,
heedless motion upon their clattering zoccoli, they
lounge with wonderful ease against the wall at the back,
or against the two pillars, unconscious of the patches on
their clothes or of their bare throats, that are knotted
perhaps with a scarlet rag. Loose and abandoned, they
lounge and talk, or they watch with wistful absorption
the play that is going on.

They are strangely isolated in their own atmosphere,
and as if revealed. It is as if their vulnerable being was
exposed and they have not the wit to cover it. There is
a pathos of physical sensibility and mental inadequacy.
Their mind is not sufficiently alert to run with their
quick, warm senses.

The men keep together, as if to support each other
the women also are together; in a hard, strong herd. It is
as if the power, the hardness, the triumph, even in this
Italian village, were with the women in their relentless,
vindictive unity.

That which drives men and women together, the indomitable necessity, is like a bondage upon the people. They submit as under compulsion, under constraint. They come together mostly in anger and in violence of destructive passion. There is no comradeship between men and women, none whatsoever, but rather a condition of battle, reserve, hostility.

On Sundays the uncomfortable, excited, unwilling youth walks for an hour with his sweetheart, at a little distance from her, on the public highway in the afternoon. This is a concession to the necessity for marriage. There is no real courting, no happiness of being together, only the roused excitement which is based on a fundamental hostility. There is very little flirting, and what there is is of the subtle, cruel kind, like a sex duel. On the whole, the men and women avoid each other, almost shun each other. Husband and wife are brought together in a child, which they both worship. But in each of them there is only the great reverence for the infant, and the reverence for fatherhood or motherhood, as the case may be; there is no spiritual love.

In marriage, husband and wife wage the subtle, satisfying war of sex upon each other. It gives a profound satisfaction, a profound intimacy. But it destroys all joy, all unanimity in action.

On Sunday afternoons the uncomfortable youth walks by the side of his maiden for an hour in the public highway. Then he escapes; as from a bondage he goes back to his men companions. On Sunday afternoons and evenings the married woman, accompanied by a friend or by a child—she dare not go alone, afraid of the strange, terrible sex-war between her and the drunken man—is seen leading home the wine-drunken, liberated husband. Sometimes she is beaten when she gets home. It is part of the process. But there is no synthetic love between men and women, there is only passion, and passion is fundamental hatred, the act of love is a fight.

The child, the outcome, is divine. Here the union, the oneness, is manifest. Though spirit strove with spirit, in mortal conflict, during the sex-passion, yet the flesh united with flesh in oneness. The phallus is still divine. But the spirit, the mind of man, this has become nothing.

So the women triumph. They sit down below in the theatre, their perfectly dressed hair gleaming, their backs very straight, their heads carried tensely. They are not very noticeable. They seem held in reserve. They are just as tense and stiff as the men are slack and abandoned. Some strange will holds the women taut. They seem like weapons, dangerous. There is nothing charming nor winning about them; at the best a full, prolific maternity, at the worst a yellow poisonous bitterness of the flesh that is like a narcotic. But they are too strong for the men. The male spirit, which would subdue the immediate flesh to some conscious or social purpose, is overthrown. The woman in her maternity is the lawgiver, the supreme authority. The authority of the man, in work, in public affairs, is something trivial in comparison. The pathetic ignominy of the village male is complete on Sunday afternoon, on his great day of liberation, when he is accompanied home, drunk but sinister, by the erect, unswerving, slightly cowed woman. His drunken terrorizing is only pitiable, she is so obviously the more constant power.

And this is why the men must go away to America. It is not the money. It is the profound desire to rehabilitate themselves, to recover some dignity as men, as producers, as workers, as creators from the spirit, not only from the flesh. It is a profound desire to get away from women altogether, the terrible subjugation to sex, the phallic worship.

The company of actors in the little theatre was from a small town away on the plain, beyond Brescia. The curtain rose, everybody was still, with that profound, naïve attention which children give. And after a few minutes I realized that I Spettri was Ibsen's Ghosts. The peasants and fishermen of the Garda, even the rows of ungovernable children, sat absorbed in watching as the Norwegian drama unfolded itself.

The actors are peasants. The leader is the son of a peasant proprietor. He is qualified as a chemist, but is unsettled, vagrant, prefers play-acting. The Signor Pietro di Paoli shrugs his shoulders and apologizes for their vulgar accent. It is all the same to me. I am trying to get myself to rights with the play, which I have just lately seen in Munich, perfectly produced and detestable.

It was such a change from the hard, ethical, slightly mechanized characters in the German play, which was as perfect an interpretation as I can imagine, to the rather pathetic notion of the Italian peasants, that I had to wait to adjust myself.

The mother was a pleasant, comfortable woman harassed by something, she did not quite know what. The pastor was a ginger-haired caricature imitated from the northern stage, quite a lay figure. The peasants never laughed, they watched solemnly and absorbedly like children. The servant was just a slim, pert, forward hussy, much too flagrant. And then the son, the actor-manager: he was a dark, ruddy man, broad and thick-set, evidently of peasant origin, but with some education now; he was the important figure, the play was his.

And he was strangely disturbing. Dark, ruddy, and powerful, he could not be the blighted son of Ghosts, the hectic, unsound, northern issue of a diseased father. His flashy Italian passion for his half-sister was real enough to make one uncomfortable: something he wanted and would have in spite of his own soul, something which fundamentally he did not want.

It was this contradiction within the man that made the play so interesting. A robust, vigorous man of thirty-eight, flaunting and florid as a rather successful Italian can be, there was yet a secret sickness which oppressed him. But it was no taint in the blood, it was rather a kind of debility in the soul. That which he wanted and would have, the sensual excitement, in his soul he did not want it, no, not at all. And yet he must act from his physical desires, his physical will.

His true being, his real self, was impotent. In his soul he was dependent, forlorn. He was childish and dependent on the mother. To hear him say, "Grazia, mamma!" would have tormented the mother-soul in any woman living. Such a child crying in the night! And for what?

For he was hot-blooded, healthy, almost in his prime, and free as a man can be in his circumstances. He had his own way, he admitted no thwarting. He governed his circumstances pretty much, coming to our village with his little company, playing the plays he chose himself. And yet, that which he would have he did not vitally want, it was only a sort of inflamed obstinacy that made him so insistent, in the masculine way. He was not going to be governed by women, he was not going to be dictated to in the least by any one. And this because ne was beaten by his own flesh.

His real man's soul, the soul that goes forth and builds up a new world out of the void, was ineffectual. It could only revert to the senses. His divinity was the phallic divinity. The other male divinity, which is the spirit that fulfils in the world the new germ of an idea, this was denied and obscured in him, unused. And it was this spirit which cried out helplessly in him through the insistent, inflammable flesh. Even this play-acting was a form of physical gratification for him, it had in it neither real mind nor spirit.

It was so different from Ibsen and so much more moving. Ibsen is exciting, nervously sensational. But this was really moving, a real crying in the night. One loved the Italian nation, and wanted to help it with all one's soul. But when one sees the perfect Ibsen, how one hates the Norwegian and Swedish nations! They are detestable.

They seem to be fingering with the mind the secret places and sources of the blood, impertinent, irreverent, nasty. There is a certain intolerable nastiness about the real Ibsen: the same thing is in Strindberg and in most of the Norwegian and Swedish writings. It is with them a sort of phallic worship also, but now the worship is mental and perverted: the phallus is the real fetish, but it is the source of uncleanliness and corruption and death, it is the Moloch, worshipped in obscenity.

Which is unbearable. The phallus is a symbol of creative divinity. But it represents only part of creative divinity. The Italian has made it represent the whole. Which is now his misery, for he has to destroy his symbol in himself.

Which is why the Italian men have the enthusiasm for war, unashamed. Partly it is the true phallic worship, for the phallic principle is to absorb and dominate all life. But also it is a desire to expose themselves to death, to know death, that death may destroy in them this too strong dominion of the blood, may once more liberate the spirit of outgoing, of uniting, of making order out of chaos, in the outer world, as the flesh makes a new order from chaos in begetting a new life, set them free to know and serve a greater idea.

The peasants below sat and listened intently, like children who hear and do not understand, yet who are spellbound. The children themselves sit spellbound on the benches till the play is over. They do not fidget or lose interest. They watch with wide, absorbed eyes at the mystery, held in thrall by the sound of emotion.

But the villagers do not really care for Ibsen. They let it go. On the feast of Epiphany, as a special treat, was given a poetic drama by D'Annunzio, *La Fiaccola sotto il Moggio—The Light under the Bushel.*

It is a foolish romantic play of no real significance. There are several murders and a good deal of artificial horror. But it is all a very nice and romantic piece of make-believe, like a charade.

So the audience loved it. After the performance of *Ghosts* I saw the barber, and he had the curious grey clayey look of an Italian who is cold and depressed. The sterile cold inertia, which the so-called passionate nations know so well, had settled on him, and he went obliterating himself in the street, as if he were cold, dead.

But after the D'Annunzio play he was like a man who has drunk sweet wine and is warm.

"Ah, bellissimo, bellissimo!" he said, in tones of intoxicated reverence, when he saw me.

"Better than *I Spettri?*" I said.

He half-raised his hands, as if to imply the fatuity of the question.

"Ah, but—" he said, "it was D'Annunzio. The other——"

"That was Ibsen—a great Norwegian," I said, "famous all over the world."

"But, you know—D'Annunzio is a poet—oh, beautiful, beautiful!" There was no going beyond this "bello—bellissimo."

It was the langauge which did it. It was the Italian passion for rhetoric, for the speech which appeals to the senses and makes no demand on the mind. When an Englishman listens to a speech he wants at least to imagine that he understands thoroughly and impersonally what is meant. But an Italian only cares about the emotion. It is the movement, the physical effect of the language upon the blood which gives him supreme satisfaction. His mind is scarcely engaged at all. He is like a child, hearing and feeling without understanding. It is the sensuous gratification he asks for. Which is why D'Annunzio is a god in Italy. He can control the current of the blood with his words, and although much of what he says is bosh, yet the hearer is satisfied, fulfilled.

Carnival ends on the 5th of February, so each Thursday there is a Serata d' Onore of one of the actors. The first, and the only one for which prices were raised—to a fourpence entrance fee instead of threepence—was for the leading lady. The play was *The Wife of the Doctor*, a modern piece, sufficiently uninteresting; the farce that followed made me laugh.

Since it was her Evening of Honour, Adelaida was the person to see. She is very popular, though she is no longer young. In fact, she is the mother of the young pert person of *Ghosts*.

Nevertheless, Adelaida, stout and blonde and soft and pathetic, is the real heroine of the theatre, the prima. She is very good at sobbing; and afterwards the men exclaim involuntarily, out of their strong emotion, "Bella, bella!" The women say nothing. They sit stiffly and dangerously as ever. But, no doubt, they quite agree this is the true picture of ill-used, tear-stained woman, the bearer of many wrongs. Therefore they take unto themselves the homage of the men's "Bella, bella!" that follows the sobs: it is due recognition of their hard wrongs:

"The woman pays." Nevertheless, they despise in their souls the plump, soft Adelaida.

Dear Adelaida, she is irreproachable. In every age, in every clime, she is dear, at any rate to the masculine soul, this soft, tear-blenched, blond, ill-used thing. She must be ill-used and unfortunate. Dear Gretchen, dear Desdemona, dear Iphigenia, dear Dame aux Camélias, dear Lucy of Lammermoor, dear Mary Magdalene, dear, pathetic, unfortunate soul, in all ages and lands, how we love you. In the theatre she blossoms forth, she is the lily of the stage. Young and inexperienced as I am, I have broken my heart over her several times. I could write a sonnet-sequence to her, yes, the fair, pale, tear-stained thing, white-robed, with her hair down her back; I could call her by a hundred names, in a hundred languages, Mélisande, Elizabeth, Juliet, Butterfly, Phèdre, Minnehaha, etc. Each new time I hear her voice, with its faint clang of tears, my heart grows big and hot, and my bones melt. I detest her, but it is no good. My heart begins to swell like a bud under the plangent rain.

The last time I saw her was here, on the Garda, at Salò. She was the chalked, thin-armed daughter of Rigoletto. I detested her, her voice had a chalky squeak in it. And yet, by the end, my heart was over-ripe in my breast, ready to burst with loving affection. I was ready to walk on to the stage, to wipe out the odious, miscreant lover, and to offer her all myself, saying, "I can see it is real *love* you want, and you shall have it: *I* will give it to you."

Of course I know the secret of the Gretchen magic; it is all in the "Save me, Mr. Hercules!" phrase. Her shyness, her timidity, her trustfulness, her tears foster my own strength and grandeur. I am the positive half of the universe. But so I am, if it comes to that, just as positive as the other half.

Adelaida is plump, and her voice has just that moist, plangent strength which gives one a real voluptuous thrill. The moment she comes on the stage and looks round—a bit scared—she is *she,* Electra, Isolde, Sieglinde, Marguèrite. She wears a dress of black voile, like the lady who weeps at the trial in the police-court. This is her modern uniform. Her antique garment is of trailing white, with a blonde pigtail and a flower. Realistically, it is black voile and a handkerchief.

Adelaida always has a handkerchief. And still I cannot resist it. I say, "There's the hanky!" Nevertheless, in two minutes it has worked its way with me. She squeezes it in her poor, plump hand as the tears begin to rise; Fate, or man, is inexorable, so cruel. There is a sob, a cry; she presses the fist and the hanky to her eyes, one eye, then the other. She weeps real tears, tears shaken from the depths of her soft, vulnerable, victimized female self. I cannot stand it. There I sit in the padrone's little red box and stifle my emotion, whilst I repeat in my heart: "What a shame, child, what a shame!" She is twice my age, but what is age in such a circumstance? "Your poor little hanky, it's sopping. There, then, don't cry. It'll be all right. *I'll* see you're all right. *All* men are not beasts, you know." So I cover her protectively in my arms, and soon I shall be kissing her, for comfort, in the heat and prowess of my compassion, kissing her soft, plump cheek and neck closely, bringing my comfort nearer and nearer.

It is a pleasant and exciting role for me to play. Robert Burns did the part to perfection·

> O wert thou in the cauld blast
> On yonder lea, on yonder lea.

How many times does one recite that to all the Ophelias and Gretchens in the world:

Thy bield should be my bosom.

How one admires one's bosom in that capacity! Looking down at one's shirt-front, one is filled with strength
and pride.

Why are the women so bad at playing this part in real
life, this Ophelia-Gretchen role? Why are they so unwilling to go mad and die for our sakes? They do it regularly
on the stage.

But perhaps, after all, we write the plays. What a
villain I am, what a black-browed, passionate, ruthless,
masculine villain I am to the leading lady on the stage;
and, on the other hand, dear heart, what a hero, what a
fount of chivalrous generosity and faith! I am *anything*
but a dull and law-abiding citizen. I am a Galahad, full
of purity and spirituality, I am the Lancelot of valour
and lust; I fold my hands, or I cock my hat on one side,
as the case may be; I am *myself*. Only, I am not a respectable citizen, not that, in this hour of my glory and
my escape.

Dear Heaven, how Adelaida wept, her voice plashing
like violin music, at my ruthless, masculine cruelty. Dear
heart, how she sighed to rest on my sheltering bosom!
And how I enjoyed my dual nature! How I admired
myself!

Adelaida chose *La Moglie del Dottore* for her Evening
of Honour. During the following week came a little
storm of coloured bills: "Great Evening of Honour of
Enrico Persevalli."

This is the leader, the actor-manager. What should he
choose for his great occasion, this broad, thick-set, ruddy
descendant of the peasant proprietors of the plain? No
one knew. The title of the play was not revealed.

So we were staying at home, it was cold and wet. But

the maestra came inflammably on that Thursday evening, and were we not going to the theatre, to see *Amleto*?

Poor maestra, she is yellow and bitter-skinned, near fifty, but her dark eyes are still corrosively inflammable. She was engaged to a lieutenant in the cavalry, who got drowned when she was twenty-one. Since then she has hung on the tree unripe, growing yellow and bitter-skinned, never developing.

"*Amleto!*" I say. "*Non lo conosco.*"

A certain fear comes into her eyes. She is school-mistress, and has a mortal dread of being wrong.

"*Si*," she cries, wavering, appealing, "*una dramma inglese.*"

"English!" I repeated.

"Yes, an English drama."

"How do you write it?"

Anxiously, she gets a pencil from her reticule, and, with black-gloved scrupulousness, writes *Amleto*.

"Hamlet!" I exclaim wonderingly.

"*Ecco, Amleto!*" cries the maestra, her eyes aflame with thankful justification.

Then I knew that Signor Enrico Persevalli was looking to me for an audience. His Evening of Honour would be a bitter occasion to him if the English were not there to see his performance.

I hurried to get ready, I ran through the rain. I knew he would take it badly that it rained on his Evening of Honour. He counted himself a man who had fate against him.

"*Sono un disgraziato, io.*"

I was late. The First Act was nearly over. The play was not yet alive, neither in the bosoms of the actors nor in the audience. I closed the door of the box softly, and came forward. The rolling Italian eyes of Hamlet glanced up at me. There came a new impulse over the Court of Denmark.

Enrico looked a sad fool in his melancholy black. The doublet sat close, making him stout and vulgar, the knee-breeches seemed to exaggerate the commonness of his thick, rather short, strutting legs. And he carried a long black rag, as a cloak, for histrionic purposes. And he had on his face a portentous grimace of melancholy and philosophic importance. His was the caricature of Hamlet's melancholy self-absorption.

I stooped to arrange my footstool and compose my countenance. I was trying not to grin. For the first time, attired in philosophic melancholy of black silk, Enrico looked a boor and a fool. His close-cropped, rather animal head was common above the effeminate doublet, his sturdy, ordinary figure looked absurd in a melancholic droop.

All the actors alike were out of their element. Their Majesties of Denmark were touching. The Queen, burly little peasant woman, was ill at ease in her pink satin. Enrico had had no mercy. He knew she loved to be the scolding servant or housekeeper, with her head tied up in a handkerchief, shrill and vulgar. Yet here she was pranked out in an expanse of satin, la Regina. Regina, indeed!

She obediently did her best to be important. Indeed, she rather fancied herself; she looked sideways at the audience, self-consciously, quite ready to be accepted as an imposing and noble person, if they would esteem her such. Her voice sounded hoarse and common, but whether it was the pink satin in contrast, or a cold, I do not know. She was almost childishly afraid to move. Before she began a speech she looked down and kicked her skirt viciously, so that she was sure it was under control. Then she let go. She was a burly, downright little body of sixty, one rather expected her to box Hamlet on the ears.

Only she liked being a queen when she sat on the throne. There she perched with great satisfaction, her train splendidly displayed down the steps. She was as proud as a child, and she looked like Queen Victoria of the Jubilee period.

The King, her noble consort, also had new honours thrust upon him, as well as new garments. His body was real enough, but it had nothing at all to do with his clothes. They established a separate identity by themselves. But wherever he went, they went with him, to the confusion of everybody.

He was a thin, rather frail-looking peasant, pathetic, and very gentle. There was something pure and fine about him, he was so exceedingly gentle and by natural breeding courteous. But he did not feel kingly, he acted the part with beautiful, simple resignation.

Enrico Persevalli had overshot himself in every direction, but worst of all in his own. He had become a hulking fellow, crawling about with his head ducked between his shoulders, pecking and poking, creeping about after other people, sniffing at them, setting traps for them, absorbed by his own self-important self-consciousness. His legs, in their black knee-breeches, had a crawling, slinking look; he always carried the black rag of a cloak, something for him to twist about as he twisted in his own soul, overwhelmed by a sort of inverted perversity.

I had always felt an aversion from Hamlet: a creeping, unclean thing he seems, on the stage, whether he is Forbes Robertson or anybody else. His nasty poking and sniffing at his mother, his setting traps for the King, his conceited perversion with Ophelia make him always intolerable. The character is repulsive in its conception, based on self-dislike and a spirit of disintegration.

There is, I think, this strain of cold dislike, or self-dislike, through much of the Renaissance art, and through all the later Shakespeare. In Shakespeare it is a kind of corruption in the flesh and a conscious revolt from this. A sense of corruption in the flesh makes Hamlet frenzied, for he will never admit that it is his own flesh. Leonardo da Vinci is the same, but Leonardo loves the corruption maliciously. Michelangelo rejects any feeling of corruption, he stands by the flesh, the flesh only. It is the corresponding reaction, but in the opposite direction. But that is all four hundred years ago. Enrico Persevalli has just reached the position. He *is* Hamlet, and evidently he has great satisfaction in the part. He is the modern Italian, suspicious, isolated, self-nauseated, labouring in a sense of physical corruption. But he will not admit it is in himself. He creeps about in self-conceit, transforming his own self-loathing. With what satisfaction did he reveal corruption—corruption in his neighbours he gloated in—letting his mother know he had discovered her incest, her uncleanness, gloated in torturing the incestuous King. Of all the unclean ones, Hamlet was the uncleanest. But he accused only the others.

Except in the "great" speeches, and there Enrico was betrayed, Hamlet suffered the extremity of physical self-loathing, loathing of his own flesh. The play is the statement of the most significant philosophic position of the Renaissance. Homlet is, far more even than Orestes, his prototype, a mental creature, anti-physical, anti-sensual. The whole drama is the tragedy of the convulsed reaction of the mind from the flesh, of the spirit from the self, the reaction from the great aristocratic to the great democratic principle.

An ordinary instinctive man, in Hamlet's position, would either have set about murdering his uncle, by reflex action, or else would have gone right away. There would have been no need for Hamlet to murder his mother. It would have been sufficient blood-vengeance if he had killed his uncle. But that is the statement according to the aristocratic principle.

Orestes was in the same position, but the same position two thousand years earlier, with two thousand years of experience wanting. So that the question was not so intricate in him as in Hamlet, he was not nearly so conscious. The whole Greek life was based on the idea of the supremacy of the self, and the self was always male. Orestes was his father's child, he would be the same whatever mother he had. The mother was but the vehicle, the soil in which the paternal seed was planted. When Clytemnestra murdered Agamemnon, it was as if a common individual murdered God, to the Greek.

But Agamemnon, King and Lord, was not infallible. He was fallible. He had sacrificed Iphigenia for the sake of glory in war, for the fulfilment of the superb idea of self, but on the other hand he had made cruel dissension for the sake of the concubines captured in war. The paternal flesh was fallible, ungodlike. It lusted after meaner pursuits than glory, war, and slaying, it was not faithful to the highest idea of the self. Orestes was driven mad by the furies of his mother, because of the justice that they represented. Nevertheless he was in the end exculpated. The third play of the trilogy is almost foolish, with its prating gods. But it means that, according to the Greek conviction, Orestes was right and Clytemnestra entirely wrong. But for all that, the infallible King, the infallible male Self, is dead in Orestes, killed by the furies of Clytemnestra. He gains his peace of mind after the revulsion from his own physical fallibility,

but he will never be an unquestioned lord, as Agamemnon was. Orestes is left at peace, neutralized. He is the
beginning of non-aristocratic Christianity.

Hamlet's father, the King, is, like Agamemnon, a
warrior-king. But, unlike Agamemnon, he is blameless
with regard to Gertrude. Yet Gertrude, like Clytemnestra, is the potential murderer of her husband, as
Lady Macbeth is murderess, as the daughters of Lear.
The women murder the supreme male, the ideal Self,
the King and Father.

This is the tragic position Shakespeare must dwell
upon. The woman rejects, repudiates the ideal Self
which the male represents to her. The supreme representative, King and Father, is murdered by the Wife and the
Daughters.

What is the reason? Hamlet goes mad in a revulsion
of rage and nausea. Yet the women-murderers only represent some ultimate judgment in his own soul. At the
bottom of his own soul Hamlet has decided that the Self
in its supremacy, Father and King, must die. It is a
suicidal decision for his involuntary soul to have arrived
at. Yet it is inevitable. The great religious, philosophic
tide, which had been swelling all through the Middle
Ages, had brought him there.

The question, to be or not to be, which Hamlet puts
himself, does not mean, to live or not to live. It is not
the simple human being who puts himself the question,
it is the supreme I, King and Father. To be or not to be
King, Father, in the Self supreme? And the decision is,
not to be.

It is the inevitable philosophic conclusion of all the
Renaissance. The deepest impulse in man, the religious
impulse, is the desire to be immortal, or infinite, consummated. And this impulse is satisfied in fulfilment of
an idea, a steady progression. In this progression man is

satisfied, he seems to have reached his goal, this infinity, this immortality, this eternal being, with every step nearer which he takes.

And so, according to his idea of fulfilment, man establishes the whole order of life. If my fulfilment is the fulfilment and establishment of the unknown divine Self which I am, then I shall proceed in the realizing of the greatest idea of the Self, the highest conception of the I, my order of life will be kingly, imperial, aristocratic. The body politic also will culminate in this divinity of the flesh, this body imbued with glory, invested with divine power and might, the King, the Emperor. In the body politic also I shall desire a king, an emperor, a tyrant, glorious, mighty, in whom I see myself consummated and fulfilled. This is inevitable!

But during the Middle Ages, struggling within this pagan, original transport, the transport of the Ego, was a small dissatisfaction, a small contrary desire. Amid the pomp of kings and popes was the Child Jesus and the Madonna. Jesus the King gradually dwindled down. There was Jesus the Child, helpless, at the mercy of all the world. And there was Jesus crucified.

The old transport, the old fulfilment of the Ego, the Davidian ecstasy, the assuming of all power and glory unto the self, the becoming infinite through the absorption of all into the Ego, this gradually became unsatisfactory. This was not the infinite, this was not immortality. This was eternal death, this was damnation.

The monk rose up with his opposite ecstasy, the Christian ecstasy. There was a death to die: the flesh, the self, must die, so that the spirit should rise again immortal, eternal, infinite. I am dead unto myself, but I live in the Infinite. The finite Me is no more, only the Infinite, the Eternal, is.

At the Renaissance this great half-truth overcame the

other great half-truth. The Christian Infinite, reached by a process of abnegation, a process of being absorbed, dissolved, diffused into the great Not-Self, supplanted the old pagan Infinite, wherein the self like a root threw out branches and radicles which embraced the whole universe, became the Whole.

There is only one Infinite, the world now cried, there is the great Christian Infinite of renunciation and consummation in the not-self. The other, that old pride, is damnation. The sin of sins is Pride, it is the way to total damnation. Whereas the pagans based their life on pride.

And according to this new Infinite, reached through renunciation and dissolving into the Others, the Neighbour, man must build up his actual form of life. With Savonarola and Martin Luther the living Church actually transformed itself, for the Roman Church was still pagan. Henry VIII simply said, "There is no Church, there is only the State." But with Shakespeare the transformation had reached the State also. The King, the Father, the representative of the Consummate Self, the maximum of all life, the symbol of the consummate being, the becoming Supreme, Godlike, Infinite, he must perish and pass away. This Infinite was not infinite, this consummation was not consummate, all this was fallible, false. It was rotten, corrupt. It must go. But Shakespeare was also the thing itself. Hence his horror, his frenzy, his self-loathing.

The King, the Emperor, is killed in the soul of man, the old order of life is over, the old tree is dead at the root. So said Shakespeare. It was finally enacted in Cromwell. Charles I took up the old position of kingship by divine right. Like Hamlet's father, he was blameless otherwise. But as representative of the old form of life, which mankind now hated with frenzy, he must be cut down, removed. It was a symbolic act.

The world, our world of Europe, had now really turned, swung round to a new goal, a new idea, the Infinite reached through the omission of Self. God is all that which is Not-Me. I am consummate when my Self, the resistant solid, is reduced and diffused into all that which is Not-Me: my neighbour, my enemy, the great Otherness. Then I am perfect.

And from this belief the world began gradually to form a new State, a new body politic, in which the Self should be removed. There should be no king, no lords, no aristocrats. The world continued in its religious belief, beyond the French Revolution, beyond the great movement of Shelley and Godwin. There should be no Self. That which was supreme was that which was Not-Me, the other. The governing factor in the State was the idea of the good of others; that is, the Common Good. And the *vital* governing idea in the State has been this idea since Cromwell.

Before Cromwell the idea was "For the King," because every man saw himself consummated in the King. After Cromwell the idea was "For the good of my neighbour," or "For the good of the people," or "For the good of the whole." This has been our ruling idea, by which we have more or less lived.

Now this has failed. Now we say that the Christian Infinite is not infinite. We are tempted, like Nietzsche, to return back to the old pagan Infinite, to say that is supreme. Or we are inclined, like the English and the Pragmatist, to say, "There is no Infinite, there is no Absolute. The only Absolute is expediency, the only reality is sensation and momentariness." But we may say this, even act on it, *à la Sanine*. But we never believe it.

What is really Absolute is the mystic Reason which connects both Infinites, the Holy Ghost that relates both natures of God. If we now wish to make a living State, we must build it up to the idea of the Holy Spirit, the supreme Relationship. We must say, the pagan Infinite is infinite, the Christian Infinite is infinite: these are our two Consummations, in both of these we are consummated. But that which relates them alone is absolute.

This Absolute of the Holy Ghost we may call Truth or Justice or Right. These are partial names, indefinite and unsatisfactory unless there be kept the knowledge of the two Infinites, pagan and Christian, which they go between. When both are there, they are like a superb bridge, on which one can stand and know the whole world, my world, the two halves of the universe.

"Essere, o non essere, è qui il punto."

To be or not to be was the question for Hamlet to settle. It is no longer our question, at least, not in the same sense. When it is a question of death, the fashionable young suicide declares that his self-destruction is the final proof of his own incontrovertible being. And as for not-being in our public life, we have achieved it as much as ever we want to, as much as is necessary. Whilst in private life there is a swing back to paltry selfishness as a creed. And in the war there is the position of neutralization and nothingness. It is a question of knowing how "to be," and how "not to be," for we must fulfil both.

Enrico Persevalli was detestable with his "Essere, o non essere." He whispered it in a hoarse whisper as if it were some melodramatic murder he was about to commit. As a matter of fact, he knows quite well, and has known all his life, that his pagan Infinite, his transport of the flesh and the supremacy of the male in fatherhood, is all unsatisfactory. All his life he has really cringed before the northern Infinite of the Not-Self, although he has continued in the Italian habit of Self. But it is mere habit, sham.

How can he know anything about being and not-being when he is only a maudlin compromise between them, and all he wants is to be, a maudlin compromise? He is neither one nor the other. He has neither being nor not-being. He is as equivocal as the monks. He was detestable, mouthing Hamlet's sincere words. He has still to let go, to know what not-being is, before he can *be*. Till he has gone through the Christian negation of himself, and has known the Christian consummation, he is a mere amorphous heap.

For the soliloquies of Hamlet are as deep as the soul of man can go, in one direction, and as sincere as the Holy Spirit itself in their essence. But thank heaven, the bog into which Hamlet struggled is almost surpassed.

It is a strange thing, if a man covers his face and speaks with his eyes blinded, how significant and poignant he becomes. The ghost of this Hamlet was very simple. He was wrapped down to the knees in a great white cloth, and over his face was an open-work woollen shawl. But the naïve blind helplessness and verity of his voice was strangely convincing. He seemed the most real thing in the play. From the knees downward he was Laertes, because he had on Laertes' white trousers and patent leather slippers. Yet he was strangely real, a voice out of the dark.

The Ghost is really one of the play's failures, it is so trivial and unspiritual and vulgar. And it was spoilt for me from the first. When I was a child I went to the twopenny travelling theatre to see *Hamlet*. The Ghost had on a helmet and a breastplate. I sat in pale transport.

"'Amblet, 'Amblet, I *am* thy father's ghost."

Then came a voice from the dark, silent audience, like a cynical knife to my fond soul:

"Why tha arena, I can tell thy voice."

The peasants loved Ophelia: she was in white with her hair down her back. Poor thing, she was pathetic, demented. And no wonder, after Hamlet's "O, that this too, too solid flesh would melt!" What then of her young breasts and her womb? Hamlet with her was a very disagreeable sight. The peasants loved her. There was a hoarse roar, half of indignation, half of roused passion, at the end of her scene.

The graveyard scene, too, was a great success, but I could not bear Hamlet. And the grave-digger in Italian was a mere buffoon. The whole scene was farcical to me because of the Italian, "Questo cranio, Signore——" And Enrico, dainty fellow, took the skull in a corner of his black cloak. As an Italian, he would not willingly touch it. It was unclean. But he looked a fool, hulking himself in his lugubriousness. He was as self-important as D'Annunzio.

The close fell flat. The peasants had applauded the whole graveyard scene wildly. But at the end of all they got up and crowded to the doors, as if to hurry away: this in spite of Enrico's final feat: he fell backwards, smack down three steps of the throne platform, on to the stage. But planks and braced muscle will bounce, and Signor Amleto bounced quite high again.

It was the end of *Amleto,* and I was glad. But I loved the theatre, I loved to look down on the peasants, who were so absorbed. At the end of the scenes the men pushed back their black hats, and rubbed their hair across their brows with a pleased, excited movement. And the women stirred in their seats.

Just one man was with his wife and child, and he was

of the same race as my old woman at San Tommaso. He was fair, thin, and clear, abstract, of the mountains. He seemed to have gathered his wife and child together into another, finer atmosphere, like the air of the mountains, and to guard them in it. This is the real Joseph, father of the child. He has a fierce, abstract look, wild and un-tamed as a hawk, but like a hawk at its own nest, fierce with love. He goes out and buys a tiny bottle of lemon-ade for a penny, and the mother and child sip it in tiny sips, whilst he bends over, like a hawk arching its wings.

It is the fierce spirit of the Ego come out of the primal infinite, but detached, isolated, an aristocrat. He is not an Italian, dark-blooded. He is fair, keen as steel, with the blood of the mountaineer in him. He is like my old spinning woman. It is curious how, with his wife and child, he makes a little separate world down there in the theatre, like a hawk's nest, high and arid under the gleaming sky.

The Bersaglieri sit close together in groups, so that there is a strange, corporal connection between them. They have close-cropped, dark, slightly bestial heads, and thick shoulders, and thick brown hands on each other's shoulders. When an act is over they pick up their cherished hats and fling on their cloaks and go into the hall. They are rather rich, the Bersaglieri.

They are like young, half-wild oxen, such strong, sturdy, dark lads, thickly built and with strange hard heads, like young male caryatides. They keep close to-gether, as if there were some physical instinct connect-ing them. And they are quite womanless. There is a curious inter-absorption among themselves, a sort of physical trance that holds them all, and puts their minds to sleep. There is a strange, hypnotic unanimity among them as they put on their plumed hats and go out to-gether, always very close, as if their bodies must touch.

Then they feel safe and content in this heavy, physical trance. They are in love with one another, the young men love the young men. They shrink from the world beyond, from the outsiders, from all who are not Bersaglieri of their barracks.

One man is a sort of leader. He is very straight and solid, solid like a wall, with a dark, unblemished will. His cock-feathers slither in a profuse, heavy stream from his black oilcloth hat, almost to his shoulder. He swings round. His feathers slip in a cascade. Then he goes out to the hall, his feather tossing and falling richly. He must be well off. The Bersaglieri buy their own black cock's-plumes, and some pay twenty or thirty francs for the bunch, so the maestra said. The poor ones have only poor, scraggy plumes.

There is something very primitive about these men. They remind me really of Agamemnon's soldiers clustered on the seashore, men, all men, a living, vigorous, physical host of men. But there is a pressure on these Italian soldiers, as if they were men caryatides, with a great weight on their heads, making their brain hard, asleep, stunned. They all look as if their real brain were stunned, as if there were another centre of physical consciousness from which they lived.

Separate from them all is Pietro, the young man who lounges on the wharf to carry things from the steamer. He starts up from sleep like a wild-cat as somebody claps him on the shoulder. It is the start of a man who has many enemies. He is almost an outlaw. Will he ever find himself in prison? He is the gamin of the village, well detested.

He is twenty-four years old, thin, dark, handsome, with a cat-like lightness and grace, and a certain repulsive, gamin evil in his face. Where everybody is so clean and tidy, he is almost ragged. His week's beard shows very black in his slightly hollow cheeks. He hates the man who has waked him by clapping him on the shoulder.

Pietro is already married, yet he behaves as if he were not. He has been carrying on with a loose woman, the wife of the citron-coloured barber, the Siciliano. Then he seats himself on the women's side of the theatre, behind a young person from Bogliaco, who also has no reputation, and makes her talk to him. He leans forward, resting his arms on the seat before him, stretching his slender, cat-like, flexible loins. The padrona of the hotel hates him— "ein frecher Kerl," she says with contempt, and she looks away. Her eyes hate to see him.

In the village there is the clerical party, which is the majority; there is the anti-clerical party, and there are the ne'er-do-wells. The clerical people are dark and pious and cold; there is a curious stone-cold, ponderous darkness over them, moral and gloomy. Then the anti-clerical party, with the Syndaco at the head, is bourgeois and respectable as far as the middle-aged people are concerned, banal, respectable, shut off as by a wall from the clerical people. The young anti-clericals are the young bloods of the place, the men who gather every night in the more expensive and less-respectable café. These young men are all free-thinkers, great dancers, singers, players of the guitar. They are immoral and slightly cynical. Their leader is the young shopkeeper, who has lived in Vienna, who is a bit of a bounder, with a veneer of sneering irony on an original good nature. He is well-to-do, and gives dances to which only the looser women go, with these reckless young men. He also gets up parties of pleasure, and is chiefly responsible for the coming of the players to the theatre this carnival. These young men are disliked, but they belong to the important class, they are well-to-do, and they have the

life of the village in their hands. The clerical peasants
are priest-ridden and good, because they are poor and
afraid and superstitious. There is, lastly, a sprinkling of
loose women, one who keeps the inn where the soldiers
drink. These women are a definite set. They know what
they are, they pretend nothing else. They are not
prostitutes, but just loose women. They keep to their
own clique, among men and women, never wanting to
compromise anybody else.

And beyond all these there are the Franciscan friars
in their brown robes, so shy, so silent, so obliterated, as
they stand back in the shop, waiting to buy the bread
for the monastery, waiting, obscure and neutral, till no
one shall be in the shop wanting to be served. The
village women speak to them in a curious neutral,
official, slightly contemptuous voice. They answer neutral and humble, though distinctly.

At the theatre, now the play is over, the peasants in
their black hats and cloaks crowd the hall. Only Pietro,
the wharf-lounger, has no cloak, and a bit of a cap on
the side of his head instead of a black felt hat. His
clothes are thin and loose on his thin, vigorous, cat-like
body, and he is cold, but he takes no notice. His hands
are always in his pockets, his shoulders slightly raised.

The few women slip away home. In the little theatre-
bar the well-to-do young atheists are having another
drink. Not that they spend much. A tumbler of wine or a
glass of vermouth costs a penny. And the wine is horrible new stuff. Yet the little baker, Agostino, sits on a
bench with his pale baby on his knee, putting the wine
to its lips. And the baby drinks, like a blind fledgling.

Upstairs, the quality has paid its visits and shaken
hands: the Syndaco and the well-to-do half-Austrian
owners of the woodyard, the Bertolini, have ostenta-
tiously shown their mutual friendship; our padrone, the

Signor Pietro di Paoli, has visited his relatives the Graziani in the box next the stage, and has spent two intervals with us in our box; meanwhile, his two peasants standing down below, pathetic, thin contadini of the old school, like worn stones, have looked up at us as if we are the angels in heaven, with a reverential, devotional eye, they themselves far away below, standing in the bay at the back, below all.

The chemist and the grocer and the school-mistress pay calls. They have all sat self-consciously posed in the front of their boxes, like framed photographs of themselves. The second grocer and the baker visit each other. The barber looks in on the carpenter, then drops downstairs among the crowd. Class distinctions are cut very fine. As we pass with the padrona of the hotel, who is a Bavarian, we stop to speak to our own padroni, the Di Paoli. They have a warm handshake and effusive polite conversation for us; for Maria Samuelli, a distant bow. We realize our mistake.

The barber—not the Siciliano, but flashy little Luigi with the big tie-ring and the curls—knows all about the theatre. He says that Enrico Persevalli has for his mistres Carina, the servant in *Ghosts:* that the thin, gentle, old-looking king in *Hamlet* is the husband of Adelaida, and Carina is their daughter: that the old, sharp, fat little body of a queen is Adelaida's mother: that they all like Enrico Persevalli, because he is a very clever man: but that the "Comic," Il Brillante, Francesco, is unsatisfied.

In three performances in Epiphany week, the company took two hundred and sixty-five francs, which was phenomenal. The manager, Enrico Persevalli, and Adelaida pay twenty-four francs for every performance, or every evening on which a performance is given, as rent for the theatre, including light. The company is completely satisfied with its reception on the Lago di Garda.

So it is all over. The Bersaglieri go running all the way home, because it is already past half-past ten. The night is very dark. About four miles up the lake the search-lights of the Austrian border are swinging, looking for smugglers. Otherwise the darkness is complete.

The Mozo

ROSALINO really goes with the house, though he has been in service here only two months. When we went to look at the place, we saw him lurking in the patio, and glancing furtively under his brows. He is not one of the erect, bantam little Indians that stare with a black, incomprehensible, but somewhat defiant stare. It may be Rosalino has a distant strain of other Indian blood, not Zapotec. Or it may be he is only a bit different. The difference lies in a certain sensitiveness and aloneness, as if he were a mother's boy. The way he drops his head and looks sideways under his black lashes, apprehensive, apprehending, feeling his way, as it were. Not the bold male glare of most of the Indians, who seem as if they had never, never had mothers at all.

The Aztec gods and goddesses are, as far as we have known anything about them, an unlovely and unlovable lot. In their myths there is no grace or charm, no poetry. Only this perpetual grudge, grudge, grudging, one god grudging another, the gods grudging men their existence, and men grudging the animals. The goddess of love is goddess of dirt and prostitution, a dirt-eater, a horror, without a touch of tenderness. If the god wants to make love to her, she has to sprawl down in front of him, bla-tant and accessible.

And then, after all, when she conceives and brings forth, what is it she produces? What is the infant-god she tenderly bears? Guess, all ye people, joyful and triumphant!

You never could.

It is a stone knife.

It is a razor-edged knife of blackish-green flint, the knife of all knives, the veritable Paraclete of knives. It is the sacrificial knife with which the priest makes a gash in his victim's breast, before he tears out the heart, to hold it smoking to the sun. And the Sun, the Sun behind the sun, is supposed to suck the smoking heart greedily with insatiable appetite.

This, then, is a pretty Christmas Eve. Lo, the goddess is gone to bed, to bring forth her child. Lo! ye people, await the birth of the saviour, the wife of a god is about to become a mother.

Tarumm-tarah! Tarumm-tarah! blow the trumpets. The child is born. Unto us a son is given. Bring him forth, lay him on a tender cushion. Show him, then, to all the people. See! See! See him upon the cushion, tenderly new-born and reposing! Ah, "qué bonito!" Oh, what a nice, blackish, smooth, keen stone knife!

And to this day, most of the Mexican Indian women seem to bring forth stone knives. Look at them, these sons of incomprehensible mothers, with their black eyes like flints, and their stiff little bodies as taut and as keen as knives of obsidian. Take care they don't rip you up.

Our Rosalino is an exception. He drops his shoulders just a little. He is a bit bigger, also, than the average Indian down here. He must be about five feet four inches. And he hasn't got the big, obsidian, glaring eyes. His eyes are smaller, blacker, like the quick black eyes of the lizard. They don't look at one with the obsidian stare. They are just a bit aware that there is another being, unknown, at the other end of the glance. Hence he drops his head with a little apprehension, screening himself as if he were vulnerable.

Usually, these people have no correspondence with one at all. To them a white man or white woman is a sort of phenomenon, just as a monkey is a sort of phenomenon; something to watch, and wonder at, and laugh at, but not to be taken on one's own plane.

Now the white man is a sort of extraordinary white monkey that, by cunning, has learnt lots of semi-magical secrets of the universe, and made himself boss of the show. Imagine a race of big white monkeys got up in fantastic clothes, and able to kill a man by hissing at him; able to leap through the air in great hops, covering a mile in each leap; able to transmit his thoughts by a moment's effort of concentration to some great white monkey or monkeyess, a thousand miles away: and you have, from our point of view, something of the picture that the Indian has of us.

The white monkey has curious tricks. He knows, for example, the time. Now to a Mexican, and an Indian, time is a vague, foggy reality. There are only three times: en la mañana, en la tarde, en la noche: in the morning, in the afternoon, in the night. There is even no midday, and no evening.

But to the white monkey, horrible to relate, there are exact spots of time, such as five o'clock, half-past nine. The day is a horrible puzzle of exact spots of time.

The same with distance: horrible invisible distances called two miles, ten miles. To the Indians, there is near and far, and very near and very far. There is two days or one day. But two miles are as good as twenty to him, for he goes entirely by his feeling. If a certain two miles feels far to him, then it *is* far, it is muy lejos! But if a certain twenty miles *feels* near and familiar, then it is not far. Oh, no, it is just a little distance. And he will let you set off in the evening, for night to overtake you in the wilderness, without a qualm. It is not far.

But the white man has a horrible, truly horrible monkey-like passion for invisible exactitudes. Mañana, to the native, may mean tomorrow, three days hence, six months hence, and never. There are no fixed points in life, save birth, and death, and the fiestas. The fixed points of birth and death evaporate spontaneously into vagueness. And the priests fix the fiestas. From time immemorial priests have fixed the fiestas, the festivals of the gods, and men have had no more to do with time. What should men have to do with time?

The same with money. These centavos and these pesos, what do they mean, after all? Little discs that have no charm. The natives insist on reckoning in invisible coins, coins that don't exist here, like reales or pesetas. If you buy two eggs for a real, you have to pay twelve and a half centavos. Since also half a centavo doesn't exist, you or the vendor forfeit the non-existent.

The same with honesty, the *meum* and the *tuum*. The white man has a horrible way of remembering, even to a centavo, even to a thimbleful of mescal. Horrible! The Indian, it seems to me, is not naturally dishonest. He is not naturally avaricious, has not even any innate cupidity. In this he is unlike the old people of the Mediterranean, to whom possessions have a mystic meaning, and a silver coin a mystic white halo, a *lueur* of magic.

To the real Mexican, no! He doesn't care. He doesn't even *like* keeping money. His deep instinct is to spend it at once, so that he needn't have it. He doesn't really want to keep anything, not even his wife and children. Nothing that he has to be responsible for. Strip, strip, strip away the past and the future, leave the naked moment of the present disentangled. Strip away memory, strip away forethought and care; leave the moment, stark and sharp and without consciousness, like the obsidian knife. The before and the after are the stuff of consciousness. The instant moment is forever keen with a razor-edge of oblivion, like the knife of sacrifice.

But the great white monkey has got hold of the keys of the world, and the black-eyed Mexican has to serve the great white monkey, in order to live. He has to learn the tricks of the white monkey-show: time of the day, coin of money, machines that start at a second, work that is meaningless and yet is paid for with exactitude, in exact coin. A whole existence of monkey-tricks and monkey-virtues. The strange monkey-virtue of charity, the white monkeys nosing round to *help*, to *save!* Could any trick be more unnatural? Yet it is one of the tricks of the great white monkey.

If an Indian is poor, he says to another: I have no food; give me to eat. Then the other hands the hungry one a couple of tortillas. That is natural. But when the white monkeys come round, they peer at the house, at the woman, at the children. They say: Your child is sick. Si, Señor. What have you done for it?—Nothing. What is to be done?—You must make a poultice. I will show you how.

Well, it was very amusing, this making hot dough to dab on the baby. Like plastering a house with mud. But why do it twice? Twice is not amusing. The child will die. Well, then, it will be in Paradise. How nice for it! That's just what God wants of it, that it shall be a cheerful little angel among the roses of Paradise. What could be better?

How tedious of the white monkey coming with the trick of salvation, to rub oil on the baby, and put poultices on it, and make you give it medicine in a spoon at morning, noon, and night. Why morning and noon and night? Why not just anytime, anywhen? It will die to-morrow if you don't do these things today! But tomorrow is another day, and it is not dead now, so if it dies at another time, it must be because the other times are out of hand.

Oh, the tedious, exacting white monkeys, with their yesterdays and todays and tomorrows! Tomorrow is always another day, and yesterday is part of the en-circling never. Why think outside the moment? And inside the moment one does not think. So why pretend to think? It is one of the white-monkey tricks. He is a clever monkey. But he is ugly, and he has nasty white flesh. We are not ugly, with screwed-up faces, and we have good warm-brown flesh. If we have to work for the white monkey, we don't care. His tricks are half-amusing. And one may as well amuse oneself that way as any other. So long as one is amused.

So long as the devil does not rouse in us, seeing the white monkeys forever mechanically bossing, with their incessant tick-tack of work. Seeing them get the work out of us, the sweat, the money, and then taking the very land from us, the very oil and metal out of our soil. They do it! They do it all the time. Because they can't help it. Because grasshoppers can but hop, and ants can carry little sticks, and white monkeys can go tick-tack, tick-tack, do this, do that, time to work, time to eat, time to drink, time to sleep, time to walk, time to ride, time to wash, time to look dirty, tick-tack, tick-tack, time, time, time, time! time! Oh, cut off his nose and make him swallow it.

For the *moment* is as changeless as an obsidian knife, and the heart of the Indian is keen as the moment that divides past from future, and sacrifices them both.

To Rosalino, too, the white monkey-tricks are amus-ing. He is ready to work for the white monkeys, to learn some of their tricks, their monkey-speech of Spanish, their tick-tack ways. He works for four pesos a month, and his food: a few tortillas. Four pesos are two American dollars: about nine shillings. He owns two cotton shirts, two pairs of calico pantaloons, two blouses, one of pink cotton, one of darkish flannelette, and a pair of sandals. Also, his straw hat that he has curled up to look very jaunty, and a rather old, factory-made, rather cheap shawl, or plaid rug with fringe. *Et præterea nihil.*

His duty is to rise in the morning and sweep the street in front of the house, and water it. Then he sweeps and waters the broad, brick-tiled verandahs, and flicks the chairs with a sort of duster made of fluffy reeds. After which he walks behind the cook—she is very superior, had a Spanish grandfather, and Rosalino must address her as Señora—carrying the basket to market. Returned from the market, he sweeps the whole of the patio, gathers up the leaves and refuse, fills the pannier-basket, hitches it up on to his shoulders, and holds it by a band across his forehead, and thus, a beast of burden, goes out to deposit the garbage at the side of one of the little roads leading out of the city. Every *little* road leaves the town between heaps of garbage, an avenue of garbage blistering in the sun.

Returning, Rosalino waters the whole of the garden and sprinkles the whole of the patio. This takes most of the morning. In the afternoon, he sits without much to do. If the wind has blown or the day was hot, he starts again at about three o'clock, sweeping up leaves, and sprinkling everywhere with an old watering-can.

Then he retreats to the entrance-way, the Zaguán, which, with its big doors and its cobbled track, is big enough to admit an ox-wagon. The Zaguán is his home: just the doorway. In one corner is a low wooden bench

about four feet long and eighteen inches wide. On this
he screws up and sleeps, in his clothes as he is, wrapped
in the old sarape.

But this is anticipating. In the obscurity of the Zaguán
he sits and pores, pores, pores over a school-book, learning to read and write. He can read a bit, and write a bit.
He filled a large sheet of foolscap with writing: quite
nice. But I found out that what he had written was a
Spanish poem, a love-poem, with *no puedo olvidar* and
voy a cortar—the rose, of course. He had written the
thing straight ahead, without verse-lines or capitals or
punctuation at all, just a vast string of words, a whole
foolscap sheet full. When I read a few lines aloud, he
writhed and laughed in an agony of confused feelings.
And of what he had written he understood a small, small
amount, parrot-wise, from the top of his head. Actually it
meant just words, sound, noise, to him: noise called Cas-
tellano, Castilian. Exactly like a parrot.

From seven to eight he goes to the night-school, to
cover a bit more of the foolscap. He has been going for
two years. If he goes two years more he will perhaps
really be able to read and write six intelligible sentences:
but only Spanish, which is as foreign to him as Hin-
dustani would be to an English farmboy. Then if he can
speak his quantum of Spanish, and read it and write it
to a very uncertain extent, he will return to his village
two days' journey on foot into the hills, and then, in
time, he may even rise to be an *alcalde*, or headman of
the village, responsible to the Government. If he were
alcalde he would get a little salary. But far more important to him is the glory: being able to boss.

He has a *paisano*, a fellow-countryman, to sleep with
him in the Zaguán, to guard the doors. Whoever gets
into the house or patio must get through these big doors.

There is no other entrance, not even a needle's eye. The
windows to the street are heavily barred. Each house is
its own small fortress. Ours is a double square, the trees
and flowers in the first square, with the two wings of
the house. And in the second patio, the chickens,
pigeons, guinea-pigs, and the big heavy earthenware
dish or tub, called an *apaxtle*, in which all the servants
can bathe themselves, like chickens in a saucer.

By half-past nine at night Rosalino is lying on his little
bench, screwed up, wrapped in his shawl, his sandals,
called huaraches, on the floor. Usually he takes off his
huaraches when he goes to bed. That is all his prepara-
tion. In another corner, wrapped up, head and all, like a
mummy in his thin old blanket, the paisano, another lad
of about twenty, lies asleep on the cold stones. And at
an altitude of five thousand feet, the nights can be cold.

Usually everybody is in by half-past nine in our very
quiet house. If not, you may thunder at the big doors.
It is hard to wake Rosalino. You have to go close to him,
and call. That will wake him. But don't touch him. That
would startle him terribly. No one is touched unawares,
except to be robbed or murdered.

"Rosalino! están tocando!"—"Rosalino! they are knocking!"

At last there starts up a strange, glaring, utterly lost
Rosalino. Perhaps he just has enough wit to pull the
door-catch. One wonders where he was, and what he
was, in his sleep, he starts up so strange and wild and
lost.

The first time he had anything to do for me was when
the van was come to carry the bit of furniture to the
house. There was Aurelio, the dwarf *mozo* of our friends,
and Rosalino, and the man who drove the wagon. But
there *should* have been also a *cargador*—a porter. "Help
them," said I to Rosalino. "You give a hand to help."

But he winced away, muttering, "No quiero!—I don't want to."

The fellow, I thought to myself, is a fool. He thinks it's not his job, and perhaps he is afraid of smashing the furniture. Nothing to be done but to leave him alone.

We settled in, and Rosalino seemed to like doing things for us. He liked learning his monkey-tricks from the white monkeys. And since we started feeding him from our own meals, and for the first time in his life he had real soups, meat-stews, or a fried egg, he loved to do things in the kitchen. He would come with sparkling black eyes: "Hé comido el caldo. Grazias!"—"I have eaten the soup. Thank you."—And he would give a strange, excited little yelp of a laugh.

Came the day when we walked to Huayapa, on the Sunday, and he was very thrilled. But at night, in the evening when we got home, he lay mute on his bench—not that he was really tired. The Indian gloom, which settles on them like a black marsh-fog, had settled on him. He did not bring in the water—let me carry it by myself.

Monday morning, the same black, reptilian gloom, and a sense of hatred. He hated us. This was a bit flabber-gasting, because he had been so thrilled and happy the day before. But the revulsion had come. He didn't forgive himself for having felt free and happy with us. He had eaten what we had eaten, hard-boiled eggs and sardine sandwiches and cheese; he had drunk out of the orange-peel *taza,* which delighted him so much. He had had a bottle of *gazoosa,* fizz, with us, on the way home, in San Felipe.

And now, the reaction. The flint knife. He had been happy, *therefore* we were scheming to take another advantage of him. We had some devilish white-monkey trick up our sleeve; we wanted to get at his *soul,* no doubt, and do it the white monkey's damage. We wanted to get at his heart, did we? But his heart was an obsidian knife.

He hated us, and gave off a black steam of hate, that filled the patio and made one feel sick. He did not come to the kitchen, he did not carry the water. Leave him alone.

At lunch-time on Monday he said he wanted to leave. Why? He said he wanted to go back to his village.

Very well. He was to wait just a few days, till another mozo was found.

At this a glance of pure, reptilian hate from his black eyes.

He sat motionless on his bench all the afternoon, in the Indian stupor of gloom and profound hate. In the evening, he cheered up a little and said he would stay on, at least till Easter.

Tuesday morning. More stupor and gloom and hate. He wanted to go back to his village at once. All right! No one wanted to keep him against his will. Another mozo would be found at once.

He went off in the numb stupor of gloom and hate, a very potent hate that could affect one in the pit of one's stomach with nausea.

Tuesday afternoon, and he thought he would stay.

Wednesday morning, and he wanted to go.

Very good. Enquiries made; another mozo was coming on Friday morning. It was settled.

Thursday was fiesta. Wednesday, therefore, we would go to market, the Niña—that is the mistress—myself, and Rosalino with the basket. He loved to go to market with the patrones. We would give him money and send him off to bargain for oranges, pitahayas, potatoes, eggs, a chicken, and so forth. This he simply loved to do. It

put him into a temper to see us buying without bargain-
ing and paying ghastly prices.

He bargained away, silent almost, muttering darkly.
It took him a long time, but he had far greater success
than even Natividad, the cook. And he came back in
triumph, with much stuff and little money spent.

So again that afternoon, he was staying on. The spell
was wearing off.

The Indians on the hills have a heavy, intense sort of
attachment to their villages; Rosalino had not been out
of the little city for two years. Suddenly finding himself
in Huayapa, a real Indian hill-village, the black Indian
gloom of nostalgia must have made a crack in his spirits.
But he had been perfectly cheerful—perhaps too cheerful—till we got home.

Again, the Señorita had taken a photograph of him.
They are all crazy to have their photographs taken. I had
given him an envelope and a stamp, to send a photograph to his mother. Because in his village he had a
widow mother, a brother, and a married sister. The family owned a bit of land, with orange-trees. The best
oranges come from the hills, where it is cooler. Seeing
the photograph, the mother, who had completely forgotten her son, as far as any keen remembering goes,
suddenly, like a cracker going off inside her, wanted
him: at that very moment. So she sent an urgent message.

But already it was Wednesday afternoon. Arrived a
little fellow in white clothes, smiling hard. It was the
brother from the hills. Now, we thought, Rosalino will
have someone to walk back with. On Friday, after the
fiesta, he would go.

Thursday, he escorted us with the basket to the fiesta.
He bargained for flowers, and for a sarape which he

didn't get, for a carved *jícara* which he did get, and for a number of toys. He and the Niña and the Señorita ate a great wafer of a pancake with sweet stuff on it. The basket grew heavy. The brother appeared, to carry the hen and the extra things. Bliss.

He was perfectly happy again. He didn't want to go on Friday; he didn't want to go at all. He wanted to stay with us and come with us to England when we went home.

So, another trip to the friend, the Mexican, who had found us the other mozo. Now to put off the other boy again: but then, they are like that.

And the Mexican, who had known Rosalino when he first came down from the hills and could speak no Spanish, told us another thing about him.

In the last revolution—a year ago—the revolutionaries of the winning side wanted more soldiers from the hills. The alcalde of the hill-village was told to pick out young men and send them down to the barracks in the city. Rosalino was among the chosen.

But Rosalino refused, said again, "No quiero!" He is one of those, like myself, who have a horror of serving in a mass of men, or even of being mixed up with a mass of men. He obstinately refused. Whereupon the recruiting soldiers beat him with the butt of their rifles till he lay unconscious, apparently dead.

Then, because they wanted him at once, and he would now be no good for some time, with his injured back, they left him, to get the revolution over without him.

This explains his fear of furniture-carrying, and his fear of being "caught."

Yet that little Aurelio, the friend's mozo, who is not above four feet six in height, a tiny fellow, fared even worse. He, too, is from the hills. In his village, a cousin of his gave some information to the *losing* side of the revolution. The cousin wisely disappeared.

But in the city, the winning side seized Aurelio, since he was the *cousin* of the delinquent. In spite of the fact that he was the faithful mozo of a foreign resident, he was flung into prison. Prisoners in prison are not fed. Either friends or relatives bring them food, or they go very, very thin. Aurelio had a married sister in town, but *she* was afraid to go to the prison, lest she and her husband should be seized. The master, then, sent his new mozo twice a day to the prison with a basket; the huge, huge prison, for this little town of a few thousands.

Meanwhile the master struggled and struggled with the "authorities"—friends of the people—for Aurelio's release. Nothing to be done.

One day the new mozo arrived at the prison with the basket, to find no Aurelio. A friendly soldier gave the message Aurelio had left. "Adiós a mi patrón. Me llevan." Oh, fatal words: "Me llevan"—They are taking me off. The master rushed to the train: it had gone, with the dwarf, plucky little mozo, into the void.

Months later, Aurelio reappeared. He was in rags, haggard, and his dark throat was swollen up to the ears. He had been taken off, two hundred miles into Vera Cruz State. He had been hung up by the neck, with a fixed knot, and left hanging for hours. Why? To make the cousin come and save his relative: put his own neck into a running noose. To make the absolutely innocent fellow confess: what? Everybody knew he was innocent. At any rate, to teach everybody better next time. Oh, brotherly teaching!

Aurelio escaped, and took to the mountains. Sturdy little dwarf of a fellow, he made his way back, begging tortillas at the villages, and arrived, haggard, with a great swollen neck, to find his master waiting, and another "party" in power. More friends of the people.

Tomorrow is another day. The master nursed Aurelio well, and Aurelio is a strong, if tiny, fellow, with big, brilliant black eyes that for the moment will trust a foreigner, but none of his own people. A dwarf in stature, but perfectly made, and very strong. And very intelligent, far more quick and intelligent than Rosalino.

Is it any wonder that Aurelio and Rosalino, when they see the soldiers with guns on their shoulders marching towards the prison with some blanched prisoner between them—and one sees it every few days—stand and gaze in a blank kind of horror, and look at the patrón, to see if there is any refuge?

Not to be *caught!* Not to be *caught!* It must have been the prevailing motive of Indian-Mexico life since long before Montezuma marched his prisoners to sacrifice.

LETTERS

EDITOR'S PREFACE

THE following letters have all been taken from the large volume, *The Letters of D. H. Lawrence,* edited by Aldous Huxley. The entire collection is so extraordinarily interesting, both biographically and critically, that it has been very difficult to choose a sampling. Greatly prodigal of energy, Lawrence put enough emotion and idea into his letters to do another writer for a lifetime of creative work.

Despite its subjectivity, the large part of Lawrence's fiction and critical writing has a certain abstraction from immediate realities. In distinction from this, the letters are chiefly remarkable, I think, for the evidence they give of a concrete awareness of the world and its people. They should be proof, if proof is needed, that far from being cut off from life, Lawrence was violently sensitive to the immediate conditions of living; that far from refusing ordinary human relations, he was brilliantly alert to every smallest tension and effort in people's connections with each other. Lawrence loved friendship, perhaps too much—he was deeply tortured by its recurrent failure. From one point of view, indeed, his correspondence can be read as a record of the offering of an affection so warm and eager and profound, so much of the heroic stature of Lawrence's best work, that it could surely have found its proper response only in a world of heroes.

TO A. D. MCLEOD

Lago di Garda, Italy.
Friday, 6th October, 1912.

Dear Mac,

Your books came today, your letter long ago. Now I am afraid I put you to a lot of trouble and expense, and feel quite guilty. But thanks a thousand times. And F. thanks you too.

I have read *Anna of the Five Towns* today, because it is stormy weather. For five months I have scarcely seen a word of English print, and to read it makes me feel tearfully queer. I don't know where I am. I am so used to the people going by outside, talking or singing some foreign language, always Italian now: but today, to be in Hanley, and to read almost my own dialect, makes me feel quite ill. I hate England and its hopelessness. I hate Bennett's resignation. Tragedy ought really to be a great kick at misery. But *Anna of the Five Towns* seems like an acceptance—so does all the modern stuff since Flaubert. I hate it. I want to wash again quickly, wash off England, the oldness and grubbiness and despair.

Today it is so stormy. The lake is dark, and with white lambs all over it. The steamer rocks as she goes by. There are no sails stealing past. The vines are yellow and red, and fig trees are in flame on the mountains. I can't bear to be in England when I am in Italy. It makes me feel so soiled. Yesterday F. and I went down along the lake towards Maderno. We climbed down from a little olive wood, and swam. It was evening, so weird, and a great black cloud trailing over the lake. And tiny little lights of villages came out, so low down, right across the water. Then great lightnings split out.—No, I don't believe England need be so grubby. What does it matter if one is poor, and risks one's livelihood, and reputation. One *can* have the necessary things, life, and love, and clean warmth. Why is England so shabby?

The Italians here sing. They are very poor, they buy two-penn'orth of butter and a penn'orth of cheese. But they are healthy and they lounge about in the little square where the boats come up and nets are mended, like kings. And they go by the window proudly, and they don't hurry or fret. And the women walk straight and look calm. And the men adore children—they are glad of their children even if they're poor. I think they haven't many ideas, but they look well, and they have strong blood.

I go in a little place to drink wine near Bogliaco. It is the living room of the house. The father, sturdy as these Italians are, gets up from table and bows to me. The family is having supper. He brings me red wine to another table, then sits down again, and the mother ladles him soup from the bowl. He has his shirt-sleeves rolled up and his shirt collar open. Then he nods and "click-clicks" to the small baby, that the mother, young and proud, is feeding with soup from a big spoon. The grandfather, white-moustached, sits a bit effaced by the father. A little girl eats soup. The grandmother by the big, open fire sits and quietly scolds another little girl. It reminds me so of home when I was a boy. They are all so warm with life. The father reaches his thick brown hand to play with the baby—the mother looks quickly away, catching my eye. Then he gets up to wait on me, and thinks my bad Italian can't understand that a quarter litre of wine is 15 centesimi (1¼d.) when I give him thirty. He doesn't understand tips. And the huge lot of figs for 20 centesimi.

Why can't you ever come? You could if you wanted to, at Christmas. Why not? We should love to have you, and it costs little. Why do you say I sark you about your letters?—I don't, they *are* delightful. I think I am going to Salo tomorrow and can get you some views of the lake there. I haven't got the proofs of my poems yet. It takes so long. Perhaps I will send you the MS. of *Paul Morel*—I shall alter the title—when it's done.

Thanks—*je te serre la main.*

D. H. LAWRENCE

TO EDWARD GARNETT

[Brescia] Lago di Garda, Italy.
14 Nov., 1912.

DEAR GARNETT,

Your letter has just come. I hasten to tell you I sent the MS. of the *Paul Morel* novel to Duckworth registered, yesterday. And I want to defend it, quick. I wrote it again, pruning it and shaping it and filling it in. I tell you it has got form—*form:* haven't I made it patiently, out of sweat as well as blood. It follows this idea: a woman of character and refinement goes into the lower class, and has no satisfaction in her own life. She has had a passion for her husband, so the children are born of passion, and have heaps of vitality. But as her sons grow up she selects them as lovers—first the eldest, then the second. These sons are *urged* into life by their reciprocal love of their mother—urged on and on. But when they come to manhood, they can't love, because their mother is the strongest power in their lives, and holds them. It's rather like Goethe and his mother and Frau von Stein and Christiana— As soon as the young men come into contact with women, there's a split. William gives his sex to a fribble, and his mother holds his soul. But the split kills him, because he doesn't know where he is. The next son gets a woman who fights for his soul—fights his mother. The son loves the mother—all the sons hate and are jealous of the father. The battle goes on between the mother and the girl, with the son as object. The mother gradually proves stronger, because of the tie of blood. The son decides to leave his soul in his mother's hands, and, like his elder brother, go for passion. He gets passion. Then the split begins to tell again. But, almost unconsciously, the mother realizes what is the matter, and begins to die. The son casts off his mistress, attends to his mother dying. He is left in the end naked of everything, with the drift towards death.

It is a great tragedy, and I tell you I have written a great book. It's the tragedy of thousands of young men in England—it may even be Bunny's tragedy. I think it was Ruskin's, and men like him— Now tell me if I haven't worked out my theme, like life, but always my theme. Read my novel. It's a great novel. If *you* can't see the development—which is slow, like growth—I can.

As for the *Fight for Barbara*—I don't know much about plays. If ever you have time, you might tell me where you find fault with the *Fight for Barbara*. The *Merry Go Round* and the other are candidly impromptus. I *know* they want doing again—re-casting. I should like to have them again, now, before I really set to work on my next novel—which I have conceived—and I should like to try re-casting and re-forming them. If you have time, send them me.

I should like to dedicate the *Paul Morel* to you—may I? But not unless you think it's really a good work. "To

Edward Garnett, in Gratitude." But you can put it better.

You are miserable about your play. Somehow or other your work riles folk. Why does it? But it makes them furious. Nevertheless, I shall see the day when a volume of your plays is in all the libraries. I can't understand why the dreary weeklies haven't read your *Jeanne* and installed it as a "historical document of great value." You know they hate you as a creator, all the critics: but why they shouldn't sigh with relief at finding you—in their own conceptions—a wonderfully subtle renderer and commentator of history, I don't know.

Pinker wrote me the other day, wanting to place me a novel with one of the leading publishers. Would he be any good for other stuff? It costs so many stamps, I don't reply to all these people.

Have I made those naked scenes in *Paul Morel* tame enough? You cut them if you like. Yet they are so clean —and I *have* patiently and laboriously constructed that novel.

It is a marvellous moonlight night. The mountains have shoulder-capes of snow. I have been far away into the hills today, and got great handfuls of wild Christmas roses. This is one of the most beautiful countries in the world. You must come. The sunshine is marvellous, on the dark blue water, the ruddy mountains' feet, and the snow.

F. and I keep struggling forward. It is not easy, but I won't complain. I suppose, if in the end I can't make enough money by writing, I shall have to go back to teaching. At any rate I can do that, so matters are never hopeless with me.

When you have time, do tell me about the *Fight for Barbara*. You think it couldn't be any use for the stage? I think the new generation is rather different from the old. I think they will read me more gratefully. But there, one can only go on.

It's funny, there is no *war* here—except "Tripoli." Everybody sings Tripoli. The soldiers howl all the night through and bang tambourines when the wounded heroes come home— And the Italian papers are full of Serbia and Turkey—but what has England got to do with it?

It's awfully good of you to send me a paper. But you'll see, one day I can help you, or Bunny. And I will.

You sound so miserable. It's the damned work. I wish you were here for awhile. If you get run down, do come quickly. *Don't* let yourself become ill. This is such a beastly dangerous time. And you could work here, and live cheap as dirt with us.

Don't mind if I am impertinent. Living here alone one gets so different—sort of *ex cathedra*.

D. H. LAWRENCE

TO ERNEST COLLINGS

Lago di Garda [Brescia].
17 Jan., 1913.

DEAR COLLINGS,

Your letters are as good as a visit from somebody nice. I love people who can write reams and reams about themselves: it seems generous. And the points are interesting. What a rum chap you are! Are you a celibate? (Don't answer if you don't want to—I'm a married man, or ought to be.) Your work seems too—too—one-sided (I've only seen a tiny bit of it, as you know)—as if it were *afraid* of the female element—which makes me think you are more or less a Galahad—which is not, I believe, good for your art. It is hopeless for me to try to do anything without I have a woman at the back of me. And you seem a bit like that—not hopeless—but too uncertain. Böcklin—or somebody like him—daren't sit in a café except with his back to the wall. I daren't sit in the world without a woman behind me. And you give me that feeling a bit: as if you were uneasy of what is behind you. Excuse me if I am wrong. But a woman that I love sort of keeps me in direct communication with the unknown, in which otherwise I am a bit lost.

Don't ever mind what I say. I am a great bosher, and full of fancies that interest me. Only these are my speculations over the two drawings. I think I prefer the Sphinx one. And then, when it comes to the actual *head*, in both cases, one is dissatisfied. It is as if the head were not the inevitable consequence, the core and clinching point of the rest of the picture. They seem to me too fretful for the inevitability of the land which bears them. The more or less of wonder in the *Sappho* I liked better. Why is the body, so often, with you, a strange mass of earth, and yet the head is so fretful? I should have thought your conception needed a little more of fate in the faces of your figures, to be expressed: fate solid and inscrutable. But I know nothing about it. Only what have you done with your body, that your head seems so lost and lonely and dissatisfied?

My great religion is a belief in the blood, the flesh, as being wiser than the intellect. We can go wrong in our minds. But what our blood feels and believes and says, is always true. The intellect is only a bit and a bridle. What do I care about knowledge. All I want is to answer to my blood, direct, without tribbling intervention of mind, or moral, or what-not. I conceive a man's body as a kind of flame, like a candle flame, forever upright and yet flowing: and the intellect is just the light that is shed on to the things around. And I am not so much con-

cerned with the things around—which is really mind—
but with the mystery of the flame forever flowing, coming God knows how from out of practically nowhere,
and being *itself*, whatever there is around it, that it lights
up. We have got so ridiculously mindful, that we never
know that we ourselves are anything—we think there
are only the objects we shine upon. And there the poor
flame goes on burning ignored, to produce this light.
And instead of chasing the mystery in the fugitive, half-
lighted things outside us, we ought to look at ourselves,
and say "My God, I am myself!" That is why I like to
live in Italy. The people are so unconscious. They only
feel and want: they don't know. We know too much. No,
we only *think* we know such a lot. A flame isn't a flame
because it lights up two, or twenty, objects on a table.
It's a flame because it is itself. And we have forgotten
ourselves. We are Hamlet without the Prince of Denmark. We cannot *be*. "To be or not to be"—it is the question with us now, by Jove. And nearly every Englishman
says, "Not to be." So he goes in for Humanitarianism and
suchlike forms of not-being. The real way of living is to
answer to one's wants. Not "I want to light up with my
intelligence as many things as possible" but "For the
living of my full flame—I want that liberty, I want that
woman, I want that pound of peaches, I want to go to
sleep, I want to go to the pub and have a good time, I
want to look abeastly swell today, I want to kiss that
girl, I want to insult that man." Instead of that, all these
wants, which are there whether-or-not, are utterly ignored, and we talk about some sort of ideas. I'm like
Carlyle, who, they say, wrote 50 volumes on the value
of silence.

Send me some more drawings, if ever you have any
quite to spare. I liked your photograph, but it wasn't
very much of a revelation of you. I like immensely to

hear about your art. Write me when you feel you can
write a lot.

> Yours,
> D. H. LAWRENCE

TO J. M. MURRY

> Golfo della Spezia, Italy.
> Thursday [1913].

DEAR MURRY,

I'm going to answer your letter immediately, and
frankly.

When you say you won't take Katherine's money, it
means you don't trust her love for you. When you say
she needs little luxuries, and you couldn't bear to de-
prive her of them, it means you don't respect either yourself or her sufficiently to do it.

It looks to me as if you two, far from growing nearer,
are snapping the bonds that hold you together, one after
another. I suppose you must both of you consult your
own hearts, honestly. She must see if she really *wants*
you, wants to keep you and to have no other man all her
life. It means forfeiting something. But the only principle I can see in this life, is that one *must* forfeit the less
for the greater. Only one must be thoroughly honest
about it.

She must say, "Could I live in a little place in Italy,
with Jack, and be lonely, have rather a bare life, but be
happy?" If she could, then take her money. If she doesn't
want to, don't try. But don't beat about the bush. In the
way you go on, you are inevitably coming apart. She is
perhaps beginning to be unsatisfied with you. And you
can't make her more satisfied by being unselfish. You
must say, "How can I make myself most healthy, strong,

and satisfactory to myself and to her?" If by being lazy
for six months, then be lazy, and take her money. It
doesn't matter if she misses her luxuries: she won't die
of it. What luxuries do you mean?

If she doesn't want to stake her whole life and being
on you, then go to your University abroad for a while,
alone. I warn you, it'll be hellish barren.

Or else you can gradually come apart in London, and
then flounder till you get your feet again, severally, but
be clear about it. It lies between you and Katherine, nowhere else.

Of course you can't dream of living long without
work. Couldn't you get the *Westminster* to give you *two*
columns a week, abroad? You must *try*. You must stick
to criticism. You ought also to plan a book, either on
some literary point, or some man. I should like to write a
book on English heroines. You ought to do something
of that sort, but not so cheap. Don't try a novel—try
essays—like Walter Pater or somebody of that style. But
you *can* do something *good* in that line; something con-
cerning *literature* rather than life. And you must rest,
and you and Katherine must heal, and come together,
before you do *any serious* work of any sort. It's the split
in the love that drains you. You see, while she doesn't
really love you, and is not satisfied, *you* show to frightful
disadvantage. But it would be a pity not to let your mind
flower—it might, under decent circumstances, produce
beautiful delicate things, in perception and appreciation.
And *she* has a right to provide the conditions. But not
if you don't trust yourself nor her nor anybody, but go
on slopping, and pandering to her smaller side. If you
work yourself sterile to get her chocolates, she will most
justly detest you—she is *perfectly* right. She doesn't
want you to sacrifice yourself to her, you fool. Be more

natural, and positive, and stick to your own guts. You spread them on a tray for her to throw to the cats.

If you want things to come right—if you are ill and exhausted, then take her money to the last penny, and let her do her own housework. Then she'll know you love her. You can't blame her if she's not satisfied with you. If I haven't had enough dinner, you can't blame *me*. But, you fool, you squander yourself, not for *her,* but to provide her with petty luxuries she doesn't really want. You insult her. A woman unsatisfied must have luxuries. But a woman who loves a man would sleep on a board.

It strikes me you've got off your lines, somewhere you've not been man enough: you've felt it rested with your honour to give her a place to be proud of. It rested with your honour to give her a man to be satisfied with— and satisfaction is never accomplished even physically unless the man is strongly and surely himself, and doesn't depend on anything but his own *being* to make a woman love him. You've tried to satisfy Katherine with what you could earn for her, give her: and she will only be satisfied with what you *are.*

And you don't know what you are. You've never come to it. You've always been dodging round, getting Rhythms and flats and doing criticism for money. You are a fool to work so hard for Katherine—she hates you for it—and quite right. You want to be strong in the possession of your own soul. Perhaps you will only come to that when this affair of you and her has gone crash. I should be sorry to think that—I don't believe it. You must save yourself, and your self-respect, by making it complete between Katherine and you—if you devour her money till she walks in rags, if you are both outcast. Make her certain—don't pander to her—stick to *your-*

self—do what you *want* to do—don't *consider* her—she hates and loathes being considered. You insult her in saying you wouldn't take her money.

The University idea is a bad one. It would further disintegrate you.

If you are disintegrated, then get integrated again. Don't be a coward. If you are disintegrated your first duty is to yourself, and you may use Katherine—her money and everything—to get right again. You're not well, man. Then have the courage to get well. If you are strong again, and a bit complete, *she'll* be satisfied with you. She'll love you hard enough. But don't you see, at this rate, you distrain on her day by day and month by month. I've done it myself.

Take your rest—do *nothing* if you like for a while—though I'd do a *bit*. Get better, first and foremost—use anybody's money, to do so. Get better—and do things you like. Get yourself into condition. It drains and wearies Katherine to have you like this. What a fool you are, what a fool. Don't bother about her—what she wants or feels. Say, "I am a man at the end of the tether, therefore I become a man blind to everything but my own need." But keep a heart for the long run.

Look. We pay 60 lire a month for this house: 25 lire for the servant; and food is *very* cheap. You could live on 185 lire a month in plenty—and be greeted as "Signoria" when you went out together—it is the same as "Guten Tag, Herrschaften"; that would be luxury enough for Katherine.

Get up, lad, and be a man for yourself. It's the man who dares to take, who is independent, not he who gives.

I think Oxford did you harm.

It is beautiful, wonderful, here.

A ten-pound note is 253 lire. We could get you, I believe, a jolly nice apartment in a big garden, in a house

alone, for 80 lire a month. Don't waste yourself—don't
be silly and floppy. You know what you *could* do—you
could write—then prepare yourself: and first make
Katherine at rest in her love for you. Say, "This I will
certainly do"—it would be a relief for her to hear you.
Don't be a child—don't keep that rather childish charm.
Throw everything away, and say, "Now I act for my own
good, at last."

We are getting gradually nearer again, Frieda and I.
It is very beautiful here.

We are awfully sorry Katherine is so seedy. She ought
to write to us. Our love to her and you.

D. H. Lawrence

If you've got an odd book or so you don't want to
read, would you send it us? There is nothing for Frieda
to read—and we like everything and anything.

TO LADY CYNTHIA ASQUITH

Greatham, Pulborough, Sussex.
Sunday, 30th January, 1915.

Dear Lady Cynthia,

We were very glad to hear from you. I wanted to send
you a copy of my stories at Christmas, then I didn't
know how the war had affected you—I knew Herbert
Asquith was joined and I thought you'd rather be left
alone, perhaps.

We have no history, since we saw you last. I feel as if
I had less than no history—as if I had spent those five
months in the tomb. And now, I feel very sick and
corpse-cold, too newly risen to share yet with anybody,
having the smell of the grave in my nostrils, and a feel
of grave clothes about me.

The War finished me: it was the spear through the

side of all sorrows and hopes. I had been walking in Westmorland, rather happy, with water-lilies twisted round my hat—big, heavy, white and gold water-lilies that we found in a pool high up—and girls who had come out on a spree and who were having tea in the upper room of an inn, shrieked with laughter. And I re-member also we crouched under the loose wall on the moors and the rain flew by in streams, and the wind came rushing through the chinks in the wall behind one's head, and we shouted songs, and I imitated music-hall turns, whilst the other men crouched under the wall and I pranked in the rain on the turf in the gorse, and Koteliansky groaned Hebrew music—Ranani Sadekim Badanoi.

It seems like another life—we *were* happy—four men. Then we came down to Barrow-in-Furness, and saw that war was declared. And we all went mad. I can remem-ber soldiers kissing on Barrow station, and a woman shouting defiantly to her sweetheart—"When you get at 'em, Clem, let 'em have it," as the train drew off—and in all the tramcars, "War." Messrs. Vickers-Maxim call in their workmen—and the great notices on Vickers' gateways—and the thousands of men streaming over the bridge. Then I went down the coast a few miles. And I think of the amazing sunsets over flat sands and the smoky sea—then of sailing in a fisherman's boat, run-ning in the wind against a heavy sea—and a French Onion boat coming in with her sails set splendidly, in the morning sunshine—and the electric suspense every-where—and the amazing, vivid, visionary beauty of everything, heightened by the immense pain every-where. And since then, since I came back, things have not existed for me. I have spoken to no one, I have touched no one, I have seen no one. All the while, I swear, my soul lay in the tomb—not dead, but with a flat stone over it, a corpse, become corpse-cold. And nobody existed, because I did not exist myself. Yet I was not dead—only passed over—trespassed—and all the time I knew I should have to rise again.

Now I am feeble and half alive. On the downs on Friday I opened my eyes again, and saw it was daytime. And I saw the sea lifted up and shining like a blade with the sun on it. And high up, in the icy wind, an aeroplane flew towards us from the land—and the men ploughing and the boys in the fields on the table-lands, and the shepherds, stood back from their work and lifted their faces. And the aeroplane was small and high, in the thin, ice-cold wind. And the birds became silent and dashed to cover, afraid of the noise. And the aeroplane floated high out of sight. And below, on the level earth away down—were floods and stretches of snow, and I knew I was awake. But as yet my soul is cold and shaky and earthy.

I don't feel so hopeless now I am risen. My heart has been as cold as a lump of dead earth, all this time, be-cause of the War. But now I don't feel so dead. I feel hopeful. I couldn't tell you how fragile and tender this hope is—the new shoot of life. But I feel hopeful now about the War. We should all rise again from this grave —though the killed soldiers will have to wait for the last trump.

There is my autobiography—written because you ask me, and because, being risen from the dead, I know we shall all come through, rise again and walk healed and whole and new in a big inheritance, here on earth.

It sounds preachy, but I don't quite know how to say it.

Viola Meynell has lent us this rather beautiful cottage. We are quite alone. It is at the foot of the downs. I wish you would come and see us, and stay a day or two. It is quite comfortable—there is hot water and a bathroom, and two spare bedrooms. I don't know when we shall be able to come to London. We are too poor for excursions. But we *should* like to see you and it *is* nice here.

D. H. LAWRENCE

TO LADY OTTOLINE MORRELL

Greatham, Pulborough, Sussex.
Monday, 1 Feb., 1915.

DEAR LADY OTTOLINE,

I must write you a line when you have gone, to tell you how my heart feels quite big with hope for the future. Almost with the remainder of tears and the last gnashing of teeth, I could sing the *Magnificat* for the child in my heart.

I want you to form the nucleus of a new community which shall start a new life amongst us—a life in which the only riches is integrity of character. So that each one may fulfil his own nature and deep desires to the utmost, but wherein tho', the ultimate satisfaction and joy is in the completeness of us all as one. Let us be good all together, instead of just in the privacy of our chambers, let us know that the intrinsic part of all of us is the best part, the believing part, the passionate, generous part. We can all come croppers, but what does it matter? We can laugh at each other, and dislike each other, but the good remains and we know it. And the new community shall be established upon the known, eternal good part in us. This present community consists, as far as it is a framed thing, in a myriad contrivances for preventing us from being let down by the meanness in ourselves or in our neighbours. But it is like a motor car that is so encumbered with non-skid, non-puncture, non-burst, non-this and non-that contrivances, that it simply can't go any more. I hold this the most sacred duty—the gathering together of a number of people who shall so agree to live by the *best* they know, that they shall be *free* to live by the best they know. The ideal, the religion, must now be *lived, practised.* We will have no more churches. We will bring church and house and shop together. I do believe that there are enough decent people to make a start with. Let us get the people. Curse the Strachey who asks for a new religion—the greedy dog. He wants another juicy bone for his soul, does he? Let him start to fulfil what religion we have.

After the War, the soul of the people will be so maimed and so injured that it is horrible to think of. And this shall be the new hope: that there shall be a life wherein the struggle shall not be for money or for power, but for individual freedom and common effort towards good. That is surely the richest thing to have now—the feeling that one is working, that one is part of a great, good effort or of a great effort towards goodness. It is no good plastering and tinkering with this community. Every strong soul must put off its connection with this society, its vanity and chiefly its fear, and go naked with its fellows, weaponless, armourless, without shield or spear, but only with naked hands and open eyes. Not self-sacrifice, but fulfilment, the flesh and the spirit in league together, not in arms against one another. And each man shall know that he is part of the greater body, each man shall submit that his own soul is not supreme even to himself. "To be or not to be" is no longer the question. The question now is how shall we fulfil our declaration, "God is." For all our life is now based on the assumption that God is not—or except on rare occasions.

. . . We must go very, very carefully at first. The great serpent to destroy is the will to Power: the desire for one man to have some dominion over his fellow-men. Let us have *no* personal influence, if possible—nor personal magnetism, as they used to call it, nor persuasion —no "Follow me"—but only "Behold." And a man shall not come to save his own soul. Let his soul go to hell. He shall come because he knows that his own soul is not the be-all and the end-all, but that all souls of all things do but compose the body of God, and that God indeed shall *Be.*

I do hope that we shall all of us be able to agree, that we have a common way, a common interest, not a private way and a private interest only.

It is communism based, not on poverty but on riches, not on humility but on pride, not on sacrifice but upon complete fulfilment in the flesh of all strong desire, not in Heaven but on earth. We will be Sons of God who walk here on earth, not bent on getting and having, because we know we inherit all things. We will be aristocrats, and as wise as the serpent in dealing with the mob. For the mob shall not crush us nor starve us nor cry us to death. We will deal cunningly with the mob, the greedy soul, we will gradually bring it to subjection.

We will found an order, and we will all be Princes, as the angels are.

We must bring this thing about—at least set it into life, bring it forth new-born on the earth, watched over by our old cunning and guided by our ancient, mercenary-soldier habits.

My wife sends her greetings and pledge of alliance. I shall paint you a little wooden box. *Au revoir.*

D. H. LAWRENCE

TO LADY CYNTHIA ASQUITH

Hampstead, London.
21st October, 1915.

My dear Lady Cynthia,

What can one say about your brother's death except that it *should not be*. How long will the nations continue to empty the future—it is your own phrase—think what it means—I am sick in my soul, sick to death. But not angry any more, only unfathomably miserable about it all. I think I shall go away to America if they will let me. In this war, in the whole spirit which we now maintain, I do *not* believe, I believe it is *wrong*, so awfully wrong, that it is like a great consuming fire that draws up all our souls in its draught. So if they will let me I shall go away soon, to America. Perhaps you will say it is cowardice: but how shall one submit to such ultimate wrong as this which we commit, now, England—and the other nations? If thine eye offend thee, pluck it out. And I am English, and my Englishness is my very vision. But now I must go away, if my soul is sightless for ever. Let it then be blind, rather than commit the vast wickedness of acquiescence.

Don't think I am not sorry about your brother—it makes me tremble. Don't think I want to hurt you—or anybody—I would do anything rather. But now I feel like a blind man who would put his eyes out rather than stand witness to a colossal and deliberate horror.

Yours,

D. H. Lawrence

I am so sorry for your mother. I can't bear it. If only the women would get up and speak with authority.

TO LADY CYNTHIA ASQUITH

Garsington Manor, Oxford.
Tuesday [1915].

My dear Lady Cynthia,

. . . Your letter makes me sad. Believe me, my feet are more sure upon the earth than you will allow—given that the earth is a living body, not a dead fact.

More tiresomeness is that a magistrate has suppressed the sale of *The Rainbow*, and Methuen's are under orders to deliver up all existing copies. This is most irritating. Some interfering person goes to a police magistrate and say¬, "This book is indecent, listen here." Then the police magistrate says, "By Jove, we'll stop that." Then the thing is suppressed. But I think it is possible to have the decision reversed. If it is possible, and you and Herbert Asquith can help, would you do so? You know quite well that the book is not indecent, though I heard of you saying to a man that it was like the second story in *The Prussian Officer*, only *much worse*. Still, one easily says those things. But I never quite know where you stand: whether the inner things, the abstract right as you call it, is important to you, or only a rather titillating *excursus*. I suppose you've got to arrange your life between the two: it is your belief—pragmatistic. I suppose it had to be so, since the world is as it is, and you must live in the world, but if you can help me about *The Rainbow*, I shall ask you to do so, because I know that the pure truth does matter to you, beyond the relative immediate truths of fact.

We've got our passports: thank you very much.

When I drive across this country, with autumn falling

and rustling to pieces, I am so sad, for my country, for this great wave of civilization, 2000 years, which is now collapsing, that it is hard to live. So much beauty and pathos of old things passing away and no new things coming: this house —— it is England—my God, it breaks my soul—their England, these shafted windows, the elm-trees, the blue distance—the past, the great past, crumbling down, breaking down, not under the force of the coming birds, but under the weight of many exhausted lovely yellow leaves, that drift over the lawn, and over the pond, like the soldiers, passing away, into winter and the darkness of winter—no, I can't bear it. For the winter stretches ahead, where all vision is lost and all memory dies out.

It has been 2000 years, the spring and summer of our era. What, then, will the winter be? No, I can't bear it, I can't let it go. Yet who can stop the autumn from falling to pieces, when November has come in? It is almost better to be dead, than to see this awful process finally strangling us to oblivion, like the leaves off the trees.

I want to go to America, to Florida, as soon as I can: as soon as I have enough money to cross with Frieda. My life is ended here. I must go as a seed that falls into new ground. But this, this England, these elm-trees, the grey wind with yellow leaves—it is so awful, the being gone from it altogether, one must be blind henceforth. But better leave a quick of hope in the soul, than all the beauty that fills the eyes.

It sounds very rhapsodic: it is this old house, the beautiful shafted windows, the grey gate-pillars under the elm trees: really I can't bear it: the past, the past, the falling, perishing, crumbling past, so great, so magnificent.

Come and see us when you are in town. I don't think

we shall be here very much longer. My life now is one
repeated, tortured, *Vale! Vale! Vale!* . . .

D. H. LAWRENCE

TO EDWARD MARSH

Porthcothan, St. Merryn,
North Cornwall.
12 Feb., 1916.

MY DEAR EDDIE,

Cynthia Asquith writes me that somebody says I
"abuse you." If ever I have abused you to anybody, I am
very sorry and ashamed. But I don't think I ever have:
though Heaven knows what one says. Yet I don't feel as
if I had. We have *often* laughed at you, because you are
one of those special figures one can laugh at; just as I
am, only I'm ten times more ridiculous. But I'm sure
we've laughed kindly and affectionately: I know the
Murrys and us, we've always laughed affectionately. I
did feel rather bitter the way you took the war: "What
splendid times we live in": because the war makes me
feel very badly, always. And I may have been furious
about that: I must be more restrained. But I don't think
I've abused you, apart from the war, which is something
special: and even for that I don't think I have.

But whatever I have said, may have said, for I can't
remember, I always feel a real gratitude to you, and a
kindness, and an esteem of the genuine man. And I'm
sorry if ever I've gone against those true feelings for
you. I have thought that it was best for us to keep no
constant connection, because of your position in the
Government, and of my feelings about the war. But that
I do out of respect for your position.

However, if ever I have abused you, though I can't

remember, then forgive me: for indeed I am not ungrate-
ful, and I never want to abuse you. If the war makes us
strangers, it does not, I hope, make us in the least enemies.

I have been seedy down here, and felt like dying. I
must not get into such states. Next month will appear
a vol. of my *Italian Sketches,* which I will send you.
Only don't say, as you said of *The Rainbow: toujours
perdrix.* Because you know one suffers what one writes.

And a little later will come a book of poems. I know
you don't care much for my verses: but I'll send them
along when they appear.

It's been a bad time, this last year. I wish it were
ended. Frieda sends her regards, I mine.

D. H. Lawrence

TO J. B. PINKER

Higher Tregerthen, Zennor,
St. Ives, Cornwall.
30 June, 1916.

My dear Pinker,

I agree, it seems to me just as well, to bring out poems
hard on the heels of a book of sketches — they support
each other. So if the *Amores* are ready by the end of
July, let them come then, by all means. At any rate, that
will perhaps ensure their appearance in September; this
intention to publish in July.

I was going to write to you. I have finished *The Sisters,* in effect. I thought of writing to Duckworth and
saying to him, the novel is done in substance, and I
would send him the typed MS. in about six weeks' time,
and would he give me some money. Duckworth is so
decent, I think it is best for him to publish all my books.

And I think probably he would give me enough money to get along with. I can manage on about £150 a year, here.

They have given me complete exemption from military service. I have come almost to the end of my stock of money. I think, if I said to Duckworth that I would offer him any books I write, during the next year or two, he might keep me going. What do you think?

I have a debt to you which no doubt I can pay after a time. Settled here at last, I can live cheaply enough. This money business disgusts me. I wish I had two hundred a year, and could send everybody to the devil.

I think the best thing to do would be to make some sort of arrangement with Duckworth. I like him because he treats my books so well; so there is no reason why we shouldn't come to terms, and I give him my writings if he give me enough to live on. I want some sort of business contract like that, to free me from this sense of imminent dependence on a sort of charity.

Tell me what you think. Perhaps I had better write to Duckworth myself, so he will not think I am trying to squeeze money out of him.

Yours,

D. H. LAWRENCE

TO LADY CYNTHIA ASQUITH

Zennor, St. Ives,
Cornwall.
12th February, 1917.

They have refused to indorse my passport. It is a bitter blow, because I must go to America. But I will try again in a little time.

How are you, and what are you doing? For me the skies have fallen, here in England, and there is an end. I must go to America as soon as I can, because to remain here now, after the end, is like remaining on one's death-bed. It is necessary to begin a new life.

You mustn't think I haven't cared about England. I have cared deeply and bitterly. But something is broken. There *is not* any England. One must look now for another world. This is only a tomb.

I must wait, and try again in a little time. I don't want to bother you with woes or troubles. Only I feel there is some sort of connection between our fates—yours and your children's and your husband's, and Frieda's and mine. I know that sometime or other I shall pull through. And then, when I can help you or your husband or the children, that will be well. Because, don't hide away the knowledge, real life is finished here, it is over. The skies have already fallen. There are no heavens above us, no hope. It needs a beginning elsewhere. That will be more true, perhaps, of Herbert Asquith and of John the Son, than of you. But it is a bit of knowledge not to be evaded even while one struggles through with the present.

I feel the War won't be so very much longer. The skies have *really* fallen. There is no need of any more pulling at the pillars. New earth, new heaven, that is what one must find. I don't think America is a new world. But there is a living sky above. America I know is shocking. But there is a new sky above it. I must go to America as soon as ever I can. Do you think I don't know what it is to be an Englishman? . . .

There is no news here, we seem as in a lost world. My health is fair. It is the old collapsing misery that kills one. Frieda sends her love.

D. H. LAWRENCE

TO LADY CYNTHIA ASQUITH

> Zennor, St. Ives,
> Cornwall.
> 12th October, 1917.

MY DEAR LADY CYNTHIA,

Now comes another nasty blow. The police have sud-denly descended on the house, searched it, and de-livered us a notice to leave the area of Cornwall, by Monday next. So on Monday we shall be in London, staying if possible c/o Mrs. Radford, 32, Well Walk, Hampstead, N.W.

This bolt from the blue has fallen this morning: why, I know not, any more than you do. I cannot even con-ceive how I have incurred suspicion—have not the faint-est notion. We are as innocent even of pacifist activities, let alone spying of any sort, as the rabbits in the field outside. And we must leave Cornwall, and live in an unprohibited area, and report to the police. It is *very* vile. We have practically no money at all—I don't know what we shall do.

At any rate we shall be in London Monday evening. You can see us if you feel like it during the week.

This order comes from W. Western, Major-General i/c Administration, Southern Command, Salisbury. They have taken away some of my papers—I don't know what. It is all very sickening, and makes me very weary.

I hope things are all right with you.

D. H. LAWRENCE

TO LADY CYNTHIA ASQUITH

13b, Earl's Court Square, S.W.
                        Tuesday [1917].

It is a pity you wouldn't come this evening—and you didn't write and say why, after all.

We are leaving here on Friday—going, I think, to Dollie Radford's cottage in the country near Newbury.

But it seems we are never going to have any peace. Today there has been a man from the Criminal Investigation Department inquiring about us—from Gray. It is quite evident that somebody from Cornwall—somebody we don't know, probably—is writing letters to these various departments—and we are followed everywhere by the persecution. It is just like the Cornish to do such a thing. But it is *very* maddening. The detective pretended to Gray that I was a foreigner—but what has the Criminal Investigation Department to do with that? Altogether it is too sickening.

Ask your man at Scotland Yard if he can tell you how I can put a stop to it—if there is any way of putting a stop to it. I hate bothering you—but really, this is getting a bit too thick. I shall soon have every department in the country on my heels for no reason whatever. Surely I can find out from the Criminal Dept. what the persecution is about?

Just write a letter to your man at Scotland Yard, will you? At least this last vileness against me I ought to be able to quash. Address me at:

        44, Mecklenburgh Square, W.C.1

will you, unless you hear from me. That address will always find me.

I hate worrying you—but perhaps you will forgive me.

Frieda sends her love.

D. H. LAWRENCE

TO KATHERINE MANSFIELD

Middleton.
Thursday [? early December, 1918].
MY DEAR KATHERINE,

I received your letter this morning. I want to write a few little things I have on my mind.

First, I send you the Jung book, borrowed from Kot in the midst of his reading it. Ask Jack not to keep it long, will you, as I feel I ought to send it back. Beware of it —this mother-incest idea can become an obsession. But it seems to me there is this much truth in it: that at certain periods the man has a desire and a tendency to return unto the woman, make her his goal and end, finds his justification in her. In this way he casts himself as it were into her womb, and she, the Magna Mater, receives him with gratification. This is a kind of incest. It seems to me it is what Jack does to you, and what repels and fascinates you. I have done it, and now struggle all my might to get out. In a way, Frieda is the devouring mother. It is awfully hard, once the sex relation has gone this way, to recover. If we don't recover, we die. But Frieda says I am antediluvian in my positive attitude. I do think a woman must yield some sort of precedence to a man, and he must take this precedence. I do think men must go ahead absolutely in front of their women, without turning round to ask for permission or approval from their women. Consequently the women must follow as it were unquestioningly. I can't help it, I believe this. Frieda doesn't. Hence our fight.

Secondly, I do believe in friendship. I believe tremendously in friendship between man and man, a pledging of men to each other inviolably. But I have not ever met or formed such friendship. Also I believe the same way in friendship between men and women, and between women and women, sworn, pledged, eternal, as eternal as the marriage bond, and as deep. But I have not met or formed such friendship.

Excuse this sudden burst into dogma. Please give the letter to Jack. I say it to him particularly.

The weather continues dark, warm, muggy and nasty. I find the Midlands full of the fear of death—truly. They are all queer and unnerved. This flu. is very bad. There has only been one flicker of sunshine on the valley. It is very grim always. Last evening at dusk I sat by the rapid brook which runs by the highroad in the valley bed. The spell of hastening, secret water goes over one's mind. When I got to the top—a very hard climb—I felt as if I had climbed out of a womb.

The week-end I was at Ripley. Going, on Sat. night, the train runs just above the surface of Butterley reservoir, and the iron-works on the bank were flaming, a massive roar of flame and burnt smoke in the black sky, flaming and waving again on the black water round the train. On Butterley platform—when I got out—everything was lit up red—there was a man with dark brows, odd, not a human being. I could write a story about him. He made me think of Ashurbanipal. It seems to me, if one is to do fiction now, one must cross the threshold of the human people. I've not done The Fox yet—but I've done The Blind Man—the end queer and ironical. I realize *how* many people are just rotten at the quick.

I've written three little essays, "Education of the People." I told you Freeman, on *The Times*, asked me to do something for his *Educational Supplement*. Will you ask Jack please to send me, by return if possible, Freeman's initials, and *The Times* address, that will find him, so that I can send him the essays and see if he will print them. It will be nice if I can earn a little weekly money.

I begin to despair altogether about human relationships—feel one may just as well turn into a sort of lone wolf, and have done with it. Really, I need a little reassuring of some sort.

D. H. L.

TO KATHERINE MANSFIELD

Middleton.

Sunday, 9 Feb., 1919.

MY DEAR KATHERINE,

I send you *I Promessi Sposi* and *Peru*. I thought you would like the other two. I am very fond of George Sand—have read only *François le Champi* and *Maîtres Sonneurs* and *Villemer*. I liked *Maîtres Sonneurs* immensely. Have you any George Sand? And Mary Mann is quite good, I think. It is marvellous weather—brilliant sunshine on the snow, clear as summer, slightly golden sun, distance lit up. But it is immensely cold—everything frozen solid—milk, mustard, everything. Yesterday I went out for a real walk—I've had a cold and been in bed. I climbed with my niece to the bare top of the hills. Wonderful it is to see the footmarks on the snow—beautiful ropes of rabbit prints, trailing away over the brows; heavy hare marks; a fox, so sharp and dainty, going over the wall: birds with two feet that hop; very splendid straight advance of a pheasant; wood-pigeons that are

clumsy and move in flocks; splendid little leaping marks
of weasels, coming along like a necklace chain of berries;
odd little filigree of the field-mice; the trail of a mole—it
is astonishing what a world of wild creatures one feels
round one, on the hills in the snow. From the height it
is very beautiful. The upland is naked, white like silver,
and moving far into the distance, strange and muscular,
with gleams like skin. Only the wind surprises one, invisibly cold; the sun lies bright on a field, like the movement of a sleeper. It is strange how insignificant in all
this life seems. Two men, tiny as dots, move from a farm
on a snow slope, carrying hay to the beasts. Every moment they seem to melt like insignificant spots of dust;
the sheer, living, muscular white of the uplands absorbs
everything. Only there is a tiny clump of trees bare on
the hill-top—small beeches—writhing like iron in the
blue sky—I wish one could cease to be a human being,
and be a demon. *Allzu menschlich.*

My sister Emily is here, with her little girl—whose
birthday it is today. Emily is cooking treacle rolly and
cakes, Frieda is making Peggy a pale grey dress, I am
advising and interfering. Pamela is lamenting because
the eggs in the pantry have all frozen and burst. I have
spent half an hour hacking ice out of the water tub—
now I am going out. Peggy, with her marvellous red-
gold hair in dangling curl-rags, is darting about sorting
the coloured wools and cottons—*scène de famille.* It is
beautiful to cross the field to the well for drinking water
—such pure sun, and Slaley, the tiny village away
across, sunny as Italy in its snow. I expect Willie Hopkin
will come today.

Well—life itself is life—even the magnificent frost-
foliage on the window. While we live, let us live.

D. H. L.

Emily's nickname was Pamela, or *Virtue Rewarded.*

TO CATHERINE CARSWELL

Thirroul,
South Coast, N.S.W. -
22nd June, 1922.

MY DEAR CATHERINE,

Camomile came last week—reached me here—the
very day I sent you a copy of the American *Aaron's Rod*.
I have read *Camomile,* and find it good: slighter than
Open the Door, but better made. Myself I like that
letter-diary form. And I like it because of its drift: that
one simply must stand out against the social world, even
if one misses "life." Much life they have to offer! Those
Indian Civil servants are the limit: you should have seen
them even in Ceylon: conceit and imbecility. No, she
was well rid of her empty hero, and all he stands for: tin
cans. It was sometimes very amusing, and really wonderfully well written. I can see touches of Don (not John,
Juan, nor Giovanni, thank goodness) here and there. I
hope it will be a success and that it will flourish without
being trodden on.

If you want to know what it is to feel the "correct"
social world fizzle to nothing, you should come to Australia. It *is* a weird place. In the *established* sense, it is
socially nil. Happy-go-lucky, don't-you-bother, we're in
Australia. But also there seems to be no inside life of any
sort: just a long lapse and drift. A rather fascinating indifference, a *physical* indifference to what we call soul or
spirit. It's really a weird show. The country has an
extraordinary hoary, weird attraction. As you get used
to it, it seems so *old,* as if it had missed all this Semite-
Egyptian-Indo-European vast era of history, and was
coal age, the age of great ferns and mosses. It hasn't got

a consciousness—just none—too far back. A strange
effect it has on one. Often I hate it like poison, then
again it fascinates me, and the spell of its indifference
gets me. I can't quite explain it: as if one resolved back
almost to the plant kingdom, before souls, spirits and
minds were grown at all: only quite a live, energetic
body with a weird face.

The house is an awfully nice bungalow with one *big*
room and 3 small bedrooms, then kitchen and wash-
house—and a plot of grass—and a low bushy cliff,
hardly more than a bank—and the sand and the sea. The
Pacific is a lovely ocean, but my, how boomingly, crash-
ingly noisy as a rule. Today for the first time it only
splashes and rushes, instead of exploding and roaring.
We bathe by ourselves—and run in and stand under the
shower-bath to wash the *very* seaey water off. The house
costs 30/- a week, and living about as much as England:
only meat cheap.

We think of sailing on 10th August via Wellington
and Tahiti to San Francisco—land on 4th September.
Then go to Taos. Write to me: c/o Mrs. Mabel Dodge
Sterne, Taos, New Mexico, U.S.A. I am doing a novel
here—half done it—funny sort of novel where nothing
happens and such a lot of things *should* happen: scene
Australia. Frieda loves it here. But Australia would be a
lovely country to lose the world in altogether. I'll go
round it once more—the world—and if ever I get back
here I'll stay. I hope the boy is well, and Don flourishing,
and you as happy as possible.

                                            D. H. L.

TO CATHERINE CARSWELL

Taos, New Mexico, U.S.A.
29th September, 1922.

MY DEAR CATHERINE,

Your letter from the "Tinner's Arms" came last night.
I always think Cornwall has a lot to give one. But Zennor sounds too much changed.

Taos, in its way, *is* rather thrilling. We have got a *very*
pretty adobe house, with furniture made in the village,
and Mexican and Navajo rugs, and some lovely pots. It
stands just on the edge of the Indian reservation: a brook
behind, with trees: in front, the so-called desert, rather
like a moor but covered with whitish-grey sage-brush,
flowering yellow now: some 5 miles away the mountains
rise. On the north—we face east—Taos mountain, the
sacred mt. of the Indians, sits massive on the plain—
some 8 miles away. The pueblo is towards the foot of
the mt., 3 miles off: a big, adobe pueblo on each side
the brook, like two great heaps of earthern boxes, cubes.
There the Indians all live together. They are Pueblos—
these houses were here before the Conquest—very old:
and they grow grain and have cattle, on the lands
bordering the brook, which they can irrigate. We drive
across these "deserts"—white sage-scrub and dark green
piñon scrub on the slopes. On Monday we went up a
cañon into the Rockies to a deserted gold mine. The
aspens are yellow and lovely. We have a pretty busy
time, too. I have already learnt to ride one of these
Indian ponies, with a Mexican saddle. Like it so much.
We gallop off to the pueblo or up to one of the cañons.
Frieda is learning too. Last night the young Indians

came down to dance in the studio, with two drums: and we all joined in. It is fun: and queer. The Indians are much, more remote than Negroes. This week-end is the great dance at the pueblo, and the Apaches and Navajos come in wagons and on horseback, and the Mexicans troop to Taos village. Taos village is a Mexican sort of plaza—piazza—with trees and shops and horses tied up. It lies one mile to the south of us: so four miles from the pueblo. We see little of Taos itself. There are some American artists, sort of colony: but not much in contact. The days are hot sunshine: noon very hot, especially riding home across the open. Night is cold. In winter it snows, because we are 7,000 feet above sea-level. But as yet one thinks of midsummer. We are about 30 miles from the tiny railway station: but we motored 100 miles from the main line.

Well, I'm afraid it will all sound very fascinating if you are just feeling cooped up in London. I don't want you to feel envious. Perhaps it is necessary for me to try these places, perhaps it is my destiny to know the world. It only excites the outside of me. The inside it leaves more isolated and stoic than ever. That's how it is. It is all a form of running away from oneself and the great problems: all this wild west and the strange Australia. But I try to keep quite clear. One forms not the faintest inward attachment, especially here in America. America lives by a sort of egoistic *will*, shove and be shoved. Well, one can stand up to that too: but one is quite, quite cold inside. No illusion. I will not shove, and I will *not* be shoved. *Sono io!*

In the spring I think I want to come to England. But I feel England has insulted me, and I stomach that feeling badly. *Però, son sempre inglese.* Remember, if you were here you'd only be hardening your heart and stiffening your neck—it is either that or be walked over, in America.

D. H. L.

In my opinion a "gentle" life with John Patrick and Don, and a gentle faith in life itself, is far better than these women in breeches and riding-boots and sombreros, and money and motor-cars and wild west. It is all inwardly a hard stone and nothingness. Only the desert has a fascination—to ride alone—in the sun in the for ever unpossessed country—away from man. That is a great temptation, because one rather hates mankind nowadays. But *pazienza, sempre pazienza!* I am learning Spanish slowly, too.

D. H. L.

TO WITTER BYNNER

110, Heath St., Hampstead, N.W.3.
7 December, 1923.

DEAR BYNNER,

Here I am—London—gloom—yellow air—bad cold —bed—old house—Morris wall-paper—visitors—English voices—tea in old cups—poor D. H. L. perfectly miserable, as if he was in his tomb.

You don't need his advice, so take it: *Never* come to Europe any more.

In a fortnight I intend to go to Paris, then to Spain— and in the early spring I hope to be back on the western continent. I wish I was in Santa Fe at this moment. As it is, for my sins, and Frieda's, I am in London. I only hope Mexico will stop revoluting.

De profundis,

D. H. L.

TO J. M. MURRY

Frau von Richthofen,
Ludwig-Wilhelmstift,
Baden-Baden.
7 Feb., 1924.

DEAR JACK,

We've just got here—all snow on the Black Forest, but down in here only wet.

Europe gives me a *Wehmut,* I tell you.

We stay here two weeks—then back via Paris. I learnt in New York that the income-tax must be paid by March 15th, and I still *have no word* from that miserable Seltzer.

I don't know if you really want to go to Taos. Mabel Luhan writes she is arranging for it. You seemed to me really very unsure. You resent, *au fond,* my going away from Europe. *C'est mon affaire. Je m'en vais.* But you, in this interval, decide for yourself, and purely for yourself. Don't think you are doing something for me. I don't want that. Move for yourself alone. Decide for yourself, in your backbone. I don't really want any allegiance or anything of that sort. I don't want any pact. I won't have anything of that sort. If you want to go to America, *bien.* Go without making me responsible.

But if you want to go with Frieda and me and Brett— *encore bien!* One can but try, and I'm willing. But a man like you, if he does anything in the name of, or for the sake of, or because of somebody else, is bound to turn like a crazy snake and bite himself and everybody, on account of it.

Let us clear away all nonsense. I don't *need* you. That

is not true. I need nobody. Neither do you need me. If you pretend to need me, you will hate me for it.

Your articles in the *Adelphi* always annoy me. Why care so much about your own fishiness or fleshiness? Why make it so important? Can't you focus yourself outside yourself? Not for ever focused on yourself, *ad nauseam?*

I met ―― ――. Didn't like him.

You know I don't care a single straw what you think of me. Realize that, once and for all. But when you get to twisting, I dislike you. And I very much dislike any attempt at an intimacy like the one you had with ―― ―― and others. When you start that, I only feel: For God's sake, let me get clear of him.

I don't care what you think of me, I don't care what you say of me, I don't even care what you do against me, as a writer. Trust yourself, then you can expect me to trust you. Leave off being emotional. Leave off twisting. Leave off having any emotion at all. You haven't any genuine ones, except a certain anger. Cut all that would-be sympathetic stuff out. Then know what you're after.

I tell you, if you want to go to America as an unemotional man making an adventure, *bien, allons!* If you want to twist yourself into more knots, don't go with me. That's all. I never had much patience, and I've none now.

D. H. L.

TO THE HON. DOROTHY BRETT

Av. Pino Suarez, 43, Oaxaca, Oax.
Monday Morning [1925].

DEAR BRETT,

Your letter with ――'s enclosed this morning. They

make me sick in the pit of my stomach. The cold, insect-like ugliness of it. I shall avoid meeting ——.

If Mexico City is so unpleasant we shall probably stay here an extra week or fortnight, and go straight to Vera Cruz. I don't like the sound of it—you are right, I think, about King.

And a word about friendship. Friendship between a man and a woman, as a thing of first importance to either, is impossible: and I know it. We are creatures of two halves, spiritual and sensual—and each half is as important as the other. Any relation based on the one half—say the delicate spiritual half alone—*inevitably* brings revulsion and betrayal. It is halfness, or partness, which causes Judas. Your friendship for —— was spiritual—you dragged sex in and he hated you. He'd have hated you anyhow. The halfness of your friendship I also hate, and between you and me there is no sensual correspondence.

You make the horrid mistake of trying to put your sex into a spiritual relation. Old nuns and saints used to do it, but it soon caused rottenness. Now it is half rotten to start with.

When Maruca *likes* a man and marries him, she is not so wrong. Love is chiefly bunk: an over-exaggeration of the spiritual and individualistic and analytic side. If she likes the man, and he is a man, then better than if she loved him. Each will leave aside some of that hateful *personal* insistence on imaginary perfect satisfaction, which is part of the inevitable bunk of love, and if they meet as mere male and female, *kindly*, in their marriage, they will make roots, not weedy flowers of a love match. If ever you can marry a man feeling *kindly* towards him, and knowing he feels kindly to you, do it, and throw love after ——. If you can marry in a spirit of kindliness, with the criticism and ecstasy both sunk into abeyance, do it. As for ———, I don't think you have any warm feeling at all for him. I know your Captain ———: there is a kind of little warm flame that shakes with life in his blue eyes; and that is more worth having than all the high-flown stuff. And he is quite right to leave his door open. Why do you jeer? You're not superior to sex, and you never will be. Only too often you are inferior to it. You like the excitation of sex in the eye, sex in the head. It is an evil and destructive thing. Know from your Captain that a bit of warm flame of life is worth all the spiritual-ness and delicacy and Christlikeness on this miserable globe. No, Brett. I do *not* want your friendship, till you have a full relation somewhere, a *kindly* relation of both halves, not *in part*, as all your friendships have been. That which is in part is in itself a betrayal. Your "friend-ship" for me betrays the essential man and male that I am, and makes me ill. Yes, you make me ill, by dragging at one half at the expense of the other half. And I am so much better now you have gone. I refuse any more of this "delicate friendship" business, because it damages one's wholeness.

Nevertheless, I don't feel unkindly to you. In your one half you are loyal enough. But the very halfness makes your loyalty fatal.

So sit under your tree, or by your fire, and try, try, try to get a real kindliness and a wholeness. You were really horrid even with ———; and no man forgives it you, even on another man's account.

Know, know that this "delicate" halfness *makes* evil. Put away all that Virginal stuff. Don't still go looking for men with strange eyes, who know life from A to Z. Maybe they do, missing out all the rest of the letters, like the meat from the empty eggshell. Look for a little flame of warm kindness. It's more than the Alpha and Omega; and respect the bit of warm kindliness there is in people,

even —— and ——. And try to be *whole*, not that unreal half thing that all men hate you for, even I. Try
and recover your wholeness, that is all. *Then* friendship
is possible, in the kindliness of one's heart.

D. H. L.

Remember I think Christ was profoundly, disastrously
wrong.

TO CURTIS BROWN

Villa Mirenda, Scandicci, Florence.
15 March, 1928.

DEAR C. B.,

Thanks for yours about Gaige. I thought that was
gone—forgotten—so when Willard Johnson—the boy
who did that *Laughing Horse* number of me in Santa Fe
—wrote and asked me if he could do that story on his
little press in Taos, I said "yes." He hasn't got a bean—
so there's no money there. But I told him if he got ahead
to fix up with the New York office. But perhaps he won't
do it. If he doesn't, I shall write a second half to it—the
phallic second half I always intended to add to it—and
send it to you for Gaige to look at. Otherwise later I'll
write a 10,000-word thing and send it. It's a length I
like—and I hate having to fit magazines. Apparently the
story appeared in the February number of *The Forum*,
but they never sent me a copy, which is tiresome. I
wanted to see it.

My novel, *Lady Chatterley's Lover*, or *John Thomas
and Lady Jane*, is at the printer's in Florence: such a
nice little printing shop all working away by hand—
cosy and bit by bit, real Florentine manner—and the
printer doesn't know a word of English—nobody on the
place knows a word—where ignorance is bliss! Where
the serpent is invisible! They will print on a nice hand-

made Italian paper—should be an attractive book. I do hope I'll sell my 1000 copies—or most of 'em—or I'll be broke. I want to post them direct to purchasers. I shall send you a few little order-leaflets, and you will find me a few purchasers, won't you? I shan't send the book unless the people send the two quid, else I'm left.

I haven't heard from ———. Maybe he's got a belly-ache. I can't help it. It's not my fault if people turn into withered sticks, with never a kick in them. I believe in the phallic consciousness, as against the irritable cerebral consciousness we're afflicted with: and anybody who calls my novel a dirty sexual novel is a liar. It's not even a sexual novel: it's a phallic. Sex is a thing that exists in the head, its reactions are cerebral, and its processes mental. Whereas the phallic reality is warm and spontaneous and—but *basta!* you've had enough.

D. H. LAWRENCE

TO JULIETTE HUXLEY

Villa Mirenda, Scandicci, Florence.
17 April, 1928.

DEAR JULIETTE,

Why do you say I laugh at you? I may laugh at some things about you. I laugh at you when you say, "What if Anthony were sixteen, and read this novel!" He'd be too bored at 16: but at twenty, of course, he *should* read it. Was your mind a sexual blank at sixteen? Is anybody's? And what ails the mind in that respect is that it has nothing to go on, it grinds away in abstraction. So I laugh at you and shall go on laughing when you say: What if Anthony were 16, and read your novel! What, indeed! But of course I don't laugh at *you*, nor at your mother either. For absurdities I laugh at everybody, including myself: and why not? But at the essential person I don't laugh. And of course, you ought to know it, and not have those silly misgivings.

I've been having a tussle with my novel: publishers, agents, etc., in London holding up hands of pious horror (because it may affect *their pockets*), and trying to make me feel disastrously in the wrong. Now the Knopfs write from New York they like it very much, and hope to be able to get it into shape to offer to the public. I doubt they can't. But it's nice of them.

I'm in the midst of the proofs—hope to finish them this week. But I still haven't chosen the cover paper. The orders came in very nicely from England. Are you risking a copy, or not?

It's been nasty weather—not really nice since we came back. But today looks promising. Tomorrow Lady Colefax is due to come to tea. I'm busy finishing off my pictures—think I shall send them to Dorothy Warren for her to exhibit in her gallery in Maddox St.—she wants to. But don't go and see them—you'd only be in a rage as you were that morning in les Aroles.

We want to leave this house on the 30th—so we've not much longer. I may stay in Florence to see my book out on the 15th, then to Switzerland, to cure. I think we'll go to Vermala Montana, above Sierre (or is it Sion?)—because it's a flat plateau and I can walk without gasping. My chest is so-so—but I'm better really.

Anyhow, we'll see you during the summer—perhaps August. Remember me to Julian, and I hope the book goes gaily, and he'll feel nice and chirpy doing it: and not try to do too many other things. Frieda has actually written too. How are the children? Is Anthony at school?

D. H. L.

I suppose your mother is back in her Neuchâtel. Remember me to her when you write.

TO ALDOUS HUXLEY

La Vigie,
Port-Cros (Var).
Sunday

DEAR ALDOUS,

I have read *Point Counter Point* with a heart sinking
through my boot-soles and a rising admiration. I do
think you've shown the truth, perhaps the last truth,
about you and your generation, with really fine courage.
It seems to me. it would take ten times the courage to
write *P. Counter P.* that it took to write *Lady C.*: and if
the public knew *what* it was reading, it would throw a
hundred stones at you, to one at me. I do think that art
has to reveal the palpitating moment or the state of man
as it is. And I think you do that, terribly. But what a
moment! and what a state! if you can only palpitate to
murder, suicide, and rape, in their various degrees—
and you state plainly that it is so—*caro*, however are we
going to live through the days? Preparing still another
murder, suicide, and rape? But it becomes of a phan-
tasmal boredom and produces ultimately inertia, inertia,
inertia and final atrophy of the feelings. Till, I suppose,
comes a final super-war, and murder, suicide, rape
sweeps away the vast bulk of mankind. It is as you say—
intellectual appreciation does not amount to so much,
it's what you thrill to. And if murder, suicide, rape is
what you thrill to, and nothing else, then it's your destiny
—you can't change it *mentally*. You live by what you
thrill to, and there's the end of it. Still for all that it's a
perverse courage which makes the man accept the slow
suicide of inertia and sterility: the perverseness of a perverse child— It's amazing how men are like that. Richard

Aldington is exactly the same inside, murder, suicide, rape—with a desire to *be* raped very strong—same thing really—just like you—only he doesn't face it, and gilds his perverseness. It makes me feel ill, I've had more hæmorrhage here and been in bed this week. *Sporca miseria.* If I don't find some solid spot to climb out of, in this bog, I'm done. I can't stand murder, suicide, rape—especially rape: and especially being raped. Why do men only thrill to a woman who'll rape them and S——on their face? All I want to do to your Lucy is smack her across the mouth, your Rampion is the most boring character in the book—a gas-bag. Your attempt at intellectual sympathy!—It's all rather disgusting, and I feel like a badger that has its hole on Wimbledon Common and trying not to be caught. Well, *caro,* I feel like saying good-bye to you—but one will have to go on saying good-bye for years.

D. H. L.

ESSAYS
AND CRITICAL WRITING

EDITOR'S PREFACE

ONE has only to glance at the section headings of Phoenix, the large volume of Lawrence's posthumous papers, to get some idea of the range of his nonfictional prose. Nature and poetical pieces; peoples, countries, races; love, sex, men and women; literature and art; education; ethics, psychology, philosophy; personalia—these are the many categories necessary to order the vast material still either unpublished or uncollected at Lawrence's death.

It has naturally been impossible, within the limits of this single volume, to make anything approaching a fair representation of Lawrence's prolific non-fictional writings. The five pieces I have chosen are intended as only the barest introduction to Lawrence as essayist and critic. But they include what I think is his most striking piece of polemics, "Pornography and Obscenity," and an excellent example of his method of literary criticism, the chapter on Poe from the brilliant *Studies in Classic American Literature*. "Christs in the Tirol" might of course have been included among Lawrence's travel writings; indeed, in altered form, it appears in the volume *Twilight in Italy*. But I place it here because it is rather less conversational than most of his typical travel pieces. "Nottingham and the Mining Countryside" I have chosen because, in addition to its autobiographical interest, it presents its courageous thinking in, for Lawrence, an unusually sweetly reasonable tone. "Men

Must Work and Women As Well" is from the amusing and provocative volume, *Assorted Articles*. I reprint it both for the soundness of its social insight and as a sample of Lawrence's informal essay style. The review of four novels is interesting, I think, not only as an example of Lawrence's unconventional reviewing style, but also as an indication of his approach to current fiction.

Christs in the Tirol

THE real Tirol does not seem to extend far south of the Brenner, and northward it goes right to the Starnberger See. Even at Sterzing the rather gloomy atmosphere of the Tirolese Alps is being dispersed by the approach of the South. And, strangely enough, the roadside crucifixes become less and less interesting after Sterzing. Walking down from Munich to Italy, I have stood in front of hundreds of *Martertafeln;* and now I miss them; these painted shrines by the Garda See are not the same.

I, who see a tragedy in every cow, began by suffering from the Secession pictures in Munich. All these new paintings seemed so shrill and restless. Those that were meant for joy shrieked and pranced for joy, and sorrow was a sensation to be relished, curiously; as if we were epicures in suffering, keen on a new flavour. I thought with kindliness of England, whose artists so often suck their sadness like a lollipop, mournfully, and comfortably.

Then one must walk, as it seems, for miles and endless miles past crucifixes, avenues of them. At first they were mostly factory made, so that I did not notice them, any more than I noticed the boards with warnings, except just to observe they were there. But coming among the Christs carved in wood by the peasant artists, I began to feel them. Now, it seems to me, they create almost an atmosphere over the northern Tirol, an atmosphere of pain.

I was going along a marshy place at the foot of the mountains, at evening, when the sky was a pale, dead colour and the hills were nearly black. At a meeting of the paths was a crucifix, and between the feet of the Christ a little red patch of dead poppies. So I looked at him. It was an old shrine, and the Christus was nearly like a man. He seemed to me to be real. In front of me hung a Bavarian peasant, a Christus, staring across at the evening and the black hills. He had broad cheek-bones and sturdy limbs, and he hung doggedly on the cross, hating it. He reminded me of a peasant farmer, fighting slowly and meanly, but not giving in. His plain, rudimentary face stared stubbornly at the hills, and his neck was stiffened, as if even yet he were struggling away from the cross he resented. He would not yield to it. I stood in front of him, and realized him. He might have said, "Yes, here I am, and it's bad enough, and it's suffering, and it doesn't come to an end. *Perhaps* something will happen, will help. If it doesn't, I s'll have to go on with it." He seemed stubborn and struggling from the root of his soul, his human soul. No Godship had been thrust upon him. He was human clay, a peasant Prometheus-Christ, his poor soul bound in him, blind, but struggling stubbornly against the fact of the nails. And I looked across at the tiny square of orange light, the window of a farm-house on the marsh. And, thinking of the other little farms, of how the man and his wife and his children worked on till dark, intent and silent, carrying the hay in their arms out of the streaming thunder-rain which soaked them through, I understood how the Christus was made.

And after him, when I saw the Christs posing on the

Cross, a la Guido Reni, I recognized them as the mere conventional symbol, meaning no more Christ than St. George and the Dragon on a five-shilling-piece means England.

There are so many Christs carved by men who have carved to get at the meaning of their own soul's anguish. Often, I can distinguish one man's work in a district. In the Zemm valley, right in the middle of the Tirol, there are some half-dozen crucifixes by the same worker, who has whittled away in torment to see himself emerge out of the piece of timber, so that he can understand his own suffering, and see it take on itself the distinctness of an eternal thing, so that he can go on further, leaving it. The chief of these crucifixes is a very large one, deep in the Klamm, where it is always gloomy and damp. The river roars below, the rock wall opposite reaches high overhead, pushing back the sky. And by the track where the pack-horses go, in the cold gloom, hangs the large, pale Christ. He has fallen forward, just dead, and the weight of his full-grown, mature body is on the nails of the hands. So he drops, as if his hands would tear away, and he would fall to earth. The face is strangely brutal, and is set with an ache of weariness and pain and bitterness, and his rather ugly, passionate mouth is shut with bitter despair. After all, he had wanted to live and to enjoy his manhood. But fools had ruined his body, and thrown his life away, when he wanted it. No one had helped. His youth and health and vigour, all his life, and himself, were just thrown away as waste. He had died in bitterness. It is sombre and damp, silent save for the roar of water. There hangs the falling body of the man who had died in bitterness of spirit, and the driver of the pack-horses takes off his hat, cringing in his sturdy cheerfulness as he goes beneath.

He is afraid. I think of the carver of the crucifix. He

also was more or less afraid. They all, when they carved or erected these crucifixes, had fear at the bottom of their hearts. And so the monuments to physical pain are found everywhere in the mountain gloom. By the same hand that carved the big, pale Christ I found another crucifix, a little one, at the end of a bridge. This Christ had a fair beard instead of a black one, and his body was hanging differently. But there was about him the same bitterness, the same despair, even a touch of cynicism. Evidently the artist could not get beyond the tragedy that tormented him. No wonder the peasants are afraid, as they take off their hats in passing up the valley.

They are afraid of physical pain. It terrifies them. Then they raise, in their startled helplessness of suffering, these Christs, these human attempts at deciphering the riddle of pain. In the same way they paint the humorous little pictures of some calamity—a man drowned in a stream or killed by a falling tree—and nail it up near the scene of the accident. *"Memento mori,"* they say everywhere. And so they try to get used to the idea of death and suffering, to rid themselves of some of the fear thereof. And all tragic art is part of the same attempt.

But some of the Christs are quaint. One I know is very elegant, brushed and combed. "I'm glad I am no lady," I say to him. For he is a pure lady-killer. But he ignores me utterly, the exquisite. The man who made him must have been dying to become a gentleman.

And a fair number are miserable fellows. They put up their eyebrows plaintively, and pull down the corners of their mouths. Sometimes they gaze heavenwards. They are quite sorry for themselves.

"Never mind," I say to them. "It'll be worse yet, before you've done."

Some of them look pale and done-for. They didn't make much fight; they hadn't much pluck in them. They make me sorry.

"It's a pity you hadn't got a bit more kick in you," I say to them. And I wonder why in England one sees always this pale, pitiful Christ with no "go" in him. Is it because our national brutality is so strong and deep that we must create for ourselves an anæmic Christus, for ever on the whine; either that, or one of those strange neutrals with long hair, that are supposed to represent to our children the Jesus of the New Testament.

In a tiny glass case beside the high-road where the Isar is a very small stream, sits another Christ that makes me want to laugh, and makes me want to weep also. His little head rests on his hand, his elbow on his knee, and he meditates, half-wearily. I am strongly reminded of Walther von der Vogelweide and the German medieval spirit. Detached, he sits, and dreams, and broods, in his little golden crown of thorns, and his little cloak of red flannel, that some peasant woman has stitched for him.

"Couvre-toi de gloire, Tartarin—couvre-toi de flanelle," I think to myself.

But he sits, a queer little man, fretted, plunged in anxiety of thought, and yet dreaming rather pleasantly at the same time. I think he is the forefather of the warm-hearted German philosopher and professor.

He is the last of the remarkable Christs of the peasants that I have seen. Beyond the Brenner an element of unreality seems to creep in. The Christs are given great gashes in the breast and knees, and from the brow and breast and hands and knees streams of blood trickle down, so that one sees a weird striped thing in red and white that is not at all a Christus. And the same red that is used for the blood serves also to mark the path, so that one comes to associate the *Martertafeln* and their mess

of red stripes with the stones smeared with scarlet paint
for guidance. The wayside chapels, going south, become
fearfully florid and ornate, though still one finds in them
the little wooden limbs, arms and legs and feet, and little
wooden cows or horses, hung up by the altar, to signify
a cure in these parts. But there is a tendency for the
Christs themselves to become either neuter or else sensational. In a chapel near St. Jakob, a long way from the
railway, sat the most ghastly Christus I can imagine. He
is seated, after the crucifixion. His eyes, which are
turned slightly to look at you, are bloodshot till they
glisten scarlet, and even the iris seems purpled. And the
misery, the almost criminal look of hate and misery, on
the bloody, disfigured face is shocking. I was amazed
at the ghastly thing: moreover, it was fairly new.

South of the Brenner again, in the Austrian Tirol, I
have not seen anyone salute the Christus: not even the
guides. As one goes higher the crucifixes get smaller and
smaller. The wind blows the snow under the tiny shed of
a tiny Christ: the guides tramp stolidly by, ignoring the
holy thing. That surprised me. But perhaps these were
particularly unholy men. One does not expect a great
deal of an Austrian, except real pleasantness.

So, in Austria, I have seen a fallen Christus. It was on
the Jaufen, not very far from Meran. I was looking at all
the snowpeaks all around, and hurrying downhill, trying
to get out of a piercing wind, when I almost ran into a
very old *Martertafel*. The wooden shed was silver-grey
with age, and covered on the top with a thicket of lichen,
weird, grey-green, sticking up its tufts. But on the rocks
at the foot of the cross was the armless Christ, who had
tumbled down and lay on his back in a weird attitude. It
was one of the old, peasant Christs, carved out of wood,
and having the long, wedge-shaped shins and thin legs
that are almost characteristic. Considering the great

sturdiness of a mountaineer's calves, these thin, flat legs are interesting. The arms of the fallen Christ had broken off at the shoulders, and they hung on their nails, as *ex voto* limbs hang in the shrines. But these arms dangled from their palms, one at each end of the cross, the muscles, carved in wood, looking startling, upside down. And the icy wind blew them backwards and forwards. There, in that bleak place among the stones, they looked horrible. Yet I dared not touch either them or the fallen image. I wish some priest would go along and take the broken thing away.

So many Christs there seem to be: one in rebellion against his cross, to which he was nailed; one bitter with the agony of knowing he must die, his heart-beatings all futile; one who felt sentimental; one who gave in to his misery; one who was a sensationalist; one who dreamed and fretted with thought. Perhaps the peasant carvers of crucifixes are right, and all these were found on the same cross. And perhaps there were others too: one who waited for the end, his soul still with a sense of right and hope; one ashamed to see the crowd make beasts of themselves, ashamed that he should provide for their sport; one who looked at them and thought: "And I am of you. I might be among you, yelling at myself in that way. But I am not, I am here. And so——"

All those Christs, like a populace, hang in the mountains under their little sheds. And perhaps they are falling, one by one. And I suppose we have carved no Christs, afraid lest they should be too like men, too like ourselves. What we worship must have exotic form.

Nottingham and the Mining Countryside

I WAS born nearly forty-four years ago, in Eastwood, a mining village of some three thousand souls, about eight miles from Nottingham, and one mile from the small stream, the Erewash, which divides Nottingham-shire from Derbyshire. It is hilly country, looking west to Crich and towards Matlock, sixteen miles away, and east and north-east towards Mansfield and the Sherwood Forest district. To me it seemed, and still seems, an extremely beautiful countryside, just between the red sandstone and the oak trees of Nottingham, and the cold limestones, the ash trees, the stone fences of Derbyshire. To me, as a child and a young man, it was still the old England of the forest and agricultural past; there were no motor-cars, the mines were, in a sense, an accident in the landscape, and Robin Hood and his merry men were not very far away.

The string of coal-mines of B. W. & Co. had been opened some sixty years before I was born, and East-wood had come into being as a consequence. It must have been a tiny village at the beginning of the nine-teenth century, a small place of cottages and frag-mentary rows of little four-roomed miners' dwellings, the homes of the old colliers of the eighteenth century, who worked in the bits of mines, foot-rill mines with an open-ing in the hillside into which the miners walked, or windlass mines, where the men were wound up one at a time, in a bucket, by a donkey. The windlass mines were still working when my father was a boy—and the shafts of some were still there, when I was a boy.

But somewhere about 1820 the company must have

sunk the first big shaft—not very deep—and installed the first machinery of the real industrial colliery. Then came my grandfather, a young man trained to be a tailor, drifting from the south of England, and got the job of company tailor for the Brinsley mine. In those days the company supplied the men with the thick flannel vests, or singlets, and the moleskin trousers lined at the top with flannel, in which the colliers worked. I remember the great rolls of coarse flannel and pit-cloth which stood in the corner of my grandfather's shop when I was a small boy, and the big, strange old sewing-machine, like nothing else on earth, which sewed the massive pit-trousers. But when I was only a child the company discontinued supplying the men with pit-clothes.

My grandfather settled in an old cottage down in a quarry-bed, by the brook at Old Brinsley, near the pit. A mile away, up at Eastwood, the company built the first miners' dwellings—it must be nearly a hundred years ago. Now Eastwood occupies a lovely position on a hill top, with the steep slope towards Derbyshire and the long slope towards Nottingham. They put up a new church, which stands fine and commanding, even if it has no real form, looking across the awful Erewash Valley at the church of Heanor, similarly commanding, away on a hill beyond. What opportunities, what opportunities! These mining villages *might* have been like the lovely hill-towns of Italy, shapely and fascinating. And what happened?

Most of the little rows of dwellings of the old-style miners were pulled down, and dull little shops began to rise along the Nottingham Road, while on the down-slope of the north side the company erected what is still known as the New Buildings, or the Square. These New Buildings consist of two great hollow squares of dwellings planked down on the rough slope of the hill, little four-room houses with the "front" looking outward into the grim, blank street, and the "back," with a tiny square brick yard, a low wall, and a w.c. and ash-pit, looking into the desert of the square, hard, uneven, jolting black earth tilting rather steeply down, with these little back yards all round, and openings at the corners. The squares were quite big, and absolutely desert, save for the posts for clothes lines, and people passing, children playing on the hard earth. And they were shut in like a barracks enclosure, very strange.

Even fifty years ago the squares were unpopular. It was "common" to live in the Square. It was a little less common to live in the Breach, which consisted of six blocks of rather more pretentious dwellings erected by the company in the valley below, two rows of three blocks, with an alley between. And it was most "common," most degraded of all, to live in Dakins Row, two rows of the old dwellings, very old, black, four-roomed little places, that stood on the hill again, not far from the Square.

So the place started. Down the steep street between the squares, Scargill Street, the Wesleyans' chapel was put up, and I was born in the little corner shop just above. Across the other side the Square the miners themselves built the big, barn-like Primitive Methodist chapel. Along the hill-top ran the Nottingham Road, with its scrappy, ugly mid-Victorian shops. The little market-place, with a superb outlook, ended the village on the Derbyshire side, and was just left bare, with the Sun Inn on one side, the chemist across, with the gilt pestle-and-mortar, and a shop at the other corner, the corner of Alfreton Road and Nottingham Road.

In this queer jumble of the old England and the new, I came into consciousness. As I remember, little local speculators already began to straggle dwellings in rows, always in rows, across the fields: nasty red-brick, flat-faced dwellings with dark slate roofs. The bay-window period only began when I was a child. But most of the country was untouched.

There must be three or four hundred company houses in the squares and the streets that surround the squares, like a great barracks wall. There must be sixty or eighty company houses in the Breach. The old Dakins Row will have thirty to forty little holes. Then counting the old cottages and rows left with their old gardens down the lanes and along the twitchells, and even in the midst of Nottingham Road itself, there were houses enough for the population, there was no need for much building. And not much building went on when I was small.

We lived in the Breach, in a corner house. A field-path came down under a great hawthorn hedge. On the other side was the brook, with the old sheep-bridge going over into the meadows. The hawthorn hedge by the brook had grown tall as tall trees, and we used to bathe from there in the dipping-hole, where the sheep were dipped, just near the fall from the old mill-dam, where the water rushed. The mill only ceased grinding the local corn when I was a child. And my father, who always worked in Brinsley pit, and who always got up at five o'clock, if not at four, would set off in the dawn across the fields at Coney Grey, and hunt for mushrooms in the long grass, or perhaps pick up a skulking rabbit, which he would bring home at evening inside the lining of his pit-coat.

So that the life was a curious cross between industrialism and the old agricultural England of Shakespeare and Milton and Fielding and George Eliot. The dialect was broad Derbyshire, and always "thee" and "thou." The people lived almost entirely by instinct, men of my father's age could not really read. And the pit did not

mechanize men. On the contrary. Under the butty system, the miners worked underground as a sort of intimate community, they knew each other practically
naked, and with curious close intimacy, and the darkness and the underground remoteness of the pit "stall,"
and the continual presence of danger, made the physical,
instinctive, and intuitional contact between men very
highly developed, a contact almost as close as touch,
very real and very powerful. This physical awareness
and intimate *togetherness* was at its strongest down pit.
When the men came up into the light, they blinked.
They had, in a measure, to change their flow. Nevertheless, they brought with them above ground the curious dark intimacy of the mine, the naked sort of contact,
and if I think of my childhood, it is always as if there
was a lustrous sort of inner darkness, like the gloss of
coal, in which we moved and had our real being. My
father loved the pit. He was hurt badly, more than once,
but he would never stay away. He loved the contact,
the intimacy, as men in the war loved the intense male
comradeship of the dark days. They did not know what
they had lost till they lost it. And I think it is the same
with the young colliers of today.

Now the colliers had also an instinct of beauty. The
colliers' wives had not. The colliers were deeply alive,
instinctively. But they had no daytime ambition, and no
daytime intellect. They avoided, really, the rational aspect of life. They preferred to take life instinctively and
intuitively. They didn't even care very profoundly about
wages. It was the women, naturally, who nagged on
this score. There was a big discrepancy, when I was a
boy, between the collier who saw, at the best, only a
brief few hours of daylight—often no daylight at all during the winter weeks—and the collier's wife, who had
all the day to herself when the man was down pit.

The great fallacy is, to pity the man. He didn't dream
of pitying himself, till agitators and sentimentalists
taught him to. He was happy: or more than happy, he
was fulfilled. Or he was fulfilled on the receptive side,
not on the expressive. The collier went to the pub and
drank in order to continue his intimacy with his mates.
They talked endlessly, but it was rather of wonders and
marvels, even in politics, than of facts. It was hard facts,
in the shape of wife, money, and nagging home necessities, which they fled away from, out of the house to
the pub, and out of the house to the pit.

The collier fled out of the house as soon as he could,
away from the nagging materialism of the woman. With
the women it was always: This is broken, now you've
got to mend it! or else: We want this, that and the other,
and where is the money coming from? The collier didn't
know and didn't care very deeply—his life was otherwise. So he escaped. He roved the countryside with his
dog, prowling for a rabbit, for nests, for mushrooms,
anything. He loved the countryside, just the indiscrimi-
nating feel of it. Or he loved just to sit on his heels and
watch—anything or nothing. He was not intellectually
interested. Life for him did not consist in facts, but in a
flow. Very often, he loved his garden. And very often
he had a genuine love of the beauty of flowers. I have
known it often and often, in colliers.

Now the love of flowers is a very misleading thing.
Most women love flowers as possessions, and as trim-
mings. They can't look at a flower, and wonder a moment, and pass on. If they see a flower that arrests their
attention, they must at once pick it, pluck it. Possession!
A possession! Something added on to *me!* And most of
the so-called love of flowers today is merely this reaching
out of possession and egoism: something I've *got:* something that embellishes *me.* Yet I've seen many a collier

stand in his back garden looking down at a flower with that odd, remote sort of contemplation which shows a *real* awareness of the presence of beauty. It would not even be admiration, or joy, or delight, or any of those things which so often have a root in the possessive instinct. It would be a sort of contemplation: which shows the incipient artist.

The real tragedy of England, as I see it, is the tragedy of ugliness. The country is so lovely: the man-made England is so vile. I know that the ordinary collier, when I was a boy, had a peculiar sense of beauty, coming from his intuitive and instinctive consciousness, which was awakened down pit. And the fact that he met with just cold ugliness and raw materialism when he came up into daylight, and particularly when he came to the Square or the Breach, and to his own table, killed something in him, and in a sense spoiled him as a man. The woman almost invariably nagged about material things. She was taught to do it; she was encouraged to do it. It was a mother's business to see that her sons "got on," and it was the man's business to provide the money. In my father's generation, with the old wild England behind them, and the lack of education, the man was not beaten down. But in my generation, the boys I went to school with, colliers now, have all been beaten down, what with the din-din-dinning of Board-schools, books, cinemas, clergymen, the whole national and human consciousness hammering on the fact of material prosperity above all things.

The men are beaten down, there is prosperity for a time, in their defeat—and then disaster looms ahead. The root of all disaster is disheartenment. And men are disheartened. The men of England, the colliers in particular, are disheartened. They have been betrayed and beaten.

Now though perhaps nobody knew it, it was ugliness which really betrayed the spirit of man, in the nineteenth century. The great crime which the moneyed classes and promoters of industry committed in the palmy Victorian days was the condemning of the workers to ugliness, ugliness, ugliness: meanness and formless and ugly surroundings, ugly ideals, ugly religion, ugly hope, ugly love, ugly clothes, ugly furniture, ugly houses, ugly relationship between workers and employers. The human soul needs actual beauty even more than bread. The middle classes jeer at the colliers for buying pianos— but what is the piano, often as not, but a blind reaching out for beauty. To the woman it is a possession and a piece of furniture and something to feel superior about. But see the elderly colliers trying to learn to play, see them listening with queer alert faces to their daughter's execution of *The Maiden's Prayer*, and you will see a blind, unsatisfied craving for beauty. It is far more deep in the men than the women. The women want show. The men want beauty, and still want it.

If the company, instead of building those sordid and hideous Squares, then, when they had that lovely site to play with, there on the hill top: if they had put a tall column in the middle of the small market-place, and run three parts of a circle of arcade round the pleasant space, where people could stroll or sit, and with handsome houses behind! If they had made big, substantial houses, in apartments of five or six rooms, and with handsome entrances. If above all, they had encouraged song and dancing—for the miners still sang and danced —and provided handsome space for these. If only they had encouraged some form of beauty in dress, some form of beauty in interior life—furniture, decoration. If they had given prizes for the handsomest chair or table, the loveliest scarf, the most charming room that the men or women could make! If only they had done this, there would never have been an industrial problem. The industrial problem arises from the base forcing of all human energy into a competition of mere acquisition.

You may say the working man would not have accepted such a form of life: the Englishman's home is his castle, etc., etc.—"my own little home." But if you can hear every word the next-door people say, there's not much castle. And if you can see everybody in the Square if they go to the w.c.! And if your one desire is to get out of your "castle" and your "own little home"!—well, there's not much to be said for it. Anyhow, it's only the woman who idolizes "her own little home"—and it's always the woman at her worst, her most greedy, most possessive, most mean. There's nothing to be said for the "little home" any more: a great scrabble of ugly pettiness over the face of the land.

As a matter of fact, till 1800 the English people were strictly a rural people—very rural. England has had towns for centuries, but they have never been real towns, only clusters of village streets. Never the real *urbs*. The English character has failed to develop the real *urban* side of a man, the civic side. Siena is a bit of a place, but it is a real city, with citizens intimately connected with the city. Nottingham is a vast place sprawling towards a million, and it is nothing more than an amorphous agglomeration. There *is* no Nottingham, in the sense that there is Siena. The Englishman is stupidly undeveloped, as a citizen. And it is partly due to his "little home" stunt, and partly to his acceptance of hopeless paltriness in his surrounding. The new cities of America are much more genuine cities, in the Roman sense, than is London or Manchester. Even Edinburgh used to be more of a true city than any town England ever produced.

That silly little individualism of "the Englishman's home is his castle" and "my own little home" is out of date. It would work almost up to 1800, when every Englishman was still a villager, and a cottager. But the industrial system has brought a great change. The Englishman still likes to think of himself as a "cottager"— "my home, my garden." But it is puerile. Even the farm-labourer today is psychologically a town-bird. The English are town-birds through and through, today, as the inevitable result of their complete industrialization. Yet they don't know how to build a city, how to think of one, or how to live in one. They are all suburban, pseudo-cottagy, and not one of them knows how to be truly urban—the citizen as the Romans were citizens— or the Athenians—or even the Parisians, till the war came.

And this is because we have frustrated that instinct of community which would make us unite in pride and dignity in the bigger gesture of the citizen, not the cottager. The great city means beauty, dignity, and a certain splendour. This is the side of the Englishman that has been thwarted and shockingly betrayed. England is a mean and petty scrabble of paltry dwellings called "homes." I believe in their heart of hearts all Englishmen loathe their little homes—but not the women. What we want is a bigger gesture, a greater scope, a certain splendour, a certain grandeur, and beauty, big beauty. The American does far better than we, in this.

And the promoter of industry, a hundred years ago, dared to perpetrate the ugliness of my native village. And still more monstrous, promoters of industry today are scrabbling over the face of England with miles and square miles of red-brick "homes," like horrible scabs. And the men inside these little red rat-traps get more and more helpless, being more and more humiliated, more and more dissatisfied, liked trapped rats. Only the meaner sort of women go on loving the little home which is no more than a rat-trap to her man.

Do away with it all, then. At no matter what cost, start in to alter it. Never mind about wages and industrial squabbling. Turn the attention elsewhere. Pull down my native village to the last brick. Plan a nucleus. Fix the focus. Make a handsome gesture of radiation from the focus. And then put up big buildings, handsome, that sweep to a civic centre. And furnish them with beauty. And make an absolute clean start. Do it place by place. Make a new England. Away with little homes! Away with scrabbling pettiness and paltriness. Look at the contours of the land, and build up from these, with a sufficient nobility. The English may be mentally or spiritually developed. But as citizens of splendid cities they are more ignominious than rabbits. And they nag, nag, nag all the time about politics and wages and all that, like mean, narrow housewives.

Men Must Work and Women As Well

SUPPOSING that circumstances go on pretty much in the same way they're going on in now, then men and women will go on pretty much in the same way they are now going on in. There is always an element of change, we know. But change is of two sorts: the next step, or a jump in another direction. The next step is called progress. If our society continues its course of gay progress along the given lines, then men and women will do the same: always along the given lines.

So what is important in that case is not so much men and women, but the given lines. The railway train doesn't matter particularly in itself. What matters is where it is going to. If I want to go to Crewe, then a train to Bedford is supremely uninteresting to me, no matter how full it may be. It will only arouse a secondary and temporal interest if it happens to have an accident.

And there you are with men and women today. They are not particularly interesting, and they are not, in themselves, particularly important. All the thousands and millions of bowler hats and neat handbags that go bobbing to business every day may represent so many immortal souls, but somehow we feel that is not for us to say. The clergyman is paid to tickle our vanity in these matters. What all the bowler hats and neat handbags represent to you and me and to each other is business, my dear, and a job.

So that, granted the present stream of progress towards better business and better jobs continues, the point is, not to consider the men and women bobbing in the stream, any more than you consider the drops of water in the Thames—but where the stream is flowing. Where is the stream flowing, indeed, the stream of progress? Everybody hopes, of course, it is flowing towards bigger business and better jobs. And what does that mean, again, to the man under the bowler hat and the woman who clutches the satchel?

It means, of course, more money, more congenial labours, and fewer hours. It means freedom from all irksome tasks. It means, apart from the few necessary hours of highly paid and congenial labour, that men and women shall have nothing to do except enjoy themselves. No beastly housework for the women, no beastly homework for the men. Free! free to enjoy themselves. More films, more motor-cars, more dances, more golf, more tennis and more getting completely away from yourself. And the goal of life is enjoyment.

Now if men and women want these things with sufficient intensity, they may really get them, and go on getting them. While the game is worth the candle, men and women will go on playing the game. And it seems today as if the motor-car, the film, the radio and the jazz were worth the candle. This being so, progress will continue from business to bigger business, and from job to better job. This is, in very simple terms, the plan of the universe laid down by the great magnates of industry like Mr. Ford. And they know what they are talking about.

But—and the "but" is a very big one—it is not easy to turn business into bigger business, and it is sometimes *impossible* to turn uncongenial jobs into congenial ones. This is where science really leaves us in the lurch, and calculation collapses. Perhaps in Mr. Ford's super-factory of motor-cars all jobs may be made abstract and congenial. But the woman whose cook falls foul of the kitchen range, heated with coal, every day, hates that coal range herself even more darkly than the cook hates it. Yet many housewives can't afford electric cooking. And if everyone could, it still doesn't make housework entirely congenial. All the inventions of modern science fail to make housework anything but uncongenial to the modern woman, be she mistress or servant-maid. Now the only decent way to get something done is to get it done by somebody who quite likes doing it. In the past, cooks really enjoyed cooking and housemaids enjoyed scrubbing. Those days are over; like master, like man, and still more so, like mistress, like maid. Mistress loathes scrubbing; in two generations, maid loathes scrubbing. But scrubbing must be done. At what price?

—raise the price. The price is raised, the scrubbing goes a little better. But after a while, the loathing of scrubbing becomes again paramount in the kitchen-maid's breast, and then ensues a general state of tension, and a general outcry: Is it worth it? Is it really worth it?

What applies to scrubbing applies to all labour that cannot be mechanized or abstracted. A girl will slave over shorthand and typing for a pittance because it is not muscular work. A girl will not do housework well, not for a good wage. Why? Because, for some mysterious or obvious reason, the modern woman and the modern man hate physical work. Ask your husband to peel the potatoes, and earn his deep resentment. Ask your wife to wash your socks, and earn the same. There is still a certain thrill about "mental" and purely mechanical work like attending a machine. But actual labour has become to us, with our education, abhorrent.

And it is here that science has not kept pace with human demand. It is here that progress is fatally threatened. There is an enormous, insistent demand on the part of the human being that mere labour, such as scrubbing, hewing and loading coal, navvying, the crude work that is the basis of all labour, shall be done away with. Even washing dishes. Science hasn't even learned how to wash dishes for us yet. The mistress who feels so intensely bitter about her maid who will not wash the dishes properly does so because she herself so loathes washing them. Science has rather left us in the lurch in these humble but basic matters. Before babies are conveniently bred in bottles, let the scientist find a *hey presto!* trick for turning dirty teacups into clean ones; since it is upon science we depend for our continued progress.

Progress, then, which proceeds so smoothly, and depends on science, does not proceed as rapidly as human feelings change. Beef-steaks are beef-steaks still, though all except the eating is horrible to us. A great deal must be done about a beef-steak besides the eating of it. And this great deal is done, we have to face the fact, unwillingly. When the mistress loathes trimming and grilling a beef-steak, or paring potatoes, or wringing the washing, the maid will likewise loathe these things, and do them at last unwillingly, and with a certain amount of resentment.

The one thing we don't sufficiently consider, in considering the march of human progress, is also the very dangerous march of human feeling that goes on at the same time, and not always parallel. The change in human feeling! And one of the greatest changes that has ever taken place in man and woman is this revulsion from physical effort, physical labour and physical contact, which has taken place within the last thirty years. This change hits woman even harder than man, for she has always had to keep the immediate physical side going. And now it is repellent to her—just as nearly all physical activity is repellent to modern man. The film, the radio, the gramophone were all invented because physical effort and physical contact have become repulsive to man and woman alike. The aim is to abstract as far as possible. And science is our only help. And science still can't wash the dinner-things or darn socks, or even mend the fire. Electric heaters or central heating, of course! But that's not all.

What, then, is the result? In the abstract we sail ahead to bigger business and better jobs and babies bred in bottles and food in tabloid form. But meanwhile science hasn't rescued us from beef-steaks and dish-washing, heavy labour and howling babies. There is a great hitch. And owing to the great hitch, a great menace to progress. Because every day mankind hates the business of beef-steaks and dish-washing, heavy labour and howling babies more bitterly.

The housewife is full of resentment—she can't help it. The young husband is full of resentment—he can't help it, when he has to plant potatoes to eke out the family income. The housemaid is full of resentment, the navvy is full of resentment, the collier is full of resentment, and the collier's wife is full of resentment, because her man can't earn a proper wage. Resentment grows as the strange fastidiousness of modern men and woman increases. Resentment, resentment, resentment—because the basis of life is still brutally physical, and that has become repulsive to us. Mr. Ford, being in his own way a genius, has realized that what the modern workman wants, just like the modern gentleman, is abstraction. The modern workman doesn't *want* to be "interested" in his job. He wants to be as little interested, as nearly perfectly mechanical, as possible. This is the great will of the people, and there is no gainsaying it. It is precisely the same in woman as in man. Woman demands an electric cooker because it makes no call on her attention or her "interest" at all. It is almost a pure abstraction, a few switches, and no physical contact, no *dirt*, which is the inevitable result of physical contact, at all. If only we could make housework a real abstraction, a matter of turning switches and guiding a machine, the housewife would again be more or less content. But it can't quite be done, even in America.

And the resentment is enormous. The resentment against *eating*, in the breast of modern woman who has to prepare food, is profound. Why all this work and bother about *mere eating*? Why, indeed? Because neither science nor evolution has kept up with the change in human feeling, and beef-steaks are beef-steaks still, no matter how detestable they may have become to the people who have to prepare them. The loathsome fuss of food continues, and will continue, in spite of all talk about tabloids. The loathsome digging of coal out of the earth, by half-naked men, continues, deep underneath Mr. Ford's super-factories. There it is, and there it will be, and you can't get away from it. While men quite enjoyed hewing coal, which they did, and while women really enjoyed cooking, even with a coal range, which they did—then all was well. But suppose society *en bloc* comes to hate the thought of sweating cooking over a hot range, or sweating hacking at a coal-seam, then what are you to do? You have to ask, or to demand, that a large section of society shall do something they have come to hate doing, and which you would hate to do yourself. What then? Resentment and ill-feeling!

Social life means all classes of people living more or less harmoniously together. And private life means men and women, man and woman living together more or less congenially. If there is serious discord between the social classes, then society is threatened with confusion. If there is serious discord between man and woman, then the individual, and that means practically everybody, is threatened with internal confusion and unhappiness.

Now it is quite easy to keep the working classes in harmonious working order, so long as you don't ask them to do work they simply do not want to do. The Board-schools, however, did the fatal deed. They said to the boys: Work is noble, but what you want is to *get on*, you don't want to stick down a coal-mine all your life. Rise up, and do *clean* work! become a school teacher or a clerk, not a common collier.

This is sound Board-school education, and is in keeping with all the noblest social ideals of the last century. Unfortunately it entirely overlooks the unpleasant effect of such teaching on those who *cannot* get on, and who must perforce stick down a coal-mine all their lives. And these, in the Board-school of a mining district, are at least 90 per cent of the boys; it must be so. So that 90 per cent of these Board-school scholars are deliberately taught, at school, to be malcontents, taught to despise themselves for not having "got on," for not having "got out of the pit," for sticking down all their lives doing "dirty work" and being "common colliers." Naturally, every collier, doomed himself, wants to get his boys out of the pit, to be gentlemen. And since this again is *impossible* in 90 per cent of the cases, the number of "gentlemen," or clerks and school teachers, being strictly proportionate to the number of colliers, there comes again the sour disillusion. So that by the third generation you have exactly what you've got today, the young malcontent collier. He has been deliberately produced by modern education coupled with modern conditions, and is logically, inevitably and naturally what he is: a malcontent collier. According to all the accepted teaching, he ought to have risen and bettered himself: equal opportunity, you know. And he hasn't risen and bettered himself. Therefore he is more or less a failure in his own eyes even. He is doomed to do dirty work. He is a malcontent. Now even Mr. Ford can't make coal-mines clean and shiny and abstract. Coal won't be abstracted. Even a Soviet can't do it. A coal-mine remains a hole in the black earth, where blackened men hew and shovel and sweat. You can't abstract it, or make it an affair of pulling levers, and, what is even worse, you can't abandon it, you can't do away with it. There it is, and it has got to be. Mr. Ford forgets that his clean and pure and harmonious super-factory, where men only pull shining levers or turn bright handles, has all had to be grossly mined and smelted before it could come into existence. Mr. Ford's is one of the various heavens of industry. But

these heavens rest on various hells of labour, always did
and always will. Science rather leaves us in the lurch in
these matters. Science is supposed to remove these hells
for us. And—it doesn't. Not at all!

If you had never taught the blackened men down in
the various hells that they *were* in hell, and made them
despise themselves for being there—a *common* collier,
a *low* labourer—the mischief could never have developed so rapidly. But now we have it, all society resting
on a labour basis of smouldering resentment. And the
collier's question: How would *you* like to be a collier?—
is unanswerable. We know perfectly well we should dislike it intensely.—At the same time, my father, who
never went to a Board-school, quite liked it. But he
has been improved on. Progress! Human feeling has
changed, changed rapidly and radically. And science
has not changed conditions to fit.

What is to be done? We all loathe brute physical labour. We all think it is horrible to have to do it. We consider those that actually do it low and vile, and we have
told them so, for fifty years, urging them to get away
from it and "better themselves," which would be very
nice, if everybody *could* get on, and brute labour could
be abandoned, as, scientifically, it ought to be. But actually, not at all. We are forced to go on forcing a very
large proportion of society to remain "unbettered," "low
and common," "common colliers, common labourers,"
since a very large portion of humanity must still spend
its life labouring, now and in the future, science having
let us down in this respect. You can't teach mankind to
"better himself" unless you'll better the gross earth to
fit him. And the gross earth remains what it was, and
man its slave. For neither science nor evolution shows
any signs of saving us from our gross necessities. The labouring masses are and will be, even if all else is swept

away: because they must be. They represent the gross
necessity of man, which science has failed to save us
from.

So then, what? The only thing that remains to be done
is to make labour as likeable as possible, and try to teach
the labouring masses to like it: which, given the trend of
modern feeling, not only sounds, but is, fatuous. Mankind *en bloc* gets more fastidious and more "nice" every
day. Every day it loathes dirty work more deeply. And
every day the whole pressure of social consciousness
works towards making everybody more fastidious, more
"nice," more refined, and more unfit for dirty work. Before you make all humanity unfit for dirty work, you
should first remove the necessity for dirty work.

But such being the condition of men and women with
regard to work—a condition of repulsion in the breasts
of men and women for the work that has got to be done
—what about private life, the relation between man and
woman? How does the new fastidiousness and nicety of
mankind affect this?

Profoundly! The revulsion from physical labour,
physical effort, physical contact has struck a death-
blow at marriage and home-life. In the great trend of
the times, a woman cannot save herself from the universal dislike of housework, housekeeping, rearing children and keeping a home going. Women make the
most unselfish efforts in this direction, because it is
generally expected of them. But this cannot remove
the *instinctive* dislike of preparing meals and scouring
saucepans, cleaning baby's bottles or darning the man's
underwear, which a large majority of women feel today.
It is something which there is no denying, a real physical
dislike of doing these things. Many women school themselves and are excellent housewives, physically disliking

it all the time. And this, though admirable, is wearing. It is an exhaustive process, with many ill results.

Can it be possible that women actually ever did like scouring saucepans and cleaning the range?—I believe some few women still do. I believe that twenty years ago, even, the majority of women enjoyed it. But what, then, has happened? Can human instincts really change?

They can, and in the most amazing fashion. And this is the great problem for the sociologist: the violent change in human instinct, especially in women. Woman's instinct used to be all for home, shelter, the protection of the man, and the happiness of running her own house. Now it is all against. Woman *thinks* she wants a lovely little home of her own, but her instinct is all against it, when it means matrimony. She *thinks* she wants a man of her own, but her instinct is dead against having him around all the time. She would like him on a long string, that she can let out or pull in, as she feels inclined. But she just doesn't want him inevitably and insidiously there all the time—not even every evening—not even for week-ends, if it's got to be a fixture. She wants him to be merely intermittent in her landscape, even if he is always present in her soul, and she writes him the most intimate letters every day. All well and good! But her instinct is against him, against his permanent and perpetual physical presence. She doesn't want to feel his presence as something material, unavoidable, and permanent. It goes dead against her grain, it upsets her instinct. She loves him, she loves, even, being faithful to him. But she doesn't want him substantially around. She doesn't want his actual physical presence—except in snatches. What she *really* loves is the thought of him, the idea of him, the *distant* communion with him— varied with snatches of actually being together, like little festivals, which we are more or less glad when they are over.

Now a great many modern girls feel like this, even when they force themselves to behave in the conventional side-by-side fashion. And a great many men feel the same—though perhaps not so acutely as the women. Young couples may force themselves to be conventional husbands and wives, but the strain is often cruel, and the result often disastrous.

Now then we see the trend of our civilization, in terms of human feeling and human relation. It is, and there is no denying it, towards a greater and greater abstraction from the physical, towards a further and further physical separateness between men and women, and between individual and individual. Young men and women today are together all the time, it will be argued. Yes, but they are together as good sports, good chaps, in strange independence of one another, intimate one moment, strangers the next, hands-off! all the time, and as little connected as the bits in a kaleidoscope.

The young have the fastidiousness, the nicety, the revulsion from the physical, intensified. To the girl of to-day, a man whose physical presence she is aware of, especially a bit *heavily* aware of, is or becomes really abhorrent. She wants to fly away from him to the uttermost ends of the earth. And as soon as women or girls get a bit female physical, young men's nerves go all to pieces. The sexes can't stand one another. They adore one another as spiritual or personal creatures, all talk and wit and back-chat, or jazz and motor-cars and machines, or tennis and swimming—even sitting in bathing-suits all day on a beach. But this is all peculiarly non-physical, a flaunting of the body in its non-physical, merely optical aspect. So much nudity, fifty years ago, would have made man and woman quiver through and through. Now, not at all! People flaunt their bodies to show how unphysical they are. The more the girls are not desired, the more they uncover themselves.

And this means, when we analyse it out, repulsion. The young are, in a subtle way, physically repulsive to one another, the girl to the man and the man to the girl. And they rather enjoy the feeling of repulsion, it is a sort of contest. It is as if the young girl said to the young man today: I rather like you, you know. You are so thrillingly repulsive to me.—And as if the young man replied: Same here!—There may be, of course, an intense bodiless sort of affection between young men and women. But as soon as either becomes a positive physical presence to the other, immediately there is repulsion.

And marriages based on the thrill of physical repulsion, as so many are today, even when coupled with mental "adoring" or real wistful, bodiless affection, are in the long run—not so very long, either—catastrophic. There you have it, the great "spirituality," the great "betterment" or refinement; the great fastidiousness; the great "niceness" of feeling; when a girl must be a flat, thin, bodiless stick, and a boy a correct manikin, each of them abstracted towards real caricature. What does it all amount to? What is its motive force?

What it amounts to, really, is physical repulsion. The great spirituality of our age means that we are all physically repulsive to one another. The great advance in refinement of feeling and squeamish fastidiousness means that we hate the *physical* existence of anybody and everybody, even ourselves. The amazing move into abstraction on the part of the whole of humanity—the film, the radio, the gramophone—means that we loathe the physical element in our amusements, we don't *want* the physical contact, we want to get away from it. We don't *want* to look at flesh and blood people—we want to watch their shadows on a screen. We don't *want* to hear their actual voices: only transmitted through a machine. We must get away from the physical.

The vast mass of the lower classes—and this is most extraordinary—are even more grossly abstracted, if we may use the term, than the educated classes. The uglier sort of working man today truly has no body and no real feelings at all. He eats the most wretched food, because taste has left him, he only *sees* his meal, he never *really* eats it. He drinks his beer by idea, he no longer tastes it at all. This must be so, or the food and beer could not be as bad as they are. And as for his relation to his women—his poor women—they are pegs to hang clothes on, and there's an end of them. It is a horrible state of feelingless depravity, atrophy of the senses.

But under it all, as ever, as everywhere, vibrates the one great impulse of our civilization, physical recoil from every other being and from every form of physical existence. Recoil, recoil, recoil. Revulsion, revulsion, revulsion. Repulsion, repulsion, repulsion. This is the rhythm that underlies our social activity, everywhere, with regard to physical existence.

Now we are all basically and permanently physical. So is the earth, so even is the air. What then is going to be the result of all this recoil and repulsion, which our civilization has deliberately fostered?

The result is really only one and the same: some form of collective social madness. Russia, being a very physical country, was in a frantic state of physical recoil and "spirituality" twenty years ago. We can look on the revolution, really, as nothing but a great outburst of anti-physical insanity; we can look on Soviet Russia as nothing but a logical state of society established in anti-physical insanity.—Physical and material are, of course, not the same; in fact, they are subtly opposite. The ma-

chine is absolutely material, and absolutely anti-physical·
—as even our fingers know. And the Soviet is established
on the image of the machine, "pure" materialism. The
Soviet hates the real physical body far more deeply
than it hates Capital. It mixes it up with the bourgeois.
But it sees very little danger in it, since all western civilization is now mechanized, materialized and ready for
an outburst of insanity which shall throw us all into some
purely machine-driven unity of lunatics.

What about it, then? What about it, men and women?
The only thing to do is to get your bodies back, men
and women. A great part of society is irreparably lost:
abstracted into non-physical, mechanical entities whose
motive power is still recoil, revulsion, repulsion, hate,
and, ultimately, blind destruction. The driving force *underneath* our society remains the same: recoil, revulsion,
hate. And let this force once run out of hand, and we
know what to expect. It is not only in the working class.
The well-to-do classes are just as full of the driving
force of recoil, revulsion, which ultimately becomes hate.
The force is universal in our spiritual civilization. Let it
once run out of hand, and then——

It only remains for some men and women, individuals,
to try to get back their bodies and preserve the other
flow of warmth, affection and physical unison. There is
nothing else to do.

Review

Nigger Heaven, by Carl Van Vechten; *Flight*, by Walter
White; *Manhattan Transfer*, by John Dos Passos; *In Our
Time*, by Ernest Hemingway

Nigger Heaven is one of the Negro names for Harlem,
that dismal region of hard stone streets way up Seventh

Avenue beyond One Hundred and Twenty-Fifth Street, where the population is all coloured, though not much of it is real black. In the daytime, at least, the place aches with dismalness and a loose-end sort of squalor, the stone of the streets seeming particularly dead and stony, obscenely stony.

Mr. Van Vechten's book is a nigger book, and not much of a one. It opens and closes with nigger cabaret scenes in feeble imitation of Cocteau or Morand, second-hand attempts to be wildly lurid, with background ef-fects of black and vermilion velvet. The middle is a lot of stuffing about high-brow niggers, the heroine being one of the old-fashioned school-teacherish sort, this time an assistant in a public library; and she has only one picture in her room, a reproduction of the Mona Lisa, and on her shelves only books by James Branch Cabell, Anatole France, Jean Cocteau, etc.; in short, the literature of disillusion. This is to show how refined she is. She is just as refined as any other "idealistic" young heroine who earns her living, and we have to be reminded continually that she is golden-brown.

Round this heroine goes on a fair amount of "race" talk, nigger self-consciousness which, if it didn't happen to mention it was black, would be taken for merely an-other sort of self-conscious grouch. There is a love-affair —a rather palish-brown—which might go into any fee-ble American novel whatsoever. And the whole coloured thing is peculiarly colourless, a second-hand dish barely warmed up.

The author seems to feel this, so he throws in a highly spiced nigger in a tartan suit, who lives off women— rather in the distance—and two perfect red-peppers of nigger millionairesses who swim in seas of champagne and have lovers and fling them away and sniff drugs; in short, altogether the usual old bones of hot stuff, warmed up with all the fervour the author can command—which isn't much.

It is a false book by an author who lingers in nigger cabarets hoping to heaven to pick up something to write about and make a sensation—and, of course, money.

Flight is another nigger book; much more respectable, but not much more important. The author, we are told, is himself a Negro. If we weren't told, we should never know. But there is rather a call for coloured stuff, hence we had better be informed when we're getting it.

The first part of *Flight* is interesting—the removal of Creoles, just creamy-coloured old French-Negro mixture, from the Creole quarter of New Orleans to the Negro quarter of Atlanta. This is real, as far as life goes, and external reality: except that to me, the Creole quarter of New Orleans is dead and lugubrious as a Jews' burying ground, instead of highly romantic. But the first part of *Flight* is good Negro *data*.

The culture of Mr. White's Creoles is much more acceptable than that of Mr. Van Vechten's Harlem golden-browns. If it is only skin-deep, that is quite enough, since the pigmentation of the skin seems to be the only difference between the Negro and the white man. If there be such a thing as a Negro soul, then that of the Creole is very very French-American, and that of the Harlemite is very very Yankee-American. In fact, there seems no blackness about it at all. Reading Negro books, or books about Negroes written from the Negro standpoint, it is absolutely impossible to discover that the nigger is any blacker inside than we are. He's an absolute white man, save for the colour of his skin: which, in many cases, is also just as white as a Mediterranean white man's.

It is rather disappointing. One likes to cherish illusions about the race soul, the eternal Negroid soul, black and glistening and touched with awfulness and with mystery. One is not allowed. The nigger is a white man through and through. He even sees himself as white men see him, blacker than he ought to be. And his soul is an Edison gramophone on which one puts the current records: which is what the white man's soul is, just the same, a gramophone grinding over the old records.

New York is the melting-pot which melts even the nigger. The future population of this melting-pot will be a pale-greyish-brown in colour, and its psychology will be that of Mr. White or Byron Kasson, which is the psychology of a shrewd mixture of English, Irish, German, Jewish, and Negro. These are the grand ingredients of the melting-pot, and the amalgam, or alloy, whatever you call it, will be a fine mixture of all of them. Unless the melting-pot gets upset.

Apparently there is only one feeling about the Negro, wherein he differs from the white man, according to Mr. White; and this is the feeling of warmth and humanness. But *we* don't feel even that. More mercurial, but not by any means warmer or more human, the nigger seems to be: even in nigger books. And he sees in himself a talent for life which the white man has lost. But remembering glimpses of Harlem and Louisiana, and the down-at-heel greyness of the colourless Negro *ambiente,* myself I don't feel even that.

But the one thing the Negro *knows* he can do, is sing and dance. He knows it because the white man has pointed it out to him so often. There, again, however, disappointment! About one nigger in a thousand amounts to anything in song or dance: the rest are just as songful and limber as the rest of Americans.

Mimi, the pale-biscuit heroine of *Flight,* neither sings nor dances. She is rather cultured and makes smart dresses and passes over as white, then marries a well-to-do white American, but leaves him because he is not "live" enough, and goes back to Harlem. It is just what Nordic wives do, just how they feel about their husbands. And if they don't go to Harlem, they go somewhere else. And then they come back. As Mimi will do. Three months of Nigger Heaven will have her fed up, and back she'll be over the white line, settling again in the Washington Square region, and being "of French extraction." Nothing is more monotonous than these removals.

All these books might as well be called *Flight*. They give one the impression of swarms of grasshoppers hopping big hops, and buzzing occasionally on the wing, all from nowhere to nowhere, all over the place. What's the point of all this flight, when they start from nowhere and alight on nowhere? For the Nigger Heaven is as sure a nowhere as anywhere else.

Manhattan Transfer is still a greater ravel of flights from nowhere to nowhere. But at least the author knows it, and gets a kind of tragic significance into the fact. John Dos Passos is a far better writer than Mr. Van Vechten or Mr. White, and his book is a far more real and serious thing. To me, it is the best modern book about New York that I have read. It is an endless series of glimpses of people in the vast scuffle of Manhattan Island, as they turn up again and again and again, in a confusion that has no obvious rhythm, but wherein at last we recognize the systole-diastole of success and failure, the end being all failure, from the point of view of life; and then another flight towards another nowhere.

If you set a blank record revolving to receive all the sounds, and a film-camera going to photograph all the motions, of a scattered group of individuals, at the points where they meet and touch in New York, you would

more or less get Mr. Dos Passos's method. It is a rush
of disconnected scenes and scraps, a breathless confusion of isolated moments in a group of lives, pouring on
through the years, from almost every part of New York.
But the order of time is more or less kept. For half a
page you are on the Lackawanna ferry-boat—or one of
the ferry-boats—in the year 1900 or somewhere there—
the next page you are in the Brevoort a year later—two
pages ahead it is Central Park, you don't know when—
then the wharves—way up Hoboken—down Greenwich
Village—the Algonquin Hotel—somebody's apartment.
And it seems to be different people, a different girl
every time. The scenes whirl past like snowflakes. Broad-
way at night—whizz! gone!—a quick-lunch counter!
gone!—a house on Riverside Drive, the Palisades, night
—gone! But, gradually, you get to know the faces. It is
like a movie picture with an intricacy of different stories
and no close-ups and no writing in between. Mr. Dos
Passos leaves out the writing in between.

But if you are content to be confused, at length you
realize that the confusion is genuine, not affected; it is
life, not a pose. The book becomes what life is, a stream
of different things and different faces rushing along in
the consciousness, with no apparent direction save that
of time, from past to present, from youth to age, from
birth to death, and no apparent goal at all. But what
makes the rush so swift, one gradually realizes, is the
wild, strange frenzy for success: egoistic, individualistic
success.

This very complex film, of course, does not pretend
to film *all* New York. Journalists, actors and actresses,
dancers, unscrupulous lawyers, prostitutes, Jews, out-of-
work's politicians, labour agents—that kind of gang. It
is on the whole a gang, though we do touch respectability on Riverside Drive now and then. But it is a gang,

the vast loose gang of strivers and winners and losers which seems to be the very pep of New York, the city itself an inordinately vast gang.

At first it seems too warm, too passionate. One thinks: this is much too healthily lusty for the present New York. Then we realize we are away before the war, when the place was steaming and alive. There is sex, fierce, ranting sex, real New York: sex as the prime stimulus to business success. One realizes what a lot of financial success has been due to the reckless speeding-up of the sex dynamo. Get hold of the right woman, get absolutely rushed out of yourself loving her up, and you'll be able to rush a success in the city. Only, both to the man and woman, the sex must be the stimulant to success; otherwise it stimulates towards suicide, as it does with the one character whom the author loves, and who was "truly male."

The war comes, and the whole rhythm collapses. The war ends. There are the same people. Some have got success, some haven't. But success and failure alike are left irritable and inert. True, everybody is older, and the fire is dying down into spasmodic irritability. But in all the city the fire is dying down. The stimulant is played out, and you have the accumulating irritable restlessness of New York of today. The old thrill has gone, out of socialism as out of business, out of art as out of love, and the city rushes on ever faster, with more maddening irritation, knowing the apple is a Dead Sea shiner.

At the end of the book, the man who was a little boy at the beginning of the book, and now is a failure of perhaps something under forty, crosses on the ferry from Twenty-third Street, and walks away into the gruesome ugliness of the New Jersey side. He is making another flight into nowhere, to land upon nothingness.

"Say, will you give me a lift?" he asks the red-haired man at the wheel (of a furniture-van).

"How fur ye goin'?"

"I dunno . . . Pretty far."

The End.

He might just as well have said "nowhere!"

In Our Time is the last of the four American books, and Mr. Hemingway has accepted the goal. He keeps on making flights, but he has no illusion about landing anywhere. He knows it will be nowhere every time.

In Our Time calls itself a book of stories, but it isn't that. It is a series of successive sketches from a man's life, and makes a fragmentary novel. The first scenes, by one of the big lakes in America—probably Superior— are the best; when Nick is a boy. Then come fragments of war—on the Italian front. Then a soldier back home, very late, in the little town way west in Oklahoma. Then a young American and wife in post-war Europe; a long sketch about an American jockey in Milan and Paris; then Nick is back again in the Lake Superior region, getting off the train at a burnt-out town, and tramping across the empty country to camp by a trout-stream. Trout is the one passion life has left him—and this won't last long.

It is a short book: and it does not pretend to be about one man. But it is. It is as much as we need know of the man's life. The sketches are short, sharp, vivid, and most of them excellent. (The "mottoes" in front seem a little affected.) And these few sketches are enough to create the man and all his history: we need know no more.

Nick is a type one meets in the more wild and woolly regions of the United States. He is the remains of the lone trapper and cowboy. Nowadays he is educated, and through with everything. It is a state of *conscious*, accepted indifference to everything except freedom from work and the moment's interest. Mr. Hemingway does it extremely well. Nothing matters. Everything happens. One wants to keep oneself loose. Avoid one thing only: getting connected up. Don't get connected up. If you get held by anything, break it. Don't be held. Break it, and get away. Don't get away with the idea of getting somewhere else. Just get away, for the sake of getting away. Beat it! "Well, boy, I guess I'll beat it." Ah, the pleasure in saying that!

Mr. Hemingway's sketches, for this reason, are excellent: so short, like striking a match, lighting a brief sensational cigarette, and it's over. His young love-affair ends as one throws a cigarette-end away. "It isn't fun any more."—"Everything's gone to hell inside me."

It is really honest. And it explains a great deal of sentimentality. When a thing has gone to hell inside you, your sentimentalism tries to pretend it hasn't. But Mr. Hemingway is through with the sentimentalism. "It isn't fun any more. I guess I'll beat it."

And he beats it, to somewhere else. In the end he'll be a sort of tramp, endlessly moving on for the sake of moving away from where he is. This is a negative goal, and Mr. Hemingway is really good, because he's perfectly straight about it. He is like Krebs, in that devastating Oklahoma sketch: he doesn't love anybody, and it nauseates him to have to pretend he does. He doesn't even *want* to love anybody; he doesn't want to go anywhere, he doesn't want to do anything. He wants just to lounge around and maintain a healthy state of nothingness inside himself, and an attitude of negation to everything outside himself. And why shouldn't he, since that is exactly and sincerely what he feels? If he really *doesn't* care, then why should he care? Anyhow, he doesn't.

Pornography and Obscenity

WHAT they are depends, as usual, entirely on the individual. What is pornography to one man is the laughter of genius to another.

The word itself, we are told, means "pertaining to harlots"—the graph of the harlot. But nowadays, what is a harlot? If she was a woman who took money from a man in return for going to bed with him—really, most wives sold themselves, in the past, and plenty of harlots gave themselves, when they felt like it, for nothing. If a woman hasn't got a tiny streak of a harlot in her, she's a dry stick as a rule. And probably most harlots had somewhere a streak of womanly generosity. Why be so cut and dried? The law is a dreary thing, and its judgments have nothing to do with life

The same with the word "obscene": nobody knows what it means. Suppose it were derived from *obscena:* that which might not be represented on the stage; how much further are you? None! What is obscene to Tom is not obscene to Lucy or Joe, and really, the meaning of a word has to wait for majorities to decide it. If a play shocks ten people in an audience, and doesn't shock the remaining five hundred, then it is obscene to ten and innocuous to five hundred; hence, the play is not obscene, by majority. But *Hamlet* shocked all the Cromwellian Puritans, and shocks nobody today, and some of Aristophanes shocks everybody today, and didn't galvanize the later Greeks at all, apparently. Man is a changeable beast, and words change their meanings with him, and things are not what they seemed, and what's what becomes what isn't, and if we think we

know where we are it's only because we are so rapidly
being translated to somewhere else. We have to leave
everything to the majority, everything to the majority,
everything to the mob, the mob, the mob. They know
what is obscene and what isn't, they do. If the lower ten
million doesn't know better than the upper ten men,
then there's something wrong with mathematics. Take
a vote on it! Show hands, and prove it my count! *Vox
populi, vox Dei. Odi profanum vulgum! Profanum vulgum.*

So it comes down to this: if you are talking to the
mob, the meaning of your words is the mob-meaning,
decided by majority. As somebody wrote to me: the
American law on obscenity is very plain, and America is
going to enforce the law. Quite, my dear, quite, quite,
quite! The mob knows all about obscenity. Mild little
words that rhyme with spit or farce are the height of
obscenity. Supposing a printer put "h" in the place of
"p," by mistake, in that mere word spit? Then the great
American public knows that this man has committed an
obscenity, an indecency, that his act was lewd, and as a
compositor he was pornographical. You can't tamper
with the great public, British or American. *Vox populi,
vox Dei,* don't you know. If you don't we'll let you know
it. At the same time, this *vox Dei* shouts with praise over
moving-pictures and books and newspaper accounts
that seem, to a sinful nature like mine, completely disgusting and obscene. Like a real prude and Puritan, I
have to look the other way. When obscenity becomes
mawkish, which is its palatable form for the public, and
when the *Vox populi, vox Dei* is hoarse with sentimental
indecency, then I have to steer away, like a Pharisee,
afraid of being contaminated. There is a certain kind of
sticky universal pitch that I refuse to touch.

So again, it comes down to this: you accept the majority, the mob, and its decisions, or you don't. You bow down before the *Vox populi, vox Dei,* or you plug your ears not to hear its obscene howl. You perform your antics to please the vast public, *Deus ex machina,* or you refuse to perform for the public at all, unless now and then to pull its elephantine and ignominious leg.

When it comes to the meaning of anything, even the simplest word, then you must pause. Because there are two great categories of meaning, for ever separate. There is mob-meaning, and there is individual meaning. Take even the word *bread.* The mob-meaning is merely: stuff made with white flour into loaves that you eat. But take the individual meaning of the word bread: the white, the brown, the corn-pone, the home-made, the smell of bread just out of the oven, the crust, the crumb, the unleavened bread, the shew-bread, the staff of life, sour-dough bread, cottage loaves, French bread, Viennese bread, black bread, a yesterday's loaf, rye, graham, barley, rolls, *Bretzeln, Kringeln,* scones, damper, matsen —there is no end to it all, and the word bread will take you to the ends of time and space, and far-off down avenues of memory. But this is individual. The word bread will take the individual off on his own journey, and its meaning will be his own meaning, based on his own genuine imagination reactions. And when a word comes to us in its individual character, and starts in us the individual responses, it is great pleasure to us. The American advertisers have discovered this, and some of the cunningest American literature is to be found in advertisements of soap-suds, for example. These advertisements are *almost* prose-poems. They give the word soap-suds a bubbly, shiny individual meaning, which is very skilfully poetic, would, perhaps, be quite poetic to the mind which could forget that the poetry was bait on a hook.

Business is discovering the individual, dynamic meaning of words, and poetry is losing it. Poetry more and
more tends to far-fetch its word-meanings, and this results once again in mob-meanings, which arouse only a
mob-reaction in the individual. For every man has a
mob-self and an individual self, in varying proportions.
Some men are almost all mob-self, incapable of imaginative individual responses. The worst specimens of mob-
self are usually to be found in the professions, lawyers,
professors, clergymen and so on. The business man,
much maligned, has a tough outside mob-self, and a
scared, floundering yet still alive individual self. The
public, which is feeble-minded like an idiot, will never
be able to preserve its individual reactions from the
tricks of the exploiter. The public is always exploited
and always will be exploited. The methods of exploita-
tion merely vary. Today the public is tickled into laying
the golden egg. With imaginative words and individual
meanings it is tricked into giving the great goose-cackle
of mob-acquiescence. *Vox populi, vox Dei.* It has always
been so, and will always be so. Why? Because the public has not enough wit to distinguish between mob-
meanings and individual meanings. The mass is for ever
vulgar, because it can't distinguish between its own
original feelings and feelings which are diddled into
existence by the exploiter. The public is always profane,
because it is controlled from the outside, by the trick-
ster, and never from the inside, by its own sincerity.
The mob is always obscene, because it is always second-
hand.

Which brings us back to our subject of pornography
and obscenity. The reaction to any word may be, in any
individual, either a mob-reaction or an individual reaction. It is up to the individual to ask himself: Is my

reaction individual, or am I merely reacting from my mob-self?

When it comes to the so-called obscene words, I should say that hardly one person in a million escapes mob-reaction. The first reaction is almost sure to be mob-reaction, mob-indignation, mob-condemnation. And the mob gets no further. But the real individual has second thoughts and says: Am I really shocked? Do I *really* feel outraged and indignant? And the answer of any individual is bound to be: No, I am not shocked, not outraged, nor indignant. I know the word, and take it for what it is, and I am not going to be jockeyed into making a mountain out of a mole-hill, not for all the law in the world.

Now if the use of a few so-called obscene words will startle man or woman out of a mob-habit into an individual state, well and good. And word prudery is so universal a mob-habit that it is time we were startled out of it.

But still we have only tackled obscenity, and the problem of pornography goes even deeper. When a man is startled into his individual self, he still may not be able to know, inside himself, whether Rabelais is or is not pornographic: and over Aretino or even Boccaccio he may perhaps puzzle in vain, torn between different emotions.

One essay on pornography, I remember, comes to the conclusion that pornography in art is that which is calculated to arouse sexual desire, or sexual excitement. And stress is laid on the fact, whether the author or artist *intended* to arouse sexual feelings. It is the old vexed question of intention, become so dull today, when we know how strong and influential our unconscious intentions are. And why a man should be held guilty of his conscious intentions, and innocent of his unconscious intentions, I don't know, since every man is more made

up of unconscious intentions than of conscious ones. I
am what I am, not merely what I think I am.

However! We take it, I assume, that *pornography* is
something base, something unpleasant. In short, we
don't like it. And why don't we like it? Because it arouses
sexual feelings?

I think not. No matter how hard we may pretend
otherwise, most of us rather like a moderate rousing of
our sex. It warms us, stimulates us like sunshine on a
grey day. After a century or two of Puritanism, this is
still true of most people. Only the mob-habit of condemning any form of sex is too strong to let us admit it
naturally. And there are, of course, many people who
are genuinely repelled by the simplest and most natural
stirrings of sexual feeling. But these people are per-
verts who have fallen into hatred of their fellow men:
thwarted, disappointed, unfulfilled people, of whom,
alas, our civilization contains so many. And they nearly
always enjoy some unsimple and unnatural form of sex
excitement, secretly.

Even quite advanced art critics would try to make us
believe that any picture or book which had "sex appeal"
was ipso facto a bad book or picture. This is just canting
hypocrisy. Half the great poems, pictures, music, stories
of the whole world are great by virtue of the beauty of
their sex appeal. Titian or Renoir, the Song of Solomon
or *Jane Eyre*, Mozart or "Annie Laurie," the loveliness
is all interwoven with sex appeal, sex stimulus, call it
what you will. Even Michelangelo, who rather hated
sex, can't help filling the Cornucopia with phallic acorns.
Sex is a very powerful, beneficial and necessary stimulus
in human life, and we are all grateful when we feel its
warm, natural flow through us, like a form of sunshine.

So we can dismiss the idea that sex appeal in art is
pornography. It may be so to the grey Puritan, but the

grey Puritan is a sick man, soul and body sick, so why should we bother about his hallucinations? Sex appeal, of course, varies enormously. There are endless different kinds, and endless degrees of each kind. Perhaps it may be argued that a mild degree of sex appeal is not pornographical, whereas a high degree is. But this is a fallacy. Boccaccio at his hottest seems to me less pornographical than *Pamela* or *Clarissa Harlowe* or even *Jane Eyre*, or a host of modern books or films which pass uncensored. At the same time Wagner's *Tristan and Isolde* seems to me very near to pornography, and so, even, do some quite popular Christian hymns.

What is it, then? It isn't a question of sex appeal, merely: nor even a question of deliberate intention on the part of the author or artist to arouse sexual excitement. Rabelais sometimes had a deliberate intention, so, in a different way, did Boccaccio. And I'm sure poor Charlotte Brontë, or the authoress of *The Sheik*, did not have any deliberate intention to stimulate sex feelings in the reader. Yet I find *Jane Eyre* verging towards pornography and Boccaccio seems to me always fresh and wholesome.

The late British Home Secretary, who prides himself on being a very sincere Puritan, grey, grey in every fibre, said with indignant sorrow in one of his outbursts on improper books: "—and these two young people, who had been perfectly pure up till that time, after reading this book went and had sexual intercourse together!!!" *One up to them!* is all we can answer. But the grey Guardian of British Morals seemed to think that if they had murdered one another, or worn each other to rags of nervous prostration, it would have been much better. The grey disease!

Then what is pornography, after all this? It isn't sex appeal or sex stimulus in art. It isn't even a deliberate intention on the part of the artist to arouse or excite sexual feelings. There's nothing wrong with sexual feelings in themselves, so long as they are straightforward and not sneaking or sly. The right sort of sex stimulus is invaluable to human daily life. Without it the world grows grey. I would give everybody the gay Renaissance stories to read, they would help to shake off a lot of grey self-importance, which is our modern civilized disease.

But even I would censor genuine pornography, rigorously. It would not be very difficult. In the first place, genuine pornography is almost always underworld, it doesn't come into the open. In the second, you can recognize it by the insult it offers, invariably, to sex, and to the human spirit.

Pornography is the attempt to insult sex, to do dirt on it. This is unpardonable. Take the very lowest instance, the picture post-card sold under hand, by the underworld, in most cities. What I have seen of them have been of an ugliness to make you cry. The insult to the human body, the insult to a vital human relationship! Ugly and cheap they make the human nudity, ugly and degraded they make the sexual act, trivial and cheap and nasty.

It is the same with the books they sell in the underworld. They are either so ugly they make you ill, or so fatuous you can't imagine anybody but a cretin or a moron reading them, or writing them.

It is the same with the dirty limericks that people tell after dinner, or the dirty stories one hears commercial travellers telling each other in a smoke-room. Occasionally there is a really funny one, that redeems a great deal. But usually they are just ugly and repellent, and the so-called "humour" is just a trick of doing dirt on sex.

Now the human nudity of a great many modern

people is just ugly and degraded, and the sexual act between modern people is just the same, merely ugly and
degrading. But this is nothing to be proud of. It is the
catastrophe of our civilization. I am sure no other civilization, not even the Roman, has showed such a vast
proportion of ignominious and degraded nudity, and
ugly, squalid, dirty sex. Because no other civilization has
driven sex into the underworld, and nudity to the w.c.

The intelligent young, thank heaven, seem determined
to alter in these two respects. They are rescuing their
young nudity from the stuffy, pornographical, hole-and-
corner underworld of their elders, and they refuse to
sneak about the sexual relation. This is a change the
elderly grey ones of course deplore, but it is in fact a
very great change for the better, and a real revolution.

But it is amazing how strong is the will in ordinary,
vulgar people to do dirt on sex. It was one of my fond
illusions, when I was young, that the ordinary healthy-
seeming sort of men, in railway carriages, or the smoke-
room of an hotel or a pullman, were healthy in their
feelings and had a wholesome rough devil-may-care attitude towards sex. All wrong! All wrong! Experience
teaches that common individuals of this sort have a disgusting attitude towards sex, a disgusting contempt of it,
a disgusting desire to insult it. If such fellows have intercourse with a woman, they triumphantly feel that they
have done her dirt, and now she is lower, cheaper, more
contemptible than she was before.

It is individuals of this sort that tell dirty stories,
carry indecent picture post-cards, and know the indecent books. This is the great pornographical class—
the really common men-in-the-street and women-in-the-
street. They have as great a hate and contempt of sex as
the greyest Puritan, and when an appeal is made to
them, they are always on the side of the angels. They

PORNOGRAPHY AND OBSCENITY   655

insist that a film-heroine shall be a neuter, a sexless thing of washed-out purity. They insist that real sex-feeling shall only be shown by the villain or villainess, low lust. They find a Titian or a Renoir really indecent, and they don't want their wives and daughters to see it.

Why? Because they have the grey disease of sex-hatred, coupled with the yellow disease of dirt-lust. The sex functions and the excrementory functions in the human body work so close together, yet they are, so to speak, utterly different in direction. Sex is a creative flow, the excrementory flow is towards dissolution, de-creation, if we may use such a word. In the really healthy human being the distinction between the two is instant, our profoundest instincts are perhaps our instincts of opposition between the two flows.

But in the degraded human being the deep instincts have gone dead, and then the two flows become identical. *This* is the secret of really vulgar and of porno-graphical people: the sex flow and the excrement flow is the same to them. It happens when the psyche deteri-orates, and the profound controlling instincts collapse. Then sex is dirt and dirt is sex, and sexual excitement becomes a playing with dirt, and any sign of sex in a woman becomes a show of her dirt. This is the condition of the common, vulgar human being whose name is legion, and who lifts his voice and it is the *Vox populi, vox Dei*. And this is the source of all pornography.

And for this reason we must admit that *Jane Eyre* or Wagner's *Tristan* are much nearer to pornography than is Boccaccio. Wagner and Charlotte Brontë were both in the state where the strongest instincts have collapsed, and sex has become something slightly obscene, to be wallowed in, but despised. Mr. Rochester's sex passion is not "respectable" till Mr. Rochester is burned, blinded, disfigured, and reduced to helpless dependence. Then, thoroughly humbled and humiliated, it may be merely admitted. All the previous titillations are slightly indecent, as in *Pamela* or *The Mill on the Floss* or *Anna Karenina*. As soon as there is sex excitement with a desire to spite the sexual feeling, to humiliate it and degrade it, the element of pornography enters.

For this reason, there is an element of pornography in nearly all nineteenth century literature and very many so-called pure people have a nasty pornographical side to them, and never was the pornographical appetite stronger than it is today. It is a sign of a diseased condition of the body politic. But the way to treat the disease is to come out into the open with sex and sex stimulus. The real pornographer truly dislikes Boccaccio, because the fresh healthy naturalness of the Italian story-teller makes the modern pornographical shrimp feel the dirty worm he is. Today Boccaccio should be given to everybody, young or old, to read if they like. Only a natural fresh openness about sex will do any good, now we are being swamped by secret or semi-secret pornography. And perhaps the Renaissance story-tellers, Boccaccio, Lasca, and the rest, are the best antidote we can find now, just as more plasters of Puritanism are the most harmful remedy we can resort to.

The whole question of pornography seems to me a question of secrecy. Without secrecy there would be no pornography. But secrecy and modesty are two utterly different things. Secrecy has always an element of fear in it, amounting very often to hate. Modesty is gentle and reserved. Today, modesty is thrown to the winds, even in the presence of the grey guardians. But secrecy is hugged, being a vice in itself. And the attitude of the grey ones is: Dear young ladies, you may abandon all modesty, so long as you hug your dirty little secret.

This "dirty little secret" has become infinitely precious

to the mob of people today. It is a kind of hidden sore or inflammation which, when rubbed or scratched, gives off sharp thrills that seem delicious. So the dirty little secret is rubbed and scratched more and more, till it becomes more and more secretly inflamed, and the nervous and psychic health of the individual is more and more impaired. One might easily say that half the love novels and half the love films today depend entirely for their success on the secret rubbing of the dirty little secret. You can call this sex excitement if you like, but it is sex excitement of a secretive, furtive sort, quite special. The plain and simple excitement, quite open and wholesome, which you find in some Boccaccio stories is not for a minute to be confused with the furtive excitement aroused by rubbing the dirty little secret in all secrecy in modern best-sellers. This furtive, sneaking, cunning rubbing of an inflamed spot in the imagination is the very quick of modern pornography, and it is a beastly and very dangerous thing. You can't so easily expose it, because of its very furtiveness and its sneaking cunning. So the cheap and popular modern love novel and love film flourishes and is even praised by moral guardians, because you get the sneaking thrill fumbling under all the purity of dainty underclothes, without one single gross word to let you know what is happening.

Without secrecy there would be no pornography. But if pornography is the result of sneaking secrecy, what is the result of pornography? What is the effect on the individual?

The effect on the individual is manifold, and always pernicious. But one effect is perhaps inevitable. The pornography of today, whether it be the pornography of the rubber-goods shop or the pornography of the popular novel, film, and play, is an invariable stimulant to the vice of self-abuse, onanism, masturbation, call it what you will. In young or old, man or woman, boy or girl, modern pornography is a direct provocative of masturbation. It cannot be otherwise. When the grey ones wail that the young man and the young woman went and had sexual intercourse, they are bewailing the fact that the young man and the young woman didn't go separately and masturbate. Sex must go somewhere, especially in young people. So, in our glorious civilization, it goes in masturbation. And the mass of our popular literature, the bulk of our popular amusements just exists to provoke masturbation. Masturbation is the one thoroughly secret act of the human being, more secret even than excrementation. It is the one functional result of sex-secrecy, and it is stimulated and provoked by our glorious popular literature of pretty pornography, which rubs on the dirty secret without letting you know what is happening.

Now I have heard men, teachers and clergymen, commend masturbation as the solution of an otherwise insoluble sex problem. This at least is honest. The sex problem is there, and you can't just will it away. There it is, and under the ban of secrecy and taboo in mother and father, teacher, friend, and foe, it has found its own solution, the solution of masturbation.

But what about the solution? Do we accept it? Do all the grey ones of this world accept it? If so, they must now accept it openly. We can none of us pretend any longer to be blind to the fact of masturbation, in young and old, man and woman. The moral guardians who are prepared to censor all open and plain portrayal of sex must now be made to give their only justification: We prefer that the people shall masturbate. If this preference is open and declared, then the existing forms of censorship are justified. If the moral guardians prefer that the people shall masturbate, then their present be-

haviour is correct, and popular amusements are as they
should be. If sexual intercourse is deadly sin, and
masturbation is comparatively pure and harmless, then
all is well. Let things continue as they now are.

Is masturbation so harmless, though? Is it even comparatively pure and harmless? Not to my thinking. In the
young, a certain amount of masturbation is inevitable,
but not therefore natural. I think, there is no boy or girl
who masturbates without feeling a sense of shame,
anger, and futility. Following the excitement comes the
shame, anger, humiliation, and the sense of futility.
This sense of futility and humiliation deepens as the
years go on, into a suppressed rage, because of the impossibility of escape. The one thing that it seems impossible to escape from, once the habit is formed, is
masturbation. It goes on and on, on into old age, in
spite of marriage or love affairs or anything else. And it
always carries this secret feeling of futility and humiliation, futility and humiliation. And this is, perhaps, the
deepest and most dangerous cancer of our civilization.
Instead of being a comparatively pure and harmless
vice, masturbation is certainly the most dangerous sexual
vice that a society can be afflicted with, in the long run.
Comparatively pure it may be—purity being what it is.
But harmless!!!

The great danger of masturbation lies in its merely
exhaustive nature. In sexual intercourse, there is a give
and take. A new stimulus enters as the native stimulus
departs. Something quite new is added as the old sur-
charge is removed. And this is so in all sexual intercourse
where two creatures are concerned, even in the homosexual intercourse. But in masturbation there is nothing
but loss. There is no reciprocity. There is merely the
spending away of a certain force, and no return. The
body remains, in a sense, a corpse, after the act of self-

abuse. There is no change, only deadening. There is what we call dead loss. And this is not the case in any act of sexual intercourse between two people. Two people may destroy one another in sex. But they cannot just produce the null effect of masturbation.

The only positive effect of masturbation is that it seems to release a certain mental energy, in some people. But it is mental energy which manifests itself always in the same way, in a vicious circle of analysis and impotent criticism, or else a vicious circle of false and easy sympathy, sentimentalities. The sentimentalism and the niggling analysis, often self-analysis, of most of our modern literature, is a sign of self-abuse. It is the manifestation of masturbation, the sort of conscious activity stimulated by masturbation, whether male or female. The outstanding feature of such consciousness is that there is no real object, there is only subject. This is just the same whether it be a novel or a work of science. The author never escapes from himself, he pads along within the vicious circle of himself. There is hardly a writer living who gets out of the vicious circle of himself—or a painter either. Hence the lack of creation, and the stupendous amount of production. It is a masturbation result, within the vicious circle of the self. It is self-absorption made public.

And of course the process is exhaustive. The real masturbation of Englishmen began only in the nineteenth century. It has continued with an increasing emptying of the real vitality and the real *being* of men, till now people are little more than shells of people. Most of the responses are dead, most of the awareness is dead, nearly all the constructive activity is dead, and all that remains is a sort of shell, a half-empty creature fatally self-preoccupied and incapable of either giving or taking. Incapable either of giving or taking, in the vital self. And this is masturbation's result. Enclosed within the vicious circle of the self, with no vital contacts outside, the self becomes emptier and emptier, till it is almost a nullus, a nothingness.

But null or nothing as it may be, it still hangs on to the dirty little secret, which it must still secretly rub and inflame. For ever the vicious circle. And it has a weird, blind will of its own.

One of my most sympathetic critics wrote: "If Mr. Lawrence's attitude to sex were adopted, then two things would disappear, the love lyric and the smoking-room story." And this, I think, is true. But it depends on which love lyric he means. If it is the: *Who is Sylvia, what is she?*—then it may just as well disappear. All that pure and noble and heaven-blessed stuff is only the counterpart to the smoking-room story. *Du bist wie eine Blume!* Jawohl! One can see the elderly gentleman laying his hands on the head of the pure maiden and praying God to keep her for ever so pure, so clean and beautiful. Very nice for him! Just pornography! Tickling the dirty little secret and rolling his eyes to heaven! He knows perfectly well that if God keeps the maiden so clean and pure and beautiful—in his vulgar sense of clean and pure—for a few more years, then she'll be an unhappy old maid, and not pure nor beautiful at all, only stale and pathetic. Sentimentality is a sure sign of pornography. Why should "sadness strike through the heart" of the old gentleman, because the maid was pure and beautiful? Anybody but a masturbator would have been glad and would have thought: What a lovely bride for some lucky man!—But no, not the self-enclosed, pornographic masturbator. Sadness has to strike into his beastly heart!—Away with such love lyrics, we've had too much of their pornographic poison, tickling the dirty little secret and rolling the eyes to heaven.

But if it is a question of the sound love lyric, *My love is like a red, red rose*——*!* then we are on other ground. My love is like a red, red rose only when she's *not* like a pure, pure lily. And nowadays the pure, pure lilies are mostly festering, anyhow. Away with them and their lyrics. Away with the pure, pure lily lyric, along with the smoking-room story. They are counterparts, and the one is as pornographic as the other. *Du bist wie eine Blume* is really as pornographic as a dirty story: tickling the dirty little secret and rolling the eyes to heaven. But oh, if only Robert Burns had been accepted for what he is, then love might still have been like a red, red rose.

The vicious circle, the vicious circle! The vicious circle of masturbation! The vicious circle of self-consciousness that is never *fully* self-conscious, never fully and openly conscious, but always harping on the dirty little secret. The vicious circle of secrecy, in parents, teachers, friends —everybody. The specially vicious circle of family. The vast conspiracy of secrecy in the press, and, at the same time, the endless tickling of the dirty little secret. The needless masturbation! and the endless purity! The vicious circle!

How to get out of it? There is only one way: Away with the secret! No more secrecy! The only way to stop the terrible mental itch about sex is to come out quite simply and naturally into the open with it. It is terribly difficult, for the secret is cunning as a crab. Yet the thing to do is to make a beginning. The man who said to his exasperating daughter: "My child, the only pleasure I ever had out of you was the pleasure I had in begetting you" has already done a great deal to release both himself and her from the dirty little secret.

How to get out of the dirty little secret! It is, as a matter of fact, extremely difficult for us secretive moderns. You can't do it by being wise and scientific about it, like Dr. Marie Stopes: though to be wise and scientific like Dr. Marie Stopes is better than to be utterly hypocritical, like the grey ones. But by being wise and scientific in the serious and earnest manner you only tend to disinfect the dirty little secret, and either kill sex altogether with too much seriousness and intellect, or else leave it a miserable disinfected secret. The unhappy "free and pure" love of so many people who have taken out the dirty little secret and thoroughly disinfected it with scientific words is apt to be more pathetic even than the common run of dirty-little-secret love. The danger is, that in killing the dirty little secret, you kill dynamic sex altogether, and leave only the scientific and deliberate mechanism.

This is what happens to many of those who become seriously "free" in their sex, free and pure. They have mentalized sex till it is nothing at all, nothing at all but a mental quantity. And the final result is disaster, every time.

The same is true, in an even greater proportion, of the emancipated bohemians: and very many of the young are bohemian today, whether they ever set foot in Bohemia or not. But the bohemian is "sex free." The dirty little secret is no secret either to him or her. It is, indeed, a most blatantly open question. There is nothing they don't say: everything that can be revealed is revealed. And they do as they wish.

And then what? They have apparently killed the dirty little secret, but somehow, they have killed everything else too. Some of the dirt still sticks, perhaps; sex remains still dirty. But the thrill of secrecy is gone. Hence the terrible dreariness and depression of modern Bohemia, and the inward dreariness and emptiness of so many young people of today. They have killed, they imagine, the dirty little secret. The thrill of secrecy is gone. Some of the dirt remains. And for the rest, depression, inertia, lack of life. For sex is the fountain-head of our energetic life, and now the fountain ceases to flow.

Why? For two reasons. The idealists along the Marie Stopes line, and the young bohemians of today, have killed the dirty little secret as far as their personal self goes. But they are still under its dominion socially. In the social world, in the press, in literature, film, theatre, wireless, everywhere purity and the dirty little secret reign supreme. At home, at the dinner table, it is just the same. It is the same wherever you go. The young girl and the young woman is by tacit assumption pure, virgin, sexless. *Du bist wie eine Blume.* She, poor thing, knows quite well that flowers, even lilies, have tippling yellow anthers and a sticky stigma, sex, rolling sex. But to the popular mind flowers are sexless things, and when a girl is told she is like a flower, it means she is sexless and ought to be sexless. She herself knows quite well she isn't sexless and she isn't merely like a flower. But how bear up against the great social life forced on her? She can't! She succumbs, and the dirty little secret triumphs. She loses her interest in sex, as far as men are concerned, but the vicious circle of masturbation and self-consciousness encloses her even still faster.

This is one of the disasters of young life today. Personally, and among themselves, a great many, perhaps a majority, of the young people of today have come out into the open with sex and laid salt on the tail of the dirty little secret. And this is a very good thing. But in public, in the social world, the young are still entirely under the shadow of the grey elderly ones. The grey elderly ones belong to the last century, the eunuch century, the century of the mealy-mouthed lie, the century that has tried to destroy humanity, the nineteenth century. All our grey ones are left over from this century.

And they rule us. They rule us with the grey, mealy-mouthed, canting lie of that great century of lies which, thank God, we are drifting away from. But they rule us still with the lie, for the lie, in the name of the lie. And they are too heavy and too numerous, the grey ones. It doesn't matter what government it is. They are all grey ones, left over from the last century, the century of mealy-mouthed liars, the century of purity and the dirty little secret.

So there is one cause for the depression of the young: the public reign of the mealy-mouthed lie, purity and the dirty little secret, which they themselves have privately overthrown. Having killed a good deal of the lie in their own private lives, the young are still enclosed and imprisoned within the great public lie of the grey ones. Hence the excess, the extravagance, the hysteria, and then the weakness, the feebleness, the pathetic silliness of the modern youth. They are all in a sort of prison, the prison of a great lie and a society of elderly liars. And this is one of the reasons, perhaps the main reason why the sex-flow is dying out of the young, the real energy is dying away. They are enclosed within a lie, and the sex won't flow. For the length of a complete lie is never more than three generations, and the young are the fourth generation of the nineteenth century lie.

The second reason why the sex-flow is dying is of course, that the young, in spite of their emancipation, are still enclosed within the vicious circle of self-conscious masturbation. They are thrown back into it, when they try to escape, by the enclosure of the vast public lie of purity and the dirty little secret. The most emancipated bohemians, who swank most about sex, are still utterly self-conscious and enclosed within the narcissus-masturbation circle. They have perhaps less sex even than the grey ones. The whole thing has been driven up into their heads. There isn't even the lurking hole of a dirty little secret. Their sex is more mental than their arithmetic; and as vital physical creatures they are more non-existent than ghosts. The modern bohemian is indeed a kind of ghost, not even narcissus, only the image of narcissus reflected on the face of the audience. The dirty little secret is most difficult to kill. You may put it to death publicly a thousand times, and still it reappears, like a crab, stealthily from under the submerged rocks of the personality. The French, who are supposed to be so open about sex, will perhaps be the last to kill the dirty little secret. Perhaps they don't want to. Anyhow, mere publicity won't do it.

You may parade sex abroad, but you will not kill the dirty little secret. You may read all the novels of Marcel Proust, with everything there in all detail. Yet you will not kill the dirty little secret. You will perhaps only make it more cunning. You may even bring about a state of utter indifference and sex-inertia, still without killing the dirty little secret. Or you may be the most wispy and enamoured little Don Juan of modern days, and still the core of your spirit merely be the dirty little secret. That is to say, you will still be in the narcissus-masturbation circle, the vicious circle of self-enclosure. For whenever the dirty little secret exists, it exists as the centre of the vicious circle of masturbation self-enclosure. And whenever you have the vicious circle of masturbation self-enclosure, you have at the core the dirty little secret. And the most high-flown sex-emancipated young people today are perhaps the most fatally and nervously enclosed within the masturbation self-enclosure. Nor do they want to get out of it, for there would be nothing left to come out.

But some people surely do want to come out of the awful self-enclosure. Today, practically everybody is self-conscious and imprisoned in self-consciousness. It is the joyful result of the dirty little secret. Vast numbers of people don't want to come out of the prison of their self-consciousness: they have so little left to come out with. But some people, surely, want to escape this doom of self-enclosure which is the doom of our civilization. There is surely a proud minority that wants once and for all to be free of the dirty little secret.

And the way to do it is, first, to fight the sentimental lie of purity and the dirty little secret wherever you meet it, inside yourself or in the world outside. Fight the great lie of the nineteenth century, which has soaked through our sex and our bones. It means fighting with almost every breath, for the lie is ubiquitous.

Then secondly, in his adventure of self-consciousness a man must come to the limits of himself and become aware of something beyond him. A man must be self-conscious enough to know his own limits, and to be aware of that which surpasses him. What surpasses me is the very urge of life that is within me, and this life urges me to forget myself and to yield to the stirring half-born impulse to smash up the vast lie of the world, and make a new world. If my life is merely to go on in a vicious circle of self-enclosure, masturbating self-consciousness, it is worth nothing to me. If my individual life is to be enclosed within the huge corrupt lie of society today, purity and the dirty little secret, then it is worth not much to me. Freedom is a very great reality. But it means, above all things, freedom from lies. It is, first, freedom from myself, from the lie of myself, from the lie of my all-importance, even to myself; it is freedom from the self-conscious masturbating thing I am, self-enclosed. And second, freedom from the vast lie of the social world, the lie of purity and the dirty little secret. All the other monstrous lies lurk under the cloak of this one primary lie. The monstrous lie of money lurks under the cloak of purity. Kill the purity-lie, and the money-lie will be defenceless.

We have to be sufficiently conscious, and self-conscious, to know our own limits and to be aware of the greater urge within us and beyond us. Then we cease to be primarily interested in ourselves. Then we learn to leave ourselves alone, in all the affective centres: not to force our feelings in any way, and never to force our sex. Then we make the great onslaught on to the outside lie, the inside lie being settled. And that is freedom and the fight for freedom.

The greatest of all lies in the modern world is the lie of purity and the dirty little secret. The grey ones left over from the nineteenth century are the embodiment of this lie. They dominate in society, in the press, in literature, everywhere. And, naturally, they lead the vast mob of the general public along with them.

Which means, of course, perpetual censorship of anything that would militate against the lie of purity and the dirty little secret, and perpetual encouragement of what may be called permissible pornography, pure, but tickling the dirty little secret under the delicate underclothing. The grey ones will pass and will commend floods of evasive pornography, and will suppress every outspoken word.

The law is a mere figment. In his article on the "Censorship of Books," in the *Nineteenth Century,* Viscount Brentford, the late Home Secretary, says: "Let it be remembered that the publishing of an obscene book, the issue of an obscene post-card or pornographic photograph—are all offences against the law of the land, and the Secretary of State who is the general authority for the maintenance of law and order most clearly and definitely cannot discriminate between one offence and another in discharge of his duty."

So he winds up, *ex cathedra* and infallible. But only ten lines above he has written: "I agree, that if the law were pushed to its logical conclusion, the printing and publication of such books as *The Decameron*, Benvenuto Cellini's *Life*, and Burton's *Arabian Nights* might form the subject of proceedings. But the ultimate sanction of all law is public opinion, and I do not believe for one moment that prosecution in respect of books that have been in circulation for many centuries would command public support."

Ooray then for public opinion! It only needs that a few more years shall roll. But now we see that the Secretary of State most clearly and definitely *does* discriminate between one offence and another in discharge of his duty. Simple and admitted discrimination on his part! Yet what is this public opinion? Just more lies on the part of the grey ones. They would suppress Benvenuto tomorrow, if they dared. But they would make laughing-stocks of themselves, because *tradition* backs up Benvenuto. It isn't public opinion at all. It is the grey ones afraid of making still bigger fools of themselves. But the case is simple. If the grey ones are going to be backed by a general public, then every new book that would smash the mealy-mouthed lie of the nineteenth century will be suppressed as it appears. Yet let the grey ones beware. The general public is nowadays a very unstable affair, and no longer loves its grey ones so dearly, with their old lie. And there is another public, the small public of the minority, which hates the lie and the grey ones that perpetuate the lie, and which has its own dynamic ideas about pornography and obscenity. You can't fool all the people all the time, even with purity and a dirty little secret.

And this minority public knows well that the books of many contemporary writers, both big and lesser fry, are far more pornographical than the liveliest story in *The Decameron:* because they tickle the dirty little secret and excite to private masturbation, which the wholesome Boccaccio never does. And the minority public knows full well that the most obscene painting on a Greek vase—*Thou still unravished bride of quietness*—is not as pornographical as the close-up kisses on the film, which excite men and women to secret and separate masturbation.

And perhaps one day even the general public will desire to look the thing in the face, and see for itself the difference between the sneaking masturbation pornography of the press, the film, and present-day popular literature, and then the creative portrayals of the sexual impulse that we have in Boccaccio or the Greek vase-paintings or some Pompeian art, and which are necessary for the fulfilment of our consciousness.

As it is, the public mind is today bewildered on this point, bewildered almost to idiocy. When the police raided my picture show, they did not in the least know what to take. So they took every picture where the smallest bit of the sex organ of either man or woman showed. Quite regardless of subject or meaning or anything else: they would allow anything, these dainty policemen in a picture show, except the actual sight of a fragment of the human *pudenda.* This was the police test. The dabbing on of a postage stamp—especially a green one that could be called a leaf—would in most cases have been quite sufficient to satisfy this "public opinion."

It is, we can only repeat, a condition of idiocy. And if the purity-with-a-dirty-little-secret lie is kept up much longer, the mass of society will really be an idiot, and a dangerous idiot at that. For the public is made up of individuals. And each individual has sex, and is pivoted on sex. And if, with purity and dirty little secrets, you drive every individual into the masturbation self-enclosure, and keep him there, then you will produce a state of general idiocy. For the masturbation self-enclosure produces idiots. Perhaps if we are all idiots, we shan't know it. But God preserve us.

FROM *Studies in Classic American Literature*

EDGAR ALLAN POE

POE has no truck with Indians or Nature. He makes no bones about Red Brothers and Wigwams.

He is absolutely concerned with the disintegration-processes of his own psyche. As we have said, the rhythm of American art-activity is dual.

1. A disintegrating and sloughing of the old consciousness.

2. The forming of a new consciousness underneath.

Fenimore Cooper has the two vibrations going on together. Poe has only one, only the disintegrative vibration. This makes him almost more a scientist than an artist.

Moralists have always wondered helplessly why Poe's "morbid" tales need have been written. They need to be written because old things need to die and disintegrate, because the old white psyche has to be gradually broken down before anything else can come to pass.

Man must be stripped even of himself. And it is a painful, sometimes a ghastly process.

Poe had a pretty bitter doom. Doomed to seethe down his soul in a great continuous convulsion of disintegration, and doomed to register the process. And then doomed to be abused for it, when he had performed some of the bitterest tasks of human experience that can be asked of a man. Necessary tasks, too. For the human soul must suffer its own disintegration, *consciously,* if ever it is to survive.

But Poe is rather a scientist than an artist. He is reducing his own self as a scientist reduces a salt in a crucible. It is an almost chemical analysis of the soul and consciousness. Whereas in true art there is always the double rhythm of creating and destroying.

This is why Poe calls his things "tales." They are a concatenation of cause and effect.

His best pieces, however, are not tales. They are more. They are ghastly stories of the human soul in its disruptive throes.

Moreover, they are "love" stories.

Ligeia and *The Fall of the House of Usher* are really love stories.

Love is the mysterious vital attraction which draws things together, closer, closer together. For this reason sex is the actual crisis of love. For in sex the two bloodsystems, in the male and female, concentrate and come into contact, the merest film intervening. Yet if the intervening film breaks down, it is death.

So there you are. There is a limit to everything. There is a limit to love.

The central law of all organic life is that each organism is intrinsically isolate and single in itself.

The moment its isolation breaks down, and there comes an actual mixing and confusion, death sets in.

This is true of every individual organism, from man to amœba.

But the secondary law of all organic life is that each organism only lives through contact with other matter, assimilation, and contact with other life, which means assimilation of new vibrations, non-material. Each individual organism is vivified by intimate contact with fellow organisms: up to a certain point.

So man. He breathes the air into him, he swallows food and water. But more than this. He takes into him the life of his fellow men, with whom he comes into contact, and he gives back life to them. This contact draws nearer and nearer, as the intimacy increases. When it is a whole contact, we call it love. Men live by food, but die if they eat too much. Men live by love, but die, or cause death, if they love too much.

There are two loves: sacred and profane, spiritual and sensual.

In sensual love, it is the two blood-systems, the man's and the woman's, which sweep up into pure contact, and *almost* fuse. Almost mingle. Never quite. There is always the finest imaginable wall between the two blood-waves, through which pass unknown vibrations, forces, but through which the blood itself must never break, or it means bleeding.

In spiritual love, the contact is purely nervous. The nerves in the lovers are set vibrating in unison like two instruments. The pitch can rise higher and higher. But carry this too far, and the nerves begin to break, to bleed, as it were, and a form of death sets in.

The trouble about man is that he insists on being master of his own fate, and he insists on *oneness*. For instance, having discovered the ecstasy of spiritual love, he insists that he shall have this all the time, and nothing but this, for this is life. It is what he calls "heightening" life. He wants his nerves to be set vibrating in the intense and exhilarating unison with the nerves of another being, and by this means he acquires an ecstasy of vision, he finds himself in glowing unison with all the universe.

But as a matter of fact this glowing unison is only a temporary thing, because the first law of life is that each organism is isolate in itself, it must return to its own isolation.

Yet man has tried the glow of unison, called love, and he *likes* it. It gives him his highest gratification. He wants it. He wants it all the time. He wants it and he will have it. He doesn't want to return to his own isolation. Or if he must, it is only as a prowling beast returns to its lair to rest and set out again.

This brings us to Edgar Allan Poe. The clue to him lies in the motto he chose for *Ligeia,* a quotation from the mystic Joseph Glanville: "And the will therein lieth, which dieth not. Who knoweth the mysteries of the will, with its vigour? For God is but a great Will pervading all things by nature of its intentness. Man doth not yield himself to the angels, nor unto death utterly, save only through the weakness of his feeble will."

It is a profound saying: and a deadly one.

Because if God is a great will, then the universe is but an instrument.

I don't know what God is. But He is not simply a will. That is too simple. Too anthropomorphic. Because a man wants his own will, and nothing but his will, he needn't say that God is the same will, magnified ad infinitum.

For me, there may be one God, but He is nameless and unknowable.

For me, there are also many gods, that come into me and leave me again. And they have very various wills, I must say.

But the point is Poe.

Poe had experienced the ecstasies of extreme spiritual love. And he wanted those ecstasies and nothing but those ecstasies. He wanted that great gratification, the sense of flowing, the sense of unison, the sense of heightening of life. He had experienced this gratification. He was told on every hand that this ecstasy of spiritual, nervous love was the greatest thing in life, was life itself. And he had tried it for himself, he knew that for him it *was* life itself. So he wanted it. And he *would have* it. He set up his will against the whole of the limitations of nature.

This is a brave man, acting on his own belief, and his own experience. But it is also an arrogant man, and a fool.

Poe was going to get the ecstasy and the heightening, cost what it might. He went on in a frenzy, as characteristic American women nowadays go on in a frenzy, after the very same thing: the heightening, the flow, the ecstasy. Poe tried alcohol, and any drug he could lay his hand on. He also tried any human being he could lay his hands on.

His grand attempt and achievement was with his wife; his cousin, a girl with a singing voice. With her he went in for the intensest flow, the heightening, the prismatic shades of ecstasy. It was the intensest nervous vibration of unison, pressed higher and higher in pitch, till the blood vessels of the girl broke, and the blood began to flow out loose. It was love. If you call it love.

Love can be terribly obscene.

It is love that causes the neuroticism of the day. It is love that is the prime cause of tuberculosis.

The nerves that vibrate most intensely in spiritual unisons are the sympathetic ganglia of the breast, of the throat, and the hind brain. Drive this vibration over-intensely, and you weaken the sympathetic tissues of the chest—the lungs—or of the throat, or of the lower brain, and the tubercles are given a ripe field.

But Poe drove the vibrations beyond any human pitch of endurance.

Being his cousin, she was more easily keyed to him. *Ligeia* is the chief story. Ligeia! A mental-derived name. To him the woman, his wife, was not Lucy. She was Ligeia. No doubt she even preferred it thus.

Ligeia is Poe's love-story, and its very fantasy makes it more truly his own story.

It is a tale of love pushed over a verge. And love pushed to extremes is a battle of wills between the lovers.

Love is become a battle of wills.

Which shall first destroy the other, of the lovers? Which can hold out longest, against the other?

Ligeia is still the old-fashioned woman. Her will is still to submit. She wills to submit to the vampire of her husband's consciousness. Even death.

"In stature she was tall, somewhat slender, and, in her later days, even emaciated. I would in vain attempt to portray the majesty, the quiet ease, of her demeanour, or the incomprehensible lightness and elasticity of her footfall. I was never made aware of her entrance into my closed study save by the dear music of her low, sweet voice as she placed her marble hand on my shoulder."

Poe has been so praised for his style. But it seems to me a meretricious affair. "Her marble hand" and "the elasticity of her footfall" seem more like chair-springs and mantel-pieces than a human creature. She never was quite a human creature to him. She was an instrument, from which he got his extremes of sensation. His *machine à plaisir,* as somebody says.

All Poe's style, moreover, has this mechanical quality, as his poetry has a mechanical rhythm. He never sees anything in terms of life, almost always in terms of matter, jewels, marble, etc.—or in terms of force, scientific. And his cadences are all managed mechanically. This is what is called "having a style."

What he wants to do with Ligeia is to analyse her, till he knows all her component parts, till he has got her all in his consciousness. She is some strange chemical salt which he must analyse out in the test-tubes of his brain, and then—when he's finished the analysis—*E finita la commedia!*

But she won't be quite analysed out. There is something, something he can't get. Writing of her eyes, he says: "They were, I must believe, far larger than the ordinary eyes of our race"—as if anybody would want eyes "far larger" than other folks'. "They were even fuller than the fullest of the gazelle eyes of the tribe of Nourjahad—" Which is blarney. "The hue of the orbs was the most brilliant of black and, far over them, hung jetty lashes of great length."—Suggests a whiplash. "The brows, slightly irregular in outline, had the same tint. The *strangeness*, which I found in the eyes was of a nature distinct from the formation, or the colour, or the brilliancy of the features, and must, after all, be referred to as the *expression*."—Sounds like an anatomist anatomizing a cat.—"Ah, word of no meaning! behind whose vast latitude of sound we intrench our ignorance of so much of the spiritual. The expression of the eyes of Ligeia! How for long hours have I pondered upon it! How have I, through the whole of a mid-summer night, struggled to fathom it! What was it—that something more profound than the well of Democritus—which lay far within the pupils of my beloved? What *was* it? I was possessed with a passion to discover. . . ."

It is easy to see why each man kills the thing he loves. To *know* a living thing is to kill it. You have to kill a thing to know it satisfactorily. For this reason, the desirous consciousness, the SPIRIT, is a vampire.

One should be sufficiently intelligent and interested to know a good deal *about* any person one comes into close contact with. *About* her. Or *about* him.

But to try to *know* any living being is to try to suck the life out of that being.

Above all things, with the woman one loves. Every sacred instinct teaches one that one must leave her unknown. You know your woman darkly, in the blood. To try to *know* her mentally is to try to kill her. Beware, oh woman, of the man who wants to *find out what you are.* And, oh men, beware a thousand times more of the woman who wants to *know* you, or *get* you, what you are.

It is the temptation of a vampire fiend, is this knowledge.

Man does so horribly want to master the secret of life and of individuality *with his mind.* It is like the analysis of protoplasm. You can only analyse *dead* protoplasm, and know its constituents. It is a death process.

Keep KNOWLEDGE for the world of matter, force, and function. It has got nothing to do with being.

But Poe wanted to know—wanted to know what was the strangeness in the eyes of Ligeia. She might have told him it was horror at his probing, horror at being vamped by his consciousness.

But she wanted to be vamped. She wanted to be probed by his consciousness, to be KNOWN. She paid for wanting it, too.

Nowadays it is usually the man who wants to be vamped, to be KNOWN.

Edgar Allan probed and probed. So often he seemed on the verge. But she went over the verge of death before he came over the verge of knowledge. And it is always so.

He decided, therefore, that the clue to the strangeness lay in the mystery of will. "And the will therein lieth, which dieth not . . ."

Ligeia had a "gigantic volition." . . . "An intensity in thought, action, or speech was possibly, in her, a result, or at least an index" (he really meant indication) "of that gigantic volition which, during our long intercourse, failed to give other and more immediate evidence of its existence."

I should have thought her long submission to him was chief and ample "other evidence."

"Of all the women whom I have ever known, she, the outwardly calm, the ever-placid Ligeia, was the most violently a prey to the tumultuous vultures of stern passion. And of such passion I could form no estimate, save by the miraculous expansion of those eyes which at once so delighted and appalled me—by the almost magical melody, modulation, distinctness, and placidity of her very low voice—and by the fierce energy (rendered doubly effective by contrast with her manner of utterance) of the wild words which she habitually uttered."

Poor Poe, he had caught a bird of the same feather as himself. One of those terrible cravers, who crave the further sensation. Crave to madness or death. "Vultures of stern passion" indeed! Condors.

But having recognized that the clue was in her gigantic volition, he should have realized that the process of this loving, this craving, this knowing, was a struggle of wills. But Ligeia, true to the great tradition and mode of womanly love, by her will kept herself submissive, recipient. She is the passive body who is explored and analysed into death. And yet, at times, her great female will must have revolted. "Vultures of stern passion!" With a convulsion of desire she desired his further probing and exploring. To any lengths. But then, "tumultuous vultures of stern passion." She had to fight with herself.

But Ligeia wanted to go on and on with the craving, with the love, with the sensation, with the probing, with the knowing, on and on to the end.

There is no end. There is only the rupture of death. That's where men, and women, are "had." Man is always sold, in his search for final KNOWLEDGE.

"That she loved me I should not have doubted; and I might have been easily aware that, in a bosom such as hers, love would have reigned no ordinary passion. But in death only was I fully impressed with the strength of her affection. For long hours, detaining my hand, would she pour out before me the overflowing of a heart whose more than passionate devotion amounted to idolatry." (Oh, the indecency of all this endless intimate talk!) "How had I deserved to be blessed by such confessions?" (Another man would have felt himself cursed.) "How had I deserved to be cursed with the removal of my beloved in the hour of her making them? But upon this subject I cannot bear to dilate. Let me say only that in Ligeia's more than womanly abandonment to a love, alas! unmerited, all unworthily bestowed, I at length recognized the principle of her longing with so wildly earnest a desire for the life which was fleeing so rapidly away. It is this wild longing—it is this vehement desire for life—*but* for life—that I have no power to portray —no utterance capable of expressing."

Well, that is ghastly enough, in all conscience.

"And from them that have not shall be taken away even that which they have."

"To him that hath life shall be given life, and from

him that hath not life shall be taken away even that life
which he hath."

Or her either.

These terribly conscious birds like Poe and his Ligeia
deny the very life that is in them, they want to turn it
all into talk, into *knowing*. And so life, which will *not* be
known, leaves them.

But poor Ligeia, how could she help it. It was her
doom. All the centuries of the SPIRIT, all the years of
American rebellion against the Holy Ghost, had done it
to her.

She dies, when she would rather do anything than die.
And when she dies the clue, which he only lived to
grasp, dies with her.

Foiled!

Foiled!

No wonder she shrieks with her last breath.

On the last day Ligeia dictates to her husband a
poem. As poems go, it is rather false, meretricious. But
put yourself in Ligeia's place, and it is real enough, and
ghastly beyond bearing.

> Out, out are all the lights—out all!
>   And over each quivering form
> The curtain, a funeral pall,
>   Comes down with the rush of a storm,
> And the angels, all pallid and wan,
>   Uprising, unveiling, affirm
> That the play is the tragedy "Man,"
>   And its hero the Conqueror Worm.

Which is the American equivalent for a William Blake
poem. For Blake, too, was one of these ghastly, obscene
"Knowers."

" 'O God!' half shrieked Ligeia, leaping to her feet
and extending her arms aloft with a spasmodic movement, as I made an end of these lines. 'O God! O Divine

Father!—shall these things be undeviatingly so? Shall this conqueror be not once conquered? Are we not part and parcel in Thee? Who—who knoweth the mysteries of the angels, *nor unto death utterly,* save only through the weakness of his feeble will.'"

So Ligeia dies. And yields to death at least partly. *Anche troppo.*

As for her cry to God—has not God said that those who sin against the Holy Ghost shall not be forgiven?

And the Holy Ghost is within us. It is the thing that prompts us to be real, not to push our own cravings too far, not to submit to stunts and high falutin, above all not to be too egoistic and wilful in our conscious self, but to change as the spirit inside us bids us change, and leave off when it bids us leave off, and laugh when we must laugh, particularly at ourselves, for in deadly earnestness there is always something a bit ridiculous. The Holy Ghost bids us never to be too deadly in our earnestness, always to laugh in time, at ourselves and everything. Particularly at our sublimities. Everything has its hour of ridicule—everything.

Now Poe and Ligeia, alas, couldn't laugh. They were frenziedly earnest. And frenziedly they pushed on this vibration of consciousness and unison in consciousness. They sinned against the Holy Ghost that bids us all laugh and forget, bids us know our own limits. And they weren't forgiven.

Ligeia needn't blame God. She had only her own will, her "gigantic volition" to thank, lusting after more consciousness, more beastly KNOWING.

Ligeia dies. The husband goes to England, vulgarly buys or rents a gloomy, grand old abbey, puts it into some sort of repair, and furnishes it with exotic, mysterious, theatrical splendour. Never anything open and real.

This theatrical "volition" of his. The bad taste of sensationalism.

Then he marries the fair-haired, blue-eyed Lady
Rowena Trevanion, of Tremaine. That is, she would be
a sort of Saxon-Cornish blue-blood damsel. Poor Poe!

"In halls such as these—in a bridal chamber such as
this—I passed, with the Lady of Tremaine, the unhal-
lowed hours of the first month of our marriage—passed
them with but little disquietude. That my wife dreaded
the fierce moodiness of my temper—that she shunned
and loved me but little—I could not help perceiving,
but it gave me rather pleasure than otherwise. I loathed
her with a hatred belonging rather to a demon than a
man. My memory flew back (Oh, with what intensity of
regret!) to Ligeia, the beloved, the august, the en-
tombed. I revelled in recollections of her purity . . ."
etc.

Now the vampire lust is consciously such.

In the second month of the marriage the Lady
Rowena fell ill. It is the shadow of Ligeia hangs over
her. It is the ghostly Ligeia who pours poison into
Rowena's cup. It is the spirit of Ligeia, leagued with the
spirit of the husband, that now lusts in the slow destruction of Rowena. The two vampires, dead wife and living
husband.

For Ligeia has not yielded unto death *utterly*. Her
fixed, frustrated will comes back in vindictiveness. She
could not have her way in life. So she, too, will find
victims in life. And the husband, all the time, only uses
Rowena as a living body on which to wreak his vengeance for his being thwarted with Ligeia. Thwarted from
the final KNOWING her.

And at last from the corpse of Rowena, Ligeia rises.
Out of her death, through the door of a corpse they have
destroyed between them, reappears Ligeia, still trying

to have her will, to have more love and knowledge, the final gratification which is never final, with her husband.

For it is true, as William James and Conan Doyle and the rest allow, that a spirit can persist in the after-death. Persist by its own volition. But usually, the evil persistence of a thwarted will, returning for vengeance on life. Lemures, vampires.

It is a ghastly story of the assertion of the human will, the will-to-love and the will-to-consciousness, asserted against death itself. The pride of human conceit in KNOWLEDGE.

There are terrible spirits, ghosts, in the air of America.

Eleanora, the next story, is a fantasy revealing the sensational delights of the man in his early marriage with the young and tender bride. They dwelt, he, his cousin and her mother, in the sequestered Valley of Many-coloured Grass, the valley of prismatic sensation, where everything seems spectrum-coloured. They looked down at their *own images* in the River of Silence, and drew the god Eros from that wave: out of their own self-consciousness, that is. This is a description of the life of introspection and of the love which is begotten by the self in the self, the self-made love. The trees are like serpents worshipping the sun. That is, they represent the phallic passion in its poisonous or mental activity. Everything runs to consciousness: serpents worshipping the sun. The embrace of love, which should bring darkness and oblivion, would with these lovers be a daytime thing bringing more heightened consciousness, visions, spectrum-visions, prismatic. The evil thing that daytime love-making is, and all sex-palaver.

In *Berenice* the man must go down to the sepulchre of his beloved and pull out her thirty-two small white teeth, which he carries in a box with him. It is repulsive and gloating. The teeth are the instruments of biting, of resistance, of antagonism. They often become symbols of opposition, little instruments or entities of crushing and destroying. Hence the dragon's teeth in the myth. Hence the man in *Berenice* must take possession of the irreducible part of his mistress. "Toutes ses dents étaient des idées," he says. Then they are little fixed ideas of mordant hate, of which he possesses himself.

The other great story linking up with this group is *The Fall of the House of Usher.* Here the love is between brother and sister. When the self is broken, and the mystery of the recognition of *otherness* fails, then the longing for identification with the beloved becomes a lust. And it is this longing for identification, utter merging, which is at the base of the incest problem. In psychoanalysis almost every trouble in the psyche is traced to an incest-desire. But it won't do. Incest-desire is only one of the modes by which men strive to get their gratification of the intensest vibration of the spiritual nerves, without any resistance. In the family, the natural vibration is most nearly in unison. With a stranger, there is greater resistance. Incest is the getting of gratification and the avoiding of resistance.

The root of all evil is that we all want this spiritual gratification, this flow, this apparent heightening of life, this knowledge, this valley of many-coloured grass, even grass and light prismatically decomposed, giving ecstasy. We want all this *without resistance*. We want it continually. And this is the root of all evil in us.

We ought to pray to be resisted and resisted to the bitter end. We ought to decide to have done at last with craving.

The motto to *The Fall of the House of Usher* is a couple of lines from Béranger.

> *Son coeur est un luth suspendu;*
> *Sitôt qu'on le touche il résonne.*

We have all the trappings of Poe's rather overdone, vulgar fantasy. "I reined my horse to the precipitous brink of a black and lurid tarn that lay in unruffled lustre by the dwelling, and gazed down—but with a shudder even more thrilling than before—upon the remodelled and inverted images of the grey sedge, and the ghastly tree-stems, and the vacant and eye-like windows." The House of Usher, both dwelling and family, was very old. Minute fungi overspread the exterior of the house, hanging in festoons from the eves. Gothic archways, a valet of stealthy step, sombre tapestries, ebon black floors, a profusion of tattered and antique furniture, feeble gleams of encrimsoned light through latticed panes, and over all "an air of stern, deep, irredeemable gloom"—this makes up the interior.

The inmates of the house, Roderick and Madeline Usher, are the last remnants of their incomparably ancient and decayed race. Roderick has the same large, luminous eye, the same slightly arched nose of delicate Hebrew model, as characterized Ligeia. He is ill with the nervous malady of his family. It is he whose nerves are so strung that they vibrate to the unknown quiverings of the ether. He, too, has lost his self, his living soul, and become a sensitized instrument of the external influences; his nerves are verily like an æolian harp which must vibrate. He lives in "some struggle with the grim phantasm, Fear," for he is only the physical, post-mortem reality of a living being.

It is a question how much, once the true centrality of the self is broken, the instrumental consciousness of man can register. When man becomes self-less, wafting instrumental like a harp in an open window, how much can his elemental consciousness express? The blood as it runs has its own sympathies and responses to the material world, quite apart from seeing. And the nerves

we know vibrate all the while to unseen presences, unseen forces. So Roderick Usher quivers on the edge of
material existence.

It is this mechanical consciousness which gives "the
fervid facility of his impromptus." It is the same thing
that gives Poe his extraordinary facility in versification.
The absence of real central or impulsive being in himself leaves him inordinately mechanically sensitive to
sounds and effects, associations of sounds, associations of
rhyme, for example—mechanical, facile, having no root
in any passion. It is all a secondary, meretricious process.
So we get Roderick Usher's poem, *The Haunted Palace*,
with its swift yet mechanical subtleties of rhyme and
rhythm, its vulgarity of epithet. It is all a sort of dream-
process, where the association between parts is mechanical, accidental as far as passional meaning goes.

Usher thought that all vegetable things had sentience.
Surely all material things have a *form* of sentience, even
the inorganic: surely they all exist in some subtle and
complicated tension of vibration which makes them
sensitive to external influence and causes them to have
an influence on other external objects, irrespective of
contact. It is of this vibration or inorganic consciousness
that Poe is master: the sleep-consciousness. Thus Roderick Usher was convinced that his whole surroundings,
the stones of the house, the fungi, the water in the tarn,
the very reflected image of the whole, was woven into a
physical oneness with the family, condensed, as it were,
into one atmosphere—the special atmosphere in which
alone the Ushers could live. And it was this atmosphere
which had moulded the destinies of his family.

But while ever the soul remains alive, it is the moul-
der and not the moulded. It is the souls of living men
that subtly impregnate stones, houses, mountains, con-
tinents, and give these their subtlest form. People only

become subject to stones after having lost their integral souls.

In the human realm, Roderick had one connection: his sister Madeline. She, too, was dying of a mysterious disorder, nervous, cataleptic. The brother and sister loved each other passionately and exclusively. They were twins, almost identical in looks. It was the same absorbing love between them, this process of unison in nerve-vibration, resulting in more and more extreme exaltation and a sort of consciousness, and a gradual break-down into death. The exquisitely sensitive Roger, vibrating without resistance with his sister Madeline, more and more exquisitely, and gradually devouring her, sucking her life like a vampire in his anguish of extreme love. And she asking to be sucked.

Madeline died and was carried down by her brother into the deep vaults of the house. But she was not dead. Her brother roamed about in incipient madness—a madness of unspeakable terror and guilt. After eight days they were suddenly startled by a clash of metal, then a distinct, hollow metallic, and clangorous, yet apparently muffled, reverberation. Then Roderick Usher, gibbering, began to express himself: *"We have put her living into the tomb!* Said I not that my senses were acute? I *now* tell you that I heard her first feeble movements in the hollow coffin. I heard them—many, many days ago—yet I dared not—*I dared not speak."*

It is the same old theme of "each man kills the thing he loves." He knew his love had killed her. He knew she died at last, like Ligeia, unwilling and unappeased. So, she rose again upon him. "But then without those doors there *did* stand the lofty and enshrouded figure of the Lady Madeline of Usher. There was blood upon her white robes, and the evidence of some bitter struggle upon every portion of her emaciated frame. For a mo-

ment she remained trembling and reeling to and fro
upon the threshold, then, with a low moaning cry, fell
heavily inward upon the person of her brother, and in
her violent and now final death-agonies bore him to the
floor a corpse, and a victim to the terrors he had anticipated."

It is lurid and melodramatic, but it is true. It is a
ghastly psychological truth of what happens in the last
stages of this beloved love, which cannot be separate,
cannot be isolate, cannot listen in isolation to the isolate
Holy Ghost. For it is the Holy Ghost we must live by.
The next era is the era of the Holy Ghost. And the Holy
Ghost speaks individually inside each individual: always, for ever a ghost. There is no manifestation to the
general world. Each isolate individual listening in isolation to the Holy Ghost within him.

The Ushers, brother and sister, betrayed the Holy
Ghost in themselves. They would love, love, love, without resistance. They would love, they would merge, they
would be as one thing. So they dragged each other down
into death. For the Holy Ghost says you must *not* be as
one thing with another being. Each must abide by itself,
and correspond only within certain limits.

The best tales all have the same burden. Hate is as
inordinate as love, and as slowly consuming, as secret,
as underground, as subtle. All this underground vault
business in Poe only symbolizes that which takes place
beneath the consciousness. On top, all is fair-spoken. Beneath, there is awful murderous extremity of burying
alive. Fortunato, in *The Cask of Amontillado,* is buried
alive out of perfect hatred, as the Lady Madeline of
Usher is buried alive out of love. The lust of hate is the
inordinate desire to consume and unspeakably possess
the soul of the hated one, just as the lust of love is the
desire to possess, or to be possessed by, the beloved,

utterly. But in either case the result is the dissolution of both souls, each losing itself in transgressing its own bounds.

The lust of Montresor is to devour utterly the soul of Fortunato. It would be no use killing him outright. If a man is killed outright his soul remains integral, free to return into the bosom of some beloved, where it can enact itself. In walling-up his enemy in the vault, Montresor seeks to bring about the indescribable capitulation of the man's soul, so that he, the victor, can possess himself of the very being of the vanquished. Perhaps this can actually be done. Perhaps, in the attempt, the victor breaks the bonds of his own identity, and collapses into nothingness, or into the infinite. Becomes a monster.

What holds good for inordinate hate holds good for inordinate love. The motto *Nemo me impune lacessit* might just as well be *Nemo me impune amat.*

In *William Wilson* we are given a rather unsubtle account of the attempt of a man to kill his own soul. William Wilson, the mechanical, lustful ego, succeeds in killing William Wilson, the living self. The lustful ego lives on, gradually reducing itself towards the dust of the infinite.

In the *Murders in the Rue Morgue* and *The Gold Bug* we have those mechanical tales where the interest lies in the following out of a subtle chain of cause and effect. The interest is scientific rather than artistic, a study in psychologic reactions.

The fascination of murder itself is curious. Murder is not just killing. Murder is a lust to get at the very quick of life itself, and kill it—hence the stealth and the frequent morbid dismemberment of the corpse, the attempt to get at the very quick of the murdered being, to find the quick and to possess it. It is curious that the two men fascinated by the art of murder, though in different ways, should have been De Quincey and Poe, men so different in ways of life, yet perhaps not so widely different in nature. In each of them is traceable that strange lust for extreme love and extreme hate, possession by mystic violence of the other soul, or violent deathly surrender of the soul in the self: an absence of manly virtue, which stands alone and accepts limits.

Inquisition and torture are akin to murder: the same lust. It is a combat between inquisitor and victim as to whether the inquisitor shall get at the quick of life itself, and pierce it. Pierce the very quick of the soul. The evil will of man tries to do this. The brave soul of man refuses to have the life-quick pierced in him. It is strange: but just as the thwarted will can persist evilly, after death, so can the brave spirit preserve, even through torture and death, the quick of life and truth. Nowadays society is evil. It finds subtle ways of torture, to destroy the life-quick, to get at the life-quick in a man. Every possible form. And still a man can hold out, if he can laugh and listen to the Holy Ghost.—But society is evil, evil, and love is evil. And evil breeds evil, more and more.

So the mystery goes on. La Bruyère says that all our human unhappinesses "viennent de ne pouvoir être seuls." As long as man lives he will be subject to the yearning of love or the burning of hate, which is only inverted love.

But he is subject to something more than this. If we do not live to eat, we do not live to love either.

We live to stand alone, and listen to the Holy Ghost. The Holy Ghost, who is inside us, and who is many gods. Many gods come and go, some say one thing and some say another, and we have to obey the God of the innermost hour. It is the multiplicity of gods within us make up the Holy Ghost.

But Poe knew only love, love, love, intense vibrations and heightened consciousness. Drugs, women, self-destruction, but anyhow the prismatic ecstasy of heightened consciousness and sense of love, of flow. The human soul in him was beside itself. But it was not lost. He told us plainly how it was, so that we should know.

He was an adventurer into vaults and cellars and horrible underground passages of the human soul. He sounded the horror and the warning of his own doom.

Doomed he was. He died wanting more love, and love killed him. A ghastly disease, love. Poe telling us of his disease: trying even to make his disease fair and attractive. Even succeeding.

Which is the inevitable falseness, duplicity of art, American Art in particular.

Some other books published by Penguin
are described on the following pages.

For a complete list of books available
from Penguin in the United States,
write to Dept. DG, Penguin Books,
299 Murray Hill Parkway,
East Rutherford, N.J. 07073.

In Canada for a complete list of Penguin
Books write to Penguin Books Canada Limited,
2801 John Street, Markham, Ontario, Canada L3R 1B4.

THE VIKING PORTABLE LIBRARY

In single volumes, The Viking Portable Library has gathered the very best work of individual authors or works of a period of literary history, writings that otherwise are scattered in a number of separate books. These are not condensed versions, but rather selected masterworks assembled and introduced with critical essays by distinguished authorities. Over fifty volumes of The Viking Portable Library are now in print in paperback, making the cream of ancient and modern Western writing available to bring pleasure and instruction to the student and the general reader. An assortment of subjects follows:

D.H. Lawrence

AARON'S ROD

APOCALYPSE

THE COMPLETE POEMS OF D.H. LAWRENCE
*Collected and edited with an introduction and notes
by Vivian de Sola Pinto and F. Warren Roberts*

THE COMPLETE SHORT STORIES OF D.H. LAWRENCE,
Volumes I, II, and III

FOUR SHORT NOVELS: Love among the Haystacks,
The Ladybird, The Fox, The Captain's Doll

JOHN THOMAS AND LADY JANE: The Hitherto Unpublished
Second Version of Lady Chatterley's Lover

KANGAROO *Introduction by Richard Aldington*

THE LOST GIRL

PHOENIX: The Posthumous Papers of D.H. Lawrence
Edited by Edward D. McDonald

PHOENIX II *Edited by Warren Roberts and Harry T. Moore*

PSYCHOANALYSIS AND THE UNCONSCIOUS and FANTASIA OF THE
UNCONSCIOUS *Introduction by Philip Rieff*

THE RAINBOW

SELECTED POEMS *Introduction by Kenneth Rexroth*

SONS AND LOVERS

SONS AND LOVERS (critical edition) *Edited by Julian Moynahan*

STUDIES IN CLASSIC AMERICAN LITERATURE

WOMEN IN LOVE *Introduction by Richard Aldington*